I0630593

# DOUBLE DARE II

## A SHAMAN APPEARS

Michael Curless

mAcinSF

Copyright © 2022 by Michael Curless

All rights reserved.

No part of this publication may be reproduced, distributed, or transmitted in any form or by any means, including photocopying, recording, or other electronic or mechanical methods, without the prior written permission of the publisher, except as permitted by U.S. copyright law. For permission requests, contact Michael@macinsf.com.

The story, all names, characters, and incidents portrayed in this production are fictitious. No identification with actual persons (living or deceased), places, buildings, and products is intended or should be inferred.

Book Cover by Joleene Naylor

Second edition 2024

eBook ISBN 9781005096823

Paperback ISBN 9798990747616

To the nurses, doctors, researchers and caregivers who worked tirelessly and often at great personal risk to care for those who fell victim to the COVID-19 pandemic.

# A Note to the Reader

THE DOUBLE DARE TRILOGY portrays a chosen family of gay men living in 21st Century San Francisco, a city long revered for encouraging its denizens to live their best, authentic lives. The men chronicled here are striving to do just that. Which means there are occasional, frank scenes of sex between men. Loving, devoted men, some of whom enjoy exploring new and growing subcultures in the modern world. As the title should imply, some of these scenes may be, for the uninitiated, a bit daring.

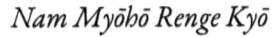

*Nam Myōhō Renge Kyō*

# One

# THREE THOUSAND MILES, GIVE OR TAKE

"Hey, buddy, you okay?" Juan, who had been leaning forward, head in his hands, sat up straight and looked up into Raymond's eyes. Juan's face mask was down around his throat, down for the first time in what ... more than twelve hours? Raymond's mask was still in place.

"I'm fine. Just really tired." Raymond sat down on the bench across from Juan, pulling his mask down as well.

"Yeah, a shift and a half of non-stop chaos will do that to you." Raymond looked intently at Juan to make sure it was just exhaustion that was responsible for Juan's posture. "You sure you're okay? Not that any of us are really okay."

"Well ... okay, considering. How's that?"

"Honest. Sounds honest. Good. None of us were ready for this, but at least some of us were more accustomed to dealing with all too frequent ER crises. What's your specialty back home?"

"OR. Yeah, this is a whole different world. Sure, we'd have an occasional crisis of our own. Gang shooting. Multi-car pileup. There was that horrible Asiana Airlines crash at SFO. But most days were pretty manageable. Mostly electives. Transplants. Joint replacements. Pretty routine. This is something else."

"You didn't have to do this, you know." Raymond leaned forward, resting his own head in his hands as he studied Juan. Juan looked across at Raymond, then slowly nodded without speaking. "You guys have this under control in California."

"That's why I came. You needed help, here in New York. The Bay Area was the first in the country to shelter in place, so we flattened the curve ... hell, we smashed it. Between that and the mandate to halt all elective surgeries, I wasn't really needed there. When I saw your governor asking for volunteers to come, when I saw how overwhelmed you guys were, I knew what I had to do."

"So, you're a fan of Andrew Cuomo, eh?"

"Well, not necessarily. He's not as handsome as our governor, but, you have to admit. He seems to be telling it like it is, which is pretty rare for a politician. Seriously, though, I felt like maybe I could help. And you guys needed help. Still do."

"No shit. None of us have been through anything like this pandemic before." Raymond sat back up, dropping his hands onto his lap, exhaustion evident in his face, too. "Thanks in part to you and the other volunteers who came, I feel like we're finally getting our hands around this. In case no one else has said anything, thanks, man. Really glad you're here."

"I appreciate it, but not to worry. I hear that about a dozen times a day. No thanks are needed."

"Good. I'm glad you know you're appreciated. You have a wife or girlfriend waiting for you back home in Frisco?"

For the first time, maybe all day, a smile graced Juan's face. He reached into the backpack next to him and pulled out his phone and pressed the power button. As it powered up for the first time since his shift started at five a.m., he directed his smile at Raymond. "No offense, but I have to set you straight regarding two parts of your question."

"Huh? Come again? Oh, was I prying? Sorry ..."

"No, no ... not at all. It's just, well, first of all, never say Frisco. You can say San Francisco. You can say Ess Eff. Or even, San Fran. But never Frisco."

"Why not?"

"I don't know. I don't make the rules. I just enforce 'em."

Raymond smiled back. Probably his first smile of the day, too. "Okay, got it. Ess. Eff. And the second thing I need to be set straight about?" Juan held his phone up to show Raymond a photo of Ricky's beaming face.

"This is who's waiting for me. I'm, uh, not all that straight." Raymond leaned forward and studied the image, longer than Juan had expected. There really hadn't been time or opportunity for any of the staff to share much about their personal lives. From the minute they entered the hospital until the moment they dragged themselves out to go home, or in Juan's case, to walk to the nearby hotel where he quarantined himself each evening, there wasn't time or energy for much in the way of small talk. In fact, despite working side by side for several weeks now, saving lives and, all too often, not, this was the first time he and Raymond had had an opportunity to talk about themselves. Raymond finally leaned back and grinned a crooked smile.

"He's adorable."

"Yeah, he majored in adorable."

"Summa Cum Laude from the looks of that picture." Juan actually laughed, for the first time in days.

"I'll tell him you said so." Juan put the phone back into his bag. "What about you? Who's waiting at home for you?"

"My wife, Gabriela, and our six-year-old daughter, Mia."

"Those are both pretty names. Okay, your turn. Do you have pic?" Raymond nodded and fished his phone out of his locker. He handed it to Juan after a moment.

"Very sweet. Both of them. Let me guess. Is Gabriela Puerto Rican American?"

"Good guess, yeah. New York born and bred, though."

"The name gave it away. Looks like you did all right in the romance department, as well."

"I did. Of course," he said humbly, "Gabriela thinks she did okay, and Mia is sure of it." Juan laughed, indulging Raymond. "In a way, I have to say I miss them, too. By the time I decontaminate when I get home and feel safe enough to actually see them, it's basically time for Mia to head to bed."

"That's got to be rough."

"Not as rough as being three thousand miles away."

"Two thousand, nine hundred and two point eight miles away. Ricky calculated it."

"He misses you." Raymond's eyes showed some of the compassion he'd had so much practice exhibiting for the past two months. "You miss him."

Juan sighed and nodded. "Yeah, we Facetime every evening after I get off, and before he starts his shift. He's kind of a front-line warrior right now, too. But, yeah, I miss him. He ..." Juan's phone chimed, interrupting him. He pulled it out to see the call was from Ricky. "Speak of the devil. Here, I'll introduce you." Juan answered the call, but before he could say anything, Ricky greeted the entire staff locker room.

"Papito! I love you! I was worried you hadn't called yet. I ... oh, are you still at the hospital?"

"Uh, yeah, mijo, I'm here with my buddy, Raymond. We just finally ended our shift. Here, say hi to the most amazing ER doc I've ever worked with. Ricky, meet Dr. Raymond." Juan handed the phone to Raymond.

"Hi, Ricky. How are things in Ess Eff?"

"Crazy, just like there. Nice to meet you, Dr. Raymond. Is Juan doing a good job for you?"

"He's doing great ... we couldn't do it without him. In fact, we're thinking about keeping him here. Is that okay with you?" Raymond looked slyly at Juan as Ricky reacted as expected.

"No. No. No. No. NO! It is NOT okay with me, Dr. Raymond ... sir."
Ricky paused, then smiled that irresistible smile through the phone that
overpowered all gay men, most women and a sizable majority of straight
men.

"I'll forward your input to the staffing committee, Ricky," Raymond
earnestly replied, then he smiled into the phone. "Nice meeting you,
Ricky. Let me hand you back to Juan."

"Nice meeting you, too, Doctor Raymond!" Juan took the phone as
Raymond stood and began pulling off his scrubs to change into the street
clothes he'd drive home in, before stripping to shower and change clothes
yet again.

"I should go, mijo," Juan smiled wanly into the phone. "It's been a
long day. You be safe tonight. I love you."

"I love you, too, Papito, and I miss you *this* much!" Juan could see
Ricky spread his arms beyond the view of the phone's camera.

"I miss you more!" Juan ended the call, and looked sheepishly over at
Raymond who was pulling on sweats. "Sorry, Raymond. I didn't intend
to slow you down. Thanks for humoring Ricky."

"You kidding? After what we've been through today, it was kind of
nice to be reminded there are sweet, healthy, people out there who love us
and are waiting to help us return to normal once this is all over. Whatever
normal turns out to be." Juan slowly nodded. As he stood and picked up
his backpack, Raymond spoke again. "Listen, Juan, thanks for opening
up tonight. For sharing Ricky with me. We, uh, need to think seriously
about getting you back home ... to Ess Eff."

"I'm here as long as you need me, Raymond."

"I know. And I really don't want to see you go, but you've been here
almost a month. Don't worry about us; we'll find more volunteers." As
Raymond headed out, he turned and said, "Try to get some rest tonight.
Tomorrow isn't looking to be any easier than today." Juan smiled, nodded knowingly and waived Raymond off. He intended to get some rest,
but sleep? Sleep had been hard to come by lately. What little of it he got
was haunted by the pain, the tragedy and the loss that surrounded him
and all his colleagues every day. The virus wasn't just a killer. It was an
accomplished torturer, one that preyed not just on its victims, but on
everyone who tried to save them as well.

Ricky pulled up on the sidewalk at the foot of the stairs leading up to
Greg and Alex's front door and killed the engine to his scooter. He gave
two quick beeps on the feeble horn to signal his arrival. He waited for

Greg and Alex to pull on enough clothing to avoid irritating the neighbors. Soon Alex came halfway down the stairs, with Greg right behind. Alex, already masked, took a seat on a step as Greg slipped his mask in place and sat next to Alex. Ricky, of course, was helmeted, masked and gloved. He had just made his last delivery for the night.

"Who is that masked man?" Greg asked in what had become their standard greeting whenever Ricky stopped by.

"Why, it's the Masked Ring Bearer!" Ricky announced, sticking to script. Then, off-script he continued, "Like I could recognize you guys behind those masks ... and all those clothes."

"Yeah," replied Alex, "seems like forever since we were all together in one room, in all our naked glory. God, I miss that."

"We all do, Alex," Greg agreed. "At least I still get to live naked with you." Greg wrapped an arm around Alex's shoulders and pulled him close. "Think of our poor Ricky here."

"I know. Sorry Ricky, I guess I shouldn't complain, huh? How's Juan doing?"

"He says okay, but I can tell he's really, really tired. Things are pretty bad there in New York."

"I know. I've become addicted to watching Cuomo on cable news. I keep waiting for him to personally thank Juan for his contribution."

"Any day now!" Ricky exclaimed. "You know, I got to meet one of the ER docs tonight when I called Juan, and he said nice things about him. Asked if Juan could stay there permanently."

"Seriously?" Greg asked.

"He wasn't serious about keeping Juan, but he was very complimentary. Kinda cute, too. Dr. Raymond."

"How much longer do think Juan will be there?" Alex asked, tugging at his mask. "He's been gone a long time. You must be awfully worried about him. Hell, I worry about you, doing deliveries every day."

"I'm really careful, Alex. Don't you worry. But, yeah, I worry about Juan. A lot. The news is so scary I can't even watch it anymore."

"I understand," Greg said. "Me, I can't stop watching. I wish it was just a scary movie. But it's not." Ricky nodded meaningfully but didn't say anything for a moment. He looked tired. Tired and lonely.

"You shouldn't be going home alone, Ricky," Greg continued. "Why don't you stay with us until Juan comes home? You could sleep in your old bed. You shouldn't be alone." Alex smized as he put a hand on Greg's thigh.

"Yeah, just like old times, Ricky," Alex agreed.

"Where would Mateo sleep?" Ricky asked tentatively.

"Next to you, amigo," Greg smiled. "He hasn't been able to see Ryan for weeks. I'm pretty sure he could use a bed buddy." Ricky laughed.

"Um, pretty tempting, but I only sleep with Juan, you know. Besides, I can't risk infecting you guys."

"But you said you're careful," Alex protested.

"I am, but you never know. I'd never forgive myself."

Greg stood up. "Well, okay, but think about it. I'm sure Juan would think it's a good idea. Ask him what he thinks." Ricky nodded. "Thanks for stopping by, Ricky. We should let you go so you can go home ... and decontaminate."

"Yeah, I will. But are you guys hungry? My last pickup gave me a bunch of food they had left at the end of the night." Both Alex and Greg looked at each other, hesitating. "It's Thai."

"In that case ..." Alex approached Ricky's scooter as Ricky stepped away to maintain a six-foot distance. Alex opened the DoorDash bag and peered inside. "Whoa. That's a lot."

"Yeah, that's why I came over. Take all you want. I can't eat it all, you know, being lovelorn and all."

"God, I wish I could give you a hug right now," Greg whined. "This is so frustrating." Alex rejoined Greg, holding three good-sized black plastic, microwaveable take-out containers.

"This is a feast, Ricky. Thanks!"

"Don't thank me. Remember what Juan said ... we owe you a thousand dinners for everything you guys did for us. I think we're down to about nine hundred and ninety-five now."

"Nine hundred and ninety-six, Ricky, but who's counting," Greg countered, grinning behind his mask.

"Okay, sorry. My bad." Ricky climbed back on the scooter and fired it up. He slid forward to release the kickstand and waved, "Always good to see you, amigos. I love you!" Both Alex and Greg blew kisses through their masks, the best they could do given the circumstances. As Ricky rolled up the hill, Alex and Greg turned and headed up the steps. Greg put his arm around Alex's waist.

"We really can't complain, can we?" Greg asked rhetorically.

"I'm still going to complain. I miss 'normal' life. A lot! But, no, we're pretty damn lucky. I don't know how Ricky and Juan can stand it." Before they got to the top of the steps, Mateo, who had been working a late shift as an 'essential' worker at the restaurant, prepping takeout, raced up the stairs to join them.

"Hi, honeys, I'm home!" he crooned. "Was that Ricky?" His English was improving by the hour.

"It was. And this is dinner, sweetie, compliments of Ricky. Sorry you missed him." Greg opened the door and held it so Alex and Mateo could file in ahead of him.

"Yeah, I miss him," Mateo said. Both Alex and Greg looked at each other, not sure if Mateo had missed the point, or had gotten it and made his own in one succinct statement. Not that it mattered. They all missed each other. But at least there was Thai to eat, as soon as Mateo had stripped, showered and decontaminated.

Alex finished loading the dishwasher and joined Greg on the couch, cuddling up close, rubbing Greg's naked thigh affectionately. Mateo was sprawled on the floor, hands supporting his head, his perky butt occasionally twitching as he stared at the television. As usual Mateo had offered to clean up after dinner, but Alex insisted he chill after having worked much of the day. Mateo was the only one in the household who wasn't totally sheltering in place. Even though both Greg and Alex worked even more hours than they would have had they been able to commute to work, they were keenly aware of the risks Mateo took each day to insure he was doing his part financially. Greg turned to Alex and delivered a full-on kiss.

"Dinner was great. Thanks."

"Hey, all I did was reheat and serve. Ricky gets all the credit." Mateo rolled over on his side to face the couch, his head supported by his left hand.

"I have a question on Ricky," he said.

"About Ricky," Alex suggested. Mateo grinned.

"Thanks. About Ricky." As he spoke, he nonchalantly fondled his cock with his right hand. He'd fully adapted to living naked with Greg and Alex and no longer gave a second thought to how he lived now.

"What's your question?" Greg asked, enjoying the view.

"Juan has been away for one month now, no?"

"Yeah," Alex agreed. "Do you miss him?"

"Si. Yeah, and Ricky, and Raphael and Luke and everbody. But I am wondering ..." Mateo paused, uncertain if his question was inappropriate. Or, if the answer was obvious to these more experienced members of the family. He didn't want to appear too clueless.

"Well?" Alex prodded.

"Who is taking off Ricky's cage for his cleaning?" Greg and Alex both immediately turned to each other in surprise.

"Damn!" Greg exclaimed. "I hadn't even thought about that!"

"Me, either!" Alex let go of Greg and sat upright. "Geez, you're right Mateo." He pondered a moment. "Don't you think, considering everything, that he's doing it himself? He does know where Juan keeps the keys ... or at least he did."

"I don't know, Alex," Greg replied. "Ricky's pretty adamant about being 'the best locked cock leather boy in the world.' Unless Juan ordered him to, I'm not so sure he would."

"Well, I'm the only other person who's ever unlocked him, but Ricky hasn't said anything."

"Would we be out of line to check with Juan?"

"It's after midnight there. Hopefully he's asleep."

"Text him. He'll see it in the morning." Alex nodded and reached for his phone and started the text. Then he stopped, looked over at Greg then resumed.

"What?" Greg asked.

"I'm texting Ricky instead. The last thing Juan needs right now is to be worrying about Ricky's hygiene."

"You're probably right," Greg agreed. Mateo nodded and rolled back over on his stomach, pleased that his concern about Ricky's hygiene routine had been valid. Alex laid his phone down and resumed his cuddle with Greg. Maybe because of the topic they'd been discussing, Greg reached down and fondled Alex's Looker 01. At least Alex's chastity cage was designed to be permanent. He felt Alex harden inside the cage, as Alex let out a low moan. But not low enough.

"Maybe I go to my room," Mateo smiled as he looked over his shoulder.

"No, sweetie, you're fine," Greg grinned back at him. "Our Alex here is just letting us know he's finally relaxing after a long day." Alex's phone chimed, and he picked it up.

"Ricky." Alex unlocked and read the text. "He says he's okay. He's been using an ear wax squeeze bulb to keep clean. Not perfect, but good enough." Alex laughed. "He says he's still the best locked cock leather boy and thanks for asking." Alex looked over at Mateo, who was staring at Alex. "I guess our services are not needed, Mateo. That was a good call, though. Thanks." They traded smiles as Alex put down the phone, placed Greg's hand back on his caged cock and resumed his cuddle.

# Two

# MAKING DO WITH ZOOM

RAPHAEL PULLED THE DINING chair out from the table and sat down, putting his cup of coffee on a cork coaster. The table, along with his company laptop, had been his ad hoc office for the past couple of months. On Saturday afternoons, like this, his personal laptop had been his and Luke's link to the family since the shelter in place mandate abruptly ended the Tuesday dinners everyone had always enjoyed. As he launched the Zoom app, Luke pulled out his own chair and sat next to him, scooting close, thigh to thigh. Luke adjusted the shoulder strap of Raphael's body harness.

"Am I ready for my close up, Sir?" Raphael smiled, as he turned and puckered, wordlessly demanding a kiss. Luke complied, then pulled back to admire Raphael's naked beauty.

"You've never been more ready, baby." He delivered another perfunctory kiss, then looked at the laptop cam and said, "Let's party."

"Party?" Niki asked from his and Steve's thumbnail on the monitor. "What's a party?"

"Hey, Niki!" Raphael greeted him. "Yeah, you remember what a party is, right? Back in 2019 B.C.?"

"B.C?" Alex asked from his, Greg's and Mateo's thumbnail. Mateo sat squeezed between Alex and Greg, and was the only one in the session so far not wearing any leather.

"B.C. Before COVID," Raphael explained. No one groaned at this newly minted nomenclature. It wasn't funny, but rather all too real. The virus had become a defining aspect of everyone's life.

"Where's Steve?" Luke asked Niki, once everyone had logged on. Ricky was also alone in his thumbnail, of course, with Juan far away in New York.

"He's here. He got a phone call from someone he works with, but he'll be here in a minute. Oh, wait, here he comes." Steve entered the frame and sat down next to Niki, revealing in the process, before he settled into place that, except for his chest harness, he was completely, and appropriately, naked, as was everyone else. It might not be Tuesday dinner, but at least the dress code was still enforced for their weekly gathering.

"Hey guys," Steve greeted the group. "Sorry, I'm here now."

"So, you're working on Saturday, Steve?" Ricky asked.

"No, amigo," Steve smiled. "It was a colleague, but it was a personal matter. My friend Ben was asking a favor."

"Okay, amigo," Ricky smiled back. "You guys all work too hard."

"I don't," Luke announced. "Like you, Ricky, I still work regular hours, on the days I go in that is, not like these 'work from home' slaves." He nudged Raphael, who laid his head on Luke's shoulder briefly, then sat back up.

"What do you mean?" Raphael questioned. "I only work, what, twelve, thirteen hours a day. That's about normal, right, Alex?"

"For a while. At first, but Greg and I decided to set limits. Five o'clock, computers down."

"Until he gets a text for help," Greg countered. "But, yeah, we're trying to moderate that."

"And what time do you log in, in the morning, Greg?" Luke asked, with a knowing look.

"What's that?" Greg said a little loudly. "You're breaking up, Luke."

"Yeah, I thought so," Luke laughed. "You know I just realized, Steve and Niki, you are the only ones, who are truly sheltering in place. Ricky has to go out and interface with the public, Mateo does too. And I have to go in, but I'm only working a couple of days a week now, and I interact with the same few people every time. Very socially distanced. Heck, we might as well all get together in person, like old times."

"At least you still have a job," Niki frowned, then whined like the sad pup he was.

"You still have a job," Raphael tried to comfort him. "You're furloughed, not fired."

"Yeah, but when will it be back? Bars will be the last thing they reopen." Steve put his arm around Niki's shoulders and nuzzled the side of his head.

"We're sorry, Niki," Alex leaned into his frame, puckering his lips into a virtual kiss. "Kiss him for me, Steve." Steve did.

"You must be able to spend more time in pup space," Ricky said, trying to cheer Niki up.

"He is," Steve confirmed as Niki nodded noncommittally. "For days at a time, sometimes. Then he feels guilty and makes up for it by being the best human husband I could ever want." Both Steve and Niki looked meaningfully at each other. Niki looked back into the camera and barked.

"See, if we were all together, we could pet Pup Niki and make him feel all better," Luke maintained. "What are they going to do, arrest us?"

"Luke, Sir," Ricky looked seriously into his cam. "We all want to be back together. But it would kill me if it turned out that I infected you guys. I look into Juan's eyes every day when we Facetime, and I see the hurt there, from what he sees every day. What he faces every day. This is real, amigos. I know it doesn't seem so bad here, but it's really bad." Everyone could see the pain in Ricky's face. He started to speak again, but just swallowed and stopped.

"God, Ricky," Luke said softly. "Now I just want to be there to comfort you. You must be so worried." It took a moment for Ricky to gather himself. Everyone gave him the space he needed.

"Yeah," is all he said at first. "I'm scared for Juan. And lonely." Again, more space. "Sorry, amigos, I don't mean to be a bummer."

"Be a bummer!" Alex shouted. "Ricky, we're here for you. If you're hurting, we need to know." Ricky managed a half smile, one not up to his usual standards. "We meant what we said the other night. You should move in with us until Juan gets back ... you shouldn't be alone."

"The other night?" Raphael asked, semi-jealously.

"Ricky stopped by with some extra Thai from his last delivery," Greg explained.

"Oh, I see," Raphael feigned hurt. "Good thing we don't like Thai, eh, Luke?" Luke just laughed.

"They were the closest!" Ricky grinned. "And there are three of them and I wanted to share it while it was still hot." He gave Raphael his fully adorable smile. "Next time, okay?"

"Don't give Ricky a hard time, baby," Luke said, looking into the cam instead of at Raphael. "I think Alex has a good idea. You shouldn't be alone, Ricky." Before Ricky could protest, Luke asked, "Tell us more about Juan. How much longer do you think he'll be gone?" Ricky took a deep breath.

"I don't know. He said things are better. Still really bad. But not as insane as when he got there. Like I said, I can tell he's working too hard. Maybe it's just the lighting or the camera, but he looks beat. He has grooves in his face from the PPE he wears all day, every day. I don't know ..." Ricky's voice trailed off.

"Damn," Niki offered.

"Ricky," Greg said in as comforting a voice as he could muster. "I know you're worried and you miss him. We all do. Maybe this doesn't help at all, but, Ricky, Juan is an amazing guy doing an incredible thing. He didn't have to volunteer to go to New York. But he did. Because he's a one in a million guy. And he loves you more than anything in the world, so he's not going to let anything happen to himself. He knows you need him back here, safe and sound."

Everyone could see Ricky was looking into Greg's eyes on his monitor, not into his camera, when he softly said, "It can't happen too soon, Greg. I'm so worried. And I miss him so much." No one spoke for a moment.

"You'll be talking to him later today, right?" Luke asked.

"Yep. Everyday."

"Make sure you tell him we all miss him and if he doesn't come back soon, we're going to go there and take him hostage for you." Ricky laughed at that idea and began to speak when something distracted him beyond his laptop. That's when he shrieked, and moved so fast the image from his camera was a blur of caramel naked skin and baby blue Holy Trainer. The audio, though, was clear as could be.

"PAPITO! ... Dios Mio! ... PAPITO!"

"Stop, Ricky!" No doubt about it. It was Juan's voice. "Don't move, mijo. I want to hug you more than anything, but I've been in two airports, two taxis and a very long plane ride. Let me strip and shower, and *then* we can touch. God, you look beautiful!" A moment later Ricky slid back in front of the laptop. He was literally bouncing in his chair.

"Juan is home! My Papito is home!"

"Yeah, we heard," Raphael said through a relieved laugh. "I think they heard it all the way back in New York. Can we say hi?"

"He's already in the shower, Raphael. He's home! I'm so happy!"

"Ricky," Greg spoke up. "We're all happy. But you know what? I think we should all log off so you and Juan can get reacquainted. Tomorrow, or Monday, or whenever you two crawl out of bed, text us and we'll all log back in so we can welcome Juan home. Okay?"

"Okay!" Ricky agreed and just like that he was gone.

"Um ... bye Ricky," Luke facetiously waved to the rest of the family.

"I wish we could have at least seen Juan for a minute," Niki frowned.

"We will, once Ricky finishes welcoming him home." Alex replied. "In a day or two. Or three." Mateo, grinning broadly, put his arms around both Alex's and Greg's necks.

"Well, guys, that was the best thing that has happened in a long, long time," Steve said, leaning into the camera. "Since we can't be together, I suggest we all follow the advice of Crosby, Stills and Nash, and log off and go celebrate 'with the one's we're with.'"

"Actually, isn't it *'love* the one you're with?'" Raphael fact checked.

"Yeah, baby, that." Luke crooned. "Let's all go love the one's we're with." And with that, Raphael and Luke disappeared. That left just Steve and Niki to wave adieu to Greg, Alex and Mateo before ending the session.

"How was that for timing?" Steve turned to Niki. "Ricky's on an emotional roller coaster today, eh, puppy?"

"No doubt. We hadn't seen Ricky this down since his roommate attacked him."

"And we haven't seen him this happy since his debut as the glitter encrusted ring bearer. I'm glad we at least got to see his face when Juan walked in."

"And his blurry Holy Trainer," Niki laughed. "I wish we'd been recording it." Steve reached down and rubbed Niki's own cage, as Niki leaned in for a full-on kiss. As they tongue wrestled, Niki gently rubbed Steve's belly. Two months of quarantine had been remarkably advantageous to Steve's mission to grow a belly for Niki. Full-time access to the kitchen combined with the closure of the gym had made it surprisingly easy to add ten pounds, all belly and love handles. Well, that and maybe a plumper butt. Steve knew he was on the right track, as Niki found it more and more difficult to keep his hands, lips and puppy tongue away from Steve's always naked body, especially the belly. Once or twice, he'd worried about whether he'd fit into pants when and if the work from home mandate ended. He doubted he'd get away with wearing the sweat pants he donned for his and Niki's once a week outing for groceries. But that concern always dissolved as soon as Niki displayed his delight in Steve's gradual transformation. So far, no one else had seemed to notice the extra weight, but again ... sweatpants. That, and the fact colleagues couldn't see below the desk during ZOOM meetings. Good thing, too, considering he didn't wear the sweatpants while working. The biggest surprise was how erotic the belly was becoming for Steve himself. He'd never had a rock-hard six-pack like Ricky, but the regular gym workouts had kept him lean enough. Never had he envisioned himself with excess body fat. In fact, he'd taken a certain amount of pride in gaining muscle over the past couple of years. He had started the belly for Niki; it was Niki's fetish he wanted to satisfy. But, oddly, he didn't mind the look or the feel of the extra padding. Nor the pleasure of Niki worshipping it. Right now, as Niki face fucked him while sliding his hands around his belly, Steve's hardon grew to full size, rising up until it brushed against Niki's wrist.

"Umm," Niki moaned into Steve's mouth. He pulled away, smiled and said, "Puppy wants his bone."

"Let's go play, puppy," Steve smiled back. He stood as Niki dropped to all fours and followed him into the bedroom. Niki was already wearing his pup tail, so it didn't take long for Steve to lock on the paw mitts and slip the puppy hood over Niki's head. Niki's tail wagged furiously as Steve adjusted the hood. For now, Steve's human husband was gone and his sexy, uninhibited puppy took his place. Pup Niki barked, jumped up against Steve to roll him over on his back and then the pup went for his favorite bone, swallowing Steve's cock to the root. Just like Raphael, Alex and Ricky, having his own cock permanently locked meant the only cock Pup Niki could enjoy was Steve's. As Pup Niki's tail wagged enthusiastically, and his hooded head bobbed up and down as he devoured Steve's cock, Steve closed his eyes and relaxed, letting his devoted pup do all the work once again.

# Three

## FINALLY, THE NEXT DARE

RAPHAEL CLOSED THE LAPTOP and stood up, pushed his chair aside and sat back down on Luke's lap, facing him, his squat-hardened thighs resting on Luke's, his cage pressed against Luke's abs, his ass conveniently settling exactly over Luke's cock. The cock that would soon have no choice but to rise up and graze the plug in Raphael's butt. Raphael leaned forward and pressed his pierced nipples against Luke's chest as he locked lips with Luke, his tongue sliding across Luke's own. He wrapped his arms around Luke's neck as Luke wrapped his around Raphael's muscled, illustrated back. Although they, too, hadn't seen the inside of the gym for weeks now, their previous dedication was still evident, and still rewarding to the touch. As they kissed, breathing through each other, as Raphael's cock strained against his steel Looker 01, he decided this might be the right time to offer himself up in the dare he'd issued to Luke weeks earlier. Once he felt Luke's cock pressing up, teasing his ass, he made his move.

"Sir," Raphael sighed as he slid his tongue free of Luke's oral embrace. "This has suddenly become a day to celebrate, wouldn't you say?"

"Indeed, baby." Luke stared into those sweet, brown, almond eyes as he licked the remnants of Raphael's deep kiss from his lips. "Something tells me you already have a celebration in mind."

"Oh, yes, Sir, I do. I've been waiting for the right time, and I think this is it."

"Ah. I see. This is beginning to sound like ... like a dare?" Raphael flashed his signature smile.

"My Braveheart ... so handsome and he's perceptive, too." Raphael leaned forward long enough to deliver another brief kiss, then he climbed off of Luke, stood and held out his hand and pulled Luke to his feet. "This way, Sir." Raphael led Luke into the bedroom and sat him at the foot of the bed. He went to the closet, rummaged a moment and returned, his left hand behind his back. He knelt in front Luke, leaned forward and kissed first one then the other of Luke's knees. Then he straightened up, looked endearingly into Luke's eyes and presented Luke with a small, brown plastic zippered case.

"Oh," Luke uttered.

"Yes. Sir. I'm ready to let you unlock me. I'm ready to let you suck me off. You have my permission. Let's celebrate!"

"I didn't know I needed your permission, baby." Raphael couldn't quite read Luke's face. He was offering Luke the opportunity he'd been longing for, apparently for months now. Luke should have been thrilled. Of course, there were consequences for Luke indulging this desire. Minor ones, Raphael thought.

"You do not need my permission, Sir. You could have instigated my blow job any time you wished. You are my Braveheart, and I am your locked cock leather boy. But, with Juan's return, this is a very special day. Also, it was my dare, after all. And I know you might be hesitant because of the price you must pay for tasting my forbidden, locked cock, so ... I thought this first time, it might be appropriate for me to make the first move. As it were." Raphael placed the case containing the hot pink Holy Trainer on the bed, then leaned forward and swallowed Luke's cock entirely in one practiced move. He slid up and down, reveling in the always rewarding taste of Luke, until Luke was sufficiently engorged. It didn't take long. Surely this would put Luke in the right frame of mind to return the favor. Luke placed a hand on either shaved side of Raphael's head and tilted it until their eyes could meet, while Raphael continued to feed. It was clear Raphael was demonstrating what he was hoping Luke was about to do to him.

"Baby, I would. I really would, but you're forgetting. The keys to your cage are locked away with the keyholder service at Mr. S." Luke had considered retrieving them at some point, after Raphael had consented to being unlocked, so he'd have them whenever this moment arose, but he had never gotten around to it before the lockdown. He expected to see Raphael's face fall in disappointment at this realization. He was a little disappointed himself, but, at least for the moment, it wouldn't be necessary to unzip that damn little brown case. Raphael pulled back, slowly releasing Luke's now slippery and gleaming cock. Luke's hands dropped, resting on Raphael's shoulders.

"Sir. It's true," Raphael replied as his tongue circled his lips. "We did turn my keys over to Mr. S for safe keeping." There was no disappointment on Raphael's face. Oh, oh, Luke thought. This is not the reaction I was expecting. "Sir, am I not your perfect locked cock leather boy?"

"Of course, baby. Perfect. Beautiful. Loving. Sexy." Luke smiled as he praised Raphael, but he wasn't sure what Raphael's point was. "And best of all, you're mine."

"Sir, I accept your praise. Have I ever challenged you to a dare you could not fulfill?" Luke thought a moment.

"Well, there was that last dare ..."

"Next to last dare ... which doesn't count," Raphael interrupted. "Remember, you fulfilled the purpose of *all* our dares by not completing that dare. And besides, the incompletion of the dare led to the last dare ... the one we are both destined to complete," and here Raphael sat up a little straighter and looked intently into Luke's eyes, "Right. Now." He picked up the Holy Trainer case, unzipped it, pulled out the brand new, hot pink Holy Trainer, the one he had purchased for just this occasion ... and two sets of keys. "These, Sir are the keys to your cage." He placed a set next to the Holy Trainer. "And these are the keys to my cage. I retrieved them a couple of weeks after I created this dare so we'd be ready whenever the time came for you to fulfill it. For me to offer you my unlocked cock for your pleasure, Sir. I didn't want you to be denied, whenever your need might arise." Raphael's mischievous smile was back. Luke let go of Raphael and fell back onto the mattress in defeat, his arms flung to either side.

"Oh, god, Raphael. I knew this day would come." Raphael crawled up onto the bed and laid down next to Luke, as he put one arm across Luke's chest and his still moist mouth next to Luke's ear.

"I can't wait to feel your mouth around my cock, Sir." Raphael whispered. There was a long pause before Luke spoke.

"And you really, really can't wait to lock me up, can you ... baby?" Luke turned his head to face Raphael. It wasn't a question.

"I can't wait!" Raphael broke up as he rolled aside in laughter. Luke's response was expected.

"Fuck!" Raphael rolled back against Luke and pulled himself up so his face was above Luke's. He was still smiling; Luke was not.

"Sir, I thought you missed being able to suck me. That's why I issued the dare." He traced a circle around Luke's lips with his forefinger as he spoke. Then he slid it into Luke's mouth and pulled it in and out, teasing Luke. "Didn't you say so? Sir?" Luke reached up and took Raphael's hand and pulled his finger out of his mouth. Slowly, teasing back.

"I do miss sucking you, yes. I did say that. I miss swallowing you, all of you, very much. I love how much you cum and how wonderful it tastes." Luke paused, staring into those dreamy eyes again. "It's the consequence of serving you after the fact that I dread. And you know it." Raphael pulled away and sat up next to Luke. He took Luke's hand in his and squeezed.

"You seem to be forgetting our dire situation, Sir." Luke's eyebrows knitted in confusion. "Sir, we're in isolation. No gym. No beach. No Tuesday dinners. No one will see you caged but me." Luke's demeanor instantly changed as he sat up, hand still clasped in Raphael's, and pushed Raphael over onto his back. Raphael grinned as Luke hovered over him as he reached for the keys still at the foot of the bed.

"I don't know why, baby, but sometimes I forget just how brilliant you are. Thank you for retrieving the keys before Mr. S was locked down. You're so right. There will never be a better time for you to lock me up, a price I'm more than willing to pay to get to finally feast on your beautiful, sweet cock. Your timing is perfect, baby!" Not wasting another minute, Luke inserted the key into Raphael's cage and pulled on the brass lock. It didn't budge. He gave Raphael a look of concern.

"Well, Sir, it hasn't been unlocked in over a year. It's probably just stuck." Luke nodded and tried again. Still nothing. And again, but still no movement. "We probably don't want to break the key off in the lock, Sir." Luke immediately stopped trying, but the thought of Raphael really being permanently locked only hardened his bobbing erection. It was pretty obvious Raphael was as hard as his cage would permit as well. They were on the cusp of a sex act they'd not shared in a year and a half. They could both practically taste it, but ... but for the damned lock!

"Sir, maybe a little coconut oil?" Luke leapt up and ran into the bath. It took him a couple of minutes to find the bottle. They hadn't needed it since changing Raphael out from his own Holy Trainer to the more permanent Looker 01. Soon he was back, waving the bottle, looking victorious. Raphael was grinning, enjoying the little wrinkle in Luke's quest to finally be able to suck his leather boy's cock. Luke hesitated, not sure how to proceed. Raphael sat up, took the bottle from Luke, pulled the key out of the lock and squeezed a few drops onto the key. Then, he squeezed a few more onto the brass cylinder in the cage and rubbed it in. He decided to torture Luke just a little bit more. He looked searchingly into Luke's eyes and said, "I'm so hard, Sir. I so wanted you to be able to eat me today." As he watched the look of concern pass over Luke's face, he slid the key into place, twisted it and pulled the cylinder out in one smooth move.

"YES!" Luke raised up on his knees in celebration. Raphael laid back down and placed the key still lodged in the brass cylinder away from himself on the bed, definitely not wanting to lose track of it.

"Sir, even though you are unlocking me, I don't want to risk accidentally touching your boy's locked cock, so you'll have to remove the cage." He placed his hands behind his head, looked sweetly at Luke and commanded, "Go ahead. Eat me, Luke!" Luke grabbed the cage with one hand and the cock ring it was attached to with the other and pulled. Once again, no movement.

'Jesus!" Luke cursed. "Why does this have to be so hard?" Raphael giggled as he lifted his head with his hands to better see what Luke was doing.

"Sir, it's okay. Just wiggle the cage back and forth, up and down. Gently. Remember it hasn't been apart for a very long time." Luke nodded and did as Raphael suggested. Finally, the cage began moving independently of the cock ring.

"Got it," Luke breathed a sigh of relief. "Finally. Dios Mio!" And with that the cage came free of the cock ring with a subtle clink. Slowly, since Raphael was clearly as engorged as the cage would permit, Luke pulled the cage free of his husband's cock. As he pulled, the urethral tube also slid out from inside Raphael's cock. The cock that had been caged from the outside and the inside for well over a year. As the urethral tube cleared the end of Raphael's glans, a dribble of precum came with it. Without hesitation Luke leaned down and licked it off the tip of his leather boy's newly freed cock.

"Oh, god!" Raphael cried, his head falling back onto the bed. "Oh, Luke, Sir. That feels amazing!" Luke gently, slowly, delicately tested Raphael's newly freed cock head with his tongue mostly, and with his lips. "Oh god ... don't ... don't stop ... please ... god ... oh ..." Not surprisingly a cock that had been imprisoned in a cage for a year and half, most of that time in a metal cage that held his cock captive inside and out, well, that cock was indescribably sensitive. Yes, the cage had pleasured and tortured Raphael endlessly, especially whenever Luke fucked him to point of mutual orgasm, but that could never compare to the warm, moist embrace of Luke's mouth.

"Mmmmm," Luke moaned as he swallowed Raphael completely, his nose sliding up onto the steel cock ring that was still in place. He had been the recipient of hundreds, maybe thousands of blowjobs from Raphael since the last time he had been able to taste Raphael's cock, and the wait had been worth it. God damn, Raphael tasted amazing. As Raphael squirmed and moaned, involuntarily moving his smooth thighs around Luke's face, his glans tickled Luke's uvula as Luke devoured his locked cock boy. Well, actually unlocked cock boy at the moment. Raphael couldn't believe how good this felt, either. Eyes closed, he reached his hands down to find the shaved sides of Luke's head. He ran his fingers along the edges of Luke's mohawk as Luke slowly, so deliciously slowly, bobbed up and down on Raphael's temporarily freed cock.

"Luke," Raphael breathed, nearly inaudibly. "Oh, man. That feels so ... I love you. Oh, god I love you." Luke was not about to let go of Raphael's cock to respond. He'd waited so long for this moment, and he was going to make it last as long as he possibly could. They both knew how to read each other's body when, normally, Luke was fucking Raphael, and Raphael was safely caged. Either one could make the other cum on command, or delay his own orgasm as needed. But this was different. Raphael hadn't been inside Luke's mouth in such a long time. He was as hard as Luke had ever seen him. Luke slowed his motion even more, wanting to delay Raphael's orgasm as long as possible. He wasn't even thinking about his own orgasm, although he'd felt his own precum smear against his thighs as his erection slapped back and forth. Funny, he suddenly realized, in a brief intellectual diversion from the purely sexual state he was otherwise engulfed in, he realized that he was playing the role Raphael usually played. He was focused solely on Raphael's cock, on Raphael's pleasure, and ultimately on Raphael's orgasm. The realization that any other time, it would be Raphael totally focused on giving Luke the best orgasm he could muster, reminded Luke of just how much he adored, treasured ... loved Raphael. Of how much he owed Raphael as a lover. As a loving husband. As Raphael's Braveheart.

So, Luke took his time. Spending a full minute or more at times, doing nothing except embracing Raphael's cock with his mouth, his tongue slowly massaging the bottom of Raphael's cock, gauging his motion by the sounds of Raphael's moans and cries. Occasionally pressing down just enough to tease the tip of Raphael's glans against the back of his throat. He would have swallowed Raphael further back if Raphael's cock had been long enough, but Raphael was not as well-endowed as Luke, certainly not as well-endowed as his brother Niki. Not that it mattered to Luke. In every other respect, Raphael's physical attributes were beyond comparison to those of any other man Luke might have ever considered. No, Raphael's cock was perfect, just as it was. The feel of Raphael's fingers pulling at his mohawk was perfect. The smell of Raphael's caramel colored, smoothly shaved pubic skin was perfect. This moment was absolutely perfect.

"No!" Raphael cried out without warning. "Sir ..." Luke felt Raphael's cock pulse at the same instant he tasted the cum rush past the back of his tongue. He pulled back enough to ensure Raphael's load would accumulate in his mouth instead of being wasted, tastelessly, down his throat. He drained Raphael, not an easy thing, given the volume of a typical Raphael orgasm. But he relished each pulse, and he did his best to give Raphael as much pleasure as Raphael always gave him. Tongue, lips, throat, Luke did his best to orchestrate the best damn blowjob he could muster. Judging by Raphael's vocalizations, it must have been sufficient.

"Oh ... god!" Raphael sighed, his chest heaving. His fingers still raking Luke's mohawk. Finally, Luke slid free of Raphael's cock and crawled up

Raphael's body, to share some of his bounty with Raphael. Lips locked, tongues embracing, Raphael's salty-sweet cum shared as both men moaned. As he had done many times before, Luke squeezed Raphael's nose shut so he was forced to breathe through Luke's nose, Luke's lungs. Total dependence. Lover's symbiosis. Breathing as one. Existing as one. Luke was not about to be the first to break the embrace. He released Raphael's nose and reached up with one hand to brush Raphael's high 'n tight, reached down with the other to caress his leather boy's cock, a cock that hadn't been touched by anyone in hundreds of days, still holding Raphael's tongue captive. Another moan from Raphael. Finally, Raphael used his tongue to lick both their lips and force a separation. He gave a little chuckle.

"So, baby," Luke whispered. "Was that so bad ... being unlocked?" A smile spread across Raphael's sweet face, as he stared into Luke's transparent blue eyes. Their faces were still close enough that, as he often did, Raphael grabbed a bit of Luke's beard between his teeth and tugged playfully.

"Well, Sir, not bad, no. ... On a scale of one to ten ... I'd say that was definitely a thousand." His grin grew even larger as Luke leaned down and locked lips once more. After a few more shared breaths, Luke lifted his head, then bent down to kiss first one pierced nipple, then the other. He looked back up at Raphael and smiled. "I'd give it an even higher score, Sir, but at the moment I don't think I can count any higher." That brought a full-fledged laugh from Luke, who wrapped himself around Raphael's body, and the two lay together, wordlessly appreciating this rare moment. A moment, Luke realized, that probably never would have happened had they never met Juan, who taught them there was nothing out of character about occasionally wanting to suck your locked cock leather boy. Luke took a deep, deep breath.

"Baby, however good it was for you, it was even better for me. Thank you, Raphael, for giving me this day. I know what a sacrifice it was for you, and I'm man enough, I'm your Braveheart enough, to now submit my cock to your lockup. I can honestly say, it was worth it." Raphael turned his head to kiss Luke's nose.

"All part of the dare, Sir, and I'm glad you are so happy to follow through. It's oh so very noble of you to willingly do this. I guess, maybe you really do love me, huh?" Luke grinned, ignoring Raphael's mockery, and gave him a noogie to affirm, that, yes, he really did love Raphael. "May I feast upon your magnificent cock, and give you one last free cock orgasm before we lock you up?

"Hmm. Baby, if you had asked me that yesterday, I would have agreed, of course. You know I love when you feast on me. But I don't think it would be in the spirit of the dare, really, for me to get off after giving you a blow job for the first time since ... what, 2018? This is all about you, so you should lock me up, without me coming." Raphael gave Luke a confused look.

"Sir, this was not about me. On the contrary, this was about giving you what you were longing for. Giving you the opportunity to suck my otherwise locked cock. This was all for you, a reward for proving your devotion the night I dared you to find another cock to suck. Remember?"

"Yeah, I do. And don't get me wrong ... sucking you just now was the best time I've had since ... well, I can't even say. But, baby, you're the one making the sacrifice by allowing me to unlock you. Being Luke's locked cock boy is so integral to you, it's actually tattooed right here above your cock." Luke traced the ink with a forefinger as he spoke.

"Okay, Sir. Let's just agree that we both benefitted from this dare. And if it makes you feel better about 'sacrificing' a last orgasm due to the sacrifice that I've willingly made, then so be it. No Orgasm For You!" The negotiation was at an end. "But, bear in mind, Sir, I will make every effort to deliver at least one orgasm to you before this week is out. Hopefully more than one."

"I'll be eager to see you try," Luke shrugged. "Either way, it was still worth it. Don't you think?"

"Are you kidding me? As much as I love you fucking me, this was at the top of the top ten. You rocked my world, Sir." Raphael grinned, leaned forward and delivered another patented Raphael kiss, one that still tasted of Raphael's seed. When they parted lips, Raphael commanded, "All right, Sir. Let's go shave and shower, and then ... for the first time ever, we lock each other up!"

"Okay, baby, but I have to warn you, it probably won't be the last time. This was definitely worth it."

"Yeah, Luke. I do give the best dares, don't I?" Raphael laughed as he wriggled in Luke's arms before they slid off the bed and headed for the shower. After getting wet and sitting down for their nightly routine, one difference was immediately obvious to both of them. As Raphael scooted up behind Luke and wrapped his legs around Luke's waist, it was his cock, not his cage that pressed into Luke's back.

"Weird," Raphael said as he reached for the razor and shaving cream.

"Yeah, but nice," Luke replied. "I kind of like the feel of your bare cock on my ass."

"Oh, is Sir thinking of becoming vers with his 'baby'?" Raphael smoothed the lather all around Luke's mohawk.

"Would my baby like that?" Luke massaged Raphael's calves which were resting on his own.

"Hmmm." Raphael pondered as he began pulling the razor through Luke's day-old stubble. "Well, maybe someday. Maybe. I don't know. I like serving my Braveheart just the way things are right now." He pulled a few more strokes, revealing more smooth skin. "If that's okay, Sir."

"It's not okay, baby ... it's perfect." Luke took advantage of Raphael rinsing off the razor to twist around and demand another kiss. He turned back around. As Raphael resumed the shave, Luke continued massaging Raphael's calves. "The only thing that matters is that at the end of the day, I find myself in bed with you." Raphael couldn't see it, but Luke was smiling. Raphael finished Luke's shave, then stood up behind him.

"Why don't you start with my pubes, Sir. It'll never be easier, with the cage off and everything."

"Should we pull off the cock ring, baby?"

"Only if you have to. But if you do ... then I'd really be totally uncaged." Luke could see the conflict in Raphael's face.

"Not necessary. I'll just pull it down a little, like this. Um, by the way, baby, have you looked at your cock?"

"No. Should I?" Knowing Raphael would never consider touching his own cock, Luke placed his hand under Raphael's balls and lifted cock and balls so Raphael could peer down at them. "Whoa. Look at that. I have a grooved cock, Sir."

"Baby, your cage has engraved a beautiful design on your cock, from all the pressure your erections have produced."

"Do you think its permanent?" Raphael asked, almost hopefully. He didn't seem the slightest bit concerned.

"Probably not. But I guess we'll never know, will we?"

"Nope. As soon as you're done here, you have to lock me back up." Luke smiled up at Raphael from his vantage point level with Raphael's grooved cock.

"Promise, baby." Luke reached for the can and lathered up Raphael's cock, balls and pubic area, and shaved the stubble in no time. Raphael's immaculately smooth Filipino body made this particular chore an easy one. As soon as he finished, he stepped out of the shower and dashed into the bedroom to retrieve Raphael's cage and keys. As he gave the cage a quick scrub with soapy water he asked, "Any last words for your unlocked grooved cock?"

"Thank you, leather boy cock for making my Sir so happy today. Now, get back where you belong." Luke laughed as he sprayed the antiseptic spray on the urethral tube before sliding the cage in place. It didn't take long, what with the cock ring already in place. Raphael sighed audibly as Luke pulled the key out of the lock and put it aside. He stood up and pulled Raphael into a damp embrace. "That's better," Raphael whispered. "Much better. Okay, my turn." He sat down, leaving room for Luke to sit down behind him so he could shave Raphael's high 'n tight. Ten minutes later, both men we're freshly shaved for another day. Almost. As Luke turned to replace the razor, Raphael took Luke's hand in his. "Sir."

"Yes?"

"As long as I'm going to be locking you up, I should probably shave you first. It has been a couple of days after all." Luke wrinkled his nose.

"Go for it, baby. Make me your all out, locked cock Sir. Like I said ... it was worth it."

"Thank you, Sir." Ten minutes later, both men stepped out of the shower, freshly shaved top and bottom, and one thankfully caged again. The other, of course, moments away from the same fate. Enjoying this novel experience more than he thought he might, Raphael took Luke's hand in his and led him back into the bedroom, where the hot pink Holy Trainer awaited. He picked it up, held it up for Luke to admire, trying his best to hide his smirk.

"Just do it, Raphael. I'm ready. Don't torture me."

"Should we video this, Sir?" Raphael suggested.

"That would qualify as torture, so ... no."

"Okay, fine. Maybe later when I catch you dancing around the living room, cage flapping in the wind." That broke the tension, and Luke laughed.

"If you catch me doing that, then by all means, capture it." Raphael nodded and reached for the keys. He unlocked the tube from the cock ring and knelt at Luke's feet. He gently fitted Luke's balls through the ring, then began folding Luke's cock through it as well. As he feared, the lack of a recent orgasm, combined with some of the hottest sex they'd had in some time, had primed Luke's cock for anything but flaccidity. Raphael jumped up, grabbed the coconut oil and resumed kneeling.

"You're not going to make this easy for me, are you?" he mumbled as he coated Luke's cock.

"Absolutely not," Luke replied. "Besides, how can I, what with this sexy caged, collared, freshly shaved leather boy at my feet. This is a moment other men fantasize about."

"Maybe if you try fantasizing me leading you around the block, naked and caged, on one of Niki's leashes for all our neighbors to enjoy." Raphael dribbled a bit more oil on Luke's cock. "Okay, good, that helps." Luke squirmed, occasionally moaned as Raphael slowly worked him through the cock ring. Finally, it slid into place. "How does that feel?"

"Like a really, really tight cock ring."

"Good. I chose the size well." Raphael looked up at Luke. "Now, for the piéce de résistance." He picked up the tube, took Luke's still not quite flaccid cock in one hand and begin working the tube up Luke's cock. Again, Luke squirmed, but after watching this same procedure applied to Raphael, Ricky and Niki, in some cases more than once, he was not about to wimp out. It didn't hurt, as such, but definitely felt different. As he watched, his cock disappeared inside what seemed to Luke to be an absurdly short hot pink Holy Trainer. It was with resignation that he watched Raphael insert the key, twist it, and then pull it out. It was done. Just like that. Luke was now officially a Locked Cock Brother. Raphael stood, tossed the key on the bed, and pulled Luke into an embrace. As Raphael slid his tongue into Luke's waiting mouth Luke got his first taste of what it feels like to have a caged erection.

"Damn!" Luke looked at Raphael with a whole new level of respect. "Fuuuuuck." Raphael grinned and flicked one of Luke's nipples.

"Enjoy it, Sir. You've earned it. Oh, and it gets even better when you're plugged."

# Four

## HOME SWEET HOME

"OKAY, MIJO, IT'S SAFE now!" Juan yelled as he pulled the shower curtain aside, expecting Ricky to still be in the living room. Not likely. Ricky was standing patiently on the other side of the curtain, unable to waste another second before throwing himself on Juan. Juan laughed as Ricky pounced, landing the two of them against the tiled wall. Ricky wrapped his arms around Juan and tilted his head back, eyes closed and lips puckered. Imagining this vision is what had sustained Juan over the past month. Finally, it was real. In the flesh, the angelic flesh, of his world's best locked cock leather boy. They kissed, they devoured one another. Slowly Juan slid down the wall, taking Ricky with him, without breaking the kiss, until they were seated, legs intertwined clumsily at first, until Ricky managed to wrap his legs around Juan's waist. Ricky rubbed his hands up and down Juan's back, a back still knotted with tense muscles. Finally, Ricky pulled his lips away and looked deeply into Juan's eyes. Eyes still slightly ringed with the imprint of PPE goggles. Juan had never looked more perfect to Ricky.

"Papito, I am so proud of you. What you did was so brave. But I am glad you are finally home."

"I missed you so much, mijo. I missed your smile ..." Juan fingered the little gold ball just below Ricky's supple, smiling lips. "I missed your kisses. Your beautiful eyes ... I couldn't sleep, not just because of the work, but because you weren't there, by my side. I don't ever want to sleep alone again, mijo."

"Well, if I have anything to say about it, you never will. It was so lonely here without you."

"I'm sure. You couldn't even be with the rest of the family, could you?" Ricky slowly shook his head as his eyes dropped and he fingered the rings in Juan's nipples. "Speaking of brave, look who's talking! You were out there five nights a week, delivering DoorDash and dealing with all kinds of people without all the PPE I had."

"Um, seven nights a week, Papito. I had nothing else to do." Ricky invoked that adorable smile Raymond had witnessed and offered, "If it's okay with you, I think I'll take a couple days off now, and pin you down to the bed."

"What? Only two days? I have to quarantine for two weeks, sweetie."

"Okay, two weeks, Papito! Maybe by then I'll have massaged all those kinky muscles out of your back." Ricky rubbed Juan's biceps in demonstration.

"That sounds pretty good to me. Come on, let me dry off, and we'll, ah, get reacquainted." Ricky unraveled himself from Juan and stood up, offering a hand to Juan. Once Juan was upright, Ricky grabbed a towel and began rubbing Juan down. "It's good to be home, mijo." Ricky flashed a grin and knelt down to be sure he didn't miss any of Juan's ample manhood with the towel. He tugged at Juan's prince albert with his tongue teasingly, and looked up at Juan from this perfect leather boy vantage point.

"Your mijo is hungry, Papito. Let's go get reacquainted."

'Okay, but first, if we're *really* going to get reacquainted ..." Juan turned away, opened a drawer in the vanity and pulled out Ricky's keys. "Hmmm, right where I left them. It looks like you haven't unlocked while I was gone, Ricky."

"Nope," Ricky proudly responded. "Only you get to unlock me, Papito. Except, you know, that one time when Alex wired up my cage for the wedding. Oh, and the strip act. But never me." He flashed a satisfied grin. "Besides, I figured out a way to keep clean without unlocking."

"That's my boy," Juan placed his free hand on Ricky's shoulder. "So, this is the longest you've gone without unlocking." Ricky nodded proudly. "You must be horny as fuck."

"Why don't you use that key, and I'll show you just how horny I am ... Sir." Juan leaned down and again pressed his lips on Ricky's. Ricky pulled close and wrapped his arms around Juan's waist. After a moment, Juan pulled free, knelt down and inserted the key into Ricky's baby blue Holy Trainer. He pulled the lock free and reached around to put the key on the vanity, then turned back, took hold of the HT tube and pulled it off. Ricky's cock bounced, clearly already erect despite the cage. Ricky giggled as Juan licked the tip.

"If it's okay with you, mijo, can we do something a little different? I've missed your perfect leather boy cock all this time, and obviously you have too." Juan squeezed Ricky's rigid cock. "I'm pretty sure you've missed mine, so why don't we start getting reacquainted with a little sixty-nine? You know, plain old vanilla gay sex. Like we did when we first met. More than anything, I just want to make love to you right now." As he spoke, Juan worked the Holy Trainer cock ring free of Ricky's anatomy, which left the stainless-steel collar around Ricky's neck as the only marker of his status as Juan's locked cock leather boy.

"I'll do anything you want, Papito. Anything. And yes, I've missed your cock. All of you. I'm so happy!" Ricky turned and raced into the bedroom and jumped on the bed. Juan was right behind, delighting in the view of Ricky's naked abandon. As a locked cock boy, Ricky most enjoyed being fucked by Juan, especially after he had finally mastered the art of the 'hands free' orgasm, which Juan (and maybe Raphael, a little) had patiently helped him discover. It had taken a lot of practice, diligent practice they had both fully enjoyed, each and every session. As much as Juan loved dominating Ricky, however, today he just wanted to revel in Ricky's presence. To touch, smell and taste every adorable inch of him. Yes, he'd indulged in sucking Ricky on occasion, although rarely, as Ricky was adamant about remaining locked as much as possible. Today, though, would be the first time, in a long time, that they would mutually suck one another. Enjoying all of each other, unfettered, on this long-awaited day just seemed right. As Juan climbed on top of Ricky, and their lips met again, he immediately noticed the difference, feeling Ricky's erect cock against his own. It was so tempting to immediately go down on Ricky, but there was no hurry. This was a homecoming they'd hopefully never have to celebrate again. No reason not to take it slowly, one inch at a time.

The kisses evolved, with Juan's lips searching every inch of Ricky's face, licking his septum ring, his labret, anointing each closed eye, brushing his dense eyebrows, sucking each pierced earlobe until Ricky moaned and squirmed under Juan's weight. When he got to Ricky's forehead, Juan had to stop and laugh.

"Mijo, your high 'n tight isn't so tight anymore. I hadn't really noticed it on Facetime."

"Yeah. You're looking at four weeks of nobody to keep it shaved and buzzed. Almost everybody else in the family had someone to keep them neat. I thought about trying to do it by myself, but it didn't really matter. Nobody could see it with my helmet on."

"I guess that's true. Well, we'll take care of it later today, or tomorrow, or whenever we get out of bed again." Ricky grinned.

"Yeah ... maybe Monday, Papito." Juan laughed.

"Atta boy." Juan smiled as he straightened up, knees on either side of Ricky's hips, and began to unscrew his prince albert ring.

"What are you doing?" Ricky put his hands on Juan's thighs. "Sir, I love your PA."

"I know, mijo, but it's been a while since you sucked me, and I want it to be just me and you. Today, I don't want anything between your lips and me." While still straddling Ricky, Juan reached over and placed the ring on the nightstand, then straightened back up, Ricky's hands still on each of his thighs. He looked down at Ricky who was looking up at Juan a little too seriously. "You are so beautiful, mijo." Ricky's smile returned. Juan lowered his head and began teasing Ricky's nipples with his lips and tongue, back and forth, one, then the other. Ricky dug his hands into Juan's hair, which had also grown to a length Ricky had never seen before. Before he could comment on it, Juan pulled away, working his way down to Ricky's trademark, washboard abs — the attribute that never escaped notice by anyone seeing him naked for the first time. Juan lingered there, worshipping, tasting, revering. If there was any part of Ricky's body that commanded reverence and envy by those who didn't know him, it was usually his abs. Juan paid them their due. Then, as his lips and tongue resumed their inventory, he found his way, finally, to Ricky's unlocked cock. Juan lifted his left leg, rotated and straddled Ricky's torso, so Ricky could fully participate in what would hopefully be a very long session of mutual fellatio. Juan felt Ricky take hold of his erection and guide it to his lips. Juan spread his knees to lower his hips for Ricky as well as his shoulders, elbows on either side of Ricky's thighs, and for the first time in many weeks, slid Ricky's cock into his mouth. Both men moaned as each gave and got what they had been denied for so long. A month for Juan, longer than that for Ricky, as he hadn't been unlocked for weeks before Juan's departure, except for brief, weekly cleanings. Both men took their time, took it unusually slowly, neither wanting to come anytime soon. For as long as possible, both men feasted. Eventually, sooner than he wanted, Ricky feared he was about to come, and he paused, releasing Juan's cock and squirming in an attempt to slip out of Juan's mouth. Juan knew exactly what was happening. He released Ricky's cock, raised up, and rotated around, lifting a leg, so that he could lay down on his side beside Ricky, face to face. Ricky turned his head and Juan took it in one hand as they began kissing again, creating a single organism, breathing as one, tongue layered on tongue. Ricky rolled to his side so he could put an arm around Juan's torso and pull himself closer. Once again, they were chest to chest, cock to cock. Finally, Juan broke the seal.

"You taste so damn good, mijo," he smiled. "Sorry if I was too, um, energetic down there."

"You were wonderful. It's just that it's been, you know, so long, that I almost lost control. I want you to come first, Papito." Again, that smile.

"Well, to be honest, I don't want either of us to come any time soon. I want to make love to you until one of us finally says 'enough!'"

"Well, that won't be me, Papito." Ricky took a deep breath and slowly exhaled as he stared into Juan's eyes. "Being here with you, like this, is all I've wanted since the day you left. And I don't ever want it to end." Juan smiled and placed a finger under Ricky's chin and tugged up on it.

"Well, having you in my life is more than I thought I would ever have. You're a dream come true, Ricky. It's one dream that will never end, no matter how many times you come." Juan pushed Ricky over onto his back again and resumed his position. He wiggled his ass as he looked back at Ricky and said, "Don't hold back, mijo. Your Papito is hungry for his leather boy's cum." Then, he dived in, taking Ricky to the root. Ricky grabbed Juan and swallowed, determined to make Juan come first. Of course, Juan, being the more experienced, had the advantage, not that it was a contest. Still, in the end, Juan won.

"I see Mateo's door is still closed." Alex returned from his and Greg's bedroom where he'd been folding laundry. Actually, folding Mateo's laundry, since he was the only one leaving the house with any regularity. The routine was for him to put his clothes directly into the washer upon returning from a shift, and then Alex would run it whenever it amounted to a full load. Otherwise, with the three of them living life naked, sheets and towels were all that accumulated during the week.

"Yeah, I assume our boy is having his nightly virtual date with Ryan," Steve said, wiggling his eyebrows. Alex set the laundry basket down and joined Steve on the couch. Steve put his tablet down and squeezed Alex's thigh. "Poor guy."

"No kidding. He gets his first boyfriend, and within weeks, a pandemic explodes and everything comes to a halt. I wish Ryan had just moved in with us when they closed the dorms and shifted all Ryan's classes to online."

"Well, I think Ryan's parents had a majority vote, Alex. Plus, don't you think it was awfully early for them to consider moving in together? They'd only had a handful of dates."

"There you go being sensible again," Alex pouted. "I mean, I know you're right, but it just seems so unfair to Mateo."

"He'll be fine. Besides, this could be a good test. Is this just a passing infatuation for Ryan ... remember his brief stint with what was his name? Clifford? Or does he really have feelings for Mateo?" Alex nodded and rubbed Greg's shoulder. He got up, went into the kitchen and returned with a bottle of Yerba Mate and two glasses. Once he'd poured, he handed one to Greg and held his out for a toast.

"Here's to Juan and Ricky. I'll bet I know what they're doing right now." Their glasses clinked.

"Probably the same thing Mateo and Ryan are doing ... only a lot more satisfying."

"You think?"

"Oh, come on. Mateo's nineteen. Plus Ryan can't keep from springing boners, even with an audience. Of course they're beating off together. I would. You sure as hell would. That cage you're wearing proves it!" Greg held his glass out, suggesting another toast.

"If you think I'm going to toast you locking me up, you can forget it, buddy." Alex took a long draught of his mate and sat the glass down. Then he laughed, picked it back up and touched glasses with Greg. "And it's a good thing you did, I guess." At that moment Mateo's door opened and he glanced at Greg and Alex, cleared his throat, then walked down the hallway to the bathroom. They could hear the water running for a longer time than expected. He returned to his room, leaving the door open.

"Called it!" Greg grinned. Alex leaned down kissed the shaft of Greg's flaccid cock, then sat back up.

"I suppose you think that entitles you to a bonus blow job tonight." Greg wiggled his eyebrows again.

"Well, yeah, if Mateo's up for it."

"You bitch!" Alex spat as he punched Greg's biceps. "You just lost your bonus BJ, mister."

"What are you guys fighting about?" Mateo asked as he entered, looking only a little flushed. "Oh, my clothes? Thanks, Alex! I was going to do that." Mateo carried the laundry basket into his room and immediately returned.

"You're welcome, Mateo, besides you were busy," Alex flashed a wicked grin to Mateo. "Anyway, we're not fighting, sweetie, we're just goofing around." Alex scooted away from Greg and patted the seat cushion between them in invitation. Mateo slipped in between them and sat. Greg handed him his glass, and Mateo sipped, then licked his lips and smiled.

"Goofing around," Mateo repeated. "I like how that sounds."

"How's Ryan?" Alex asked, treating his and Greg's almost certainly correct assumption as a reality.

"He wishes to be here. I, too, wish he was here. But what can we do? At least we can see and talk almost every day. Is okay."

"Does he get naked for you when you talk?" Alex asked, with the same wicked grin.

"Alex!" Greg reacted. Mateo laughed.

"Si. When he calls, he is already naked, just like me. Just like all of us. 'Fair is fair,' he says. He is jealous, I think." Mateo smiled. "Jealous ... right?" Alex nodded. "I laugh with him about it sometimes. He has to lock his bedroom door ... in case, you know ... his mamá."

"I'll bet he is jealous of Alex and me, getting to be with you all the time, Mateo. Do you know if his parents know about the two you?" Greg asked.

'Not sure, Greg." Mateo reached out for another sip of Greg's mate. When he handed the glass back, he sighed. "Wish he was here." Alex couldn't help himself. He put his left arm around Mateo's shoulders and squeezed, while putting his right hand on Mateo's lightly furry thigh. Mateo let out a quiet little sigh and leaned his head against Alex's shoulder. Mateo, wonderfully, innocently, reached down and played with himself, not self-conscious in the slightest around his adopted family, his thoughts with Ryan still. Greg gave him a moment before speaking.

"Mateo, this is a terrible time for all of us, but it won't last forever. We still don't know for sure what the fall semester will be like. Hopefully Ryan will be back, even if most of his classes are online. If so, I have an idea."

"¿Qué? Mateo's hands ceased their activity as he lifted his head and turned to Greg.

"Well, actually Alex gets credit for this, but it's something to think about. If Ryan is able to return in the fall, even with most of his classes online, maybe he should live here with you, off campus. His parents would save money. We'd charge a lot less than the school does for his room and board. A win-win."

"Sorry. Room and board? Off campos?" Alex offered a quick translation.

"Could we?!" Mateo's face lit up. "That would be ... okay?"

"As long as he obeys the house rules," Alex squeezed Mateo's thigh. "You know ..."

"Strip or starve!" Mateo laughed. "I remember. You sure?" Greg leaned forward to peer around Mateo at Alex. They both nodded.

"We're sure. If, and it may be a very big if, Ryan is even allowed back for classes in the fall. Everything is still unknown," Greg answered. "It would be a good idea to talk to Ryan about it before his parents commit to dorm fees. Give them time to decide. It'll give Ryan a reason to tell them about you if he hasn't already."

"Does he have a picture of you?" Alex asked.

"Yeah ... but I'm naked."

"Of course you are," Alex laughed. "Okay, so maybe you can send him a more modest one, or better yet he can introduce you to them over Facetime ... with a shirt on, of course. They won't be able to say no to you. If they want to meet us too, to feel comfortable, I guess we can put on shirts for a call, too. Whatever it takes, Mateo."

"Thank you, amigos! You are ... wonderful. You really are, um ... los mejores hermanos!"

"Greg," Alex laughed, learning forward again around the suddenly beaming Mateo. "That'll be our first tattoos, ala Raphael and Luke. 'Los Mejores Hermanos.' I like it!"

"I have no idea what it means, but I'll defer to Mateo any day."

"It means," Alex began, but Mateo interrupted.

"It means ... the bestest brothers!"

"Close enough, muchacho," Alex laughed. He stood up, reached for Greg's empty glass and started for the kitchen. Mateo jumped up and reached for Alex.

"Wait. Alex ..." As Alex turned, Mateo put one arm around him and kissed him, a real kiss, full on the mouth, for the first time ever. "Thank you. I love you both so much." Then he turned to Greg and spread his arms, inviting Greg to stand up for his own embrace. He did, and he was duly rewarded by a very happy Mateo.

## Five

## ADVENTURE ON NOE STREET

IN SOME WAYS MONDAY mornings in the age of COVID weren't quite as brutal as the Mondays of yore. Niki hadn't had to work a late shift the night before, and Steve didn't have to get up early to commute, so they now awakened naturally, without an alarm. This particular Monday Steve awoke in bed alone. Niki had refused to let himself come while playing with Steve on Saturday, wanting to ripen his erotic puppy state as fully as possible, his favorite way of coping with the loss, hopefully temporary, of his job as puptender at the Powerhouse. He'd remained in full pup gear, and in full pup headspace all weekend, and just like at Obedience School, he spent the entire time as Steve's pet. Eating, drinking as a pup. Barking, whining when he wanted his favorite bone, sleeping in the dog bed Saturday and Sunday nights. Some guys might have considered this selfish on Niki's part, but by now it was simply one aspect of a very rewarding marriage. Afterall, Pup Niki's favorite bone was always handy, right there between Steve's thighs. And whether as an obedient pup or as a loving human husband, Niki's devotion to Steve was unconditional.

Steve pulled himself out of bed and walked over to where Pup Niki was curled up. He reached down and rubbed his ass and tugged on his tail. Pup Niki stirred, raised up on his front paws and barked a cheery good morning. Steve knelt down and addressed Pup Niki. "Should I make Pup Niki a puppy breakfast or a cute husband breakfast?" Pup Niki rotated his head back and forth, considering. "Let me know." Steve stood and headed for the bathroom. As he relieved himself, Pup Niki trotted in and sat back on his haunches, lifting both mitted paws, indicating Steve could unlock them. "Ah, good, a handsome husband breakfast it is." Pup Niki barked affirmatively. Both returned to the bedroom where Steve retrieved Pup Niki's keyring, and he knelt again. Pup Niki held out one paw, then the other so Steve could unlock and remove the

mitts. Then he gently pulled the hood over Pup Niki's head. The
collar and cage were permanent accessories, suitable for pup or man.
The pup tail was optional for Niki the human, depending on his
mood. Since he didn't turn and present, Steve knew it wasn't coming
out, at least not yet. Steve stood and held out a hand to assist Niki
in standing. Once upright, Niki embraced Steve wordlessly for a long
moment, before tilting his head for a kiss.

"Thank you for indulging me," Niki muttered after their lips parted, his first words in almost two days.

"Of course, Niki. Anytime. I know you miss puptending. I know
you miss all the other pups, and the puppy park. It's actually fun
for me, too, so don't worry about it. Let's eat. You must be ready
for something besides puppy food, right?" Niki nodded, took Steve's
hand and led him into the kitchen.

"You sit, I'll make breakfast," Niki said as he started filling the
teapot with water. Steve didn't object. Besides, he knew Niki had a
not so veiled ulterior motive. Whatever he was fixing was bound to be
a little more fattening than what Steve might have suggested. As Steve
sat, Niki portioned coffee grounds into the French press pot, pulled
frozen waffles out of the freezer, then a carton of eggs from the fridge.

"Three waffles or four?" Niki asked over his shoulder.

"What happened to two?"

"Four it is." Niki's tail wagged wickedly. Steve watched silently as
Niki labored, toasting, brewing and scrambling. Within minutes he
was done, placing a plate in front of Steve, along with a cup of coffee.
While Steve took his first bite, Niki scurried to the fridge for the
cranberry juice, then sat down at his place next to Steve. Steve leaned
over and offered a grateful kiss.

"This is great, Niki." He took another bite. "How soon until my
belly is as big as Jake's?"

"It's measured in calories, not time, my sexy stud muffin," Niki
smiled. "I don't think we should go to that extreme. If that's okay."

"Good. If we did, I wouldn't be able to tie my shoes."

"I'd do it for you. Gladly."

"Except when you're in pup mode and mitted."

"Good point. So, we'll stop short of that. I kind of like your belly
like it is now. Don't you?"

"Well," Steve paused to chew and swallow. "I admit I like it more
than I ever thought I would." He took another bite and chewed. "I
guess what I like best about it is how much you like it ... how much
you like playing with it." Niki smiled, licked some syrup from his lips
and leaned over for another kiss. One accompanied by a gentle belly
rub.

"It's only fair, really. You turned me into a pup. It's only fair that I get to turn you into a bear."

"You have point," Steve said. "Although, it wasn't really my idea to make a pup out of you. You already were a pup ... inside. We just helped you come out of the pup closet. Or kennel. Or whatever."

"And I'm forever grateful," Niki laughed. "I ..." He was interrupted by the doorbell.

"Did you order something?" Steve asked as he pushed back his chair and stood.

"I don't think so ... Let me go, I'll get it." Niki rounded the corner, walked to the door and opened it. A masked and gloved courier was standing on the other side. Niki, caged, collared, mohawked and sexy as ever, and totally unabashed, asked, "Can I help you?"

"Umm, ah, I, ah ... I have a parcel for Steve Phillips."

"He's here. I'll take it." The courier was not so subtly glancing at Niki's cage.

"Oh, I'm sorry. I can only release it to Steve Phillips."

"Steve!" Niki turned as he called out, revealing his wagging tail to the courier. "Can you come here?" Steve walked up, compounding the courier's unease.

"Hello," Steve smiled, looking the courier directly in the eyes, enjoying the fact that he and Niki were no doubt making the courier's day. Or, at least providing him with some racy gossip.

"Steve Phillips? I have a package, but I need an ID and a signature."
"ID?"

"Yeah, sorry." The poor guy was clearly uneasy, not being as experienced as the mailman. Or the DoorDash guys. Steve disappeared.

"Wanna come in?" Niki offered, stepping aside.

"It's okay." The courier didn't budge. Before Niki could respond Steve returned with his driver's license. He was wearing a mask now, partly to put the courier at ease and partly as a subtle joke. The courier took the license, jotted something on his manifest, handed it Steve and asked, "If you could sign here, sir." Steve took back his license, signed, and returned the clipboard. The courier pulled a large manila envelope out of his pouch, handed it to Steve and very politely said, "Thank you gentleman. It was a pleasure." He nodded once, turned and headed down the steps.

"Okay, that was weird," Niki said as he closed the door.

"More weird for him than us, I'm sure," Steve replied. "I'm guessing you're the only caged guy he'll encounter all week."

"So far as he knows," Niki laughed. "Who is this from?" Steve looked at the label and shook his head.

"I have no idea. Let's find out." He and Niki walked over to the couch and sat. As Niki rubbed Steve's thigh, Steve ripped open the envelope. He pulled out a sheaf of papers and sat the envelope on the coffee table with a clunk. As he began looking at the papers, Niki picked up the envelope and pulled out a set of keys. He studied them as Steve skimmed the cover letter.

"It's a law firm." Niki leaned over and Steve positioned the papers so Niki could read along. "Ohhhh. Now I understand."

"Good, 'cause I have no idea what this is." Niki set the keys on top of the envelope. Steve sat up straighter and turned to Niki.

"I guess we haven't had a chance to talk since Saturday, when Ben called. Just before our meet up with the family."

"Oh, yeah. So, what's going on?" Niki picked up the keys again.

"You remember Ben, right? The guy who transferred to our Melbourne office in Australia last year?" Niki looked uncertain. "Anyway, he called to ask if I'd help him out. His grandfather died, and I guess Ben is the executor of the estate, and the principal beneficiary."

"And he wants you to help him spend all the money? That sounds like fun."

"Not even close. His grandad left him his house. At least that's what Ben wants help with. Apparently, it's been in the family for generations, and Ben asked if I'd keep an eye on it and work with a realtor to sell it. He could have his grandad's attorney do it, but, of course, that'll cost thousands of dollars. Maybe it was a mistake, but I said yes."

"So, he's not coming back himself? Not even for the funeral?"

"No, he isn't. Not with this pandemic. And there really wasn't a funeral. I guess there wasn't much family, which is why Ben is in the will and everything. It's an old house obviously. So, my guess is it will sell for only a million or so at today's prices. That explains why he wanted someone like me to handle it so there'll be more left for him after the sale. He said if he was still living here, he'd hang on to it, you know, for sentimental as well as investment reasons. But it's looking like he may make Australia his home."

"This sounds like a lot of work, Steve. And you said yes?"

"I may be sorry, but, sweetie, houses sell themselves in this town, so I doubt it'll be that much work." Steve looked through the remaining pages. "According to this I'm officially the designated caretaker of the property herein detailed ... you gotta love legalese ... so what do you say we go check it out over lunch. Right now, I have to log in and do some work. Why don't you look through all this and see if I've overlooked anything."

"Okay. I'll clean up the kitchen, too."

Just after one p.m., Steve closed his laptop and walked into the bedroom, where Niki was finishing changing the sheets on the bed. Laundry was an even lighter chore for them than for Alex, Greg and Mateo. He and Steve no longer did it on a schedule, but whenever the hamper was full.

"I pre-ordered lunch, Niki. We can pick it up on our way to the house. It's on Noe. It'll be a nice walk." He approached the closet as Niki opened a dresser drawer. "When was the last time we wore clothes?"

"Let me see," Niki pondered. "When was the last time we went grocery shopping? Was that last week? No ... two weeks ago?"

"I guess. Feels weird, huh?" Niki nodded as he pulled on his caged cock tee from Raphael before going into the bath. He'd put off removing his pup tail until the last minute. It just felt strange not feeling it wag, like something was missing, which of course, it was. He came back, pulled on a pair of shorts. Once both were dressed, they slipped on matching masks. Steve pocketed the keys and the cover letter and they headed out. They made a slight detour to grab lunch, which was bagged and ready at Castro Tarts. Then they headed back to Noe and climbed the hill for a few blocks.

"Let's see. It should be right about ... here?" Steve and Niki stopped at the bottom of a flight of slate steps leading up to a massive, three-story Victorian. Not just any old Victorian, but arguably the grandest house on the block. Steve pulled the cover letter out of his pocket and checked. "Damn. This is it." He started up the steps with Niki right behind, lunch in hand. They reached the porch, crossed to the massive double doors and stopped. Steve consulted the letter again. "We have to enter this code on the security system once we open the door." He showed the code to Niki. "Here goes." Steve tried a key, but it wasn't the right one. He tried another, this one a bit larger than the others, and it worked. He pushed the door open and entered ahead of Niki. The security panel was to the right, and it was beeping. Niki entered the code but the beeping continued. Then, he pressed the # key. The beeping stopped.

"Nice instructions, Mr. Lawyer," Niki chided.

"No matter. You figured it out. I knew there was a reason I brought you."

"You're welcome. So, this guy Ben ... did you know he was rich?"

"No. I don't think he is. This was his grandparents' house. And his great-grandparents' before that. And so on, I guess. But, yeah ... wow. Let's check it out." They were standing in a wide foyer that reached half-way back into the house. There were large pocket doors on either side, a curving staircase further back and a multicolored parquet floor at their feet. Niki slid open the door to the right to reveal a living room half the size of their apartment. It was tastefully, classically furnished.

"Multiple sofas, check," Niki noted. "Crystal chandelier, check. Cove moldings, check. Oh, built-in seating in the bay window ... check."

"Grandpa Ben had good taste, huh?"

"Ben's grandpa was also named Ben? Not terribly original, just like the interior design. But very tasteful, yeah. Nice living room."

"More properly called a parlor, or sitting room," Steve opined. "Let's try next door," he suggested. They crossed the foyer and Steve slid that pocket door open.

"Okay ... this will be my favorite room," Niki purred. They entered a den or library, about half the size of the 'parlor.' Except for the bay window, fireplace and the door, the walls were lined with bookshelves, and the bookshelves were filled with books. There was a large desk, two chairs arranged in front of the fireplace, with a low table between them. "This is where we'll relax in the evening, with our glasses of cognac," Niki proclaimed as he tried out one of the chairs. "Oh, Jeeves, another cognac, please," he looked longingly at Steve, already delegating the role of Jeeves to him. Steve sat down in the other chair and stretched out his legs so they could warm before the imaginary fire.

"So, you're ready to move in without even seeing the rest of the house?"

"I'm sold, Mr. Caretaker. Where do I sign?"

"Yeah, I have to admit. This place feels pretty homey, doesn't it? Come on." Steve stood. "Let's see the rest."

"So ... you think this will only fetch a million dollars, huh?"

"A slight misjudgment, Mr. Buyer. I was a bit premature in my calculations. We'll need to renegotiate. Have your broker call mine." Steve took Niki's hand and led him back into the foyer and toward the back of the house.

"Wait," Niki stopped moving. Steve turned to face him. "If this is going to be a tour of my new house, I need to see it properly dressed." Steve gave Niki a clueless look. "As in, undressed." Niki began pulling off his shorts. Steve laughed, but didn't object. He was just pleased to see Niki happy and excited about something for a change. As soon as both were comfortably naked, Niki took Steve's hand and led the way. Beyond the staircase, on the left was an open doorway, leading to a dining room, at its center a long table with ten chairs. In addition to a matching buffet, several more chairs were against two walls. Somewhere there must be a few leaves to expand the table even longer.

"Dining for ten, check," Steve said, mimicking Niki's earlier inventory.

"Another crystal chandelier, check," Niki chimed in. Steve nosed around in the drawers and doors of the buffet.

"Silver service for ... twenty. Check," Steve reported. Niki wandered over to what he thought was the door to the kitchen, but what turned out to be a butler's pantry between the two rooms. He opened a beveled glass door and took out a champagne flute and flicked it with a finger. The glass sang.

"Crystal service to go with the silver. Check." Steve joined Niki and put a hand around one butt cheek as Niki replaced the flute. "Looks like we won't have to do a lot of shopping before we move in, Steve."

"Nope. Ready for immediate occupancy. Okay, dreamer, let's check out the kitchen." The kitchen beyond was in stark contrast to the rest of the house, so far. The nineteenth century was left behind, and before them was an up-to-date, no, more like a designer kitchen. Stainless steel, composites, an eight-burner gas range, wall mounted ovens and no crystal chandelier. Just recessed lighting and LED spots.

"Where's the fridge?" Niki wondered aloud. "I suppose it has its own room."

"I'm guessing ..." Steve walked over to a solid, or seemingly solid, wood paneled wall. He pushed against the wall in two or three places before finding the sweet spot, where the wall bounced open, revealing side by side restaurant sized chillers. "I think Grandpa Ben liked to cook."

"And high-tech gadgets," Niki agreed. "Did Ben say anything about the house, or his grandpa to you?"

"Not really. He talked like it was just an ordinary family house. Maybe Grandpa made a few improvements since my Ben was last here. This all looks pretty state of the art. Kinda sad, if he didn't get to enjoy it very long."

"Well, we'll make the most of it for him," Niki said, continuing his fantasy. "Oh, look, here's a back stairway. Let's check out upstairs." Steve grabbed Niki's hand and pulled him close.

"My puppy's not taking the back stairs, not the first time anyway." He led Niki through another door leading directly to the foyer and up the grand staircase. On the second floor they found four bedrooms. Upon entering the first, Niki decided it must be the master bedroom, since it had its own bath. But, as they soon discovered, so did each of the others.

"Okay, we're going to have to hire help, Steve. I'm not cleaning all these toilets and showers."

"We'll just use a different bed and bath each week, so you'll only have to clean one at a time. You'll be fine." Niki laughed.

"What if we can't remember which bedroom we used last week?" Steve pulled Niki into a side hug without responding. He had to admit, dreaming was kind of fun. Niki hadn't been this animated in a long time. Neither of them had been.

"I wonder what's upstairs. A ballroom, maybe?" Steve pondered as he led Niki to the continuation of the staircase. The walls of the third floor were set back a bit, allowing for a dramatic oval balustrade that circled the entire floor, allowing an open view of the floor below. There were only three doors on this floor. One opened to another bedroom, much like the others. The other revealed the largest of the bedrooms, with the most dramatic view, of not just the street below through more bay windows, but from the side of the house, much larger and obviously more modern windows revealed the city skyline and bay beyond.

"This must have been Grandpa's room," Steve surmised.

"Yeah." Niki opened a double door expecting a closet, but was greeted with yet another bath. "Um, yeah, this is definitely the master bedroom. Check this out." Steve joined him in admiring another nod to the twenty-first century. Toto toilet, bidet, walk-in shower so big there was no need for a door or curtain, double sink vanity and a jacuzzi tub under a nearly floor to ceiling window replicating the downtown view from the bedroom. Niki turned to Steve, pressed his lips to Steve's ear and whispered, "I'm not leaving until I make sure this tub still works."

"We'll do that, I promise, but not right now, sweetie. I have to get back to work. I wasn't expecting to take this long, and we haven't even eaten our lunch. So many rooms..." Niki whimpered, despite the lack of pup gear, but he followed Steve out of the bedroom and back toward the stairs.

"Wait, where does this door go?" Niki asked as they passed the third door.

"Okay, but let's be quick," Steve relented. He opened the door, again expecting to find a closet, but it revealed yet another, narrow winding staircase. "Jeez, this is like the House on the Rock." He motioned for Niki to go first, then they began climbing the stairs. There was no door at the other end, just an open, circular room at the top of a turret they hadn't noticed earlier, with windows all around.

"Perfect," Niki said softly.

"Perfect?" Steve asked.

"Yeah. When we have the family over, this is where we'll have our Tuesday dinners. With the city lighting up at dusk."

"Wouldn't it be more appropriate to dine in the formal dining room, Mr. Malaluan-Phillips?"

"When have we ever been formal? Okay, maybe. But we should at least retire here for dessert. And cognac. Don't forget the cognac."

"Okay, dreamer. Whatever you say. Come on, we really have to go." Niki took his time wandering back down the three flights of stairs to the front door. Taking in every detail he could as he passed doors, console tables, artwork. He was falling in love with the house. When they reached the foyer, both men dressed, then Steve picked up their lunch and pointed to the security panel. "I'm leaving the security system to you, since you did so well before." Niki punched in the code, and the # key, generating three quick beeps. They opened the door and Niki took one last look back before pulling the door closed. Aware of how Niki felt, Steve handed the keys to him, so Niki could lock up. They made their way down the steps to the sidewalk below and headed home.

# Six

## A Socially Distanced Reunion

RAPHAEL WAS WRAPPING UP a couple of loose ends at his workstation. It was nearly six p.m. and he was aiming to close up shop early for once. Monday was not one of the days Luke worked, so he was in charge of dinner, which usually meant delivery or take-out. Not that Luke was outright intimidated by Raphael's prowess in the kitchen, and Raphael always complimented every dish he made, but Luke felt cooking was the one endeavor where he'd never measure up to Raphael. Tonight, however, he was giving it his best with a quiche and salad. He'd cheated, of course, with a frozen crust. Even Raphael had trouble with a scratch crust, so he didn't feel it was that much of a compromise. With the salad done, and in the fridge, the quiche prepared and ready to slide into the oven, Luke poured two glasses of Fumé Blanc and carried them to the dining room slash office. He set them down next to Raphael's mouse pad, moved behind Raphael and slid his hands under the straps of Raphael's harness to rub his shoulders.

"Umm, that feels nice," Raphael sighed. "And I'm just. About. Done." He closed the laptop, picked up the glasses, handed one to Luke and they toasted. "I don't smell anything. What are we having?"

"Quiche. I didn't want to put it in the oven too soon. Now that you're done, I'll do it."

"How about a little more back rub first, Sir ... we have all evening. For once. In fact ..." Raphael stood and turned his chair so that it faced away from the table, then sat back down. "Here, Sir, sit on my lap facing me, so you can massage my shoulders from the front." Luke looked at Raphael curiously, but set his glass down and settled onto Raphael's lap. As soon as he slid his hands under the harness straps Raphael reached down and cupped Luke's locked cock.

"Now I get it," Luke reacted, giving Raphael a look of disdain. "You just want to rub it in."

"Whatever do you mean?" Raphael feigned innocence. Then he grinned and leaned forward, demanding a kiss. As they tongue wrestled Luke's erection grew, but of course it had nowhere to go.

"Fuck," he grimaced as he pulled his lips away. "Ricky was right. You are mean. Does it ever get any easier?" Raphael massaged Luke's balls with his fingertips. "You bastard!"

"I can't believe you locked me up, for life, never having been locked yourself. I'm enjoying The Education of Mr. Luke Mitchell. And remember, you agreed to be locked up." Luke leaned forward for another kiss, since the torture inside his cage was probably already at maximum intensity. After a few shared breaths, he pulled away to respond.

"First of all, it was never my intention for you to be permanently caged. That, Mr. Malaluan, was all your doing. And I agreed to be locked only because you dared me. You know I can't refuse a dare. By the way, I only have five more days to go."

"This time around," Raphael grinned as he tweaked Luke's handy nipples. "If you enjoyed blowing me as much as I enjoyed your doing it, it won't be long before you are my locked cock Braveheart again."

"Don't hold your breath. I went more than a year and a half between BJs this time." Luke leaned back and displayed his best Cheshire Cat grin.

"Yeah, but you didn't even think it was an option until I offered it. Now you've tasted the forbidden fruit." Luke laughed as he took Raphael's hands in his, defending his nipples, and in the process, his caged cock.

"Yes, baby, you're a fruit all right. My tasty fruit. My beautiful, sexy, but definitely not forbidden fruit." At that he delivered one quick peck and rose up and headed into the kitchen to finish dinner. Raphael's phone chimed just as Luke was returning to rescue his wine.

"It's a group text from Ricky asking when we're all available to see Juan. I guess they finally climbed out of bed." Luke handed Raphael his glass and offered his own in another toast.

"To Juan. Tell Ricky ASAP works for us." Raphael thumbed a reply. It wasn't until they were nearly finished with dinner, which was actually pretty tasty, that Ricky responded with an eight o'clock invite.

"Ricky's in a good mood ... no surprise. It says BYOLCB. Which is really kind of funny since he doesn't even know that at the moment, you, Sir, are among the Locked Cock Brotherhood."

"And we're going to keep it that way. Remember? It's our little secret." Raphael gave a half-hearted pout, not really wanting to display a locked cock Luke over Zoom anyway. It would be much more fun to do it in person, something he was reasonably certain he could arrange when the time came. "Let's clean up dinner, then 'clean up' ourselves so we look great for Juan."

"Agreed. You haven't cleaned up my high 'n tight since Saturday and your mohawk will soon look like a faux-hawk. This shelter in place business is leading to lackadaisical hygiene for both of us." Luke reached over and rubbed the stubble on the side of Raphael's head.

"Yeah, but I kind of like you scruffy once in a while, baby. Nice change of pace." Raphael rolled his eyes as he carried the dishes into the kitchen. Once the dishwasher was loaded, they assumed their positions in the shower and perfected one another's appearances. Not that Juan or anybody else would care or probably even notice over the internet. Really, it was more the time together, legs wrapped around waists, intently grooming each other, that mattered in these nightly sessions of head shaving and buzz cutting. It was really all about the ritual, about the act of devotion.

Freshly showered, at eight on the dot both men were in place, eager to finally see Juan with Ricky. They were prepared, with glasses of bubbly at the ready. Raphael launched the app, logged in and turned to Luke in anticipation. Obviously, everyone else was eager, too, as the screen filled immediately with all four images.

"JUAN!" Everyone greeted the guest of honor almost in unison.

"Hi, guys!' Juan looked great. Like several other family members his hair was longer than anyone had ever seen before, but it actually flattered his sultry good looks. "Boy, have I missed you guys!" Ricky had one arm around Juan's neck, and was beaming at Juan, not at the camera. His bliss clearly not dampened after having spent the past two days no doubt glued to Juan.

"Ricky, we're over here," Niki kidded.

"Yeah, but you're not my Papito," Ricky laughed, turning to the camera briefly. "Doesn't he look amazing, amigos?"

"Welcome home, Juan," Greg said. "We've all missed you. How *are* you?"

"Hey, Greg, thanks. You all look great, too. I'm ... I don't know. I'm just so glad to be home. So, so glad to be back with Ricky." There was a seriousness behind Juan's smile that didn't escape anyone's notice.

"You're our hero, Juan," Alex said. Mateo, sitting between him and Steve, nodded gravely. "Since we can't hug you, how about a round of applause." Everyone clapped, including Ricky. Luke picked up his flute, handed one to Raphael.

"To Juan!" Raphael shouted as he and Luke clinked their glasses in front of the camera.

"Oh, man, why didn't we think of that," Steve cried. "Raphael is always front and center with the bubbly."

"Actually, it was Luke's idea," Raphael admitted. "But, sure, I'll take the credit." He set his glass down and looked intently into the camera. "Juan, you *are* our hero. Ricky has told us some of what you went through. So, what was it like? Seriously, because we're all family ... really, how are you?" Juan took a long, deep breath, then spoke with a somewhat forced smile.

"Raphael ... all of you. I really appreciate your concern. Tell you what, after my isolation is up, maybe we can figure out a way to all be in the same place, socially distanced, and I'll tell you all about it. But, to be honest, it's still pretty raw. Let me just say ... well ... I've never seen so many people die before. And not all older people, guys." He took another deep breath. Ricky laid his head against Juan's shoulder and rubbed out a sniffle. "Right now, all I want to do, what I need to do, is be with you guys and be happy, however we can do that." Juan turned to Ricky, chucked him under the chin and delivered an enviable kiss.

"Go for it, Ricky," Alex cooed. Both Ricky and Juan looked back at the camera with renewed smiles.

"Juan, forgive me," Raphael said quietly. "I wasn't thinking."

"No, no ... you're fine, Raphael. Don't apologize. I appreciate how concerned you are, and I really do want to talk about it ... soon. This pandemic is really, really serious. Not everyone is taking it as seriously as you guys are. So, and I'm not kidding, I'm very proud of how all of you are handling it. Including this guy, here." Juan planted a kiss on top of Ricky's head. "We have enough sanitizer and face masks to outfit the hospital."

"Well, you know," Ricky grinned, "we are both on the front line here."

"How much time off do you have before you have to report back to work, Juan?" Steve asked.

"I'm not a hundred percent sure. I'm in isolation for two weeks. I was tested before I left. I'll get tested again at the end of the two weeks. Electives are still not being scheduled, but there are still a few emergencies now and then ... so maybe in two weeks. They told me my job right now is to decompress. I don't know, maybe I'll help out with some testing stations or something if there aren't enough surgeries. Maybe pitch in down in ER if they need it. We'll see. Right now, as far as I'm concerned, my job is to put a smile on my very patient mijo here." Ricky bounced a little, grinning wider.

"Something tells me DoorDash is going to be short a driver for the next couple of weeks," Greg surmised. Mateo nodded firmly.

"You think?" Ricky laughed. "I threatened to handcuff myself to Juan, but he said that wouldn't be necessary."

"You have handcuffs?" Raphael asked with fake surprise. "Gee, Ricky, maybe before the two weeks are up you can change his mind."

"If not, can we borrow them?" Alex pleaded. Greg looked at him with genuine surprise while Mateo put both hands over his mouth, probably in honest embarrassment. "What? I'm still evolving." Alex ruffled Mateo's hair which, at this rate, would soon be on its way to shoulder length.

"Mateo, you've been awfully quiet," Juan leaned into the frame. "¿Comó te va?"

"I'm good," Mateo answered in accent-free English. "Alex and Greg are good to me. I'm happy. And very happy to see you, Juan."

"He's working too much," Greg offered. Mateo shook his head in disagreement.

"Looks like you've adapted well to living naked. I'm proud of you," Juan grinned and winked.

"Yeah. Is nice. Really nice."

"He's even going on naked video dates with Ryan," Alex revealed to everyone's delight. Mateo gave Alex a dirty look. "What? It's a *good* thing, amigo." Alex turned to the camera. "Right guys?" Everyone agreed. Everyone was happy for Mateo, happy for Juan, happy to have the family, as much as it could be, back together again.

"We had almost talked Ricky into staying with us until your return when you showed up, Juan," Alex continued in his revelations. "We were worried about him, too."

"I know," Juan replied. "I can't tell you how much that means to us. My time away reinforced for me just how much this family we seem to have created means to Ricky and to me. How much I missed you all. It's worth, what?" Juan turned again to Ricky. "Nine hundred and ninety-five dinners, right?"

"Well, like Greg said, who's counting?" Alex laughed. "Nobody's alone now, and that's the most important thing."

"Cheers to that," Luke said, lifting his glass. "We've got to figure out a way to physically get together. And soon. I think Raphael's getting bored with me." Raphael looked down at the hot pink holy trainer locked onto Luke's cock, then up at Luke's face and smiled. The evil smile. Then he turned to the camera.

"Oh, I don't know. I wouldn't call it bored ..." Luke immediately changed the subject.

"What about you two, Steve and Niki? Neither of you have to leave the house. Are you walking? Suffering cabin fever?"

"I'm not sure it's clinical yet, but, yeah. Pretty much. Niki's been pupping out a lot ... and you know how puppies are. They sleep a lot." Niki barked in affirmation, licked Steve's cheek and turned to the camera.

"I miss working," Niki sighed. "A lot. Kinda depressing. And I miss us all getting together, the dinners, the beach, Ricky's awesome pancakes. OH! We did do something really fun earlier today, though."

"Oh, yeah," Steve agreed. "You should have seen Niki."

"What did you guys do?" Raphael asked. "You two go to an outdoor puppy park?"

"Nothing like that," Niki said. "You guys might think it was no big deal, but ..."

"Niki went on kind of a daydream staycation. We toured a very cool house on Noe."

"This house is awesome!" Niki enthused. "I wish you guys could see it. Man. It has a library, a butler's pantry, a turret room with windows all around."

"So, what's this, now?" Luke asked. "Are you guys thinking of moving?"

"No, no, not at all. A colleague of mine, who moved to Australia last year to open our office there, asked me to take care of it for him. His granddad died and left it to him. I'm going to work with a realtor, and everything, so he doesn't have to come back. He's executor of the estate."

"And Steve's the designated caretaker," Niki said.

"Yeah, and Niki's the designated imaginary Lord of the Estate. He's all but moved in. I have to admit, it's a showplace."

"I want to see it!" Raphael pleaded. "I mean, if you're the caretaker, you can show it to me, can't you?"

"Oh, yeah!" Niki nodded furiously, clearly getting excited all over again. "You won't believe how cool it is, Raffie. Let's do it!"

"Well," Steve introduced a dose of reality, "we are supposed to be sheltering in place and everything. Maybe if you're available next time I go over ..." Raphael and Niki subtly nodded to each other over Zoom, and wordlessly initiated a plan, as only two brothers could do. Steve seemed oblivious, but it didn't escape Luke, who squeezed Raphael's thigh. Raphael, he knew, would not be denied. Luke decided to change the subject again.

"Juan and Ricky, is there anything we can bring you, since you're in total quarantine? Modelo, Dos Equis? Lip balm?"

"Energy bars?" Alex suggested. Both Juan and Ricky laughed.

"We're good, guys, but thanks. If we think of anything, we'll let you know. What do you say, Ricky?"

"I have everything I need ... right here," he beamed, wrapping his arm around Juan's neck again.

"Spoken like the best little leather boy in the world," Luke toasted again, although his glass was tragically empty. "And on that note, we should probably let you two go for now. Juan, you're probably still a little jet lagged ... it's after midnight in New York."

"Yeah, a little. Ricky's been pretty generous with the back rubs, though, and that helps."

"Oh, is that what we're calling it now?" Alex laughed "Backrubs?" Ricky stood up, pushed his chair aside, moved halfway behind Juan, and began demonstrating how to give a back rub, his baby blue Holy Trainer moving in and out of sight behind Juan's shoulder as he worked over Juan's defined deltoids.

"On second thought, why don't we all get a refreshing beverage and sit back and watch the Juan and Ricky show," Greg suggested.

"Yeah, they do a good show," Mateo seconded. Alex turned to Mateo in wonder.

"Have you seen the Juan and Ricky show before, Mateo?" he asked, before turning to the camera and wiggling his eyebrows.

"Umm ... I have to go pee," Mateo punted, as he got up and walked out of the view of the camera, giving everyone a show of his own as his perky brown butt exited upstage center.

'Ricky? ..." Alex pressed on fruitlessly. Juan leaned forward with his right arm towards the laptop.

"It was great seeing you all. I love you ... let's do this again soon." Blip. Juan and Ricky's thumbnail went dark.

"Alex, go get Mateo," Niki laughed. "We want details."

"Sorry, Niki," Alex smiled. "Mateo, and I speak from experience, is the epitome of discretion. He hasn't spent enough time around us yet to be otherwise. Just be patient, Niki. We'll get the story one way or another."

"If there even is a story, guys," Greg said.

"Oh, there's a story. Mateo ran off and Juan logged off. There's a story," Raphael asserted. "And I'm betting it's a doozy."

"We all have our stories, Raphael. I think Alex would agree, right Alex?" Luke posed. "It's best to let the storytellers decide when and where to share them. Huh, boys?"

"What?" Niki perked up. "How many stories are there?"

"There are eight million stories in the naked city," Steve intoned in his best voce basso.

"What?!" Niki repeated. "I'm only interested in ... well, two at the moment."

"All in good time, Niki," Luke smiled, mimicking Ricky by putting his arm around Raphael's neck. "That, Niki, is what we call a cliff-hanger." Blip. Luke and Raphael disappeared.

"What just happened?" Niki turned to Steve.

"You'd better ask Alex fast before he ..." but it was too late. Alex and Greg's thumbnail went dark.

"Fuck," Niki muttered. "We were so close."

"I don't think you were close at all, puppy. Not yet anyway. You'll just have to wear Raphael down when you get a chance. You know how to work him better than anybody."

"I guess. It sure was good to see Juan, though. I kinda like his hair longer. It reminds me of how Raphael used to wear his, don't you think?"

"It does, yeah. You should tell him. Maybe he'll keep growing it."

"I will. It would be nice if Raphael grew his long again, too. I always liked it long."

"Good luck with that, Niki. I have a feeling his transformation, like yours, is permanent. And, I might add, all for the better." Steve ruffled Niki's mohawk.

"Speaking of better," Niki turned his attention to Steve's belly, which he rubbed, then gently kissed. "I like your transformation, too." He sat back up and leaned in for a kiss. When they parted, Niki suggested, "I think we still have brownies, don't we?"

"I thought we decided that this was the right belly size, sweetie." Niki thought a moment.

"Just one. I'll split it with you."

Seven

# LUKE, MEET BRUTUS

"WELL, THAT WAS FUN," Raphael said, as he lifted his glass and drained the last drops of his sparkling wine. He sat the glass down and turned his full attention to Luke. He toyed with Luke's left nipple. "It's too bad Jake's shop is closed. I'm sort of in the mood to have him pierce you again. This nipple looks awfully lonely."

"Lonely? It's one of a matched pair, baby, and they're both happy just like this. Well, they're even happier when you're licking them, but you know what I mean."

"Did I say lonely? I meant to say plain and unadorned. Besides, I'm feeling a little dare deprived."

"Are you kidding? Look at my once proud and mighty cock, Raphael. It was your dare that got me locked up like this."

"Yeah, but that dare was issued a long time ago, Sir."

"I'm locked up right now, baby. If anyone's proposing a dare, it should be me." Raphael leaned in to lick Luke's nipple. Luke took Raphael's head in his hands, and closed his eyes. As Raphael nursed, Luke slowly exhaled.

"Is this what you meant by happier?" Raphael teased before returning his attention to Luke's hardening nipple. Unfortunately for Luke, that wasn't the only part of his body that was hardening.

"Oh, here we go again," he said through gritted teeth. "You really know how to torture me, don't you? Ow, ow ... I never thought I'd regret an erection." Raphael released Luke's nipple and raised his lips to Luke's ear.

"Torture sounds like a good idea, Sir," he whispered. "If I don't get to issue a new dare, at least I should get to fully realize this one. Come with me." Raphael stood and held out his hand to Luke. Foolishly, Luke took it and followed Raphael into the bedroom. "Take off your harness, Sir, and sit at the foot of the bed."

"This sounds like a dare," Luke said suspiciously as he did as he was told.

"Um ... like I said, the continuation of a dare ... issued months ago," Raphael replied as he kneeled at the side of the bed. He pulled out the toy bag located there, unzipped it, reached in and found what he was looking for. "Or, you might call it ... torture." He stood and presented an intimidatingly proportioned strap-on. "Sir, may I re-introduce you to Brutus."

"Oh shit! I forgot!" Luke fell back on the bed, his feet still on the floor, his hot pink Holy Trainer on full display. Raphael's Braveheart never looked so vulnerable to him. The reversal in their power exchange was oddly titillating to Raphael. This, he decided, would be fun.

"I'll be gentle, my sweet, little Braveheart," Raphael teased. "Tell me, my dear, are you a virgin?"

"Oh, are we compounding this with role play?" Luke accused as he raised up on his elbows. "What's next, live-stream video?" Raphael laughed. A bwaa ha ha kind of laugh, as he retrieved the lube pump and a cum towel from the night stand, then positioned himself at Luke's feet.

"As I said, I'll be gentle. I want you to enjoy this as much as I do when you fuck me. Now, lay back." It took a minute for Raphael to buckle on the strap-on. Once it was secure, he looked down and laughed.

"What's so funny?"

"It looks ridiculous on me." Luke again raised up long enough to see what Raphael was seeing, then fell back, laughing.

"Oh, baby, maybe you *should* be filming this. You really do look ridiculous."

"Next time. Sir. Consider this a dress rehearsal. Now lift those sexy legs!" Raphael lubed up Brutus, then slid the towel under Luke's ass and began lubing him up. He'd played around Luke's butt hundreds of times, rimmed him into ecstasy, but this was going to be a first. It almost felt taboo. But, exciting at the same time. Luke flinched initially, but quickly assumed a stoic stance, and true to his word, Raphael took his time, inserting just one lubed up finger at first, then two. He wanted to be sure Luke was as lubricated as possible, and he wanted Luke to adjust to the feeling of Raphael's fingers. Actually, he wanted Luke to enjoy it. Then, a little awkwardly, Raphael positioned Brutus. He gently pressed the tip against Luke's rosebud. Luke sucked in a breath, but maintained his stoic face. "Deep breaths, Sir ... deep breaths." Luke nodded slowly and breathed in. Since Raphael couldn't feel how Luke's ass was responding, he could only judge the situation by Luke's expression and by any acceptance of Brutus by Luke's ass. He applied the least amount of pressure he could while still trying to advance. After a couple more breaths, Brutus moved. Only a centimeter, but he moved. After another advance, Raphael felt confident enough to pull back ever so slightly, then advance again, giving Luke a preview of what it felt like, not just to be entered, but to be fucked. Lovingly fucked. Luke gently moaned ... a good sign, Raphael thought. So, he continued.

Luke had determined that he would get through this. Somehow. After all, how many times had he fucked Raphael? And Raphael loved it. Hell, he often begged for it. It can't be that bad, can it? But as soon as he felt the tip of Brutus against his butt, he immediately thought, sure it can. Be that bad. Some guys are made to top. Some are made to bottom. And a few can flip. But, I'm a top. This is going to be hell. But I can't let Raphael know that. Keep a calm face. Don't cry out. Remember the pain Raphael went through to impress me with that awesome tattoo on his back? I can be that brave. I can do it. La la la la la. Breathe, Raphael says to breathe. Yeah, breathe. Just. Don't. Show. Pain.

Brutus moved another centimeter. Raphael pulled back half that and advanced. He continued watching Luke's face. His eyes were squeezed tight, contradicting the calmness Luke was forcing the rest of his face to exhibit. Raphael smiled. His Braveheart was trying so hard to be brave. With Luke's next exhale, he went for two centimeters. A little back and forth. A couple more breaths. Another centimeter. And so on until Brutus finally made his way past Luke's internal sphincter. It surprised both Raphael and Luke. Luke gasped. Raphael paused. And waited. Then, ever so slowly began pushing and pulling Brutus, very, very gently. Luke moaned. His eyes relaxed. And for the first time Raphael became aware of his own breathing. Surely he hadn't held his breath all that time, but now he took a deep, satisfying breath and began properly fucking Luke. Gently, but definitely, with determination. Luke was silent at first, but eventually a moan escaped his lips. The best sign, though, was what was happening inside that hot pink Holy Trainer. Luke was clearly aroused, and unlike during his previous caged erections, he wasn't complaining, at least not yet. Not wanting to break the spell, Raphael was very measured in his motion, wanting to give Luke's prostate plenty of attention without overburdening the rest of his virgin ass. Luke could not have been in better hands.

Once Raphael was confident that Luke was under his spell, he leaned forward, putting his hands on either side of Luke's chest. Raphael wasn't tall enough for his lips to reach Luke's, but that wasn't his target anyway. He lowered his lips to Luke's left nipple as Brutus took care of Luke's prostate. He kissed, he licked, he teased with clenched teeth, first the left, then the right. Brutus kept at it. Luke's occasional moans came more frequently, then slowly morphed into plaintive cries. Was Luke mimicking Raphael when Raphael was on the receiving end of Luke's cock, or was this natural for him ... a new natural? Either way, Raphael was entranced. Gratified that he was, on his first effort, giving Luke what appeared to be a fantastic fuck. Just as Raphael was wondering how he could make this even better for Luke, Luke's breath caught and Raphael knew, shit! This is it. Luke grabbed both of Raphael's biceps as he cried out. As he came, all over himself. Raphael was stunned. He looked down at Luke's belly and chest in disbelief. Then up to Luke's smiling face, where there was even a gob in Luke's beard.

"Son of a bitch, Sir. You came on your first fuck!" Luke laughed through his heavy breaths and let go of Raphael. As Raphael pushed himself back up to a standing position, Luke again put his hands behind his head and lifted it enough that he could see Raphael in all his Brutus-accessorized glory. Raphael unbuckled Brutus, gently pushed him a bit further up Luke's ass and then crawled up the bed and laid down next to Luke. He leaned down, licked the gob off Luke's beard and shared it with Luke in a long, deep, kiss. Both men breathed deeply. Raphael settled down next to Luke, put an arm across his chest and sighed.

"Okay, that wasn't at all what I expected," Luke admitted. "Not even close."

"I can't believe you came. Your first time."

"The credit goes to you, baby. Nobody fucks like you do."

"Oh, yeah. It was my first time, too. On top, I mean. Good point, Sir. I guess we're good together no matter who's on top."

"Except when I'm on top we usually cum together."

"Uh, well, Sir..." Raphael reached down, curled his finger around the tip of his Looker 01, and brought it up to Luke's lips and swirled. Luke parted his lips and accepted Raphael's finger and the gift it bore.

"When did that happen?"

"Not long before you, Sir. While Brutus was taking care of you, my plug was taking care of me. That and the view I had of my new Bottom Braveheart." Raphael replaced his arm around Luke's chest and snuggled in. Then he sighed, the kind of sigh that often preceded a nap.

"Um, baby. Shouldn't you pull Brutus out? Baby?"

"Mmmmm. Nap time, Sir."

"Baby?"

"Hush. My dare, Sir. After the nap." Luke issued a slightly perturbed sigh. "I love you, Sir."

"I love you, too, baby," Luke whispered, then pulled Raphael close.


Tuesday morning as Luke and Raphael were having their 'going to work' shower together, Raphael squatted down behind Luke as he lowered the soapy loofah down Luke's back and onto his no-longer-virgin ass. He diligently scrubbed each cheek, then stood, rotated Luke so he could do his front, and asked, "How's my Braveheart's butt this morning. Sir?"

"It's fine, baby. You were true to your words. Very gentle." Luke leaned down and kissed Raphael, allowing the spray to drench both of them.

"I did my best, Sir," Raphael smiled once Luke released him. "As did you. I still can't believe you came your first time."

"You shouldn't be surprised." Raphael gave Luke a questioning look. "Baby, how could I not cum while being fucked by someone as erotic, exotic and sexy as you. I didn't have a chance."

"Still," Raphael responded, ignoring Luke's praise. "That was quite a feat. Maybe I'm not the only one in this marriage with an amazing prostate."

"Maybe. But you're certainly the only one with a fourteen-inch cock." Raphael laughed and wrapped his arms around his soapy, wet Braveheart. He pulled his head back and looked up into Luke's clear blue eyes.

"Yeah, but you'll always have the 'dick of death' hanging between your legs. Or, locked up between your legs in this case." Raphael jiggled Luke's Holy Trainer.

"Four more days, baby. Four more days." Luke gave Raphael a quick scrub down, then they rinsed and toweled each other off. As was now standard, Luke, after dressing in civvies, would be heading out to work, grabbing a latte-to-go on his way, but Raphael, along with nearly everyone else in the company would be working from home. Most of them would be working in jammies or sweats, maybe a dress shirt if a Zoom meeting was on their schedule, but Raphael, like Alex, would be working naked, caged, harnessed and plugged. And in Raphael's case, also collared, like Ricky and Niki. Thinking of their shared states of undress, while he poured steaming water into the Chemex, made Raphael's cage feel a bit heavier. Which reminded him again of Luke's amazing feat the day before. Which made his cage even heavier. Not that he could do anything about it right now. He settled in front of the laptop and began tackling the first of several projects demanding his attention.

Niki was busy cleaning the bathroom when Steve stepped into the doorway.

"Niki, one of the realtors I've tried to contact wants to see the house this morning, so I'm going to head out at ten for a bit." Niki turned to Steve with a look of disappointment. "Hey, don't look so sad. It's going to sell eventually, so we might as well put it behind us sooner than later." Niki didn't look placated. "I kind of wish you'd never seen it."

"No, it's okay. I'm being silly, I know. Right now, all I have are dreams ... and you."

"And Raphael and Luke and Alex and Greg and Juan and Ricky. And Mateo. You have a lot to be grateful for, puppy." That brought a half smile to Niki's face.

"I know." Suddenly his face brightened. "Say! You promised to let Raphael see it. If he's free, can we come over with you? You know, in case it sells right away?"

"Did I promise?" Niki nodded solemnly. "Well, not while the realtor is there. Tell you what, that shouldn't take more than an hour. I'll text you after the realtor leaves. If Raphael is free, you can come over then. Okay?" It was definitely okay with Niki.

The door had barely closed on Steve at nine forty-five when Niki texted Raphael. As he suspected, Raphael was happy to make time. This would be the first time they'd seen each other in the flesh for weeks. They planned to meet at the corner near the house at ten forty-five.

They arrived within minutes of each other. Not surprisingly, both were wearing caged cock t-shirts and shorts. The brotherhood was alive and well.

"Niki!" Raphael enthused as he bowed, several feet away. "God, I really want to hug you!"

"Yeah, me too," Niki agreed. "What the hell ..." he started for Raphael, who backed away.

"No ... no. Let's be good. Luke is out just often enough to possibly become infected. I don't want to risk passing it on to you. But, God, you look great, Niki."

"Is Luke working today?" Raphael nodded. "How is Luke?"

"Luke is ... good. Really good." Raphael was tempted to share more about Luke's current status, but immediately thought better of it. "You know, considering. So, where's this house?"

"Up the hill here. We're just waiting for the realtor to leave. As soon as Steve texts we can go up."

"Well, meantime let's walk. It's so good to see you." The two of them began ambling. Niki didn't want to wander too far from the house, so they circled a couple of blocks several times, catching up, one-on-one. It was time well spent. Finally, Niki's phone chimed.

"Follow me!" Niki's enthusiasm was back in full force as he took the lead, Raphael barely six feet behind. When they reached the foot of the steps to the house, Niki stopped and looked up at it, then turned to Raphael. "What do you think?"

"Well, I'm not going to buy it until I've seen the inside but, yeah ... very nice." Niki laughed and, without thinking, broke protocol, grabbing Raphael's hand and pulling him up the steps. Raphael didn't resist. It felt right. Before they got to the front doors, Steve opened one and greeted them with a wave.

"Raphael! Come on in!" Steve stepped aside. "So ... so much for social distancing, eh, Niki?"

"Oh!" Niki reacted. "I wasn't thinking. Sorry, Raphael." He let go of Raphael's hand and moved toward the center of the foyer.

"I'm sure it's fine, Niki. Fuck this pandemic!" Raphael had a genuinely pained look on his face. Touching Niki, even briefly, had been cathartic.

"I'm sure it's fine, too, Raphael," Steve assured him. "It really is good to see you, though."

"Both of you," Raphael agreed. "So ... when does the tour start?" Not that he needed one, but that was Niki's cue. He was so eager to show Raphael around, he completely forgot to strip first, as he had the first time. He led Raphael and Steve through the entire house, in the same order in which he and Steve had explored it days earlier, ending in the turret room, each of the three of them sitting on the floor, socially distanced and sufficiently impressed with their surroundings.

"Okay. I can see why you fell in love with it," Raphael pronounced. "Words don't do it justice." Niki nodded. "Why doesn't your friend want to keep it? Who wouldn't want to live here?"

"It's not that he doesn't love the house," Steve replied. "He does. But, he's also happy where he is in Melbourne, and he doesn't plan to move back here anytime soon. He never lived in the house, but his dad did, and of course his grandparents. And great grandparents. There's some sentiment there. He said he'd considered keeping it, as an investment maybe, but thought it would make more sense to let it go." Raphael didn't respond at first, deep in thought.

"So," he finally spoke. "He's open to keeping it?" Steve tentatively nodded. "Did the realtor think it would sell quickly?"

"Probably. The market is a little weird right now, with the pandemic and the economy. Prices are flat, or even a little down right now, but still, this would go for millions."

"No doubt. And it belonged to his grandfather?" Steve nodded again, wondering what Raphael was thinking. "And you're in charge of selling it, through a realtor, of course." Steve nodded yet again. "So, you must have the property tax assessment." It wasn't a question.

"Maybe. The attorney sent a packet of documentation. Niki, was that in that stack of papers?" Niki shrugged. "Raphael? Are you thinking of trying to buy this place?" A look of glee flashed across Niki's face.

"No. No. But I do have an idea. Can you text me the assessment when you find it?"

"Seriously?" Steve gave Raphael a non-judgmental, but suspicious look. Raphael just stared back calmly. "Um, sure," Steve consented. "Okay." Niki was looking back and forth between the two of them. When his gaze settled on Raphael, Raphael returned the look as an undetectable smile graced his face, hidden by his mask. Had Niki been wearing his tail, it undoubtedly would have been wagging furiously.

"I knew you'd love the house," Niki said. "It's perfect, isn't it?"

"Almost," Raphael replied. "It's missing just one thing." Steve looked surprised.

"Like what? A sauna?" he asked.

"No. Although that's not a bad idea," Raphael smized. "Let me check on a couple of things, and I'll let you know."

"Let me know?" Steve turned to Niki. "Is this what drives Luke crazy all the time?"

"One of them, yeah," Niki invisibly grinned. He wasn't sure what Raphael was thinking, but whatever it was, he knew it would be worth waiting for.

# Eight

## RAPHAEL'S BIG IDEA

MATEO WAS PLAYING WITH his scrambled eggs, more like torturing them, but barely eating them. His sourdough toast was going begging, too. This hadn't escaped Alex's notice, who wasn't taking it personally. Usually, Mateo was full of praise for anything Alex put before him. Even frozen waffles, since Alex wasn't willing to try to compete with Ricky's pancakes, even though some of the ingredients were still in the cabinet. The recipe, however, was not. Alex set his mug down and focused on Mateo.

"Sweetie, what's wrong?" Mateo looked up guiltily, then took a big bite of now tepid egg.

"Is okay," he replied after swallowing. His smile didn't fool a former thespian.

"Spill. You remember what 'spill' means, right, amigo?" Mateo put his fork down and made eye contact with Alex.

"Is Ryan. I think he is afraid to ask his mama and papa about what you and Greg said. Him to live here with me ... with us."

"Why do you think he's afraid. Did he say so?"

"No." Mateo took another bite and swallowed. "I don't think he ask."

"When did you two last talk about it?"

"Maybe two days ago."

"Well, here's what I think, Mateo. This is very important to you. Right?" Mateo nodded. "Do you think it's important to Ryan?"

"I think. I hope is so."

"Well, Mateo, Ryan knows his parents better than anyone. And he's a teenager, so he knows how to work his parents." Mateo looked a little confused. "What I mean is, he knows when and how to approach them about something really important that he wants them to agree to. I think he's just waiting for the right time. For the best time for them to say yes!" Alex sat back with an air of certainty.

"Hmmm." Mateo took another, bigger bite. "You think?" Alex nodded. "Maybe you are right. Thanks, Alex!"

"Mateo ... it's okay to ask Ryan what's going on, you know. Don't be afraid to let him know what you are thinking. What worries you. What makes you happy. He will appreciate it." Mateo smiled and nodded.

"Thanks, Alex. Thank you for everything."

"Anytime, amigo." Alex got up, put his mug in the sink and headed to his laptop for another day of working from home. On his way, he stopped by Greg's 'office,' the bay window in the living room, where they had converted a console table into a desk. The arrangement totally violated Alex's former perfect feng shui, but pandemics have a way of doing that.

"I overheard," Greg looked up at Alex. "Good advice."

"Thanks. I was channeling you, after all."

"Ha!" Greg laughed. "If only." Greg lowered his voice despite the fact they could hear Mateo running water in the kitchen sink. "I'm kind of having second thoughts. I hope we didn't set Mateo up for disappointment. Maybe Ryan would rather be on campus. It's still really early between them, after all."

"Maybe. Hopefully Mateo will grow from this. It is his first relationship ... hell, his first boyfriend. Maybe it's love. Maybe just infatuation. The good news is, either way, we're here for him."

"That's right, you are his fairy godmother."

"Um, that would Raphael. He's the one who introduced the two of them at the wedding."

"Okay, fairy godfather, then."

"What does that make you?"

"An innocent bystander?"

"Hardly. You're the one who sealed the deal for him moving in with the half-rent bait."

"Fine, I'm the queer uncle, then. There's always a queer uncle." Alex leaned down and kissed Greg's cheek.

"I don't know," he said as he walked away, "you're pretty studly for a queer uncle." Greg issued a quiet snort and returned to work.

When Luke arrived home that evening, he stopped by Raphael's chair for a mandatory 'I'm home' air kiss before heading into the bedroom to strip, drop his street clothes in the hamper, then shower away any lingering, covert corona virus before inviting Raphael in for their nightly shave and shower ritual. Raphael interrupted him in mid-stride.

"Wait, Sir!" Raphael slid out of his chair. "Don't move." Luke gave him a questioning look, but did as he was told. Humoring Raphael almost always paid generous dividends. "Let me just ..." Raphael leaned over, his fingers dancing across his keyboard. "There. That'll buy some time." Then he stood and grinned at Luke. "I'm taking you on a quick field trip, then you can strip and shower."

"Okey doke. Where are we going?" Raphael was already in the bedroom pulling on sweats and a caged cock tee over his harness. He reappeared and used the door frame as support as he slipped into a pair of sandals. He picked up the bottle of hand sanitizer on the dining table, applied a squirt to his own palm and handed it to Luke. He pulled on a mask while Luke decontaminated both hands, then he took Luke's hand in his and headed both of them for the door. "You still haven't said ..."

"I know. Sometimes visuals are better than words. Ask me again in five minutes." Raphael was clearly on a mission as they hustled through the Castro, doing their best to socially distance from others as they out-paced most of the other pedestrians. Once they turned onto Noe, and headed up hill, Luke forced Raphael to slow down.

"Baby, I haven't done decent cardio in months."

"Sorry, Luke. You're right. Sorry. I guess I'm kind of excited."

"So ... clue me in!" Raphael gave Luke a sly smize, finally walking side by side with Luke instead of pulling him behind like a reluctant toddler. Soon they reached the slate steps.

"No clues necessary, Sir. I just wanted you to see this, to put into context my possibly hairbrained scheme. But one I think could actually be, well, monumental!" Raphael turned to face The House.

"So, what's the scheme?"

"How would you like to live here?"

"Here?" Luke looked up the steps at the imposing Victorian. "In that house?" Raphael grinned behind his mask and nodded.

"As what? The butler?"

"Oh, Sir, you can be the butler if you really want, but, ah, that shouldn't be necessary."

"You mentioned context. What am I missing?" Raphael led Luke up the steps to the entrance, then he turned and sat down as if he actually did live there. Luke followed suit. He waited out Raphael, knowing sooner than later Raphael would 'splain everything.

"I wish I could show you the inside, and if you agree, then we'll make that happen, but first I wanted your opinion. Sir. If you aren't interested, then ... I won't pursue it any further."

"Any further?" Raphael turned his gaze from the street below and gave Luke his full attention.

"This is the house that Steve is supposed to sell. The one Niki fell in love with. I got to see the inside today. I've fallen in love with it, too."

"Ohhhh. That's nice, I guess. But ... really ... why are we here? We can't buy it."

"No, but I have a better idea." Luke looked at Raphael expectantly and squeezed his hand in encouragement. "Maybe I'm dreaming. Maybe I'm the only one, aside from Niki, who would even consider this, but, Luke, what if all of us, the family, rented it from Steve's friend. He told Steve he'd like to keep the house. If we all moved in, we could cover the taxes, so Steve's friend wouldn't be out anything. He keeps possession of the house, we live in the lap of luxury, all of us, together. No more social distancing."

"When you say all of us ..."

"All nine of us. Luke, the house is huge. Six bedrooms, all with their own baths. Giant, modern kitchen. Hell the dining room table is so big we wouldn't even need all the chairs. It'd be Tuesday dinner every night. And after dinner we'd have plenty of privacy in our separate bedroom suites. Not that this family requires a lot of privacy."

"I still don't see how we could afford it."

"Forget that right now ... I've done the numbers. I just want to know how you would feel about all of us living together under one roof. Like the family that we are. Like I said, if you don't like the idea, I'll understand and that'll be the end of it. I said it was kind of hair brained, didn't I?" Raphael rested his case. Luke looked out over the street below, taking in what Raphael had said. He twisted around and looked up at the double front doors. Then he stood up, let go of Raphael's hand, and descended a couple of steps so he could get a better look at the front of the house. And of Raphael, posed in front of it. Raphael patiently waited. Luke returned to his side and took Raphael's hand in his again.

"I'm trying to think of reasons why it might be a bad idea." After a moment, Raphael widened his eyes to silently ask, 'And?'

"Of course, I'd like to see the whole house, like you have." Raphael's hopes rose. "Do you think everyone else would think it's a good idea?"

"I don't know, Sir. Right now, all I'm interested in is your opinion. It's why we're here."

"Hmmm. I don't know. Could I live with seven other naked, sexy guys? In a Victorian mansion with five bedrooms?"

"Six, Sir. One has a bathroom bigger than our apartment. And a library. A Viking range. Sir. A butler's pantry. Sir." Luke tugged on the masked beard at his chin in mock deep thought. A good sign. Then, he gave Raphael's hand a squeeze.

"Based on what I know so far ... it sounds like an idea worth pursuing to me!" Raphael wrapped his arms around his still not decontaminated

Braveheart and delivered an awkward, masked, signature Raphael cheek kiss. When he pulled away, Luke inserted a simple note of realism. "Of course, you still need seven more votes."

"Eight, counting Steve's friend, but I don't know why he'd object. It's a win-win for him."

"You really think you could live with seven other guys? I mean, I know we all love each other, but at the end of the day, we all head off in different directions. At least we used to, when ... you know."

"Let's just see what everybody else thinks. Okay?" Luke nodded. "Come on. Let's go shave and shower. I'm all contaminated now, too, Sir." They stood and headed down the steps to the sidewalk, where Luke stopped and turned to look back up at the house.

"I don't know. It kinda feels like a fantasy, baby."

"That's how I felt about you, Sir. And look at us now ... husband." Luke laughed and pulled Raphael close as they headed down the hill. Raphael was right, he thought. It never hurts to dream.

Greg was standing in front of the refrigerator, the door open, surveying its contents when Alex walked in. He brushed past Greg, patting him on his bare ass, on his way to the sink.

"Trying to cool down the apartment?" he scolded.

"No, smart ass. Doing research ... trying to decide on dinner." Greg closed the door and took a seat at the island. "Do we know when Mateo will be off tonight? I need a break from the computer. I wonder if I have time to make a lasagna."

"A lasagna? That sounds yummy. And overly ambitious." Alex walked up behind Greg and massaged both shoulders, then slid his hands down Greg's chest to find two neglected nipples. "Or ... we could maybe better spend that time in the bedroom. You could make me scream with no Mateo here to hear. But to answer your question, I'm not sure. His hours seem to be pretty erratic these days." He nibbled an ear to further motivate Greg to abandon the lasagna idea. As he slid his right hand away from Greg's nipple in search of a hopefully erect-by-now uncaged cock, Alex's phone chimed. Alex wasn't deterred, having found exactly what he was hoping for, so Greg reached for the phone instead.

"Saved by the bell," Greg said as Alex's right hand paid homage to his erection.

"How so?"

"Mateo says dinner's on him. He'll be home in forty-five minutes."

"I wonder what he has in mind?" Alex mused as he continued his shoulder and cock massage. Greg shrugged.

"All I know is we have some time to kill. So, what was that idea you had a moment ago?"

"Follow me." Alex slid his hand off Greg's shoulder, but kept a firm grip on Greg's captive cock as Greg stood up and allowed himself to be led into the bedroom, where Alex pushed him onto his back on the bed. Greg had barely scooted up to get fully on the bed before Alex pounced, straddling Greg's hips with his knees, once again attending to Greg's nipples, only this time using his lips and tongue instead of his fingertips. Alex was energized, and rambunctious, as usual, his cage occasionally tapping Greg's balls while he worked Greg's nipples. After several minutes, he reached down to ensure Greg was still hard. He was. And Alex was hungry. He whipped around, abandoning Greg's nipples, and devoured Greg's cock. While Alex began paying his respects, Greg reached up and grabbed Alex's ass with his right hand. As he rubbed each cheek, his thumb found its way to Alex's rosebud. Now it was Greg's turn to massage Alex, and eventually to find purchase, as his thumb slid in as far as possible. Alex began to moan around the girth of Greg's fully erect cock. With his other hand Greg rubbed Alex's thigh. It was about the only other body part he could reach in this position. He couldn't reach Alex's nipples, and this was pretty much Alex's show at the moment, so he wasn't too concerned about underperforming. Alex was awfully skilled at the phallic flute, so, why not just enjoy it? For quite some time, he did. Until inspiration struck and Greg slid his thumb free and with both hands lifted Alex's left leg up and over Greg's chest and head without dislodging his cock from Alex's oral grasp. Huh, he thought. I'll have to remember that. He then placed both hands on Alex's ass cheeks and pulled down, until his tongue could find its way into Alex's ready ass. At first contact Alex moaned again and he rewarded Greg with double suction. He freed his right hand and found Greg's balls, and began pulling them toward Greg's knees as he swallowed his cock even deeper. Greg was now helpless. Alex knew how to treat Greg's balls, and he showed them no mercy. Each advance of Greg's tongue resulted in his balls moving further away from the root of his cock. It was abuse of the most rewarding kind. Greg's breathing quickened as Alex continued to torment his balls and pay homage to his cock. This was exquisite, a loving torture that only Alex could provide. No one else had ever understood how this worked, or why this worked for Greg. All that mattered, really, is that it did. And only with Alex. By now both men were drenched in their own and each other's sweat. Both had been moaning, although neither was aware of it. For them, it was all about sensation, taste, pain, agony, ecstasy. Alex was feasting on precum, as well as dripping plenty of his own onto Greg's torso from the nozzle of his Looker cage. His only regret was that Greg's cock couldn't be in his ass at the same time it was in his throat. Greg's tongue was talented, but it wasn't his cock. Finally, after a considerable amount of time and effort, Alex squeezed and pulled just enough that Greg cried out as he exploded. Alex immediately released his balls, but maintained possession of his cock, sliding up Greg's pole in order to savor his reward. Once the pumping ended, Alex collapsed on top of Greg, his chin on Greg's balls, his face between Greg's thighs, his own thighs on either side of Greg's head. Both men still breathing heavily.

After a moment of silence, Greg said, "That was amazing."

"It was, amigos," Mateo agreed with a giant smile. "It was even better than the Juan and Ricky show." Then he slowly pulled shut the bedroom door that Alex and Greg had forgotten to close.

# Nine

_____ ⟡ _____ ⟡ _____

# STAGE TWO OF THE BIG IDEA

As STEVE AND NIKI were engrossed in the third episode of Sense8 on Netflix, a text arrived on Niki's phone. Since Niki was in full pup headspace, tailed, hooded, mitted and curled up on the couch next to Steve, it was up to Steve to check it out. Ever since Niki's once secret obsession with puppyhood had been discovered by Steve, eventually making it possible for Niki to live a portion of his life in his current state, Niki had shared his screen lock password with Steve, giving him the ability to stand in for the human Niki when Pup Niki was in full form. Steve patted Pup Niki's back as he leaned forward and picked up the phone.

"It's your brother, puppy." Pup Niki lifted his head and licked Steve's thigh. He looked up at Steve expectantly. "I don't think it's urgent. We'll deal with it when you're ready to transmogrify from puppy to husband." Pup Niki barked once in affirmation and laid his head back down on Steve's thigh, panting quietly. Steve texted a short reply, set the phone aside and resumed streaming.

"Huh," Raphael put his phone down and continued stripping off his street clothes. Luke was already naked. As soon as Raphael was suitably unattired, Luke began unsnapping Raphael's harness from behind, so they could shower and shave. "Steve said he'd get back to me later. Niki must be a pup this evening."

"Feeling ignored, baby? What were you texting him about, anyway?"

"Are you kidding? About the house. I want you to see the inside as soon as possible."

"What's the rush? You said only one realtor has seen it, and that was just today."

"So far as I know! News travels fast in the realtor world, Sir. They'll be climbing all over each other to list that house. I don't want to take any chances." Raphael walked into the bath and started the water, giving the hot water time to find its way from the heater to the faucet. "I'll bet we won't have to wait ten minutes for hot water in our new house." He embraced Luke from behind as Luke began carefully pissing into the toilet. Luke hadn't fully adapted to pissing with a locked cock, and he half squatted, refusing to pee sitting down, to avoid making a mess. As he turned, Raphael dropped to his knees and licked the last few drops from the end of Luke's Holy Trainer.

"All you had to do was ask ..." Luke laughed, reaching down and ruffling Raphael's soon to be perfected high 'n tight.

"I just wanted a taste, Sir. Didn't want to spoil my appetite." Midway through the soaping and shaving, as Luke was finishing the sides of Raphael's head, he finally verbalized what he'd been thinking about since they'd left the house.

"Baby, what you're contemplating is incredibly ambitious. I mean, it has a dozen moving parts. You aren't going to be too disappointed if it doesn't work out. Are you?" Raphael remained silent, eyes closed, as Luke manipulated his head. "I can tell this means a lot to you." Finally, Raphael turned to meet Luke's gaze.

"First of all, it's going to work out. I can feel it." He gave Luke a moment for his certainty to sink in. Then he reached around and placed a hand just under Luke's left armpit, his thumb massaging Luke's left nipple. "But if I'm wrong ... and that would be a first, wouldn't it? Then ... I'll be fine. I'll be fine." He leaned in and helped himself to a long, savory kiss.

When Greg and Alex finally opened their bedroom door, Mateo was in the bathroom, the shower running, where he was no doubt decontaminating. They both slinked into the kitchen to find Mateo had laid out placemats and flatware on the island. A large pizza box was in the oven, on low heat, plates on the counter. Alex pulled a Modelo out of the fridge for Mateo, while Greg opened a bottle of Syrah.

"I'd kinda like to shower myself before eating, but ... ah..." Alex's voice trailed off.

"Yeah. This is going to be awkward. But we have no one to blame but ourselves."

"It's kind of funny, in a way."

"Then why am I not laughing?" Greg poured two glasses from the bottle and inserted a glass stopper. Alex walked over, sat the Modelo at Mateo's place then wrapped an arm around Greg's waist as he picked up his glass and toasted Greg.

"It's funny because we've been working on loosening up Mateo. Helping him accept, hell, to revel, in his sexuality. Today's little show can't hurt ... I mean we're not his parents. Biologically anyway."

"Yeah, but what if we've traumatized him, you know, for life?" Alex cackled.

"Greg, you heard what he said. He thought it was funny." The bathroom door opened. "Let me handle this." A moment later Mateo entered the kitchen, his mop still damp and haphazardly tucked behind his ears. He looked shyly at both Greg and Alex, but was unable to suppress a smile. One that grew as he crossed the room to the oven.

"Amigos, I got a deep dish at Little Star for us. Are you ... hungry?" The smile grew into a laugh. He pulled the box out of the oven, set it on the stovetop, then turned to face them both. "Don' be embarrass, amigos. That was sexy as fuck!" Greg turned to Alex.

"His English is coming along nicely. Did you teach him that?"

"I did not. He must have picked it up on the street." Then Alex turned back to Mateo.

'We're really sorry, Mateo. We weren't thinking."

"Don' be sorry, Alex. Is okay. Really." Then Mateo's grin grew again. He couldn't help it.

"Did you mean it?" Greg, feeling relieved, asked suddenly. "Was it really better than the Juan and Ricky show?" Alex pulled away from Greg.

"Greg!" He looked back at Mateo, eyes widening. Mateo wordlessly nodded slowly, then turned to begin dishing up the pie. It wasn't until they were each into their second slice before Alex broke the silence.

"So, Mateo, what's the occasion ... you treating us for dinner. It's delicious by the way." Greg nodded, in the midst of a big bite.

"I want to say thank you for this morning. When we talk. You help." Greg nodded again.

"You don't need to thank me, Mateo. It makes us feel good to see you happy. Even if Ryan can't move in with us ... I'll bet he still sleeps here more often than in some crummy old dorm. Either way, you won't be lonely." Mateo pondered that thought.

"Crummy?"

"Sucio ... Old. Dirty. Not Nice. Worn out." Mateo nodded his understanding. "But I shouldn't have said that. The dorms are fine. I just meant not as nice as being here with us. Don't listen to everything I say."

"I listen to everything you say. And to Greg. It is how I learn." Mateo flashed a smile before draining his Modelo. He stood and cleared his place. Force of habit from his day job. He was eager, no doubt, for his virtual date with Ryan.

"Mateo," Greg said. Mateo paused and turned as he headed out of the kitchen. "When you tell Ryan about ... you know ... this evening ... try not to laugh too much." Mateo's face lit up.

"I try amigos." He pursed his lips in an air kiss, then disappeared around the corner. When his door clicked shut, Alex turned to Greg.

"Well, the good news is, he'll probably make it sound sexier than it was."

"I don't think that's possible, sweetie," Greg replied. Alex looked confused. "Because, Alex ... it was ... sexy as fuck!" Alex raised his glass and smiled. Because it was.

"Papito," Ricky called out from the kitchen, "looks like it's either beans and rice or delivery. Or, I make a run to the store." Juan wandered into the kitchen where Ricky was facing away, staring into the cabinet, wearing his apron, the only article of clothing Juan had ever seen him wear at home. Juan put his arms around Ricky from behind and kissed the top of Ricky's head, where normally there'd be a nearly hairless landing strip. They still hadn't taken the time to shave and buzz Ricky's high 'n tight back into regulation shape, much less tackled Juan's increasingly abundant mane.

"Beans and rice sounds fine to me, mijo. While you do that, I'll order groceries for delivery. Remember, you're quarantining with me. I don't want you going anywhere." Without fully breaking the embrace, Juan turned Ricky around so they were facing one another. "I don't want you out of my sight. Not yet anyway." The next kiss was lips on lips.

"Well, if you insist, Papito," Ricky grinned. His hands slid down Juan's back to find his ass, and he pulled Juan tight, so tight Juan's hardening cock pressed against Ricky's equally hard abs. Both men moaned into another, longer kiss. When it ended, Ricky reached down to grasp Juan's cock in both hands before squatting down and sliding it into his mouth. He worked it for just a minute before releasing Juan and standing back up. "My favorite appetizer." Then he grinned, turned and reached into the cabinet for the frijoles negros. Juan looked down at his disappointed cock, sighed and went in search of his phone. He returned to the kitchen and leaned against the counter as he began adding items to the shopping app.

"How are we on toilet paper? I've heard that's a thing now."

"We're fine, Papito. But tonight we'll finish the salsa." Juan nodded and continued tapping. He had just set the phone down when it chimed. Ricky looked over his shoulder as he stirred the beans.

"Hmm. Raphael wants to know when for sure I'm out of quarantine."

"Maybe he's planning a welcome home party," Ricky grinned. "That'd be fun."

"And illegal. Not to mention ill advised." Juan tapped out a response and set the phone down again and sidled up behind Ricky at the stove. "It would be nice to see everyone again, though." Ricky turned around to pull Juan close. He spoke into Juan's taut chest. "I miss everyone, but as long as I finally have you back, I'm happy. For now."

"That makes two of us, mijo." He ruffled Ricky's hair before breaking the embrace. "I'll get the plates."

"Ten more days!" Raphael exclaimed. "That's just too long."

"What?" Luke asked as he dished up the coleslaw to accompany Raphael's broiled salmon filets. "What's ten days?"

"Juan says he's in quarantine for ten more days."

"Yeah, he said he'd be in quarantine for two weeks last Saturday, so that's about right. Why? What are you doing ... texting everybody tonight?"

"Not yet." Raphael set his phone down and peeked in the oven. "Okay, dinner's ready." He donned an oven mitt, and retrieved the cedar plank, the filets popping salmon fat into the air. Unlike Ricky, he was willing to brave a hot stove in just a harness. Luke came around with the two plates so Raphael could slide the filets in place, then they sat at the non-office end of the dining table, where Luke had set places with wine and water for them. They were several bites into dinner when Raphael got up to grab his phone. He tapped out a text, then picked up his fork again.

"Who are you bugging now, baby?"

"Juan, still. Trying to sweet talk him into coming out of quarantine. For just a teeny tiny while."

"I have a feeling you've met your match on that score, Raphael. This time you just may be denied. I'm not sure your powers of persuasion are as effective over text. It's not your words that melt men's resolve, baby ... it's that face." Luke wiggled his eyebrows and leaned over for a kiss.

"We'll see. Sir." Raphael said confidently before he obliged Luke's kiss, then returned to his filet. It wasn't until dinner was finished and cleaned up before Raphael's phone announced Juan's response. Luke could tell by Raphael's expression that he'd been right. Raphael sighed.

"You were right." Raphael whined, then read the text, "'I can't wait to see you, either, but I love you too much to risk it. I'm sure I'm negative, but I want to be absolutely sure. The minute I'm cleared, you'll be the first to know. XOX' I guess I've lost my superpower. One of them anyway."

"He's just looking out for us, baby. He was in one of the most dangerous places on the planet, after all."

"Yeah. I guess." Raphael and Luke took their regular places, each at opposite ends of the couch, feet in each other's crotch. Luke nudged Raphael's cage with his foot playfully.

"Cheer up, baby. I think you're letting this house bum you out before you even know if your 'hairbrained scheme' is feasible." Raphael stared into Luke's eyes a moment, then glanced down at Luke's pink Holy Trainer, his face brightening. He nudged Luke's cage with his own foot.

"You're right. I should be enjoying this moment ... this whole week. Here, let me get another pic of you." He reached for his phone again, but Luke was up and on top of Raphael before he could unlock it. He pressed Raphael into the couch, chest on chest, lips brushing lips.

"No photographic evidence, baby. It's in the contract." Raphael giggled at that.

"Where the hell is this contract you keep talking about ... the one I've never signed."

"In a safe place. And ... what do you mean 'another' pic?"

"Oh that? It's in a safe place, too." Raphael giggled again, as Luke climbed off, stood and reached down to scoop up his locked cock boy and carry him into the bedroom. Raphael was cheered. Mission accomplished.


It wasn't until after breakfast that Pup Niki signaled he was ready to transition from puppy to husband. He'd slept the night in full puppy mode, snuggled up against Steve, his tail between Steve's thighs. Steve took the rubber bone Pup Niki was offering out of his hooded mouth and slid out of his chair to nuzzle with him a moment before heading into the bedroom, Pup Niki trotting behind, tail wagging. As Steve picked up the keyring, Pup Niki sat up on his haunches to present his mitted forepaws, so Steve could unlock them. As soon as the puppy hood was off, Niki spoke.

"Thanks for breakfast, Steve."

"You're welcome. Did you get enough to eat?"

"Yep. Let's shower, then let's find out what Raphael wanted last night."

"Any guesses?" Steve prompted. They both had a pretty good idea it had something to do with Niki's dream house.

"Not for sure, but if I had to bet ...."

"Yeah. No doubt. Come on, sweetie. I have enough time before logging into work to shave around your mohawk if you want." Steve rubbed the side of Niki's stubbly head as he pulled him in for a long-awaited kiss. Kissing was the thing he missed most when Niki was pupped out, so it was a long one. After they'd shaved, showered and toweled off, Steve sat down in front of his laptop to begin his day. Niki plopped onto the couch, retrieved his phone and opened Raphael's text, then replied. The screen hadn't even dimmed before Raphael's reply arrived. After a couple of back-and-forth texts, Niki cleared his throat, wanting Steve's attention, but not wanting to interrupt anything too important. Steve turned in his chair.

"Were we right?"

"Yep. Actually, he wants to know when we can go back to the house so he can show it to Luke."

"Because ..."

"He didn't say. You know Raphael. He loves being mysterious." Steve had turned back around without further comment when Niki sat up straight. "I know! I'll tell Raphael you won't let us go back to the house unless he tells us what he's up to first. What do you think?"

"I think you're making me the bad guy," Steve replied without turning around. After he typed a few more characters, he continued, "And I think it's brilliant." Niki giggled and slouched back down to send off one more text. This time Raphael's response wasn't as prompt. When Niki's phone finally did chime, Steve reacted again without turning. "Did it work?"

"Sort of." Steve turned to give Niki his full attention. "He said he'll tell us, but at the house, with Luke and today. He's a pretty good negotiator, you know."

"I remember. Hang on." Steve turned back to his laptop where Niki could see several windows opening and closing. Steve typed a bit. Then, again over his shoulder his instructions were precise. "Tell him five o'clock at the house, and if he's a minute late the deal is off. My final offer."

"That's funny. Yippee, I get to see my house again!"

"Mmm humm. Now, I really have to get to work, sweetie." Niki tapped out another text, followed by an almost instantaneous reply chime. Steve didn't need to ask what it was. He just needed to be able to wrap up everything by four forty-five.

As Steve and Niki rounded the corner, they could see Raphael and Luke half a block away, sitting on the bottom step. Raphael had made sure they wouldn't be one minute late.

"Luke!" Steve greeted him and bowed in lieu of a hug, as they approached. "Good to see you in the flesh. Is that a new kilt?"

"This old thing?" Luke laughed. "God, it's good to see you guys, too. This was worth it just to lay eyes on you both. I see you're keeping the mohawk clean and tight, Niki."

"Just like you. You look great, Luke. Wait until you see the house!" Steve looked at Raphael who was looking only slightly sheepish.

"We kept our part of the bargain. Are you keeping yours?"

"Yes, but I didn't really want to talk about it yet. I hope this doesn't jinx it."

"Jinx what?" Steve asked.

"His hairbrained scheme," Luke laughed. "This one's a doozie. Let's go inside so I can see what Raphael is so excited about." Steve nodded and extended his arm toward the house. Niki took the lead, with Raphael and Luke following. Steve brought up the socially distanced rear. Niki unlocked the door and swung it open, then stepped aside to allow Raphael and Luke to enter. Once they were in the middle of the foyer, Niki and Steve entered. As Steve closed the door, Niki disabled the alarm.

"Okay, Raphael," Steve smiled. "Why are we here again?"

"Let me show Luke around, then ... I promise ... I'll reveal all." Raphael let go of Luke's hand long enough to take a step toward Steve. "Thanks for letting me do this, Steve. If I could hug you, I would."

"I'll collect that hug later," Steve smized. "You're welcome, of course. Okay, why don't you start the tour."

Raphael took Luke's hand again and began dragging him from room to room. It wasn't long before dragging was no longer necessary, as Luke, too, became enchanted with the house. Soon he was moving ahead exploring with Raphael, and on occasion Niki, who narrated the selling points of various features. Steve, for the most part, listened and observed. He'd never seen Niki or Raphael show so much interest in any material object before. Steve held back while Niki and Raphael took Luke up to the turret room, to insure social distancing. After they filed back down the narrow stairway, Raphael widened his eyes above his mask with excitement and a bit of nervousness as he looked at Steve.

"Okay, let's go down to the dining room and I'll explain," Raphael said as he led the way down the two flights of stairs. Once each of them had taken a chair around the table, Steve leaned forward toward Raphael, his hands clasped and resting on the table top, as he gave Raphael his full attention. Niki, seated nearby, was focused on Raphael, too.

"Let me start by confirming a couple of things, Steve." Raphael was in corporate mode, with Steve his client. "Your friend inherited the house from his grandfather, correct?" Steve nodded. "And he's the sole beneficiary?" Another nod. "And he is open to keeping the house if that could make practical sense for him. For sentimental reasons, and as an investment?"

"Yes," Steve affirmed, "I think so, but it really doesn't seem practical given his circumstances."

"What if we could make it not just practical, but easy for him to keep the house?" Steve unclasped his hands and sat back in his chair. He knew Raphael well enough to know whatever he was leading to had been well thought out. But he had no idea how any such idea could be 'practical.'

"Enlighten me, Raphael."

"The reason I didn't want to discuss this yet, is because it involves the entire family. All nine of us." Niki looked back and forth between Steve and Raphael, unsure but increasingly excited. Raphael stood up, taking control of the room. He wanted Steve to be reminded of just how spacious the place was as he revealed his proposal. He pulled down his mask to ensure Steve heard every word as he walked around the room, ending up behind Luke, where he put both hands on Luke's shoulders. "I propose that we all move into this house and make it our home. The whole family, here, under one roof. We'd each have our own suite for privacy, and tons of common space to come together, not just on Tuesday for dinner and Sunday for Ricky's pancakes, but every day. We could cover the utilities and property taxes with our rent payments ... and still end up paying less than we're all paying now for four separate apartments. Steve ... your friend could keep the house at no added expense. And we can truly be a family. In one of the grandest houses in the 'hood." As if on cue Niki leapt out of his chair and danced over to Steve. He got down on his knees, ready to beg, not as Pup Niki, but as one ecstatic husband. Steve put a hand on Niki's shoulder, but continued looking at Raphael, who concluded with, "What do you think?" Luke reached up to put a hand over Raphael's hand to silently say 'well done.' Raphael squeezed Luke's shoulders, then returned to his chair. As he sat, he smiled at Niki before replacing his mask, knowing he'd made Niki's day, at least for the moment. The duration of Niki's glee, of course, would be contingent upon Steve's reaction. Steve looked over at Luke for any indication of Luke's opinion. Luke just winked.

"Wow," Steve finally said. "You, ah, you've given this a lot of thought." Raphael smiled with his eyes, but remained silent. Steve looked down at Niki who made full use of his adorable brown puppy eyes. There was no doubt what Niki thought of the idea. Still, Steve had to ask. "Did you know this was coming?"

"Not exactly. I mean, no! I knew Raphael was up to something, but I didn't know it was this incredible. I vote yes! You know I love this house! And to be living with Raphael again ... and the whole family. Steve, we'd be together ... the whole family!" Steve looked back at Luke, still wanting to hear his take on the idea. Luke took his cue.

"It's kinda crazy, Steve. I mean I look around and can't imagine living in a place like this ... can you? But Raphael's got it all figured out. If, that is, everybody ... including your friend ... agrees. Like I told Raphael, you and Niki are one thing. But Juan and Ricky haven't been family for all that long. They may not want to live with us. Even Alex and Greg may decline, although I don't think they would. Alex and Raphael have a pretty special bond. Then I think about all the great times we've had together, and I think, it just might work. In a way ... it seems too good to be true." Luke stood and unconsciously mimicked Raphael by walking up behind him and putting both hands on Raphael's shoulders. He decided to finish with words inspired by Raphael's declaration a day earlier. "When we first met, I thought Raphael was too good to be true, too. So, maybe it's not so crazy an idea after all." He leaned down and kissed Raphael's landing strip through his mask. Then straightened up to face Steve again.

"Steve," Raphael spoke softly. "you don't have to decide right this minute. But, please ... don't sell the house until we know whether the whole family is up for it." Steve smized in response to Raphael's earnest plea.

"I haven't even chosen a realtor, Raphael. When do you plan to reveal this idea to the others?"

"The minute Juan is released from quarantine. Well, the first minute we can get everybody here after that. Ten, eleven days. I tried to talk him into sneaking out sooner, but he's so damn adamant." Raphael's eyes smiled to show he wasn't really condemning Juan.

"Juan's a nurse," Steve replied. "He'd be upset with us if he knew we were here right now like this."

"I'm not telling," Raphael smized. Steve looked down at Niki, then back at Luke, then Raphael.

"It's an intriguing idea," he said. Niki, growing more confident, stood up at Steve's side and put his arm around Steve's shoulders in a loose hug. "Can I imagine living in this house?" He paused, looking around the room. "Why not? We all work hard." He looked deferentially up at Niki. "When we're allowed to." He put his arm around Niki's waist and tugged. "But we do. We're good people. We deserve a few good breaks coming our way." He turned his gaze back to Raphael. "You're sure about the math, Raphael? I want all our ducks in a row before I propose this to Ben."

"Totally sure. Because Ben is the previous owner's grandson the house won't be reassessed for taxes. Kind of unfair, but that's the law. Do you want to approach him before or after we talk to the rest of the family?"

"Oh, before. If he isn't on board, we don't want to needlessly get anybody else's hopes up. Living with this guy here for the next ten days will be hard enough as it is." He tugged tighter on Niki's waist. "Let's be sure before we risk disappointing the whole family. You must be dying to tell Alex." Raphael laughed.

"Yes and no. You know me, I like the big reveal. So, yeah, I can wait. We have to wait. Ten whole days." Steve stood and pushed his chair back into place. As Raphael stood, he asked, "Steve, is there anything more I can do to help you persuade Ben to agree?"

"No, Raphael, I don't think so. I'll let you know if Ben has any concerns, but like I said, you did your homework already. My guess is he'll be relieved. Unless he was already counting on the proceeds of a sale, but I didn't get that impression." Raphael held up both hands, crossing fingers on both for good luck, then he turned to hug Luke.

"I want to hug you both, too!" Raphael turned back to Niki and Steve.

"Let's do!" Niki started toward Raphael, but Steve grabbed his arm.

"Let's not jinx it, sweetie. If this works out, we'll all be cohabiting and there'll be hugs aplenty. Every day, right Raphael?"

"Just like old times," Raphael agreed. "Only better."

# Ten

## COUNTING DOWN THE DAYS

"WHAT DO YOU SAY we take a hike today," Steve suggested to Niki as they cleared their breakfast dishes. It was Saturday morning, and a rare, perfectly clear morning at that. Ever since the lockdown, with traffic nearly non-existent, only the fog hampered visibility, and today there was no trace of Karl the Fog, even on Twin Peaks. "Since we were already out earlier this week at your 'dream house,' we might as well break the stay-at-home order again for a little exercise."

"Are you trying to take my mind off the fact you still haven't heard back from Ben yet?" Niki replied, stating the obvious.

"No. Well, maybe. A little. We do need the exercise. You have been awfully quiet." Steve shook out the place mats at the sink, folded them on the counter, then turned to Niki and pulled him into a hug. "We'll hear from Ben any minute. I'm anxious too, to be honest."

"I don't think we'll hear from him anytime soon. It's two a.m. on Sunday morning there." Steve pulled his head back a bit with a look of surprise.

"So now you're an expert on time zones?" Niki laughed.

"Just one ... Melbourne, Australia. For obvious reasons. Okay, let's hike. Might as well make it a workout; let's do Corona Heights."

They each pulled on shorts and tops, a long-sleeved tee for Steve and a gray locked cock hoody tee for Niki. They passed through the Castro, up Castro Street itself to 14th, then up 14th to Roosevelt and then to the trail and steps leading to the crest of Corona Heights. They were midway up to the top when Niki, in the lead, stopped dead. There, ten feet ahead, was a coyote. She was off to the right, in the tall grass, eyeing two young kids on the trail, twenty feet ahead of Niki. One was maybe eight years old, the other younger, and they seemed as entranced with the coyote as she was with them. The coyote was wary, but not exactly skittish. She looked hungry.

"What should we do?" Niki asked, turning to Steve.

"Where the hell are these kids' parents?" Steve asked rhetorically. "Let's just hang here a minute." And so, they did, until the coyote finally admitted she was out-gunned and slinked away from the kids. Satisfied, Niki and Steve continued up the path, greeting the kids as they passed, who appeared to have no idea the coyote's interest in them was purely gustatory. Once they reached the top, Niki and Steve found a large boulder with a view of the skyline and bay, and sat, arms around each other's waists. After a few minutes, Niki sighed.

"It's beautiful, but it looks so quiet," he observed.

"Yeah. Look down Sixteenth. Hardly any cars. I guess that's not all bad."

"I wonder if we can see our new house from here." Niki craned his neck.

"So much for diverting your attention from the house," Steve muttered. Niki laughed.

"Sorry. You're right. Look! There's Mount Diablo!"

"Ha, ha. So, can you see the house?" Niki shook his head.

"Too many trees. Just as well, I guess."

"Yeah, just as well. Should we walk on over to Buena Vista as long as we're here?" Niki agreed, and they retraced their steps back down the trail to flatter ground. As they approached Roosevelt, Niki took Steve's hand. The walk to Buena Vista Park was quick and steep. But not as steep as their trek into the park on their way to the popular viewing area at the top. They shared much huffing and puffing, but little conversation. They found an isolated spot on the low block wall with a view of the Golden Gate Bridge and the Bay, with the headlands and Mt. Tam beyond, and sat, still holding hands. After a few minutes of comfortable silence, Niki took Steve's hand in both of his and spoke, still looking at the view, and not at Steve.

"What you said yesterday started me thinking." Steve turned to Niki, but didn't speak. "You know, about us working hard, deserving some reward." Niki turned to look into Steve's eyes. "I really do have a lot to be thankful for. I was thinking about where I'd be right now, who I'd be right now, if my parents hadn't thrown me out, if I hadn't gone to Angel and Raphael's home. If I hadn't been adopted by Mama and Pop." He paused a moment, but continued looking into Steve's eyes. "If you hadn't found me. And rescued me a second time." Steve smized but remained silent, not about to interrupt this rare soliloquy from his husband. Niki turned back to the view. "I am so fortunate, Steve. To live here. With you in my life ... with a whole family I love ... not just Angel and Mama, but Raphael and Luke, Alex and Greg, Ricky and Juan, and now Mateo." He turned back again to Steve. "Yeah, I miss puptending,

I miss my job, but I really am fortunate compared to so many people right now in this fucking pandemic. So, if we don't get the house, I'll be disappointed, but, Steve, I'll be okay. Better than okay. We'll be fine." Steve pulled his hand free of Niki's and wrapped his arm around Niki and pulled him closer.

"That's right, puppy, we'll be fine."

"So, I've decided that since I've been so fortunate, I want to better myself. I want to do more, to give more. To contribute more than I can as a pup pulling drafts in a dark and noisy gay bar. Not just to the household, although that would be nice. But, to the community at large."

"I thought you loved being a puptender. Lots of people sure appreciate what you do."

"I do love it. Maybe I won't give it up entirely, but ... Steve, like I said, I've been thinking. I did a little research. I want to go back to school and get a degree in nursing. Like Juan. Actually, I think I'd like to become a respiratory therapist, something I never heard of before the pandemic." Steve pulled down his mask, then Niki's and leaned in and planted one on Niki's sexy, full lips. Then he pulled Niki's back into place, grinning.

"Do it. You know you can. You'd be a great nurse, no matter what you specialize in, with that big heart of yours. Niki, if that's what you want, I'll do whatever I can to help you. We all will. Juan will be thrilled."

"Well, don't say anything to anyone yet," Niki pleaded, adjusting his mask. "Please. Not until ... unless I get accepted. Okay?" Steve nodded, still grinning.

"Promise. It'll be our little secret. You know, we may not have many more of those if we really do end up all living together in your dream house."

"Oh, Steve," Niki smized coyly as he reached over and replaced Steve's mask. "We'll always have our little secrets. One way or another. I promise."

"Today's the day," Luke whispered in Raphael's ear as he snuggled up tighter behind him, his cage pressed into Raphael's plugged ass. They'd stayed up late watching TV. Raphael yawned as he stretched, still entangled in Luke's arms. He rolled around to face Luke, automatically puckering up for a kiss without even opening his eyes yet. He absentmindedly reached down for Luke's cock, when his eyes popped open.

"Oh," he grinned as he pulled his lips away from Luke's. "That's what you meant. Yeah, I guess today is the day. Unless ..."

"Oh, no, baby. No 'unless.' Today. Is. The. Day. It's Free Willy Day."

"Let's think about this, Sir. That pink Holy Trainer ... it's you. It's really you." Luke put his right hand on the back of Raphael's shaved head and pulled him into another kiss to stop the flow of insanity. When they parted, Luke looked into Raphael's twinkling almond eyes.

"Baby there's nothing you can say, or do that will keep me caged any longer. I got what I wanted. I paid my dues. You got what you wanted. So, a dare's a dare. I don't know what my next dare for you will be, but I will do my best to make sure it measures up to this." He reached down and jiggled his locked cock. He let go of Raphael and crawled out of bed and stood, looking down at Raphael, who was doing his best to look alluring, angelic even, to coax Luke back into bed. "Admit it, Raphael, haven't you missed my cock, just a little bit?" Raphael sat up and crawled to the edge of the bed where he raised up on his knees and reached out for Luke. Luke moved forward just enough for Raphael to wrap his arms around Luke's waist. He buried his head between Luke's pecs a moment, then pulled his head back and looked up at Luke.

"Get the keys, Sir, and I'll show you just how much I've missed your cock." Luke grinned, pulled out of Raphael's embrace and did as he was told.


Sunday evening, the sweet and spicy smell of Greg's postponed lasagna was wafting through the apartment, causing Alex's stomach to growl. Mateo was expected anytime, so Alex unfolded himself from the couch and sauntered into the kitchen to do his part — the Caesar salad he'd promised to make. Greg was at the sink, doing cleanup.

"It takes longer to clean up the mess than it does to eat," Greg complained over his shoulder. Alex piled the components for the salad on the counter, closed the fridge door, and crept up behind Greg to put a hand on either hip as he squatted down and buried his tongue between Greg's plump cheeks. "Oh, are we doing a repeat of the other night, Alex? Another free show for Mateo?" Alex freed his tongue and stood, caressing Greg from behind still.

"No, just giving my husband a distraction from his arduous labor. So, so arduous."

"Well, if complaining gets this kind of attention, prepare for an onslaught." He turned around and wrapped his arms around Alex. "Ever since we adopted Raphael's and Luke's clothes-free lifestyle you've been even hornier than ever. I like it."

"I can't help it. I mean ... there you are, all day, every day, on display. It's like living in a virtual reality porn movie. Especially with Mateo around, too. I hadn't thought about it like that, but it's true. I'm living in a porn movie." He leaned in for a kiss. When they separated, he looked down at Greg's erection and smiled. "Of course, if this was a real porn movie I'd be squatting down right now and sucking you dry instead of ..." and he let go of Steve and returned to the salad station, "... making you a healthy Caesar salad." Before Greg could reply they heard Mateo coming through the front door.

"Good thing it's not a movie, sweetie," Steve replied, attempting to suppress his boner. "We'd run the risk of corrupting Mateo, the innocent minor character ... and by minor, I mean under twenty-one, not insignificant." Alex brushed past Greg, intentionally rubbing up against him in his effort to access the sink, to rinse off the romaine. As he scrubbed, he turned to Greg, who had refused to budge and smirked. They could hear Mateo starting his decontamination shower.

"I think we've done a pretty good job of corrupting Mateo regardless, I'm proud to say. He's coming along nicely don't you think? If Ryan does move in with us, it's only a matter of time before one, or both of them, end up collared and caged."

"I'm not so sure. Maybe they're both vanilla through and through. Like you almost were."

"Not my fault. Plus, I didn't have sexy role models like Raphael, Ricky, Niki ... and me." Alex's smirk was accompanied by wiggling eyebrows. "What do you say we make a bet ... or better yet, issue a dare, like Raphael and Luke. Yeah, a dare ... that's a good idea."

"How would that work?" Greg asked as he set up places on the island for the three of them. "You mean if you're right I have to do something you decide, and if I'm right you have to do my bidding?"

"Exactly. See! You're smarter than you look, big guy."

"Are you guys teazhing each other again?" Mateo appeared, freshly showered, his still damp hair pulled back in the shortest of ponytails.

"Tea zing, the z sound, even though it's really an ess," Alex coached. "Teasing. Yes, we like to tease each other. Don't you tease Ryan?"

"Maybe," Mateo grinned as he reached for the open Modelo Greg had automatically placed at his spot. Greg pulled the lasagna out of the oven and placed it on the stove top to setup, while Alex slid a salad plate in front of Mateo as he climbed on his stool. Then he and Greg followed suit, with their salads. "Dinner smells good, Greg. Thank you, guys." Greg lifted his glass of Soave and toasted.

"To our happy and healthy home. May it ever be so." Two glasses and a bottle clinked. Mateo looked thoughtful as he took his first bite. He looked over at Alex.

"May ... it ... ever ... be ... so?"

"Greg was being poetic ... people don't really talk like that. It means, let's hope it never changes."

"Ah. Si. For sure!"

Greg laughed. "For sure, indeed." Once the salad was consumed, Greg served up the lasagna, which had cooled enough to hold together on the wide spatula. After the first bite, Alex held up his left hand, making the 'okay' sign to show his approval, while still chewing. Mateo was making approving sounds of his own. Finally, after swallowing, Alex pronounced dinner a success.

"This is your best lasagna yet, sweetheart." He leaned over to deliver a commendation kiss. Mateo nodded while watching them. Greg noticed and leaned over and puckered up for Mateo, who giggled and gave Greg a quick peck.

"I didn't want you to feel left out Mateo," Greg said. "And thanks, guys, lasagna is always iffy." Conversation lagged as all three concentrated on dinner. Mateo was the first done, but took up Greg's offer for more, 'a tiny bit more.' Alex set his fork down in surrender and picked up his glass and sipped.

"Did you get the sense that something is up during our Zoom get together yesterday?"

"What do you mean?" Greg asked, sipping from his own glass.

"Well, it's hard to put into words. I know Raphael pretty well by now. I think he's up to something. I can always tell. I don't know if he's launching a major dare on Luke, but he had this kind of preoccupied air about him."

"I didn't notice that. But I thought Niki was happier than he's been in a long time. He's been pretty morose about the bar closing, but he didn't seem bummed out at all yesterday."

"Yeah," Mateo said. "He was happy. I'm glad."

"Maybe he's in on whatever you suspect Raphael is up to," Greg speculated. "Raphael has been known to involve other people in these dares ... as we well know." Alex nodded absentmindedly.

"Yeah ... good times. I miss those days." He looked sadly at Greg, who put a comforting hand on Alex's thigh.

"There will be more good times ahead, sweetie. I promise." Greg turned to Mateo and said, "Right, muchacho?"

"Si!" Mateo nodded emphatically, then climbed off his stool, placed his plate in the sink and headed to his room, for a good time of his own, no doubt, with Ryan. While they wrapped up the leftover lasagna and loaded the dishwasher, Greg and Alex could hear Mateo giggling. He and Ryan really were making the best of their now long-distance relationship. As he wiped his hands on a dishtowel, Alex patted Greg on the ass.

"Not exactly a dare, but let's have a little fun with Mateo and Ryan."

"Oh?"

"We know he had to tell Ryan about ... you know. Let's do the scene from 'When Harry Met Sally' outside Mateo's door. Follow my lead." Alex left the kitchen and whipped around the corner, leaving Greg no choice but to 'follow' him, at least that far. Once they were both in the hallway, Alex started moaning. "Oh ... oooooh, ooooh Greeeg ..." Then he nodded at Greg, encouraging him to join.

"Aaah .... Aaaahhhhh, oooooh," Greg did his best.

"Yes .... Oh yeeeesss ... oooooh Greeeg," Alex followed up.

"STOP IT. YOU GUYS!" Mateo shouted from the other side of the door.

"Oooooh ... Greg .... Yessss." Mateo yanked the door open with one hand, phone and erection in the other.

"Oh, hi, Mateo." Alex innocently said. "We were just trying to set the mood for you and Ryan. Tell him we miss his irrepressible boner."

"Tell him yourself," Mateo laughed, handing the phone to Alex, who could see Ryan repositioning his own phone in a failed attempt at modesty.

"Now, Ryan ... you know the rules. No hiding boners in this house ... even virtually." Everyone could hear Ryan laughing, as Greg peeked over Alex's shoulder at Mateo's phone.

"We miss you, Ryan," Greg waved.

"Not as much as I miss Mateo. And all you guys. It's boring and lonely here."

"It's boring everywhere, Ryan," Alex agreed. "You look good, though. Nice haircut."

"Yeah, I'm this close to getting some clippers and giving myself a cut like Raphael. Or maybe even like Luke's. Nobody'll see it but Mateo. And my parents, but they don't count." Greg took his cue.

"Yeah, Ryan, have you had a chance to talk to your parents about our offer? To live here with Mateo this fall?" It was a little presumptuous, but the opportunity was there, and Greg didn't want it to slip away.

"Yeah, we talked. They're 'thinking about it.' I think they're worried that Mateo and I are just a fling and if we break up, then what? Plus, they may worry that I wouldn't have any 'adult supervision' if I'm living off campus."

"How about it, Mateo?" Alex looked at Mateo. "Are you just using Ryan for his body, and then you'll toss him aside when you're done?" Mateo thought a moment, processing the concept.

"No, Alex." He took the phone from Alex's hand and looked directly at Ryan. "You are my sweetheart, Ryan." Then he looked at Alex. "Sweetheart, right?" Ryan was laughing from his end.

"Sweetheart indeed," Alex nodded. "Ryan, tell your parents they have nothing to worry about. Not about Mateo, and not about 'adult supervision.' Greg and I run a tight ship." That phrase threw Mateo for a loop, but Ryan understood.

"I'll keep working on them, Alex, thanks," Ryan said. "Now, if you 'adults' don't mind ... "

"Oh, sure, you guys go back to what you were doing," Alex smiled. "What*ever* it was ..." Mateo grinned and slowly closed the door. Greg took Alex by the shoulders.

"Alex," he quietly said, "promise you'll never do that again." Alex wiggled his eyebrows and leaned up for a kiss.

"It's not like they don't have virtual sex every night. We gave them something to laugh about. But I promise. So, it's still early ... sex or Netflix?"

"How about Sexflix?" Alex cocked his head. "Let's watch an episode of Schitt's Creek, and every time someone says 'Moira,' you have to suck me for two minutes."

"Oh, sure. It'll take us what, three hours to watch one episode?"

"Yeah, but it'll be a great three hours ... at least for me."

"Okay. But, tomorrow, I get to pick." Alex took Greg's hand and pulled him into the living room. "If Mateo walks in on us again, remember, it's your fault." So, innocently enough, they sat, Alex cuddling Steve as Steve picked up the remote and navigated to their 'Continue Watching' menu on Netflix. Alex had hardly gotten comfortable before Johnny Rose uttered the magic word, 'Moira.'

"On your knees, Deep Throat," Greg smiled as he spread his knees. Alex sighed as he slid down off the couch and slipped into place between Greg's thighs. He reached both arms up and cupped his hands behind Greg's butt as he swallowed his cock. He really didn't consider this punishment, anyway, and the thought of being caught by Mateo again made his cage a little heavier than usual. Greg was finally getting nice and hard when he reached down and lifted Alex's head. "Okay, times up." Alex whined, but climbed back up on the couch, knowing it wouldn't be long before someone said the magic word again. Sure enough, not three more minutes passed before Alex was off the couch and into position. In fact, Greg was still tumescent, so Alex picked up right where he left off. When Greg tried pulling his head up this time, Alex resisted. Screw Schitt's Creek, he thought, this is far more entertaining. Greg did succeed in breaking Alex's vacuum, but this time Alex remained between Greg's thighs, resting his head just below Greg's balls. Good thing too, as barely a minute passed before the next utterance of 'Moira.' Alex swallowed Greg all the way to the pubes, determined to not be denied his intent to wrest a full orgasm from Greg this time. He was soon in that cocksucker headspace he often enjoyed with Greg where only Greg's cock and his mouth existed, all else was banished from his awareness. This was better than any sitcom. It took a while, but eventually Alex realized that more than two minutes had passed. Way more. No matter. That is, until, he heard Mateo speak.

"Oh, sorry." Alex started to lift his head, but Greg used both hands to force it back down, to the root of his cock. He heard Greg reply.

"No, it's okay, come on back in. Sit down. Don't be embarrassed."

"I'm not embarrass. I ah …"

"Cool, then have a seat. Alex and I were playing a TV game is all." Alex was pushing with both hands to elevate his head off Greg's cock, but Greg was stronger. Greg briefly explained the game. As he talked his cock grew even stiffer in Alex's mouth. So, tonight Greg's an exhibitionist, Alex thought. Briefly, only briefly, he considered using his teeth, but thought better of it.

"Sounds fun. Sure looks like fun. I will remember it. Maybe play with Ryan." Mateo sighed deeply.

"Hey, don't be so sad, muchacho. You and Ryan will get to play soon. Meanwhile, if you want, you can watch. Alex always loves to put on a show." Alex tried protesting verbally, but nothing intelligible made it around Greg's cock. Alex decided to stop giving Greg any satisfaction, hoping he'd lose interest and free Alex. He relaxed his mouth, and just let his mouth and head rest idly on Greg's boner.

"Mateo, looks like Alex needs a little motivation to perform. Go into our bedroom. You'll find something on the floor of the closet. Bring it in here."

"Are you fucking kidding me!" is what Alex shouted around Greg's cock, but what came out was muffled gibberish.

"This?" Alex heard Mateo ask.

"That's it."

"You going to spank me?"

"No, Mateo. You are going to spank Alex." Alex applied every ounce of strength he could muster into his biceps, but could not overcome Greg's headlock.

"¿Que?" Mateo looked genuinely shocked.

"Mateo, it's okay. Alex loves to be spanked. He's never been spanked by a sexy boy like you while sucking my cock before. He will thank you later. Go ahead. Please." Mateo didn't know what to think. He'd never seen anyone spanked sexually before, let alone been involved a such a scene. His only experience with spanking involved an angry father and a frightened child. Surely Greg was just messing with his head.

"Mateo … have I ever lied to you? Trust me. Spank Alex." Mateo approached the couch. He swung the paddle, but stopped short of making contact with Alex's exposed ass. He looked at Greg warily. Greg just nodded toward Alex's ass. Finally, Mateo swung half-heartedly and landed a tap.

"No, Mateo. Harder. Alex likes it really hard." Mateo wished he could ask Alex for confirmation, but the sounds coming out of Alex's mouth, whether English or Spanish, were unintelligible. "Harder, Mateo. As hard as you can." Mateo, as if asking for forgiveness, reached down and rubbed Alex's ass with his left hand, the first time he'd ever touched Alex there, then, with his right hand, swung the paddle with all his might. The sound surprised him. Alex jumped, but not enough to free his and Greg's hold on Greg's cock. Mateo looked at Greg for a reaction. "More, Mateo. Just like that!"

Mateo struck again. Then, again. Then on the other cheek. After a dozen blows Alex began to engage his bliss, actually a new found bliss that combined the blows on his ass with the taste and feel of Greg's cock ... the only active cock in their marriage. Soon, as Alex's ass blushed, it was no longer necessary for Greg to hold down Alex's head. Alex was once again devouring his cock, and his cock loved it. It grew harder with each of Mateo's blows, and Alex could taste the flow of precum each time he pulled free enough to be able to taste it. As Mateo's blows landed his cage grew heavier as well.

Greg had been right, Mateo soon realized. Alex was completely horned out. Greg's head was lolling back on the couch now, his hands resting on Alex's shoulders. This was overload for Mateo, who suddenly realized he was sporting his own erection, despite having jerked off with Ryan only half an hour earlier. He thought he should be embarrassed, but he wasn't. In a way he was serving his two friends who were mentors in many ways. He was doing them a favor, right? He was making Alex happy, and Greg, too. And the scene, he had to admit, was too fucking hot. Greg lifted his head and looked blearily at Mateo, saw his swinging boner and came. Alex lifted his head enough to allow some of the cum to splash off his face, then dived back to swallow the rest. He nursed Greg until there was no more cum to be had. Mateo, uncertain what to do next, stood by, the paddle dangling from his right hand, still erect. Alex raised up his upper body and turned to face Mateo, cum dripping from his cheek. Mateo looked down away from Alex's face, a bit embarrassed, only to see that cum was also dripping from Alex's cage and had pooled beneath him.

"Thank you, Mateo," Alex croaked. "That can't possibly have been your first spanking."

"Not my first to get. But first to give." Alex laughed as he collapsed into Greg's lap. He looked back up at Mateo, taking in his erection, and smiled.

"Well, I hope it's not your last. You have a gift, muchacho." Mateo nodded, then padded down the hall to return the paddle. He then slipped into his room and quietly closed the door. He laid down on his bed, took his erection in hand and picked up his phone with the other. He was about to text Ryan, to tell him about his amazing new experience, then reconsidered. Would Ryan be jealous? Or, worse yet, offended? It wasn't really a three-way was it? No one had touched him. He hadn't come, though he really wanted to right now. He put the phone back down and began rubbing out his second orgasm of the evening. Maybe it would be better to save this story for later, once Ryan was living with the three of them and knew them better. Yeah, maybe when Ryan could have the opportunity to spank Alex himself.

Eleven

# RAPHAEL'S BIG REVEAL

NIKI WAS BUSY FILLING out the online application form for San Francisco State's undergrad nursing school. After doing the same for CCSF, he'd already located his transcripts and other data, so it wasn't a challenge, just tedious and time consuming. But one thing Niki had an abundance of these days, was time. Steve was sitting at his workstation, hoping to wrap things up in time to start thinking about dinner. Just another day in lock down, until. Steve's phone vibrated an incoming call. Steve looked at the screen, then over at Niki who was still intent on his own screen. Steve cleared his throat and took the call.

"Hello, Ben. Good to hear back from you." Niki instantly materialized at Steve's back, apparently without having walked across the apartment. He placed both hands on Steve's shoulders as Steve continued. "How are things in the Melbourne office?" Niki was whispering prayers and spells to himself as Steve continued with, "Uh huh ... uh huh ... sounds good. Yeah, we're doing okay at working remotely here, too." Niki squeezed Steve's shoulders in an effort to steer the conversation to a more important topic. "You got my email about the house?" Niki let up slightly. "Good. Good. I hope I didn't throw you for a loop. Uh huh ... yeah, like I wrote, we've all known each other for a long time. In fact, we're in-laws with Raphael and Luke. Alex works for the same company as Niki's brother Raphael. Yeah, that's how we met him and his husband Greg." Niki started applying more pressure again and whimpering very quietly. "It's kind of hard to explain, but we're more of a family than friends, really. Before the pandemic we were all together several times a week, dinner, the beach, brunch on Sundays. Uh huh ... that's why we thought of the idea, so we could spend even more time together." Steve stopped talking for what seemed like forever to Niki. Steve nodded a couple of times but didn't speak. Finally, "Well, we just thought if you really were interested in keeping the house, especially with the market being so iffy right now ... uh huh." Niki leaned forward and rested his forehead on the top of Steve's head to keep his own head from exploding. "Okay. Thanks, Ben. I appreciate that. Talk to you in a couple of days. Take care." Niki backed away as Steve set his phone down and turned in his chair.

"Well?!"

"He wants to run the idea by a couple of other people." Niki's face started to frown up, when Steve reached out and took his hands. "But, Niki ... he thinks it's a great idea!"

"YES!" Niki pulled Steve up into a breath-defying bear hug. Steve wrapped his arms around Niki and held him tight. Niki wriggled free enough to look up at Steve with those puppy brown eyes.

"Niki, we're one phone call away from you getting your dream house for real. I mean, I can't believe it, but there's a chance you really may get your dream house!"

"I can't believe it either. But, somehow, I knew ... I just knew. It was so right. As soon as I saw it, Steve. I just knew it."

"Ben promised to get back to me in a day, two at the most. Now you realize, puppy, we haven't talked to the others yet ... Greg, Alex, Juan or Ricky. So, even if Ben says yes, it's not quite a done deal." Niki didn't seem concerned.

"We'll leave that to Raphael. Nobody's ever said no to Raphael." Niki wasn't going to let any what-ifs dim his ecstasy. He started for his own phone, then turned back. "Maybe you better put me in pup mode right now, so I can't text Raphael until we hear back from Ben. I know I can't trust myself."

"You sure?" Steve took Niki's face in both hands and presented a momentary kiss. "It could be a couple of days."

"It's either that ... or hide my phone." Niki looked up at the ceiling for guidance. Then, without a second thought he dropped to all fours and trotted into the bedroom, with Steve following.

"Ricky, work wants me to confirm a time for my follow-up COVID test," Juan wandered into the bathroom with his phone in hand. Ricky was at the sink, engaged in his twice a week shave. Juan sidled up behind him and pressed his flaccid cock between Ricky's invitingly perky cheeks and wiggled his hips. Ricky pressed his ass back in answer. "Why don't you come with me. You're a front-line worker, so you qualify for testing."

"Can I? You sure?"

"I'll tell them there'll be two of us."

"When is it?"

"Friday morning. nine a.m. Kinda early, I know." Juan tapped out a confirmation on his phone.

"It's okay. So, I guess we'll finally be free, huh? Sorta, kinda free. Back to work at least." Ricky put the razor down and splashed water on his face as Juan handed him a face towel.

"Yeah, our little holiday is coming to an end, mijo. It's been good, huh?" Ricky turned away from the sink and pulled Juan into his arms. He pressed his damp cheek into Juan's pecs. Juan reached up and rubbed the back of Ricky's head. "Say, we never have taken care of your high 'n tight. Should we do that now, or have you decided to grow it out?"

"Oh, no Papito, your world's best locked cock leather boy has to have a perfect high 'n tight, don't you think?" Juan tossed his head back with a short laugh.

"I guess you're right. You do keep me on my toes, don't you? Okay, you spread a couple of towels on the floor, I'll go get a chair." Once Ricky was seated, Juan retrieved the clippers from the bottom of the vanity and plugged them in. "I'm a little rusty at this, mijo, so don't be surprised if we end up just shaving it all off." Ricky giggled and looked up over his shoulder at Juan.

"Papito, do your best. If we have to shave it off, then fine. But, you know, then I get to shave yours off, too."

"Well ... in that case I'll make damn sure I do a good job."

"Good. But, seriously, Papito, I'll do you next if you want. Except ..." Juan snapped the clippers on and began running them up the back of Ricky's head, the correct guard still in place from the last time he'd shaved Ricky's high 'n tight over a month ago.

"Except what, mijo?" He tilted Ricky's head to the side for a better angle.

"Well, Sir, I don't know how appropriate it is for a handsome, Leather Daddy, but I kinda like your hair longer like this." Juan snapped the clippers off and came around to face Ricky. He squatted down to Ricky's level and brushed off some of the hair that had fallen on Ricky's thigh. Ricky looked questioningly at Juan.

"You like my hair longer, mijo? Seriously?" Ricky nodded, then smiled.

"You look sexy as fuck. Sir." Juan laughed and slapped Ricky's thigh.

"Well, you know. When I was a teenager, I had a ponytail halfway down my back. I loved it."

"Really? No ..."

"I have pictures to prove it." Ricky took Juan's hand in his own, raising it to his lips for a kiss. He looked at Juan with a whole new appreciation for him.

"Was my Papito a skater dude?" Juan grinned, looking down at Ricky's feet, then back up.

"I guess I was, yeah, for a while anyway."

"Why'd you cut it. It must have looked amazing."

"I cut it for my first interview at the hospital. I didn't want anything to prevent me from getting the job."

"It obviously worked."

"It did, yeah. My grades and references probably had nothing to do with it." Another big smile.

"I'll bet you could have gotten the job even with your epic ponytail."

"Maybe so. Nowadays nurses have shaved heads, ponytails, earrings and high 'n tights just like yours."

"Good. Then it's decided." Juan gave Ricky a look inviting follow-up. "We're going to grow your hair, Papito." The way Ricky said it left no room for further discussion. Juan stood up, lifted Ricky's chin with one hand and delivered a quick, firm kiss before moving back behind Ricky, picking up the clippers and snapping them on.

"I guess we are, mijo. Whatever you say."

Raphael's Friday had been one of those Fridays. He'd spent more time dealing with other people's issues than managing his own. Since he'd hardly touched his own To Do List, it probably meant another lost weekend. He was considering logging out to take a walk around the block to clear his head when his phone chimed. It was a text from Steve. A simple one, showing a thumbs up emoji and the words, 'Call Me.'

"LUKE!" Raphael yelled as he stood up and pressed Steve's contact icon.

"What?" Luke rounded the corner to see Raphael looking happy, flustered, and anxious all at once.

"Steve ..." Luke knew exactly what he meant. Raphael had his phone on speaker.

"That was quick," Steve laughed. "I didn't want to interrupt your work day or I'd have just called."

"Interrupt!" Raphael put an arm around Luke who was now at his side. "So ... "

"Ben says yes, Raphael." Luke hugged Raphael who whooped from his end as Niki joined in from his. "So ... what's next?" Steve asked.

"As soon as Juan is cleared from quarantine, I'll be in touch. Thank you, Steve, thank you, thank you. You did great!"

"I was only following orders, Raphael. Now I know how Luke feels."

"You don't know the half of it, Steve," Luke agreed. "But you have to admit, Raphael always pulls these schemes off. Let me add my congrats to you, though. Ben must really trust you."

"I guess. He's a good guy. Now it's up to us to not let him down."

"Never fear," Raphael assured. "We'll be the best tenants anyone could ever hope for. Right, Niki?"

"We'll show our house more tender loving care than it's ever seen before, Raphael," Niki promised.

"Luke did offer to be the butler," Raphael grinned as he turned around in Luke's arms. "You did, didn't you?"

"No fair," Luke protested. "That was before I knew you had a plan to get the house without any of us becoming indentured servants. So, no, Raphael, I will not be the butler. But I do know where we can get a friendly puppy for the house." On cue, Niki barked his assent.

"We'll wait to hear from you, Raphael," Steve said, ready to end the call.

"Thank you, again, Steve. For everything." Raphael put his phone down, the need for a walk forgotten. Luke patted his shoulders as he sat back down, newly energized to wrap up as many tasks as possible in anticipation of a very special weekend after all.

Later that evening, Raphael nearly knocked Luke over as he whipped out of the shower to grab his phone. It had chimed a text notification as the two of them were in the midst of their shave and shower routine. Luke stood up in the shower, razor in hand, as Raphael scooped up the phone, lather dripping off the side of this head. He turned to face Luke as he unlocked the phone. Luke didn't have to ask if it was good news. Raphael grinned, tossed the phone on the vanity and rubbed his hands together as he resumed his place, seated at Luke's feet.

"Well? Was that ..."

"Juan. As he promised, we're the first to know. He and Ricky are out of quarantine." Raphael clapped his hands, then whipped around and raised up on his knees to face Luke, who hadn't moved. "Sir! Tomorrow we'll finally get the whole family together. And it won't be on Zoom ... it'll be in our new home." Raphael tugged briefly on Luke's handy cock, then resumed his normal shavee position.

"What if ..."

"No what ifs. Sir. This. Is. Happening." Luke resumed his position, legs wrapped around Raphael's waist. He smoothed a bit more lather on Raphael's head.

"I guess we'd better do an extra good job on each other, then, if we're going to be showing the house tomorrow." Raphael patted Luke's calf in affirmation.

"Good point. Make me beautiful, Sir. But not too beautiful. We don't want to distract them from the house, do we?" Luke laughed as he pulled the razor down the back of Raphael's head.

"I don't know, baby. Between you and that house ... I think it'd probably be a draw."

"I knew it!" Alex set his phone down. Greg was still holding the remote he'd used to pause the episode of 'Hollywood' the three of them were watching when Alex's phone had vibrated. "I knew he was up to something."

"Care to elaborate?"

"That was a group text from Raphael, to the family. Instructions on where to meet tomorrow for an in-person meet up instead of online."

"Really?" Mateo sat up from his prone spot on the floor. "Is okay?"

"That's a gray area, Mateo," Greg said professorially. "Depends. On where and for how long." He turned to Alex. "What makes you think Raphael is up to something."

"One. He has us meeting in person. Two. At an odd location, not at their place. Three. 'Cause I know Raphael."

"Oh. Okay. Where are we meeting?" Alex picked up his phone again and reread the text.

"On the street. At the corner of Noe and 20th."

"Yeah, that is weird. Were Juan and Ricky included on the text?" Alex nodded. "Cool. They're finally out of quarantine." Alex nodded again and squeezed Greg's thigh.

"An adventure!" Mateo offered, then returned to his prone viewing position, Greg's cue to press play.

So it was, fittingly, that Juan and Ricky's first foray into the outside world in two weeks was to finally see the rest of the family face to face. Well, masked face to face. As they trudged uphill on Noe, hand in hand, they could see several figures standing on the corner at what must be their destination. One of them left the group and ran downhill to greet them.

"Mateo!" Ricky shouted. Mateo came to a stop almost six feet short and spread his arms.

"Amigos! I miss you!"

"We've missed you, too, Mateo," Juan said as he and Ricky released hands and gave Mateo air hugs. Very unfulfilling air hugs. "What's going on?"

"Don' know. Come on!" Mateo began walking backwards up to the rest of the group, not wanting to take his eyes off Ricky and Juan. The remainder of the climb was made in silence. Once they arrived at the corner, they could see that everyone was there ... everyone but Raphael. Muffled greetings and compliments were exchanged, along with earnest desires to 'fuck the pandemic' and seriously hug one another. But, no one did. Then, Greg asked the obvious.

"Where's Raphael, Luke, and why are we here?" Luke smiled, but no one could see it. Although they could see Niki wriggling in Steve's casual embrace.

"Follow me, boys, and all will be revealed." Luke turned and headed up the block, the rest trailing in semi-socially distanced manner. It wasn't long before Luke stopped and turned. "Right this way. Go on up the steps, Juan, Ricky ..." Juan and Ricky, in front of the pack, looked up the steps to see a magnificent Victorian house, not an unusual sight, except, in the doorway, was a figure, a well-built, Pacific Islander, almost naked but for a face mask and a sheer, glittery mankini. A waving, mischievous Raphael. Hand in hand, Juan and Ricky started up the steps. Greg looked questioningly at Luke, who simply smized and motioned him and Alex to follow Juan and Ricky. Luke took Mateo's hand and held him back. Steve and Niki were next, then Luke and Mateo, hand-in-hand, headed up the rear.

When Juan and Ricky arrived at the front doors, Raphael stepped aside, inside, so they could enter the foyer. As each couple entered, they found a spot as socially distanced as possible. Once Luke and Mateo entered, Raphael closed the doors and turned to face his family.

"It is so good to see you all! Juan, welcome home. God, I want to hug all of you. You all look so amazing."

"You're the one who looks amazing," Alex said. "You forgot to tell us this was going to be formal."

"Oh, this old thing?" Raphael laughed. "This was a last-minute thought. I just wanted to make this a little festive."

"Make what a little festive?" Greg asked, "Is there more going on than getting the family together in person? Why here? Whose house is this?" Juan, his arm around Ricky's shoulders, pulled him close as he gazed around the foyer.

"Whose house, indeed." Raphael teased. "Let's all get comfortable, and I will tell you everything." He gestured toward the sitting room and said, "Niki ..." On cue, Niki slid open the pocket doors; he and Steve led the rest of the group in. Everyone found a place to sit, with Steve and Niki taking the bay window seat. There was certainly plenty of other seating to accommodate social distance for everyone. Raphael gave them a moment to take in their surroundings. Once everyone had had a look, and returned their attention to Raphael, he pulled down his mask so they could see his face as he said with his most irresistible smile, "Welcome to your new home guys. Our home. All of us together, for real."

Not surprisingly, that was met first with silence, then outbursts from all the uninitiated in the room, all at once, so none of it was intelligible. Raphael raised his hands to quiet everyone.

"We'll explain everything in detail. But, first, you should see the place. To keep social distance, Niki is going to take Juan and Ricky on a tour starting down here. I will take Alex, Greg and Mateo on a tour starting in the turret room upstairs. Then, we'll all meet back in the dining room and we'll explain everything. Okay?" Raphael slipped his mask back into place.

"Wait ... so Niki is in on this? A turret room? What is ...?"

"Alex, hold your questions. Juan, Ricky ... Niki will start your tour with his favorite room. The rest of you, follow me." And so, they did. Meanwhile, Steve and Luke prepared the dining room, setting out cheeses, crackers, olives and cream cheese stuffed dates, along with flutes from the butler's pantry. The bubbly was already chilling in the kitchen's hidden fridge. Whether everyone was onboard with the idea or not, just being together, in person, for the first time in nearly two months, was reason enough to celebrate. After nearly half an hour, members of the family began filing into the dining room. Raphael led Alex, Greg and Mateo in from Niki's library shortly before Niki descended the stairs, with Juan and Ricky trailing. Even though it was a large table, they weren't exactly six feet apart, but at this point no one, not even Juan, was objecting.

"Did everyone enjoy the tour?" Raphael asked as he wandered around the room in his sparkly wedding mankini. Naturally, Alex was the first to speak.

"I'm still trying to figure out what kind of dare this is. Raphael, what have you been smoking?"

"Okay ... no more questions from Alex, and no Alex, this is not a dare," Raphael pronounced before looking at Greg. "What do *you* think, Greg?"

"Well, I'm not sure what to think. It's a great house. It would make an amazing home, you're right about that. But ... how would that even work? It would cost a fortune."

"Actually Greg," Raphael moved as close to him as he dared, "it will cost less than you're paying now." Even with the mask, Raphael could tell Greg thought he was crazy. "Let me explain. This is the house Steve's friend inherited, you remember? He and Niki talked about seeing it over Zoom a couple of weeks ago?"

"Oh yeah! Duh ... on Noe Street. Of course," Alex made the connection. "But ..."

"Alex, let me finish before you accuse me of being stoned again. We're not buying the house. We're renting it from Ben. Guys, we, well actually, Steve, offered his friend Ben a deal he couldn't refuse. He gets to keep the house his dad and grandad grew up in, and we get to live here, all under one roof, as the family we really are. We only have to pay the property taxes and utilities. Divided four and a half ways ... it's less than we're each paying now." Raphael stopped, letting that sink in.

"That can't be right," Alex, the doubter, said. "it's ... it's too good to be true." Raphael kneeled near Alex to drive home his response.

"Alex. It's not 'too good.' It's perfect. Look around. You belong here. We all do." He stood back up and looked at Juan and Ricky. "Juan, we haven't heard from you and Ricky." Ricky put an arm around Juan's neck and looked intently at Juan, who made eye contact with Ricky long enough to know what Ricky thought. Then Juan looked over at Luke, then at Niki, before addressing Raphael.

"Ah, well ... I didn't realize ..." he took a deep breath. "I guess I'm just surprised that you never mentioned the most ... interesting ... feature of the house." Raphael cocked his head questioningly. "Oh ... you mean you don't know?"

"Know what, Juan?" Raphael asked.

"You haven't been downstairs?" Raphael looked at Steve and Niki. All three shook their heads.

"There's a basement?" Niki asked. Juan climbed out of Ricky's embrace and his chair.

"Maybe it's gone now," Juan said cryptically. "You guys wait here. I'll be right back." He started for the butler's pantry.

"Papito, I'm coming, too." Ricky was right behind him.

"Okay, but the rest of you ... wait here." Steve, who was sitting at the end of the table nearest the pantry, leaned back to see them head into the kitchen then take a left toward the back stairs.

"What could be so interesting about a basement?" Raphael asked the room at large. Before anyone in the room could respond, Ricky shrieked from below.

"DIOS MIO!" As one, ignoring Juan's request, the family leapt out of their chairs and followed Steve into the kitchen, then back past the stairs and through a door no one had noticed before. As a very non-socially distanced cluster they plowed down a flight of stairs to find Juan and Ricky standing in the middle of an elaborate, fully equipped dungeon.

"Holy Shit!" Luke spoke first. It had everything. A St. Andrews Cross. Not one, but two slings. A puppy cage. A low table with cutouts that could function as a surface for mummification, bondage and plenty more. And walls displaying all the toys and equipment expected in a full-service dungeon. Niki immediately walked over to the puppy cage and lovingly brushed his hand across the top of it.

"It's beautiful," he purred. Steve joined him and put a hand on his shoulder.

"It's nicer than the ones at BPOS, isn't it," he agreed. Niki nodded. Meanwhile Mateo wandered over to one of the many assortments on the walls, this one offering a variety of whips, floggers, cat o' nine tails and paddles. He selected one paddle in particular and turned to Alex.

"Look, Alex!" His eyes telegraphed that he was undoubtedly grinning beneath his mask. Raphael burst into laughter. Alex rolled his eyes and tossed his head back simultaneously in embarrassment, causing Steve to lean over and whisper in Niki's ear.

"What was that you said about keeping secrets?" Niki shrugged.

"How did you know this was here?" Ricky asked Juan. "It's amazing, Papito!"

"Let's go back upstairs, and I'll tell you." Juan stood at the base of the stairs until everyone but Ricky had filed back up. He took a last look around, then urged Ricky ahead of himself up the stairs. Everyone was seated, except for Raphael who was opening the bubbly. As he poured, Luke distributed the filled glasses.

"So, Juan, it seems Steve and Niki weren't the first of us to appreciate what this house has to offer," Luke prodded.

"I guess so," Juan chuckled. "Thanks," he said as Luke placed glasses for him and Ricky at his elbow. "Well, I do have to say being here right now, contemplating making this a home with all of you is, well, it's bittersweet." He waited until Luke and Raphael took their seats and everyone raised their glasses together.

"I know we haven't voted yet," Raphael stood back up, "so, for now, I'd like to make a toast to us, the family, together again, and may it soon be ... together always." Cheers were offered, masks were pulled down, and everyone sipped. "Go on, Juan, about this being bittersweet."

"So, yeah, I've been here before, but never in this room. Only in the hall on my way to the dungeon. See, Ben, the grandfather, not your friend, Steve, was a very respected member of the leather community. It was only moments ago, when Raphael was explaining, that I realized Ben was the person who had died and left the house to your friend. We weren't close friends, but he was someone I admired and looked up to. I learned a lot from him. Many of us did. It was at his dungeon parties that I learned so much of what I know about leather and kink and all that goes with it. They were always small groups, six or eight guys, not always the same guys. They weren't orgies. He knew how to select the right people to create amazing dynamics. He was a craftsman. He took it seriously, but at the same time he made sure we all had fun. Lots of fun. Gosh, I'll miss him." Ricky put his arm around Juan's neck and tugged. At first no one spoke.

"Juan," Raphael quietly said, "I'm sorry. I didn't know."

"Don't be, Raphael. Of course, you couldn't know. It's all a freaky coincidence. But in a way, like it was meant to be. I don't know what more you wanted to say about the house, Raphael, but for me, for us," he looked at Ricky, "it would be an honor to make Ben's home our home. I think he'd be very pleased."

"Why didn't you say something right away?" Luke asked.

"Well, I didn't know why we were here ... what was going on. I didn't want to derail The Raphael and Niki Show. I thought maybe you also knew Ben, Luke, and that he'd loaned you guys the house so we could all physically get together today."

"No, Juan, I didn't know him. From what you've said, I wish I had, though."

"Yeah, you'd have liked him. You all would have. He was one of a kind."

"Maybe you can step into his shoes, Juan," Steve offered. "I mean, if we all do move in. I certainly wouldn't know where to start downstairs, except, of course, with the puppy cage."

"Thanks for the vote of confidence, Steve," Juan nodded to Steve. "Sure, I'd be happy to do what I can. But, uh, I could never fill Ben's shoes. Er, boots, I should say. He knew how to dress the part."

"Well," Raphael again took control of the discussion, "back on that topic ... of moving in ... since Alex is not allowed any more questions, do you have any Greg?"

"Wait," Alex interrupted. "If I can't ask questions ... bitch ... can I make a comment, or two?"

"That was a question," Raphael corrected him. "Take back the 'bitch,' and ... sure."

"I take it back. Raphael, you know I love you more than all the See's Black Forest Truffles in the world. Okay ... let's see. Can I say this without a question mark ... I eagerly await your plan for how we go from living where we are to living here, given that we all have various leases." Raphael looked over at Steve, but before he could speak Alex continued. "Secondly, I am also eagerly awaiting your recommendation on how we would address the issue of maintenance on this beautiful, massive, but potentially demanding edifice." Raphael laughed.

"Well put, Dr. Practicality. Greg, how do you bear living with this wild and irresponsible guy?"

"As you well know, Raphael," Greg deadpanned, "he has his charms."

"Yeah, he does, doesn't he? I'll take the first non-question and let Steve take the second. I see at least three ways we can take possession. We can stay in our current apartments until each lease is up, and then move in, we can stay where we are until we find someone to sublet, then move, or ... and this is what I think Luke and I will do, and probably Niki and Steve, if I know Niki at all, is to move in now and keep paying on our current place until the lease is up. Our lease is up in just two months anyway." Alex raised his hand, but before he could speak, Raphael spoke over him, "Remember, we're not really paying rent here, we're paying utilities and property taxes. The taxes for this year are already paid, so we won't be writing any checks for that again until well into next year. So, we can move in now, and continue paying our current rent until the old lease is up, or until we find someone to take it over, which should be pretty easy, even with the pandemic." Alex nodded, accepting Raphael's logic and turned to Steve.

"We made an agreement," Steve said, "with Ben ... my Ben ..." He turned to Juan. "Juan, I'm sorry this is how you learned about your Ben." Juan nodded wordlessly. "Our agreement is that we would cover any incidental maintenance. A leaky toilet, that sort of thing. Beyond that, Ben's grandad didn't just leave him the house. He inherited a fair amount of money, too, which is probably why he wasn't highly motivated to sell the house. He expects us to stay on top of any significant maintenance issues, and he'll pay for them. He wants us to keep the place pristine. Niki promised we would."

"Yeah," Niki nodded. "Tender loving care."

"So," Raphael began wrapping up. "Everyone has voted except you, Greg, Alex and Mateo. You had good questions, er, non-questions. You don't have to decide right now. But can we get your answer in the next couple of days?"

"Why don't we conference for a minute," Greg stood. "Alex and Mateo, come with me into Niki's library." After the three had quietly closed the pocket door, Raphael also stood and started slowly pacing around the room.

"It's kind of weird, isn't it?" He posed to no one in particular. "Niki immediately knew this was his dream house, while all the while, downstairs was a perfectly good puppy cage going begging. It's almost as if the house was barking to him, quietly and undetected."

"Are you suggesting the house is supernatural ... that it has powers?" Steve asked. Niki, at least his eyes, looked conflicted.

"Heavens no," Raphael replied. "Just that it's all too, too perfect in a way."

"Raphael," Juan spoke up, "I think we should accept that this was meant to be. Not that there's anything surreal about it, but that it's only right that a family that lives the kind of life that Ben loved and promoted would carry that tradition on. It's like he passed it on, through his grandson, thanks to the intervention of Steve and Niki, and you. What I'm trying to say is, maybe it really was meant to be."

"Yeah," Raphael sat back down next to Luke. "Destiny." The pocket door could be heard sliding open, followed shortly by the return of Greg, Alex and Mateo. They didn't need to verbalize their vote, as all three were naked.

"What! Are you guys crazy?" Alex announced. "Why are you all wearing clothes ... at home?" As if on command, everyone else stood and stripped. As he was pulling off his shorts, Niki spoke first.

"This is funny. The first time we toured the house, I made Steve and me get naked, so it would feel like home. And now it is home!" He pulled Steve into a hug.

"Which brings up a good point," Raphael said. "This is not just any house. It has character. It's stands out on this block. This house deserves a name. Like Filoli, or the Hearst Castle. I suggest we call our home, Niki's Dream House." Steve nodded, along with a couple of others.

"No, Raphael," Niki protested. "it's not just my house now. It's all our home. I know! You guys, you know how the different groups who compete in the ballroom culture call themselves the House of This or the House of That? This should be 'The House of the Locked Cock Brotherhood.'"

"Perfect!" Alex clapped. "It's kind of a mouthful, but it says it all. Raphael?"

"I want to hear what Ricky thinks," Raphael replied, wiggling his eyebrows.

"Well, you know," Ricky bowed toward Niki, "I think it sounds *legendary!*"

"Well, that's settled," Luke laughed. "I have another suggestion for rewarding Niki, though, and I hope none of us will vote down this one." All eyes turned to Luke. "As a finder's fee for Niki and Steve, I suggest they get the master bedroom for the first year."

"Here, here," Juan seconded. Everyone agreed, so there was no debate.

"Now that that's all settled, is it okay ... *Raphael* ... if I can ask a question?" Alex looked slightly menacingly at Raphael, who bowed and extended his left arm toward Alex in a princely fashion. "Thank you. Since we're all naked, and we're all about to be cohabiting in this, our home, can I please, please have a long-awaited group hug?!" Everyone converged on Alex, including Juan, for what might still be the longest group hug in family history.

## Twelve

# DECISIONS AND DISCOVERIES

THE NEXT DAY, SUNDAY, was to be the first of many pancake break-fasts prepared by Ricky in The House of the Locked Cock Brother-hood. Since social distancing had gone out the window the previous day, the family had declared themselves a COVID-19 bubble, which limited their exposure to others, but guaranteed mask-free, unfet-tered access to one another. Another slice of the new normal. Luke and Raphael were, as if it was tradition, the last to arrive. They put the bag of groceries on the floor of the foyer and stripped and piled their street clothes along with all the others before padding back to the kitchen to find Ricky aproned and hard at it. Mateo was juicing oranges, while Alex was trying to figure out how to work an espresso machine. He turned at Raphael's greeting.

"Guys, this kitchen has everything!" Luke removed his mask and then peeled Raphael's off, permitting a quick, husbandly kiss.

"Where did you find that?" Raphael asked as he wandered over and rubbed Alex's paddle prone ass. Luke was unloading the berries and melon at the island, where Niki and Steve were lounging after having set the table in the dining room.

"In the cabinets behind that 'wall' over there. This house is full of secrets. It took me five minutes to find the fridge."

"Yeah," Ricky said over his shoulder. "Everywhere you look there's something cool. Mateo found that juicer in the butler's pantry."

"Fresh-squeezed oj, espresso drinks, Ricky's pancakes ... something tells me we're all going to have bellies like Steve's here in no time," Luke stated the unstated obvious. He moved over next to Steve, put one hand on his shoulder and rubbed Steve's belly with the other. "Be honest. This isn't just a COVID belly, is it?" Steve looked at Niki, who rolled his eyes up in a failed attempt to declare innocence. "Good for you, Niki. I knew you'd get your belly sooner or later."

"What?" Alex asked. "What have I missed now?" He flipped the on switch and the espresso machine lit up. "Yes!"

"Alex are you the only one in the family who didn't know Niki is turned on by bellies? Sexy bellies like Jake's and now Steve's?" Raphael asked. He looked over at Steve and Niki and winked. "How big are you guys going to go?"

"We're thinking about stopping now, right Niki?" Steve said. "While I can still tie my shoes." Greg and Juan wandered in from the back stairs.

"Tying shoes? What's going on?" Greg asked. "Got that thing figured out yet, Alex?" Alex nodded, deep in concentration, with Raphael's arm around his shoulder. Juan joined Ricky at the stove top and stirred the batter.

"We were just complimenting Steve and Niki on the belly Niki had Steve grow," Luke explained.

"Ah," Greg said, as if that made perfect sense. "Juan and I were scoping out the bedrooms, trying to decide which to put dibs on."

"What did you decide?" Steve asked, happy to change the subject from his own anatomy.

"Well, they're all great," Juan set the batter bowl back down and turned toward the island. "I was thinking the one on the front left, under Steve and Niki's room for us. I've never had a bay window before. But, if any of you guys were thinking of taking it ..."

"And I thought Alex and I would take the room on the left, near the back," Greg followed up. "I like that view better than the street view."

"What about you, Mateo," Raphael asked on his way to the butler's pantry, hoping to find espresso cups. "Have you picked out a room?"

"Me? No, Raphael. Whatever is left is good for me. Very good, amigo." Mateo turned off the juicer, and poured the last of the fresh juice into the large glass pitcher he'd been filling.

"Come with me, Mateo," Luke took Mateo's hand and headed for the back stairs. Raphael placed the espresso cups in the island sink and rinsed, then dried them. They hadn't been used in a while. Niki was rinsing and pitting strawberries at the other sink, while Steve was putting melon in a serving bowl. There were to be no store containers on this inaugural brunch table. It wasn't until Juan started distributing the plated pancakes in the dining room that Luke and Mateo returned and everyone found a seat.

Alex raised his juice glass. "Our thanks to Ricky for the 'cakes, to Mateo for the juice, to Raphael and Luke for the fresh fruit. And, most assuredly, thanks to Niki and Steve for the roof above our heads. Here's to our first Sunday brunch in the House of the Locked Cock Brotherhood."

"Cheers!" was the response. After a few bites, Raphael turned to Luke.

"What did you and Mateo decide, Sir? Which room will be ours?"

"Mateo decided that since the room in the front has a bigger closet, it should be ours. Don't tell anyone, but I think he wants the room towards the back because it's closer to the kitchen." Mateo laughed, covering his not quite empty mouth and nodded. "Is that okay, baby?"

"As long as you and Mateo are happy, I'm happy, Sir," Raphael scrunched up his face, then puckered for a slightly syrupy kiss. Luke obliged.

"Guys," Juan spoke, enjoying the sight of the kiss. "I'm still not sure this has sunk in. Sitting here ... I know all of this is real. But part of me still doesn't believe it."

"I know what you mean," Greg said as he took Alex's hand in his, pausing Alex's enjoyment of Ricky's pancakes. "I'll admit I wondered last night, after we'd committed to this, if it was the right thing to do. But truth is, I'm never happier than when we're all together. It must be a lot to adjust to, after everything you've been through over the last six weeks, but Juan, it is real, and if I haven't said it before, let me tell you now, we are honored, and frankly humbled, to have you as part of our family." Juan swallowed, despite not having taken any bites lately.

"Juan," Niki said, "it's okay. You're home now." Juan nodded to Niki and sniffed, took a deep breath. Then he picked up his juice glass.

"We are ... all home now," he toasted. "Salud!"

"I have a question," Alex said as he freed his hand from Greg's grasp. "That is, if I'm allowed a question." He gave Raphael an indignant look, but didn't wait for an answer. "What are these little boxes for?" He pointed to one of the small, black boxes, wrapped in a bow, at each place setting. Steve nodded to Niki.

"Go ahead and open them," Niki grinned. Everyone dropped their utensils and picked up a box.

"Wow!" Raphael effused. "How did you know? It's just what I wanted!" Each box contained a set of keys to the house. Ricky dangled his set in front of Juan.

"Does this make it seem more real, Papito?" Juan grinned and nodded, then followed Raphael and Luke's example with a quick lip lock with Ricky. Everyone resumed eating. After a few more bites, Greg spoke.

"I have a question, too. Maybe some of you have already figured this out. This house is fully furnished, with great stuff. What do we do with our furniture? Most of it doesn't quite measure up, if you know what I mean."

"Yeah," Steve replied. "All of this stuff is Ben's property now. Not that he wants it in Melbourne, but we certainly can't sell it or anything."

"We just got a pretty expensive mattress last fall," Luke said. "We were thinking of moving that in and putting the mattress here in storage."

"Yeah, I love that mattress," Raphael said. "We might put a couple of other things in storage with the mattress and sell the rest of our furniture."

"Maybe we should all sleep here in our new rooms a night or two to decide what we want to do," Juan suggested. "I'm guessing the mattress in our room here is at least as good as ours, maybe better."

"Good idea, Juan," Greg replied, "Luke has a good idea, too. If Alex and my storage unit isn't big enough, maybe we can all go together on an upgraded unit for anything we want to keep, and sell or donate the rest."

"Why get another storage unit?" Alex asked.

"To ... store stuff," Raphael replied, looking at Alex as if he wasn't familiar with the concept.

"Oh," Alex grinned back. "So, I guess there are still some things you don't know about our new house. Follow me." Alex stood and held his hand out to Raphael. Just like old times, hand in hand, Alex led Raphael out of the room through the butler's pantry. First Luke then Juan, then everyone else followed, through the kitchen, down the stairs to the dungeon.

"Shouldn't we let brunch digest before we indulge in wild, kinky sex?" Raphael asked.

"You wish," Alex laughed, pulling Raphael around a corner to yet another door Raphael hadn't encountered. Still holding Raphael's hand, something he hadn't done in months, Alex opened the door, reached around to flip a light switch, then pulled Raphael through into a large utility room. "Here's your storage room." Everyone else trailed in. "Greg and I discovered this earlier when we were, uh, familiarizing ourselves with the dungeon."

"Huh," Luke said. "Now we know where the water heater is. Yeah, we could probably store all of our stuff that we don't sell down here, from all our apartments."

"Or ..." Raphael remarked, as he broke free of Alex and strode around the room, "What if ... I don't know about you guys, but I really miss the gym. What if we set up a gym in here? You know, a couple of benches, a couple of barbells, some dumbbell handles and some plates. Not a lot, but enough to stay in shape."

"Maybe yoga mats?" Juan suggested.

"An elliptical?" Niki added.

"You guys might be on to something," Steve agreed. "Who knows when the gym will open again, or how easy it'll be to work out when it does. They're talking about a reservation system to keep the numbers down."

"Yeah," Raphael agreed. "This way we maintain our bodies and our social distancing bubble."

"This was your idea, Raphael," Luke asserted, "so you're in charge of researching the cost and sourcing. But my guess is we could set up a serviceable gym for the cost of three or four months of all our gym dues."

"Not only that," Raphael said as he walked back to Alex and lifted Alex's right arm and squeezed his biceps, "we might even buff up Alex here." Alex wrested his arm free of Raphael's grip.

"What? And ruin my perfect dancer's body?" Raphael planted one on Alex's cheek, another first in lo these many months.

"We love you just the way you are, Alex," he cooed. "But if you want any pointers, we'll be here to help." Alex rolled his eyes and headed for the door. As they were passing through the dungeon Juan paused.

"So, Alex, what were you and Greg familiarizing yourselves with down here when you discovered the utility room?"

"Oh, uh ... you know ... just stuff," Alex mumbled. Greg caught Juan's eye and grinned.

"Were you planning your next birthday, Alex?" Raphael asked with a giggle. Alex shook his head in dismay.

"Okay, that comment demands follow up," Juan said, sitting down on the edge of the bondage platform, clearly interested in hearing more.

"No, it doesn't," Alex replied as he started up the stairs. Alone. Everyone else remained in place. After a moment Alex retreated back down the stairs and looked pleadingly at Raphael. "Raphael ... please."

"Allow me," Luke walked over to Alex and put an arm around his shoulders. "On his birthday Greg arranged a special night for Alex in Jake's dungeon. Raphael and I played a small part in it. That's all you need to know unless Alex decides to share more in the future. It was his special night." Alex looked gratefully at Luke.

"Yeah, that's right. Thanks, Luke."

"This family is full of secrets, and great ideas today," Juan stood up. "We should make that a tradition. On each member's birthday, he gets to celebrate with a night in the dungeon with the rest of the family providing the party favors."

"You're not talking about balloons, are you?" Niki asked.

"No." Juan grinned.

"Cool," was Niki's reply. Steve ruffled his mohawk as they followed Alex and Luke up the stairs. As everyone began carrying plates and utensils from the dining room into the kitchen, Ricky continued the conversation that had been interrupted by the trip downstairs.

"So ... are we all sleeping over tonight?" he asked.

"Why not?" Steve placed a stack of plates on the counter where Alex was loading the dishwasher. "Maybe we can get Alex buzzed enough to tell us about his birthday." Alex straightened up and gave Steve a resolute look.

"Steve, maybe ... after your next birthday."

"Oooooo," Ricky responded. "I think I'm gonna like living here."

No one was surprised when Niki and Steve were the first to move in. Mentally, Niki had moved in weeks earlier. He'd even dreamed about living in the house, although that dream occurred before the discovery of the puppy cage, proving that real life can be better than some dreams. The following Saturday Luke and Greg went together on a rental and the two households moved all the things they were keeping into the storage unit Greg had rented earlier, when Mateo moved in. Luke had agreed to be the 'agent' in charge of handling the sale of all the items still left in both apartments, since he had most days free. They agreed that whatever didn't sell before lease end would go to Community Thrift. Two weeks later Juan finally arranged a sublet and he and Ricky, along with Luke, transported their keepsakes to the storage unit, and their personal stuff to the House. Finally, the House was home to everyone. That night, after dinner, to celebrate, Niki invited everyone into the library, where he had lit a fire in the fireplace. Well, to be honest, he'd pushed a button. It was a gas insert, but a realistic one. The lights were dimmed. Once everyone was settled, surprising even Niki, Steve entered with a serving tray laden with nine snifters and a bottle of Remy Martin XO.

"Seriously?!" Niki jumped up. "My dream is complete."

"Everyone, when Niki declared this to be his favorite room before he'd seen the rest of the house," Steve explained, "he vowed his evenings would be spent here, in front of the fire, with a glass of cognac. It turns out he knew exactly what he was talking about. Who wants cognac?" Eight hands went up. Steve poured; Niki distributed. Ricky was the first to raise his glass.

"Can I toast?" he asked. Steve hoisted his snifter toward Ricky in invitation. Ricky cleared his throat dramatically and looked into Juan's eyes. "Never in a million years would I have dreamed that one day I would be sitting here, next to the handsomest man in the world, as his lover. As his perfect locked cock leather boy. As a member of a family of locked cock leather boys and their husbands." Ricky looked at Mateo. "With another brother bravely navigating his way through a long-distance relationship, a relationship that hopefully won't be long distance much longer." Alex raised his snifter and swirled it to signal that the toast was maybe a wee bit too long. "All together in a house to die for! Take that 2020!"

"Here, here!" Steve affirmed. Everyone sipped. Except Mateo, who immediately bent forward, coughing. Juan, sitting next to him, rapped him on the back a couple of times.

"Easy, muchacho. This isn't Modelo. Don't gulp it, sip veeer-ry slowly, and let it warm your tongue before you swallow," Juan coached. Mateo, unable to speak, nodded and wiped at his eyes.

"So, Niki," Raphael spoke. "Is your dream really complete? If so, no one is happier for you than me."

"Well, let's just say my dreams are coming true. Amazingly so. I do have more dreams." He glanced at Steve. "I'm working on them, too. So, stay tuned." He raised his snifter to Raphael, then sipped.

"Here's to dreams," Greg raised his snifter. "May they all come true."

"I'm afraid to ask what you're dreaming, sweetie," Alex joked.

"You've already committed to one of them," Greg replied, then looked over at Luke and Raphael. "Right guys? Folsom? Next year ... if there is a Folsom next year."

"Oh, yeah!" Raphael responded. "Not fair! COVID gave Alex a year's grace."

"What's that?" Juan asked.

"Alex promised he'd do Folsom naked this year, but ... no Folsom," Greg explained. "He was just an uptight Midwesterner last year."

"Uptight?" Alex disputed. "I *was* naked, except for a chest harness and bare-assed codpiece. You call that uptight?"

"And look at you know," Luke grinned. "You've come a long way, baby." Alex had to smile and nod.

"It's been a fun ride ... yeah," he agreed. "At least next Folsom I won't be naked alone. I'll have seven naked brothers and a husband with me."

"How about it, Mateo?" Juan asked. "Will you do Folsom naked with Alex?" Mateo hesitated.

"If Ryan is, yes." Juan squeezed Mateo's thigh in affirmation and looked over at Luke.

"Alex isn't the only one who's come a long way," he winked.

"Time for Ryan," Mateo said as he stood. "Okay?"

"Of course, it's okay," Alex said. "You can show him the proper way to enjoy cognac. Make him jealous he's not here yet." Mateo, snifter in hand, started for the door.

"Say 'hi' for all of us," Greg added. Mateo nodded as he exited.

"Are we rushing things for Mateo?" Raphael asked once Mateo was gone. "Sometimes I forget how little time he's been out as gay, let alone dealing with us."

"Us?" Luke probed.

"You know ... perpetually naked, caged kinksters. With a dungeon no less. Apparently he's familiar with Alex's affinity for paddles." Alex flipped Raphael the bird. Affectionately, of course.

"Guys, we're fine," Juan said. "We've never coerced him to do something he doesn't want to do. As long as we keep it that way, he'll let us know his boundaries. I'm actually kind of jealous of him, being exposed to us at his age. If he does gravitate to a leather lifestyle, none of it will be so much a fetish for him as it'll be, just ... natural. Something he grew up with."

"Yeah," Niki agreed. "Now I'm jealous, too." Steve laughed and stood up, reaching for Niki's hand.

"Come on, puppy," he said. "Bring your cognac, and let's go to our room. We'll see who else we can make jealous tonight."

"That's a good idea," Greg stood. "'Night, guys." Alex leaned down and kissed Juan, Ricky, Raphael and Luke in turn on his way out.

"Damn," Juan said softly.

"Yeah," Raphael agreed as he stood. "It's real, Juan. Enjoy it." Once Juan stood, Raphael hugged him, then kissed him, then Ricky. Luke followed suit before he and Raphael headed for the stairs.

"You okay, Papito?" Ricky noticed Juan's eyes glistening before he wrapped his arms around Juan in front of the fire.

"Mijo, I've never been more okay in my life. Here, lay down." Ricky sat back down as Juan knelt next to him, then lowered Ricky onto his back. "I want to make love to you here in front of the fire. If that's okay with you." A broad smile grew across Ricky's face as he reached up for Juan and nodded.

"Yeah, Papito. It's fine by me."


It was one of those rare and precious days, a Saturday no less, with no wind, no fog, just strong, steady sunshine bringing the temperature in the Castro close to 80 degrees. Which is downright toasty in a city unaccustomed to 'balmy.' The gym equipment had not yet arrived, so Alex and Greg had been on a long walk, from which they returned bearing loot. After stripping in the foyer, Greg headed for the kitchen while Alex bounded upstairs. Not long after moving in it had become customary for everyone to leave their bedroom doors open, except when needing to work undisturbed, or when indulging their partner's needs. So, it wasn't much of challenge for Alex to stand in the middle of the second floor and announce an impromptu picnic.

"Hey, guys, Greg and I brought home a treat!" he shouted. "Luke, do you still have the beach blankets? Party in the back garden!" He headed down the back stairs to help Greg unpack. "We haven't had a back yard since we moved out here." Alex said in his indoor voice. "This'll be fun."

"Yeah, I've only been back there once so far. A day like today demands it," Greg agreed. Luke and Raphael were first in the kitchen, each holding a beach blanket. Raphael handed his to Luke, who headed for the back door.

"How can I help?" Raphael asked, sliding his arm around Alex's waist. He pulled a grape off a bunch Greg had just slid into a bowl and popped it in Alex's mouth.

"Do you know how to slice a watermelon?" Greg suggested.

"Wedges or disks?" Raphael replied.

"Your choice, maestro," Greg smiled as he handed Raphael a ten-inch chef's knife. By the time the rest of the family had made it into the kitchen, Alex had filled nine glasses with ice, and arranged them on a tray. Steve took possession and headed to the door, with everyone else trailing with bounty that included fresh fruit, lemonade and a platter of cookies from Hot Cookie. Raphael was the last to exit the house with the wedges of watermelon. He sat down between Luke and Steve, who handed him the last glass of lemonade.

"Thanks Greg and Alex," Niki toasted. "Great idea!"

"Yeah, I'll second that," Juan agreed.

"Well, this is the first Saturday afternoon we've all been home," Alex acknowledged. "We thought it was a perfect day to pay homage to the garden."

"This is my first time back here," Juan said as he took stock of the landscaping. "Ben was smart ... not surprisingly. All drought tolerant. Lots of stone work. No need for a lawn boy."

"I'll be your lawn boy, if you want," Ricky kissed Juan's shoulder. Juan chuckled.

"That would be the least of your duties, mijo."

"Where should we spit the seeds?" Niki asked. "I don't want to make a mess here."

"That's what this cup is for," Alex pointed. "We'll leave them near the birdbath over there for the birds." Mateo sheepishly began picking up seeds he'd spit behind him. After a few minutes of idle chatter, Luke moved away from the food far enough that he could stretch out flat to soak up the sun. Raphael rubbed Luke's left thigh, then brushed his hand across the ink that declared Luke's cock to be Raphael's property.

"Man, why can't every day be like this," Luke sighed.

"Yeah," Greg agreed. "If we tried to do this back home, we'd be battling flies, gnats, ants and ninety-eight percent humidity.

"Not to mention we'd never get away with being naked and har-nessed, either," Alex asserted. Greg nodded and smiled at the irony of Alex luxuriating in being naked, not to mention harnessed, out in the open in his own back yard. But, before he could point that out, a creak emanated from the middle of the privacy fence. Part of the fence moved inward a few inches and the face of an older Asian man peeked around what was obviously not solid fence, but a gate. As Luke quickly sat up, the man spoke.

"I do not mean to intrude, dear friends, but I thought I might say hello and welcome you to the neighborhood." Juan stood immediately and bowed gracefully to the man as Ricky looked on in surprise.

"Kon'ichiwa, Hiroshi-san," Juan intoned. The man stepped through the opening to reveal a very fit, and nearly naked masked man with a neat gray ponytail. He bowed to Juan then stood up straight, eyes twinkling.

"Kon'ichiwa, Juan-san. I did not recognize you! How wonderful! May I?"

"Please, come and meet my family," Juan enthused as he moved closer to the man, "Should we ... should I go get our masks?"

"No, please, as you were. One moment ..." The man retreated back to the other side of the gate, revealing a large circular tattoo on his back as he did so. He then immediately reappeared with a tray of his own. "I do not mean to intrude, but when I saw you all together from my upstairs window, I wanted to take this opportunity to be neighborly. I brought a gift of sake." As he approached the blanket everyone stood, still uncertain as to what was happening or how to act. Violating social distancing, Juan reached out and took the tray from Hiroshi, bowed once more and set it down on the blanket before straightening up and placing his arm around Ricky's waist. Considering how the man was dressed no one, except perhaps Mateo, was terribly self-conscious about their total nudity. From a distance he appeared to be wearing a red print thong, but the back was constructed of intricately braided cloth, with a bit of loose fabric tucked into the back of the waist band on each side. The costumer of the group was intrigued.

"Hiroshi, please, join us in the enjoyment of your sake. For just a few moments, let's forget about COVID-19." Juan's invitation didn't give him an option. Hiroshi nodded, his eyes still twinkling. There was probably a smile beneath his mask. "Everyone, this is Hiroshi. I'll tell you more in a moment, but first, Hiroshi, I want to introduce you to my family. This is Ricky, my lover, and the best locked cock leather boy in the world." Hiroshi bowed to Ricky, who awkwardly bowed back.

"It is an honor to meet the one who has chosen Juan for his own," Hiroshi said.

"Always so perceptive, Hiroshi," Juan laughed. "Yes, Ricky chose me, and I was helpless to resist." Juan then introduced the rest of the family one by one. Then he indicated the blanket to encourage Hiroshi and the rest to sit. Once they had, Hiroshi reached for the sake bottle and began opening it.

"Juan, if you please, hand each of these beautiful men a choko?" Once everyone had one of the small, intricately decorated ceramic cups, Hiroshi poured sake into each, then he set the bottle down. Juan leapt up and moved over behind Hiroshi. He picked up the bottle and poured sake into Hiroshi's empty choko. Once Juan was back at Ricky's side, Hiroshi pulled down his mask to reveal a salt and pepper goatee, lifted his cup and said, "Kanpai!"

Juan, and then everyone else responded with "Kanpai!" Mateo looked cautiously at how Hiroshi sipped the sake before putting it to his lips, not wanting to repeat his first experience with cognac. Juan raised his choko toward Hiroshi again and said, "To Ben." Hiroshi nodded, with a slight smile. Juan looked somberly at Hiroshi.

"I'm so very sorry for you, Hiroshi. I know you and Ben were very close. As close as we are as a family."

"Yes, I loved him dearly. We had many wonderful times together. And not just in the dungeon."

"Whoa!" Alex couldn't help himself.

"Yes, Alex," Juan turned to him, "that's how I know Hiroshi. He helped Ben mastermind most of the dungeon parties. Hiroshi is a very skilled practitioner of kinbaku, the art of Japanese rope bondage." Niki, who was sitting next to Hiroshi, spoke for everyone.

"Awesome! I'd love to see that." Hiroshi turned to Niki with a smile.

"If your husband has no objections, I would be delighted to bind you sometime, Niki. You would make a beautiful subject."

"Yes, please," Niki responded, confident in Steve's agreement.

"I didn't know about Ben until recently, Hiroshi, when we first visited the house a few weeks ago," Juan explained. "With everything going on, I guess I've really been out of touch. It was a shock."

"For everyone, yes," Hiroshi nodded. "I'm sure with this pandemic you have been a very busy nurse."

"It's been a challenge for all of us," Juan agreed.

"Papito ... Juan ... spent a month in New York helping with their crisis there," Ricky spoke up. "He's our hero." Juan looked down, embarrassed, then wrapped an arm around Ricky's shoulders and pulled him close.

"I am so happy to see you in love, Juan," Hiroshi said. "Especially with such a charming and apparently collared and devoted lover." Ricky reached up to touch his collar and smiled. "And a big family, too."

"One day I'll explain all this," Juan smiled. "But, yeah, I am one lucky guy."

"I was worried who might take over Ben's house," Hiroshi set his choko down, and picked up a wedge of watermelon. "I cannot think of anyone I would rather see living here than you, Juan, and your family. This makes losing Ben a little easier to accept. He would be delighted to know his house is home to a family of naked, caged, harnessed and collared young men such as yourselves."

"Well, Hiroshi," Raphael broke his silence, "we are lucky to have such a generous, kind and sexy neighbor as you. I hope you will consider joining our COVID bubble, so we can spend more time with you. Except maybe for Juan, I'm sure there is much we could learn from you." Hiroshi looked around the group, all of whom were smiling and nodding. He landed back on Raphael. One pair of almond eyes silently sharing a moment with another.

"Raphael, just as your husband was no doubt powerless to resist your beauty, I too, cannot resist your charm and would be humbled to join your 'bubble.'" He looked around the group again, then stopped with Juan. "How is it possible that you are here?"

"I think that is best explained by Steve," Juan replied. "He and Niki made this possible." Steve proceeded to explain the highlights as Hiroshi munched his wedge of watermelon, nodding at times.

"It was meant to be," Hiroshi pronounced when Steve concluded. "It was meant to be."

"Sir. Hiroshi," Alex sought attention. "It's really none of my business, but I'm fascinated by what you're wearing. I've never seen anything like it."

"This?" Hiroshi looked down at his crotch. "This is just a fundoshi. An all-purpose Japanese garment. Worn as underwear, for swimming, festival wear. It's really about the simplest garment ever created, except maybe the loincloth."

"I love it," Alex praised.

"Would you like to see how it works?" Alex nodded, as did Niki and Raphael. "Wait here." Hiroshi stood, and disappeared around the gate that was still ajar.

"You've been holding out, Juan," Luke said as he moved over behind Juan on his knees and draped his arms around Juan's neck and down his pecs, his cock pressed against Juan's back. "What else haven't you told us about this house? Hiroshi is fascinating."

"I can't tell you everything all at once, guys," Juan protested. "Give me a break!" Juan tilted his head back and looked up Luke, enjoying the feel of Luke's fingers on his nipples. "If I told you everything, there'd be nothing left to tell."

"You tease!" Luke laughed, slapping Juan's pecs. He returned to Raphael's side. "First a dungeon. Then a sexy rope bondage master. I can't wait to see what comes next."

"I said it before," Ricky piped up, "and I'll say it again. I'm gonna love living here. I already do." Juan planted one on Ricky's cheek, then began gathering up the empty choko. Hiroshi came back through the fence with a canvas bag in one hand. He set it down next to the blankets and pulled out a white folded cloth decorated with a navy blue check.

"Alex, come be my model. Juan, will you be my assistant ... like old times?" Juan and Alex joined Hiroshi while everyone else scooted around to watch. Hiroshi unfurled the cloth which was about twelve inches wide and maybe ten feet long.

"This is a fundoshi?" Alex asked. Juan nodded. "And it'll end up looking like that?" he touched Hiroshi's fundoshi at the waist. "Incredible." Hiroshi and Juan went to work, folding the cloth in half width-wise, then draping it part way down Alex's back, then down his torso and over his caged cock. Juan held the cloth at Alex's shoulder while Hiroshi twisted it into a very tight braid as he passed it through Alex's legs and up his ass, then around his waist over the strip of cloth draped down his torso, back around to his ass crack again, then, still twisting, he threaded the cloth through what was snuggling up Alex's ass, then wrapped the remaining cloth around the waist band to the left until it was used up. Raphael, whose own back always drew admiring comments, focused on Hiroshi's tattoo each time he turned his back. When he finished, Hiroshi nodded to Juan who pulled the length of cloth that had been draped over Alex's shoulder down over his crotch, then, like Hiroshi, he twisted it into a braid as he passed it between Alex's legs and then wrapped it around the braided cloth between Alex's cheeks, again and again and again until it reached the waist band, where he wrapped it around and around the waist band in the opposite direction from the way Hiroshi's cloth was wrapped, until it was all used up. Juan tugged a bit on the pouch that had been formed around Alex's cage, then he stood back and admired it.

"And that," Juan announced, "is how you wear a fundoshi."

"How does it feel, Alex" Hiroshi asked.

"Cool. Snug. A lot like wearing a harness. It makes my ass happy." Greg stood up and looked Alex over.

"Turn around, sweetie," he instructed. Alex pirouetted. Of course.

"How does it look?" Alex coyly begged for praise.

"Pretty damn sexy," Greg complied. "If you aren't going to be naked, this is the way to go." He turned to Hiroshi. "Guys really wear this to the beach ... to festivals?"

"Oh, yes. Mostly only Americans are ashamed of the body. Well, and maybe the Brits. But I guess that explains it."

"Alex used to be embarrassed about nudity, but we cured him of that," Raphael laughed. "It does look sexy on you ... just like it does on Hiroshi." Alex turned to Hiroshi and spread his arms, encouraging a hug. Hiroshi smiled and took Alex into his embrace.

"Thank you for sharing this with me, Hiroshi," Alex said. "I just might have to get one of these for myself."

"It is yours, Alex," Hiroshi bowed as he released the embrace. "I selected that one to compliment your eyes."

"Oh, no, I couldn't," Alex protested.

"I have one here for each of you," Hiroshi said as he emptied the canvas bag onto the blanket. "I just ask one favor in return."

"Anything," Raphael promised as he scattered the fundoshi apart from one another. He looked up into Hiroshi's eyes.

"Just don't wear them out here. Your naked beauty ... your joyful celebration of your sexuality and your chastity ... fills the garden with joy ... and brings me great happiness." Raphael stood, a blue and white fundoshi, the reverse of Alex's fabric, in his hand. He wrapped his arms around Hiroshi in his own grateful embrace.

"Since we never wear more than these harnesses, Hiroshi, and we always wear our collars and cages, that will be an easy promise to keep. Right, guys?" Raphael looked around for consensus and got it.

Thirteen

# Black Lives Matter

After Hiroshi had taken his leave, everyone pitched in to cart the remains of their surprisingly rewarding pop-up picnic into the house. As they were each heading off in different directions, Luke noticed Raphael heading down into the dungeon instead of upstairs. Luke carried the fundoshi he'd picked out up to their room, then decided to find out what Raphael was up to. When he arrived at the bottom of the dungeon stairs, he found Raphael standing in front of the collection of ropes, fingering a length of bright red rope he'd taken off the wall. Luke quietly padded up behind him and pressed up on his butt plug.

"Aaaugh," Raphael jumped before turning around, still holding the Shibari quality rope. "You're sneaky, Sir," he laughed.

"Not really, baby. You were kinda lost in thought." Raphael nodded. "Did Hiroshi pique your interest in bondage?"

"Maayybe," Raphael smiled, brushing the rope against Luke's bearded chin. "I have no idea what it's all about."

"Remember what it felt like to be trussed up in the bondage harness the night Jake and I transformed you from sexy gym bunny to locked cock leather boy?"

"Hmmm, yeah. But there was a lot more than a little bondage involved that night."

"Well, there's more to the experience than just the feel of rope snuggly caressing your body, baby." Luke leaned forward and pressed his lips on Raphael's as he wrapped one arm around his back to pull him close, close enough that Raphael could feel Luke's hardening cock press against the ink above his cage.

"Just talking about it seems to have a pretty wonderful affect, Sir," Raphael mumbled through the kiss. "I can hardly wait to try it." Luke pulled back enough to look Raphael in the eye, to determine how serious he was.

"Then, let's not wait, baby. I'll be right back." Luke bounded up the stairs as Raphael sat down on the end of one of the slings. He held the rope against his cheek. It felt somehow comforting. He closed his eyes and imagined Hiroshi in his fundoshi, wrapping and braiding this very rope around a naked and blindfolded Juan and felt his cage tighten inside and around his own erection. So, it was a double shock when he heard Juan's mellow voice coming down the stairs.

"It's been a while," Juan was saying, "but, sure if you guys want, we'll give it try." He appeared at the bottom of the stairs, with Luke behind him, and Ricky trailing Luke.

"What's this?" Raphael stood, still holding the rope.

"Baby, I asked Juan if he'd do the honors, since he has more experience with this than I do. And Ricky asked if he could watch."

"I'm no expert," Juan deflected. "I've watched Hiroshi many times, and assisted on occasion, but I can at least give you a feel for what it's like, if you want, Raphael. At least enough for you to know if you'd like to submit to Hiroshi sometime."

"Oh, I was just curious, Juan. You probably have other things you and Ricky would rather be doing." Raphael gave Luke a WTF? look.

"No, I'm happy to give it a go, Raphael," Juan said as stepped up to Raphael and took the bundled rope from him. "You don't want to disappoint Ricky, do you?" Ricky grinned, and gave Raphael a 'who me?' look.

"Okay, if you want," Raphael relented. "Sure. Tie me up, Sir Juan." Juan leaned down and delivered a chaste kiss. Raphael returned it, then cleared his throat self-consciously.

"Luke," Juan instructed, "why don't you remove Raphael's harness." Juan grabbed a couple more bundles of rope while Luke unsnapped Raphael's body harness and Ricky sat at the foot of the St. Andrew's cross. "Okay, Raphael, we'll start with a simple body harness for you, and maybe bind your arms as well, to give you a sense of being immobilized." Raphael looked at Luke, then back at Juan and grinned. Luke stood back and watched as Juan carefully formed a web of rope around Raphael's upper body, shoulders, chest, waist, and down and around his thighs, all without actually tying any knots. The web was tight, constricting Raphael, but apparently not painfully so. For Raphael, the feeling was similar to his ubiquitous leather body harness, only better, even tighter, and involving more of his body. Feeling Juan's constant touch made it exquisite. The pressure from his cage was tighter than anything Juan was doing, but it was Juan's touch that was tightening the cage, come to think of it.

"That looks so cool," Ricky said as Juan finished the harness and began binding Raphael's wrists. Luke walked around Raphael, admiring Juan's work from every angle, while also noticing that Juan had a raging hardon. Then, as he and Ricky watched, Juan bound Raphael's already bound hands to the harness, in position over his chest.

"I feel helpless, Juan, Sir," Raphael smiled. "Snuggly, hugged all over, but helpless at the same time."

"Yes, Raphael, that's a lot of it," Juan agreed. "Giving control over to the bondage master." He turned to Luke. "What do you think Luke?" He walked up to Raphael and fingered the rope in several places. It was indeed very tight on Raphael's body. He smiled at Juan, then turned back to Raphael and, as Juan had done, delivered a gentle, brushing, barely-there kiss to Raphael's lips.

"It's beautiful, Juan. He looks incredible, and I think it's finally time for Raphael's next dare." Raphael's eyes widened. "A flash dare, as Raphael would say. A variation on Raphael's last dare to me. You won't say no, will you, baby?" Raphael, not certain what Luke had in mind, nevertheless, responded as he always had.

"Of course not, Sir. Dare me." Ricky had stood and walked over to Juan's side, curious to finally see what this dare business was all about. He slid his left arm around Juan's waist and placed his right hand on Luke's back, just above his ass. Luke turned to Juan.

"You did a beautiful job, Juan. Raphael has always been a work of art, and you've created a worthy frame for his art. Don't you think, Ricky?"

"Yeah, he looks beautiful."

"I think we should reward Juan, Raphael. If it's okay with Ricky."

"I don't understand, Sir," Raphael replied.

"Juan, let's pick up Raphael and place him on the bondage board over there, on his back." Ricky released Juan so he and Luke could scoop Raphael off his feet and place him on the board. "Now, let's turn him so his head is just beside that cutout there." They positioned Raphael sideways on the board, his ass just at the edge of one side, his head next to the cutout. "Juan, Raphael's last dare to me was to find someone to suck off, since I was jealous of your ability to suck off Ricky. It's a long story and I'll explain later, but let's just say it's my turn to dare Raphael ... to suck you off. While I fuck him."

"Oh, but, we've never ..." Juan didn't finish his sentence.

"Ricky," Luke interrupted, "if you climb up on here and straddle Raphael's chest on your knees, facing Juan, you can kiss Juan and play with his nipples while Raphael sucks him off and maybe, just maybe, Raphael can move his fingers enough to play with your ass while I play with his."

"Raphael," Juan looked down at Raphael's placid face level with his crotch, "are you okay with this?"

"It's a dare, Juan," Raphael smiled. "I prove my devotion to Luke by submitting to his dares." To prove the point, he opened his mouth and wiggled his tongue. Ricky gasped.

"Okay, while I remove Raphael's plug and lube him up, go ahead and lower his head into the cutout, so you have a better shot at deep throating him. Ricky, you know what to do." Luke, reflecting back on his week of being caged, was not to be denied. He lifted Raphael's legs and worked the Thunderplug out of Raphael's ass, then applied lube to Raphael and himself. Ricky straddled Raphael as ordered, while Juan, always conscious of his patients' comfort, positioned a towel around the cutout before lowering Raphael's head down into it. As Luke had anticipated, doing so created the perfect angle for Juan to face fuck him easily. Juan paused to unscrew and remove his PA ring. His erection had faded with the surprise of Luke's dare. Ricky leaned forward and pulled Juan's tongue deep into his own throat. As soon as he began teasing Juan's nipples, Juan began hardening again, giving Raphael something to work with. Luke had already found purchase at his end, and he slowly began giving Raphael's notorious prostate something to work with as well. This was supposed to be a reward for Juan, but it was Raphael who was benefiting the most. He'd never sucked anyone in this position before, and found it distracting at first, to have Juan's balls brushing against his eyes and forehead, but soon that distraction gave way to Luke's skill and Juan's foreign but lovingly applied cock. What was initially odd soon became erotic. He was sucking off Juan, arguably the handsomest and sultriest of the family. It was several minutes before he remembered he was supposed to be trying to play with Ricky's ass. He lifted his hands as far from his chest as possible, barely an inch, not enough to reach Ricky's ass, but there, that must be his balls. He wiggled a finger and Ricky moaned. Yep, his balls. Juan had spent many nights in this dungeon, engaged in many different acts, some more fringe than others, but never with men he had an emotional bond with; with men he loved. Raphael was clearly an accomplished cocksucker, and Ricky ... nobody could treat his nipples more erotically than Ricky. Juan sucked Ricky's tongue again, imagining it fucking him just as he was fucking Raphael. Ricky moaned as Juan pulled him in deep.

Luke had the best view of anyone. Ricky's ass wiggling above Raphael's bound body, his shaved high 'n tight buried beneath Juan's bronze hands holding their heads together in another form of bondage. Juan's cock sliding in and out of Raphael's oral grasp. When he knew he couldn't last much longer, he looked down, gratified to see seed spilling from Raphael's cage, all the trigger he needed to spill his own. As he was finishing, Juan pulled away from Raphael's grasp to avoid choking him with his orgasm, his cum splashing off Ricky's belly, cage and then

Raphael's face. Juan was breathing heavily as Raphael lifted his head slightly and scoffed.

"Hey!" He looked up at Juan. "I could have taken that!" Juan squatted down so his face was level with Raphael's.

"I've intubated enough people to know what is and isn't a good idea, you amazing little cocksucker. You weren't in the best position for that." He kissed Raphael's forehead and licked his own cum off Raphael's nose. "But thanks for offering." Juan then stood, reached out and lifted Ricky up and over Raphael's head. Luke lowered Raphael's legs, then looked over at Juan and Ricky.

"Welcome to your first dare, guys. You did great." He looked down at Raphael, then back to Juan. "Should we just leave Raphael tied up here for the night?"

"Well, Sir," Raphael responded, "if you do, your next dare will blow your fucking mind."

"Here," Juan laughed, "I'll help you get him up." Juan and Luke lifted Raphael to a standing position, then Luke wiped the rest of Juan's cum off Raphael's face, before kissing him. A long one, giving Luke a little taste of Juan, who stood by, ready to release Raphael from his bonds. But, first, he grasped each of Raphael's biceps in his hands and looked intently into his eyes.

"Raphael, you're amazing. You definitely have what it takes to be the second-best locked cock leather boy in the world." Raphael looked at Ricky, and smiled, taking the compliment exactly the way it was intended.

"Thanks, Juan. There's nobody I'd rather play second fiddle to than Ricky." Ricky embraced Raphael, holding him for a moment to appreciate the feel of a rope encased brother. It felt really good, more erotic than he'd anticipated. Then he stepped back to allow Juan to release Raphael. Meanwhile Luke had been cleaning Raphael's Thunderplug in the lavatory. Juan wrapped the rope into bundles and hung them in place on the wall. Luke returned with Raphael's plug wrapped in paper towels. He handed the plug to Raphael, then pulled both Juan and Ricky into a group hug.

"I hope that wasn't too weird for you guys," he said quietly. "I probably overstepped my bounds. Ha! Bounds, get it?" Raphael groaned. Juan put a hand on the back of Luke's neck and squeezed.

"We're a family, yes, but a kinky leather family, Luke." He was looking into Raphael's eyes as he spoke from within Luke's embrace. "I expected something like this to happen eventually. Maybe just not this soon." He pulled out of Luke's grasp and pulled Ricky to his side. "I hope it wasn't too weird for you, mijo."

"Maybe, a little," he admitted with a smile. "But it was fun, too. It's just ..."

"Just what, mijo?"

"Everybody came but me." Ricky batted his brown eyes at Juan in a realistic pout.

"Well, let's see if we can't do something about that," Juan replied. As he led Ricky past Luke and Raphael toward the stairs, he warned, "Our bedroom door will be closed for a while, gentlemen." Luke retrieved Raphael's harness and the two headed up the stairs themselves.

"I'm impressed," Raphael said as he and Luke slowly mounted the stairs, arm in arm. "You came up with a revenge dare, a flash revenge dare, no less, on the spot, with two other members of the family. Who actually complied."

"So, now we have revenge dares, too?"

"Hey, you invented it, not me. How will I ever top that?"

"Maybe we should let this become the pinnacle, baby. You know, not even try to top it."

"In your dreams."

It wasn't until their walk on Tuesday, after Luke had returned from his shift, that Raphael had a chance to complete a mission he'd been contemplating. He'd been moved by Hiroshi's generosity on Sunday, not just the sake, but the nine fundoshi as well. He wanted to reciprocate, so he steered their walk so that they neared the end of it on 18th Street, at the flower shop near Castro. Dozens of buckets of cut flowers spilled out onto the sidewalk.

"We need to stop here a moment, Sir," Raphael slowed as they approached the entrance. San Francisco was still in a phase of the stay-at-home order that forbid entering retail establishments, but 'curbside' was finally allowed.

"Oh, you shouldn't have," Luke joked, squeezing Raphael's hand.

"Sorry, Sir, not for you. For Hiroshi." The clerk approached and interrupted Luke's attempt to learn more. "This will be a gift for a Japanese-American friend who has elevated aesthetic tastes. What orchid would you recommend?" As the clerk reentered the shop, Luke snorted.

"Elevated aesthetic tastes? Explain that one, baby."

"I can just tell, Sir," Raphael smiled. "His single, minimalist, artistic tattoo. His tasteful fundoshi, and not just his, but all the ones he gifted us as well. That's why I want to do this. To thank him for his generosity.

And his total acceptance of us as neighbors. We really lucked out in that department."

"No shit," Luke laughed. "He's the perfect neighbor for us."

"And we're the perfect neighbors for him. I hope having us around will help him heal from Ben's death."

"Well, if anyone can do that, you can, baby. And Juan. He obviously has a soft spot for Juan."

"Who doesn't?" Raphael teased, but Luke wisely didn't take the bait. The clerk returned with a potted orchid in each hand.

"This Phalaenopsis is pretty loaded with buds, and if maintained well will bloom at least a couple of times a year. But I really like this one." He held out a specimen with bright yellow blooms with ragged edges dotted with red freckles. "It's a Psychopsis. The blooms tend to last forever with this one."

"You had me at Psychopsis," Raphael released Luke's hand and reached for the plant. "We'll take it." He handed the clerk his debit card, then turned to Luke. "What do you think?"

"I think Hiroshi would appreciate anything you gave him." Luke took the plant from Raphael for a closer look. "It is beautiful. You and Niki both have big hearts. Must be Mama's influence, huh?"

"I don't know, Sir. I thought it just comes naturally, but you may be right." The clerk returned Raphael's card. Hand in hand, the two resumed their walk. After they'd entered the front door, Luke placed the orchid on the console table. Before either had pulled off their shoes, they heard a quiet sobbing coming from the library. Raphael gave Luke a questioning look as he slid the pocket door open. Niki was sitting in one of the fireplace chairs, tablet in hand. He turned at the sound of the door, tears in abundance.

"Niki!" Raphael rushed to his side and squatted down level with him. "What ... what's wrong?"

"It happened again!" Niki moaned as he handed the tablet to Raphael. By now Luke was at his side, leaning down to look over Raphael's shoulder.

"Fuck! Oh, fuck!" Raphael spat out. He tilted the tablet so Luke could see better. As soon as he grasped what had happened, Luke went to the other side of Niki and squatted down to put his arm around Niki's shoulder.

"Niki," he said softly, "I'm sorry. So sorry."

"God dammit!" Raphael swore again as he read. "Nine minutes! They suffocated him for nine minutes! In broad daylight in the middle of the street. In front of a crowd!" He continued reading as Luke whispered in Niki's ear, comforting him. "It happened yesterday. It looks like there's a huge protest forming in Minneapolis." Luke let go of Niki and pulled out his phone. He checked social media while Raphael continued tracking breaking news.

"There's a protest forming here, a couple of them," Luke reported. "Niki, we should go." Luke stood up and held out his hand to help Niki up. Raphael stood as well, and put the tablet on the desk.

"I'll go see who else is home," Raphael said over his shoulder as he headed for the stairs. Within a minute he was back. "Everybody's getting dressed, except Juan and Ricky. They must both be working. I'll text them so they know what's up." Niki ran upstairs to put on clothes as well. He returned with Steve in tow, just behind Alex, Greg, and Mateo. He'd managed to find his two Black Lives Matter t-shirts and was wearing one and carrying the other. Of course, both Alex and Raphael were wearing caged cock tees.

"Is that another Black Lives Matter shirt?" Alex asked Niki, who nodded. "Can I wear it?" Niki nodded again and smiled as he handed it to Alex, who peeled off the caged cock and pulled on the BLM shirt. "Thanks." Then he hugged Niki, who was more composed now but still sniffling.

"You guys are awesome," he said.

"No," Greg replied. "We're family. And we're human beings. Let's go make a scene." Luke opened one of the front doors and everyone headed out, just in time to encounter Juan heading up the steps in his scrubs. "You guys go on, I'll fill in Juan," Greg directed. It apparently didn't take him long, as Greg and Juan jogged up and joined the family within a block.

"I already texted you and Ricky about what we're doing," Raphael said when he noticed Juan pulling out his phone. Juan nodded and slipped it back into his pocket. "There's a protest forming at Civic Center." By the time they'd reached Market Street, it was obvious they wouldn't be making the trek alone. They found themselves in the midst of dozens initially, then hundreds headed for the Civic Center District. A number had taken the time to make signs: Black Lives Matter, BLM, George Floyd, I Can't Breathe, Say Their Names, Breonna Taylor, and some listing multiple names, including Ahmaud Arbrey and others. Long before they reached Market and Van Ness, the group was too big to estimate but reasonably organized, shouting slogans back to a man in dreadlocks, sporting a megaphone.

By the time they made it to City Hall, the crowd had grown to thousands. Young and old, Black, White, Asian, Latino/Latina, Native American and all the variations in between that made living in San Francisco so inspiring. Most were masked, too many weren't. There was a lot of shouting, some speeches, singing and a lot of tears. Lots of hugs. And really no social distancing. For the moment, for the first time in months, the coronavirus had been upstaged by a threat more pervasive, yet more immediate, more personal, this one man-made and seemingly just as unbeatable. After about an hour, after the sun had dipped below Twin Peaks, Greg turned to Luke.

"I think things could start to get a little out of control once it's dark. There's a lot of anger here. I think we should head home."

"Agreed," Luke replied. He and Greg corralled the family and spent the next fifteen minutes making their way through the crowd back to Market Street. As they were passing Octavia, Juan pulled his phone out and paused. He thumbed a moment, then caught up.

"Ricky was asking where to meet us, but I told him we're on our way home ... to meet us there. Is everybody hungry? I'm thinking of making a detour to Jasmine Garden."

"I'll go with you," Greg volunteered. "It'll take two of us to carry all the food this crew can eat." Luke handed Greg a couple of twenties.

"Get plenty of imperial rolls," Luke requested.

"And garlic noodles," Niki said. Their spirits weren't exactly lifting, but the thought of food was a welcome distraction. Greg and Juan peeled off at Church and Fourteenth, while the rest continued up Market. Once they arrived at home, as they were peeling off their street wear in the foyer, and Ricky appeared from upstairs, Alex took charge.

"Let's all get together in our room since we have a TV. I'm sure we all want to know what else is going on. It'll be like Tuesday dinner used to be at Raphael and Luke's."

"Sounds good," Luke agreed. "Steve and I will round up a coffee table or two and some cushions. Raphael, you, Ricky and Alex are in charge of the beverages and such." Everyone scattered. Alex and Niki rearranged a couple of chairs in the bedroom to clear a bigger space, and soon everything was ready for the main attraction. Until then, Alex switched on the TV and tuned in CNN. When they heard the front door open, Ricky ran down so Juan and Greg knew what was up. He transported the four bags of containers to the bedroom while Juan and Greg dutifully stripped. When they entered the bedroom, they found everyone mesmerized by what they were seeing on screen. Juan and Ricky unloaded the containers as Greg moved to a spot next to Alex, who was still holding the remote.

"Protests are everywhere," Alex reported. "Everywhere. We've been switching back and forth between CNN and MSNBC." As each of them helped himself to a little of this or that, mechanically feeding themselves, their full attention remained on the screen. Minneapolis was out of control. Most other cities were mainly peaceful, but there was looting and rioting in some other cities, too.

"I've never seen it this big, this wide-spread, this fast before," Steve said. "This is different."

"It's the third or fourth execution by cop, or former cop, in what, three weeks?" Juan replied. "Like that sign says," he motioned toward the screen, "everyone agrees, enough is enough. This does feel different."

"I just wish they weren't looting," Niki moaned. "That doesn't help."

"Those aren't protesters," Steve put an arm around Niki's neck and handed him an imperial roll. "Protests always bring out the criminal element ... they use the protests as cover."

"Guys," Luke, who'd been multitasking, looked up from his tablet. "There's another protest tomorrow afternoon at Mission High."

"I'm going," Niki asserted.

"Me, too," Greg seconded. Everyone, except Juan, who couldn't opt out of his shift this late, volunteered as well.

"If I can get away early, I'll be there," he offered.

"Alex, can you make a run to the office tomorrow?" Raphael asked. Alex gave him a questioning look, his mouth too full of garlic noodles to respond. "I want to upload some files to the large format printer. To make signs for the protest." Alex nodded, then swallowed.

"Sure. I'll load it with heavy stock. Just let me know when. There shouldn't be anyone else there."

"Cool," was Raphael's response.

By eleven, the food and wine were gone, and it was clear the protests weren't winding down, even in some East Coast cities. Everyone decided they might as well call it a night. Everyone rose as Alex and Greg filled the carryout bags with empty containers. Raphael sought out Niki and pulled him into long, long hug.

"It's going to be different this time, Niki," he whispered. "I can feel it. Can't you? We saw it tonight here, and on TV. Everyone on TV was saying it, too. All four cops were fired already. They were actually fired. This time it's different. We'll make sure of it."

"Maybe," Niki replied, sounding less than convinced. "I hope you're right, Raffie."

"And we're going to do our part. Us ... and a few hundred thousand others." Raphael squeezed Niki once more and released him. Kissing his forehead just below the mohawk. Steve then took over.

"Come on, Niki. Let's go to bed," he nodded gratefully to Raphael, then put an arm around Niki and led him out the door and up the stairs to their floor. Within minutes, everyone else had retreated to their rooms, and the house was silent.

# Fourteen

# GRATITUDE AND THERAPY

BREAKFAST HAD BEEN A somber affair, taken in ones and twos, after which most everyone retreated to their work from home stations, except for Juan, of course, who, as usual, was out the door before anyone else was up. One of the 'benefits' of being a surgical nurse. Niki had ensconced himself in the library, glued to his tablet, following news updates and monitoring social media. Mateo spent an hour with him, silently for the most part, offering support, before he left for his shift. Around eleven, Alex dressed and left for the office, to take care of the print run Raphael had initiated. He was back by one with a stack of twenty by twenty-four-inch signs that he left on the dining room table. He'd run out enough to weather several protests, if it came to that. Raphael thanked him, then took the interruption as an opportunity to check on Niki. As he walked through the foyer on his way to the library, he saw the orchid on the console table. He'd totally forgotten about it.

"Sweetie," he said, kneeling at Niki's feet. "Any new news?"

"More protests. I guess with the economy shut down, people have all day free. Still pretty tense." Niki laid the tablet on his thighs as he looked at Raphael.

"I thought I'd deliver the plant I got for Hiroshi, to thank him for the fundoshi. Why don't you take a break from that and come with me?"

"Okay, that's probably a good idea, Raphael. Thanks. I'll go dress."

"Why? He's already seen us both naked and harnessed. We'll go through the garden fence, like he did." Niki smiled at the thought.

"Naked delivery men. I like it."

"Actually, now that I think about it, let's wear our new fundoshi. He'll be impressed." Niki brightened at the suggestion.

"Except, I'm not sure I remember how to put it on," Niki wavered.

"Hey, we'll help each other. Come on." Raphael stood and reached out for Niki's hand. Niki left his tablet on what had by now become his chair, and they headed upstairs. Someone should have shot video of their attempts to turn the long strips of fabric into sexy garments. It wasn't as easy as Juan and Hiroshi had made it look. First there wasn't enough to make it around Niki's waist, then, too much, resulting in the tail end ending up over his belly. The twisting part was not exactly intuitive, either. Alex heard them laughing and swearing, so he wandered into Raphael's room to see what was up.

"Going to a party?" he asked.

"We thought we'd wear our fundoshi to take Hiroshi's orchid to him, but I think if he sees how we look in them, he'll ask for them back," Raphael sighed. "I wanted to impress him."

"Here, let a pro help you," Alex chirped.

"Pro? You've worn one precisely once," Niki recounted, stepping out of his mess of a fundoshi and handing it over to Alex.

"Yeah, but I was clearly paying more attention than either of you, from the looks of it."

"Alex," Raphael said, dramatically putting a hand on one hip and doing his best Evangelista impression. "Honey, you had one naked hunk and one nearly naked hunk wrapping cloth around your naked body. *That* ... is what we were paying attention to."

"And it felt mahvelous," Alex grinned. "Here, Raphael hold this on Niki's shoulder for me." In less than five minutes, Alex had Niki's cage safely under wraps in a very passable, authentic fundoshi. "Okay, Niki, your turn to assist." In moments Raphael's cage was also beautifully concealed.

"You're amazing," Raphael praised. "Wow, this feels pretty good, doesn't it, Niki?" Raphael circled Niki to inspect him from all sides. "Thanks, Alex. Want to come with us?"

"I better get back to work. That field trip you arranged for me has put me a little behind schedule, and I want to be able to join the protest later. Say hi to Hiroshi for me, though." Raphael, and then Niki, each gave Alex a lips on lips thank you kiss on their way out of the bedroom. Once downstairs, Raphael scooped up the orchid and they dashed out the back door. It took Niki a moment to locate the unobtrusive latch on the gate in the fence that Hiroshi had entered from.

"Someday, when we know him better, we'll have to ask Hiroshi what this secret gate is all about," Raphael said furtively.

"Duh," Niki responded "It's all about sex." Raphael telegraphed doubt with his eyes, but had to admit Niki was probably spot on. They walked up the short flight of steps to Hiroshi's back door and Raphael knocked. In just a few seconds Hiroshi opened the door, smiling broadly, wearing only a fundoshi of his own, not surprisingly.

"Raphael, Niki! How wonderful to see you both."

"Please forgive us for the intrusion, but we don't have your phone number," Raphael held out the orchid as he attempted a bow. "We wanted to thank you for your generosity Saturday."

"How lovely," Hiroshi enthused as he took the orchid from Raphael and bowed in turn. Then he stepped aside and waved an arm inviting them in. "Please, come in, and we'll rectify that phone number issue here and now. May I offer you some tea?" Raphael and Niki looked at each other briefly. Niki needed the diversion from all the angst emanating from his tablet, but Raphael was basically playing hooky.

"We can't stay long," Raphael said apologetically. "I should get back to work, but we can stay a few minutes. Tea would be nice." Hiroshi nodded then directed them to the living room before disappearing back into the kitchen. The room was tastefully furnished, with a minimalist aesthetic. Just as Raphael had predicted. Raphael and Niki were still taking it in, when Hiroshi returned with the same tray he'd used to serve them sake. This time it bore a small iron teapot and squat porcelain cups. There was also a small dish with several little wrapped packages on it. Hiroshi poured, Raphael and Niki each took a cup. Hiroshi picked up his cup and held it towards Raphael and Niki.

"To new friends." Raphael and Niki repeated the toast, then sipped. The tea was hot, aromatic, a bit peaty, but not bad. "These," Hiroshi touched one of the little packages, "are senbei ... savory crackers. Please help yourselves." Niki picked one up and tentatively tore it open to discover something unlike any cracker he'd seen before, but he had totally forgotten about lunch, so he was more than game. He popped the entire cracker in his mouth and munched.

"Oh my god," Niki muttered through the crumbs. "That's really good. This is a cracker?" Raphael reached for one and followed suit. Once he'd swallowed, he nodded and smiled.

"Seaweed and rice, right?" he speculated.

"And lots of flavorings," Hiroshi laughed. "I'm glad you like them. By the way, you both look very stunning ... you didn't need to dress for your visit. Your everyday nudity will always be welcome here."

"We almost did that," Raphael smiled, "but we wanted to show our appreciation for your kindness."

"You did very well putting them on," Hiroshi nodded. "I'm impressed."

"We had a little help from Alex, who says 'hi' by the way," Niki explained. "Our first attempt was pretty pathetic."

"That is true for everyone, Niki. But you will soon master it. As you have no doubt already discovered, it is always easier if another naked man assists you." Hiroshi wiggled his eyebrows meaningfully, then, more seriously, he focused his attention directly on Niki. "How are you doing, my friend ... with all that is happening in Minneapolis and elsewhere?" Niki set his tea cup down and leaned forward, forearms on his thighs and returned Hiroshi's gaze. He sighed before speaking.

"I honestly don't know. We've been here before, so many times." Hiroshi nodded. "It's horrible. Every killing is horrible. So, I'm upset. I'm angry. I feel defeated." He paused, then sat up straighter. "But at the same time, I'm so gratified ... shocked really ... at the reaction this time. It's like people finally noticed. Finally woke up. I feel a little bit of hope, I guess. If I dare ..."

"Dare, my lovely young friend. Dare!" Hiroshi was clearly taking the situation very seriously himself. "Did you participate in last night's protest?"

"Yes," Niki replied. "We all did. It was kind of cathartic really. We left before things got rowdy."

"We're going to the one at Mission High today, too," Raphael said. "It may be even bigger."

"May I join you?" Hiroshi turned to Raphael. "I would not feel so out of place if I were with my 'bubble.'" Bright smiles widened across Raphael's and Niki's faces.

"That would be great!" Raphael enthused. Niki nodded, eyeing another cracker.

"It's been some time since I 'got rowdy'," Hiroshi grinned. "Raphael, I haven't complimented you on your backpiece. It's remarkable. South Pacific inspired?"

"Very good!" Raphael twisted around to display his back. "Yes, it's Bornean, I borrowed it from a Filipino-American tattoo artist I admire. And not just because he's also Filipino-American."

"And not just because he is also a very beautiful man," Hiroshi complimented both Raphael and Leo Zulueta. "I know his work. It was made to adorn your muscular back, just as the puppy paws are utter perfection on Niki. Pup Niki, I'm guessing?" Both Raphael and Niki laughed as Niki nodded. "Please, puppy, have another treat. Each one is different." Hiroshi motioned to the crackers. Niki complied instantly.

"Hiroshi," Raphael continued, "I was admiring your back, too, Saturday. It's beautiful ... like Japanese brush art. I assume it has special meaning."

"You are very perceptive as well, Raphael. It is called Enso, a Zen Buddhist symbol that can have several meanings. The one I prefer is 'total enlightenment.' A worthy goal, would you not agree? And yes, it is rendered in one or at most two simple brush strokes. Ethnic tattoos are not all that we have in common, you know." Raphael cocked his head in anticipation of a further explanation. Hiroshi stood and began unwrapping his fundoshi. As he nearly finished, he turned to face away, then allowed the cloth to drop to the floor. He turned back to reveal smoothly shaved pubes above a stainless-steel chastity cage.

"Whoa," Niki reacted.

"Very nice," Raphael approved. "It looks great on you, Hiroshi."

"I installed it, for the first time in years, when Ben died and vowed not to remove it until my grieving has faded to a dull ache." Raphael swallowed hard.

"That is incredibly noble of you, Hiroshi," he said quietly. Niki slowly nodded, looking up at Hiroshi with his big brown puppy eyes. Raphael continued, "I hope ... I hope having us here, to carry on some of the tradition you and Ben enjoyed in his house, will somehow help you. Not that we could ever replace Ben ..." Hiroshi walked over between Raphael and Niki and spread his arms in invitation. Both stood and wrapped their arms around Hiroshi.

"No, Raphael, you cannot replace Ben. But you have brought new energy and new joy into his house ... and into mine. And, dare I say, into my heart." He pressed a kiss on each of their foreheads, then pulled away from their embrace. "This has been a wonderful visit. You and the rest of your family are welcome anytime. Now, we must let you get back to work, Raphael, and Niki, please take the rest of the crackers. I have plenty. And here ..." He picked up a small piece of paper on the tray. "You obviously did not bring your phones with you, so here is my number. Now you have it! Just let me know when you are leaving for the protest. I look forward to it." Raphael took the number, then bowed, with Niki, clutching a handful of packaged crackers, following his example. Hiroshi bowed in turn, then led the way to the back door to see them out. Once they were inside their own back door, Niki held out the crackers to offer some to Raphael. He took just one, then pulled Niki into yet another hug.

"Hiroshi is a very special guy, Niki."

"Yeah. He makes you feel so good just being with him."

"He does. He's mysterious and yet totally open at the same time. I could learn a lot from him."

"So could I. I hope we do." Niki broke the embrace. "Now, go get your work done so we can go protest." Raphael grimaced, but started up the back stairs. Part way up, he called back to Niki.

"Don't binge on bad news, Niki. Go spend some time in the puppy cage instead." Niki barked in response, then headed up the stairs himself. He found Steve in their room, on his laptop at the desk.

"Hey," Steve said over his shoulder, then turned to see Niki sporting his fundoshi. "Hey!" he repeated more enthusiastically. "That looks really cute on you."

"Thanks," Niki smiled as he did a three-sixty to feature his nearly bare ass. "Raphael and I took the orchid over to Hiroshi. Here, try one of these." He spilled the crackers onto the desk.

"What are they?" Steve sorted through the pile. "They're all in Japanese." Niki picked one up and tore it open to reveal the treat inside.

"They're Japanese crackers. They're really good. Hiroshi is so cool. He wants to go to the protest with us today."

"Mmmm," Steve mumbled through the cracker. "This is really different. But I like it." Niki nodded.

"Listen, as long as I've disturbed you, can you pup me up? I need some time in the puppy cage. You know. To cope." Without waiting for an answer, Niki pulled off the fundoshi and dropped to all fours, tongue out. Steve cupped a hand under Niki's chin and ruffled his mohawk with the other.

"Sure thing, puppy." Steve pulled open the puppy drawer and proceeded to install Niki's hood, mitts and tail. "Come on, puppy, I'll open the cage for you." Steve walked and Pup Niki trotted down the hall to the back stairs. It took Pup Niki longer than Steve to maneuver down to the first landing where Steve was waiting. "Why don't you finish the trip down on just two legs, puppy. I won't tell anyone." Pup Niki looked up at Steve and whined, but then held out a forepaw for help in standing up. The rest of the trip did go much faster.

"Okay, in you go." Steve said once they'd reached the dungeon and he had unlatched the cage door. He affectionately patted Pup Niki on the ass as he crawled in. Steve latched the door shut, then squatted down and asked, "How many hours, pup?" Pup Niki barked twice. "Have a nice nap." Steve left the dungeon and headed up the stairs as Pup Niki circled the inside of the cage three times before settling into place, hopefully for a reality-free nap.


Mateo asked to leave early from his shift so he could join the family at the protest. A couple of other employees overheard and indicated a desire to do the same, convincing the manager to close the restaurant early so they could all join in. Normally that would have never happened, but business being what it was, and the now international participation in the protests, these were not normal times. Mateo was hoping everyone was still home when he entered the foyer. He glanced into the library as he pulled off his street clothes and saw Niki's tablet on his chair and immediately thought, oh oh, they've left. I should have stayed dressed.

Then he heard voices in the dining room. He wandered back to find Alex and Greg sorting through the protest signs.

"Hey, muchacho," Alex greeted him. "Which sign do you want to hold at the protest?" Mateo walked up to the table and put an arm around Greg's waist as he looked over the selection. Greg ruffled his ever-lengthening mop of black hair.

"Maybe this," Mateo posed, picking up one that read, 'Say Their Names.'

"Good choice," Greg approved. Steve wandered into the room from the other door leading to the butler's pantry. "Picking out our signs," Greg said to Steve.

"Cool," Steve approached. "Let's see what the organizers have for us." As he looked them over, he said, "I'll do this one. I'm pretty sure Niki will want this 'Stop Killing Us' sign. Speaking of whom, I was on my down to let Pup Niki out of his cage."

"Can I?" Mateo eagerly offered.

"Okay, but Pup Niki won't be able to climb the stairs in pup mode. You'll need to remove his hood and mitts first. The tail can stay in, of course." Mateo nodded his willingness. "Here," Steve held out the keys to Pup Niki's mitts. Mateo set his sign on one of the chairs against the wall and headed through the butler's pantry into the kitchen where he dutifully scrubbed his hands before he bounded down the stairs, then crept up to the cage. The puppy was asleep. He sat down in front of the cage, reached through the bars and patted Pup Niki's thigh.

"Wakey el perrito ..." he cooed. Pup Niki lifted his head and turned to see not Steve, but Mateo. Pup Niki bounced up and excitedly barked, pressing his puppy snout against the bars, panting.

"Does puppy want out?" Pup Niki barked excitedly again. Mateo scooted over and unlatched the door and swung it open. Pup Niki bounced out and jumped on Mateo, forcing him over onto his back. As Mateo giggled, Pup Niki straddled Mateo and licked his face up and down, barking every few licks. Mateo was half-heartedly trying to fend him off. Then, for the first time, Pup Niki pulled his favorite puppy trick on Mateo. He whipped around and swallowed Mateo's bone. Mateo shrieked as Pup Niki growled, shook his head back and forth and sucked. Clearly being the best, naughtiest pup he could be was desperately need-ed therapy for Pup Niki. And considering it had been months since Ryan had sucked his cock, this moment was therapeutic for Mateo as well. He didn't really resist much at all. Just enough to say he had resisted, not that anyone would have asked. Just enough to further energize the puppy. This was total abandon for both of them. A boy and his pup. Having good clean fun together. Well, good fun, anyway. As good as it felt, as fun as it was, Mateo wasn't sure how far to let this go. He was thinking back to the night he'd spanked Alex into an orgasm and how torn he'd felt. It had been sexy and fun. Like this. He looked over at the wall of paddles, and the ropes, then down at Pup Niki's bobbing puppy hood and that's when he lost it. He reached for Pup Niki's hood, but it was too late. He came, and to his surprise, Pup Niki didn't pull away. Didn't object. Didn't stop sucking. Not until he'd sucked Mateo dry. Had this been Steve, Pup Niki would have pulled away then, and once freed of his hood, shared his prize in a long, sloppy kiss. But even puppies have boundaries. Especially with a near virgin like Mateo. Once he was finished, Pup Niki released Mateo and backed up, sitting on his haunches. He barked, then lifted his paws, signaling it was time to remove his mitts. Mateo sat up and pulled his legs into a cross-legged position. He looked at Pup Niki for a moment with a crooked smile, appreciating the blow job, but uncertain how to acknowledge it too. He leaned over to his left to retrieve the keys, then raised up on his knees and unlocked Pup Niki's mitts. Pup Niki bent his head down to make it easier for Mateo to remove the puppy hood. Once it was off, Niki raised back up and smiled at Mateo, who could finally see his human face.

"I hope I didn't offend you, Mateo," Niki said quietly, still smiling. "Pup Niki really needed that. It's not my fault you're so damn cute." Mateo laughed, looking down at his now flaccid cock, then back at Niki.

"Is okay. It felt pretty good. You suck good, Niki." Now it was Niki's turn to laugh.

"Well, I've had more practice than you. Again, if I went too far, I apologize."

"No, is okay. But," and Mateo's gaze intensified, "can it be our secret? For now?"

"Sure." Niki made the universal zipping of the lips gesture. "It's our secret." Mateo's smile grew. Niki picked up his mitts and hood and stood, then reached down and took Mateo's hand to help him up. "We better go get ready for the protest, muchacho." Mateo nodded and they headed up the stairs and on into their respective rooms to dress.

Fifteen

# 'I Promise'

Everyone but Juan, who was still at work, had gathered in the foyer, clothed and with signs in hand. Raphael pulled out his phone and texted Hiroshi. He also texted Juan, telling him they'd meet him at the protest. By the time they had all filed out and down the steps, Hiroshi was there waiting at the bottom, wearing an all-black ensemble of knee length shorts and a long-sleeved tee. Raphael offered him a choice of signs, as he had brought three, one for himself, one for Hiroshi and one for Juan. Hiroshi chose 'Black Lives Matter.'

"I hardly recognize you in your masks and clothes," Hiroshi joked.

"Yeah," Niki replied, "we prefer you in a fundoshi, too. Or less." Steve gave Niki a questioning look, but didn't pursue it.

"Juan will join us as soon as he can, Hiroshi," Raphael advised. "We should go now. I think the protest is already in full swing." The 'bubble' headed down the hill, then took a right at Eighteenth Street, where there was already a stream of people heading east. By the time they crossed Sanchez, it was so crowded people were spilling into the street. At Church Street it was clear this was way bigger than the night before. Eighteenth Street in front of Mission High was packed solid. They veered up into Dolores Park, past the tennis courts and into the soccer field, joining thousands more. Overhead a news helicopter circled. Raphael kept an eye on his phone off and on, and after a couple of speeches from the steps of the school entrance he finally saw Juan's text. Juan was still at Eighteenth and Sanchez, so he texted back their approximate location. Fifteen minutes later Juan was finally in sight. He approached, gave Ricky a hug, kissing out of the question with the masks, then hugged Hiroshi, greeting him with words Raphael couldn't hear over the crowd and speaker. Raphael held out the remaining sign to Juan, who took it and responded with a nod of thanks. Raphael had kept the 'No Justice, No Peace' sign for himself. The speeches and chants went on for over an hour after they had arrived. Then, the crowd, which they later learned exceeded fifteen thousand, was encouraged to march to either the Mission Precinct Station or the Hall of Justice on Brannon. It was no contest. The 'bubble' opted for the Mission Station, a much shorter walk.

Once they reached the station, it was clear the police had been expecting them, with a cordon of uniformed officers surrounding the building and parking lot. Signs were lofted, chants rang out, but there was no violence. No threats. No tear gas. Niki maneuvered his way to the front of the throng, Steve doing his best to keep on his tail. There, along with much of the rest of the leading edge of the crowd, Niki took a knee. Steve followed suit, just behind him. Amongst the shouting and chants, several officers approached the front line of protestors, and Niki prepared himself to be arrested or assaulted. Instead, some of the officers knelt with them, facing them. Surprised, Niki started to tear up. He held firm eye contact with the officer opposite him. It was hard to read expressions or emotions with the masks on everyone, but Niki didn't feel threatened by this man, still on one knee. After a moment of this eye-to-eye encounter, the cop signed in ASL, 'I promise.' Niki didn't understand at first, and he glanced down pondering this development. That was when he remembered the sign leaning against his knee read 'Stop Killing Us.' He looked back up at the officer, who had not broken his gaze, and signed back over the noise, 'Please.' The officer repeated, 'I promise.' This was what Niki needed. A little humanity. Official recognition that, yes, Black Lives Matter. Niki began to openly weep. He was not alone. A protestor on his right, reached over and squeezed his shoulder, tears running down into her mask. The officer stood, nodded to them both and stepped back as the other officers followed suit. Steve placed a hand on top of the protestor's hand, comforting both her and Niki. It was just one moment in what would be days, weeks and months of resistance and frustration, grief and determination. And change. Real change, sooner than anyone would have thought possible. But this had been Niki's moment. To realize that with people like this officer, change might be possible.

Steve stood and put his hands under Niki's armpits, lifting him to a standing position. Niki turned and wrapped his arms around Steve, who was nodding to the sympathetic protestor to confirm that she was okay. She nodded back, and no doubt smiled to know Niki was in good hands. Technically he was a basket case, but in a good way. At least for the moment, a hopeful way. It took a few minutes, but Steve finally was able to navigate their way back to the rest of the 'bubble.' Although, at the moment, the concept of a COVID-19 bubble was kind of irrelevant. Once they were all together, they agreed it was time to head home. As they slowly made their way to the edge of the crowd and headed north on Valencia, they naturally coupled up, husbands and lovers holding hands. Mateo, who normally would have ended up between Greg and Alex, holding their hands, positioned himself next to Hiroshi and tentatively slid his hand into Hiroshi's, who squeezed Mateo's hand in acknowledgement. Once they had advanced far enough from the main crowd that speaking in an outdoor voice was possible again, Hiroshi spoke.

"Thank you for including me this evening. This was a spiritual experience for me, I think."

"And for Niki," Steve spoke over his shoulder to Hiroshi. "You made a connection there, didn't you?" he turned back to Niki.

"Yeah, I guess. He was cool. Imagine that, a cool cop."

"All I know is, I'm glad we came," Steve continued. "I'm glad you could join us, Hiroshi. By the way, thank you for the crackers. They're awesome."

"I am glad you like them," Hiroshi replied. "Sadly, you cannot get them here."

"Crackers?" Alex piped up. "Now what have I missed?"

"You could have gone with us, Alex, but ... noooo," Raphael chided. "You preferred to work."

"No ... I had to work," Alex pouted. "Anyway, I missed lunch. Is anybody else hungry?"

"No, Alex," Greg continued abusing Alex, "we all filled up on crackers." Just about everyone but Alex found that funny.

"Say," Greg said. "I baked a lasagna yesterday that I was planning to heat and serve tonight. Hiroshi, why don't you join us. We'd love to have you."

"Yes, Hiroshi," Alex pleaded. "Greg makes a pretty good lasagna." Mateo shook their joined hands up and down.

"Yes, Hiroshi," Mateo added his voice. "Please?"

"How can I say no?" Hiroshi looked into Mateo's eyes. "First an orchid. Then a protest, and now dinner? I will be in your debt for a long time."

"Except for Juan and Ricky we don't do debts," Raphael said matter-of-factly. "Hiroshi, we only do dares. And double dares."

"I'm not sure what that means," Hiroshi replied.

"Maybe Raphael and Luke will explain it over dinner," Alex suggested. "If you're lucky, that's as close to one of their dares as you'll ever get."

"Okay, now I am very intrigued," Hiroshi laughed.

"You've been warned," Alex continued. Raphael shook his head. Once they began filing into the foyer, everyone in the family automatically began stripping off their street clothes and stuffing them into the stacked cubbies along the stairwell. Hiroshi was not surprised, given the picnic he had attended, but he was amused. Clearly nudity was more than casual in this house, it was apparently mandatory and organized as well. As a good guest, Hiroshi followed suit, although this would hardly be the first time he'd been naked in this house.

"Juan, you and Mateo have both already put in a full day, and Niki, you've had your share of stress," Greg said. "Why don't the three of you take Hiroshi into the sitting room or the library and relax. The rest of us will see to dinner." Juan nodded and led the way into the library, with Hiroshi following, then Mateo and Niki, arms around each other's waists. Niki indicated one of the fireplace chairs to Hiroshi as he pulled his tablet from the other before he sat down in his chair. Juan and Mateo sat on the floor together in front of the fireplace, facing Niki and Hiroshi. They were discussing reactions to the protest when Raphael entered with a tray with four wine glasses that he put on the low table between the two chairs.

"It's Soave, guys, since we're eating Italian." Then he left.

"To Black Lives," Juan toasted after Hiroshi handed Juan his glass.

"And Brown Lives," Niki responded. Then, he turned to Hiroshi, "To the lives of all people of color." Hiroshi chuckled.

"Yes, when it comes to protests, we usually seem to be overlooked, even here, where we are one third of the population."

"That's because you don't make enough 'trouble.'" Niki suggested. "I kept waiting for you to get rowdy today ..."

"One day, my friend," Hiroshi smiled at Niki. "Juan has seen me get rowdy, have you not?"

"If that's what you want to call it," Juan laughed. "Yeah, you do know your way around a dungeon. As well as a few other things." He and Hiroshi exchanged a meaningful look.

"So, Juan," Hiroshi said as he looked down at Juan, "you promised to tell me the story of your unique family. Is this a good time?"

"Sure," Juan set his glass on the hearth. "I'll give you highlights since I am really the newest member of the family, except for Mateo here." He put a hand on Mateo's thigh. "Luke and Raphael are really the anchors of the family, and they can tell you more." Juan proceeded to tell the story of how Ricky had seduced him, not once but twice, resulting in him becoming initiated into the Tuesday dinners that led to beach outings, a rescue of Mateo, and ultimately not one but two double wedding ceremonies. Ricky had wandered in and sat down on the other side of Juan midway through the tale, so he was there when Juan described Ricky's starring role in the second wedding ceremony.

"I wish I could have been there to see you," Hiroshi said, genuinely captivated. "You must have broken a lot of hearts that evening."

"Oh, I don't know," Ricky shyly responded, looking first at Hiroshi, then at Niki.

"Don't listen to him," Niki leaned forward. "He. Was. Legendary."

"He was," Juan agreed. "He must have gotten half a dozen marriage proposals that night. I could deal with that. The worst part came later ... when we spent an hour in the shower getting all the glitter off his body."

"It was worth it," Niki turned to Hiroshi. "It was definitely worth it."

"And you had no idea about this second ceremony?" Hiroshi asked.

"None. It was a lot like a dare, I guess, only not one concocted by Raphael or Luke for once."

"I keep hearing about these dares," Hiroshi look around at the others. "Do they still happen?"

"That's a good question," Ricky said. "We should ask Raphael or Luke."

"Ask me what?" Raphael appeared once again at the door. "Dinner's ready, boys." Everyone rose and followed Niki out the door and down the hall to the dining room, where the table was candlelit and set for ten.

"Oh, my," Hiroshi uttered. "Do you always dine like this?"

"Oh, no," Alex replied. "We thought we'd just go casual tonight."

"Funny guy," Raphael said. "No, you're our first dinner guest, Hiroshi, what with the pandemic and everything. And ... we wanted to celebrate, no, wrong word ... we wanted to acknowledge the importance of the awakening of our community to the realization that Black Lives Matter."

Everyone found a seat and Greg dished up portions of lasagna onto plates stacked at the end of the table and then passed them around. Salad and bread were passed around as well and everyone dug in. Dinner was tasty and convivial, making Hiroshi feel at home, which was strange and bittersweet, considering he'd shared so many meals at this very dining table with Ben, and sometimes Ben and a few others.

When there was a lull in the conversation, Hiroshi addressed Raphael. "Alex suggested you and Luke would explain about your practice of dares, Raphael. I am very curious." Raphael put his fork down and wiped with his napkin. He took a sip of wine first, then looked mischievously at Hiroshi.

"We owe pretty much everything to the power of the dare, wouldn't you say, Luke?" He turned to Luke who made a 'who me' face at Hiroshi. Then he smiled.

"Hiroshi, you should have seen Raphael when we were first dating," he said. "You would hardly recognize him. He had almost shoulder length hair, no piercings, no tattoos, no collar, no cage, no butt plug ... oh, sorry."

"Jesus," Raphael scolded.

"Anyway, we were dating, we both wanted to get serious but we both were unsure how serious the other guy wanted to be, and so we kind of clumsily landed on the idea of gauging each other's commitment by testing it with a dare. Back and forth. The first guy to fail to do the other's dare would therefore prove his devotion was lacking. Like I said, when we started Raphael was a beautiful, studly guy, but totally vanilla. But I had a feeling there was a locked cock leather boy in there somewhere. He just needed to be freed. Against his will, granted." Luke turned to Raphael and flashed his Cheshire grin. "It turned out I was right."

"What were some of these dares?" Hiroshi was intrigued. "The concept is fascinating."

"There've been a lot," Raphael pondered. "The mandatory kilts for Luke, which led to the mandatory caged cock shirts for me."

"Which is what begin our friendship," Alex interjected. "If Raphael hadn't been forced to wear caged cock polos to work, I'd have never known he was caged."

"Yeah, that's right," Raphael continued. "Our ink, our septum rings, my first ... since Luke already brought it up ... my first butt plug and this collar and the harness I usually wear."

"Our short-lived career as strippers," Alex added. Niki and Ricky both hooted and nodded at that.

"Strippers!?" Hiroshi raised his wine glass. "This story gets more interesting by the minute! Do you have a favorite dare?" Raphael looked at Luke, then leaned over and planted a solid, lip on lip kiss.

"I think I have two," he turned to Hiroshi. "One was when I proposed to Luke and presented him with an engagement ring on the night he pierced and caged me. And the fact that he accepted."

"And the second?" Hiroshi prodded. Raphael looked devilishly at Luke whose eyes suddenly widened.

"Oh. I can't talk about that one. Yet. Maybe soon, though."

"I love a good mystery," Hiroshi leaned back. "Something to look forward to. Okay, then let me ask this, if I may. What was your last dare?" Raphael looked across to Juan and Ricky, and cocked his head and raised his eyebrows to silently ask permission to share. Juan slowly nodded, having shared plenty with Hiroshi in the flesh.

"Well, that would by one inspired by you, Hiroshi." Hiroshi looked wide-eyed at Mateo on his left and Alex next to him.

"Inspired by me? You must tell."

"That would be the other night when Juan tied me up in rope bondage then Luke and he fucked me from both ends while Ricky played with Juan's nipples, and I played with his balls. That's as much as I could reach because of the bondage." Luke rolled his head back in utter despair. Juan slyly grinned. Ricky looked guilty. Niki looked left out. But it was Alex who reacted with the utmost dismay.

"WHAAAT!! Are you kidding me?" He looked at Raphael and Luke, then over at Juan and Ricky. Then at Hiroshi who had pretty much decided this was the best dinner party he had attended in quite some time. "And I thought I'd missed out on the crackers!" That brought guffaws around the table. Which did little to amuse Alex. "Seriously?"

"Alex," Luke said very calmly leaning forward ever so slightly. "You will undoubtedly have many memorable experiences in our dungeon. Each of us will. We can't all be present at every spontaneous opportunity." Alex did not look very appeased. "Alex ... remember your birthday?" Alex blushed, looked down at his cage, and made an 'oh yeah' face.

"What's this?" Steve asked.

"Yeah," Juan added. "The birthday ... again?" Alex, blushing still, made an 'I didn't do it' face.

"Um. I have nothing more to say," was all Alex would share.

"Okay then," Luke responded. "Thank you, Raphael, for making this True Confessions dinner so very special."

"Luke," Hiroshi came to Raphael's defense. "I should not have encouraged Raphael to share so much."

"I'm kidding, Hiroshi," Luke grinned. "It's okay. Really. You had no idea what he was going to say. Neither did I. I'm just glad that's all he shared." Raphael, having long ago shed any sense of shame when it came to sex, just smiled beatifically.

"You created me, Sir," he turned to Luke. "You said it yourself. When you found me I was vanilla. Now, I'm your proudly naked, collared and caged locked cock leather boy and I don't care who knows it. Hell, our brother knows it. The CEO of my company knows it. I'm certainly not going to hide anything from my beloved family here."

"Here, here," Juan lifted his wine glass. "To openness and honesty." Everyone else raised their glasses.

"So," Niki spoke up. "Is this really True Confession time?"

"What do you mean?" Steve asked, unsure of what was coming.

"Well," Niki glanced over at Mateo. "Pup Niki was a little bit bad today." Mateo tried not to smile, but failed. "When Mateo let me out of the puppy cage this afternoon ... well, he looked *so* cute." He paused but no one interrupted him. "Uh ... Pup Niki buried his bone." Ricky looked clueless.

"He sucked his cock," Juan explained. Then, to the rest of the group, "Looks like the dungeon is getting plenty of action, guys." Niki looked sheepishly at Steve. Steve just shook his head.

"Was Niki a bad puppy?" Ricky asked.

"Sounds like it, doesn't it?" Steve replied. "I think we're going to have to discipline him, don't you think?"

"Uh huh," was Ricky's response. Then he turned to Hiroshi. "Didn't you offer to tie him up in rope bondage, Hiroshi?"

"I did, yes." Hiroshi grinned. "But that does not seem like much of a punishment."

"It depends on what happens once he's tied up, wouldn't you say?" Juan looked over at Steve. Steve grinned and looked at Niki.

"Hiroshi," Steve asked, "are you free this Saturday?"

"I would be honored," Hiroshi replied.

"I shouldn't have said anything," Niki whined, a little unconvincingly. "I promised Mateo I wouldn't tell, so if anybody should punish Pup Niki, it should be you, Mateo." Niki looked guiltily at Mateo.

"Is okay, Niki," Mateo smiled. Alex put an arm around Mateo's shoulders.

"Niki's right, muchacho," he said. "You should start off Pup Niki's punishment Saturday, after Hiroshi binds him up."

"What do you mean, 'start off'?" Niki looked at Alex.

"I don't think it would be respectful to Hiroshi if we 'wasted' his skills at Shibari for just one go at punishing Pup Niki."

"I don't know ..." Niki leaned back in his chair, looking a little glum. "I only want Mateo to punish Pup Niki." He looked around at the rest of the family for support. He didn't get any. Finally, Steve spoke.

"How about this? We'll let Mateo decide who else, if anybody, has a hand in Pup Niki's punishment. I trust Mateo to make a fair decision. How about it, Mateo?" Mateo locked a gaze with Niki for a moment, then he looked at Hiroshi who smiled in his wise and gentle way. Then Mateo took a dramatically deep breath.

"I will decide. With Hiroshi." Hiroshi laughed as he leaned back in his chair.

"Oh my," he said. "I am not just the bondage master for this, then? If you wish, Mateo. I will assist you." He looked over at Juan and winked. This was indeed a memorable dinner party for him. "May I ask a favor, however? I would like to spend some time with Pup Niki. I would like to get to know this puppy better before deciding the best 'punishment' for him." Niki's glum face broke into a smile. "Niki, when might Pup Niki be available to spend time with me?" Niki shrugged.

"Tomorrow ... any day this week. My schedule is wide open, except for any more protests that come up."

"Thursday then?" Hiroshi asked. Niki nodded enthusiastically. "If a protest comes up, just let me know."

"This is so cool," Ricky spoke up. "I've said it before ... I really love living here with my family." He raised his nearly empty glass, as everyone followed his lead.

"I have no complaints," Alex chimed in. "Except maybe ... about those crackers." Niki rolled his eyes and got up, exited through the butler's pantry and headed upstairs. A moment later he was back, and gingerly placed a wrapped senbei on Alex's empty plate.

"Now maybe we'll get some peace and quiet around here," he said as he sat back down. Alex grimaced and looked at Niki.

"Thank you," he squeaked without making a move. After a moment, Raphael spoke for everyone.

"Eat the damn cracker, Alex." Greg started laughing, soon followed by Hiroshi, then Luke and Steve. Chastened, Alex tore it open and bit. After a few crunches he pushed the rest of the cracker in and finished it off, to an audience of nine. He made the most of his drama training. He licked his lips. Smacked a couple of times. Licked his lips again. Took a sip of water. Then turned to Hiroshi, eyes squinting with a big smile.

"Best fucking cracker I ever tasted." Greg reached over and pulled Alex's head into his lap and shook him by the shoulders in a modified 'you can suck my cock while you're down there if you want' sideways bear hug. When Alex raised back up, he looked around at his audience and finished his mini-performance with, "Now. What's for dessert?"


Dessert was Mitchell's Mango ice cream, and it did not take long to finish it off. Hiroshi was the first to rise.

"Thank you, my friends, for an exciting, entertaining and, I must add, delicious evening. Niki, whenever Pup Niki is ready on Thursday, I'll look forward to spending some quality time with him." Then he addressed Mateo. "Once I've gotten to know the puppy better, you and I can discuss his discipline." Mateo grinned and nodded. "Thank you again, and now I must go. Goodnight, everyone." As he walked to the foyer to retrieve his clothes, Mateo joined him, then saw him out. He returned to the dining room and sat, sneaking peeks at Niki. Juan noticed.

"You were wise, Mateo, to recruit Hiroshi for Pup Niki's discipline session. He will guide you well." Mateo nodded.

"Juan," Luke asked. "I couldn't help but notice Hiroshi is caged. Was he always?"

"No, never. That's new, at least to me."

"It's new," Niki explained. "He told Raphael and me about it. He locked up after Ben died, and he says he'll stay locked until the pain of losing him eases."

"Oh, man," Luke responded. "I'm glad I didn't say anything."

"I guess they were even closer than I knew," Juan said. He pondered a moment, then continued. "You know, I'm really glad we're here, in this house, I mean, glad for him. I think being around us is good for him right now."

"Just so long as he doesn't get so attached to Pup Niki that he wants to adopt him," Steve joked. "You know how puppies are."

"Not to worry," Niki patted Steve's belly. "I'm yours, all yours, and I always will be." Greg stood and began collecting dishes. Everyone else followed suit, eventually all ending up in the kitchen, some scraping into the compost, some rinsing, Alex loading the dishwasher.

"You know," Greg said, turning to the group as he attacked the lasagna pan in the large sink, "all this dungeon talk this evening reminded me. Who has the next birthday? Remember our vow?"

"Oh, yeah, that's right!" Luke plopped the ice cream dishes in front of Alex. "Hang on ..." He dashed into the foyer to retrieve his phone from his cubby. "Okay," he announced upon returning, "Alex, I know when your birthday is." He tapped briefly into his phone. "So, you're safe for a while. I know Raphael's ... and mine." More tapping. "Greg?" One by one, Luke recorded each birthday. "I'll figure out a calendar or something we can post, so we know whom to celebrate and when. But it looks like Juan, you'll be initiating the Dungeon Birthday Celebrations."

"Oh, good," Juan deadpanned. "Let's not call them celebrations. More like Dungeon Birthday Sessions. Or, knowing this group, Dungeon Birthday Ordeals."

"Dungeon Birthday Fuckfests?" Alex suggested.

"Classy, Alex," Raphael banged him hip against hip. "How about Dungeon Birthday Ceremony?"

"I like it!" Juan agreed. "Dungeon Birthday Ceremony. It evokes candles, masks ..."

"Human sacrifice?" Steve offered. "Of the sexual kind, I mean."

"Yeah," Juan continued. "You got it. If we're going to do this, it might as well be" And before he could finish, Ricky piped up on cue.

"Legendary!" he exclaimed. "I love it!"

## Sixteen

# PROTEST AND A PICNIC

WEDNESDAY AFTERNOON NIKI WAS in his chair, following news coverage of what were by now daily, global protests. He was also tracking social media to keep up on any local action. Between San Francisco, Oakland and several other Bay Area cities, there were multiple protests being planned every day. Some more general, some more thematic. Today's best opportunity seemed to be a march on wheels being organized by a younger crowd, much like the huge event at Mission High School had been. Thinking back, Niki was reminded again of his encounter with the officer. He kind of hoped he'd see him again, although it would be tough to know if he did, given the masks they were both wearing. His reverie was interrupted when Raphael, taking a break from work, wandered in and plopped into the other chair.

"Planning our next protest?" he asked.

"Actually, yeah," Niki laid the tablet on his lap and engaged with Raphael. "I know what I want to do, but I'm not working. You guys all are, so you don't have to do every protest that comes along. It's not really your fight, anyway." Raphael climbed out of his chair and knelt next to Niki, taking his hand in both of Raphael's.

"Don't even think that. And not just because I'm your adoptive brother. Your skin may be darker than mine, but I'm still a person of color." Raphael gestured to his chest with one hand. "Asian to some, Pacific Islander to others. But even that is irrelevant. You saw the crowd yesterday. The vast majority were white. This *is* my fight. I guarantee you it's Luke's fight. It's every thinking, moral human being's fight. Niki, you are not in this alone. Not in this family, and not ... not even ..."

"Okay ... okay, you're right. You're right. The whole world seems involved this time. But really, I don't expect everyone to feel obligated to participate in every protest. You know ... burnout."

"Well, when's the next protest?"

"There's one later this afternoon, that'll go from the Civic Center to Castro, up Market Street. On wheels."

"Wheels?"

"Yeah, bikes, skateboards, scooters, probably those electric unicycles."

"Sounds crazy."

"Yeah. That's why I want to do it."

"Let me check with everybody. When's it supposed to start?"

"I think four o'clock." Raphael nodded and let go of Niki's hand, stood and exited. Twenty minutes later, when Niki was viewing coverage of a protest in D.C., Raphael returned.

"Well, you get part of your wish. Alex and I will join you, but Ricky needs to Dash and the others prefer more stationary protests. Juan and Mateo are both working, anyway, so it'll be the three of us. We need to go nab three Lyft bikes before they're all gone."

"You sure? You won't get in trouble?"

"Hardly. I guess I didn't tell you. Cynthia put out a message this morning, telling us to log any time protesting to our community service number. You have her support too, Niki." That choked up Niki just a little, noticeably enough that it prompted Raphael to pull him up and into a hug.

"Am I interrupting," Alex kidded from the doorway.

"Yes, Alex, you've discovered our secret, mad, incestuous love affair. Promise you won't tell." Alex, who was the only one in street clothes, walked up and joined the hug.

"We could make it a torrid threesome, you know, to keep me quiet." Raphael looked at Niki, then turned back to Alex, who's lips were inches from his own.

"That would be rather awkward, wouldn't it? Seeing as how we're all three caged."

"That didn't stop us before," Alex smirked, then planted one on Raphael's lips.

"What?" Niki asked.

"Alex's birthday," Raphael said, as if that explained everything. Which it did not. But before Niki could pursue it, Alex broke free of the hug.

"You boys protesting naked or are you going to go get dressed? We need to grab those bikes." Both Niki and Raphael dashed out of the library and up the stairs. Meanwhile Alex checked his phone to identify the nearest locations for bikes. None of them had used one since their ride to the beach eons ago. He then opened the front door and sat on the top step, enjoying the view of the neighborhood. He watched several cyclists head down the hill and wondered if they were heading to the protest or just going about their business.

"What do you think, Alex?" Raphael in shorts and a locked cock tee like Alex's, asked as he approached the door. "Should we try to carry signs on our bikes?"

"I think I'll pass. I never mastered riding no-handed. I'll just use my big mouth."

"You're probably right." He leaned the signs against the cubbies just as Niki arrived in his Black Lives Matter tee and shorts. "Okay, team, let's go make good trouble." They tried a nearby, but relatively out of the way, rack first in hopes of getting three bikes. There were four left, two electric and two standard.

"You older guys take the electric ones," Niki teased. "I'll take one of these." Raphael looked at Alex, who was usually the snark artist, but when Alex didn't react, he did.

"Okay, Twink Boy. But seriously, let's trade off after a while. Just let me know when you get tired." Niki shook his head as if that would be unlikely. They headed down to Market and rode several blocks before encountering increasing traffic. Not cars, but bikes. First dozens, then hundreds of bikes. And electric scooters. All of which slowed them down, but at least indicated they weren't going to be the last to arrive at Civic Center. This was sizing up to be another big turnout.

Many in the march were already progressing up Market when they arrived at City Hall. People on wheels of all kinds, including even skateboards, were making their way west, many holding signs, but most just chanting along with leaders with megaphones. The march was big enough that there were numerous contingents. There were carts with sound systems playing music pulled by bikes. There was a drum corps on foot. Occasionally someone pushing a stroller. Yes, one-year-olds contributing to the cause. They sat on the sidelines for a while, enjoying the diversity of the march, until they saw an obvious group of queer protestors, which they melted into and proceeded west. Occasionally Niki saw officers along the way, holding back traffic at side streets. After scoping out a dozen or more over several blocks, he realized he would never recognize 'his' cop, especially while moving and from a distance. Instead, he decided to pay full attention to the protestors around him, and the people cheering them on. Raphael had been right. Most of them were not Black, but they were just as animated, just as earnest as the Black participants.

"Is this what you expected?" Raphael shouted over the crowd. He was on Niki's left, while Alex was on his right.

"I didn't know what to expect," Niki replied. "But this is nice. No speeches, just a lot of people making noise. At this pace we could have ridden a lot longer."

"Maybe that was the plan ... to not tire everyone out," Alex said. "My guess is there will be speeches at Harvey Milk Plaza, though." Niki nodded. As they passed Van Ness, they heard a familiar voice over the crowd.

"AMIGOS!" Mateo pushed up next to Alex on his skateboard.

"Mateo!" Alex grinned. "Where'd you come from?"

"I wait here. I hope to find you. When I was home from work Greg tol' me where you are."

"I can't believe you found us," Niki shouted. "Thanks for coming."

"De nada," Mateo maneuvered around to get between Alex and Niki. They made room for Mateo to keep pushing his board alongside them. Mateo's presence reminded Niki of both indiscretions he'd committed yesterday, and of the consequences to come. Pupping out with Hiroshi would no doubt be enjoyable, but he wasn't sure about the discipline that was to follow. As they passed Church Street, Niki made a suggestion.

"Guys, I'm not really up to hearing more speeches today. Why don't we break off at Sanchez? We can dock the bikes there and walk home."

"Sure, Niki, if that's what you want," Alex replied. He accelerated to take the lead and peeled off at the corner. As Niki and Raphael pulled up to the bike station, Alex had already docked his bike and Mateo was at his side, skateboard in hand. They paired off to head home, Raphael and Niki hand in hand, Alex holding Mateo's free hand. Once they had ventured far enough away from the crowd that normal conversation was possible, Niki spoke.

"Thanks for coming guys. Especially you, Mateo. I hope you didn't wait too long for us."

"Not long," Mateo patted Niki on the shoulder. "It was fun." The fact that Mateo had taken the time and effort to join the protest meant more to Niki than he was comfortable saying. He looked over his shoulder at Mateo as he apologized again.

"I really am sorry I broke my promise yesterday, Mateo." Raphael looked at Niki, aware of the mix of emotions he was dealing with. He squeezed Niki's hand tighter.

"Is okay," Mateo assured him, no doubt smiling behind his mask. "Sex is easy for you amigos, more than me." No one said anything, not sure what to say. Then Mateo continued, "I want to do sex as much as you sometime ... but I am not sure. I think about Ryan."

"Wait," Alex responded. "Are you saying you think you should only have sex with Ryan?"

"Si. I think. I don' know." It was clear, even with the mask, that Mateo was conflicted. Alex pulled him into a sideways hug.

"Mateo," Raphael laughed, "you're in love with Ryan, aren't you?" He looked back to see Mateo nod silently. "I hope you understand that what we do with each other is ... fun ...it's play ... it's just sex. I love Niki, and Alex and you ... but I'm *in love* with Luke. But don't let us pressure you into doing anything you aren't comfortable doing.

"Oh, great," Niki moaned. "Make me feel even worse."

"No, no, Niki," Raphael squeezed Niki's biceps. "That's not what I mean. I'm saying what you did was just playing ... having fun. You were relieving stress. This is the point I was trying to make ... sooner than later ... I predict ... Mateo will see sex play as separate from making love to a significant other."

"Yeah," Alex turned to Mateo, "just you wait. Living with us will corrupt you in no time."

"Alex!" Raphael scolded. "I'm trying to make it sound like a virtue."

"I know! I meant corrupt in a good way."

"Yeah," Raphael snarked. "That'll surely translate well."

"How's this?" Alex defended himself. "Sex ... good. Making love ... better."

"Whatever ..." Raphael gave up.

"Speaking of making love," Alex turned to Mateo again. "Any word from Ryan about school?"

"No. It may be all online. So, he may have to stay there. To save money."

"That sucks," Alex stated the obvious. "When will he know?"

"Nobody knows," Mateo whined. He turned to Alex with sad eyes. "I miss him."

"I know, muchacho," Alex pulled him close again for a few steps.

"Maybe it would help if you sent him pictures of the fabulous house he'd be living in," Raphael suggested, turning to walk backward so he could face Mateo.

"I did." Mateo's eyes brightened briefly. "He thought it was fake. So I did video."

"We'll just have to hope he has some in-person classes," Alex said. "Then we can work on his parents."

"Until then," Raphael asserted, before turning back around, "Pup Niki will be happy to suck you off in the meantime." Niki pulled his hand away from Raphael in protest, but Raphael managed to wrestle it back for the remainder of the walk home.

Everyone else was home by the time they made their entrance. As they were stripping down in the foyer, Steve walked in.

"How was it?" he asked. "I see you found Mateo."

"Actually, Mateo found us," Niki smiled as he pulled off his mask, still grateful Mateo had made the effort. "It was good. A good crowd. Good energy. Very diverse."

"Yeah," Alex agreed. "We fell in with one of the queer contingents."

"We figured you guys would have worked up an appetite," Steve said as Niki wrapped him in a hug, "so we put together a little picnic in the garden. It's ready now." Everyone trailed behind Steve through the kitchen, except Raphael, who made a stop in the powder room off the foyer. After which, he slid into place next to Luke, who handed him a stemless glass of wine.

"Did I miss the toast?" Raphael asked.

"Allow me," Niki raised his glass. "To Mateo. And his big, forgiving heart." Juan laughed out loud.

"Nice try, Niki," he chuckled. "Hiroshi will be consulting with Mateo on your discipline, and I speak from experience. He may look sweet and speak gently at the dinner table, but ..." He didn't need to say more.

"All I can say, Niki," Alex interjected, "and I might as well, since Mateo revealed my secret in the dungeon the other day, is that Mateo definitely knows his way around a paddle."

"Oh, man," Niki whined. Steve leaned over and mumbled something into Niki's ear, then kissed his cheek. A slight smile blossomed on Niki's face.

"I'm sorry I didn't ride with you guys today," Luke said to Niki. "Where's the next protest?"

"Not sure," Niki replied as he reached for a wrap. "I'm sure there's at least one every day this week. It depends on when Hiroshi and I finish tomorrow what I will do."

"I doubt he'll take up your whole day," Luke continued. "If you want to participate tomorrow, I'm with you." Everyone else nodded, munching away.

Dinner was relatively quick, since the temperature began to fall as the sun dropped behind Twin Peaks. They gathered things up as a group and retired into the house to load the dishwasher and disperse. Raphael and Luke wandered into Alex and Greg's room, where they began watching protest coverage on TV. Pretty soon Juan and Ricky joined them and they all watched a couple of hours of coverage of national and international protests in support of Black Lives Matter. Mateo was in his room, sexting with Ryan, while Steve and Niki had gone up to their room to spend some alone time together.

"I think I underestimated the reaction to George Floyd's killing," Greg admitted.

"It's about time," Raphael said. "Part of me can't believe it's taken until now for people to see what's been happening, especially to Black men."

"I think we can thank the pandemic to some extent," Alex proposed. "People are working from home or not working at all. They have time to read, to watch TV. To think. Like tonight, to get out and show their outrage."

"I agree," Luke patted Alex on the thigh. "I've certainly felt more engaged than I otherwise would have been, even being part of a multi-racial family."

"Guys, I'm glad we're doing this thing with Niki Saturday," Raphael said. "Even with all of us here with him. Because none of us are Black, I worry he feels alone in dealing with what's happening. I mean we grew up together as a family, but not during his formative years. You know what I mean? I guess I'm asking everybody to kind of look out for him as much as we can. Being unemployed on top of everything else just makes it worse for him."

"You're right, Raphael," Alex mumbled, then scooted closer to Raphael. "You're a good brother. Did uh … did you or Angel ever have to deal with racism growing up?" Raphael looked at Alex and smiled, gave a short, muted laugh as he rubbed Alex's thigh. Alex held eye contact with Raphael.

"Of course. I mean, not a lot, nothing like what Niki probably experienced, but, yeah, as a kid I got called a 'chink' more than once. Idiots. If you're Asian, you must be from China, right? But it was pretty rare. I guess we were lucky growing up here."

"Juan, Ricky, what about you?" Alex pressed.

"Oh, a little, now and then … petty stuff," Juan replied. "Nothing like most Black people experience. Ricky?"

"Most of my friends, my school mates were Latino, so not too much, no. Like you said, Raphael, we were lucky to grow up here."

"So, what are you suggesting about Niki's discipline session?" Luke asked Raphael.

"I don't know. I guess we'll see what Mateo and Hiroshi come up with. I just want to be sure when it's done, that Niki feels loved and supported, not ganged up on. Know what I mean?"

"You make a lot of sense," Greg agreed. He turned to Alex. "Did you feel ganged up on, on your birthday, sweetie?"

"I did. Yeah, I did. And I loved every minute of it." He looked at Raphael and made a face.

"On that note," Raphael stood, "why don't we go to our room, Luke, so you can gang up on me." Luke stood, wrapped an arm around Raphael's waist and led him toward the door. As they passed through it,

Luke patted Raphael on the ass as he looked back at the group and licked his lips. Juan stood and reached down to assist Ricky.

"I agree with Raphael," Juan said. "I'll talk with Hiroshi and Mateo to be sure Niki gets the best kind of discipline, as if that's even necessary. Mateo's not looking for revenge."

"No," Greg agreed. "I think that's why he asked Hiroshi to help. He'd just as soon let it go. 'Night guys." Juan nodded and he and Ricky headed into the hallway. Before they got far Mateo opened his door.

"Juan ... Ricky ... can you talk?" Juan waved him to follow them into their room where the three of them plopped onto the bed. Juan and Ricky pushed pillows aside and sat with their backs to the upholstered headboard. Mateo sat facing them, his legs intertwined with theirs.

"What's up?" Juan asked in English. The rest of the conversation was in Spanish, as Mateo was concentrating more on his emotions than his vocabulary.

"I want to talk to you about sex ... if that's okay." Ricky hooted, but immediately saw that Mateo was troubled.

"Is this about Saturday ... with Niki?" Juan asked.

"No. Yes. Yes, but more than that. Living here with all of you is wonderful, so wonderful. But sometimes confusing. And frustrating. Sex is so easy for all of you."

"Said the naked cutie playing with my foot," Ricky smiled. Mateo let go of his foot. "Don't stop, Mateo! I was kidding. It's nice, I like it." Mateo half smiled and resumed playing footsie.

"I want to be like you guys. I think. I mean I kind of was when Niki sucked me in the dungeon. It was nice. Really nice. I like Niki ... all of you. But part of me felt guilty. About Steve. And Ryan." Juan was listening intently. He didn't interrupt, but gave Mateo time to organize his thoughts and express them. When Mateo had been silent for too long, he moved his leg over to rub against Mateo's, to encourage him to continue.

"What I'm trying to say is I think I want to do more sexy things with all of you, but I don't want to feel like I'm cheating on Ryan. You know I'm practically a virgin, so there's a lot I don't know, and a lot I'd like to do, to try, to learn about. But not if it would hurt me and Ryan." Mateo fell silent again, looking down.

"Mateo," Juan spoke, then waited until Mateo looked up into his eyes. "You said you enjoyed Niki sucking you." Mateo nodded. "Okay. Last night Alex said you gave him a pretty good spanking." Mateo nodded again and this time he couldn't suppress a smile. "Did you enjoy spanking Alex?"

"Not at first. It was weird, I thought. But Greg wanted me to. Pretty soon I could tell Alex wanted me to, so I did. And he and Greg were so into it, pretty soon I was, too. So, yeah, I guess I did enjoy it."

"Why did you enjoy it?"

"I don't know." Juan remained silent and let Mateo think. Finally, he looked up again and said, "I guess maybe because Alex liked it so much. I felt good making him feel good."

"So, Mateo, is that good or bad ... to make Alex feel good. With Greg right there?"

"I guess it's not bad," Mateo said seriously. Juan laughed.

"No, Mateo, it's not bad. Alex felt good. You felt good because he felt good. I'm guessing Greg felt good?" Mateo grinned and nodded. "Did it hurt Ryan?"

"Ryan doesn't know."

"Why not?"

"I didn't tell him." Again, Mateo was silent a moment. "I was afraid to. Afraid it would make him sad. That he would think I was cheating."

"By spanking a friend?"

"It wasn't just spanking. He had Greg's cock down his throat the whole time. Greg came. Alex came."

"Did you come?" Mateo shook his head.

"Well, I got really hard and dripped a little." Juan grinned.

"Why do you think that was cheating if you didn't come? If neither Greg nor Alex touched you?"

"Because it was sex. Kinky sex. With friends."

"Do you know if Ryan has kinky sex with friends while you two are separated?" Mateo looked stricken.

"Ryan? No, Juan. He wouldn't." As soon as he said it, Mateo knew what Juan's next words would be.

"How do you know, Mateo?" Mateo gave Juan a pained look.

"I just ... I ... I don't ... "

"Ryan doesn't have a kinky bone in his body ... yet." Ricky offered.

"Oh, so you know Ryan better than Mateo?" Juan scolded. Ricky gave Juan an 'excuse me!' look.

"Mateo, my dear sweet, adorable Mateo," Juan reached down and grabbed Mateo's foot, then paused until Mateo made eye contact again. "You're trying to deal with too much too fast under very unfair conditions. You finally got the courage to come out, that's good. You did so surrounded by a bunch of guys who love you and made it easier for you. That's really good. You somehow managed to get a boyfriend almost immediately, which is not just good ... it's incredible. Then he was taken away from you by a pandemic. Now, while you're trying to keep the boyfriend and be true to him long distance, you're living with a bunch of kinksters in a house with a dungeon and you're being tempted every day to, as you put it, cheat on him."

"Wow," Ricky sighed.

"Did I get that about right?" Juan continued with Mateo. Mateo nodded and raised his eyebrows.

"Yeah, amigo. What do I do?" Juan held his arms out to encourage Mateo to move closer. Juan pulled him into sitting hug turning him so that Mateo's back rested against Juan's chest, their legs splayed out together. Juan wrapped his arms around Mateo's torso one hand across his chest, one hand just above Mateo's cock. Mateo's heart was beating fast.

"Mateo, it may not be easy, at least at first, but it will all be easier when you learn to separate sex and love. Sex is fun. Love is serious. Love includes sex, but sex doesn't have to include love. Now, in the House of the Locked Cock Brotherhood, we kind of have three flavors of all that. Ricky and I are in love. We're committed to each other." He turned to face Ricky as he wiggled his eyebrows and said, "Hopefully for life! We love you. We love Raphael and Luke, and yes, we had sex with Raphael and Luke, but it was for fun, actually a dare, but it was not for love, even though we do love them. Confused yet?"

"Not yet," Mateo laughed. "I think I get it."

"Good. What you did with Niki, what you did with Alex and apparently Greg ... that was fun sex. That wasn't necessarily cheating on Ryan."

"Necessarily?" Mateo asked. Juan patted Mateo's chest.

"Good boy. You're listening. 'Cause this is my real point. You and Ryan need to talk. About what you each want. What you expect from each other and from your relationship. At this point you don't know if Ryan is fooling around with other guys or not. You aren't telling him everything. You haven't made any long-term commitments to each other. Therefore, you're a very frustrated guy. There's an easy way to fix that ... talk to Ryan. Be honest. Be open. And listen to him. If you do that, I promise, everything will be easier."

"Huh. That's kind of what Alex said to me one day. To share more with Ryan."

"Alex is a smart guy. So are you."

"But what if I tell him about Niki or Alex, and he gets mad."

"Well, I wouldn't start with that, but if he does, and if you want to be leading a more sexual life, then Ryan's not the right guy for you. Better to find out now, don't you think?

"But I really like Ryan," Mateo whined. "I ... I love him."

"Mateo, if he loves you, he'll want you to be happy. It's really that simple." Mateo fell silent, his head resting near the top of Juan's chest.

"You're lonely, aren't you, muchacho," Ricky whispered. Mateo didn't respond. "Everybody goes to bed with someone they love but you."

"Yeah," Mateo barely spoke, staring at the ceiling.

"Mateo, I was sleeping in my bed alone at Greg and Alex's. My last night there, the night before I told Juan I wanted to be his locked cock leather boy for life, Greg could tell I was a wreck." Juan turned to give his full attention to Ricky. "He invited me to share his and Alex's bed, to comfort me. I didn't at first, but then, I went to them. We didn't have sex. We just cuddled all night, you know? Mateo, it was just what I needed. Any night you feel lonely, please ... come and cuddle with us." Ricky looked up at Juan, who grinned at him, then winked. Ricky smiled back, then reached over and squeezed Mateo's shoulder. "Anytime, muchacho." Mateo pulled himself up onto his knees, then turned, facing Juan, and leaned forward and planted a lip-on-lip kiss. He pulled back, and leaned over to give Ricky the same treatment. He definitely looked less conflicted than when he entered the room. He even reverted to English.

"Thank you. I will think about it ... the cuddle ... ever'thing. Thank you, amigos!" He padded out, both Ricky and Juan admiring the sight of his perky brown butt receding into the distance. Once they heard his door close, Juan turned to Ricky and followed Mateo's example, only for a lot longer, and with tongue. When they separated, Juan spoke, using his most sexy voice.

"That was very generous of you, mijo."

"Well, you know, I feel sorry for Mateo," Ricky said quietly, looking a little too serious. "I hope it was okay for me to invite him to sleep with us, Papito."

"Of course, it's okay. You have a big heart, mijo. In fact, I think you deserve a reward. Do you remember where we put your keys?" Ricky smiled that adorable smile, planted another lip-on-lip on Juan, then bounded out of bed and into the bath.

Seventeen

# THE DISCIPLINARIANS

AFTER BREAKFAST, NIKI SPENT a good portion of the morning in the library, again catching up on coverage of the protests around the world, events regarding arrests and charges of officers, the reactions of civic and political leaders. He wanted to know as much as he could absorb. Once he was sated, he wandered up to ask Greg to prepare him for his time with Hiroshi. Greg texted Hiroshi to inquire about timing, and Hiroshi responded almost immediately that anytime was fine. It didn't take long to install Pup Niki's mitts, tail, hood and chest harness. For good measure, Greg pulled out his leash and clipped it to his permanent collar. He led the pup downstairs and out the back door. Once Niki touched ground, he dropped to all fours, looked up at Steve and barked, tail wagging happily. Greg led him over to the gate in the privacy fence, opened it, and let go of the leash as the pup dashed off. Before he even fully closed the gate, he saw Pup Niki mark his territory.

Luke, Juan and Mateo were all working, as was Ricky, doing an earlier than usual DoorDash stint in case Niki would suggest a late afternoon protest. Just the work-at-home crew of Steve, Greg, Alex and Raphael were left in the House of the Locked Cock Brotherhood. Around eleven-thirty, Steve logged off and went to the kitchen to ponder lunch. Alex heard him stirring around and came down the back stairs to see 'what's cooking.'

"Hungry?" Steve greeted him.

"I could be," Alex smiled, as he opened the hidden fridge in search of something cold and wet.

"I'm thinking comfort food," Steve suggested. "Grilled cheese and tomato soup."

"That sounds perfect," Alex agreed. "Want me to check with the others?" Steve nodded as he pulled ingredients out of the fridge. Twenty minutes later the four of them were stationed around the island, chowing down on a simple but satisfying lunch.

"I wonder how Pup Niki and Hiroshi are doing?" Alex mused.

"Yeah," Steve said. "Pup Niki hasn't had a chance to pup out around anyone outside the family for a long time now. I'll bet he's loving it."

"I hope so," Raphael looked toward the window that faced on Hiroshi's house. "Anything that can distract him from life as we currently know it is good."

"He's okay," Steve looked at Raphael, knowing how concerned he was about his little brother. "I mean, as well as anyone. Being here, in his dream house, helps a lot, Raphael, and you really made that happen. And all of us supporting him at the protests means everything to him. We had a good night last night, if you know what I mean. So, he's doing okay."

"No, Steve," Alex looked slyly at Steve. "I don't know what you mean. Do go on."

"Use your imagination, Alex," Steve smiled, then took a big bite of sourdough grilled cheese.

"Everybody knows my secret, but I get left guessing," Alex pouted.

"I think more secrets will be revealed as time goes on," Raphael said coyly.

"Oh?" Alex prodded.

"Well," Raphael grinned. "We do have the power of the dare. That's all I'm going to say for now."

"Is this what we call foreshadowing?" Greg asked. Raphael wiggled his eyebrows.

"Maaaybe."

"Speaking of dares, I have no idea what to expect on Saturday, Steve," Greg said.

"Join the club. It's entirely in the hands of Mateo and Hiroshi."

"And Juan," Greg added. "He said he'd make sure it's a good experience for Niki."

"That's good," Steve replied, "although I totally trust Hiroshi and Mateo to keep things sane."

"Yeah," Raphael added, "we told Juan we want this to be more of an affirmation than a punishment."

"A disciplinary affirmation ceremony," Alex said. "This is getting complicated."

"Maybe I'm wrong," Raphael looked at Alex, "but I think the 'discipline' part is just an excuse to let Niki know he needs to be more thoughtful, even as a pup, about whom to suck and when. Mateo is still young and reasonably innocent."

"Mmmmm, not that innocent," Alex countered. "I think he's coming along pretty nicely, at least in the corporal punishment department."

"Alex knows of which he speaks," Greg laughed. "But, yeah, he's still figuring out a lot of things. And you have a good point, Raphael. We know he's willing to watch and explore to some extent ... remember his reference to the Juan and Ricky show? We still don't know what that's about. But, still, none of us knows what his boundaries are." Greg climbed off his stool and placed his empty dishes in the sink. "One thing we can be sure of ... living here with us is certain to expand his horizons, whether he wants it or not." Raphael nodded as he, too, bussed his dishes before heading upstairs and back to work.

When Steve returned to his desk, before logging on he checked his phone and saw a text from Hiroshi telling him he could retrieve Pup Niki anytime, although there was no hurry. Steve texted back that he'd take a break and come over at three. It was just after three when he opened the gate and walked into Hiroshi's garden for the first time. He found Hiroshi, wearing a solid black fundoshi, sitting in the shade in a blue Cape Cod chair, reading a book, Pup Niki curled up at his feet.

"Well," Steve said, "this looks like something Norman Rockwell might paint." Hiroshi laughed as he put his book down. Pup Niki stirred, then yapped happily as he bounded toward Steve, who knelt down and simultaneously patted the pup on the head and butt. Pup Niki rolled over, inviting Steve to rub his belly, his cage glinting in the sun. Steve indulged Pup Niki for a moment, then stood. "Did you two have a good time together?"

"We did, indeed," Hiroshi also stood. "May I have a moment before you take Pup Niki home?" Steve nodded. Hiroshi knelt and whistled to get the pup's attention. Pup Niki rolled over onto all fours and trotted over. Hiroshi took his hooded face in both hands as he spoke. "You stay here, boy. We'll be back in a minute. Okay? Stay." Pup Niki gave a brief, low bark and collapsed on the spot. Hiroshi stood and motioned for Steve to follow him into the house.

"Is everything okay?" Steve asked once they were inside, concerned about the need for a conference. "Was he a good boy?"

"He was an excellent companion," Hiroshi assured Steve. "We had a grand time. One of the things I wanted to explore was whether the puppy persona is more cosmetic and play-acting, or is it more deeply ingrained. Pup Niki is a pup, through and through. He inhabits puppy space."

"Yeah, he does. We spent a week at obedience school, which was good training for both of us. Sometimes, when he's been a pup for a while, it seems like it takes effort for him to shed the puppy persona and become my husband again."

"That's very perceptive of you, Steve. I'm not surprised. It's a very safe place for Niki, to be a pup. Similar, perhaps, to mediation for many others. He's lucky to have a husband as understanding as you."

"He's been a much happier guy since we gave him permission to explore his puppy side, so it's been good for all of us."

"Permission?"

"A long story ... one of many, I guess. We have a lot of stories."

"Something else to look forward to. Speaking of which, I wanted to ask you of any triggers or fetishes to consider or actions to definitely avoid on Saturday, since I've been chosen by Mateo to counsel him."

"Hmmm. Let's see ... the pup thing is obvious."

"Yes, since he committed his indiscretion as a pup, he should definitely be 'disciplined' as a pup. Since his infraction, not that I would call it that, but at any rate, was to give Mateo oral gratification, I assume Pup Niki enjoys fellatio?"

"Loves it. Definitely a favorite. Obviously he enjoys anal ... he often wears a puppy tail even when upright and talking. Wears one to bed sometimes, too. This is getting awfully personal, but ... I think he likes pee. I guess most pups do." Hiroshi nodded thoughtfully.

"Do you engage in group sex?"

"Not really. Well, not exactly sex, but he had a great time with the other pups at obedience school, and when we go to the puppy park, but that's really just pup play, even though they are all naked and caged."

"So, would you say group sex would be something we should avoid Saturday?" Steve thought a moment.

"No, I wouldn't say that. It's something we've just never pursued. We've always been enough for each other. But I guess his attack on Mateo indicates it might be something he's open to, now that I think about it."

"Well, thank you, Steve. I will do my best to counsel Mateo and to make sure Pup Niki appreciates his 'discipline' as much as possible. You've been very helpful."

"I should thank you, Hiroshi. You're very generous with your time."

"Not at all. This was a delight for me. Pup Niki, in fact all of you, are welcome anytime. Next, I will need to meet with Mateo, whenever he wishes." Hiroshi walked to the door and stood aside, allowing Steve to exit first. Steve turned at the bottom of the stairs.

"Thank you again, Hiroshi. I'll let Mateo know you're ready to meet with him." He headed for the gate, and Pup Niki bounced up and followed on his heals. At the gate, the pup turned toward Hiroshi and barked twice, tail wagging furiously. Hiroshi bowed. Pup Niki barked once more, then dashed through the gate. Once they were in their own garden, Pup Niki raised up on his haunches, lifting his forepaws to indicate he was ready to revert to human form.

"Okay, puppy, the keys are upstairs." Steve reached down and took one mitted paw to help Pup Niki stand. Then he took the leash in one hand and wrapped the other around Pup Niki's waist and led him up to their room.


Niki, back in human form, was in his chair, glued to his tablet, when Mateo returned from his shift. He noticed Niki as he stripped in the foyer, tossed his clothes in the washer off the kitchen, then headed up the back stairs to decontaminate in his shower. When he returned, Niki hadn't moved, but he looked up as Mateo entered the library.

"Hola, muchacho," Niki smiled.

"Hola. More protests?"

"Yeah. Everywhere. It's really amazing."

"How was Hiroshi?"

"It was fun. He taught Pup Niki a new trick. He's so cool."

"Yeah. I like him."

"So, you and Hiroshi are really going to plan my discipline, huh?"

"More Hiroshi ... I hope." Mateo sat in the other fireplace chair. "I don' know about these things." He stared at the unlit fireplace for a moment, then resumed eye contact with Niki. "I was okay with you, Niki. I don' want you to be ... discipline." He looked distraught. Niki reached over and rubbed his knee.

"No, no, Mateo, it's okay. Nobody is really upset with me. Seriously, they're just using this as an excuse to tease me. It's really just a game. For fun."

"Really? A tease? Like what Alex and Greg do?"

"Well, I don't know what Alex and Greg do, but probably, yeah. It keeps things interesting, I guess. But, please ... don't feel bad. Just cook up something fun with Hiroshi."

"Cook?"

"Um ... plan, prepare, sorry I don't know the Spanish for it. Maybe you should have Juan or Ricky with you when you meet with Hiroshi, to help with the language. Otherwise, I may really be in trouble!" Niki laughed, further putting Mateo at ease. He hadn't seen Niki laugh in a long time.

"Okay, I will ask." Mateo looked at the tablet. "Is there another protest ... for us?"

"Oh, sure ... every day. I don't want us to burn out, though. It looks like there's going to be a really big one on Saturday, so I think we should do that. If you and Hiroshi are done disciplining me, that is."

"Okay. I will ask Saturday off." Mateo smiled at Niki. "Discipline *and* a protest. A good day for Niki, yes?"

"I guess that's up to you, Mateo. But, yes, a good day." Mateo stood and spread his arms, inviting a hug. Niki stood and made it a good one. When they separated, he thought about making a comment about Mateo's tumescent cock but thought better of it. Clearly Mateo was missing Ryan.

Over dinner Niki announced his hope to participate in Saturday's protest, inviting anyone who was interested and setting the stage for an early enough 'discipline ceremony' so that he would be free to attend. Everyone agreed to both.

"Mateo, Hiroshi said he's available anytime you want to talk about Pup Niki's discipline," Steve said. "I think he has some ideas."

"Good," Mateo replied.

"Mateo, is it okay if I go, too?" Juan suggested.

"I was hoping," Mateo agreed, looking at Niki for approval. Niki smiled.

"Let's try for tonight, when we're done here." Juan looked meaningfully at Niki as he continued, "you know, in case we need time to build scaffolding or something."

"Oooooo," Alex enthused.

"Just remember, guys," Niki tried making eye contact with everyone around the table, "we're all going to a protest march afterwards, so go easy on me. Okay?" There was general, ambivalent, and totally noncommittal agreement around the table.

As dinner was being cleared, Juan texted Hiroshi, who agreed to meet immediately. Juan and Mateo headed out the back door as Niki watched them go.

"What are you thinking?" Raphael came up behind Niki and pulled him into a hug from behind.

"Nothing. Everything." He turned around in Raphael's embrace and the two lowered their arms to the other's hips so they could look into each other's eyes. "I know I should be so, so happy living here in my dream house, with the family. And I am. But ... "

"I know. I kind of feel the same way. It's like *A Tale of Two Cities* on steroids ... you know, 'the best of times, the worst of times.' We can't do anything about the pandemic, or your furlough, or police brutality or any of that, but at the same time we have this house. We all have each other. Don't ever forget that you're loved, Niki. We all stand with you. You're not in this alone. Okay?" Niki smiled and nodded.

"Nice speech!" Alex called from across the kitchen. As they let go of one another Raphael bowed to Alex, who was walking over to them. Alex put an arm around Niki's waist in solidarity. "Seriously, though, I think we're all a little messed up right now. Maybe not as bad as we were when Juan was in New York, but, damn." He pressed an index finger into Niki's chest. "This discipline session Saturday is just what we need to reignite our esprit de corps."

"Oh, brother," Raphael scoffed. "You just want a chance to try out that selection of paddles downstairs. You don't need an excuse for that."

"You're right," Alex pressed the same finger into Raphael's chest. "I don't. And don't you forget it." He flexed his eyebrows before turning face and wiggling his ass on his way to the stairs.

"Was that an invitation?" Niki asked.

"Sure felt like one." Raphael rubbed his chest. "Maybe we'll make the session a double ceremony. It wouldn't be the first time, would it?" Niki laughed. Then he put an arm around Raphael's shoulders and the two headed for the stairs themselves.


Ricky was laying on his stomach on the furry rug at their bedside, ear-buds in, listening to a playlist. He hadn't really had time to himself since Juan had returned, and he wasn't sure what else to do. He knew he'd be welcome in Alex and Greg's room, watching protest coverage, but by now it had become depressingly repetitive for him. He was almost in a half-awake, half-asleep dream state when he sensed movement, and raised up to see Juan and Mateo arrive. He pulled the earbuds from his ears and grinned.

"Papito! Mateo! Did you get it all figured out?" Juan stretched out on the bed sideways, on his stomach, positioning his head near where Ricky was now sitting. He motioned Mateo to join him.

"Yeah, it's going to be ... let's call it appropriate for the crime."

"Tell me. Tell me!" Ricky scooted over so his face was nearly touching Juan's.

"I think you'll enjoy it more if it's a surprise," Juan proposed. He reached over and ruffled Ricky's high 'n tight. Meanwhile Mateo sat next to Juan, legs crossed, his hands in his lap, watching Juan and Ricky interact.

"Mateo, you'll tell me ..." Ricky prompted. Mateo shook his head no, but grinned.

"I get in trouble," Mateo said. Ricky leapt up on the bed and tackled Mateo, pushing him onto his back as he squealed.

"Are you ticklish?" Ricky teased. As he did his best to torture Mateo, Juan rolled away and sat up to watch. Within seconds Mateo had Ricky pinned to the bed.

"Are *you* ticklish?" he countered. Turns out Ricky was and Mateo took full advantage. When he'd finished, Ricky raised up on both elbows and looked first at Mateo, then Juan.

"Man, I've got to start working out. Everybody's stronger than me." Juan squeezed Ricky's biceps.

"Seriously?" Juan asked. "I think you're pretty sexy just as you are, Legendary Ring Bearer." He looked over at Mateo. "What do you think, Mateo?"

"Yeah, he is sexy." Mateo tentatively brushed a hand along Ricky's calf next to him, but didn't make eye contact. No one said anything for a moment. Ricky looked at Juan, then moved his leg to rub up against Mateo's thigh.

"Muchacho. Maybe tonight you will sleep with us? To keep away the loneliness?" Mateo looked over at Juan for guidance. Juan just smiled. Mateo took a deep breath.

"Okay. I brush my teeth!" He rolled off the bed and dashed out the door. Ricky moved over to lay his head on Juan's thigh, where he could look up into Juan's face.

"He's a lonely boy, Papito," Ricky justified.

"Yeah, and it doesn't hurt that he's always had the hots for you."

"And for you!" Ricky contended. Juan snorted.

"Let's go brush our teeth, mijo." When they finished and returned to the bedroom, Mateo was back, standing awkwardly at the foot of the bed. As Ricky crawled in, Juan walked to the door and closed it, then approached Mateo. From behind, he put his hands on Mateo's shoulders and gently massaged.

"Mateo," Ricky suggested, "the night I slept with Greg and Alex, I slept in the middle. It was very nice." Mateo nodded then crawled onto the bed from the foot as Juan walked around to his side and pulled the covers back to invite Mateo in. He and Mateo crawled in together. Ricky was on his side, facing Mateo, Juan was on his side, facing Mateo and Mateo was on his back, not sure what to do. Juan laid an arm over Mateo's torso and gently kissed his cheek.

"Sweet dreams, Mateo," Juan muttered. Ricky followed Juan's lead. After about five minutes, Mateo rolled over on his right side and wrapped an arm around Ricky's waist. Ricky, eyes closed, wrapped an arm around Mateo's waist and pulled him close enough that his cage was pressed into Mateo's cock. Juan completed the picture, wrapping an arm across both their waists, his cock snugged up against Mateo's ass. Mateo feared he wouldn't sleep at all like this, but he was wrong. Ricky was right. This was nice. After only a few minutes of fantasizing about what he, Juan and Hiroshi had discussed, and comforted by the touch of not one, but two beautiful men he adored, he fell into a deep and satisfying sleep.

Juan's alarm quietly chimed at five a.m. Friday morning, startling Mateo, who sat up as Juan slid out of bed. Juan leaned over and pushed Mateo back onto the pillows.

"Sorry. Go back to sleep, Mateo," he whispered. As Mateo laid back down, Ricky, used to the routine, stirred just enough to flop an arm across Mateo's chest. Mateo blearily looked up at Juan, who smiled before padding away to the bathroom. Mateo rolled onto his side, wrapped an arm around Ricky's waist and nodded off.

Two hours later, long after Juan had left, Mateo woke again, for good this time. He pulled away from Ricky who muttered 'buen día' without even opening his eyes. Mateo sat on Juan's edge of the bed for a moment, before standing, turning toward Ricky to see he was already asleep again, then heading for the door. As he quietly pulled it closed, he turned to see Alex top the back stairs, a glass of juice in hand. For a nanosecond he felt embarrassed but then immediately felt empowered to, instead, be proud. Or at lease nonchalant. Empowered, perhaps, by yesterday's conversation with Hiroshi and Juan, compounded by recent conversations with Juan and Ricky, the story of Raphael's experience in the dungeon with Luke, Juan and Ricky, and even his own experience with Alex and Greg before the move. And more than anything, his long simmering desire to be more like the rest of the family. At any rate, he ambled toward his own door, making eye contact with Alex. "Buen día," he smiled.

"Buen día, lucky boy," Alex smirked as he pulled Mateo into a one-armed hug and pecked him on the cheek. Mateo's smile grew as he continued on to his room. Once Alex closed his door, he walked to the side of the bed, where Greg was listening to NPR before his shave and shower, and announced, "Our boy is coming along nicely." Then, without further explanation, Alex walked into the bathroom and closed the door.

Two unexpected arrivals continued the noteworthiness of this particular Friday. Around eleven a loud chime erupted throughout the house. Niki stepped into the foyer from the library at the same time Alex leaned over the railing near his room. They looked at each other.

"What was that?" Niki asked. Alex shook his head, clueless. As Niki headed back toward the kitchen it erupted again. He turned around to see something move beyond the curtained floor to ceiling side window at the front doors. He approached the doors and looked through the peep hole. A uniformed man was on the other side. He opened the door and said, "Hi. Sorry, we've never heard the doorbell before." Which, from the UPS driver's perspective, was not the most notable part of Niki's greeting.

"Hi. I have twelve boxes here for a Raphael Malaluan?" Niki turned and yelled.

"Raphael! Delivery!" A few seconds later a second naked, pierced, collared and caged tattooed man came rumbling down the staircase.

"Hi."

"Raphael Malaluan?" The driver did his best to maintain eye contact. Raphael nodded. "I have a bunch of boxes to deliver. It'll take forever to get them up these steps with my hand truck. Can you guys help?"

"Sure!" Raphael looked at Niki. "It's our gym!" He started out the door, then thought better of it. "Yeah, we'll help. We'll be right back." Then, to Niki, "Let's put on some shorts." A couple of minutes later Raphael returned with Luke in tow, and they headed down the steps to the street. Soon Niki was back and before they were done, Greg and Ricky had also arrived. None of the boxes weighed more than sixty pounds, but several were awkwardly long. The driver, initially dumbfounded by what greeted him at the door, was soon merely amused by this unconventional but cheerful group of guys living in a fabulous house. After all, the Castro was his territory, and today wasn't the first time he'd been greeted by a naked recipient. They made quick work unloading the shipment, and for that he was grateful.

"Thanks guys," he said as he handed Raphael his copy of the manifest. "I trust you'll enjoy your workouts."

"Thanks, yeah," Raphael replied. "We've already had the first one and we haven't even opened the boxes." As Raphael headed up the steps the driver admired the ink on his back. He thought to himself, there's got to be a story here.

Everyone pitched in to lug the boxes down to the utility room slash gym. As Ricky set down one of the boxes that probably contained weight plates he looked over at Raphael.

"Amigo, how long before I look like you?" Raphael walked over, squeezed his left biceps, then dramatically looked Ricky up and down.

"Do you seriously want to beef up? You look good now."

"Well, you know, next time I wrestle Mateo, I want to win."

"Well, if you're serious ... and dedicated, maybe in a year and a half, maybe two." Raphael knew it would take longer than that, but he didn't want to discourage Ricky if he was truly interested.

"Really? Will you help, Raphael?"

"Sure. But it won't be easy, Ricky. You know what they say ... no pain, no gain."

"Maybe you should figure out a dare routine," Alex suggested. "Set a goal and if you don't meet it, you have to do a dare." Raphael looked at Alex as if he'd just solved the mystery of the universe.

"That's brilliant, Alex." He turned to Ricky. "Are you that serious?"

"Yep," Ricky nodded. "I like it!" Raphael turned back to Alex.

"What about you, Alex. Are you game? Or, are you keeping the perfect dancer body?"

"Umm," Alex dithered. "Let me give it a try first. I'm not sure about that gain pain thing." Raphael laughed.

"This, from the guy who gets off on being paddled," he said, looking at Ricky, lifting one eyebrow. "The first time he notices the sleeves of his locked cock tees are getting a little tighter, he'll be hooked. Mark my words." Alex, not convinced, just shrugged.

Since it was nearly noon, and everyone who worked from home had already abandoned their computers, the group headed to the kitchen for lunch. Unpacking the gym would have to wait.


After lunch everyone scattered. Niki planned to go back to what would hence forth be known as the gym to start unboxing everything, but first he wandered up with Steve to their room. As Steve settled in at the desk to log back in, Niki picked up his tablet and sat on the bed, facing Steve's back.

"Oh," he said. For a moment he said no more, and Steve thought nothing of it. But then Niki followed up with, "It's here." Steve swiveled his chair to face Niki.

"What?" he asked. Niki glanced up, a serious look on his face.

"It's an email from SF State."

"What does it say?" Steve rolled closer, knees to knees.

"I'm afraid to look."

Steve reached for the tablet. "Here, let me."

"NO! I'll do it ... I'll do it." Steve watched Niki's face, watched his eyes track back and forth as he read. After a brief moment he looked up, a smile breaking out, "I'm in!" Niki handed the tablet to Steve, who read just enough to confirm, then tossed the tablet on the bed and pulled Niki into a celebratory hug. Followed by a kiss. Both were beaming.

"See!" Steve exclaimed. "I knew you'd get in. Niki you'll be a great nurse!"

"Sssshh," Niki whispered. "They'll hear you. I want to wait until Juan is here to tell everyone."

"Okay, sorry," Steve whispered back. "So ... tonight? At dinner?"

"Yeah."

"We'll make it special." Niki nodded, then sat back down and picked up his tablet again, the tablet that had been delivering mostly excruciating news until this moment. After he'd read the entire email twice more, he rose, kissed Steve on the back of the neck and headed back downstairs to the gym.


Much like the formal invitation Niki had sent inviting Raphael and Luke to the surprise dinner where he announced his engagement to Steve, Niki left a note on each bedroom door requesting that every member of the family plan to appear for dinner at seven p.m. Further, he admonished them to avoid the kitchen and dining room between six and seven p.m.

"Sounds like Niki is hoping to convince us to cancel tomorrow's discipline ceremony," Luke speculated as he handed the note to Raphael, who hadn't left his desk all afternoon. Raphael read it and laughed.

"Good luck with that," he said. Alex poked his head in just then, note in hand.

"So?" he asked. "This is intriguing ..."

"Yeah, Luke thinks he's trying to bribe us so we won't discipline Pup Niki tomorrow."

"Oh, but we must!" Alex replied. "Really? You think that's it?"

"Who knows," Luke replied. "We'll find out soon enough. If nothing else, it's a labor free dinner." Alex nodded and slipped away.

Apparently, Niki was serious. The kitchen and dining room doors to the foyer and the kitchen door to the back stairs were closed shortly before six. They'd never been closed before. When Juan returned from work, he noticed the closed kitchen door as he stripped in the foyer, blocking direct access to the washer, but he didn't think too much of it, until he found the note on his and Ricky's door. He wandered into Raphael and Luke's room as he read it.

"Did anyone text Ricky about a seven p.m. command performance?" he asked.

"Oh shit," Raphael replied.

"I'll do it," Juan turned to leave. He stopped to ask, "Do you guys know what this is about?"

"Nope," Luke smiled. "Niki likes mysteries. We're all in the dark." Juan nodded with a slight smile, then left. He texted both Ricky and Mateo, although he expected Mateo to be home long before seven. And he was. He stuck his head in Juan's door at six-thirty, note in hand.

"Come on in," Juan, lounging on the bed, said as he put his book down. He motioned Mateo to climb aboard. Mateo sat cross legged, near the foot of the bed. "Did you sleep okay last night?" Mateo nodded, a satisfied smile appearing on his face.

"Yes. I did. Did you?"

"I did, muchacho. I'm glad you finally did it. It was nice having you here. We don't want you to feel all alone."

"Ricky is right. It was good. Thank you."

"Did you tell Ryan?"

"I tell him tonight."

"So, you're ready to start talking about important things with him?"

"Si. Yes. I think is time." It was at that point that Ricky bounded in.

"Papito!" He grinned at Mateo as he rushed to Juan and delivered a major kiss. "I got your text. What's up?"

"I'm not sure, mijo. It's a surprise, I guess."

"Okay, don't move, anybody. Let me decontaminate ... I'll be right back." Less than five minutes later, a slightly damp Ricky returned from the bathroom and sat next to Juan, but looked over at Mateo as he addressed Juan.

"Mateo sneaked out this morning. I guess he doesn't like sleeping with us."

"You're wrong, mijo," Juan smiled. "When I left, you two were wrapped all around each other. You looked so sweet." Ricky rolled his eyes.

"I was telling Juan you are right, Ricky," Mateo said earnestly. "I like it. It was nice."

"Good!" Ricky smiled as he reached across and rubbed Mateo's thigh. "I was kidding. I could tell you liked it. You even snored." Mateo knitted his brow. "Roncaste." Mateo looked shocked.

"No ... not me." Juan laughed and nodded slowly. Mateo fell back and groaned.

"It's okay," Juan said as he stood up and took Ricky's hand to lift him up. "Everybody does it once in a while. Especially when they are really, really comfortable. Come on, let's round everyone up and head down to the sitting room. It's almost time for our surprise dinner." Ricky reached out for Mateo's hand and the three headed across the hall to recruit Raphael and Luke. Greg and Alex weren't in their room, but they found them downstairs in the library. They were all headed for the sitting room when the door to the dining room opened and Steve stepped into the foyer.

"Gentlemen ... dinner is served." He stood aside and motioned for everyone to enter. The chandelier was dimmed, candles were lit on the table and sideboard. Steve and Niki had set the table with the good china, silver and stemware, not the everyday stuff. There was a tureen of cucumber yogurt soup and platters of Mediterranean food ... baba ghanoush, tabuleh, stuffed filo, kebabs, hummus and pita. There were a couple of opened bottles of wine on the table and, on the sideboard, the sterling ice bucket with a bottle resting on ice. Once everyone was seated, Steve pulled the bottle of bubbly out of the ice bucket and began pouring, with each of them passing their flute around so Steve could fill each one. Finally, everyone was armed for the obvious forthcoming toast. Rather than sitting, Steve stepped next to Niki, who was struggling to keep a placid face, and raised his glass.

"Gentleman ... it is with great pride that I introduce to you San Francisco State's newest nursing student, Niki Maricel Raphael Angel Malaluan-Phillips."

"Whoa!" Raphael exclaimed before anyone else could react. As Raphael pushed his chair back and rushed over to Niki, Niki looked over at Juan, who gave him a broad smile and a thumbs up. Once the clamor died down and Raphael had returned to his seat, Steve sat as well.

"Niki," Juan spoke first. "I doubt you will, but if you ever need my help with your studies, I would be honored to mentor you in any way I can." Niki looked humbled.

"I ... I didn't want to say anything to anyone, except Steve, of course, in case I didn't make it. I have a confession ... I did list you as a reference, but obviously they didn't contact you."

"Actually, they did, Niki. But I can keep a secret, too. I told them they'd be crazy not to admit you." Niki's face fell into a jumble of smiling, teary gratitude.

"Hey! No tears!" Ricky exclaimed. He raised his flute again, "To our newest nurse!" Ricky's toast was followed by the passing of platters and dinner began in earnest. A few minutes into the feast, as he held his soup bowl out to Greg for another ladle of soup, Alex posed a reasonable question.

"So, does this mean tomorrow's discipline ceremony is out? Has Niki redeemed himself?"

"Hmmm," Luke replied. "That's a good question. What do you think, Mateo?" Mateo looked at Juan, then Niki.

"Okay for me!" He made a funny, undecipherable face at Niki. Juan laid down his fork and turned to Mateo, pretending to be quite serious.

"Mateo ... after all the planning you and Hiroshi have done?"

"Oh," Mateo sighed. The last thing he wanted to do was disappoint Hiroshi. "I don' know ..."

"How about this?" Luke suggested. "We make it a congratulatory discipline ceremony." Juan smiled and nodded. "Would that work, Juan?"

"With a little modification of Hiroshi's and Mateo's meticulous planning, I'm sure it would." He turned his grin on Niki.

"Oh, man," Niki sighed. He picked up his flute and drained it. He knew whatever was coming would be as big a surprise as the one he'd sprung on everyone else. He also knew it would most likely be more good than bad. Pretty sure, anyway.

Once dinner was over, Raphael and Alex insisted that they'd do cleanup so Steve and Niki could celebrate in whatever fashion they chose. Juan and Mateo headed out for an impromptu visit to Hiroshi to discuss Plan B for tomorrow's session. Luke, Greg and Ricky went downstairs to continue unpacking the gym. Juan joined them after he and Mateo returned, while Mateo retired to his room to hook up with Ryan. All in all, everyone thought, it had been a very good day. A relief, really, to have had something to celebrate.

Like most Saturday mornings, this one started slowly and later than a weekday. Mid-morning, Raphael and Luke finished assembling the two benches and the rack for the weight plates, and Raphael did an inventory to insure everything had arrived.

"Well, Sir, it won't make the cover of Muscle Mania, but it's a good start," Raphael pronounced as he surveyed their setup.

'Muscle Mania?"

"I made that up. Here, help me load this barbell. You can spot me as I do the introductory bench press." Not surprisingly, Raphael had lost a little strength. After only a few reps, he lowered the bar into the supports. "Don't laugh, Sir."

"You did fine, baby. I've probably lost more definition than you. But it won't take us long to get it back. Heck, we can work out every day now, if we want. This was another great idea of yours." Luke bent over and rewarded Raphael with a lip-on-lip kiss.

"Well, if this is how we're supposed to work out, count me in," the ever-timely Alex announced as he entered. "This looks pretty cool, guys." Raphael sat up.

"Sit here, Alex," Raphael patted the end of the bench. As Alex sat, Raphael rose and configured a twenty-five-pound dumbbell then sat next to him. "Here, do this." He showed Alex how to do a biceps curl.

"Give me a break, Raphael. We had gym class in the Midwest, too, you know." Raphael placed the dumbbell in Alex's grip and watched as Alex did a couple of reps, then paused.

"Don't stop now," Luke encouraged. "Let's see how may reps it takes to fatigue your muscle." Alex rolled his eyes but resumed reps. When he got to twelve, Raphael put a hand on his forearm to stop him.

"Okay, good, rest in place ten seconds then do another ten." Alex did. "Repeat." Alex did seven more, then stopped. "No ... you're doing great! Force three more. Three more. Come on ..." Alex grunted, clenched his teeth and got first one, then one more rep in. He tried, really tried, but couldn't manage the third.

"Excellent!" Raphael clapped, then lifted the dumbbell out of Alex's grip. "How does that feel."

"Like I'm done," Alex half-laughed.

"That's how you do it. When you can't do any more, you've fatigued the muscle, and the muscle will grow. Now the other arm ..." Alex tried to resist, but Raphael wouldn't have it. He got down on his knees next to Alex and cheered him on, rep after rep until once again he'd reached muscle fatigue. As Raphael set the dumbbell aside Alex actually looked pleased.

"Maybe ... uh ... you could show me some other exercises? But I want to watch you guys first." Raphael and Luke both laughed.

"You bet," Luke clapped Alex on the shoulder. "You'll find it becomes kind of addictive, but in a good way." Alex nodded as he watched Raphael's back ... and ass ... as he squatted down and assembled another dumbbell set. Sure, he thought, why not. If my back ever gets to looking like Raphael's, maybe I'll consider a sexy tattoo, too.


At noon, per Mateo's instructions, Steve pupped out Niki and led him down to the dungeon, locking him in the puppy cage. He was to spend the next half hour there, contemplating his indiscretion. Or, more likely, enjoying a nap. At twelve-thirty Hiroshi knocked on the back door, clad only in a deep red fundoshi, with a tiny dog bone print. In other words, dressed for the occasion. Mateo greeted him and the two bowed gracefully, something that amused Mateo, but made him feel more sophisticated each time he did it. Mateo dashed up the back stairs to corral the rest of the family. Soon all were present in the dungeon. As Hiroshi directed, they moved the bondage table into the center of the room and lowered it on its adjustable legs to just a few inches off the floor.

"Ordinarily I would request everyone to remove their clothing before we proceed, but that will never be necessary for this family, will it?" Hiroshi joked. He turned to Steve. "Is Pup Niki ready to offer his recompense to Mateo?"

"He is," Steve answered with a smile.

"Then bring him forth." Steve nodded then went to the puppy cage, unlatched it and coaxed Pup Niki out. He'd had plenty of time to get deeply into pup head space. As usual, Steve had installed his puppy hood, tail, mitts and knee pads, but, per instructions, had left off his chest harness. Pup Niki trotted over to Hiroshi, who knelt down on his knees. He caressed Pup Niki's hood as he calmed the pup. "You are not a bad puppy, you are a good puppy, excellent puppy. But you did do something bad. Understand, puppy?" Pup Niki barked once, then whined. "Yes, it's okay, puppy, but we need to make sure you never do it again ... without permission. Understand puppy?" Pup Niki barked once, more enthusiastically. "Good boy. Gooood boy." Hiroshi looked up at the family. "Niki indicated an interest in Shibari, so as part of his discipline, first I'm going to bind him." Pup Niki's tail began wagging. Hiroshi turned to Mateo. "Mateo, the blue ropes please." Mateo went to the collection of ropes on the wall and removed several bundles and returned to Hiroshi. "Steve, since puppies can't stand, if you could help hold Pup Niki up on his hind legs ..." Steve pulled the pup up by his shoulders, and held him so that he was essentially standing from the knees up. "Perfect. Thank you, Steve." Then, for the next twenty minutes, as everyone watched in silence, Hiroshi constructed a web of rope around Pup Niki's torso, from shoulders to groin and around his sides, creating an intricate body harness, more beautiful and tighter than any leather harness. When he was done, Hiroshi nodded to Steve to lower Pup Niki onto his forepaws. Hiroshi reached under the pup's snout and lifted his hooded head so they were making eye contact. "Does that feel good, puppy?" Pup Niki barked and wagged his tail enthusiastically. Hiroshi smiled and stood.

"Now, let's place the pup on the bondage board with his forepaws here." He indicated a spot near the edge. Steve, Luke and Mateo lifted the pup onto the board. As they positioned Pup Niki, Raphael realized why the board had been lowered. Pup Niki's snout was level with Mateo's crotch as he stood next to him. "Mateo, two bundles of the black rope please." Hiroshi proceeded to lash Pup Niki's four paws to the bondage board, using the cutouts. Once he was done, the pup was essentially immobilized. Once again, being the pro that he was, Hiroshi leaned down and addressed Pup Niki, checking to make sure he was not in discomfort. Then he turned to the group.

"Mateo, Pup Niki took advantage of you without your permission. Is that correct?" Mateo stepped forward, directly in front of Pup Niki and nodded to Hiroshi. "What will rectify this transgression?" It was soon clear to everyone that what they were about to witness, and to some extent participate in, had been carefully choreographed.

"Pup Niki should only suck my cock when I present it to him." Ricky made a barely audible 'whoa' sound.

"And how would you do that?" Hiroshi asked. Without speaking Mateo stepped forward and inserted his cock into Pup Niki's snout. As Pup Niki's tail began wagging, and he made low, muffled woofing sounds, Pup Niki buried Mateo's bone once again. As they obviously had planned, Juan and Hiroshi moved to either side of Mateo and caressed his back and ass to help encourage him to relax and perform before an audience. Juan leaned down and chewed on Mateo's ear, making him moan and apparently bone up more, as Pup Niki began moving back and forth on Mateo's bone, making decidedly louder sucking sounds. Hiroshi began to play with Mateo's nipples as Juan slid his right hand down between Mateo's cheeks. This was beginning to look less like discipline for Pup Niki and more like a four-way for Mateo's benefit. Which maybe made sense since Mateo was the 'victim' of Pup Niki's indiscretion. Mateo began to moan, then whimper.

"Dios Mio," he muttered. "Ohhh ... ohhh..." He turned and looked up at Hiroshi, who smiled as he continued to pay homage to Mateo's nipples. Mateo closed his eyes, his head still cocked toward Hiroshi, and he puckered his lips. Juan looked over at Hiroshi, grinned and nodded down at Mateo. Hiroshi leaned down and kissed Mateo, who moaned even louder just as he shot into Pup Niki's throat. Mateo buckled, but Juan and Hiroshi kept him upright. Ricky looked over at Raphael and Alex, astounded, then grinning. First Greg, then the rest of the observers began clapping. Juan and Hiroshi pulled Mateo out of Pup Niki's mouth and guided him to a sitting position on the floor. He was breathing heavily. As Juan retrieved something from the shelves from near the slings, then walked up behind Pup Niki, Hiroshi stood and addressed the family again.

"Puppies learn best when offered positive reinforcement, as Mateo just illustrated. Negative reinforcement, while not ideal, is sometimes employed as well. Such as when a very young pup undergoes the trials of becoming housebroken. Allow me to demonstrate." Hiroshi stepped in front of Pup Niki, his caged cock level with the pup's snout. He slowly leaned in, and Pup Niki reflexively leaned forward too. When he was about to touch his snout to Hiroshi's cage, Juan loudly slapped a rolled newspaper against his free hand just over the pup's bound body, startling the pup and everyone else, except Mateo and Hiroshi. Mateo giggled.

"Originally, we intended to have each of the free cock members of the family follow Mateo in orally 'disciplining' Pup Niki, by giving him permission, or not, but given yesterday's announcement, about which we are all very proud, we have decided to limit such discipline to only two. Mateo, of course, deserved to go first. Steve, as Pup Niki's guardian, you should go next and last, unless you choose to defer to someone else."

"Hmmm ..." Steve hesitated. "I have the pleasure of enjoying all of Pup Niki's skills anytime I wish. I would like to defer to the man who has inspired Niki to follow in his chosen path. I defer to Juan." Juan's eyes widened, clearly indicating this was not in the script. Pup Niki barked, then barked again more enthusiastically.

"Well," Juan said. "In that case ..." He moved towards Pup Niki's snout. Juan looked over at Ricky, to make sure Ricky was included, but this would not be the first time Ricky watched someone else in the family suck him off. Grinning, Ricky walked up next to Juan, wrapped his left arm around Juan's waist and placed his right hand on Pup Niki's shoulder, reinforcing the fact that, this time, going for the 'bone' was permissible.

Once he finished, Juan gingerly extracted himself, knelt down to eye level with Pup Niki and spoke.

"Good boy. You're a good boy." He patted the pup's other shoulder then stood and embraced Ricky fully.

"Mateo," Hiroshi instructed, "please help me remove the black ropes from our puppy." Once he was freed, Pup Niki bounded around the bondage board a bit, happy to be done with his 'discipline.' "Steve, if you would hold up Pup Niki again, I'll release his bonds." As Hiroshi undid the intricate Shibari, everyone else gathered around the board to watch and to praise the pup.

Steve removed the mitts, then the hood, so that Niki, and not Pup Niki, was back and could walk up the three flights of stairs. Once he was standing, Niki took a deep breath and looked kindly at Hiroshi.

"Thank you, Hiroshi," Niki bowed. Then he turned to Mateo and smiled. "That wasn't as awful as I feared."

"Did you enjoy the Shibari?" Hiroshi asked.

"I did. I didn't want you to take it off, to be honest."

"We will do it again, sometime. I meant it when I told Pup Niki he is a good pup."

"I'd like that. By the way, would you like to join us at the protest this afternoon? We're leaving around four. We'll be marching on Mission." Hiroshi turned to Raphael.

"Do you still have enough signs, Raphael?"

"We sure do," Raphael smiled. "You can take your pick."

"Then I shall see you all this afternoon." Hiroshi handed the ropes to Mateo, walked to the foot of the stairs, then turned and bowed. "Thank you for including me. It felt good to be back in the dungeon again ... and with such inspirational men around me." He nodded at Juan, then headed up the stairs. Steve and Niki followed him.

"Well," Alex whined as he looked plaintively at Raphael, "I didn't get to participate, but at least I got to witness a little dungeon action this time. I guess it's a start."

"What?" Raphael exuded innocence. "I didn't plan any of this."

"No ... but, you know." Alex looked unfulfilled.

"Alex, just enjoy it," Raphael smiled, lovingly punching Alex's slightly tender left biceps. "There will be more to come. It's only going to get better." Alex had to smile.

"Promise?" he asked.

"I promise." Raphael caught Luke's eye. "Sir, I need a shower, before lunch."

"You go ahead, baby," Luke replied. "Take Mateo with you, to save water. Alex, Greg, and I will clean up the dungeon."

"You sure?" Juan asked, his arm already around Ricky's shoulders.

"You guys go get cleaned up," Greg insisted. "We've got this." Juan squeezed Greg's shoulder as he led Ricky toward the stairs, but before he hit the first step, Greg continued, "Remember, handsome, you're our first birthday victim ... er, celebrant."

"Yeah," Juan answered, turning at the foot of the stairs. "I remember. I trust you'll all make it memorable." He grinned, and pulled Ricky up the stairs and out of sight.

"That sounded like a challenge," Luke looked at Greg as the two of them lifted the bondage board..

"Uh huh," Greg nodded. "Looks like we may be consulting with Hiroshi ourselves."

## Eighteen

# FANCY MEETING YOU HERE

JUAN AND RICKY, FRESHLY showered, wandered into the kitchen to find Mateo sitting alone at the island, eating a sandwich. Ricky opened the fridge and began pulling out ingredients to fix his and Juan's lunch, as Juan sat down next to Mateo.

"What do you think, Mateo? About Pup Niki's discipline?"

"Good," Mateo smiled, wiping his mouth with a napkin. "Better than I thought. And a surprise ... you!"

"Yeah, that wasn't planned, was it? But, the best scenes ... or discipline ceremonies ... are the ones that surprise you. I thought you did very well. Especially with everyone watching."

"Si. I just close my eyes and think of Ryan."

"So. Last night ... did you tell Ryan about today? And about sleeping with us?" Mateo nodded, but didn't speak, munching on his sandwich. Finally, he turned to look at Juan who was patiently waiting.

"I think is okay," Mateo finally pronounced. Again, Juan remained silent, forcing Mateo to speak. "First he was ... quiet ... like you now." Juan smiled. "But then he say, 'I understand.'"

"Did you tell him you love him?" Ricky asked, always one to get right to the heart of things. Mateo nodded, then laughed.

"I said 'if you was here I be sleeping with you.' Then he start to cry. Then I cry. We talk a long time." He looked directly at Juan. "I tried to 'splain fun sex and love sex like you and Raphael say."

"Did he understand?" Juan asked. Mateo nodded slowly.

"He say yes. He wish to be here, naked and all sexy like us, I think." Juan squeezed the back of Mateo's neck, then ran his hand down Mateo's back all the way to his butt, which he patted.

"He will be, Mateo. It will all be fine." Mateo nodded, looking almost but not entirely convinced. Ricky slid a plate in front of Juan and sat down with his own next to him. He leaned back to look at Mateo over Juan's back.

"Juan's always right, muchacho. Ryan will be here."

"Okay," Mateo replied, hoping both were right.


The family met Hiroshi at the foot of the steps at four, some in BLM tees, some in locked cock tees. Ricky had run across the crop top locked cock tee that Raphael had created for his audition with Juan, and he was sporting it, killer abs on full display. They shuffled through and selected which signs each would carry just before heading out. For this march they headed east on 20th Street, the most direct route to Mission, which meant climbing a hill or two. As usual they were paired off, with Mateo and Hiroshi holding hands once again as well. The youngest and the oldest together in solidarity. The sidewalks became more crowded, as before, the closer they came to Mission Street. Once there, the crowd was so massive the lead marchers were out of sight, with the entire throng moving slowly, but peacefully. Most were on foot, but there were bikes and skateboards and scooters mixed in as well. There weren't obvious contingents as at the last march they'd attended, so they simply slipped into the stream and followed along. A news copter buzzed overhead, hopefully providing footage to be amalgamated live or on tape with protests from other cities on major networks, reinforcing the breadth and depth of civic engagement across the country.

It was about a half an hour into the march when they heard it. Amongst all the other chanting, shouting and singing, a voice, from behind, calling out "Nicholas!" Then, "Nicholas! Nicholas JOHNSON!" Niki stopped dead and turned. He put his arm around Steve's waist and pulled him close, as the woman worked her way through the interspersed bodies to reach them. Once he realized what was happening, Raphael pulled Luke and the others away and to the side, off the street and onto the sidewalk where they could stand still without being swept along. Luke looked at Raphael, who just shook his head, not taking his eyes off of Niki.

"Is that you, Nicholas?" the woman exclaimed as she finally came face to face with Niki. She looked him up and down, then looked at Steve briefly, then back at Niki.

"Well, what do you know," Niki replied. "Hello, Mother." Niki looked up at Steve, then cocked his head to the woman. "Steve, this is my birth mother. Mother, this is my husband, Steve."

"Husband?"

"Yes, that's what married men call each other." She glanced again at Steve before turning to Niki.

"Look at you, Nicholas! You're so ... and what kind of hairdo is that?"

"It's called a mohawk. It's very stylish. And, by the way, my name is not Nicholas."

"What do you mean? It certainly ..." Niki cut her off.

"I changed my name when we got married. My name is Niki Maricel Raphael Angel Malaluan-Phillips."

"All of that, huh? My, my ... So, you're not a Johnson anymore?"

"I stopped being a Johnson the day you threw me out. It just took me a while to make it legal." She continued to study Niki, with brief glances at Steve who, not knowing what to do, did nothing except hold onto Niki. Niki squeezed Steve's waist tighter, signaling his anxiety.

"You, uh ... so you're okay." It sounded more like a statement than a question.

"Oh, I am so much better than 'okay'. In fact, let me say this." Niki was quickly becoming more animated. "Thank you ... Mother. Thank you ... for throwing me out. I can't imagine who I'd be or where I'd be right now if you hadn't, except that I'd probably still be the miserable, frightened, closeted person I was then. But, thanks to you, I'm not. Instead, I have a loving, compassionate family. A family that loves me for who I am. Do you know how empowering that is? Look!" Niki indicated Steve. "I have a smart, talented, handsome husband. I live in a fabulous home. A house with eight bathrooms! I'm surrounded by people who look out for me. Who have made me who I am and are helping me become what I dream to be. I have an exciting and meaningful career ahead of me. It's funny. I guess I hadn't really thought about this before now, but you did me the greatest favor you could possibly have ever done. So ... thank you." Niki stopped and waited, but his mother just stared at him. "Enjoy the march," Niki concluded, then pulled Steve away as they turned and moved forward, not knowing where the rest of the family was by now.

"You certainly got that off your chest," Steve said as he tugged Niki's waist to signal support.

"I'm not even sure what I said," Niki half laughed with relief. "I didn't swear at her, did I?"

"You might as well have," Steve replied. That's when the family surrounded them. Raphael broke from Luke's grasp and pulled Niki into a walking hug. He leaned in and kissed him on the cheek, then looked back to see Niki's mother still standing there, staring at them as they marched away.

"Are you okay?" Raphael asked, knowing this encounter had to be traumatic. Niki continued looking forward intently for a moment, not

at Raphael. Then, he looked over at him and grabbed Raphael's waist
and pulled him close.

"You know what? I'm VERY okay. Seeing her made me realize how
lucky I am to be me, to be your brother and Steve's husband." And then
he shouted, "I'M VERY OKAY!" Another marcher, not in on the context of the conversation shouted back, "YOU'RE VERY OKAY!" Niki,
now euphoric, tossed caution to the wind and high-fived the marcher.

A couple of hundred feet back his mother began walking again, but
more somberly than before. Until the crowd closed in, she watched
Nicholas and the group of men around him. There were so many of
them, none of them Black. They were white, Asian and Latino, different
ages, but judging by how they were acting and touching one another,
all obviously close to each other and to Nicholas. Especially the younger
Asian kid. Ah, she thought. Yeah. That's where she'd heard that name
before. Malaluan. His best friend was named Malaluan ... Angel Malaluan. Huh. So that's where he went. I always liked that name ... Angel.

"So that was your mother?" Juan asked a couple of hours later, after
they'd left the march behind and were walking home, away from the
crowd now and able to converse.

"My birth mother, yeah," Niki replied. "Mama is my mother now,
Raphael's, Angel's and mine." Juan nodded. He understood the intensity of Niki's emotion. Everyone did, except for Hiroshi, who didn't know
all of Niki's story, but was piecing it together from what he saw and was
hearing.

"And that's the first time you've seen her since ..."

"Since she threw me out of the house, yeah. I'm surprised she even
recognized me."

"Mothers have special powers," Hiroshi spoke. "Even those who do
not deserve them."

"Niki handled it extremely well," Steve said. "He spoke very highly of
all of you."

"As he should," Raphael laughed. "We all made him the amazing man
he is today. Right, Niki?" Niki couldn't resist. He barked. Everyone was
quiet the remainder of the walk, on a day that had been far more eventful
for Niki than anyone had expected.

Sunday morning, as tradition demanded, found Ricky at the stove; however, it was Niki at the juicer. Mateo was nowhere to be seen yet. He didn't appear until everyone had already seated themselves and started eating.

"Sorry," he greeted everyone as he slipped into his chair and passed his plate to Ricky. "I slept over."

"Overslept," Alex coached. "Big night with Ryan?" Alex handed Mateo his plate of pancakes as Juan passed him the bowl of fruit.

"Si ... yeah. He wants to be here so bad."

"It would be a lot easier if classes weren't going to be online for at least the fall semester," Steve stated the obvious. "I feel badly that Niki has to start his first semester online, but at least he's here with us."

"Yeah," Juan said, "I've been trying to come up with a rationale for why Ryan would be better off here than downstate, but there really isn't one ... other than satisfying this guy's libido." He ruffled Mateo's bedhead. "I don't think that carries a lot of weight with Ryan's parents." Everyone fell into silence for a few minutes as they continued eating. Until Alex decided on a way to check in with Niki.

"Did you really like the Shibari Hiroshi did for you yesterday, Niki?" he asked.

"Yes!" Niki replied. "It felt really cool. It must have looked cool, too."

"It did," Alex affirmed. "I liked the way it felt, too. I know you'll laugh, Raphael, but I kind of felt more muscular when Hiroshi did it to me."

"No, I get it," Raphael winked at Alex. "It's similar to why I like wearing this full body harness. It hugs the body. Makes me more aware of different parts of my body."

"You mean like how it tugs on your butt plug when you sit down?" Luke asked, not so innocently.

"You always have to bring up butt plugs when we're eating," Raphael scolded. "Jesus."

"Well, am I right?" Luke pursued. Raphael rolled his eyes, and refused to answer.

"I hope what we did yesterday wasn't ... hurtful," Alex revealed his concern. "Niki, you understand?"

"Oh," Niki sat upright, noting the concern on Alex's face. "It's okay, Alex. That was not the first time I've been on display. You know ... BPOS."

"Oh ... yeah." Alex looked around the table to assess everyone's reactions. "I just wondered ..."

"Well, don't worry about it," Niki said. "I thought it was fun." Okay, Alex thought. I guess I can stop worrying about Niki. After breakfast everyone scattered while Alex and Raphael handled cleanup. Mateo headed out for his shift at the restaurant, Niki settled into the library to catch up on the protest coverage and Luke and Juan headed down to the gym.

"I'm going to go workout, too," Raphael said as he hung up his dishtowel. "Want to get in some reps?"

"Maybe I'll watch for a few minutes," Alex replied. "I'm not sure I'm ready for an audience."

"Don't be silly ... we were all ninety-six-pound weaklings when we started."

"Bitch."

"Come on." Raphael grabbed Alex's hand and dragged him to and down the stairs and into the gym.

About an hour later, Mateo was back, slamming the front door and running up the stairs. Niki barely caught a glimpse of him passing through. Mateo didn't even stop to strip first. Then, Niki heard a muffled anguished scream from upstairs. He ditched his tablet and ran up the stairs, not sure where to turn. At the same time Ricky came out of his room and hurried towards Niki.

"That wasn't you?" Ricky asked.

"No, I think it was Mateo."

"He's at work."

"No ... he just came back." Niki and Ricky walked over to Mateo's door and knocked.

"Don' come in!" Mateo shouted. Niki tried the door anyway, but it was locked.

"Mateo. What's wrong?" Ricky called out. "Let us in!"

"No! I can'. I might have it." Niki and Ricky looked at each other, confused.

"Mateo, what is wrong?" Ricky repeated.

"COVID!" Mateo wailed. "They close the restaurant and send everybody home."

"Shit!" Niki reacted.

"Wait here," Ricky said as he grabbed Niki's biceps with both hands, then fled down the back stairs. He made the trip down two flights in seconds, raced into gym and yelled, "Papito! It's Mateo ... he might have COVID!" Juan dropped the dumbbell he was curling and stood up from his end of the bench and followed Ricky. Everyone else followed Juan. They were soon crowded around Mateo's door, along with Greg, who had come out of his and Alex's room to see what the commotion was about. Juan sat down and knocked.

"Muchacho, it's me."

"Juan," Mateo yelled. "Estoy esustado!"

"I know," Juan yelled back. "Mateo, come sit next to the door so we don't have to shout." Everyone else sat, too. After a moment, Juan continued in a more soothing tone, "Are you there?"

"Si."

"Okay, tell me everything."

"Everything was okay 'til Ramon got a call. He hang up and say everbody go home. Eduardo has tested positive. I have to close. Go get tested. Stay safe."

"So, Eduardo was not there today?"

"No."

"Was he there Friday?"

"Si ... yes. Sorry."

"Did he seem okay?"

"Yes. I think so."

"Did Eduardo say why he got tested?"

"No." He paused, then, "I don' know. Ramon did not say."

"Does Eduardo have family or roommates?"

"Roommates, yeah. I don' know how many. ¿Por qué?

"I'm just trying to figure out how serious this is, muchacho. Everybody wears masks all the time at work, right?"

"Yes. Always."

"Were you closer than six feet to him for a long time Friday?" Once again, Mateo didn't answer immediately.

"I think so. Yeah. I am sure. We all are close ... a lot."

"And you always wear gloves?"

"Always." Juan looked around at the serious faces on everyone listening. No one else had spoken a word.

"Okay. Mateo. I think everything will be fine, but just to be safe. Just to be sure, you should not come out of your room until we know your status. Everybody out here wants to hug you right now, but ..."

"I know. I know..."

"So, listen. We'll bring you food and leave it outside your door. You can leave the dishes outside your door when you're done. I'm going to leave a thermometer out here in a couple of minutes and I want you to take your temperature for me every time I ask. I'm going to see if I can get a test kit so we can test you here."

"¿Mañana?"

"I'll try. But, Mateo, even if I can, we won't get the results for a couple of days, maybe longer. Mateo, if you were infected Friday, it probably won't register this soon anyway. We will need to do another test in three or four days."

"Dios Mio!"

"Yeah, muchacho, I know. I'm sorry."

"Is okay ..."

"Yes. It will all be okay. We're all with you, you know." With that, everyone chimed in to confirm their concern.

"Sorry, amigos!" Mateo responded.

"Mateo!" Raphael moved closer to the door. "This isn't anybody's fault. Don't be sorry. Just be brave. Anything you need, knock on the door. Or text us. Day or night. Okay?"

"Okay! Thank you!" Everyone stood. Juan motioned for everyone to follow him into his and Ricky's room. He closed the door.

"Fuck!" Niki whisper-swore.

"Listen, guys," Juan counseled, "we'll get through this. We're in a much better situation than a lot of people. With his own bathroom Mateo is essentially quarantined. If I can get the test kit and PPE, tomorrow's test may not tell us anything, like I said, but it might. To be honest, I'm most worried about Hiroshi. He and Mateo were both masked yesterday, but they spent a lot of time together, most of it holding hands. Just to be safe, we shouldn't get close to Hiroshi until we know Mateo's negative. I'm going to let him know the situation so he can monitor himself in the meantime."

"Can you test him, too?" Alex asked. "Test all of us?"

"Wouldn't that be nice?" Juan replied sarcastically. "Alex, testing in this country still sucks, as you know. I'll be very lucky to get a test kit for Mateo. Right now only essential workers or people who have symptoms can get tested. It's pathetic, but that's where we are."

"So, why test Mateo tomorrow if it won't be conclusive?" Luke asked.

"Two reasons. If he tests positive, then we all need to quarantine and get tested ourselves."

"And the second?" Ricky asked.

"To make Mateo feel better. To show we're taking care of him." Niki nodded.

"That makes sense," he smiled at Juan. "I do have a lot to learn from you." Juan smiled back. He walked into the bath, then returned a moment later and handed Niki a glass containing a digital thermometer that smelled of rubbing alcohol.

"Here, Nurse Niki. Deliver this to the patient in the room at the end of the hall." Niki took it, and with great ceremony, opened the door and exited. Juan picked up his phone and texted Hiroshi. As Niki was returning, Hiroshi texted back. "Okay, I'm going to go talk with Hiroshi through the garden gate. I'll be back in a bit."

"I'm going upstairs to tell Steve," Niki said, "then I'm going downstairs to see Hiroshi." Taking Niki's cue, everyone else headed downstairs to observe Juan. Alex and Raphael were the first to the back door. Juan was sitting on the ground in front of the open gate, but they couldn't see Hiroshi on the other side.

"Screw this," Raphael said, "I'm going out." He opened the back door and led the rest of the family into the garden. Juan looked over his shoulder at the group, not surprised at their inability to await his return.

"So, this sucks, huh?" Niki was the first to greet Hiroshi, who was sitting cross-legged on his side of the gate. Typically, he looked serene in the face of what Juan had just shared with him.

"Not as well as you, Niki," he responded. Niki shook his head, amused, despite his angst.

"Okay, I asked for that," Niki replied. "We're worried about you."

"Let us all worry about Mateo," Hiroshi insisted. "I have taken all precautions, even after holding Mateo close yesterday. He must be very distraught."

"He is," Alex said. "He needs a hug right now, but we can't."

"One moment," Hiroshi held up a hand, then stood and walked toward his house. A moment later he was back with a rectangular box wrapped in intricately decorated paper. He slid it across to Juan.

"What's this?" Juan asked as he picked it up.

"It is a box of Alex's favorite crackers," Hiroshi replied, producing much needed laughter from everyone except, of course, Alex. "Please give them to Mateo. Ask him to think of good health each time he eats one. Tell him to think about how soon he will receive a hug from each of us again with each one he eats."

"Are you suggesting we tell him they're magical crackers?" Juan asked.

"Magical? No. Just tell him they are imbued with love. Which is sometimes more powerful than germs. Tell him whatever you think will give him courage. As you well know, Juan, stress lowers immunity. We need Mateo to be strong."

"You be strong, too, Hiroshi," Juan smiled. "And keep me posted on your vitals, okay?"

"Yes, doctor. As ordered." Hiroshi stood and bowed, receiving multiple bows in return, then he headed back to his house. Juan stood and closed the gate. He handed the box to Ricky.

"Here, mijo, you heard Hiroshi. Take these to Mateo and give him something to smile about." Ricky took the box and ran up the steps and into the house.

"Why do I always end up the butt of every joke?" Alex asked as the family began moving toward the house.

"You're not, Alex," Greg offered, "it just happens so often it seems that way." Raphael broke into laughter once again and pulled Alex into a side hug.

"Isn't that what I just said?" Alex genuinely asked.

"Alex," Raphael explained, "you usually set yourself up for it. You make it too easy."

"I don't know what you mean."

"Next time, we'll point it out to you. Like right now ... you said butt. Reddened butt? Paddled butt? Need I go on?"

"No, you need not."


"I'm going to run out and get a super veggie burrito for Mateo," Alex announced as he entered the kitchen in street clothes, where Luke and Raphael were pondering their options for dinner. "That's his favorite comfort food."

"Why don't I go with you," Raphael offered. "We're having trouble figuring out what to fix, anyway."

"Yeah," Luke chimed in. "I don't seem to have much of an appetite. Maybe I'll come, too." Moments later, dressed for the outside world, they found Alex sitting on the top step just outside the front door. There was little conversation as they walked, each in his own thoughts, mostly morose ones. As they waited outside the taqueria for their order to be filled, the silence became too awkward.

"This is really thoughtful of you," Raphael turned to Alex. "Mateo's lucky to be with us. Imagine if he were still in that apartment with those brutes."

"No kidding," Alex agreed. "He'd be totally on his own. Yeah, he's in a good place, all right. Like Thursday night ..."

"Thursday night?" Luke asked.

"Yeah, I forgot about that," Alex's eyes brightened, probably along with a grin behind his mask. "Early Friday morning I caught him coming out of Juan and Ricky's room. I think he spent the night."

"No!" Raphael protested. Alex nodded definitively.

"I love it!" Luke said. "I'm kind of surprised, though." He thought a moment, then continued, "I wonder who's more likely to give us the details ... Ricky or Juan?"

"Ricky!" Alex and Raphael responded simultaneously.

"We just have to find the right time," Alex added.

"Well, I'm glad," Raphael said. "He's the only one sleeping alone, even if he is sleeping with his phone." The server arrived at the table blocking the door with their food and Alex insisted on paying for the entire order. On the walk back Raphael posed the question on everyone's mind.

"So, what do we do if Mateo's COVID positive?"

"We let Juan take charge," Luke answered. "Like he already has."

"This could get really complicated, and a little scary if Hiroshi is, too," Alex worried.

"Not to mention maybe all the rest of us," Raphael topped Alex's concern.

"Okay, guys," Luke intervened. "Let's not go there. We need to stay upbeat … for Mateo." Once they entered the foyer, they stripped and headed into the kitchen. Alex pulled a Modelo out of the fridge as Raphael unpacked the order and put Mateo's burrito, a cup of salsa and a bag of tortilla chips on a plate and handed it to Alex. By the time Alex returned with Greg, Juan and Ricky, Raphael and Luke had arranged everyone's order on plates in the dining room.

"Niki and Steve aren't eating?" Juan asked as he sat.

"Not eating Mexican," Alex replied through the tortilla chip he was demolishing. "Not sure what they're doing."

"Well, thanks for thinking of Mateo … and us," Juan dipped a chip of his own in the salsa verde.

"How's he doing?" Luke asked.

"No temp so far," Juan smiled. "Hiroshi, too. Not that that means a lot, but it's all we have to go on so far."

"How … how likely is it that Mateo may be infected," Raphael asked, ignoring Luke's earlier suggestion.

"Raphael," Juan set his burrito down, "that's the problem with this virus. The answer to almost every question is 'we don't know.' We learn more every day. It's good he and Eduardo were masked, but not good that they were working closely for hours. It depends on how much virus Eduardo was carrying. And how long he'd been positive. How good the ventilation was. And did Mateo touch his eyes, regardless of the mask and gloves." He gave Raphael a 'who knows' look.

"I hope this isn't giving you flashbacks, Juan," Greg tried to sound comforting. Juan shook his head.

"I, uh, flash back a lot, guys, especially in the hospital, without any obvious reason. Probably somewhat like what a soldier who's been in combat experiences, but just not as intense. Not that it wasn't intense. But I didn't have bullets whizzing over my head." He picked up his burrito again and began to chew. For a moment everyone was silent, just eating. Then, Ricky reached over and put a hand on Juan's shoulder.

"You're here now, Papito. And a good thing, too, for Mateo." Juan smiled, turned and wordlessly solicited a locked cock leather boy kiss.

"I think Mateo has eight nurses in attendance, from what I can tell," Juan looked around the table. He rolled up the aluminum foil from his burrito and stood. Raphael signaled to him to leave his plate for Raphael to buss later. "I'm going to check Mateo's temp once more. Oh, also, I'm leaving our bedroom door open tonight in case Mateo starts coughing. Let me know if anyone hears anything, okay?" Everyone nodded, then Juan and Ricky headed upstairs. Once they were gone, Greg looked over at Luke's plate. He'd only eaten one of his two tacos.

"You feeling okay, Luke?" he asked.

"Just not hungry," Luke replied.

"He always loses his appetite when he's worried," Raphael explained, reaching for the orphaned taco.

"I don't know who I'm more worried about," Luke watched as Raphael crunched away. "Mateo, Hiroshi or Juan."

"Or Niki," Raphael muttered after swallowing. "Let's face it, guys ... 2020 sucks."

Nineteen

# TESTING, UNO, DOS, TRES

RAPHAEL WOKE FIRST. BUT he wasn't the only one up for long, as Luke had his right arm wrapped around Raphael's waist from behind. It was impossible for Raphael to free himself to go the bathroom without disturbing Luke, who stirred, rolled over onto his back and yawned.

"Baby, come back," he muttered, eyes still closed.

"In a sec," Raphael replied. Dutifully, mission accomplished, he slid back under the covers and snuggled against Luke, who rolled onto his side to re-wrap the sir/leather boy package, his eyes still closed. "Happy Monday, Sir," Raphael whispered. Luke's eyes opened as reality, as in the reality of the day before, dawned on him.

"Mateo ..." Luke croaked, then cleared his throat.

"I didn't hear any coughing. Did you?"

"No. Good. I guess."

"I'll start the coffee." Raphael unraveled himself from Luke once again and shuffled out of the room, glancing at Mateo's door as he passed on his way to the back stairs. Not surprisingly Alex and Greg's door was partially open. Juan and Ricky's was closed with Juan already at the hospital by now. Raphael hadn't even finished pouring water into the coffee maker when Alex wandered in.

"Did you sleep?" Alex asked through a yawn as he closed the fridge and shook the jug of everyday orange juice.

"I did," Raphael replied, pulling down three mugs from the cabinet. "I was exhausted. You?"

"Off and on. I kept listening ... you know. Which is silly, I guess. According to Juan, *if* Mateo is infected it's probably too early for him to have symptoms anyway."

"Maybe you can take a nap later. No sense making yourself sick worrying about Mateo."

"Hey, I like that idea. Is that third mug for Mateo?"

"Yeah. I thought I'd leave it outside his door and text him in case he's awake."

"You're sweet," Alex said as he put an arm around Raphael's waist. Raphael gave Alex his best, eyes scrunched, 'yeah, I know' look. "Don't forget ... extra sugar."

"Yuck," Raphael dropped the look.

"I know, but that's how he likes it." Raphael followed Alex back up the stairs and left one heavily doctored mug of coffee in front of Mateo's door.

Because everyone was eagerly waiting to see if Juan was able to obtain a test kit, the day dragged by slowly. Niki had contemplated spending some time pupped out in his cage but thought better of it. He didn't want to be out of the loop when Juan returned. He did spend some time in the gym for the first time, doing a light workout. It had been so long since the gyms closed that he couldn't even remember what weight he normally curled. But it helped pass the time. He was back in his chair in front of the fireplace, checking on protest coverage, when he heard Juan coming through the front door.

"Did you get it?" Niki was at the library door before Juan had even pulled off his shoes. Juan had an unfamiliar plastic bag with him.

"I scored, yeah," Juan half-laughed, holding up the bag. "But don't tell anybody. With the help of a friend ... I broke protocol."

"For a good cause," Niki smiled back. He followed Juan upstairs and into Juan's and Ricky's room. Ricky was out Dashing. "Can I watch?"

"Okay, but stay back." Niki knitted his brow in confusion. "Sometimes the test causes people to cough, or sneeze or gag, expelling excessive droplets and aerosol. That's why I'll be using this." He pulled several PPE items out of the bag. "I'd be wearing a disposable gown in a normal test environment, but here in the House of the Locked Cock Brotherhood, I'll just shower when we're done. I will need these, though." Juan put on an N-95 mask, adjusted it, then positioned a clear face shield on his head. He pulled on a pair of nitrile gloves, then picked up his phone and texted Mateo, who had probably heard him and Niki in the hallway and had been expecting the text. He responded immediately. Juan handed Niki a face mask, then headed out of the room and over to Mateo's door. Niki followed, but frustratingly, Juan positioned Niki a good ten feet away from Mateo's door, but still in the line of sight. Juan knocked, two quick taps. Mateo opened instantly.

"Muchacho. Good to see you. How are you doing?"

"Okay. Nervous? Bored." Juan laughed.

"That's good. It probably means you're going to be just fine." Apparently, everyone was on alert. At the sound of Mateo's voice, Alex, Greg, Raphael and Luke all appeared from their rooms and congregated near Niki. Juan looked over his shoulder to see who was where. "Mateo, looks like we have an audience. Is that okay?" Mateo beamed and waved at everyone, happy to see and be seen.

"Is okay," he smiled.

"All right, then." Juan looked over his shoulder at Niki. "Niki, make sure no one gets any closer." Niki nodded seriously. Juan turned back to Mateo.

"Okay, why don't you sit down here in the doorway." Juan sat, too, and pulled the test implements out of his bag and prepared them. He explained to Mateo what he was going to do, and warned him to expect it to be irritating but not painful. He asked Mateo to tilt his head back and 'relax.' As he guided the swab up first one and then the other nostril, Mateo reacted, groaning a bit and stifling a cough. Everyone in the hall winced along with him in sympathy. When he was finished, and the swab was securely encapsulated, Juan sat back and smiled at Mateo. "You did great."

"That's all?" Mateo shook his head and rubbed his nose.

"That's all for now. We'll need to do this again in a few days, like I said. To be sure. Meanwhile, you need to stay here. I know it's boring. But it's very important. Okay?" Mateo nodded, but didn't look thrilled.

"Mateo!" Raphael called out. Mateo looked over to where everyone was clustered. "What's your favorite flavor of Mitchell's?" Mateo smiled and stood up. Juan picked up his bag and stood as well, moving away from Mateo's door.

"The mango was good."

"Mango will be on tonight's menu, muchacho!" Mateo nodded, met everyone's gaze and closed his door. Everyone followed Juan back into his room, where he secured the test kit in a biohazard ziplock, then tossed the PPE into the waste basket, pulled the liner and immediately tied it shut.

"I need to shower, from work as well as Mateo," Juan said. "Both Mateo's and Hiroshi's temps are still good, so ... so far so good."

"When will we know?" Niki asked, examining the test kit without touching it.

"Hopefully within a couple of days on this test, but it could be longer. We'll do a repeat on Thursday, unless ..."

"Unless what?" Alex asked.

"Unless this one comes back before then ... positive. If it does, we'll already have our answer." Alex looked stricken. "But, let's count on it being negative." Alex and Raphael both nodded hopefully. Juan walked into the bathroom, cueing everyone else to disperse.

Tuesday came and went without incident. No coughing, anyway. Just a lot of nervous anticipation. Wednesday evening, too, Juan returned home with no news. Dinner passed quietly, with Luke not the only one exhibiting a depressed appetite. Finally, late Thursday afternoon, Juan arrived with another plastic bag. Niki was in the library, tablet in hand, while guarding the foyer, and he again met Juan as soon as the front door opened. He gave Juan an expectant look.

Juan held up the bag, "Time for test number two." He quickly stripped then headed upstairs, Niki on his heels. Niki was in place, ten feet from Mateo's door when Juan exited his room, outfitted in his PPE. He knocked just once. Mateo opened the door, grinned at Juan, then at Niki, and immediately sat.

"I have good news and bad news, muchacho," Juan said, resulting in panicked faces on both Mateo and Niki. "Oh, sorry," Juan almost reached out to comfort Mateo. "I shouldn't have put it that way. The good news is your test was negative!" Mateo's smile returned as Niki fist pumped in the distance. "The bad news is we need to do another test to confirm your status. Enough time has passed now. If you were infected this test will confirm it." Mateo nodded thoughtfully, his smile fading a bit. Juan prepped the test and Mateo tilted back his head without any prompting. It was all over in a minute. "Okay," Juan said as he stood up, "this will be over soon, Mateo. I'm sorry we have to keep you quarantined, but I'm pretty confident you're fine. We'll keep checking your temperature, though, until we get the results back."

"¿Mañana?" Mateo gave Juan a pleading look, which pained Juan as well as Niki.

"No ... I wish. You know what? I'm going to take this back to the hospital now instead of waiting until tomorrow. But we still won't know tomorrow. Maybe sometime this weekend. Or Monday. Hang in there muchacho." Mateo tried a smile as he closed his door and Juan headed back into his room. Niki followed.

"Can I come to the hospital with you?" he asked, holding out the trash liner for Juan, who dropped his PPE in, piece by piece.

"Ordinarily, yes, but, Niki, no one is allowed in except staff and patients right now. Even family of patients can't enter. It's draconian, but it's policy. It's necessary." Juan slipped the biohazard bag into a shoulder pouch and headed down to the foyer, where he pulled on the same scrubs he'd worn home. Before he closed the front door, he turned to Niki. "I'll be back soon. Just think, Niki ... in a couple of years you could be doing this instead of me. Thanks for your help." After the door closed Niki walked back into the library and picked up his tablet. A smile flickered as he powered it up again. Within seconds he was back in the world of Black Lives Mattering across the country.

Late Saturday morning, with still no news, found Niki and Raphael in the gym. Workouts were still hit or miss for everyone, unlike pre-COVID, when Raphael, Luke, Steve and Niki worked out together on an established schedule. Niki was spotting Raphael, who was finally managing to bench press three sets of twelve reps, but about twenty pounds shy of the weight he'd previously pressed. When Raphael lowered the barbell into the supports and sat up, he gave Niki a smile of accomplishment.

"I think I miss the cardio as much as the weights," Niki said.

"It's important," Raphael nodded. "Your suggestion of an elliptical was a good one, but *man* they're expensive." Niki sat down on the bench next to Raphael.

"We could go old school," he looked at Raphael. "Running shoes cost a lot less. Instead of taking walks for exercise, what if we jogged instead ... on alternate days from the weights."

"You do realize, in this part of the city, there are maybe six blocks of flat ground," Raphael challenged him.

"Exactly. It'd would be like putting the elliptical on an 'intermittent' mode. Uphill one minute, downhill the next. It would be great cardio." Raphael studied Niki a moment, judging his seriousness.

"I'm trying to find an argument against your suggestion, but ... I can't. It's actually a pretty good idea. Doctor Niki."

"Not Doctor. Not even Nurse Niki, yet. Just 'I don't want to get fat' Niki. Especially with all these runs to Mitchell's you've been making."

"That'll end as soon as Mateo's out of quarantine," Raphael replied, as he put an arm across Niki's shoulders. "I think you're on to something. Weights one day, jog the next. Tell you what. Let's walk over to On the Run this afternoon. I'll spring for our running shoes and you can be in charge of mapping out our jogging routes. You know, start out with maybe a two-mile course and gradually increase it."

"Walking over to On the Run sounds like a major trek already."

"Yeah, it does, doesn't it? Fat boy." Raphael pinched Niki's waist. "Are you with me?"

"On one condition." Raphael raised his eyebrows questioningly. "You can never call me fat boy again."

"Deal. Come on. Let's get dressed. We can stop for lunch on Ninth Avenue afterward. That'll break up the walk."

As Raphael was heading for the stairs from his room, clothed, so obviously going out, Alex came to his own door.

"Off to adventure?" Alex asked.

"Kinda. Niki and I are going to start jogging, so we're walking over to 9th Avenue to get running shoes." Alex looked a bit thoughtful. "Wanna come along?"

"That's a long walk."

"Yep. The kind dancers are built for. There's lunch involved." Alex gave a short laugh.

"Give me a sec. I'll be right down." Raphael and Niki were waiting in the rarely used sitting room when Alex appeared, interestingly enough in the Black Lives Matter t-shirt he'd borrowed from Niki.

"Good idea!" Niki leapt up. "Be right back." He headed up the two flights of stairs to trade his locked cock tee for his BLM shirt.

"That gives me an idea," Raphael said to Alex. "I should go on-line and design locked cock tees with Black Lives Matter on the back." Alex nodded.

"If you do, let me know. I'll order a couple with you."

"Okay, but don't tell Niki. We'll surprise him." Alex agreed.

Despite the fact non-food retail stores were limited to 'curbside' service, it wasn't all that difficult to select running shoes from the assistant on duty at the door. She was happy for the business and took her time showing the three prospective joggers several models available. They all knew their sizes, so the inability to try them on wasn't a problem. In the end, they each selected a slightly different shoe. Newly equipped they headed across the street to Marnee Thai for the promised lunch, which they carried two blocks north into Golden Gate Park for an impromptu picnic. As they were finishing up lunch all three phones signaled a text. Raphael was the first to react.

"YES!" He nearly lost his phone as he threw both arms into the air. "Mateo's negative!"

"That means Hiroshi's okay, too!" Niki cheered.

"Guys, we need to celebrate." Raphael turned to Alex. "Do you know what Mateo's favorite dish is?"

"He'll eat anything. And thank you for it."

"Do you think he likes sushi?" Niki suggested. "We should have Hiroshi over, too."

"Oh, man, you're full of good ideas today," Raphael slapped Niki's thigh. "What do you think, Alex?"

"I think Mateo would eat anything to celebrate this. At least sushi would mean green tea ice cream for dessert instead of mango ... for a change."

"I'll ignore that remark," Raphael replied. "I'm texting Luke so he can let everyone but Mateo know our plan. Niki, why don't you text Hiroshi." Texts sent, they cleared their space, deposited the recycling and compost on their way out of the park and made especially quick work of the long walk home, refreshed by lunch and energized by Juan's text.

The three hadn't finished stripping when Mateo bounded down the stairs, Greg and Luke on his heels. They'd all been in Greg's room, drinking a celebratory Modelo and watching TV.

"AMIGOS!" Mateo yelled as he hit the bottom stair and all three jockeyed for a hug, which devolved into one big group hug.

"Is Juan here?" Niki asked.

"No," Luke replied. "He texted us from the hospital as soon as he got the results. He'll be home in time for dinner. We're aiming for seven. Ricky will wrap up DoorDash a little early. In fact, we'll be his last delivery."

"Just like old times," Raphael grinned. "So, we don't have to run out. Brilliant!"

"Actually," Luke said as he idly opened the shoe box Raphael had set on the floor, "I am going to pick up some Asahi ... in keeping with the theme." Then he looked at Raphael. "You guys joining a team?"

"I'll go with you," Raphael smiled, as he started putting his clothes back on. "I'll explain. Go get dressed, Sir."

"Yes, baby, er, Sir." Luke winked at Greg and headed up the stairs.

"You must be sooo happy!" Alex pulled Mateo into another hug.

"Si ... yes. Eks static!" Everyone laughed and Alex saw no reason to coach Mateo this time.

"I'll bet Ryan's eks static, too," Niki said.

"He is! He was so sad with me, before. He wants to come to see me. He is begging his parents."

"That would be awesome," Raphael finished tying his new running shoes. "Just make sure he gets tested first." He saw the look on Mateo's face as he stood up. "I'm kidding Mateo. He should come!"

Just like Mateo, Hiroshi was greeted with hugs, individual and group, as soon as he entered the back door. The longest one from Mateo.

"You've been in my thoughts, Mateo," Hiroshi smiled as they pulled apart. "My mantra the past few days has been directed to you."

"Thank you, Hiroshi," Mateo said tentatively, a bit shyly in fact. "Mantra for me? What is mantra?"

"It's like praying ... but different. 'Nam Myōhō Renge Kyō' is the mantra I've been reciting. It was a way of helping ensure that you would overcome this." He put his hands on Mateo's shoulders. "And you did." Hiroshi looked around at the rest of the family. "Not that you needed my help. Obviously, you were in very good hands."

"Juan was great!" Mateo agreed. Juan laughed.

"And Niki assisted," he said. "It was a group effort. We were all very concerned about you, too, Hiroshi. It was a close call. A reminder, I guess, for us all to stay vigilant."

"Indeed, Juan," Hiroshi agreed. "We must protect the bubble, eh?" He pulled Mateo in for one last hug. Mateo brightened as they pulled apart.

"Thank you for the crackers, Hiroshi. I ate every one." Hiroshi responded with a single nod.

"Speaking of crackers, are you hungry, Hiroshi?" Luke asked. Hiroshi nodded again. "Ricky has brought us a celebratory feast. Shall we?" Luke motioned toward the butler's pantry entrance to the dining room. The table settings were of the fancy variety, as expected, except chilled pilsner glasses stood in place of wine glasses and the utensils included enameled chopsticks at each setting. As everyone took their places, Luke and Greg poured Asahi for everyone. Then Luke ladled miso soup into small bowls that Greg delivered one by one.

"We've been feeding Mateo every kind of comfort food he likes for the past week, Hiroshi, so we wanted to honor you with tonight's dinner," Raphael said as he picked up his bowl and held it toward Hiroshi, then tilted it and sipped.

"Honor me?"

"Like I said," Juan lifted his bowl toward Hiroshi, "we were concerned about you, too." Hiroshi looked a bit embarrassed.

"If I knew how to blush, I would," he laughed as he lifted his bowl in kind. "Thank you for your concern, and most especially for your company ... and this food. Kanpai!"

Alex was right. Mateo made quick work of every piece of sushi and nigiri put in front of him. Luke's appetite seemed restored as well. For an hour, the worry of the past week and the pain and unrest associated with the Black Lives Matter protests were set aside, and relief and camaraderie took their place.

After breakfast Sunday, in which Ricky's pancakes seemed to taste even better than usual, Alex, surprisingly, was the one to suggest the first Team Locked Cock run. Mateo, who still hadn't been out of the house for a week, asked to go along. Once they'd departed, Ricky asked Juan to show him some pointers in the gym. It wasn't long before Luke, Greg and Steve joined them. Juan started out by giving Ricky the most important lesson he would need in the gym.

"It's important to develop good habits, mijo, and the most important thing is: it's not how much weight you're lifting, it's how you're lifting it ... your form. You'll see some guys lifting lots of weight really fast ... literally pumping iron. That isn't good form. You want to move slowly. Let the muscle do the work, not momentum. Let's start with a simple biceps curl." Juan assembled a twenty-pound dumbbell for Ricky, a forty-five pounder for himself. Diligently, Ricky mimicked Juan for the next hour. Biceps curls. Chest presses. One arm rows. Flys. And at the end, without the weights, planks, crunches and pushups. Juan didn't want to overdo it and sour Ricky on the concept the first time out. Juan was rusty anyway and Ricky, sweating and breathing hard, was definitely ready for a rest after his last pushup.

"What do you think, Ricky?" Steve, spotting Luke on the bench, asked as Ricky collapsed into Juan's lap.

"Fun! But now I know why they call it a workout."

"It'll get easier," Luke said, unconvincingly, through gritted teeth, as he pressed one more rep.

"I'm not sure I'm ready for Ricky and Alex to bulk up," Greg said, doing his own biceps curls on the other bench. "I kind of like being able to have my way with Alex." Juan laughed.

"I don't know about you, Greg, but I plan to stay at least one step ahead of Ricky in the he-man department. That okay with you, mijo?" He squeezed Ricky's seemingly unchanged biceps.

"I just want to be able to wrestle Mateo and win, Papito," Ricky responded as he reached up and fingered the ring in Juan's nipple. "Hey, you know, is it normal for lifting weights to make you horny?" Juan laughed, along with everyone else, but he was the one lucky enough to be able to lean down and suck Ricky's tongue into his mouth. He reached down and wiggled Ricky's locked cock and balls.

"I think Ricky and I need to go take a shower, guys. Enjoy your workout." Juan slid free of Ricky and stood, his growing erection on display as he reached down and helped Ricky up. Ricky grabbed Juan's boner and led him toward the door.

"Yeah," Steve grinned. "Enjoy the rest of your 'workout,' too."

"Now, that's something I never saw at the gym," Luke wiggled his eyebrows. "Did you, Steve?"

"Only in the steam room. By Raphael and you."

"Oh, yeah," Luke grinned. "But only once. Good times."

## Twenty

# A Performance Dare

"I HAD AN IDEA," Alex announced to the room, over a dinner of panko breaded tilapia fish sandwiches, potato salad and roasted asparagus.

"Do tell," Raphael responded, making his big grinned, squinty-eyed face that begged elaboration but threatened disdain. Alex gave Luke a 'how do you live with him' look in response. Taking the harassment one step further, Niki chimed in.

"Did it hurt?"

"It's clear you two are brothers," Alex sniffed. "No, seriously. Mateo, what is Ryan's major?"

"¿Que?"

"¿Corso de Estudio?"

"Ah. He is not sure. Archology, anth ... anthro..."

"Archeology? Anthropology?"

"Yes! Thanks, Alex. He is not sure yet."

"Well ... I was thinking," Alex gave Raphael and Niki a quick defensive glance, but forged ahead, "if he signs up for a lab course, if there's one available this coming semester, and if it's not too late to change his schedule, he would need to be on campus this fall semester. Well, attending a lab on campus, but living here, of course. With you."

"That's not a bad idea," Juan agreed. "It's worth considering. Like you say ... if it isn't too late."

"I will ask him," Mateo smiled at Alex. "Thanks, Alex!"

"What was that you used to call me, Raphael?" Alex pressed. "You know ... like when I wired up Ricky for our strip act?"

"Gosh," Raphael pretended to struggle to remember. "I, uh, can't quite ..."

"Genius, Raphael, you called me a genius."

"Actually, it was *evil* genius, as I recall."

"Ah, so you do remember. Let me hear you say it again." Alex gave Raphael the same squinty-eyed grin.

"Alex is an evil genius," Raphael barely whispered. Which motivated Greg to weigh in.

"Seems to me you two are clearly brothers, too." Both Alex and Raphael, grinning, nodded, the faux disdain and competition over. For the moment.

Later that evening, phone in hand, Mateo wandered into Greg and Alex's room where they were watching yet another episode of Schitt's Creek, but without the oral gratification element.

"Alex, can you 'splain for Ryan your idea?" Mateo held his phone out to Alex, as Greg paused the video.

"Sure, muchacho." Alex turned to Greg, "Raphael ruined Mateo forever on the pronunciation of 'explain,' didn't he?"

"I wouldn't worry ... we all have our quirks," Greg replied as Alex took Mateo's phone. It only took a minute to share his idea with Ryan, who didn't even try to hide his nudity this time.

"It's worth a shot," Ryan agreed. "I'll see what I can come up with. Thanks, Alex."

"Let us know, Ryan. And if you can arrange the lab, let us know what the campus housing costs would be. I think Mateo mentioned to you living here would cost a lot less, and that may help you convince your parents, too. And don't forget to tell them there's a nurse in the house, as well."

"Yeah ... right! How can they say no?" Ryan looked more hopeful than ever. Alex handed the phone back to Mateo, who padded away, already re-engrossed in Facetime.

"Was he naked," Greg casually asked.

"Of course. He'll fit right in."

"There is a down side ... for Juan and Ricky."

"What? Oh, you mean ..."

"They'll lose their cuddle buddy."

"Orrrr ... they might end up with two."

"I don't see that happening. At least not for a long time. Mateo and Ryan have a lot of catching up to do."

"Yeah, but they'll be doing it in the House of the Locked Cock Brotherhood."

"I see your point, but they may turn out to be incorruptible."

"Have you forgotten who led off Niki's discipline session?"

"Oh, yeah." Greg turned, giving his full attention to Alex. "Maybe we should bet on it."

"Or, like we said before, make it an opportunity for a dare."

"You mean you and me, or Mateo and Ryan?"

"Hmmm." Alex looked intently at Greg. "What *do* I mean?"

"I think we should leave the dares to Luke and Raphael."

"I'll think about it," was Alex's noncommittal reply. "Press play."

Alex and Raphael were in the gym, several jogs and workouts now behind them. Alex had added an additional plate to the dumbbells and two to the barbell in his routine, and Niki had slowly been adding distance to their routes. Progress was being made. It might have been wishful thinking, but Raphael was sure his locked cock tees were getting tighter again.

"Greg and I were talking a couple of weeks ago ... when was the last time you and Luke did a dare?" Alex asked as he and Raphael were racking their weight plates.

"Let's see," Raphael pondered. "Jeez, it's been a while. All the fun businesses are closed, and sharing life here with all of you guys has been kind of a distraction, I guess. I mean a good distraction! But it has kind of put a damper on the dares. To answer your question ... it must have been Luke's dare in the dungeon. To have him and Juan spit roast me. With Ricky as the secret sauce, as it were."

"Raphael, you make a mini-orgy sound so ... so poetic." Raphael slapped Alex on the bare ass, a gesture that conveyed multiple messages when applied to Alex.

"No one's ever accused me of being a poet before, so thanks. Why do you ask?"

"Oh, I don't know. They've always been kind of entertaining. Even the one's Greg and I haven't been involved in. So ... it's your turn. To dare Luke, I mean."

"It is. Yeah. But it's so hard now ..."

"You'll think of something. I'm not the only evil genius in the family." Raphael laughed and nodded in agreement. "With all of us living here, you've certainly got an audience for whatever you come up with."

"Hmmm, an audience-oriented dare. That could be fun." Raphael draped an arm around Alex's neck and the two headed through the dungeon and up the stairs to their respective showers. Just as Raphael was preparing to start his, Luke entered the bedroom, having just arrived home from work.

"Perfect timing, Sir," Raphael grinned, but kept his distance. "I just finished my workout. Wanna catch up on our buzz and shave?"

"Let's do, baby. We've been slipping a little lately, haven't we?"

"Well, a lot of our routines have changed, Sir, and working though Zoom makes it less important, too. Most other people haven't had a haircut in months, so nobody notices a couple of days' stubble."

"Well, I do, baby, so we'd better take care of that. Let me decontaminate, first ..." Raphael gave Luke five minutes alone in the shower, then he peeled off his body harness and joined him. Once both were wet, Luke turned off the water, Raphael sat and Luke took up position behind him, legs around Raphael's waist. Raphael, eyes closed, treated these moments almost like meditation, the warm water, the minty lather, Luke's breath on his neck, the intermittent feel of Luke's pecs against his back as he moved back and forth. The means, sharing this intimate time with Luke was as gratifying as the end, a perfectly formed high 'n tight for Raphael and a crisp mohawk for Luke. Once Luke finished shaving the sides and back of Raphael's head, he flicked on the shower briefly to rinse off Raphael, then rubbed his horseshoe dry with a towel so he could buzz the remaining hair and landing strip nice and tight. As he finished, Raphael chuckled subtly.

"What's funny?"

"Oh, I was just thinking about the first time you did this to me. Now I love it, but ..."

"I remember. I thought maybe I'd gone just a bit too far. That maybe that night would be our last date."

"And look at us now. A hundred dares later."

"You've been counting?" As Luke sat the clippers on the floor, Raphael raised up and flipped around on all fours so he was facing Luke.

"Okay, Sir, I may be exaggerating a little, but we've racked up more than a few along the way." Raphael stood and moved around behind Luke, switching places so he could perfect Luke's mohawk. After he wrapped his legs around Luke from behind and began spreading lather around Luke's head he continued, "Alex reminded me today that it's been a while. Since our last dare."

"Oh, it hasn't been that long, has it?" Luke turned his head so he could half see Raphael, sensing that this conversation was not just idle chatter. "Has it?" Raphael repositioned Luke's head and began shaving.

"Maybe not." He paused for effect as he continued shaving the sides of Luke's head. "A few weeks since your last dare, a few months for mine."

"Is there something you want to tell me? Baby?"

"No." Raphael's answer was short, but not curt. Just matter of fact. After another long pause, "Just, thinking about the past. How lucky I am." He leaned forward and kissed the freshly shaved side of Luke's head.

"Thanks for the warning, baby," Luke almost chuckled himself.

"You know me so well, Sir."

"I do, and baby, I'm the lucky one."

"Yes, Sir. And don't you forget it."

"What's this?" Greg asked Mateo, who had slipped a piece of paper across the table as the family was enjoying another Sunday Pancake Breakfast.

"From Ryan. Room and board at school." Mateo grinned. "He tol' me last night."

"Does this mean he got the lab course?!" Alex was ready to celebrate. Mateo shook his head.

"Not yet. He wanted Greg to know ... in case." Alex leaned over and Greg shared the number with him. Alex whistled.

"No wonder his parents are happy to have all his classes online."

"Yeah," Raphael agreed. "Tuition may be reasonable, but they get you with the fees, room and board." Greg nodded as he turned his attention back to Mateo.

"Tell Ryan if he lives here, the cost would be one third. Here, I'll write it down for you." He slid off his chair and walked into the kitchen to get a pen, before returning and handing the paper back to Mateo.

"Looks good!" Mateo beamed. "His parents will be happy, no?"

"Less unhappy, maybe." Alex laughed. "Let's just hope he gets that lab course." Mateo nodded as he folded up the note. "Mateo, we're going for a run at one o'clock. Wanna come?"

"Yes!" Mateo's schedule interfered about half the time with Alex, Raphael and Niki's runs. "I want to look good for when Ryan comes." Greg pointed at Mateo with a pancake laden fork.

"You have nothing to worry about, muchacho. He wouldn't be messing with his class schedule if he wasn't dying to taste those syrupy sweet lips of yours." Mateo took Greg literally and licked his lips in case he'd missed something. He then stood and carried his dishes into the kitchen before heading up the back stairs, note in hand, no doubt eager to share Greg's offer with Ryan.

"I hope we're not setting up Mateo for disappointment," Juan cautioned.

"Maybe Ryan can talk his parents into it, whether he gets the lab or not," Luke speculated. "He's already being robbed of the normal college experience with online classes. Maybe he can guilt them into it."

"Greg," Steve said, as he, too, stood after finishing breakfast. "Did you remember to factor in the savings on laundry expenses Ryan will enjoy if he's living here?" Niki laughed as he looked to Greg for his answer.

"No ... and now that you mention it, I didn't factor in the savings on Ryan's data plan either."

"That could be the biggest savings of all!" Niki said, before he stood and walked over to Ricky and planted one on Ricky's cheek. "Thanks for another legendary breakfast, Ricky." Ricky smiled and turned to encourage a second, lip on lip kiss of gratitude.

"It's my pleasure," Ricky smiled.

"Hey!" Raphael suddenly exclaimed. "I just realized. Ricky ... are you expecting these breakfasts to count toward the thousand dinners you and Juan owe us?" Juan and Ricky looked at each other as Luke laughingly picked up Raphael's dishes.

"Juan, Ricky ... may I answer for you?" Luke said over his shoulder as he headed for the kitchen.

"Um ... okay?" Juan responded tentatively. Luke returned and stood behind Raphael, placing both hands on top of Raphael's harnessed shoulders. He leaned down close to his right ear.

"Of course not, baby. It wasn't in the contract." Raphael turned his head so he could meet Luke's gaze.

"I see," he said with a steely grin. "As we know, Sir, our 'contract' is iron-clad." He turned back to Juan and Ricky and winked.

"What does that mean, baby?"

"Oh, Sir, I'm so glad you asked," Raphael continued looking at Juan, as he winked again. "I'll elaborate tomorrow afternoon, after our workout. I'd rather show you than tell you." Juan looked up at Luke and smiled. Luke lifted his hands from Raphael's shoulders and walked toward the foyer.

"I do not like the sound of this," he said, apparently to himself.


Since Mateo's restaurant was still a couple of days away from reopening, Ricky was the only member of the family scheduled to be out late on a Monday afternoon, but his schedule was easily adjusted so he could be home in time for what Raphael hoped would be an entertaining way to start the new week. Raphael, Luke, and Alex had been working out together since Raphael and Alex had logged out from work around four thirty. Juan had joined them once he'd decontaminated after getting home from his shift. It was a good workout, now that each of them had had a few weeks to develop a personal program. Raphael and Alex were finishing up with planks as Luke racked his weight plates and headed for the door.

"Where are you going, Sir?" Raphael looked up as he lowered his body to the mat.

"To our room. I'll wait for you to shower." Raphael leapt to his feet as Alex slowly stood.

"Actually, Sir, we have to put our shower off for a little while," Raphael said as he walked up and put his arms around Luke's waist, pressing his cage just under Luke's balls. He leaned up for an easily obtained kiss. "First, it's time for your next ... contract mandated dare." Luke leaned back, but didn't break Raphael's hold on his waist.

"Oh, really?" He smiled at Raphael, then glanced at Juan and Alex. "Well, let's go up to our room and you can tell me all about it."

"Actually, Sir, the dare starts now ... a flash dare. A flash, repeat, collaborative, performance dare." Raphael batted his eyes.

"Oh, really," Luke repeated, his smile fading. "Sounds complicated. You mean here, in the gym?"

"Oh no, Sir. This way," Raphael coached. He led Luke into the dungeon as Alex flew up the stairs to notify everyone else that the dare was commencing, since everyone, except Luke, of course, had been clued in. Raphael walked Luke over to the St. Andrews cross, as Juan stood idly in the middle of the room. Luke assumed that meant this dare would involve him being bound on the cross, which actually excited him.

"Should I stand here," he asked cheerily, stepping up on the platform the cross was mounted on.

"No, Sir. For now, just sit here." Raphael motioned to the platform. Luke looked a tad disappointed, but sat, then glanced up at Juan, who averted his eyes as the rest of the family descended the stairs. Once everyone was assembled, Raphael walked over next to Juan and spoke.

"As you all know, Luke and I have cemented our love for each other with tests of our devotion, also known as 'dares.' Over time we've invented different kinds of dares. Flash dares. Mutual dares. And, apparently ... revenge dares." Raphael looked over at Luke as he spoke the last two words. "Some of you have been recruited into participating in the occasional dare. With gratifying results." He grinned at Steve and Greg. "This evening marks yet another new dare. It's a flash dare, meaning it happens with no notice. It's a performance dare, which is why you're all here. As you'll soon see, it's a collaborative dare, not one executed solely by me. It's also, and this is a first ... a repeat dare. Does that make it by definition not a first? No ... it's a first. Anyway, I hope you enjoy it as much as I intend to. Get comfortable, we're about to start."

"You're really milking this, baby." Luke looked around the room. "He forgot to say this is the wordiest dare we've ever had."

"Well, Sir, it is my expectation this dare will leave you speechless." As Raphael walked back over to Luke, where he leaned down and planted a long, noisy, lip on lip kiss, Greg, Steve, Ricky and Niki moved the two benches from the gym into the dungeon so everyone could get comfortable. Once they were seated, Raphael walked back to Juan and said, "Rope Master, bind me please." Juan nodded, then walked to the wall and selected a couple of bundles of rope. Over the next thirty minutes he created a web of Shibari around Raphael's torso, front, back and sides and around his crotch, ending by binding his arms across his chest as he had before, to ensure Raphael couldn't move his hands. When he'd finished, Raphael walked over to the bondage table and sat at the edge. Juan stepped up onto the table and, from behind, pulled Raphael completely onto the table, positioned him on his back, bound his legs spread-eagled, then bound Raphael's already encased torso to the table as well. During all of this, Luke was at a loss as to how this amounted to a dare for him. It was fascinating, sexy, but it was all about Raphael and Juan. Every once in a while, Alex glanced his way to see how he was reacting. Luke was relaxed, appreciative, clueless. Once Raphael was immobilized, Juan placed a rolled-up towel under his head so Raphael could see the rest of the room along with his own body. Juan stepped away and joined the rest of the family. Raphael smiled at Luke, then said, "Alex, if you please."

Alex stood and walked over to Luke and held out a closed fist. Luke instinctively held out his right hand as Alex dropped a set of keys into it. Luke's eyes widened as he looked up at Alex, who flashed an evil genius smile before he walked away.

"Please, Sir," Raphael implored, "suck me dry." Luke slowly stood, looked down at the keys, then over to Raphael. He didn't move. No one spoke, most not understanding what was happening. Luke made a speechless, pleading look at Raphael. Raphael, completely bound but totally in charge, said, "Oh, Sir, did I forget to say this is a both a repeat dare and a revenge dare as well?" Luke gave a very short, low laugh and slowly approached the bondage table. He looked back at the family briefly. "Oh, come on," Raphael teased, "you love an audience. Remember, that's how we met." Luke shook his head, climbed up on the table on all fours, straddled Raphael's left leg, his face above Raphael's. He gave Raphael an undecipherable look, then raised up on his knees and inserted the key into Raphael's cage.

"Oh, no!" Mateo moaned. Juan pulled him into a sideways hug. Ricky looked up at Juan with something of a knowing smile. Niki was entranced, but also speechless. Luke pulled the brass lock out of the cage effortlessly this time and set it aside. He separated the tube from the cock ring with only a bit more resistance, slowly slid it towards himself, then set it aside as well. Then, with no fanfare, he backed up a bit, lowered his head and swallowed Raphael's newly freed, grooved cock.

"Juan," Mateo whispered. "I don' un'erstand."

"It's okay. There will be more. Just watch."

"This is crazy," Niki caught Ricky's gaze. Ricky nodded. Juan leaned over to Niki and whispered back.

"It's about to get even more crazy, Niki." As Luke sucked, Raphael began moaning, wriggling as best he could in his bonds, his eyes closed. He grew hard in Luke's mouth, and Luke, despite the situation, savored the taste of Raphael's precum when it arrived. He decided he might as well enjoy this moment, knowing what almost certainly would follow all too soon. To that end, he made sure to play Raphael as masterfully as he could, edging mercilessly, and backing off to delay as long as possible the inevitable orgasm, and the price he himself would surely pay. It took a while, but eventually Luke realized Raphael must be doing his damnedest to delay the orgasm as well. Aspiring for some semblance of control in this situation, Luke, without breaking his hold on Raphael's cock, rotated around, straddled Raphael's head and lowered his cock to Raphael's mouth. As his pierced glans brushed across Raphael's lips, Raphael opened his mouth and swallowed.

"Is this the crazier part?" Niki asked.

"Not even close," Juan replied. Soon both Luke and Raphael were moaning around tender oral obstructions. Luke, however, still had the upper hand over his unlocked cock sucker and it wasn't long before Raphael finally surrendered, pulsing into Luke's warm, moist, demanding mouth. Once Raphael was spent, Luke raised his head, releasing the cock that had never been seen unlocked before by anyone but Niki and Steve. He looked at the family, then wordlessly, raised up on his knees, drawing his own cock out of Raphael's oral grasp, still rigid, his own seed unspent.

"Please, Sir, I haven't fed yet," Raphael protested. Luke moved away from Raphael and climbed off the bondage table. He leaned over and kissed Raphael's moist lips. Then straightened up. He looked down at Raphael with a mixture of respect and defeat.

"You bet I'm still hard, baby. If you think I'm going to make this next part any easier for you, you are sadly mistaken." He looked across to Juan, assuming how this was going to go, and said, "Okay, Juan. Do what you have to do." Everyone else turned to Juan expectantly. Juan walked over to the bondage board, untied the bonds that held Raphael down and asked Luke to help him lift Raphael off the board and back onto his feet. Once he was upright, Raphael turned first to Luke, then to Juan, wordlessly demanding a kiss from each. He was absolutely wresting every bit of drama out of the moment that he could. He smiled at the family, landing on Ricky, with a wink. Then he heaved a heavy sigh.

"Juan, please introduce Luke to the joys of bondage, while Alex assists me." Luke turned to Juan who smiled and wordlessly cocked his head toward the St. Andrew's cross. As Juan walked Luke over and positioned him on the cross, Alex began unbinding Raphael's arms. Mateo and Ricky were focused mostly on Raphael's grooved and exposed cock. A cock they'd never fully seen before. Before Juan had finished lashing Luke's wrists and ankles in place on the cross, Alex had freed Raphael's arms. Raphael took the opportunity to dash into the lavatory to pee, clearing his urethra of any remaining cum, then he walked back through the dungeon and stopped in front of the now immobilized Luke.

"Did you really have to tie me up for this?" Luke asked, having now fully accepted his fate. Although he was not looking forward to the finale, he did seem willing to face it with grace.

"Well, Sir, since the dares have become harder to do, I figured why not go for broke? Oh, I just realized. We're both bound, so this was also a mutual dare." He paused and turned to the family before turning back to Luke. "And this next part is mutual, too!" Raphael giggled, uncharacteristically.

"Just do it, baby," Luke shook his head.

"Alex," Raphael commanded, holding out his right hand as he knelt in front of Luke. Alex walked over to the cross and reached under the rear of the platform and retrieved the small brown translucent plastic zippered case. He placed it ceremoniously in Raphael's hand. Alex then withdrew and walked over to the bondage board to retrieve Raphael's cage, lock and key, which he then took into the lavatory to rinse while all eyes were focused on Raphael and Luke.

"Okay, Niki," Juan leaned over and murmured. "This is the crazier part."

"Whoa," Ricky whispered, recognizing the Holy Trainer case. Despite his intent to remain steely hard, Luke's erection had subsided substantially. Still, Raphael had to work to get Luke's package through the cock ring. He then maneuvered the hot pink tube, rotating it back and forth a bit before finally muscling it into place. Luke looked over to the family, chagrined and not surprised to see both Greg and Steve grinning at him. Raphael inserted the brass lock, twisted the key, then slowly withdrew it. He then stood and untied Luke's wrists, then his ankles. As he finished, Alex walked up with Raphael's cage, lock, key and the spray bottle of sterilizer in a small basket. Raphael turned to face the family.

"Please, Sir, I've been unlocked for far too long." Alex offered the basket to Luke, then returned to Greg's side. Luke sprayed the cage and attached urethral tube, knelt at Raphael's feet and slid the cage in place. In less than a minute, both husbands were securely locked. Luke stood and Raphael pulled him into a fierce hug.

"Are we done, baby?" Luke looked over Raphael's head at the assembled family. Everyone was smiling, except for Mateo and Niki. "Mateo, do you know what just happened?" Mateo slowly shook his head. "It's all

Juan's fault." Juan snorted in disagreement, smiling nonetheless. Luke freed himself from Raphael's embrace and knelt in front of Mateo. In abbreviated form, he explained how Raphael had agreed to allow Luke to unlock him so that Luke could once again enjoy sucking him, as Juan sometimes did with Ricky. However, violating the permanence of Raphael's chastity would always come with a price, a dare, requiring Luke to be locked for a week each time.

"That's harsh," Niki said.

"Which?" Luke asked. "The cage or the duration?"

"Um ... both." Niki looked to Steve for his reaction.

"Niki," Raphael looked inquisitively at Niki. "Do you want to be unlocked? Like, right now?"

"No, of course not," Niki asserted.

"Exactly." Raphael joined Luke at Mateo's feet. "See, Mateo, like all our dares, this is how we've decided to show our love, our devotion, and in some cases, our submission to one another. I make a sacrifice for Luke and he makes one for me." Raphael reached down and lifted Luke's caged cock and balls with his right hand. "Luke's sacrifice is just a lot prettier than mine!"

"He's got you there, Luke," Greg laughed. Luke took a deep breath, smiling with gritted teeth.

"One other thing, Mateo," Luke said, looking at Juan, not Mateo. "Some of our dares involve other people, right Greg? Sometimes those other people ... especially people who have been accomplices in a previous dare ... find themselves on the receiving end of a subsequent dare."

"You've been warned," Greg turned to Alex.

"I think we all have been," Alex replied. "So, Luke ... a week?"

"Yes, Alex. A week." Alex looked at Greg.

"It'll be worth it."

## Twenty-One

⟨⊙⟩————•————⟨⊙⟩

# NIKI'S BIGGEST CAGE YET

MOSTLY FOR A LAUGH, but also just to see if he could get away with it, Luke ambled into the kitchen Tuesday morning wearing the fundoshi Hiroshi had given him. Ricky, at the stove, turned to say good morning but just laughed instead.

"Oh no you don't!" Alex proclaimed. He stepped away from the espresso machine and, just as Raphael had done in their first impromptu strip performance, he knelt in front of Luke and yanked the fundoshi down around Luke's ankles. Then he reached up and shook the hot pink Holy Trainer along with its contents. "This baby must be on display at all times, Mister."

"What are you?" Luke asked as he stepped out of the unfurling fundoshi. "The chastity police?"

"What's the rule, Mateo?" Alex asked as he stood.

"Strip or starve!" Mateo responded. Alex nodded knowingly at Luke then returned to his barista duties. He handed the first steaming cup to Luke.

"Besides, Luke," he said with a genuine smile. "It really looks cute on you." Luke inhaled deeply.

"It's going to be a long week," he sighed, then sipped.

"Especially since you won't be having any sex," Niki predicted.

"What do you mean?" Raphael feigned shock.

"Well ... you know ..." Niki made a 'duh' face.

"I guess you should have said something sooner, Niki, 'cause we already had amazing sex last night," Raphael said regally. "Was it good for you, Sir?"

"As always, baby," Luke grinned at Niki.

"I guess I'll have to reread my copy of the *Joy of Gay Sex*," Niki conceded as Alex handed him his cup.

"Or I can share my CliffsNotes with you later," Alex stage whispered. Niki nodded along with the joke as he sipped.

"Okay, sex fiends, the scrambled eggs are ready," Ricky announced as he headed into the dining room with the platter. After the eggs, fruit and brioche toast were passed around and everyone had begun eating, Greg looked over at Luke in all seriousness.

"I have to admit, Luke, you didn't hold back when you picked out that cage. Does it glow in the dark?" Then, unable to help himself, he broke into a broad grin.

"I'm the one who picked it out," Raphael proudly announced. "No it doesn't."

"I can fix that for you, Luke, right Ricky?" Alex to the rescue.

"Alex," Luke gave Alex his full attention, "you're already on the revenge dare list, and Greg," he turned to Greg, "one more word out of you and I'll expand that list." Greg couldn't tell if he was kidding or not.

"That's okay," Greg replied, after a short pause. "I'll be in good company. Hell, you might as well put all of us on that list. I'm pretty sure we're all going to end up on it anyway. Pretty as pink sure." Luke, shaking his head, could only laugh. Raphael was grinning, too, relieved that Luke was adapting to his new status as the most recent, if only temporary, locked cock brother.

"Luke, about this revenge dare list ..." Alex pursued, "remember the dare that forced two innocent young men to be involuntary strippers at the Powerhouse?" Luke nodded as he chewed. "Yeah ... well, I think we're even. You can take me off the list."

"Hmmm," Luke looked thoughtful. "I'll think about it." He took another bite, then looked back at Alex. "You know, Alex, that dare ended up generating a lot of good for the Trevor Project, so I'm not so sure it was such a sacrifice after all."

"Um, Sir, that was my doing, not yours," Raphael respectfully clarified.

"But it all started with the most crowd-pleasing strip show this town has ever seen, so Greg and I get half the credit, baby."

"Figures," Raphael turned to Alex. "We do all the work and they get half the credit." Alex nodded.

Raphael wandered into the library late that afternoon to see if Niki was up for a run. Niki looked up from his tablet and screwed up his face.

"There's a protest soon, and I haven't done one in a while ... if that's okay?"

"When and where?"

"Mission, again, to Civic Center, in an hour. Or sooner, if it's like all the others."

"I'll go with you. Let me check with the others." He started for the door, then turned. "I have something special for you, too." Niki nodded as he returned to his tablet, happy that Raphael was game. Half an hour later as Niki headed up to his room to dress, Raphael poked his head out of his and Luke's door, catching Niki midway up the next flight.

"We'll meet you in the foyer. Don't put on a shirt." Five minutes later Niki and Steve arrived in the foyer, Niki, as instructed, in just shorts and shoes. They found Raphael, Luke, and Alex waiting, all of them in new matching black locked cock tees. As Niki stepped off the last stair, the three turned to reveal the Black Lives Matter imprint on the back.

"Cool!" Niki exclaimed. "Where'd you get them?" Raphael pulled another out of one of the cubbies and handed it to Niki.

"They were inspired by you, Niki, so you can advocate for two causes at once." As Niki pulled the shirt on, Raphael draped an arm around Luke's shoulders. "Fortunately, we ordered a couple of extras, so our newest locked cock brother wouldn't feel left out."

"Is it karma or justice, Luke?" Niki asked. "Since you're the one who forced Raphael into a locked cock wardrobe?"

"No comment, Niki." Luke unwound Raphael's arm from his shoulder so he could pick out his sign and they could make their exit. As Alex opened the door, Luke issued a warning. "You guys better hope no wind gusts blow up my kilt, or your previously secret caged cock emblem will be revealed to all for what it really stands for." Raphael nudged Alex and wiggled his eyebrows as they shared a grin.

Niki had been right. They were hardly the first to arrive at Mission and 20th. There were thousands of marchers, as far up and down Mission as could be seen, and here and there a few police to control traffic from the side streets. The crowd was as diverse as all the other marches, just as loud and apparently peaceful. Which was the best part of doing daytime protests. It wasn't long before the family had picked up on the chants being called and they joined in. The crowd was moving along, often in step with someone drumming.

About half an hour in, as they were approaching South Van Ness, some kind of drama broke out to their right, on the sidewalk. A small group had stopped marching and were surrounding an anti-protestor who might have been a homeless person. He was apparently causing a scene, but he was on the edge of things so most marchers were unaware of him. It was Niki, looking back again, who saw the guy land a punch on a young black kid, with a 'No Justice No Peace' sign, who crumpled immediately. Niki was out of Steve's grasp, across the street and down on his knees, leaning over the kid, before anyone else knew what was happening. The kid was unresponsive, and there was blood on the sidewalk under his head, scaring Niki, who wasn't sure what he should or shouldn't do. Just as he looked up, the man kicked the kid. Without thinking, Niki jumped up and shoved him hard with both hands, sending the guy off his feet and over onto his back away from the kid. Because they were at a major intersection, there were several cops nearby and they soon surrounded Niki and the kid before any of the family could react. One pulled Niki off the kid as two cops knelt down beside the attacker. A fourth knelt over the kid, who still appeared unresponsive. A bigger crowd, attracted by the cops, immediately formed around them as Raphael started for Niki. Steve grabbed him.

"Wait, Raphael," he shouted over the crowd. "Let's see what's happening first." It was hard to see through the throng.

"I want to go to Niki," Raphael protested, trying to wriggle out of Steve's hold. Luke took Raphael's other arm to further subdue him.

"They're either going to let him go, or take him in," Luke shouted. "If they do that, we'll be more help to him if we aren't in custody with him."

"Custody!" Raphael freaked out. Alex put an arm around Raphael's waist from behind. The four of them moved as close to the situation as they could, and out of the still moving mass of protestors. They were finally able to get onto the sidewalk, maybe fifty feet from the scene, just as most of the protestors who had encircled the commotion began to disperse. That's when they saw two cops walking Niki, hands zip-tied behind his back, toward a police van at the corner. Another was walking the attacker, also handcuffed, away as well. The kid was still on his back, but appeared to be conscious, a cop staying with him. An approaching siren announced the arrival of the EMTs.

"He didn't do anything!" Raphael protested. Alex wrapped his other arm around Raphael's waist.

"I know," Steve leaned down into Raphael's face. "We need to stay calm. Let's get closer. Maybe we can explain what happened to the cops."

"Yeah," Luke agreed, "but let's not let them know we know Niki, or they may not listen to us."

"Stupid cops!" Raphael was in no mood to be reasoned with.

"Luke, Alex, keep Raphael here," Steve loosened his grip on Raphael. "I'll go see what I can learn." Raphael again tried wrestling out of Alex and Luke's holds, but they had him out numbered.

"Baby, let Steve handle this. Let's keep an eye on that van ... see which way it goes."

"I never should have taught you how to work out," Raphael turned his head to address Alex.

"And I've only just started," Alex said through gritted teeth. They watched as the fire department rescue van arrived on Van Ness, unable to navigate the marchers on Mission. One EMT ran up, knelt down and conferred with the cop still with the kid. He said something into his radio, then began checking out the kid, who tried to sit up, but the EMT held him down, conferred with the cop again, then stood up and ran back to the ambulance. As he returned with another EMT and a gurney, one of the cops who'd taken Niki away also returned. Steve approached him, and the two spoke. The cop nodded a couple of times. Several other protestors approached and talked to him and Steve as well.

"Looks like Steve's doing okay," Alex tried to console Raphael. "Maybe they'll let Niki go now."

"I don't think so," Luke said. "Look." He pointed toward South Van Ness, where they could see the van pulling away.

"FUCK!" Raphael broke free, but now had nowhere to go. He took a very deep breath and turned to Luke. "Now what? Sir?" Luke closed his eyes, not wanting to fuel Raphael's rage. He opened them and just stared at Raphael, brows knitted, but silent for a moment, waiting out Raphael's next outburst. Raphael could see Luke wasn't going to say anything until he himself spoke again. In a quieter tone, but one that could still be heard over the crowd, Raphael earnestly asked, "I mean, what. Do. We. Do?"

"Baby, first we find out what Steve knows." Raphael slumped against Luke's side, wrapping an arm around Luke's waist. Alex, confident that Raphael was under control now, jogged over to the where Steve and a couple of other protestors were talking with the cop. The EMTs had the kid on the gurney and were wheeling him through the crowd to the corner, heading for the ambulance. Steve, Alex and the others spoke with the cop for a few minutes more, then Steve looked their way. He said something else to the cop before heading back to Luke and Raphael. He had a non-committal expression as he and Alex approached.

"What do we know?" Luke asked as they returned.

"Several of us were able to explain what happened, that Niki was trying to protect the kid. A couple thought Niki was attacking the guy, but I think the rest of us were able to counter that." He looked appreciatively at Alex.

"So, what do we do?" Raphael pleaded.

"We go bail him out. If that's what it takes. They took him to Mission Station. Anyone else want to go?" Raphael's eye widened, clearly

telegraphing 'you have to ask?' As one, they turned and headed
south, against the crush of protestors.


Niki was numb. He'd almost gotten sick in the police van, he was so
traumatized, but he was able to keep it together. So far. He looked
around himself in the holding cell and counted. There were seven
other people there, all masked, two of them obviously with masks
provided by the cops, and all young guys like himself, except for the
guy who had assaulted the kid. He was clearly homeless, Niki could
see now, and therefore of indeterminate age. He could be anywhere
between early thirties and early fifties. Niki just wished he wasn't
in his proximity. The guy didn't seem to recognize Niki as the one
who'd pushed him; for that he was grateful. Fuck! he thought, his
forearms resting on his thighs, looking down at his feet. If I end up
with a record, will it prevent me from being in school? From getting
a nursing job? Any job? The thought of nursing school brought his
thoughts back to the poor kid, laying on the sidewalk. He'd only
wanted to help him. He glanced up as a couple of cops walked past
the wide wall of chain-link separating the cell or pen or whatever
it was called from the corridor. One of them turned his head and
looked in as they walked past, and did a double take. He paused
slightly, then continued on.


"Sarge, you have the paperwork on the new crew in holding?" the
Captain asked as he approached the duty desk. The sergeant looked
up and reached into a stack of trays.

"Right here. Nothing's been processed yet. Most of them just
arrived." He passed the handful of papers to the Captain.

"Thanks. I'll be right back." He looked over the papers as he
walked back to the holding cell, where he stopped and turned, looking over the confined group. Niki sensed something was up and sat
up and looked at the cop. The Captain, looking directly at Niki,
held out his right hand and crooked his index finger in the universal
'come here' signal. Niki looked left and right, hoping it wasn't him
he wanted. When he looked back at the cop, the cop nodded. Niki
took a deep breath and stood; the cop motioned again. Niki walked
over and stopped a couple of feet shy of the barrier.

"Hi," the cop said. "What's your name?"

"Niki Malaluan-Phillips," Niki replied quietly, and almost as a question, as if he wasn't sure if that was the right answer. Mainly because he wasn't sure what was happening. If this encounter was a good sign or a bad one. The cop shuffled the papers he was holding, then nodded and looked up at Niki.

"Thank you, Niki. Stay here. I'll be right back." He walked away. Maybe, Niki thought, Steve's here and he's bailing me out. Please let that be what's happening. He looked back at the other detainees, a couple of whom were looking at him. Then, the cop was back.

"I'd like to speak to you privately, Niki, but I need your permission to do that without a lawyer present." Niki gulped. A lawyer? Oh ... shit! His heart sunk and it showed in his eyes. "Niki, you don't need one. I'm not going to charge you. I just want to talk." Niki didn't speak. Didn't move. Then the cop put the piece of paper under his left arm to free both hands and signed, 'I promise.' Niki looked up at the cop's face. *His* cop's face. With the mask, both today and that day before, it was hard to recognize him, but it had to be him. A slight smile, hidden by his own mask, crossed Niki's face as he nodded ascent.

"Okay," he said. The cop turned and signaled to someone out of sight, who turned out to be another cop who walked up and unlocked the door. As he opened it, Niki's cop walked around the other cop and motioned Niki to come out into the corridor. The cop ushered him halfway down the hall in the opposite direction from where most of the action seemed to be concentrated. He opened a door and stood aside and motioned Niki to enter. As Niki did, his cop motioned something to the cop who'd unlocked the cell door, then followed Niki into the room.

"Have a seat. Make yourself comfortable, Niki." The cop took the chair opposite Niki across from a small, metal topped table. The door opened again and the other cop entered, wordlessly placed two bottles of water on the table and closed the door as he left. Niki's cop pushed one bottle in front of Niki and picked up the other, unscrewed the cap, lowered his mask below his chin and took a swig. Niki looked at his bottle but kept his hands in his lap. He glanced furtively at the cop, finally able to see his face. A surprisingly friendly, open face. Handsome, actually, in an indeterminate, multi-ethnic way.

"Please, help yourself," the cop nodded to the water bottle. "You've had a rough day. I know. My name is Captain Fuentes, Niki. We've met before."

"Yeah, I remember," Niki finally spoke, as he reached for the water. He pulled down his own mask and drank. "I thought you were pretty cool." Fuentes gave a short laugh.

"Thanks. That's what I'm always going for." It was Niki's turn to chuckle.

"I can't believe you remembered me."

"Well, Niki, and this not a judgement, you understand, but you do have a very distinctive haircut." Niki nodded and smiled, a smile that was finally visible. Fuentes picked up the sheet of paper, back to business. Niki's smile faded.

"Tell me what happened out there." Niki took another sip of water, then leaned forward, forearms on his thighs, hands clasped, putting his head closer to the table top. He looked up at Fuentes, who smiled, placed the paper back on the table and leaned back in his chair. "Everything exactly as you remember it." So, Niki told him what he saw. What he remembered seeing and doing. Everything was pretty clear up until the moment the cops took him into custody. That's when emotions overwhelmed his observational skills. Fuentes didn't interrupt or ask any questions, remaining silent whenever Niki paused. When he felt he was finished, Niki sat up straight and asked his own question.

"Is he going to be okay ... the kid? He wasn't moving." Fuentes smiled.

"You're in police custody, and you're worried about the victim." Fuentes almost unperceptively shook his head. "Hang on ..." He went to the door, opened it and stepped into the corridor. He stopped someone, spoke briefly, then closed the door and sat again.

"What do you do ... for a living," he asked.

"I'm furloughed right now. COVID. But I start nursing school in a couple of weeks."

"Really? I'm not surprised. I'm sure you'll be a terrific nurse. Out of the thousands of people on the street, you were the one who tried to render aid to that kid. Yeah, I was right."

"Right about?"

"About you. You're what I like to call 'good people,' Niki. I could tell the first time we met. That's why I was surprised to see you here today, but I'm not surprised now that I know the whole story. Niki, you don't need to worry about being detained. What you told me is corroborated by several witnesses. Also, the individual you decked is ... well, he's well known to us. My officers should have spent more time getting the facts before detaining you, but that's really hard to do in the middle of a protest. What we really should do is issue you a commendation." The door opened and a cop handed Fuentes a piece of paper, then exited. Fuentes quickly scanned it, then looked at Niki and smiled. "It looks like your patient is going to be okay. They're keeping him overnight for observation. He has a nasty laceration and he appears to have a concussion, but he should be fine." Niki smiled, and took a deep breath. Fuentes reached into a chest pocket and pulled out a card, then scribbled something on the back before sliding it across the table to Niki. Niki picked it up.

"Niki, don't stop protesting." Niki looked up and engaged eye contact with Fuentes. "But, please, be careful out there. Okay? We need all the good nurses we can get. If you find yourself in trouble, and if you can't reach me at the number on the front of the card, my personal number is on the back." Fuentes stood, and Niki did the same, pocketing the card in his shorts. "Can we give you a ride home?" Niki genuinely smiled as he pulled his mask into place.

"Thanks, Captain, but it's not that far." Captain Fuentes might be cool, but he really didn't want to be seen getting out of a police car in front of the House of the Locked Cock Brotherhood.

"Okay, let me show you out." Fuentes opened the door, stepped out into the corridor and waited for Niki to follow. The two walked side by side, through the station to the entry vestibule and out to the street doors. Niki turned to Fuentes.

"I was right, too, Captain Fuentes."

"Oh?"

"You really are cool. Not just cool, but you're a cool cop. We need more of those, too." Fuentes could have taken that as criticism, or even condemnation of his fellow officers, but he took it in the spirit it was offered. He pushed open the door for Niki. "Take care, Captain. Thanks for the card."

"Stay safe, Niki." As Niki started onto the sidewalk, another cop walked up beside Fuentes.

"Trying to recruit another Black officer, Captain?"

"I wish. He'd make a good one. No, he's going to be a nurse."

"Oh, well, we need more of those, too, I guess." As they watched, Niki didn't get more than a few feet before he was surrounded by Steve, Luke, Raphael, and Alex. Steve lifted him a few inches off the ground in a fierce hug. Raphael leaned in and planted one on Niki's cheek.

"Looks like he has a fan club, Captain."

"More like a family. He was wearing a wedding ring. Pretty sure that's his husband trying to squeeze the life out of him."

"Damn. Black and gay. We really could use him on the force." Fuentes looked at the cop and shook his head.

"That's what I most appreciate about you, Benson. Always looking out for the force."

"Right ... Cap'n. Ready to find out what today's issue is for our old friend, 'slugger'?" Fuentes sighed, closed his eyes and nodded. They turned away from the happy reunion and headed back to the holding cell.

Ricky was waiting outside a taqueria to pick up his next delivery when he saw the text from Juan. 'Close your app as soon as you can & bring home the order in my name from Sushi Time. I'll explain over a Spicy Tuna Roll.' Ricky smiled. A mystery. And sushi, no less. Did this mystery involve Hiroshi? Once he'd delivered the burrito order, he doubled back to Sushi Time. It was a big order, nearly filling his insulated carrier. At home, he parked the scooter and lugged dinner up the steps. He was surprised when he entered to find everyone in the sitting room, instead of the kitchen, or dining room.

"Dinner's here. Oh, and Ricky, too!" Luke kidded. "Raphael, Alex, you guys pick out some wine. Greg and I will corral a couple of these coffee tables. Since it's Tuesday, let's do 'Tuesday Dinner' like old times."

"So, what's going on?" Ricky asked as he stripped.

"Niki will tell us all about it over dinner," Juan said as he took possession of the DoorDash bag. "You run and decontaminate as fast as you can." When he came back downstairs, everyone was waiting, including Hiroshi, so he had been right. Juan handed him a glass of wine as he settled in between Juan and Mateo. The food was arranged over two coffee tables that had been moved together, with everyone sitting around them, almost tatami style.

"Thank you for joining us, Hiroshi," Steve said. "Niki had quite a day today, and we wanted you to help us honor him."

"Honor him?" Ricky was still in the dark.

"Let me make a toast, then we'll tell you all about it." Steve lifted his glass and turned to Niki. "To Niki. Future nurse and current day super hero. Protector of the young and defenseless. Oh, and mascot to the cops of the Mission Station. Cheers!" Everyone chimed in on 'cheers' while Ricky and Hiroshi shared clueless looks.

As they ate, the story unfolded, mostly by Niki, but with numerous interruptions by Luke, Steve, Raphael and Alex. Everyone had their own interpretation of events. Some more embellished than others.

"Luke and I had to hold Raphael back," Alex spun. "He was this close to tackling a cop and getting himself arrested along with Niki."

"I wasn't arrested," Niki corrected.

"Yeah, but Raphael sure as hell would have been," Alex asserted. Luke nodded as he turned to Raphael.

"I have to say, you have an ardent defender in your brother here," Steve agreed. "I've never seen Raphael so worked up before."

"Well, I was pissed," Raphael defended himself. "They just assumed ..." His unfinished thought was fully understood by everyone.

"Captain Fuentes agreed they overreacted." Niki explained. "But he said it was hard in the middle of a protest to sort things out. He actually apologized, Raphael." Niki looked at Raphael, appreciating that Raphael had been so eager to defend him. "In fact, he said I deserved a commendation." He looked a tad sheepish. "I think he was kidding."

"I don't think so," Alex offered. He turned to Hiroshi. "The cop gave him a 'get-out-of-jail-free' card!"

"Everyone should have one of those," Hiroshi smiled. "Seriously?" Niki was rolling his eyes.

"He gave me his card."

"With his personal phone number!" Alex continued. "Niki has a new boyfriend!" Alex looked very pleased with himself.

"I prefer to think of him as a fellow first responder," Niki played along. "Who admires my 'distinctive' haircut." On cue, Steve ruffled Niki's mohawk.

"Were you scared?" Mateo asked. The thought of detention was far too close and personal for Mateo to contemplate joking about it. Niki gave him a sympathetic smile.

"Not exactly, Mateo. I mean, okay ... a little scared, but I was worried ... mostly. Worried that if they arrested me, it could end my nursing career before it even began." Juan nodded as he placed a piece of yellowtail sushi in Ricky's mouth.

"You have my number, too, Niki," Hiroshi spoke. "If you get detained again, call me first. I know a very good lawyer." Niki laughed.

"Thanks, Hiroshi, but I have no intention ... absolutely *no* intention of ever seeing the inside of a holding cell again," Niki promised. He looked around at the family to reinforce his intent.

"I guess you'll have to content yourself with the puppy cage downstairs, then," Raphael deadpanned. Niki nodded, but maybe less than enthusiastically.

"Hiroshi," Juan gave Hiroshi a knowing look. "Have you ever been detained by the police?" Hiroshi chuckled.

"How else do you think I got to know a good lawyer?"

"Really?" Ricky looked awestruck.

"It was not as honorable as what got our favorite puppy here in trouble, I must admit." Hiroshi took a sip of wine, suddenly sensing himself at the center of attention. "But it was 'good trouble' of another kind. During the White Night Riots. I was young. Like my good friend Raphael here, I was pissed. We were all pissed. We could not believe we had been so betrayed." Mateo looked at Juan, then Raphael, then Luke, hoping he wasn't the only one who had no idea what Hiroshi was talking about. Raphael caught his eye and read his reluctance to speak.

"Hiroshi, I know a little about that night. But not as much as someone who was there. Can you tell us about it?" Hiroshi turned to Mateo.

"Mateo, do you know who Harvey Milk was?" Mateo shook his head.

"I know the MUNI station is named for him ..." was all he knew.

"Okay, let's start there." He looked around the group. "This could be a long story. Are you sure?"

"Absolutely," Greg said. "I'll get another bottle of wine." He jumped up and headed for the kitchen as Hiroshi began. By the time he finished, Hiroshi had delivered a primer on Harvey Milk's long sought pursuit of representation of the gay community on the Board of Supervisors, his close working relationship with Mayor George Moscone, and the subsequent brutal murders of Moscone and Milk in their City Hall offices by Dan White, a former cop and disgruntled former Supervisor himself. And the shockingly light sentence handed down to White at the conclusion of his trial, which sparked protests, peaceful at first, but which ended in violence and destruction at City Hall. Everyone had stopped eating, hanging on Hiroshi's recounting of cinema worthy events that had been all too real.

"What got you arrested?" Ricky asked.

"Well, as a Buddhist, I am ashamed to say I knocked a cop out cold."

"Whoa!" Alex reacted."

"But I stopped him from beating the crap out of a fellow gay protestor, so it was for a good cause." Mateo smiled at Hiroshi and put a hand on his thigh. Hiroshi put a hand on Mateo's shoulder as he looked at Niki. "Sometimes we do not think, we just act, right Niki?" Niki smiled.

"And your lawyer friend?" Niki asked.

"Another protester, but one smart enough not to get arrested," Hiroshi smiled. "He got the charges dropped."

"Wow," Luke raised up on his knees so he could reach a California roll. "He really is a good lawyer."

"And a good friend to this day," Hiroshi grinned as he noticed again Luke's new adornment. "Enough of my much too long story. I would love to hear Luke's now." Luke looked confused as he settled back in place.

"He means this, Sir," Raphael prompted as he jiggled Luke's hot pink Holy Trainer. Luke leaned his head back in dismay.

"Oh, yeah," he half laughed. "Hiroshi, it's temporary. Another one of our dares. It comes off next Saturday ... Friday if we get to use my calculations." Raphael mouthed 'Saturday.'

"Well, it is very becoming Luke," Hiroshi sounded serious, until he continued, "the color is totally you." Alex cackled.

"See! I told you it looks good on you!" Alex looked at Greg as he said, "There's something irresistibly hot about a hunky guy in a locked cock."

"Which is why," Greg replied, "I still haven't totally agreed to us joining Luke and Raphael in this whole 'dare' thing." He looked at Luke. "I know exactly what my first dare would be ... a revenge dare, no doubt." Alex put an arm around Greg's shoulders as he laid his head against Greg's chest.

"You think you know me so well," he muttered. Steve leaned over and whispered in Niki's ear, who nodded. He and Steve unfolded themselves and stood, Steve's arm around Niki's shoulders.

"Guys, Niki's had a big day, so I'm going to be rude and take him up to bed now. Thank you for dinner, Juan and Ricky. Hiroshi, good to see you as always. Good night all." Everyone wished them goodnight. Hiroshi, too, stood.

"Thank you for inviting me." He bowed slightly. "Every meal I share with you is an adventure." Mateo stood and pulled Hiroshi into a hug, then a brief, but earnest kiss. Hiroshi beamed to the group. "And dessert is always the best part." He kissed Mateo on the forehead, then he and Mateo walked into the foyer where Hiroshi slipped into his sandals before Mateo showed him out the back door. When Mateo returned, everyone else was up, collecting trays, plates, chopsticks and glasses.

"You know," Ricky said, "I can't tell who your real boyfriend is, Mateo ... Ryan or Hiroshi." He made a face to show he was only kidding. Mateo looked thoughtful for a second, then smiled.

"Maybe I have two boyfriends?" he asked.

"Ha!" Juan reacted as he walked past Mateo and gripped his shoulder, shaking it in agreement. "He's got you there, mijo."

"And ... the corruption of Mateo is complete!" Alex announced.

# Twenty-Two

# A LONG AWAITED KISS

JUAN AND RICKY WERE standing side by side at the sink, brushing and flossing before bed. Ricky slyly bumped Juan's bare hip with his own and furtively glanced at Juan in the mirror once or twice, trying to be coy. Ricky was being less than subtle and his intent did not escape Juan's notice. He didn't say anything in response. Juan knew exactly what was coming. As they slid into bed, Ricky kept sliding until he was on top of Juan, legs straddling Juan's, chest resting on firm chest, his hands on either side of Juan's head. He buried his fingers in Juan's now lush mop as he lowered his lips to Juan's, extracting Juan's minty-fresh tongue deep into his own allegedly submissive, but clearly demanding mouth. Juan wrapped his arms around Ricky's back, then slowly slid his right hand down to Ricky's apparently hungry ass. For a time neither spoke, just breathed through the kiss, heartbeat echoing heartbeat. Finally, Ricky lifted his head enough to break the seal.

"Papito, I know you have to get up early tomorrow, but it would be so nice to feel you inside me right now." Juan looked up into Ricky's adorable brown eyes.

"Let me guess, mijo" Juan smiled. "Sushi makes you horny?"

"Being your locked cock leather boy makes me horny, Papito. You make me horny." Ricky leaned down and teased Juan's lips again with his own. "Just for a little while?" Then, for emphasis, Ricky employed his most irresistible smile. Juan, incapable of denying Ricky, nodded and reached his left arm out, in search of the bedside lube. Ricky leaned over and grabbed it for him, keeping Juan's legs captive between his own. "Here," Ricky whispered, "let me." Ricky raised up on his knees to expose Juan's erection. He liberally coated it, then rubbed the remainder of lube into himself. Not wanting to waste a minute, he tossed the pump bottle aside and, with one hand guiding, settled into place, slowly impaling himself as Juan maintained eye contact with his most prized possession. Juan reached up and captured a hairless, brown nipple in each hand as Ricky slowly raised and lowered himself, giving a sweet, little moan each time his buttocks touched Juan's hips. As both breathed more deeply, Juan swelled further, enhancing satisfaction for both of them. Juan began to punish each of Ricky's nipples between thumbs and forefingers, gently at first, then more intensely. Ricky's breathing came more loudly, his mouth open now, the breaths more forced. Up and down, Ricky worked Juan's cock, his sphincter doing its best to punish Juan, just as Juan was punishing him. Soon Ricky's breaths were intersected with little cries. He'd broken eye contact, eyes closed now, his focus directed to his tortured nipples and to a lower chakra. This could not go on forever, and it didn't. Without warning, Ricky came, shooting onto Juan's belly and chest, but, ever the perfect locked cock leather boy, he maintained his rhythm in pursuit of Juan's orgasm. He opened his eyes now, reengaged contact with Juan, his beatific smile blooming across his face. That was all Juan had to see to come himself. He released Ricky's nipples and buckled, making the most of this impromptu orgasm. As it subsided, Ricky laid forward, not quite all the way down on Juan's chest, not wanting to free Juan's cock just yet. Giving each of them a little more pleasure. When Juan pursed his lips in hope of a kiss, Ricky released Juan and repositioned himself, smearing his cum between them as he pressed his lips to Juan's. It had been more than 'just a little while,' but it had been time, and bodily fluids, well spent. When Ricky lifted his head enough to allow it, Juan whispered.

"Thank you, mijo." Ricky closed his eyes shyly in response. "I love you." Ricky's eyes opened.

"I love you, Papito. Thank you for indulging me." His hands found Juan's mop again.

"I hope I wasn't too hard on your beautiful nipples." Ricky lowered his head and nestled in, his lips next to Juan's ear. He made a little moaning sound.

"I think I kind of liked it, you know?" Juan was silent a moment. Then he rolled over onto his side, causing Ricky to slide off, so that they were facing each other, on their sides. Juan put his left arm around Ricky's waist and pulled him close, faces nearly touching again. Ricky was gazing into Juan's eyes.

"Mijo, we've never really talked about this, I mean, not seriously, but are you ready to explore more of the world of leather? Of domination and submission?" He gently rubbed the gold labret beneath Ricky's supple lip. "Loving domination. And willing submission?" Ricky's lips slowly curled into a wordless response. "I know you're caged, collared and harnessed; you rock the high 'n tight, and you bottom like you've been doing it all your life. But tonight, it just felt right to punish your nipples. I don't want to rush you ..." Ricky's smile fully bloomed.

"I thought you'd never ask, Papito." He moved his right hand up to finger the ring in Juan's left nipple, without breaking eye contact. "I'm ready to submit, Papito. Totally. What luck! We have a dungeon right downstairs!" Juan gave a short laugh, followed by another, longer, wetter, fiercer kiss. When they parted, practicality returned.

"Let's get a quick shower, then I do need to sleep." Juan raced Ricky into the bathroom where he opened the middle drawer of the vanity and retrieved Ricky's keys. He always insisted on doing a thorough cleaning of Ricky's cage and its contents after each of Ricky's orgasms. The shower and the re-lockup of Ricky took just long enough to allow for one more unplanned development. They returned to the bed to find it not quite empty.

"Hola, amigos. I heard your shower." Mateo was on top of the covers, on his side, head propped up on one arm, like a '20's silent film starlet. "Is okay?"

"Is everybody horny tonight?" Juan asked as he climbed onto the bed and over Mateo, rolling him onto his back in the process.

"Not horny," Mateo said seriously, propping himself back up on his elbows. "Jus' lonely."

"It was either us or Hiroshi, huh, muchacho?" Ricky kidded as he crawled under the covers on the other side of Mateo. Mateo grinned.

"I pick you!" He turned to Juan, still uncertain. "Is okay?"

"Is okay, Mateo," Juan lifted the covers so Mateo could climb under. "Just no wrestling tonight, okay? I have to sleep." Mateo nodded, climbed under and wrapped himself around Ricky. Juan followed, sliding over until his back and butt rested against Mateo's. By his count, he decided as he doused the bedside lamp, Mateo had at least four boyfriends. Before he fell asleep, Ricky reached across Mateo to rub Juan's waist, just above his hip.

"Papito, do you think what Niki did today, trying to help that kid, was the right thing to do? I mean, he's not really a nurse ... yet." Juan didn't respond immediately. Mateo and Ricky exchanged glances in the dark. Juan yawned and placed a hand on top of Ricky's.

"It was the only thing to do, mijo. Niki has good instincts. He'll be a wonderful nurse, and we should all be proud of him." Both Mateo and Ricky smiled in agreement.

Wednesday evening, after dinner, Steve and Niki were in the fireside chairs in the library, each focused on his own tablet, Niki's feet resting on top of Steve's. Raphael and Luke, were on one of the couches in the sitting room, reading, like old times, each with a foot in the other's crotch, except this time both cocks were locked. Luke's for only two more days by his count, three by Raphael's. Raphael, of course, had possession of the keys, so ... three. Ricky and Juan were in the gym and Alex and Greg were in their room, watching TV. Mateo was doing what Mateo did every evening, chatting, laughing, sexting with Ryan. Until he burst out of his room and ran across the hall to Alex and Greg. The ensuing commotion was heard downstairs, bringing Raphael and Luke into the foyer, where they saw Mateo bounding down the stairs, skipping every other step. Alex and Greg were following more slowly.

"He got it!" Mateo shouted, bringing Niki and Steve out of the library. "Ryan got the lab!" A group hug formed around Mateo who still had his phone in hand.

"Hold still!" came Ryan's voice over the speakerphone. "You're making me dizzy."

"Congratulations!" Alex plucked the phone out of Mateo's hand. "So, are your parents on board?" As they spoke, Juan and Ricky arrived, having heard the shouting. Mateo threw himself at them as he repeated his news.

"Conditionally, Alex," Ryan reported. Alex raised his hand to request everyone's attention.

"What does that mean, Ryan?" Alex asked as he walked into the sitting room, taking Ryan and the rest of the family with him. He propped the phone against the stack of books on the main coffee table and sat on the couch in front of it as Mateo and Ricky joined him on either side. Everyone else gathered in the background.

"I've told them about the house, about all of you guys, but I'm not sure they believe how awesome you all are. I mean, they've met Mateo virtually, and they love him, but ... well, with COVID and everything, they want to be sure I'd be safe there."

"So where do we stand?" Greg leaned into the field of view.

"They want us to drive up together so they can meet you and see the house themselves. That's the good news."

"Good news?" Alex asked. "What's the bad news?"

"You guys would all have to put clothes on." Raphael fake screamed.

"Sorry, Ryan, not possible," he maneuvered around to see Ryan's face. "Sorry ... can't be done."

"Yeah," Juan agreed. "That's just too big an ask. Too bad, it would have been nice having you here." Mateo looked over at Juan in disbelief as Juan winked, restoring Mateo's smile. Raphael picked up the phone to enable a more intimate exchange with Ryan, who was grinning himself at this cute, but not that cute, of a performance.

"When are you coming?" Raphael asked. "It'll take us a week to dust everything. I assume your mother will be wearing her white cotton gloves."

"Oh, no, don't do anything ... just don't be naked and we'll be fine. They'll love you guys. I'm hoping for Saturday. I plan to bring my stuff and just stay ... if that's okay."

"Oh, don't worry, Ryan. We have plenty of rope downstairs in case they try to take you back with them," Raphael asserted.

"Uh ... okaaay?" Ryan replied. "Like I said, they'll be fine. Unless Mateo gave me a virtual tour of an imaginary house and you're all living in a one-bedroom walkup in the Tenderloin."

"Here," Raphael said, handing the phone back to Mateo, "give him another tour on your way back to your room." As Mateo headed for the foyer, everyone shouted goodbye to Ryan.

"Seriously," Alex said as he drew a finger across the top of the coffee table, "we probably should dust."

"I never should have let Luke out of his commitment," Raphael pretended dismay. Greg raised his eyebrows, encouraging elaboration.

"He offered to be the butler if we moved in here."

"Well, he is dressed for the part this week," Steve teased. "Where would you like to start, Luke?"

"In the dungeon," Luke replied. "With you. Follow me." Steve laughed

"Speaking of the dungeon," Raphael mused, "I got the impression Ryan doesn't know about it."

"Yeah," Greg agreed. "That'll be a nice surprise, won't it?"

"I can hardly wait," Alex stood and put an arm around Greg's waist.

"We should probably let Mateo initiate him, sweetie," Greg suggested. "Don't you think?"

"It all depends on when his birthday is," Alex declared as he led Greg toward the foyer. "We may get to resort to those ropes after all."

Luke's first words upon waking Saturday morning were no surprise. Before Raphael had even opened his eyes, Luke whispered his command into Raphael's ear.

"Baby, unlock me." Raphael rolled around and fingered Luke's closest nipple. He took a dramatically deep breath before responding.

"Orrrr, Sir, you could give me another blowjob and go for two weeks." He batted those amazing eyes. Luke stared into them for a moment before responding, testing Raphael's early morning endurance. Yes, Raphael was being cute, but Luke had soldiered through the week without a single complaint this time. A dare is a dare, after all, and he'd done his part, bravely he thought.

"Orrrr," was all Luke said as his face telegraphed an unstated, but abundantly clear 'promise.' Raphael nodded and leapt out of bed, opened the closet door and closed it behind him. Luke could hear him humming loudly in an attempt to mask the sounds he was making as he retrieved the keys from their hiding place. Seconds later, as Raphael straddled Luke's thighs, pulling the brass lock out of Luke's cage, Luke shook his head, a wry look on his face.

"What?" Raphael asked.

"The things we do for the one's we love." Raphael tilted his head, much like Pup Niki would do, indicating he didn't follow. Raphael had pulled the Holy Trainer tube free, but hadn't yet touched the cock ring when Luke smiled and raised his arms, pulling Raphael onto him, demanding a kiss, and interrupting the very action he'd endured a week to attain.


By this morning the dusting, vacuuming and putting-away-of-things had been accomplished, with each of them having taken responsibility for a different room. Niki, of course, had called dibs on the library, and boy was he sorry, not realizing how much time was involved in dusting each and every volume, and the shelves they rested on. In the end, Steve, Juan and Raphael came to his rescue after finishing the sitting room, dining room and butler's pantry themselves. Fortunately for Steve, regular use and the glass doors in the butler's pantry kept the stemware and china reasonably dust free. That left enough time Saturday morning for Raphael and Alex to begin preparations for what they hoped would be a confidence building lunch for Ryan's parents. They were just washing up when Mateo bounced into the kitchen from the back stairs.

"Ryan texted." He looked down at his phone so he could read the text verbatim. 'Just turned off 101. Put on your CLOTHES!'" Mateo giggled. "Look!" Mateo held out his phone so they could see he'd put 'clothes' in all capitals.

"Ten minutes to curtain, people!" Alex announced as he headed for the stairs, wiggling his photogenic dancer's butt on the way out.

"Better butch it up for the parental units!" Raphael called after him. Then he put an arm around Mateo's waist and walked him toward the stairs. "You nervous?" he asked as he squeezed Mateo's waist.

"Scared to death," Mateo replied. "Is that right?"

"Your words are right, but the sentiment is all wrong, muchacho. They'll love you. Just be you, okay? You must be excited to see Ryan." Mateo made a whimpering sound.

"I have no words for it," he honestly said.

"Actually, that was very well said, Mateo." They'd reached Mateo's door. Raphael kissed him on the forehead. "Meet you downstairs."

Mateo was sitting in the bay window seat in the sitting room, his body twisted so he could see the street, when Greg and Alex entered. Greg was in a polo and shorts, as was Alex, his polo adorned with the caged cock logo, which he knew Raphael would be sporting as well. Mateo was in his finest: a pressed collarless long-sleeved white shirt with a subtle floral embroidery, also in white, and black slacks. His hair, like Juan's lately, pulled into a short ponytail. He looked like an altar boy, one anxious as hell. Alex and Greg wandered over to watch with him, as Greg began massaging Mateo's shoulders. Mateo turned to Alex.

"What do I say?"

"What's Ryan's last name?"

"Riley."

"You might go with 'Hi, Mr. and Mrs. Riley. It's a pleasure to meet you. Ryan welcome to your new home.' You can't shake hands with his parents, of course, but you probably should give Ryan a big ol' deep French kiss." Mateo looked doubtfully at Alex before turning to Greg.

"Just ignore that last part, Mateo, and you'll be fine." Mateo smiled and nodded before turning back to the window. Then after a moment, without turning his head he cracked both Greg and Alex up.

"Don' you worry ... I'll kiss him ... and strip him as soon as his madre and padre are gone." The statement was matter of fact. Clearly, Mateo was dead serious. At the same time that Raphael and Luke entered, a car coasted to a stop in the street, pointed up hill on the other side of the street. Mateo raised up on his knees on the seat.

"Nice car," Alex stated the obvious.

"Maybe we should have held out for more room and board," Greg agreed. The car headed on up the block, out of sight, then reappeared after having done a U-turn. It took them a moment, and a couple of tries to get fully parked on the steep grade. Greg noticed that Ryan's dad hadn't chocked his wheels, so he reached out for Mateo's hand. "Come on, muchacho, let's go teach Ryan's dad how to park in San Francisco." As the two masked up and headed out the door and down the steps, Juan and Ricky arrived in the foyer.

"Nice kilt, Luke," Juan praised. "Seriously. A pinstripe. Never seen that one."

"I only wear it for weddings and funerals," Luke joked as he installed his own mask. "And to impress Mateo's future in-laws. You should probably be wearing scrubs."

"That's what I said," Ricky exclaimed. "See?" He gave Juan a peeved look.

"We don't want to overdo it, guys," Juan objected. "Better to just be ourselves."

"Then, I guess I'd better strip," Raphael countered, pretending to unbuckle his belt.

"Let's just go for the happy medium, baby," Luke took hold of Raphael's hands. "You look perfect." Raphael turned to Juan with a royal smile.

"He says that a lot." Then he batted his lashes. Because he really did look perfect.

"Here they come," Alex warned. "Act natural. On second thought, just act cool." He opened the right-hand door so that both doors were open, giving the arrivals a grand view of the foyer and the family assembled there. Niki and Steve were descending the stairs as Ryan's parents followed Greg into the foyer. Ryan and Mateo, holding hands, were in the rear, masks still in place, indicating Mateo had kept his word. So far.

"Ryan!" Alex, Raphael and Niki all shouted at once. Ryan's eyes were beaming over his mask.

"Guys!" he greeted back. "We made it!"

"Ryan," Greg, who had now assumed the role of MC, closed the doors and asked, 'do you want to make the introductions to our little family?"

"Yeah, sure, thanks," Ryan replied still somewhat breathlessly. "Um, Mom and Dad, this is Alex, Greg's husband. The handsome guy in the kilt is Luke, his husband is Raphael, here. That's Juan and Ricky. Juan's a surgical nurse. See I told you I'd be in good hands. This is Niki, Raphael's brother, and his husband Steve. And, just because once isn't enough, this is Mateo. He's quiet, but deep." During the introductions everyone had nodded, made eye contact and sized up one another. As best one can do while masked.

"Welcome to our home, Mr. and Mrs. Riley," Mateo enunciated perfectly.

"It's lovely," Mrs. Riley responded. "Forgive me if it takes me a time or two get everyone's name right. You have us outnumbered," she laughed. "Ah, I know it's protocol, and all, but I have to ask, you don't all wear masks at home do you?"

"No ... but ..." Greg started.

"Then," Mrs. Riley peeled off her mask, "I'm perfectly fine if we take these things off. I want to see your faces!" Mr. Riley chuckled, unsurprised by his wife's unorthodox suggestion. "Please, call me Beth." Perhaps to reinforce his wife's comfort with her surroundings, Ryan's father removed his mask, too.

"I'm Tom," Ryan's father followed up. Soon, gratefully, everyone was barefaced and smiling.

"That's better," Beth surveyed the group. "I appreciate all of you taking the precaution, but we all have to get to know one another, don't we?" As if by habit, Beth took Tom's mask and dropped it into her handbag along with her own.

"You can be assured we take every precaution," Juan said. "We maintain a very tight bubble, and except for us 'essentials,' everyone works from home." He saw no reason to mention the occasional fifteen-thousand member protest march.

"Do any of you need to use the powder room after your long drive?" Raphael asked. When she nodded, Raphael walked Beth down the foyer and opened the door for her.

"Nice place, guys," Tom said looking up at the staircase and into the open sitting room. "Ryan said it was a mansion, but we thought he was probably overselling."

"Thanks," Niki responded, a bit shyly. "It's not really a mansion ... it just looks like one." That got a good laugh, and began what would be a warm, rapport building experience with Ryan's parents over the course of the next couple of hours. Beth rejoined the group, squeezing Luke's biceps as she passed him, causing Raphael to smile. It was probably the kilt, he thought, and for which he took full credit.

"Mateo," Greg suggested, "why don't you and Ricky give the Riley's a tour of Ryan's new place. When you're done, we'll have lunch ready." To give the tour group some space, everyone else headed up stairs and into their respective rooms. About half an hour later, when they heard them entering what would be Ryan and Mateo's room, Raphael and

Alex headed back down to the kitchen. They were wrapping things up when they heard Ricky finishing the tour at the foot of the back stairs.

"And this is the way to our back garden. When we can, we sometimes like to have a picnic back here." He'd opened the back door.

"Wow," Tom said. "You must have a gardener?"

"No," Ricky laughed. "We do it. With a lot of help from our next-door neighbor, Hiroshi. He knows his stuff."

"He's very nice," Mateo offered. Alex and Raphael, safely out of sight, shared a knowing glance and chuckle as they heard Ricky close the door.

"And this goes ...?" Tom asked. The knowing glance devolved into one of angst.

"Oh, that ... just the basement," Ricky replied. "It's just a basement. Let's go this way." Ricky immediately led them into the kitchen where Alex and Raphael were plating lunch.

"Ricky ... show everyone into the dining room. Lunch is ready," Alex instructed. He raced up the back stairs to ask Greg to corral everyone while Raphael carried the tureen into the dining room and placed it on the sideboard. As soon as Luke arrived, he joined Raphael, delivering cups of soup to each place as Raphael ladled them. Greg was helping Alex deliver plates of burgers and coleslaw. The burgers were open, with the fixings on the side, so each could dress their burger to their taste.

"It looks like you boys know your way around a kitchen," Beth complimented as Raphael and Luke took their seats.

"Well, we do like to eat," Raphael laughed, his soup spoon in mid-air. "Everyone pitches in and we each have our specialties." He took a sip, confirming that the soup was a success.

"What kind of soup is this?" Ryan asked. "I love it."

"Artichoke," replied Raphael. "It's Niki's and my Mama's recipe." Tom looked at Niki first, then at Raphael, a thoughtful smile settling on his face.

"Is the burger hers, too?" he asked. "Is this Niman Ranch beef?" Alex laughed.

"These are Impossible Burgers, Tom." Tom knitted his brow. "They're vegan ... not beef."

"No." Tom was unconvinced. He took another bite and chewed. "Seriously?" Alex nodded proudly.

"Everything is delicious," Beth said. "I kept meaning to try the Impossible Burger, but it's never happened. Besides, I wasn't sure Tom would be up for it."

"Well, I'm up for it now, dear," Tom affirmed. "You should give me more credit."

"You heard him, boys," Beth laughed. "Tofu, here I come."

"Well, let's not go crazy," Tom countered. Clearly, they were at ease, enjoying the food, enjoying the company, the house, and the whole idea of trusting Ryan to the care of the House of the Locked Cock Brotherhood.

"Do you guys still do pancakes Sunday mornings?" Ryan asked hopefully.

"We sure do!" Ricky grinned. Ryan turned to his mother.

"That's Ricky's specialty. They're really good."

"And we serve them just the way you remember," Ricky grinned wider. Ryan looked down at his plate, trying not to blush.

"Cool," was all he could muster.

"Well, you have an enviable kitchen to work with," Beth nodded to Ricky. "I don't know which I like better, the kitchen or the library." The usually quiet Niki found his moment.

"The library, for sure. It just feels like home, don't you think?" Beth nodded.

"Yes, it does, Niki," she agreed. "I can see myself reading a big, fat novel in front of the fire on a chilly winter evening." Ryan rolled his eyes, but Niki was in total agreement.

"Which reminds me, how will you get to campus from here, Ryan?" Beth asked. Ryan hesitated, so Niki spoke up again.

"We can take the M, from Market street, just a few blocks down the hill, or we can use the E-bikes around the corner. I did a test ride on the bike, Ryan, so I know a good route. We can ride together once or twice if you'd like."

"Niki, you're a student at SF State, too?" Beth looked pleased.

"Yes," Niki smiled. "Nursing school."

"Following in Juan's footsteps?" Tom speculated.

"He's been my inspiration, yeah," Niki confirmed. "Like most of Ryan's, my classes will be online for now, but I'm still looking forward to the semester beginning." From there the conversation drifted to how the pandemic had changed everything, not just school. More questions about what everyone did, how they spent their free time. At one point Beth issued a blanket compliment by voicing a concern.

"Ryan, how will you manage to focus on your studies in a house full of so many handsome men?" Ryan didn't have an answer for her right away, so Mateo came to the rescue.

"I will make sure he studies ... Beth," he declared, still hesitant to address her so familiarly. She seemed pleased and amused.

"Most days here are pretty full," Luke offered. "Those who aren't working outside the house are in their rooms, working from home. We usually have dinner together, but otherwise ..." Beth nodded.

"Honey," Tom turned to Beth, "there'll be fewer distractions here than in a dorm with a hundred or more other undergrads. I don't think we have anything to worry about. Right, Mateo?" Mateo nodded enthusiastically.

Everyone lingered over the empty plates for a few minutes, with no clear agenda. Alex and then Raphael rose and began collecting dishes, which was apparently Tom's cue. He stood, pulled a folded envelope out of his pocket and laid it on the table.

"I'm not sure who the treasurer is, so I left the name blank, but here's a check for the first six months of Ryan's room and board. If all your meals are anything like what we just enjoyed, we're getting a real bargain." Beth rose as well and pushed her chair into place.

"Do me a favor Raphael," she requested, "and teach Ryan how to make artichoke soup. In fact, Ricky, teach him how to make pancakes, too. I've tried, but I haven't had much luck with him in the kitchen."

"Not a problem," Alex grinned. "We have house rules that make cooking, cleaning and eating extra appealing, right Ryan?"

"Yeah, I guess," Ryan mumbled, avoiding eye contact. Then, he gave himself away flashing a big grin at Mateo.

"Well ... whatever works," Tom concluded. "We probably should hit the road, Beth. Ryan, let's get your things." He and Ryan led the group into the foyer where Beth paused to gaze one last time into the library, exchanging smiles with Niki. Steve and Luke followed Tom and Ryan down to the car, completing the chore in just one trip back up the steps. Then Tom and Beth, followed by Ryan, then the rest of the family, returned to the car. Initially Tom and Beth pulled Ryan into a hug, but after a moment, Beth loosened her hold on Ryan and motioned Mateo into the circle between her and Ryan. Mateo was clearly touched, unable to hide a sniffle. Tom broke away and opened Beth's door then closed it after her. As he walked around and climbed in, Beth issued her last instructions to Ryan, and maybe the rest.

"Be good. Study hard." Then with a smile, "And don't forget to have a little fun." Ryan nodded, then as the Tesla quietly glided away, he and Mateo waved. As they rolled down the hill Beth adjusted her side mirror and watched.

"Are they kissing?" Tom asked.

"Passionately."

"I wonder what took them so long?"

"Us, of course. We probably should have left a while ago."

"What, and missed our first Impossible Burger?" Beth readjusted her mirror and sighed. Then, before they had reached Market Street she reached over and began manipulating the monitor.

"What are you doing?" Tom casually asked as he maneuvered through Castro traffic.

"We're not in any hurry, are we?"

"Nooo ...?"

"I thought I'd reset the navigation. I thought we'd stop in Big Sur."

"Big Sur? Hmm." He was silent a moment. "When were we last there?"

"Well, let's just say Ryan was too young to remember it."

"Oh, yeah. Well, he's old enough now, isn't he? I admit, until today I wasn't too keen on him returning so soon, but I'm happy for him. I'm actually glad he manipulated us into letting him return to San Francisco. This way he's going to have some semblance of a college experience, and I'd much rather have him in that house with his friends than on campus with thousands of other students."

"Plus ..." Beth put a hand on Tom's thigh.

"Plus?"

"We'll have the house all to ourselves again." Tom smiled without taking his eyes off the road. When he realized navigation wasn't leading them back to 101, he turned to Beth.

"Highway 1?" he asked, knowing the answer. She grinned.

"We're not in a hurry, right?" She busied herself for another moment on the monitor, then leaned back, her hand back on Tom's leg, as The Beach Boys' 'Pacific Coast Highway' flowed through the cabin.

Mateo had one arm around Ryan's waist, the other under his arm, his hand gripping the back of Ryan's neck. Ryan had wrapped both arms around Mateo's shoulders. Lips were locked, eyes were closed and apparently, for them, time had stopped advancing. Several members of the family exchanged glances and knowing smiles in anticipation of the kiss breaking. After a moment, Ricky, unconsciously jealous perhaps, wrapped an arm around Juan's waist. Greg cleared his throat. It was the arrival of Hiroshi that finally broke the seal.

"Is there another protest today?" Hiroshi asked as he approached. He was wearing gardening gloves and holding a short-handled trowel.

"No," Niki replied. Then he realized the reason for Hiroshi's question. "Oh, you mean because we're dressed? We had guests."

"Ryan," Greg said a little louder than he otherwise would have, "I'd like to introduce our friend Hiroshi." It was then that Ryan finally pulled his lips free. He lowered his left arm so he could turn toward Greg, but kept Mateo in his grip with the other.

"Sorry." He seemed to be addressing Greg, but maintained eye contact with Mateo. "I've been waiting a long time for that." Mateo was the one who broke eye contact as he turned to Hiroshi.

"Hiroshi, my boyfriend, Ryan," Mateo beamed. He walked Ryan over to Hiroshi. "Ryan, this is my friend, Hiroshi. And our very good neighbor!" Hiroshi slipped the glove off his right hand and reached out. Ryan, like everyone, was unused to shaking anyone's hand, and he hesitated.

"It's okay, Ryan," Hiroshi smiled. "I'm in the bubble!" He reached out further. "Also, I've been tested." Mateo slipped out of Ryan's grasp, freeing Ryan's right arm. Mateo hugged Hiroshi, genuinely happy to see to Hiroshi and partly to show Ryan it was okay, then he pulled the two together. Ryan reached out and shook Hiroshi's hand.

"Very good to meet you," Ryan said.

"The pleasure is all mine," Hiroshi responded a little formally with a slight bow as he released Ryan's hand.

"Ryan's parents brought him up today, for school," Alex explained. "He's going to be staying with us ... with Mateo. They just left." Hiroshi looked at Mateo.

"You must be very happy today, Mateo," Hiroshi smiled more with his mouth than his eyes. "I know you were worried this might not happen."

"Oh, I was." Mateo wrapped an arm around Ryan's waist. "But, is okay now!"

"Okay?" Raphael chided. "Mateo, try this: 'Everything is perfect now!'"

"Yeah! Like you said," Mateo beamed, uninterested in a vocabulary lesson at the moment. "Come, Ryan. We get your things." Mateo pulled Ryan up the steps. Just before entering the foyer Mateo turned and waved. "Bye Hiroshi!"

"Let's give them a hand," Greg said to Alex. They climbed the steps a bit more slowly than Mateo had done. Hiroshi watched them go.

"He seems very nice," he said to no one in particular.

"It was kind of love at first sight," Raphael explained. "At least on Mateo's part. Although I think Ryan took to him right away. They met at our wedding, so, in a way, love was in the air."

"A lot of first encounters happen at weddings," Hiroshi agreed. "Or, so I understand." He smized wistfully. Juan put an arm around Hiroshi's shoulders.

"We wouldn't know first-hand, would we, Hiroshi? We haven't had much experience at weddings yet." Hiroshi gave a short laugh.

"Not yet, no." He looked at Niki. "Like I said before, I really wish I could have been at that wedding myself." Then with a sly smile he winked at Ricky. "Since it was legendary." Juan rocked Hiroshi's shoulders with a one arm hug.

"I should get back to it," Hiroshi pulled away from Juan and slipped on his glove. Before he turned, Raphael spoke.

"Hiroshi, we're thinking of celebrating Ryan's arrival with a little bubbly later this afternoon, if you're available. We'd love to have you join us." Hiroshi nodded.

"That would be nice," he said quietly. "Thank you." He walked to his steps, turned, waved and then disappeared as he began climbing.

"I know I should be all happy, happy, but I feel kind of sad for Hiroshi," Niki whispered, looking up at Steve. Steve nodded knowingly as he took Niki's hand and started for the steps. Once everyone was in the foyer and the door was closed, as everyone began stripping, Juan offered his thoughts.

"Hiroshi has a good heart, Niki. He'll be fine. I know I shouldn't speak for him, but I think the bond he and Mateo have developed is because he knew Mateo was the odd man out here. He knew Mateo was lonely. As long as I'm speaking for others, I think Mateo felt that same way for Hiroshi. They were there for each other when they needed it. I think ... I hope ... it's a bond that will endure even with Ryan here."

"I think you're right, Juan," Luke affirmed. "More than anything, it will be Ryan who tests their bond."

"Yeah," Raphael agreed. "Let's hope Ryan understands."

Alex wandered into the library later in the afternoon, finding Niki in his chair as he'd expected. Niki lowered his tablet as Alex plopped into the companion chair.

"I wonder if Mateo and Ryan will come out of their room today?"

"They already did, Alex. They went out about a half an hour ago."

"You're kidding. I didn't hear a thing." Alex wiggled Niki's thigh. "You made a good impression on the Riley's today, Niki." Niki smiled, yet showed surprise with a short laugh.

"How so?"

"I think they were glad to hear you're also taking classes at SF State, and you'll be able to help Ryan figure things out. And studying nursing doesn't hurt either." Niki nodded.

"I think we all made good impressions. It's cool Beth liked the library, too."

"What's not to like?" Alex said as he stood and walked over to the nearest bookcase. In all this time he really hadn't paid attention to what this private library had to offer. He tilted his head and began to scan titles and authors. The conversation died and Niki went back to his tablet. Alex slowly explored, working his way around the perimeter, finding more and more titles he thought he might want to read. It was an eclectic collection, one that had obviously grown over years, decades, maybe generations. History, biographies, science, philosophy, politics, including reasonably contemporary politics. Grandpa Ben clearly didn't like Donald Trump. And fiction. Mysteries, classics, thrillers and more than a few gay titles, some Alex hadn't seen before.

"Have you actually looked at these books, Niki?" Alex was holding a copy of a recent David Sedaris work. Niki turned to look over his shoulder.

"Uh, yeah. I dusted almost every one of them yesterday."

"Have you read any of them?"

"A couple so far. I know it seems like I'm addicted to this," he shook the tablet, "but I love books, too." Their conversation was interrupted by the sound of the front door opening. Once it closed, they could hear Ryan's voice.

"Immediately?"

"Yes. Only naked past the foyer." Alex chuckled as he walked to the doorway to find Mateo stripping and Ryan holding a large ponytail palm.

"Oh, darn," Ryan uttered.

"Hi, guys," Alex grinned. "Learning the house rules again, eh, Ryan?" Ryan screwed up his face.

"Yeah." Ryan approached Alex. "I wanted to surprise you, but I guess this is still a surprise. This is for you." He held out the plant, but Alex stood firm.

"For me? What? Why?"

"I'm here thanks to you, Alex. The lab idea. I owe you, big time."

"Ohhh," Alex nodded. "This is really sweet, Ryan. It's beautiful. But I can't accept it like this ..." Ryan looked a little crestfallen. Alex cast his gaze to Mateo, who, fully stripped now, sidled up next to Ryan and relieved him of the plant.

"You have to be naked first," Mateo instructed. Ryan bit his lower lip.

"Sorry. Duh ..." Alex and Mateo, and then Niki who had joined Alex, patiently watched Ryan strip. Mateo guided him to the cubbies, where he saw everyone else's clothes from earlier in the day, apparently each outfit in its designated cube. Ryan stuffed an empty one then turned and took possession of the palm, holding the pot just below waist level. He once again approached Alex and offered the plant.

"Much better, Ryan," Alex grinned. "Again, this is very sweet. We're all just glad you're back." As he took the plant from Ryan, he looked down, then back up at Ryan's face. Ryan shook his head.

"I'm still me," he shrugged. Alex handed the plant to Niki, then he pulled Ryan into a hug, letting Ryan's erection slide between his thighs. He patted Ryan on the back.

"We missed you, Ryan, boner and all," Alex comforted him. Once they separated, Alex took back the plant.

"I know it's kinda big," Ryan seemed to apologize. "But, if it's too much for your room I figured in this big old house you'd find a good spot for it somewhere."

"I have a couple of ideas already, no worries, Ryan," Alex said as he admired the plant. "Oh, you know, speaking of this big house ... Mateo, you should probably take hold of that handy boner there and lead Ryan down stairs. You know ... show him the gym." Niki nodded knowingly.

"Okay!" Mateo agreed. He grabbed Ryan's ample handle and led him toward the kitchen. Alex turned to Niki.

"I wish we had a camera down there."

"It's good thing we don't," Niki countered. "God, we need at least a little privacy around here."

"Privacy is overrated," Alex contended. Niki's look indicated he wasn't convinced. "Come on, help me find a home for my new pet." As they headed for the stairs, they heard Ryan's reaction, despite Mateo having closed the basement door. They exchanged amused looks. As they had suspected, it was clear Mateo hadn't given Ryan a complete video tour of the house after all.

Twenty-Three

# GETTING TO KNOW YOU

NIKI WAS IN THE library, but sitting at the desk, not his usual place in front of the fireplace. He was attending class, logged into a Zoom session, on his second day of distance learning. Steve had offered to relocate from their room for him, but Niki preferred the more studious surroundings of the library anyway. He not only felt inspired by it, but thought it might convey a more impressive, and real, backdrop for his instructor and fellow classmates. Ryan was 'in class,' too, at the desk in his and Mateo's room, while Mateo was at work. Since Ryan's session wasn't interactive, he was in regulation HLCB dress ... naked. Niki was wearing a single item, a BLM tee.

Once he'd finished his class, Ryan rose and ambled down to the kitchen for another cup of coffee. He approached the library to see how Niki was doing, listening out of sight a moment in case Niki was actively participating. A typical move in a house that was home, work space and school, all at the same time. After hearing nothing, he peeked in to see Niki was typing on the laptop rather than interacting. Niki looked up, smiled and sat back in the leather chair.

"Hey," Niki waved Ryan in. Seeing Ryan starkers reminded Niki of his own atypical status, so he leaned forward and pulled the tee up and over his head. "You done for the day?"

"Done with class. I have some homework left but ..." Ryan climbed into Niki's chair, but on his knees and facing backward so he could make eye contact with Niki.

"Same here."

"Are you liking it?" Ryan asked. "Being back in school?" Niki nodded. "I am. It's been a while, but yeah. It's probably better this way."

"You mean online?"

"No, I wish it wasn't online. No, I mean, it's better that I didn't go right from high school to college. I'm so much more motivated to pay attention, to participate, and hopefully to study hard. I mean ... I have a goal now. It's not just school for school's sake." Niki paused thoughtfully. "I know where I'm going, Ryan, if that makes sense."

"I get it," Ryan shifted around and sat in the chair facing the fireplace as Niki got up and moved to the chair next to Ryan. "I know a lot of students who, like you said, are in school just for school's sake. Mostly to party and maybe sample a few courses, but some of them don't really have a plan. I don't know ... some days I worry I might be a little like that."

"What do you mean?" Niki put his elbow on the arm of the chair and rested his head in his hand, giving Ryan his full attention. "Mateo wasn't sure exactly what your major is, maybe anthropology or archeology?"

"Exactly. I haven't been able to narrow it down. I'm still undeclared, taking classes in both, and loving both. Last semester I volunteered at the Academy ... California Academy of Sciences Museum in Golden Gate Park. Have you been?"

"Sure. It's very cool. Steve and I have a membership. I love the rainforest. The planetarium is cool, too."

"Yeah, visitors usually only see the cool museum part, but they do amazing, ground breaking research there, too. I met some awesome scientists and even got to help out on some of the research. Not any of the field research ... out in the ocean or on other continents, but stuff in the labs. It was great, and I'd be volunteering now, but ... COVID." Niki nodded knowingly.

"Tell me about it," Niki sympathized. Then, he sat up straight. "But you know ... I guess, for me, COVID hasn't been all bad. If it hadn't happened, I wouldn't have been furloughed, and I'd still be bartending and I probably wouldn't have been motivated to go back to school." Ryan made a 'how about that' face. "Ryan, do you have to choose one over the other? Archeology or anthropology?"

"What? You mean a double major?"

"Yeah. Or two degrees? You know, an extra year or so?"

"Huh. Think I should?" Ryan seemed to be asking himself more than Niki as his gaze wandered to the bookshelves behind Niki for a second. Then he resumed eye contact with a smile. "Thanks, Niki. Something to think about."

"You'll figure it out," Niki grinned. "Speaking of ... I offered to show you the best route to campus. When's your first lab?"

"Friday."

"How much homework do you have? We could ride over today if you want? Or, tomorrow morning. My only live class tomorrow is in the afternoon."

"Today works. Besides I could use the exercise."

"Said the guy with what ... zero bodyfat?"
"And zero muscles. Put your shirt back on, and let's go."


Of course, Ryan didn't have 'zero muscles,' but by the time they'd arrived on campus he was glad they'd chosen electric bikes. San Francisco boasts fifty-two major hills, and Ryan was pretty sure they had crested half of them on the way to school. When they docked the bikes on the edge of campus, Ryan made no bones about being out of shape as he stretched each leg.

"Man, I could hardly keep up with you, Niki," he protested, massaging his thighs. "It wasn't a race, you know."

"Sorry, I didn't know I was racing," Niki laughed. "You okay?"

"I'm all right," Ryan straightened up. "You must ride a lot."

"No, but I run three times a week. Raphael, Alex and I, and sometimes Mateo. You should join us, Ryan. It's fun." Niki reached over and patted Ryan's thigh. "You don't want Mateo getting the better of you, do you?" Ryan made a non-committal 'hmm,' so Niki changed the subject.

"Ryan, why don't you show me around the campus, so I'll know where everything is." They set out, side by side, with Ryan narrating a tour of buildings and points of interest. At first, it felt awkward to Niki to be walking with a member of the family, even a new one, without holding hands. He didn't want to put Ryan in an uncomfortable position, not knowing how out Ryan might be on campus, so he slipped his left hand into his pocket, not sure what else to do with it. The campus was larger than Niki had anticipated, but Ryan was clearly happy to be back and grew more animated as the tour progressed. As if he'd saved the best for last, they finally came upon the HSS building, the College of Health and Social Services, where hopefully sooner than later Niki would be attending classes in person. They found a spot to sit and rest, side by side.

"I can tell you miss being here," Niki turned his gaze to Ryan.

"Yeah ... I do. There was always something going on." Ryan was wistful. Niki smiled as he watched Ryan possibly relive some moment. "But!" Ryan made eye contact with Niki. "I'm back in San Francisco! In a lot of ways being with you guys must be like living in a frat house, so it's really not so bad." Finally relaxing in Niki's presence, perhaps, Ryan reached over and squeezed Niki's thigh. Taking advantage of the moment, Niki put a hand on top of Ryan's, to reinforce the welcomeness of intimacy.

"Ryan, you don't know how right you are. Has Mateo told you our official name for the house?" Ryan shook his head, his eyes indicating he was anticipating something good.

"Ryan, you are living in the House of the Locked Cock Brotherhood." Niki pressed down on Ryan's hand to drive the point home. "Which probably sounds weird, since neither you nor Mateo is locked." Ryan pursed his lips as if this idea demanded further contemplation. "I guess that means you two are the pledges, right?" At that, Ryan had to laugh.

"I guess! I like it! I often thought about what it would be like to pledge a fraternity." He squeezed Niki's thigh again. "But I never heard of one as unique as the House of the Locked Cock Brotherhood." He held Niki's gaze a moment longer. "So, are you saying one or both of us will end up locked in this kinky fraternity house?"

"That'll be up to you two." Niki liked where the conversation was going, and didn't want to say anything that might intimidate Ryan. "You remember our conversation in Alex and Greg's living room? About how each of us ended up locked, right?" Ryan nodded, smiling at the memory of his first experience of mandated nudity with the family. "Nobody will force you or Mateo to do anything you don't want to do. Believe me ... I know what can happen if any of us does."

"Oh, yeah ... are you talking about you and Mateo?" Niki nodded solemnly.

"Did Mateo tell you about that?" Niki broke eye contact and looked down, embarrassed.

"Yeah, he did. And about what happened afterward." Niki gave a short laugh, not one of mirth. Then he sighed and looked back at Ryan.

"I apologize. I hope you won't hold it against me. But you know as well as anyone how damn cute Mateo can be. I was in full pup mode. It almost wasn't my fault!" It was Ryan's turn to laugh.

"Niki, it's okay." Another squeeze of Niki's thigh. "I'll admit, I was a little hurt ... maybe a little jealous when Mateo told me about the things he's done with some of you guys. But we talked it out, and I think I understand the kinds of relationships you all have. I think. He kind of gave me a lecture about sex and love and the intersections of the two. It was pretty cute, actually."

"Wait ... 'things' he's done?" Niki looked confused. "You mean more than with me? I'm ... I'm impressed."

"I shouldn't say any more about that." Now Ryan seemed a bit embarrassed. "So, does, uh, does everybody use that dungeon in the basement?" Niki leaned into Ryan, touching shoulder to shoulder momentarily.

"I'm not sure. I do know everybody's witnessed activities there ... you know, the situation Mateo's apparently already told you about. Including Hiroshi, our neighbor, who's actually spent more time there than any of us. But, yeah, several of us have, uh ... taken advantage of it." Niki wasn't sure how much detail he should share with Ryan yet, figuring it was up to Mateo to continue to share any gory details. "It came with the house, you know."

"No!" Ryan pulled back. "You guys didn't build it?" Niki shook his head.

"Does it scare you? Having it in the house?" Ryan slowly shook his head.

"No." He looked intently at Niki, his mask making it hard to interpret what he was thinking.

"Does it intrigue you?" Ryan paused before responding.

"A little. Maybe." His hand was still on Niki's thigh. "I don't have any experience with that stuff. Like you guys. Listen, as long as we're talking about all this, can I ask you a personal question?" Niki nodded. "I've never seen you as a puppy. What does it do for you?"

"Wow." Niki shifted around so he was facing Ryan, as he put his right leg up on the low retaining wall they were sitting on. "That's a hard question to answer. First of all, it started as a fetish, I admit. I used to look at pictures and videos online of guys in pup gear. It was pure porn for me. It was the main thing I jerked off to. That was before I was caged, obviously. But when Steve, and Raphael and Luke, made it possible for me to try it, it went beyond a fetish, beyond sex. I don't know, Ryan, it's hard to explain. It's kind of like a psychotropic drug for me, maybe. I forget about all the human issues I have to deal with, and I just see and treat everything like a puppy would. I don't know, maybe a state of meditation is a better metaphor? It makes me happy and at peace. That's the bottom line. I really like being Steve's puppy." Niki paused and looked intently at Ryan, who didn't say anything. "Okay, I've totally weirded you out." Ryan looked shocked and reached out and grabbed Niki's left hand that was resting on his knee.

"No!" Ryan protested. "Not at all. Niki ... that sounds, I don't know ... kind of inspirational." He paused, looking down at the ground at their feet. After a moment, he looked back into Niki's eyes. "Can I ask you another question?" Niki smized his assent.

"I remember you saying that the thing you most liked about your chastity cage is that it makes your cock look so much smaller. Not that it looks all that small now." Niki involuntarily looked down at his uncharacteristically clothed crotch. "So, now that everything's closed, the gym, the bar and the only people seeing you naked are the family, why do you stay caged?" Niki gave Ryan a bemused look.

"Huh. I guess it never occurred to me to have Steve take it off. It's just a part of me now. I like how it feels, and not just when I'm aroused and it presses against my cock. I do like how it looks, just for myself, regardless of what anyone else might think." He paused a moment to consider any other benefits. "To use what has become a very over-used expression these days, it's my new normal. Make sense?"

"Yeah. I was just curious." Ryan shifted self-consciously. "I can't wait to see you as a puppy, Niki. I can't wait to ..."

"You can't wait to ...?"

"Umm, to be fully initiated into the fraternity of the House of the Locked Cock Brotherhood."

"Well," Niki stood and kept hold of Ryan's hand, testing Ryan as he also stood. "If you have any more questions, all you have to do is ask, Ryan. I'm not an expert in the dungeon, for example, but Hiroshi and Juan are, and Luke pretty much, too. Anything you want to know, one of us can help. Whenever you want. I think Mateo is slowly expanding his horizons, too, so it should be fun for both of you." Ryan nodded enthusiastically. "So, Ryan, should we find a couple of bikes, or take MUNI back?" Surprisingly Niki still held Ryan's hand in his.

"Let's ride back, Niki," Ryan smized. "You can follow me ... see if I remember the route." He squeezed Niki's hand as he led him toward a nearby dock of bikes.


Mateo crept up behind Ryan, who was at the desk in their room, deep in homework, and, throwing COVID caution to the wind, kissed Ryan's bare shoulder, producing the desired effect.

"Don't Do That!" Ryan spun around in his chair, flustered, but happy to see Mateo. He reached forward, but Mateo backed away.

"Huh uh," Mateo scolded. "First, I decontaminate."

"Five minutes, then I'm coming in after you," Ryan promised. Mateo smiled, blew an air kiss and dashed into the bath. Ryan hurried to finish up what he could, hoping he would have something better than homework to do for the rest of the evening. By the time he slipped into the shower his notorious boner was at full staff. Mateo, shampoo still streaking his hair, dropped to his knees and swallowed it as if on command. Ryan took a deep breath and buried his fingers in Mateo's mane, massaging the back and sides of Mateo's head. Mateo held Ryan captive as he slid his soapy, slippery hand up and into Ryan's perky crevice, his middle finger finding its way to Ryan's prostate.

"Ah, cariño," Ryan sighed. He let Mateo suck and probe a moment, something he was getting awfully good at, before he moved his hands onto Mateo's shoulders, tapping them to get Mateo's attention. Mateo looked up without releasing Ryan cock, to see Ryan looking down, air kissing him. Mateo released Ryan's cock and ass and stood so he could swallow Ryan's tongue instead. Ryan's erection rode up Mateo's belly as Mateo's slid between Ryan's thighs. Mateo's arms wrapped around Ryan's back. Ryan had his left arm around Mateo's back, while he buried his right hand deep into the hair on the back of Mateo's head, pressing their lips more firmly together. Both were whimpering between deep, grateful breaths. Months of separation made each shared breath a gift given and treasured. Eventually they separated, just enough to soap each other down quickly, then rinse. As they were toweling each other off, Mateo again dropped to his knees and kissed each of Ryan's ass cheeks, before standing again. Ryan spun around.

"I still can't believe I'm actually here with you. Finally."

"Yo también. I miss you, Ryan."

"Missed, my love. No more missing. I'm here now." Mateo shook his head, trying to understand. Ryan explained the present and past tense in Spanish.

"We're together now." That, Mateo understood. They exited the bath, Mateo holding Ryan from behind with both arms around his waist, headed for the bed when they heard a quiet woofing from the other side of the bedroom door that Mateo had left ajar when he snuck up on Ryan earlier. Ryan looked confused, but Mateo grinned, released Ryan and moved to the door. He peeked out, then, grinning even more, pulled open the door.

"Hey, perrito!" Pup Niki bounded into the room. First, he sniffed then licked Mateo's feet, then he trotted over to Ryan, whose feet were similarly inspected. Pup Niki looked up at Ryan and began barking enthusiastically. Ryan just stood there, flabbergasted. He couldn't believe what he was seeing. This was not what he'd imagined a Pup Niki would look like. Niki's eyes were the only part of his face visible behind the puppy hood, complete with snout and floppy ears. Niki's hands were gone, covered in paw mitts. And a tail ... a furiously wagging tail ... was sticking out of Pup Niki's butt. With the permanent dog collar, the chest harness and Niki's beautiful, cocoa skin, he was, for all intents and purposes, a playful Labrador. Ryan's mind was blown. Mateo, more familiar with the pup, walked over, dropped to his knees and began petting him. Pup Niki immediately turned to give full attention to Mateo and pounced. Within seconds Mateo was on his back, giggling, while Pup Niki was slathering him with puppy kisses. Ryan, catching on, dropped to his knees.

"Here puppy," Ryan called. He whistled, a surprisingly powerful whistle. Pup Niki abruptly stopped assaulting Mateo, looked over at Ryan, barked once and bounded to Ryan, who began rubbing behind

Pup Niki's rubber ears. Mateo sat up and watched. As any curious pup would, Pup Niki began sniffing this new person from toe to head, licking frequently. Ryan looked over at Mateo, amazed, amused and maybe a little turned on, although it was hard to tell with him. Pup Niki, always craving attention, rolled over onto his back, paws up, and yapped. Ryan looked to Mateo, who scooted over and began rubbing Pup Niki's belly. Pup Niki made happy whimpering sounds, panting joyfully.

"He's like a real puppy!" Ryan acknowledged, as he knelt and rubbed alongside Mateo. This was the most intimate contact he'd had with Niki/Pup Niki and he couldn't help taking note of Pup Niki's cage, and how well packed it was.

"He is real puppy," Mateo agreed. "He does not talk, but he listens." Mateo moved his head up over Pup Niki's snout. "Good boy. Are you good boy?" Pup Niki barked twice, then rolled over onto all fours again. Ryan raised up on his knees, his boner stiffer than ever, taunting both Mateo and Pup Niki, who was eye level with it. He whimpered with frustration. He sniffed it, backed up a step, looked up at Ryan, then back at the boner with another whimper. Mateo laughed.

"He wants your bone. He likes boner bones." Ryan reached out and rubbed behind Pup Niki's ear again. Pup Niki approached and pressed the side of his head against Ryan's thigh. Then, he backed up a step, lowered his back haunches until his tail was on the floor, his forelegs stiffly holding his chest and head up for Ryan to admire. Pup Niki tilted his head to the side, then whimpered again.

"He's begging for your bone, Ryan," Steve said from the doorway, where he'd been watching for a couple of minutes. Ryan looked guiltily at Steve.

"What do I do?" Ryan asked. "You know I can't help it."

"He understands you. If you don't want him to have it, just tell him. He's a good puppy. He'll obey." Pup Niki barked once, looked over at Steve, then looked back at Ryan and whimpered again, tilting his head.

"God ... he's so adorable," Ryan conceded. He looked back at Steve who made a 'it's up to you' face. Ryan looked back at Pup Niki, then at Mateo, who was enjoying Ryan's awkward first encounter with the puppy, then back to Pup Niki. He turned toward the pup, his boner swaying, and said, "Okay, puppy, but only for a minute." Pup Niki pounced and swallowed Ryan's bone in one eager gulp. He began, as usual, shaking his head back and forth, growling around the cock, while sucking intensely. Ryan's eyes widened. "Whoa!"

Mateo raised up on his knees, hands over his mouth. "Dios Mio ..." Mateo reached out and grabbed Pup Niki's furiously wagging tail, which only added to the pup's gratification. Ryan, not sure what else to do, put both hands around the pup's hooded head, rubbing behind his ears.

The growling increased, along with the suction. Suddenly Ryan's eyes widened and he pulled free, sitting back on his calves, his cock glistening with saliva and precum. He lowered his face level with Pup Niki's and stared into his eyes. For a moment, that's all they did. Stare. Mateo released Pup Niki's tail and rubbed his ass, then patted it. Finally, Pup Niki tilted his head again, maintaining eye contact with Ryan. Ryan reached out and brushed Pup Niki's chest.

"You. Are. Fucking. Amazing." That was only the second time anyone, including Mateo, had heard Ryan swear.

"Okay, boy," Steve commanded. "Let's go, puppy. Come on." Pup Niki turned and trotted over to Steve, looked up, barked once, then headed into the hall. "Dinner will be ready in about half an hour, boys. If you're, uh, not too busy." Steve pulled the door closed, leaving Ryan and Mateo looking at each other. Mateo scooted over and pressed his lips to Ryan's briefly. Ryan still seemed taken aback. Then, Mateo leaned down and swallowed Ryan's slippery bone. He worked it for only a minute or so, then raised back up to face Ryan.

"I finish what Pup Niki start ... okay?" Ryan smiled as he leaned forward and kissed Mateo again. "Go ahead, muchacho." Mateo pushed Ryan onto his back, straddled his torso and held Ryan down until he'd finished what Pup Niki had started.


It wasn't until dessert that Pup Niki's latest escapade came up. Niki had played it cool all through dinner.

"I hear you got to meet Pup Niki today," Luke looked at Ryan.

"I did!" Ryan put down his fork and looked at Niki while answering Luke. "It was amazing. Niki and I had talked about the whole puppy thing this afternoon after we biked over to campus. I guess he wanted me to see the real thing for myself." Niki displayed a smile tinged with mischief.

"I thought you might get a kick out of it," Niki said. "What did you think?"

"Like I said, it was amazing. You were ... cute, fun, really expressive and realistic. And ... sexy. I've never seen anything like it."

"That's our Pup Niki," Raphael laughed. "You should see him when he's with a bunch of other pups. He's definitely an alpha pup."

"I can believe it," Ryan looked across at Raphael. "He makes it pretty clear what he wants, without any words." Then he turned to Steve. "He must be a handful at times." Steve laughed.

"If you let him, yeah, but he's also pretty well trained. Sometimes you have to be firm. And consistent. You have to be consistent with pups, otherwise they get confused." Ryan turned back to Niki.

"Is it weird, hearing us talk about Pup Niki in front of you?" Niki shook his head.

"No, not really. Not that I'm clinical or anything, but when I'm a pup, I'm a pup, not me. So, anything you say about Pup Niki applies to him, not to me." Ryan slowly nodded his understanding.

"Like you said earlier," Ryan speculated. "It's kind of like meditation for you." Niki nodded.


Mateo loudly flopped on the bed after brushing his teeth, signaling to Ryan that it was time to shut down his laptop and come to bed. Ryan turned and smiled, but turned back to the screen.

"One more minute, Mateo. I promise." Mateo sighed dramatically, making Ryan laugh. "Hey, school is what got me here, and doing well is what will keep me here." As he continued slowly scrolling through his text, Mateo rolled onto his side, supporting his head in his raised left hand, in what was becoming his signature come hither alluring pose. When he hadn't heard anything for a moment, Ryan looked behind him at Mateo. "Oh man ..." Score one for Mateo. Ryan closed his laptop and pounced, wrapping himself around Mateo. Ryan reached up and pulled the hairband off Mateo's mini ponytail, slid one leg between Mateo's and pulled him close as he pressed their lips together. Mateo sighed again, this one muffled by Ryan's kiss. When they parted, they stared quietly into each other's eyes, Ryan running his left hand up and down Mateo's side, from thigh to armpit.

"You have such beautiful skin." Mateo blinked, never having been told that before.

"Me?" Ryan nodded and brushed lips with Mateo again.

"You. You're beautiful. And sweet. And brave. And beautiful." Mateo snorted at the surprising praise.

"Brave? Me?"

"Yeah, you. You're out there almost every day on the front lines, feeding people in a pandemic. Risking your health." Mateo rocked his head back and forth, wordlessly acknowledging Ryan's point.

"Okay. And ... I am lucky," Mateo asserted. Ryan raised his eyebrows in a silent question. "To be loved by you." Ryan smiled.

"No, I'm the lucky one," Ryan countered. "I get to love you. I get to make love to you. Like right now. I owe you one ... for this afternoon." As he spoke, Ryan rolled Mateo over onto his back and scooted down. He lifted Mateo's legs onto his shoulders so he could bury himself between them, sucking and licking Mateo's balls, his cock, his taint, his ass. Back to his cock. The more he tasted the more ravenous he became. Every touch of Ryan's tongue, every lick delivered a subtle but seminal charge to Mateo, who'd never really had sex before Ryan. He'd never fantasized being rimmed because it wasn't even a concept until Ryan had first done it to him, so many months ago. And now here it was again, Ryan submitting himself to what intellectually seemed to Mateo to be beneath Ryan ... beneath anyone, but it felt so good. And Ryan liked it so much. And did it so well. So very well. Mateo was not just sighing anymore, he was moaning. He reached down to touch the top of Ryan's head and brushed his own cock as he reached, and was shocked to feel how hard it was. Everything about this, what Ryan was doing, felt so good. He slid his hand up from Ryan's hair to grab his own cock. He started to jack it, but then felt Ryan's hand on his.

"That's my job, my sweet prince," Ryan said, as he pulled Mateo's hand away, and grabbed hold of Mateo's cock and began slowly pumping as he drove his tongue back into Mateo's ass. As Mateo raised his arm back up, his left hand brushed across his right nipple, releasing a surprising pulse that raced straight to his prostate. Huh. That was nice, he thought. He circled the nipple with his finger. Oh god. He raised his right hand, and soon, both forefingers found their way to both nipples. He was barely touching them, but that combined with Ryan's tongue and Ryan's grip was taking Mateo somewhere he'd never been before. He and Ryan were both making love to his body and it was a thousand times better than any time he'd ever masturbated, even when Ryan was on the other end of the phone masturbating with him. Somehow Ryan was able to reach his other hand up and brush Mateo's hand away from this right nipple, so he could take possession of that part of Mateo's body, too. For a time, Ryan gently teased it with his thumb, maintaining focus on Mateo's cock and ass, until finally Mateo cried out and came. Ryan squeezed Mateo's cock hard, not jerking anymore, just squeezing, as Mateo pumped, dug his heels into Ryan's back and quietly whimpered. Once Mateo finished, Ryan pulled back, slid out from between Mateo's legs and spread them flat beneath him. He put a hand on either side of Mateo's waist, leaned down and licked up most every drop of Mateo's gift. He swallowed Mateo's cock and sucked, making sure it was empty, then crawled up Mateo's sweaty, smooth, brown body, lowered himself, put a hand on either side of Mateo's head and buried his tongue in Mateo's waiting mouth. They laid there, lips sealed with Mateo's cum, breathing together for a small eternity. When they did finally separate, Ryan smiled down at Mateo.

"Did I make my prince happy?" Mateo didn't speak, just nodded slowly, licking his own residue off his lips. Ryan took a deep breath and exhaled slowly. His right hand slid down and caressed Mateo's left ear. "I think you own me, Mateo. You are my prince. And I am your devoted servant."

"But I should be your servant, no?"

'No ..." Ryan continued to slowly caress Mateo's ear. "Do you want to be my servant?" Mateo stared into Ryan's eyes, looking for a clue to the right answer. Ryan's eyes were listening, not talking.

"I don' know. I mean ..." Ryan waited for more, but Mateo wasn't able, or willing, to finish his thought.

"Mateo, I don't want this to sound weird, but I do worship you. Like you're my Mayan Prince, and I am your servant. I take pride in having the honor to be your chosen and devoted love slave. I probably shouldn't be saying any of this, but I want to be honest with you, always, and this is how I feel. Seeing you makes me happy. Touching you makes me ecstatic. Serving you makes me complete. Being away from you made me miserable. How can I not worship you?"

"Can we still be boyfriends?" Ryan laughed, then leaned down and pressed his lips to Mateo's, his hands buried again in Mateo's mane. When he pulled free, Ryan stared again into Mateo's eyes, seeing the uncertainty there. He probably had said too much, too soon.

"We will always be boyfriends, my love. Until, someday ... I hope, we're husbands. Whether you like it or not, Mateo, I will always worship you." Mateo's smile returned. The uncertainty faded from his eyes. He reached up and pulled Ryan tightly into a full body embrace.

"Okay," he whispered into Ryan's ear. "I be your prince."

# Twenty-Four

# DAD'S TRUTH SERUM

As THEY SOMETIMES DID, Alex and Raphael were taking a lunch break together in the kitchen on Friday, sitting across from one another at the island. They were talking shop when Mateo entered from the back stairs.

"You guys busy?" he asked as he took a stool. Raphael nodded a silent order to Alex as he slid the jug of iced tea toward Mateo. Alex jumped up and grabbed a glass for Mateo from the cabinet.

"What's up, muchacho?" Alex asked as he retook his seat. Mateo sighed through a deep breath as he poured.

"I maybe really happy or ... maybe nervous? Is nervous right?"

"En español, amigo," Alex prompted. They decided 'nervous' was good enough.

"Ryan tol' me he worships me," Mateo confessed. Alex and Raphael exchanged amused looks. "There is more."

"Spill," Alex commanded, putting down his glass and giving Mateo his full attention.

"He say I am his Mayan prince and he wants to be my servant. My love slave."

"ooooOOOooo," Alex looked wickedly at Raphael.

"You say that like it's a bad thing," Raphael responded.

"I don' know what it is," Mateo replied uncertainly.

"When did he say this?" Alex probed. "What were you talking about when he said it?"

"Not talking ... doing sex." Mateo couldn't help but smile at the memory. "Really good sex." Both Raphael and Alex broke into laughter, hearing this confession from the normally discrete Mateo.

"Okay, in that case, maybe it was just the hormones talking," Alex offered when he recovered.

"I don't know," Raphael countered. "Ryan studies this stuff. He probably sees more in Mateo's Latin good looks and demeanor than we do." Raphael leaned back and made a show of examining Mateo more critically. "Yeah, I can see it."

"And what do you see, he asked," asked Alex.

"Mayan royalty. I can't believe I didn't see it before." Alex looked at Mateo and rolled his eyes.

"Enter the academician," Niki announced as he entered from the foyer, his tablet in hand. "Not that I'm complaining, but I overheard what you guys were saying from my study." He pronounced the words 'my study' with an imperious affectation. He sat next to Mateo and rotated his tablet so Mateo could see the screen. "Here's a map of Mexico and Central America. Where did your parents immigrate from, muchacho?"

"Ummm, here. Mérida."

"Aha," Niki said, meaningfully. "And where else do you have family there?" Mateo pointed to several other spots in the Yucatan. Niki looked up at Alex and wiggled his eyebrows. "Ryan's right. Mateo is Mayan. He might as well be from Chichén Itzá." As the other three talked, Niki quietly continued his research on his tablet.

"Have you talked to Ryan about being from the Yucatan?" Alex asked. Mateo shook his head.

"No. I don' think ..."

"Well, either Ryan's just guessing or," Alex turned to Raphael, "once again, you were right." Raphael flashed his Cheshire grin.

"I don' know how to be Ryan's prince," a slightly troubled Mateo muttered, looking at Alex as he sipped his tea.

"Remember what we've talked about, muchacho," Alex counseled. "Talk. Listen. Ask questions. Obviously, you two are communicating a lot more than you used to ... so let Ryan guide you."

"Raphael," Mateo turned his way. "Umm, oh never mind."

"What?" Raphael leaned forward. "Don't do that to me ... what?"

"Umm," Mateo took another deep breath, "are you Luke's love slave?" Alex shrieked while Niki gave Raphael a sly look. Raphael's eyes widened, before he grinned.

"I get it. Hey ... it's a valid question, guys. The cage, the collar, the harness. I do call him Sir, and he is my Sir. Credit Mateo for deductive reasoning." Alex reached over and patted Mateo's hand.

"That was a very good question," he intoned, humoring both Raphael and Mateo.

"You know, Mateo, I never thought about it that way, but ... in some ways, yeah, I am Luke's sex slave. I'm also his lover. I'm his husband. And ... sometimes he's *my* sex slave." That got Niki's attention. "Mateo, we're lucky to be alive here and now. We can be whatever we want to be, when we want to be it. It's not like a couple thousand years ago, when, if Ryan was your sex slave, he could never be anything else. He can be your sex slave one day, and you can be his the next." Mateo looked thoughtful. "Mateo, a lot of what we do is just role-playing. You know ... pretend. To make things interesting. I mean, yeah, I'm Luke's Locked Cock Boy, like my tattoo says, and I always will be, but most of all I'm his husband. His partner. His equal." Mateo nodded. "Would you like to be Ryan's sex slave?" A slight smile appeared on Mateo's heretofore all too serious face.

"Maybe. Sometimes?" Raphael flashed Mateo a thumbs up.

"Muchacho, just have fun," Alex advised. "Like I said, follow Ryan's lead." Mateo nodded, slid off the stool and placed his glass in the sink.

"I go to work," Mateo said. As he passed back behind Alex, who confirmed Mateo would be home in time for dinner, he put a hand on either of Alex's shoulders and kissed his neck just below his curls. He flashed a grin at Raphael, then Niki on his way to the back stairs.

"Guys," Niki looked up from his tablet, "this is all really pretty interesting. You'll like this, Raphael ... the Mayan's perfected chocolate." Raphael wiggled his eyebrows at Alex in acknowledgment. "And Ryan is right ... Mayan princes did have sex slaves. Get this ... they wore only loincloths, not just the slaves, but usually even the princes, except for ceremonial purposes. Kind of like our fundoshi." He looked up from his tablet. "This could be kind of cool, to have a prince and his sex slave in the house. Along with the locked cock leather boys and ... a puppy."

"Sure," Raphael stood and carried his dishes to the dishwasher. "As long as we don't practice any of those ceremonial rituals."

"What do you mean," Alex asked, joining Raphael.

"Sweetie, the Mayan appeased their gods with human sacrifice." Alex tossed his hands in the air.

"Don't tell me any more. I was happy just knowing about sex slaves in loincloths." As Alex headed for the back stairs, Niki continued his report.

"They were cannibals, too."

"La la la la la," Alex chanted loudly as he climbed the stairs.

Luke, Raphael, Juan and Ricky were steaming up the gym, when Alex appeared at the door. It was his and Greg's turn to be in charge of dinner.

"We're thinking of doing a twist on Greg's lasagna, stuffed cannelloni. It'll be faster. Sound good?"

"Sounds yummy," Raphael replied, standing over Luke's bench, spotting him. "Is Greg secretly Italian?" Alex laughed.

"No, he just loves pasta. Besides, he found a hand crank pasta maker in one of the kitchen cabinets and he's been dying to try it out.

"Home made fresh pasta?" Juan said. "Count me in. You guys need any help?" Alex shook his head and disappeared. Thirty minutes later, as they finished their workouts and gathered their towels, Raphael stopped Juan on his way out of the gym.

"Juan, maybe I shouldn't say anything, but Mateo didn't say not to talk about it ..." That sounded serious to Juan, who sat back down on the nearest bench. Ricky sat on his lap, wrapping an arm around Juan's neck. Luke sat on the other bench, wondering what was coming. Raphael sat cross legged on his towel on the floor in front of Juan and Ricky and told them about Mateo's conversation.

"A Mayan prince," Juan repeated. He took a deep breath as he rubbed a hand up and down Ricky's slick torso. "If I didn't know Ryan, and his history with Mateo, I would think that was ... racist."

"I know." Raphael agreed. "But we know he's not. He wouldn't be here, with all of us, if he was. He adores Mateo. He wants to be the sex slave, not Mateo. I think it's his way of not just loving him, but introducing an element of power exchange into their relationship, like he sees in all of ours."

"Otherwise, he and Mateo are the boring 'straight' gay guys in the house?" Juan asked. Raphael made a 'maybe' face.

"It may not be that calculated," Luke suggested. "He's an anthropologist in the making. Maybe it's a culture, if that's the right word, that he's studied and admires. Besides, lots of straight men call their wives and girlfriends 'princess.'

"Ahem," Raphael darted a look at Luke. "Not to mention everyone here has witnessed you calling a certain locked cock boy 'princess' as well." Luke looked like he was having trouble recalling said incident. Raphael looked back up at Juan. "So, maybe it's not such an odd thing after all. I just bring it up because it threw Mateo, and I know he looks to you for guidance, just like he does with Alex. I thought you should know. I really don't think it's a big deal." Juan nodded.

"I'll, uh, I won't say anything." He looked at Ricky, "*We* won't say anything. If Mateo brings it up, we'll listen. But I agree. I don't think it's a big deal. I don't know what privileges Mayan princes enjoy, but it might be kind of fun for Mateo." Ricky chuckled.

"Yeah, Papito," he said to Juan. "If you were Mayan, I'd want to be your sex slave." Juan grasped Ricky as he stood up.

"You *are* my sex slave, mijo. And my prince." He looked back at Luke. "It's complicated ..."

"This was a keeper, Greg," Steve said as he laid his fork across his plate. "That was probably the first time I've had fresh homemade pasta, except maybe in a couple of high-end restaurants. We should never do dried pasta again." Alex grinned at Greg as he placed a hand over Greg's.

"Yeah, sweetie, you've spoiled us now. You're doomed."

"Not bad for my first attempt, I'll admit," Greg smiled. "Actually, it wasn't that hard, so, sure, maybe we'll try homemade fettucine next time. After all, we do have the technology."

"If anything with a hand crank can be called 'technology,'" Alex, the IT guy, contended.

"Call it what you like, I give it five stars," Luke pronounced. "Listen, guys, unless Niki and Ryan have pressing homework, I was thinking of instituting a new, periodic event in the turret room after dinner. It's the one room we really haven't taken advantage of yet. Is that okay?" Curious glances were exchanged, including from Raphael, but no one objected. "Let's clear the table first. Raphael and I will do the clean up later. This'll take maybe half an hour." As everyone stood and began gathering plates and utensils, Alex leaned into Raphael.

"What's up?"

"I have no idea."

"Think it's a dare?"

"You think? No ... well, I guess we'll find out." In the kitchen, it was Luke's turn to lean into Raphael and mutter.

"Hang back, baby, I'll need your help to carry something up with us." Raphael nodded silently. Everyone else climbed up the three flights of stairs and positioned themselves, most cross-legged, on the floor in a circle around the room, their backs to windows revealing a dusky evening. It was Ryan's first time up the narrow flight of stairs.

"This is pretty cool," he said as he walked around the circle, checking out the view, before settling down next to Mateo. "How come we've never been up here before?"

"We come up every night after you two go to bed," Niki confided. "We perform our secret rituals up here." Ryan pretended to believe him.

"That's what I've been hearing ..." Ricky laughed, reached over and slapped Ryan's thigh. Raphael topped the stairs, carrying a tray with ten 'rocks' glasses, followed by Luke bearing a bottle and a carafe. As Raphael walked around handing each family member a glass, Luke sat in the open space between Steve and Ryan. As soon as Raphael joined him, all eyes fell on Luke, who held up the bottle 'show and tell' style.

"This is what my dad and I call 'truth serum.'" At that Raphael reached over and grabbed the bottle from Luke and began examining it. Clearly, he was not in on whatever this was. "It was on an evening much like this that my dad poured us each a glass of his favorite single malt Scotch, one that his dad had introduced him to, and had a heart-to-heart talk with me. He toasted me and we each took a sip, and then he asked me if I was gay. He said I had to tell the truth because I'd just downed truth serum." Luke looked around the circle for reactions, but everyone was taking him at face value, at least so far. "Like all dad jokes, it was kinda lame, but at the same time it made it pretty obvious he wanted me to be honest and he wasn't judging. It worked. We talked. We laughed. I cried. We hugged." Luke took the bottle back from Raphael and began to open it. "Anyway, ever since, I've always tried to have a bottle of this stashed away."

"What is it?" Juan asked.

"Aberlour A'bundah Alba," Luke looked up at Juan and smiled.

"Easy for you to say," Greg laughed. Luke, who'd sounded pretty intense so far, laughed, too.

"Well, it's Scotch. It's Gaelic for 'The Original.' This particular whiskey is made exactly the way the original founder made it. So, Alex, not too much 'technology' goes into it." Luke poured an inch into Raphael's glass, then into Ryan's on his right. Then he reached across Ryan to Mateo for his glass, and so on until everyone had been served. Luke held up his glass. "Even though we all live together, we've all been awfully busy lately, so I thought it would be good if we took a moment to stop and check in with one other. Instead of using a talking stick, I thought 'truth serum' would be tastier and a lot more fun." Luke raised his glass a bit higher, then put it to his lips and sipped. As Juan sipped, he made eye contact with Mateo, who was watching Juan. Juan winked as Mateo gingerly took a sip. After he'd tasted, Steve held his glass toward Luke.

"Mmmmm. Very, very nice. This was a capital idea, old boy." Niki rolled his eyes.

"Steve," Niki said, "it's Scotch. From Scotland, not England. You've watched too many Sherlock Holmes movies."

"It's okay, Niki," Luke replied. "He likes it, and that's all I care about. I may be wrong, but I don't think you can watch too much Sherlock Holmes, whether with Basil Rathbone, Jeremy Brett or Benedict Cumberbatch." Raphael mouthed 'Jeremy Brett.'

"Thank you, Luke," Ryan said as he casually rubbed Mateo's back, their thighs touching. "I've never tasted Scotch before. Yet another first for me here in the House of the Locked Cock Brotherhood."

"You're welcome, Ryan," Luke replied. "I brought water in case anyone wanted to add a few drops. Some people think it helps bring out more flavor." He set the carafe in the middle of the circle. "So, who wants to go first?"

"Based on our conversation yesterday," Niki spoke up, "I think Ryan should go first. We joked about how the House of the Locked Cock Brotherhood is like a fraternity and Ryan and Mateo are our pledges. This could be part of his initiation."

"Fraternity?" Alex interjected. "Yeah! I never thought of it that way, but with two undergrads under our roof, it kind of is." He smiled and took another sip.

"How about it, Ryan," Niki pressed. "What does Luke's truth serum compel you to share with us?"

"Do I really have to go first?" Ryan resisted. He looked painfully at Mateo. "I'm not sure what we're doing ... besides tasting this." As a delaying tactic he put his glass to his lips and took another sip.

"I'll go, but you have to go next, Ryan," Greg said. "I'm not sure what we're doing either, but I have a question." He turned to Juan. "How long are you planning to grow your hair, Juan?" He turned to Luke. "I've been wanting to know for weeks now, but I didn't have the balls to ask." He raised his glass of truth serum to support his contention, then sipped. Juan took a sip and savored it, making Greg, and everyone else, wait for his answer. After he swallowed and smiled at Luke in appreciation, he turned to Greg as he put his arm around Ricky's shoulders.

"You'll have to ask this guy here. He asked me to let it grow, so that's what I'm doing. It's up to Ricky." Greg turned his gaze to Ricky, who looked briefly guilty before beaming back at Greg.

"When he was a teenager, Juan had a ponytail down to here," Ricky put his hand halfway down Juan's back. "He was a sexy skater dude!" A surprised look came over both Juan's and Greg's faces.

"How do you know I was sexy?" Juan, smiling coyly, asked Ricky.

"Like that's even a question," Alex said. Ricky nodded in agreement.

"I didn't know I get to decide how long we'll grow it," Ricky continued, "so, I'm not sure, Greg. I guess we'll all find out, you know?" No one spoke immediately, each sipping, savoring. Greg turned back to Luke.

"Well, Luke, I think your dad's serum works. Now we know Juan was a sexy skater dude with a ponytail." Luke nodded approvingly as Greg focused on Ryan. "Okay, Ryan, you're up!" Ryan cleared his throat, then set his glass down on the floor in front of him. He looked around the circle before speaking, then landed on Niki.

"This really is how I imagine an initiation might be, without the hazing ... which I really appreciate, guys." Luke nudged Ryan.

"The night's still young," he kidded.

"Umm, anyway," Ryan kept his gaze on Niki, "I wanted to ask my fellow underclassman about school. How's it going? Do you like your instructors? Made any friends yet?" Niki grinned.

"School's great! I aced my first quiz." Steve reached over and clinked glasses with Niki. "Yeah, instructors are smart, and nice. New friends? Not yet. It's not gonna happen, probably, over a laptop. That's my only complaint ... not being in an actual classroom."

"It'll happen," Steve consoled him. "Until then, you have us. And the most impressive study hall of any of your classmates, I'll bet." Niki clinked glasses with Steve again in agreement. Steve turned to Luke.

"It's funny, but the day Niki and I discovered this turret room he fantasized about the family coming up here after dinner for dessert and cognac." He turned back to Niki. "What do you think? Is your dream still intact with a rare Scotch and revelations instead?"

"Even better," was Niki's reply. "So, I guess it's my turn, huh?" Luke nodded. Niki looked at Raphael, mischief dancing in his eyes.

"I've been wanting to ask this for weeks, so, thanks for the truth serum, Luke. Raphael ... how were you and Luke able to have great sex when you were both locked up?" Raphael's eyes widened as he turned to Luke, who looked up at the concave ceiling, pretending innocence or ignorance, or maybe hoping someone would change the subject. Fat chance. Ryan turned in his spot, giving his full attention to Raphael, clearly interested in the answer. Mateo leaned forward, his right arm over Ryan's right shoulder, resting his chin on Ryan's left shoulder, apparently just as intrigued.

"I guess we're done with the warm up questions," Steve laughed. Luke shook his head helplessly.

"Well, Sir, since this little séance was your idea, I think *you* should answer Niki's question." Raphael was leaning against Luke, his lips centimeters away from Luke's ear, the Scotch already loosening his inhibitions.

"Umm, I'd rather hear you tell it, baby," Luke said as he turned to face Raphael, their lips now tentatively touching.

"I think they're going to give us a demonstration instead," Alex said hopefully. Both Raphael and Luke began chuckling before Raphael turned to Alex, eyebrows wiggling.

"No demos tonight, Alex, sweetie. Okay, fine, Sir, you may be sorry, but I'll 'splain how it's done. One more sip." Raphael made a show of savoring another sip of his Scotch, then he described how he and Brutus managed to induce a hands-free orgasm in Luke on the very first try.

"WHAT!?!" Ricky exclaimed. "Your first time, Luke?" He turned to Juan. "Man, that's just not fair!" Juan wrapped an arm around Ricky's neck and nuzzled him.

"I want to meet this 'Brutus,'" Alex insisted. "Did you say fourteen inches?" He looked down at Greg's currently flaccid cock, then back at Raphael. "I'm serious. As soon as we're done here." Greg made eye contact with Luke, who once again simply shook his head.

"Hey, Alex," Ricky grinned. "Maybe there's one in the dungeon?"

"Sorry, guys," Steve said, "I did a pretty thorough inventory one day when Niki was asleep in his cage. No Brutus. No Son of Brutus, even." To hopefully put an end to this topic, Luke picked up the bottle and held it out, offering a refresher to anyone. Juan held out his glass, followed by Alex, then Greg. Luke poised it over Raphael's glass, who put his hand over it, palm down, indicating 'I'm good.'

"So, it's my turn?" This time Luke nodded affirmatively. Raphael took a sip, then a long, deep breath. He leaned forward to look around Luke. "Ryan, since this is your and Mateo's 'initiation' ceremony into the House of the Locked Cock Brotherhood fraternity, do you have any thoughts ... hopes ... plans on how you and Mateo might ... evolve, to use one of Alex's favorite words ... as the semester goes on?" They made eye contact. Raphael looked curious, encouraging. Ryan screwed his face up thoughtfully, perhaps a little uncertain. "Or, are you happy with things just the way they are?" Alex leaned forward, putting both elbows on his knees, cupping his face in his hands, focused on Ryan and Mateo, who let his arm drop down around Ryan's waist as he lifted his head off Ryan's shoulder. More than anyone else, he, too, was curious to hear what Ryan might say. No one spoke as Ryan took a moment to think. He turned from Raphael to look into Mateo's eyes, which produced an involuntary smile for both. When Ryan turned back to Raphael he was still smiling.

"Wow. That is a really deep question. Is it okay if I don't have a specific answer, Raphael?" Raphael nodded silently. After another pause, Ryan glanced at Luke before resuming eye contact with Raphael. "I guess the truth is, I've never been happier than I am right now. I mean, being here. Waking up every morning next to Mateo seems unreal ... I waited so long for that to happen and now it is my reality. Our reality. And to be able to share this house with all of you." He looked around the circle, aware that everyone was listening to his every word. "Am I happy with the way things are, Raphael? No ... happy doesn't begin to describe it. Do I want more for us ... for Mateo and me? Yes ... yes." He turned back to Mateo, whose slightly parted lips, still wet from the Scotch, reflected the dimming light coming through the windows, distracting him enough that he couldn't help himself. He pressed his lips to Mateo's, blotting away the shine and, to no one's surprise, producing a trademark Rigid Ryan boner. Without looking away from Mateo, he finished his answer. "I have some ideas, Raphael, on how we might evolve, and living with all of you, the possibilities are kind of endless, if you know what I mean. This is one kinky fraternity. But for now, if you don't mind, that's between Mateo and me. You'll just have to wait and see. I know you, and everyone here, will support us." Mateo nodded somberly. "We're counting on you. All of you." Ryan again pressed his lips to Mateo's, indicating his answer was complete.

"Well said," Juan spoke. "I think Mateo is in good hands, Raphael."

"That was never in doubt," Raphael replied, then lifted his glass to drain the last few drops.

"You're right, Juan," Luke raised up on his knees and reached for the still full water carafe. "That was what is known as a cliff hanger, and a good note to end on this evening. Thank you, everyone, for indulging me."

"So, are we going to do this again?" Niki asked.

"I hope so," Ricky voted.

"How about it?" Luke looked around the circle. "I'll bring the truth serum."

"Count me in," Greg said." Alex nodded as he stood, then reached down to offer an assist to Greg. As everyone else began to stand, Niki looked over at Ryan and smiled as he spoke.

"Since we're all here, we might as well begin the nightly ritual." Ryan grinned back.

"That was funny the first time," Alex said over his shoulder as he began descending the stairs. "The secret to comedy, Niki, is knowing when to stop."

"Everybody's a critic," Niki whined to Steve, who ruffled Niki's mohawk as he guided him toward the stairs. Raphael and Luke gathered the remaining glasses and headed to the kitchen to do the clean up as promised. As Raphael was rinsing dishes and loading the dishwasher, Luke was scraping remnants from the baking dish into the compost bin.

"You didn't get what you were hoping for, did you, baby?" he teased as he joined Raphael at the sink.

"What?"

"Ryan ... he didn't really answer your question."

"In a way he did. Sir ..." Raphael gave Luke a coy smile. "He wouldn't have asked for our support if he was hoping he and Mateo were going to be picture perfect vanilla lovers forever. Don'tcha think?" Luke landed a peck on Raphael's cheek.

"That's my boy ... the eternal optimist."

"Realist ... I keep telling you. Now, go finish up in the dining room. Sir. After all, volunteering KP duty was your idea."

# Twenty-Five

# PLANNING A BIRTHDAY CEREMONY

LUKE WAS WALKING BEHIND Raphael, his arms around Raphael's waist, his cock teasing Raphael's butt, as they entered their room. Raphael was in mid-sentence ... something about buying it by the case ... when he stopped short. Surprisingly, well, maybe not that surprisingly, Alex was sitting on their bed, patiently waiting.

"Can Brutus come out and play?"

"Alex!" Raphael reacted. "Jeez. Seriously?" Alex stood, grinning.

"Yes, Raphael. I was serious. I can't wait to meet this fantastic lover who induces first time locked cock orgasms. Can you blame me?" Luke freed Raphael.

"Baby, you know Alex. He isn't going to let this go." He gave Alex a faux condescending look as he patted Raphael's butt. "It's just a toy, Alex." Raphael opened the closet and rummaged a moment, then turned and presented Brutus, splayed across both hands as if it were a precious, magical dagger. Alex's eyes widened as he approached Raphael and reached out to take hold of it.

"A toy?" He turned to Luke. "If this is a toy, then the Queen Mary is a dingy. Holy crap! No wonder you came the first time. I'm surprised you lived to tell the tale!" He turned back to Raphael. "Man, you guys don't kid around, do you?"

"What?" Raphael was genuinely confused. "It's just a strap-on."

"Yeah, and the Salesforce Tower is just a building." He turned back to Luke. "Luke, you took this? Your first time? I. Am. Impressed." He turned Brutus around a couple of times, gauging its girth. He handed it back to Raphael and adopted an almost little boy tone of voice. "Would it be okay if I borrowed him sometime?"

"Are you saying Greg isn't always enough for you?" Luke asked. "I mean ..."

"Oh hell, yes," Alex laughed. "I, uh, well, I was thinking of using it on *him*." Both Luke and Raphael looked at each other, further confused. "For a special occasion. A surprise. Don't say anything. If, uh ... boy ... if he can even take it." He reached out and once again curled his fingers around Brutus." Raphael chuckled.

"Here, take it, sweetie. I'm not planning on locking up Luke in the very near future." He looked past Alex at Luke again and winked. Luke sat on the bed, bowing out of any further discussion.

"Um ... Greg may step out of the shower any minute and I don't want to risk him seeing Brutus yet."

"Here," Raphael walked over to Luke and bent down and slid Brutus under the bed, between Luke's feet. "We'll leave him right there. When the time is right, you'll know where to find him." When he stood up, Alex pulled him into a hug. He looked over Raphael's shoulder at Luke.

"Thanks. You guys are great. And always an inspiration." He landed a quick peck on Raphael's cheek, and then he was gone. Raphael sat down next to Luke.

"Hmmm," Raphael sighed.

"So now we're sharing toys with Alex and Greg?" Raphael turned and gave Luke a frustrated look.

"What was I supposed to do? It was the only way to get rid of him."

"Actually, now that I think about it ..." Luke gave Raphael a sly grin.

"Oh, no, Sir. We're not giving up total custody of Brutus." Raphael stared noncommittally at Luke a few seconds before a knowing smile expanded across his face. "You have to admit, Brutus has been awfully good to you." Luke tried to maintain a straight face, but staring into Raphael's eyes soon made that impossible. He turned, wrapped an arm around Raphael's chest and forced him onto his back. He hovered his face above Raphael's a moment, taking in the beauty he found there, before leaning down and administering a quick, gentle kiss. The kind that usually inspired more to follow. He lifted his face to break the seal.

"It's you, baby, who's been awfully good to me. Brutus was quite incidental." Raphael smiled and batted his 'fuck me' eyelashes.

"Well, Sir, since we've been drinking truth serum, I guess I'll have to take you at your word. Now, why don't you close the door, so you can take me ... well, just take me ..."


Greg was watering plants in the back garden Sunday afternoon, which some might have considered a chore, but he enjoyed it. He didn't, for a minute, miss having to mow a lawn, shovel snow, or clean out gutters like he and Alex had been obligated to do before moving from the Midwest to San Francisco. Keeping the drought tolerant plantings healthy and happy was a breeze by comparison. Hiroshi still liked to handle the more intricate transplanting and pruning, but he was happy to delegate the regular hydration to Greg. At the sound of the back door, he turned to see Steve approaching, two iced teas in hand.

"Thanks," Greg said as he took one with his free hand. He nodded to the 'shrub' he was watering. "Where Alex and I come from a jade plant like this would strictly be a houseplant and a fraction of this size."

"Yeah, everything thrives here," Steve nodded. "Including you and Alex. Do you miss the seasons?"

"It was always so extreme. A hundred and twenty-degree shift in temps between summer and winter. Ice storms. Ninety-eight percent humidity. Have you ever shoveled snow?" Steve shook his head. "You haven't missed anything. I guess maybe I do miss the occasional thunderstorm. Those can be cathartic."

"Cathartic? Don't they usually portend disaster in movies?"

"Yeah, but in real life, they're dramatic and kind of fun sometimes. Mother nature puts on a show, lowers the temperature, cleans the air, and the ground. I'm talking a good thunderstorm, not a violent one. I haven't heard a clap of thunder or seen a bolt of lightning since we moved here."

"You haven't seen much rain either for that matter. Let's hope we have an El Niño winter. You won't have to do this so often if we do." Greg nodded before moving on to the Mexican Fan Palm. Steve followed along. "So, Greg ... next week is Juan's birthday, and if you remember, it was his idea to 'celebrate' birthdays in the dungeon." Greg released the trigger on the hose, stopping its flow, then dropped it. He polished off his tea, revealing a broad grin as he lowered the glass.

"I take it you have an idea of how we should celebrate?"

"Not exactly. When it comes to the dungeon, Juan's really the most experienced in the family, with maybe Luke as runner up." He paused, not sure at first if what he was about to propose was reasonable, but then decided to say it. "But we do know someone who not only has plenty of dungeon experience, but knows Juan pretty well, too." It only took Greg half a second to react.

"Hiroshi!" He looked over the privacy fence at the second story of Hiroshi's house, then back at Steve. "Do you think he'd have any ideas?"

"He handled Niki's discipline pretty well. I think it's worth asking him."

"You know him better than I do. Let me know what he says. This could be good ..." Steve nodded and headed back into the house as Greg picked up the hose and resumed tending the garden. As he finished and was cranking the hose onto the storage reel, Steve returned, phone in hand.

"Hiroshi can see us now," he announced.

"I'm kind of grubby," Greg looked down at his muddy feet.

"He's meeting us in the garden. You're fine." Steve headed to the gate and opened it, while Greg hosed off his feet before following. Steve held the gate open for Greg, who found Hiroshi spreading a cloth in the shade, not quite as naked as the two of them. The fundoshi he sported was solid black.

"Greg! Steve ... good to see you, my friends. What would you like to drink?"

"We're fine, Hiroshi," Steve said as he sat. "We don't want to take too much of your time. And I should apologize for not seeing more of you lately. Niki's studies are dominating everything, and there hasn't been much time for anything else."

"I understand," Hiroshi sat, cross-legged, facing Steve. Greg positioned himself with his butt on the cloth, but his feet in the grass, still worried about making a mess.

"Yeah, but we need to have you over for dinner again," Greg offered. "I'm sure Mateo misses you, too."

"How is he?" Hiroshi inquired with a twinkle in his eyes. "And his budding romance."

"When they're together, they're inseparable," Steve said. "But Ryan is a serious student, too, and of course Mateo works, too much sometimes. But, it's actually Juan that we wanted to talk to you about." Hiroshi didn't say anything, just looked at Steve patiently. "I hope this doesn't come across wrong ..." Hiroshi said nothing, but his patient continence invited Steve to continue. "Ummm ..."

"What Steve is trying to say," Greg spoke up, "is we could use your advice on how to celebrate Juan's birthday in the dungeon next week." A slight smile appeared on Hiroshi's face.

"Ahh. I see."

"It was Juan's idea, many weeks ago, that we should celebrate birthdays in the dungeon," Steve was now more comfortable sharing with Hiroshi. "You know the dungeon better than any of us, and you know what Juan might enjoy, if you know what I mean." Hiroshi's smile grew. "We want whatever we do to be worthy of Juan." Hiroshi didn't respond immediately, seemingly lost in thought. Greg began to worry if their request was out of line. Hiroshi shifted in place before speaking, making eye contact with both of them.

"As I think you know, I consider the dungeon as something of a sacred space ..."

"Oh, we know," Steve said, reaching his right hand out in show of peace. "If this seems like a bad idea ..."

"On the contrary, Steve," Hiroshi interrupted, "I am honored you thought of me. Juan and I have shared some memorable times in the dungeon, you are right. This celebration ... would everyone in the family be present?"

"That's the idea, yeah. Why?"

"Well, Juan does have some remarkable talents, shall we say, and I do enjoy helping him achieve the kinds of ecstasy he has been known to revel in. But I would not want to frighten the younger ones."

"What are you suggesting?" Greg looked worried. "Ritual piercing? Knife play?"

"No, no, Greg. Nothing like that. Perhaps I'm being overly protective." Hiroshi paused again, thinking. "Are you looking for suggestions, or are you inviting me to 'show Juan a good time' myself?" Greg looked at Steve for guidance.

"We want this to be special for Juan," he said. "I don't think we necessarily expected you to have to do anything ... but if you want to, that would be amazing. I'm sure Juan would enjoy sharing his birthday with you, Hiroshi. We don't want to burden you ..."

"It would be a pleasure and an honor, not a burden, my friend. Let me give it a little thought. I have something in mind already. So, the idea is to make this a rewarding experience for Juan." Both Steve and Greg nodded. "Let's talk again. When is the celebration?"

"His birthday is Thursday. But we don't have to do it that exact day," Steve replied.

"Without revealing any plans," Hiroshi conspired, "find out if Thursday works for everyone. It is okay if Juan knows you are planning something for him ... since this was his idea, he probably expects it, but let us keep my involvement a secret from him. That will make it all the more special." Hiroshi winked, clearly becoming more motivated with each passing moment.

"Ah ... a conspiracy!" Steve said smiling. He nudged Greg. "I like where this is going." He turned to Hiroshi. "Thank you, Hiroshi. I'm glad we talked. I really didn't know what we might do, but with you in charge, I know it'll be special."

"Yes," Hiroshi agreed. "A special day for a very special friend."


At dinner that evening, Steve decided to start the ball rolling.

"Has anyone looked at the birthday list in the kitchen lately?" he casually asked. Juan smirked but said nothing.

"Juan's birthday is next Thursday!" Ricky announced, beaming at Juan. He had probably been counting the days.

"So, Juan, how do we celebrate birthdays in the House of the Locked Cock Brotherhood?" Steve prodded.

"I think we all know the answer to that," Juan replied, leaning back in his chair as Ricky turned his beaming smile to everyone else around the table.

"I don't," Ryan volunteered. He turned to Mateo, who just smiled and wiggled his eyebrows, leaving Ryan still clueless.

"Ryan," Luke said, "you're in for a treat. It was Juan's idea that we celebrate birthdays in the dungeon. I don't know if he realized at the time that he would be first celebrant, but I think it's pretty fitting, don't you Juan?"

"Uh ... yeah, sure," he replied, half smiling. "So ... Steve, it sounds like you might have a plan on how this will go?" Steve simply smiled at Juan, poker faced. "Is that a yes?"

"Let's just say," Steve relented, "that the committee is utilizing all available resources to ensure your birthday will be one for the ages." At the same time he and Greg exchanged knowing glances, Raphael and Luke exchanged clueless ones.

"The committee?" Juan and Raphael asked in unison. "Available resources?" Juan continued.

"We need to confirm everyone's availability," Greg said. "Is everyone free next Thursday evening?" No one, it seemed, had a conflict. As if anyone had anything approaching a social calendar in 2020.

"Unless something unexpected happens at the hospital," Juan cautioned, maybe serious, maybe teasing.

"Well, if so, we'll reschedule, Juan," Steve pronounced. "This isn't happening without you."


Juan and Ricky were often the first to turn in, given Juan's insanely early mornings. Ricky always slid into bed with Juan, snuggling, until Juan drifted off, then sometimes he would slip away for another hour or more, socializing with other family members or watching something on TV in Greg and Alex's room. Yet another advantage to having everyone under the same roof. Later, he'd silently return, wrap himself around Juan and drift away himself. Tonight, Juan had a pressing question as they curled up together, facing each other, legs intertwined.

"Mijo, I assume you are on the 'committee' with Steve ... and whoever else for this birthday celebration?" Ricky grinned and fingered Juan's right nipple ring. He answered honestly as they gazed into each other's eyes.

"I know nothing, Papito."

"You expect me to believe that? You certainly knew my birthday is next week."

"Of course I know when your birthday is. I've been looking forward to it. Maybe more than you! But, really ... I don't know what Steve was talking about. Are you excited, Papito?"

"Am I going to have to tickle it out of you?" Juan slid a hand down Ricky's side, his thumb bumping along the ridges of Ricky's abs.

"Honest! I really don't know," Ricky laughed in anticipation of Juan's next move. "Even if I did, I wouldn't tell you. That would spoil the surprise. Best Locked Cock Leather Boys don't spoil surprises, you know." He gave Juan a stern look, at the same time he released Juan's nipple and reached down and wrapped his hand around Juan's cock. "We do things like this ..." He began to slide down under the covers, intent on swallowing Juan. Juan pulled him back up to eye level.

"No, Mijo, it's too late. I need to sleep." He wrapped a hand around the shaved back of Ricky's head and pulled until their lips met. After a couple of mint flavored moments, he pulled free. "Tell you what, though. Now that you mention it, we still haven't taken the next step of your leather boy training that we talked about. Maybe tomorrow evening, if the dungeon's free, we can do something. What do you think?"

"Yes, Sir!" Ricky leaned forward on his own to deliver another kiss. "I'll start my deliveries early so I can end early. Now, go to sleep Papito." Ricky playfully pushed Juan away. "I love you."

"Love you more," Juan replied as always, then rolled over on his side, facing away. Ricky snuggled up, wrapped an arm around Juan's waist and patiently waited until Juan's breathing signaled that it was time to find out more about Juan's birthday celebration. He first crept upstairs to Steve and Niki's room, but the door was open and they weren't there. Two flights down he found them in the library, in front of the fire and, not surprisingly, sipping cognac. Steve was in the chair that had the best view of the doorway.

"Ricky!" He waved him in. "Would you like a snifter?"

"No thanks," Ricky smiled as he slid into place on the floor at Niki's feet. "I don't mean to interrupt."

"You're not interrupting," Niki said. "We're just relaxing in front of the fire, sipping cognac in our grand old house, like a grand old married couple." Ricky ran a hand up and down Niki's calf as he looked over at Steve.

"Yeah. It's pretty wonderful, isn't it." He looked up at Niki. "Not that you're really an old married couple. That's only half right." No one said anything for a moment. "The fire feels good." After another pause, Ricky got to his point. "Juan thinks I know what you're planning for his birthday." Steve chuckled. "So ... what are you planning? I won't tell ..."

"Ricky, I guarantee you won't tell. Because, I won't tell. Because I don't know what we're doing either." Ricky scooted around to face both Steve and Niki, his back to the fire.

"So, who does know?"

"You won't tell?"

"Promise."

"Greg and I are working with Hiroshi." Ricky leaned back, supporting himself with both hands on the hearth behind him.

"Oh, wow. You guys are wicked. Of course ... he and Juan used to ... this is perfect!" Steve nodded before taking a sip.

"So, none of us will know what will happen?"

"We're going to meet with Hiroshi before Thursday, so, yeah we'll know before then. I think. We'll probably need to do some kind of preparation. Niki and I were talking, we should have some food afterward, don't you think? Maybe a cake? Juan's not big on sweets, is he?"

"Just me," Ricky grinned. Niki reached his right foot out and tapped it on Ricky's left foot.

"Maybe Hiroshi's planning on having Juan 'eat you up' for his birthday," Niki speculated. He turned to Steve. "That could be fun to watch."

"I was thinking more like carrot cake," Steve deadpanned. "Maybe cupcakes?"

"Let's do cupcakes," Ricky replied. "I know the perfect bakery for them. Also, unless someone has found my stash, I have some Mexican Chocolate ice cream hidden in one of the freezers."

"Okay, then," Steve said, "dessert's covered. Maybe I can get Raphael and Alex to be in charge of the savory part." Ricky nodded.

"This is going to be a weird birthday celebration ... not even knowing what we're doing," Ricky mused.

"Well, this was Juan's idea originally, remember," Niki pointed out.

"Yeah, I guess," Ricky replied as he stood and turned to Steve "Listen, don't tell me what Hiroshi comes up with. Juan was going to try to tickle it out of me, so, you know, it'll be better if I don't even know."

"Our lips are sealed, Ricky." Ricky paused at the door and turned.

"Thanks for doing this, Steve. I can hardly wait!" And before Steve could react, he was gone. Upstairs Ricky crept back into their room and slid under the covers. He inched up next to Juan, forming himself around Juan's slightly curled body, his arm back around Juan's waist. He settled his head into his pillow and took a deep breath.

"So did you find out anything?" Juan quietly muttered. Ricky pressed his chin between Juan's shoulder blades, issuing a subtle snort.

"Nope. Now go to sleep, Papito." Juan took a deep breath, then muttered one last time.

"Love you more ..."

Shortly before noon, Steve descended the stairs from his 'office' and tapped on the open door to Greg and Alex's room as he entered.

"Hey," Greg swiveled his chair away from his laptop.

"Hiroshi has a plan. Will you have time to go over with me before Juan gets home ... we don't want him to know we're conspiring with Hiroshi."

"I can take a break anytime ..."

"Let's get it over with. I'll go text Hiroshi and meet you downstairs in five." Greg nodded and spun back around to his keyboard.

Hiroshi opened his back door before they reached the top step, and showed them into the living room, where he had a casual tea service set out on the coffee table. Greg and Steve took places on the couch while Hiroshi poured tea into three cups before pulling up a side chair. Today's fundoshi was a nearly sheer gauzy white, one of the more traditional fabrics, that clearly featured his cage.

"You shouldn't have gone to so much work, Hiroshi," Steve said, "but, um, I see you have some of those incredible crackers."

"Help yourselves, please. Yes, my cousin in Tokyo sends me regular care packages, so I always have them on hand." Both Greg and Steve eagerly reached for a packet. Hiroshi cradled a tea cup, sipped, then continued. "I have debated how best to honor Juan on his birthday, and, well, for better or worse, I have decided to approach it as my gift to Juan ... how I would celebrate his day with him if it were only Juan and me in the dungeon." Steve and Greg exchanged confused glances.

"So, you don't want us to be there?" Greg asked.

"No, no ... on the contrary. What I mean is, I do not want to hold back on *my* contribution to the evening, given we will have an audience. Some of whom, well ... have not had as much experience as Juan and me." Both Greg and Steve still looked uncertain. "Let me explain. If you agree, there will be two parts to the evening. First, all of you will treat Juan to a delightful dungeon experience. I suggest binding him to the St. Andrew's cross and having your way with him. I think Luke has had a little experience with that."

"Um, so have I, Hiroshi," Greg said. Steve looked surprised. Greg looked at him and smiled. "A little, anyway." A light went on for Steve.

"Oh ... Alex's birthday ... that we have all heard so little about?" he guessed. Greg nodded.

"Excellent, I will leave to you what you want to do with Juan. Make it intense, but don't allow him to reach orgasm. Let him think what you're doing is all that he will experience." Hiroshi ceremoniously unwrapped and munched a cracker, then took another sip of tea. "Then, the real fun will begin." Both Greg and Steve leaned forward as Hiroshi detailed his own part in the celebration.

"Seriously?" Steve asked. He looked at Greg, who widened his eyes, before returning his attention to Hiroshi.

"So, you and Juan have done this before?" Greg asked.

"Many times. Juan is something of a legend among the old crowd."

"Now I know why you were concerned about frightening the 'younger ones,'" Steve realized. He turned back to Greg. "Mateo ... Ryan ... what do you think?" Greg looked at Hiroshi.

"Will Juan be in pain? I mean will there be screams?"

"No, my friends. Juan will be transported. His cries will be of joy, of pure pleasure."

"This I have to see," Steve said. He looked over at Greg. "This was Juan's idea, after all."

"Again, I would suggest keeping this just between us, if possible," Hiroshi advised. "For maximum dramatic effect." His grin disappeared behind his tea cup.

"And here, Hiroshi, I thought you were this sweet, gentle, Zen centered man of the world," Steve teased. Hiroshi lowered his cup to reveal that smile.

"Oh, but I am, my friend. What Juan and I will be doing has been described by some as metaphysical."

"Yeah," Steve smiled back. "Like I said ... this I have to see."

## Twenty-Six

# WBLCLB

JUAN STASHED HIS SCRUBS in the washer, then headed up the back stairs, expecting to find Ricky impatiently waiting. But the room was empty. He stepped into the shower to decontaminate, while reviewing mentally how he was going to train/entertain Ricky in his first official leather boy lesson. He was rinsing off when Ricky slipped in behind him, flashing his irresistible smile. Juan maneuvered out from under the spray without making contact with Ricky, so he could begin his own decontamination. Once Ricky had scrubbed his hands, forearms and head and face well enough, and rinsed off the suds, Juan moved in and began scrubbing the rest of Ricky's body down. Which would have been easier if Ricky hadn't been wrapping himself around Juan at the same time.

"I wanted to get home before you, Papito, but my last delivery was crazy. And slow."

"You're here ... I'm here. That's all that matters, mijo." Juan endowed Ricky with his first kiss of the evening. "Are you ready for your first Best Locked Cock Leather Boy test?" Ricky's grin began to fade.

"Test? I thought it was going to be a lesson."

"A lesson that's also a test, mijo." He placed a hand on each of Ricky's shoulders. "Don't worry. I'm confident you'll do fine." Juan stepped out of the shower, pulled a bath sheet off the rack and held it out for Ricky to step into. Once they'd toweled each other off, Ricky started for the bed, but Juan reached out and grabbed him around the waist from behind. "We'll be doing your training in the dungeon, mijo, remember? But first, we're going to need those restraints you used to wear before we moved in with the family."

"Oh, yeah," Ricky's grin returned as he pulled free of Juan and opened a couple of dresser drawers in search of the wrist and ankle restraints. "I put them away when we moved in and totally forgot about them. Maybe I should start wearing them again, don't you think, Papito?"

"I like the way you think, mijo, but it's really up to you. They do look sexy on you, but right now they're going to be more functional than decorative." Ricky sat on the floor, where It took him a couple of minutes to buckle the ankle restraints in place, then he held out both arms, the wrist restraints clasped in each hand, for Juan to buckle them in place.

"This is exciting!" Ricky enthused. "I've been thinking about it all day."

"Me too, mijo," Juan smiled. He finished buckling Ricky up, then pulled him to his feet, hooked a forefinger through the D-ring on Ricky's left wrist restraint and led him out the door and toward the stairs. As they passed by Alex and Greg's door, Alex looked up.

"Hey! I didn't know you guys were home." Then he caught sight of Ricky's restraints as both he and Juan kept walking. Alex jumped up and leaned out of the doorway. "Playtime, boys?"

"Training!" Ricky called out over his shoulder. "My first leather boy lesson." Then as he and Juan descended the stairs, "And ... a test!"

"Have fun!" Alex called out. "I hear Juan grades on a curve!" He retreated back into his room, happy to see Juan and Ricky were taking some time for themselves.

Downstairs, Juan pulled the door closed at the top of the basement stairs as they descended, the signal to the rest of the family that the dungeon was 'occupied.' When they stepped off the last step, Juan walked Ricky over to one of the slings.

"Okay, mijo, sit here." Juan stepped around to the other end, reached out and pulled Ricky's shoulders down and into place. Without speaking he lifted first one arm and then the other, securing the restraints to the chains suspending the sling. Ricky, looking pensive, in fact, a little apprehensive, didn't take his eyes off Juan's face, which was focused and determined. Juan walked to the other end of the sling and lifted each of Ricky's legs, securing each ankle restraint to the chains, rendering Ricky immobile and vulnerable. Juan rubbed Ricky's left leg from just below the ankle restraint down to Ricky's groin. "Is that okay, Ricky? Are you comfortable?"

"Yeah ... it's weird, though. If someone else was doing this to me, I'd be scared right now." Juan leaned in from the side of the sling to deliver another kiss.

"But it is me, mijo. This is what we both signed up for, right?" Ricky smiled bravely and nodded. "Remember the other night when I played with your nipples and you said you liked it?" Ricky nodded again. "A lot of guys, straight guys usually, never explore their nipples. They don't know what they're missing. Just like their asses. We're going to pay special attention to your nipples ... to see just how erotic yours are ... how erotic they might become if we train them. So, we're going to start there." Ricky expected Juan to begin squeezing one or both of his nipples, but instead, Juan moved away a moment, then came back holding something. He held up what looked like a lipstick and circled each of Ricky's nipples. Ricky's naturally smooth chest eliminated any need for Juan to shave around the nipples first.

"What's that?" Ricky asked.

"Chapstick." Ricky's brows knitted in confusion. Juan then ran the Chapstick around a couple of objects in his left hand before he reached down and positioned one over Ricky's right nipple. He rotated it back and forth briefly, the pressed it into Ricky's chest and squeezed. As he followed suit on Ricky's left nipple, Ricky could feel the first one begin tugging on his nipple.

"So, you're not going to play with my nipples?"

"Can you feel anything?"

"Yeah, a little."

"Just wait. A half an hour from how you'll really feel their effect. These are nipple suckers. They'll keep your nipples occupied while I play with the rest of you." A slight smirk appeared on Ricky's face and his eyebrows went from knitted to wiggling. He took a deep breath as he lifted his head to scope out the suction cups. Juan moved away again and returned with another toy.

"Raphael always liked this little item before he graduated to the Thunderplug he and Alex often wear now. This is a Master butt plug, just like his. Think you can handle it?" Ricky's grin was confident, if not smug.

"I handle you just fine, don't I, Papito?" Juan laughed.

"I thought so." He lubed up the plug and then lubricated Ricky, slowly and thoroughly, making the most of the moment, producing satisfied moans from his leather boy. Once he was convinced Ricky was relaxed, he positioned the plug and rotated it back and forth as he pushed it home. Once the crown passed Ricky's internal sphincter the plug was sucked into place, securely home. Juan pushed against the base and wiggled it gently, producing the desired result, a gasp from Ricky.

"Did I pass the test, Papito?" Ricky asked between moans.

"Oh, mijo, we haven't even gotten to the test yet. This is just your warmup." Juan toyed with the butt plug a little longer, stimulating Ricky and noting how much he was enjoying the experience. Ricky had clearly relaxed now, the plug and nipple suckers taking his mind off the fact he was restrained and helpless. Once again Juan walked away from Ricky momentarily. When he returned, he surprised Ricky by inserting the key in his cage.

"You're unlocking me?" Ricky exclaimed.

"This is the test, mijo." Juan calmly replied. He pulled the brass lock out of Ricky's Holy Trainer, then pulled the tube free of Ricky's already hard cock. He placed both aside then slowly grasped Ricky's naked cock and squeezed. "You're a leather boy ... restrained, plugged, nips engorged. Your lover, your Sir, your Papito has your cock in his control. How long can you resist him? How long can you control your leather boy cock? How long before you submit ... and come? Mijo, if you can hold off for twenty minutes, you'll pass the test. Can you do that?"

"I don't know!" Ricky looked panicked. "I haven't come in days! Twenty minutes?"

"Starting now, mijo ..." Thus began the longest twenty minutes, so far, of Ricky's life. He'd been locked for months now, aside from the periodic unlocking for hygiene, when, on even rarer occasions, Juan had sucked him dry. He could count those blow jobs on one hand. If Juan simply stood and watched, sure, he could avoid an orgasm for twenty minutes, despite the plug, despite the nipple suckers, despite the restraints and having his ass on display in this sling ... but if Juan did anything? Anything at all? Twenty minutes? This didn't feel like a test. With Juan holding his cock, this was more like a final exam. Before he could respond again, to Ricky's dismay, Juan immediately began massaging Ricky's cock. At first, Juan took things very slowly. At first, he concentrated on the shaft and avoided Ricky's glans. Ricky had laid his head back down on the sling, his eyes were closed now, no doubt enjoying the sensations Juan was providing, but at the same time, trying not to succumb. At least, not yet. Once Juan felt he'd lulled Ricky into a false sense of control, he began to finger his hard, shiny glans. Ricky's breath caught and his lips tightened, his eyes still closed. He wriggled a bit, but thanks to the restraints there was no way he could pull away from Juan's devious hand. A hand that was soon moistening the glans with Ricky's precum. Ricky began to moan. And to wriggle more. Juan was confident that by now the suction cups were producing novel sensations in Ricky's nipples. A combination of tingling and tightness, no doubt, adding to the overall sensual experience and making it that much harder for Ricky to delay orgasm. That was the plan, anyway. About ten minutes into the 'test,' Juan, without abandoning the hand job, began playing with the Master plug again. Ricky whimpered and offered Juan a bit more precum.

"Papito," he whispered. It wasn't a warning, nor a demand. More like an expression of gratitude. After a couple minutes of butt plug play, Juan ran his hand up and down Ricky's restrained leg, massaging first his calf, then his thigh, inching back toward Ricky's crotch and ass. Then, another round with the plug. Then, for variety, Juan ran his free hand up and down Ricky's washboard. Slowly, gently, admiringly. Ricky hadn't known it, of course, but all along Juan had wanted to insure he'd pass the test. He'd purposely avoided taking Ricky too far too soon. It was now well past twenty minutes, and time to give Ricky his release. Juan let go of Ricky's glistening cock, reached up and pulled both nip suckers free, letting them fall down between Ricky and the sling. Then he grasped each nipple and began kneading them. Ricky caught his breath, experiencing sensations he'd never known before. Many men in long term chastity rely on their ass for sexual stimulation. Some find their nipples become hardwired to their prostate. Some are lucky enough to benefit from both. At this point, so early in Ricky's training, the only certainty was that he loved being fucked by Juan and could come from it. So, maybe it was the Master plug. Or the hand job. But, arguably, this time, it was Juan's attention to his freshly pumped nipples that fired off the orgasm that splattered over both of them.

"NO!" Ricky cried out. "Papito ... nooo."

"It's okay, Ricky ... mijo ... you passed. Just enjoy it."

"Oh," Ricky sighed. His demeanor instantly changed, as he relaxed and a smile spread across his face. His eyes slowly opened and he focused on Juan's face hovering just above his own. "That was amazing."

"What did you like best? The butt plug, the nipple suckers ... the hand job?"

"Umm," Ricky paused as he tested the butt plug, which wiggled under his control. "Can I say all of it?" Juan laughed, then leaned down and pressed his lips to Ricky's.

"Sure, mijo. As far as I'm concerned, that was the right answer. Why don't you lay here and relax a moment. I'll be right back." Juan straightened up, retrieved the nipple suckers and headed up the stairs, leaving Ricky alone in the sling. As Juan passed by Alex and Greg's door on the way to his room Alex looked up again.

"Did he pass?"

"He passed," Juan grinned.

"Where is he?" Alex asked.

"He's kind of tied up right now. He's in the sling." Juan continued on into his room. Alex, being Alex, couldn't resist. He slipped out the door and headed for the stairs.

"Alex ..." Greg called out. Fruitlessly. Then, he, too, headed out the door and down the stairs. When Juan returned to the dungeon, he found Alex and Greg on either side of Ricky, still restrained, still plugged, wearing his own cum and still smiling.

"Once again, I've missed what must have been some hard-core dungeon action," Alex said.

"Talk to Greg," Juan laughed. "Nobody's stopping the two of you." He had a small black shopping bag in one hand and a wash cloth and towel in the other. As he began wiping Ricky down, he made a point to pay special attention to his nipples, producing involuntary moans.

"Wow, Ricky ... your nipples," Alex observed. "They're ... huge."

"Impressive," Greg agreed. Ricky lifted his head to look, but couldn't really see well from his position. Juan handed Ricky's Holy Trainer to Alex and asked him to clean and dry it off for him. Since Alex had invited himself into their session, Juan thought, he might as well make himself useful. Juan cleaned up Ricky's still tumescent cock and was ready when Alex returned. Once Ricky was safely locked up, Juan began unfastening his leg restraints from the chains. He nodded to Ricky's arms and Alex and Greg moved in and unfastened them. Once Ricky's arms were free, Juan reached down and pulled him out of the sling and stood him up. Now Ricky could look down at his nipples.

"Whoa," he reached up and fingered them. "Dios Mio ... that feels so good." He grinned at Juan. "Is this permanent? Will they stay like this?" Juan pulled him into a loose hug.

"No, mijo, it's not permanent." Ricky uttered a slight whimper into Juan's chest. Juan pulled back to look Ricky in the eyes. "But ... it can be. If you want. You just need to train them. We'll talk about that later. First, congratulations! You passed Best Locked Cock Leather Boy 101. You get a prize."

"Ooooh," Ricky looked over at Alex and Greg. "I didn't know there'd be a prize. You know, besides the one in my butt." He wiggled his deadly ass to punctuate the obvious. Juan reached down and pulled something out of the shopping bag.

"Here, mijo, is your next piece of leather gear." Juan held up a leather vest, then turned it to display the back, which was emblazoned in the letters 'W B L C L B' spelled out in rainbow-colored rhinestones in homage, perhaps, to a certain former glitter-encrusted ringbearer. "You can wear it on your deliveries and no one will know what it means. Unless you wear just the vest, I guess." Ricky turned away from Juan and stuck out his left arm, inviting Juan to slip it on him. He worked his right arm through the other arm opening and turned back. Juan placed both hands inside the vest, just under Ricky's arm pits, a thumb gently rubbing each nipple. Ricky whimpered again.

"Don't stop doing that, Papito." Greg turned to Alex.

"We should probably ..."

"Yeah," Alex agreed as he led Greg toward and up the stairs. Juan pulled Ricky into yet another embrace, one reminiscent of the one that started their journey together so many months ago on the patio of the Eagle. With Ricky's face buried in Juan's chest. Only this time, Ricky was wearing the leather vest, and no one else was present to witness what was obviously something much deeper than simply pure physical attraction between two very sexy leather men. Ricky lifted his face far enough away from Juan's chest to make eye contact again.

"Thank you Papi ... Sir," Ricky caught himself, thinking, hoping that their relationship had evolved ever so slightly this evening. "Thank you for the leather boy lesson. For these super sexy nipples. And this ..." Ricky wiggled his ass much like Pup Niki would have done. "For this studly vest. But most of all, for saying yes that day at the Eagle."

"No, mijo, I should be thanking you. For not taking no for an answer. For giving me the opportunity to say 'yes' at long last. And mijo ... you can still call me Papito if you want. Even after a hundred lessons. Okay?" Ricky nodded, then he squeezed Juan tightly one more time before letting go and heading for the stairs, with Juan in tow. When they topped the basement stairs, their newly realized hunger was met with a spicy fragrance. They were surprised to find Raphael and Luke still preparing dinner in the kitchen.

"Enter the dungeon masters," Raphael quipped as he looked over at Ricky and Juan. "Hey! Somebody's all dressed up!"

"Yeah," Ricky grinned. "Check it out." He turned to display his back as he once again wrapped his arms around Juan.

"Like ... a ... rhinestone ... leather boy ..." Luke crooned.

"Very cool!" Raphael said as he parked his wooden spoon and walked over to admire Ricky's vest. "Pretty sure I know what 'WBLCLB' stands for." Both Juan and Ricky nodded.

"He earned it, Raphael," Juan smiled. "I thought we'd probably missed dinner." He and Ricky followed Raphael back to the stove to see what he was stirring.

"No, Alex and Greg clued us in earlier, so we sort of rescheduled," Luke said. "Raphael's green curry with prawns and brown rice. If you guys want to shower, we'll be ready in ten minutes." Ricky and Juan headed up the back stairs.

"Well, one thing's for sure," Raphael said as he taste-tested the curry. When he said no more, Luke come up behind him and rested a hand on the small of his back.

"What's that, baby?"

"You'll never have to worry about paying any royalties to the Glenn Campbell estate." He turned and flashed his mischievous smile, within striking distance of Luke's lips. Luke struck first with a quick peck.

"My talents lie elsewhere, and those, my dear, are royalty-free." He patted Raphael on the ass, then headed to the sink to wash up.

## Twenty-Seven

# HAPPY BIRTHDAY, JUAN

NIKI SLIPPED A BOOKMARK into his text book, plopped it on the other fireplace chair and rose for the first time in nearly two hours. It was nearing noon and he needed a break from studying. He wandered into the kitchen where he found Ryan seated at the island, a coffee mug and a sheaf of papers in front of him.

"Do archeology students have to keep studying, even on a coffee break?"

"They do when they think maybe they scheduled too many semester hours," Ryan smiled, laying the papers aside. "Sit down ... force me to take a break." Niki pulled a bottle of kombucha from the fridge and sat.

"Sure, I'll be the bad influence, if you want." He shook the bottle carefully, just enough to stir the sediment without causing it to effervesce, then unscrewed the top and sipped. "What are you engrossed in today?"

"Mesoamerica."

"Ah ... the Aztecs and Maya." Ryan's eyes widened.

"You know that?" Niki gulped, only partly thanks to the kombucha. He didn't want Ryan to know what he'd learned from Mateo's 'out of school' conversation, at least not without Mateo's consent.

"Yeah ... a little. From high school, I guess. Pretty fascinating, really."

"It *is*." Ryan folded his arms on the counter and grew more intense as he spoke. "In some ways they were more advanced than many European cultures, with cities populated in the tens of thousands. And amazing architecture, including some of the tallest pyramids in the world, some of it still standing. In fact, we continue to find new cities to this day. They invented writing, hieroglyphs a lot like the Egyptians used and made books on a special kind of bark instead of paper, most of which the Spanish invaders destroyed ... unfortunately."

"You're kidding? Why?"

"They thought the writings must be sacrilegious, is one theory. Don't get me started. So, we've lost a lot of what might have told us more. There are so many mysteries, still, about them. That's what fascinates me, I think. What happened to their civilizations? They appeared to just abandon thriving cities, but nobody is sure why. Famine? Drought? Disease? War? There was some warring at times between different city states, but probably nothing like we have experienced in modern times." Niki was pleased to see how enthralled Ryan was with his subject matter. He decided to probe beyond Ryan's academic interests to see what he might be able to coax from Ryan. Maybe something that could be useful for Mateo.

"I think Mateo's people are from the Yucatan. Or somewhere like that."

"He is, yeah. Isn't that awesome?" Niki nodded. So far, so good.

"Have you guys talked about it much?"

"A little. Not too much. I think Mateo considers himself more Mexican, more Hispanic than Mayan, but I can see it in him sometimes."

"What do you mean?"

"I don't know ... a humble but regal quality. His beautiful skin. He has a Mayan nose, don't you think?" Niki laughed.

"I'll take your word for it. Do you think you'll ever get to go down and do some archeological exploration yourself in Mesoamerica?"

"Oh, Niki, I hope so." He stared into Niki's eyes a moment before continuing. "There's so much more to learn. To discover."

"I'm guessing there's still more to learn and discover about you and Mateo, too." Ryan looked down at his coffee, smiling shyly. He looked back into Niki's eyes.

"I like what I'm discovering so far ..." Niki sat back. He wanted the conversation to continue.

"Do you guys talk as much as you did when that was about all you could do, when you were separated?"

"Sometimes. Sometimes we don't talk at all ... to make up for all times that's all we could do." Ryan's face made it clear that he was talking about sex.

"You can tell me to shut up if you want, but ... I think it's great you and Mateo found each other. You know ... the fact that you're his first love. He deserves someone as caring and gentle and intelligent ... okay ... I am going to shut up now."

"Why?" Ryan grinned. "Keep going ... I don't get compliments like this very often. What makes you think I'm so gentle ... I mean, sure the intelligent part is clearly obvious ..." Niki laughed.

"I don't know. I've always been a pretty good judge of people. And Mateo wouldn't be so devoted to you if you weren't caring and everything."

"I'm probably the one who feels devoted." Ryan cleared his throat. "Just between you and me?" Niki nodded and leaned forward, eager to hear more. "In a way, when I'm in bed with Mateo, it's a lot like how you described being a pup." Even though he wasn't in pup gear, Niki instinctively tilted his head questioningly. "I kind of lose myself. I just want to do whatever I think will make Mateo happy. It's hard to describe. It's almost like I become a part of Mateo, that I lose myself in him. That I am whatever he needs me to be in that moment. I've done things with Mateo I've never done with anyone else." Ryan stopped, without breaking his intense eye contact. "I hope that doesn't sound demented." Niki paused before speaking, afraid to say the wrong thing and curtail this moment.

"Demented? Not even close. Okay ... I don't want to put words in your mouth, but ... are you saying you feel submissive to Mateo, you know, like Raphael often is with Luke? Or Ricky with Juan?" Ryan looked up and away, in thought for a moment.

"Maybe. But I think it's more than that. I don't know. I'll have to think about that."

"Have you guys done any exploring in the dungeon together?" Ryan shook his head, perhaps just a bit disappointedly.

"No. Not yet anyway. I wouldn't know where to start."

"But you'd like to?" Niki liked where this was going.

"Yeah, I think so. I mean ... it's right there. How many fraternities have a dungeon on site? Right?"

"Are you waiting for Mateo to say something? Or do something?"

"Probably. To your point earlier, we haven't really established specific roles like everybody else in the family. Umm, not to brag, but so far we seem to have plenty of fun without any ... accoutrements." Niki nodded to show his approval.

"Well, you do have a handy one on you at all times, Ryan. Your irrepressible boner ... Anyway, just remember, you're in a family here. Juan would be happy to guide you guys in the dungeon any time you ask, I'm sure. Or Hiroshi, next door, if you're too embarrassed to ask Juan. Now that I think of it, Luke might be good, too." Ryan made a 'good to know' expression in response. "I'm guessing we'll see some interesting action Thursday for Juan's birthday. Maybe that'll spark some discussion with Mateo. Okay, once again ... I'll shut up now."

"Stop it. Niki, it's nice to know you care. Really. But, so far, I have no complaints. None. Or should I say, nada." With perfect timing, Steve entered from the foyer.

"Are you ready for that grilled cheese sandwich I promised?" Steve rubbed Niki's shoulders from behind.

"Yeah," Niki replied, his tongue caressing his upper lip in anticipation.

"Can I fix you one, Ryan?" Steve headed for the fridge.

"Thanks, but no. I just had some yogurt."

"You should say yes," Niki advised. "This isn't just any old grilled cheese. Steve makes it with grilled onions and tomato, two kinds of cheese, lettuce, sourdough ..."

"Okay. You talked me into it." Ryan looked coyly at Niki. "Another advantage of being a part of this family, eh, Niki?" Niki nodded sagely before getting up and heading to the cupboard for plates.


"Whatcha do-in?" Steve straightened up and turned to face Luke, just as he was about to slip the envelope under Juan and Ricky's door.

"Hey, Luke." Steve gave Luke a conspiratorial grin. "Just following orders ... for Juan's celebration. Here, since Juan knows I'm on the 'committee' why don't you slide this under his door. To give me deniability." Luke looked a bit confused but did as Steve requested.

"What do you mean, following orders? I assumed you and Greg were in charge of this whole thing. Except for Ricky and Raphael."

"Ricky and Raphael?" A worried look came over Steve's face. "Do you have a minute? Maybe we should compare notes." Steve headed for Greg and Alex's door, with Luke following. Steve stuck his head in the open door, to see Greg facing away at his laptop at the desk. Alex was elsewhere. "Can we bug you minute?" Greg turned in his chair and waved them in. "Where's Alex?" Steve asked as he closed the door, so they wouldn't be overheard. Luke sat on the edge of the bed, all ears.

"He's in his remote, remote office ... the guest room upstairs. He's had to do a lot of talking today and didn't want to distract me."

"This house has everything, even spare offices," Luke laughed as Steve sat in the side chair.

"I just got a text from Hiroshi with some suggestions including a final request he wanted us to give Juan prior to the ceremony, so I printed it out and slipped it under his door. Thanks to Luke, if he asks, he won't know for sure who was responsible." He glanced at Luke. "Also, I think Luke knows something we don't know, so I thought we should touch base." Greg nodded.

"What did Hiroshi say?"

"Not a surprise, I guess. I hope it doesn't give anything away. It's a request that Juan do a deep cleaning when he gets home from work on Thursday."

"What?" Luke reacted. "Deep cleaning?"

"A douche. A good one." Luke gave Steve a clueless look, so Steve filled him in on Hiroshi's plan. Luke glanced back and forth between Steve and Greg, not sure he believed Steve, but he could tell Steve wasn't joking.

"So, Juan won't know about Hiroshi until after we've put him through a fake ceremony first?" Both Greg and Steve nodded. "This sounds kind of intense. And a little complicated."

"Hiroshi says Juan's a pro," Greg said. "And Juan will be deliriously happy about it."

"Uh huh ... and Ricky will be totally freaked out," Luke said, concerned.

"We ... uh, we talked about that," Greg replied. "Hiroshi is confident that Juan will be in ecstasy, not agony, and that should allay any fear for Ricky or Mateo. Or Ryan. I guess we have to trust Hiroshi's judgment. In some ways he knows Juan better than we do. Obviously." Luke took a deep breath.

"Okay ..." Luke seemed less than convinced. "Don't you think we should warn Ricky at least beforehand?"

"I don't think so. Juan already tried to force him to reveal our plans, so we need to keep him in the dark. We just need to be ready to ease any concerns he might have Thursday evening. Speaking of, what's this about Ricky and Raphael?" Steve asked. "Are we going to run into competing birthday ceremonies?"

"All I know is they're conspiring about something. I caught them returning together from somewhere last week and I wouldn't have thought anything about it, except they both looked guilty as hell. Naturally, I assumed they were plotting some kind of dare, but when I tortured Raphael about it later, he confessed they were on a mission for Juan's birthday. But he wouldn't tell me what it was. He was 'sworn to secrecy.'"

"Like all the rest of us," Greg muttered. "This *is* getting complicated."

"And we need to complicate it further," Steve laughed. "That's another reason I brought Luke in. We really need to figure out what we're going to do with Juan tomorrow in the lead up to Hiroshi's appearance. That was something else he texted me. I have instructions on how to orchestrate, literally, his entrance. But first, what are we going to do? Luke ... you know a dungeon better than I do." Luke smiled at Greg.

"Well, Greg knows about as much as I do. How about it, Greg. Should we shackle him to the St. Andrew's cross?" Greg rubbed the underside of his chin in thought.

"We could ..." He reached back on the desk for a pad and pen and began to jot ideas down as they came up. Fifteen minutes later, Alex opened the door, laptop in hand.

"Oh ... hey, guys," he stopped short of entering the room. "Am I interrupting?"

"No, hon," Greg stood. "We're just ..." He paused as Alex made a 'yes???' face.

"What Greg's trying not to say is we were plotting secrets and we can't tell you," Steve confessed.

"Ah," Alex grinned. "So, this is the committee, huh?" He looked at each of them. "This is going to be good, isn't it?" Greg nodded.

"Finally!" Alex laid his laptop on the bed next to Luke.

"Finally?" Luke asked.

"I'm finally going to see some serious dungeon action," Alex said as he headed for the bathroom.

"Alex ... are you forgetting Niki's discipline session?" Steve asked.

"I'm talking *serious* dungeon action," Alex said as he closed the bathroom door. Then he opened it and stuck his head around. "You guys better not disappoint me." He closed the door again. Then opened it again. "Or Juan!"

"Something tells me neither Juan nor Alex is going to be disappointed," Luke whispered.

After depositing his scrubs in the washer, Juan sprinted up the back stairs, ID badge in hand. He opened his door and entered, nearly slipping on something. He almost picked up the white number ten envelope that bore only his name, but decided to decontaminate first. He placed his badge on the desk and headed for the shower. It had been a busy, intense day and he took his time wetting down, turning off the spray, navy shower style, scrubbing hither and yon, then leisurely rinsing off. Once he was dry, he returned to the bedroom, having forgotten the envelope in the interim. Smiling, he scooped it up, suspicious of what it might pertain to, since it clearly hadn't arrived in the mail. He tore it open and pulled out a single sheet of paper and read.

*Good evening, Mr. Reyes:*
*Your mission, and let's be honest, you have no choice but to accept it, is to appear in the dungeon tomorrow evening to partake in a celebration of your birthday.*

*To ensure your utmost enjoyment of the festivities, you are hereby in-structed to not only decontaminate upon returning home, but to also execute a thorough and complete colonic cleansing. We trust you know what that entails. Get it? Tails!*

*As always, should you or any other members of the House of the Locked Cock Brotherhood be caught or otherwise embarrassed, the Secretary will disavow any knowledge of your actions. This note will not self-destruct ... duh ... it's a note. Just recycle it responsibly. Thank you for your attention to this, Juan, and have a good evening.*

Juan's laughter could be heard, even through the closed door. This was undoubtedly Steve's doing, although the note wasn't signed. Juan was reasonably sure he knew what the committee might have in store, too, after the 'truth serum' conversation in the turret room. Who, he wondered, would be wielding Raphael's strap on? He laid the note aside, pulled a fresh towel out of the closet and headed for the gym. Luke and Steve were already there.

"Guys ..." Juan greeted them as he walked over to the dumbbell rack. "Where's everybody else?"

"Hey, Juan!" Luke smiled, glancing briefly at Steve. "Raphael, Alex and Niki are on a run. How was your day?"

"Challenging. I thought this might help me relax." Juan took a seat at the opposite end of the bench where Steve was sitting and began his biceps curls. After a moment of silence, Juan glanced at Steve who was intent on his own workout ... or pretending to be. "So, Steve," Juan finally said, "I didn't know you were a Mission Impossible fan." Steve chuckled in spite of himself.

"Me? What's that?" Juan just looked at Steve, his tongue poking into his right cheek, his eyes smiling. After a moment of this silent interroga-tion, Steve buckled. "Yeah, okay. A guilty pleasure." Juan nodded.

"Well, message received, Mr. Secretary." Juan transferred the dumb-bell to his left hand and proceeded to concentrate on his workout. When he caught Luke and Greg glancing at one another, he stood, but before racking his dumbbell, he turned and asked, "I'm going to be sorry I ever suggested birthday celebrations in the dungeon, aren't I?" Steve turned and gave Juan his full attention.

"Well ... I'd say there's an eighty-five percent chance you won't be sorry, Juan."

"Luke?" Juan turned to Luke.

"I'm kinda new to the committee, so I'm thinking ... maybe ... ninety percent. Ninety percent chance you won't be sorry."

"Hmmm. Okay then," Juan said as he selected a heavier dumbbell plate. "Maybe I'll sleep tonight after all."

Juan did sleep well. Apparently better than Ricky did, because as he extinguished the alarm, he wasn't the only one to stir.

"Happy Birthday, Papito!" Ricky's greeting was cheerier than his sleepy face, the only thing visible above the bunched covers. He yawned before muttering, "I wanted to be the first to say it." Juan leaned down and kissed his forehead.

"Thank you, mijo. Go back to sleep."

"'kay." Ricky rolled over, then back to say, "I can't wait for tonight."

"That makes two of us," Juan replied softly on his way to the shower.

Raphael and Alex took an extended lunch hour to make a run to Whole Foods. Raphael had talked Alex into a menu for Juan's dinner that sounded elegant, but tricky. Raphael was confident they could pull it off. As they unpacked their haul, he explained that like most seafood, the prep would be the most time consuming, so they made a plan to meet back in the kitchen around five. Once the prep was done, they'd only need about twenty minutes to finalize before serving, and they figured they could do that while everyone else entertained Juan with bubbly and, no doubt, a post mortem on the dungeon scene ... whatever that was going to be. Raphael had already pressed the 'pledges' into service to set up the dining room at their convenience, and he had set one place as a template for Ryan and Mateo.

"I don't know why everything has to be a big secret, Raphael," Alex complained. "I caught Greg, Steve and Luke conspiring in our room, but they wouldn't tell me anything."

"Maybe they don't realize how good you are at keeping secrets, paddle boy."

"Or Halloween. Or Ricky's surprise appearance at our last strip show. Or the most legendary wedding in San Francisco history! I can be discrete."

"You certainly can. For what it's worth, they're not the only ones harboring secrets for tonight." Raphael wiggled his eyebrows.

"Oh?" Alex stared into Raphael's eyes ... patiently.

"Sorry ... sworn to secrecy," Raphael smiled. "All I'll say is, it'll be worth the wait. Not that we have to wait much longer." He put his arms around Alex's waist and pulled him into a cage to cage embrace. "I'm glad we're doing this. This is the first party we've had in a long time.

And I'm glad you and I are doing Juan's dinner. We haven't collaborated on anything together in forever, either." Alex leaned forward to deliver a quick peck.

"Me, too." As they parted, he continued. "The dares have been pretty sparse lately, too."

"Is that a complaint? Maybe I'm waiting for you to initiate one. You know ... challenge Greg with one all on your own." Alex looked a little wistfully into Raphael's eyes.

"It's more fun plotting them with you. Weddings, I can do, But dares ... I was always better taking direction."

"Something to work on," Raphael smiled. Then both headed upstairs and back to work.

Juan entered the house Thursday not knowing exactly what to expect. He'd been feted at the hospital by a few of his socially distanced colleagues in the staff breakroom with a cake that, off and on during the day, slowly disappeared as the hours and the random breaks took their toll. He was carrying a Safeway bag filled with mostly gag gifts that he'd now have to either find places for or regift as opportunities presented themselves. But he had to admit it had been fun, and it was nice to know how much, and how sincerely, he was appreciated. But now, now that he was home, he knew he was in for recognition of a very different kind. He wasn't too worried about what might happen in the dungeon. Even Luke, who was probably the most familiar of the family with leather scenes, wasn't nearly as experienced as Juan, so whatever they'd cooked up wasn't going to be all that difficult to endure. In fact, Steve's note yesterday pretty much gave away what to expect. They probably thought a little anal action with a strap on would be uncharacteristic for him, and therefore a bit of a challenge. He knew they'd put some effort into whatever was coming, and he was prepared to make sure they knew he was grateful for their love. Even if it did turn out to be something he could easily endure, even with one hand, or both, tied behind his back. After depositing his scrubs, Juan carried his loot up to his and Ricky's room only to find that Ricky was apparently still out on deliveries. And there, on the bed, was yet another birthday gift. Sort of. A shower shot nozzle on top of another note, which read:

*Fresh off the store shelf. Never used. Enjoy.*

Again, no signature. Okay, then, Juan thought. It's been a while since I've done this, so I might as well get it over with. He carried the nozzle into the bath, unscrewed Ricky's nozzle and began the process. It was nearly an hour later when Ricky appeared. He looked more excited than Juan did.

"Papito, Happy Birthday ... again! You get a kiss, but that's all you get until I shower." He leaned down to Juan, who was lounging on the bed with his current book, and delivered the hottest hands-free kiss he could muster. Then he bounded into the bathroom. Ten minutes later he stepped into the doorway.

"Am I going to have to dry myself off?"

"Uh, whose birthday is it? Shouldn't you be the one attending to me?" Juan said as he climbed off the bed and joined Ricky in the bath. He began patting Ricky down.

"Oh, don't worry, I'll take care of you later, after, you know ..."

"Actually, I don't know," Juan chuckled as he made sure each armpit was completely dry. "Do you?"

"A little, but not much. I don't think anybody knows everything."

"Oh, really?" Juan squatted and worked on Ricky's cage and the space between it and his divine derriere. "So, you didn't know about this?" Juan stood and held up his nozzle.

"My shower shot?" Ricky looked confused.

"Actually, my shower shot. This is yours." Ricky gave Juan a shocked look that confirmed his innocence. "I was instructed to 'prepare' for whatever is going to happen tonight." A mischievous look washed across Ricky's face as he took the towel from Juan and finished the job.

"This is going to be better than I thought," Ricky said. "No wonder they wouldn't tell me anything." The two of them returned to the bedroom where Juan began showing Ricky his birthday loot. They were deciding which items were keepers when Steve knocked on the frame of the open door.

"Hey Steve," Juan turned and smiled.

"Happy Birthday, Juan," Steve bowed in the traditional COVID era non-contact greeting. "Are you ready for your mission? I mean 'really' ready?"

"Yes, Steve, I'm ready. Spic and span." Steve nodded.

"Good, then follow me, please." Steve led Juan and Ricky to and down the back stairs. Juan noticed, as they passed near the kitchen door, an enticing, garlicky smell.

"Yum. Can we skip right to dinner?" Steve looked back and grinned.

"What, and miss all the fun? Tonight, my friend, you have to earn your dinner." He headed down the dungeon stairs. When Juan hesitated, Ricky pushed him from behind.

"You aren't afraid are you, Papito?"

"No, mijo, but maybe I should be. Come on." Down they went. There, in subdued lighting, with house music quietly throbbing in the background, were all the family members, each man clad in his own unique fundoshi, except for Steve, who'd remained naked so as not to give anything away.

"Happy Birthday, Juan!" everyone exclaimed as they bowed.

"Oh, you didn't tell me this would be semi-formal."

"The first of many surprises for our guest of honor," Steve said. "You'll excuse Ricky and me for a moment, so we can get into the spirit of things." He and Alex corralled Ricky and headed into the gym. Meanwhile Luke and Greg ushered Juan over near the St. Andrew's cross and began buckling restraints on each of his ankles.

"This looks kind of serious," Juan joked, already impressed with what they were up to.

"Did you expect any less of us?" Greg grinned from his vantage point at Juan's feet. Juan shook his head, returning Greg's smile. As Luke and Greg stood up, Raphael and Niki moved in with restraints of their own, one for each of Juan's wrists. By the time they'd finished, Alex returned with Ricky and Steve, each of whom were now sporting a fundoshi of their own. As Niki pulled away, Raphael ran his hand up and down Juan's side pausing at this hip.

"Are you feeling a little vulnerable?" He cooed in the sexiest voice he could muster. Juan laughed.

"Please be gentle with me," he replied. Raphael wrapped his hand around Juan's right butt cheek and squeezed before moving away.

"Juan," Luke approached, "as a handsome and devious man once said to us, 'I'll be your escort this evening. Do as I say and no one will get hurt.'" Juan momentarily closed his eyes and nodded, remembering that night in the wedding van. He started to move toward the slings. "No, no, birthday boy. We need you over here, at the cross." Juan showed surprise as he swung around and positioned himself. Now he really was confused about what he was in for. "Okay, that's good ... just raise your arm ..." Luke and Greg proceeded to fasten Juan's restraints to the cross, immobilizing his arms and legs. Then Steve approached. At first Juan thought he was going to kiss him, but instead, Steve produced a blindfold which he gently fastened in place.

"How's that?" Steve asked.

"Dark. Very dark." Steve turned to the family.

"He's tied up and blindfolded, and he's telling jokes." Ricky cackled.

"Don't worry, Papito! I'll protect you!"

"I'm counting on you, mijo!" Juan shouted back. Clearly, they'd put some planning into this, Juan thought. I need to play my part as earnestly as they do. Of course, there had been no rehearsal and very little collaboration except between Luke, Steve and Greg. The hurried pow wow they'd had with the rest of the family was going to have to get them through. That, and a little improvisation, no doubt. Basically, the plan was to get Juan hot and bothered without bringing him to a climax.

They began with Niki and Mateo each licking an armpit while Luke got behind Juan, reached around and began playing with Juan's pierced nipples. He'd had plenty of practice with Raphael's, so he had a pretty good idea what would and wouldn't work. Transferable skills, as it were. Greg positioned a block on the platform in front of Juan's spread feet and helped Ricky up onto it, so his lips were level with Juan's. Ricky leaned forward, wrapped his arms around Juan's neck and his lips around Juan's, who moaned appreciatively. Raphael squeezed between Luke's legs in order to scoot around and perch on the same block Ricky was standing on, between his legs, allowing him to swallow Juan's cock. Raphael had the distinct pleasure of accommodating Juan's PA while simultaneously bumping the back of his head on Ricky's Holy Trainer. Not ideal, but not all that bad, either. Yet another first. Juan's PA was definitely more of a challenge than Luke's ampallang, but Raphael's mission was to be sure Juan didn't come anyway, so he didn't approach his task with quite the gusto he otherwise would have brought to it. Very little of Juan's body was now accessible to Alex and Ryan, but they did their best to fondle Juan and lick, kiss and teasingly bite whenever and wherever possible, basically to provide as much sensory overload as they could. Ryan was tentative at first, intimidated not only by the situation itself, but by the idea of intimately touching Juan, of whom he'd always been somewhat in awe. After a while, inhibition fell away, and he began to explore new parts of Juan as they became available. Which, of course, energized his rambunctious cock, which had been relatively well behaved of late, as he had slowly grown accustomed to living naked with nine other variously kinky guys. The fundoshi he wore wasn't as snug as it probably should have been, and half his cock found its way out of its confines in no time. Not that anyone cared.

Greg waited a few minutes to allow everyone else to do their best, which he deduced was more than adequate based on Juan's moans and squirms, and what little audible deep breathing Ricky permitted him, before he decided it was time to execute the first of Hiroshi's instructions. He first increased the volume of the music, then slid behind the cross, next to Luke. He held up the seriously sized butt plug Hiroshi had recommended, eliciting a wicked grin from Luke, who moved to the side while maintaining contact with Juan's left nipple. Luke began rubbing just above Juan's ass with his right hand as Greg lubed up the plug. When he began lubing Juan, the reaction was instantaneous and not unexpected. Despite Ricky's lip lock, Juan yelped. Ricky doubled down, as did Raphael, and Greg began his quest to find a home for the plug. At first Juan didn't make it easy ... at all. But Greg didn't back off, and after a couple of minutes, probably because Juan knew he really had no choice, he relaxed and Greg was able to complete his mission. When he stood, Luke gave him a wide-eyed look. He leaned over to whisper, "I can't believe you got that in."

"Remember," Greg whispered back, "Hiroshi said he's a pro, so ..." Luke nodded and moved back into position so he could pleasure both of Juan's nipples again. Hiroshi had suggested they keep Juan plugged at least twenty minutes before his arrival, so they continued. Raphael actually released Juan a couple of times, fearing he might be getting too close. Juan had been under siege longer than he had anticipated. Finally, however, Greg put an arm around Ricky's waist and pulled him away from Juan. Everyone else retreated as well, while Steve tapped out a text on his phone. Juan, smiling, took several long, deep breaths.

"That was incredible," he said. "Thank you, guys. I mean that. This was a unique birthday treat." Greg and Steve moved in and unfastened his ankle restraints from the cross, then released his wrist restraints. Juan reached up for the blindfold, but Steve grabbed his wrist in time.

"Whoa, whoa, birthday boy," he laughed. "We're not done with you yet. We're here to celebrate you in ways you richly deserve. This was only act one of two." Ricky grabbed Steve's free arm and raised his right hand and shook it in front of Steve, extending three fingers. "Correction, act one of three." Ricky grinned and nodded.

"Three, huh?" Juan responded, then sniffed dramatically. "You sure we can't just cut right to dinner?"

"There'll be plenty of time to enjoy Raphael and Alex's gift to you. First, Act Two." Steve nodded to Greg, and the two of them each took an arm and walked Juan over to a sling. They turned him around and backed him into the sling. As soon as he felt the leather against the backs of his thighs, Juan knew what was happening. He slid into place without any help and raised his arms in anticipation of being restrained yet again.

"That's a good boy," Greg teased as he secured Juan's right arm to the chain. Steve and Luke each took a leg and presently Juan was once again immobilized, horizontally this time, and even more vulnerably displayed. Ricky now saw how he must have looked to Juan just days earlier. He liked what he saw.

"So ..." Juan prompted.

"So ... Act Two begins," Steve intoned. He walked over to his tablet and tapped a button, initiating Hiroshi's soundtrack through the sound system. At the same time Hiroshi appeared at the base of the stairs, surprising everyone but the committee. Mateo raised his hand and was about to greet him when Greg clapped a hand over Mateo's mouth at the same time Hiroshi put a finger to his smiling lips. A finger, a whole hand in fact, encased in a black latex elbow length opera glove. Pink Floyd's 'Time' from the *Dark Side of the Moon* album began, startling everyone with its clanging, chiming timepieces. Several in the room had never heard this track before. Juan, of course, had, and he began chuckling.

"Oh nooo ..." A smile grew below his blindfold on his recently abused, luscious lips. Hiroshi approached the sling and pulled Juan's blindfold away.

"Happy Birthday, Juan-san."

"Thank you, Hiroshi-san. This is indeed a surprise. I was expecting to meet Brutus this evening."

"Are you disappointed, my friend?"

"What do you think?" Hiroshi placed his gloved hand on Juan's chest.

"It has been a while, Juan. But I would like this to be my gift to you." They maintained eye contact until Juan responded.

"And I graciously accept." Hiroshi turned away, put his hands on Ricky's shoulders and leaned in to him.

"Do not worry, my friend. What we are about to do has made your Papito famous in some circles. He will be fine." Hiroshi continued to the end of the sling. He spread a small plastic mat on the floor, positioned a stool, sat and gently pulled out Juan's butt plug. As the music intensified, he poured a thin, viscous liquid on his gloved hand and began, first with one finger, then two, then three ... to enter Juan. It was then that Raphael looked at Luke with widened eyes. Silently asking "Is he ... he isn't, is he?" Luke nodded and smiled as he wrapped an arm around Raphael's shoulders. Raphael reached out and pulled Ricky into an embrace from behind, not sure how Ricky was going to take this. Within moments, as the soundtrack transitioned to 'Us and Them,' intensifying further, Hiroshi slid his entire hand in. Ryan gasped and clung to Mateo, who wrapped an arm around Ryan's waist. Unthinkingly, he reached down with his other hand and began playing with Ryan's exposed erection.

Hiroshi played Juan as if he were another instrument in the soundtrack. He was focused totally on Juan's face, which reacted in time to Hiroshi, or to the music ... or both. At times Juan's moans could be heard, at times the music overpowered them, or they subsided. As Hiroshi had promised Ricky, Juan appeared to be in ecstasy, not agony. Everyone else had overcome their surprise and concern by now, rapt, watching Hiroshi playing his instrument, Juan. The two of them were as well orchestrated as the soundtrack Hiroshi was accompanying, or perhaps conducting from inside Juan's abdomen. 'Us and Them' transitioned into 'Brain Damage,' then 'Eclipse' and then 'The Great Gig in the Sky.' Hiroshi had timed his efforts with Juan so that his cries of utmost phrenzy coincided with Clare Torry's orgiastic vocalizations. Almost as if Juan was trying to harmonize with her. Then, suddenly, Juan's cock began leaking all over his abdomen. At first Ricky thought he was coming, but ... no, it was piss, being forced out of Juan by Hiroshi's efforts. Ricky couldn't hold back any longer. He pulled away from Raphael and took Juan's restrained right hand in both of his. Juan opened his eyes, looked up at him and smiled, from a distance, from a place Ricky had never seen him before. There were tears leaking from Juan's eyes, but not of pain or grief. Rather of pure otherworldliness. He was there physically, but also, he wasn't. As if he'd taken a hallucinogen. The track faded and a new one began, first with just a guitar and a voice, a beautiful, deep voice. As Greg Lake began to sing 'You Turn Me On' Juan smiled at Ricky as Hiroshi slowly withdrew his hand. He peeled off the glove and began to massage Juan's vertically restrained thighs. He nodded to Steve, who nudged Greg and the two began to uncouple Juan's wrist restraints from the chains. Ricky continued to hold Juan's hand. As Hiroshi wiped Juan down, Greg and Steve released Juan's ankle restraints and lowered Juan's legs. Ricky walked toward the end of the sling as Greg took Juan's other hand and helped Ricky pull Juan into a standing position. Juan was still breathing deeply. He pulled Ricky into an embrace, then reached out and pulled Hiroshi into the same embrace. After a respectful moment, Ryan spoke up.

"So that's what fist fucking looks like." Hiroshi chuckled as Juan looked over Ricky's head at Ryan.

"That's what Hiroshi's fist fucking looks like. No one does it quite like Hiroshi." Hiroshi pulled out of the embrace and turned to Ryan and Mateo.

"And no one takes it quite like Juan, my friends." He turned back to Juan and bowed. "My most sincere happy birthday to you, Juan." Juan nodded and smiled, still looking a little dazed, then turned to Steve.

"Well ... okay. Is it time for Act Three?" Steve walked over to Ricky who was still wrapped around Juan and tapped him on the shoulder.

"You're up, Ricky." Ricky pulled away and rubbed his nose.

"I ... uh ... wow, that was um ..." He paused and glanced at Hiroshi. "I don't think I can top your act, Hiroshi." Raphael, fearing Ricky was getting cold feet, spoke up from behind him.

"Ricky ..." Ricky nodded without looking at Raphael, his eyes locked on Juan.

"Tell me if I'm doing this right, Raphael ..." Ricky knelt down on one knee in front of Juan. "Papito ... Juan ... I love you more than you will ever know. I can't find enough of the right words to say it, but maybe this will help." He reached into his fundoshi and pulled out the little black box that Raphael had used to present Juan with his HT keys. He opened it and pulled out a gold band, which he held up to Juan. "Juan, will you marry me?" Juan, already in a vulnerable, emotional state, began to lose it. As tears welled up, and a crooked smile spread across his face, he knelt down to Ricky's level. No one else, it appeared, was breathing. Juan held out his left hand, but just as Ricky moved to slide the ring on, Juan pulled his hand back.

"Ricky ... Enrique ... I will marry you. On one condition." Ricky straightened up in confusion. He started to speak then stopped. Then Juan spoke again. "You have to promise our engagement won't be as long as Raphael and Luke's was." Ricky burst out a blubbery laugh, accompanied by a chorus of cheers behind him as Juan again presented his left hand. Ricky slid the ring on as the two of them were surrounded in a clumsy, half-kneeling group hug.

"Ricky," Alex declared, "you sure know how to put together a Third Act." Juan wiped away his tears.

"Well, all of you certainly know how to put together a birthday ceremony. I'm speechless. I'm spent." He slowly stood, bringing Ricky with him. He reached out and again pulled Hiroshi into a side hug. He looked into Hiroshi's eyes and shook his head in appreciation. "Now," he addressed the room. "I was told there would be dinner."

"As promised," Greg said. "Ricky, take Juan up and give him a quick shower. Hiroshi, follow me. You can shower in our room. Alex and Raphael will have dinner ready in ..." He looked at Raphael.

"Twenty minutes, guys," Raphael announced. "Don't get too distracted by your new fiancé, Juan." Juan pulled Raphael into a brief hug and kiss as he and Ricky headed for the stairs. Once Ricky, Juan, Hiroshi and Greg had left, Luke turned to Ryan and Mateo.

"So. Ryan. How was your first dungeon experience?"

"Fuuuuuuck." Luke laughed and pulled the two of them into an embrace of his own.

"Glad you enjoyed it."

# Twenty-Eight

# PILLOW TALK

WHEN JUAN AND RICKY entered the dining room, everyone else was already seated. No one had really expected Juan's shower to take just twenty minutes, and it hadn't. Besides the shower, and whatever activities besides scrubbing had occurred under the spray, they'd obviously spent a few minutes getting Juan into his fundoshi as well. As they took their places, Alex, Raphael and Niki jumped up and headed into the kitchen while Luke rose and opened the first bottle of bubbly. Greg began retrieving glasses and handing them off to Luke, then returning them to each diner's place, freshly filled. Niki placed several small ramekins filled with a thick white pudding-like substance around the table while Alex distributed four bread baskets. Raphael lugged in an oversized tureen and set it on the sideboard. Alex made yet another trip into the kitchen and returned with a platter of roasted asparagus.

"Everything smells great," Juan praised, his left hand on Hiroshi's thigh and his right hand captured in both of Ricky's. "What are we having?"

"Roasted garlic goat cheese dip ... that's what the baguette slices are for," Alex detailed, "roasted asparagus and Raphael's soon to be famous mussels in white wine, shallots and butter sauce."

"Oh, so that's what the little forks are for," Greg held his up. "This house has everything."

"It does now," Niki declared as he took his seat. "The first time he saw the place Raphael said it lacked just one thing ... us! So, yeah, now we can say it has everything." Raphael was ladling mussels and broth into shallow bowls and handing them to Alex to distribute.

"And just think," he tossed over his shoulder to Niki, "at the time I had no idea it even had a dungeon ... or a gym." Once the mussels were served, Alex and Raphael took their seats, and Steve raised his glass.

"To you, Juan, Happy Birthday, and to you, Ricky, congratulations on ensnaring your man ... twice. We love you both." Glasses were raised, waived, clinked and pressed to hungry lips around the table.

"Is it true?" Juan asked as he set his glass down and took the platter of asparagus from Hiroshi as it made its rounds. "None of you knew everything that was going to happen tonight?"

"I didn't tell, did you, Raphael?" Ricky asked as he took the platter from Juan.

"Nope. Not even Luke."

"Raphael took me to the same jeweler where he got Luke's ring. When he proposed. In a dungeon. Just like us." Ricky looked very satisfied with himself.

"Well, everyone, you surprised me on all counts. A proposal. A mauling on the cross. And you Hiroshi. Obviously, you were on the committee. I didn't think anyone here knew about ... your talent."

"I was more of a consultant to the committee," Hiroshi smiled as he forked a mussel free of its shell and plopped it into his mouth. "Juan, let's be serious. My 'talent' would be nothing without your gift."

"I think it's safe to say the two of you make beautiful music together," Luke said. "I, for one, was in awe." Several around the table nodded in agreement.

"About the music," Ryan spoke up, "That was unexpected. I think I've heard some of it before."

"You probably have, but those selections were a little before your time, Ryan," Hiroshi smiled. "When I was your age, and we indulged in certain substances ... Pink Floyd and Emerson Lake and Palmer, along with so many others, accompanied many of our, shall we say, astral trips. The journey Juan and I took this evening was of a much more physical nature, of course, but also one that deserved an appropriate accompaniment. Would you agree?"

"For sure," Ryan nodded. "I don't know how it was for you Juan, but I thought the music really made the whole experience complete. And the guy on the last track ... he has a really nice voice."

"Yes, he did, Ryan. Greg Lake. Sadly, he is no longer with us. Keith Emerson, the keyboardist, too, has died." Hiroshi took a deep breath as he picked up his wine flute. Juan put a hand on his shoulder, figuring theirs' weren't the only deaths noted in that sigh.

"You're right about the music, Ryan. Tonight wasn't the first time Hiroshi has accompanied a session with that sound track. For me, it does make the experience better. More stimulating, more enveloping."

"Well," Alex offered, "I thought Raphael and I were kinky by wearing Thunderplugs regularly. I don't know how you did it, Juan. You kinda blew me away." Alex looked at Raphael, with raised fork. "Compliments to the chef, by the way ... the mussels are perfect." Raphael smiled and bowed his head in appreciation.

"I don't think you were the only one blown away, Alex," Luke glanced over at Ryan and Mateo before turning to Alex. "Ryan's boner made an unscripted appearance I noticed." Ryan and Mateo exchanged glances, Ryan's a bit sheepish, but Mateo in full grin.

"He can' help it," Mateo stated the obvious.

"Not that you mind, I'm sure," Niki kidded. Mateo gave him a shy, but knowing look.

"As long as we're talking about this ... umm, over dinner," Ryan posed, "I'm guessing it takes a lot of time and training to learn how to ..." he hesitated to say it, "fist?" Both Hiroshi and Juan exchanged glances, chuckling. Juan dipped his head, deferring to Hiroshi.

"We can discuss this in detail anytime you wish, Ryan, but ... yes. It is not something you and Mateo should try tonight on your own." Mateo turned to Ryan, eyes widened.

"Oh, I wasn't ..." Ryan trailed off. "Thanks, Hiroshi. I thought so." The topics of conversation became a bit more elevated after that, through dinner and into dessert, compliments of Ricky's cupcake bakery and his semi-secret stash of Mexican Chocolate ice cream. It didn't take long for Juan to blow out the sole candle centered in his carrot cake cupcake.

"So, you've been holding out, mijo," Juan kidded as he spooned a bite of ice cream. "I had no idea we had any Mexican Chocolate in the house."

"I was hoarding it specially for tonight, Papito." Ricky heaved a slight sigh.

"It is really good," Alex said. "And chocolate's not my favorite ice cream flavor."

"Well, savor it," Raphael cautioned. "Three Twins has closed for good."

"No!" Alex reacted. "Damn. Another one?"

"FTP," Niki grumbled to Alex.

"FTP?"

"Fuck This Pandemic." Alex nodded in response, actually licking his spoon clean. Once dessert, including the last known serving of Three Twins Mexican Chocolate had been consumed, Steve made a suggestion.

"Why don't we all retire to the sitting room. We can toast Juan one more time with a snifter of cognac. I know it's traditionally served in the library, but seating there is kind of limited."

"Actually," Hiroshi rose, "I brought a special bottle I would like to contribute to tonight's celebration, if I may ..."

"Even better," Steve replied. As the family headed for the sitting room, Hiroshi, Greg and Alex went into the butler's pantry to corral glassware and, at Hiroshi's request, a decanter. Hiroshi also retrieved a small decorated bag he'd placed there earlier. When they joined the family, Alex and Greg placed the glasses and decanter on a coffee table, and Hiroshi presented the bottle for Juan's inspection.

"Oh, wow," Juan smiled at Hiroshi. "Are you sure?"

"I can't think of a better occasion or more deserving recipients." Raphael leapt up and put an arm around Hiroshi's waist, as he looked over his shoulder. Hiroshi turned the bottle so he could see the label.

"Ricky, you aren't the only one with a secret stash," Raphael said as he rejoined Luke.

"What is it?" Ricky asked. Sitting on a couch next to Juan, he'd glanced at the label but hadn't appreciated what he was about to experience. Hiroshi knelt down next to the coffee table and began cutting through the foil. Instead of a standard corkscrew, he carefully slid a two-pronged cork puller into the bottle and gently worked the fragile cork out. As he began pouring through the silver strainer into the decanter to trap sediment, he answered Ricky's question.

"This is 1994 Ware's Porto. It was considered by many to be the vintage of the century. I was lucky to lay back a few bottles when it was released." He looked up at Ricky as he slowly emptied the bottle. "I think you'll like it." He then poured an inch and a half into each of the port glasses as Alex distributed them. Once everyone was served, Hiroshi settled into place on the floor and raised his glass to Juan and Ricky.

"To young love. May it grow stronger with each passing year." Juan smiled back at Hiroshi as Ricky focused on Juan, each tilting their glass to their lips.

"Perfecto," Juan judged, licking his lips. "Thank you for sharing, Hiroshi." Everyone fell under the spell of Hiroshi's port for a few moments, sipping and making happy sounds.

"So, this is twenty-six years old?" Ryan marveled.

"Yes, Ryan. Older than you and Mateo," Hiroshi grinned. "What do you think, Mateo. Do you like it?" Mateo nodded and smiled appreciatively at Hiroshi.

"I do."

"Do you like it better than cognac?" Juan asked.

"Maybe," Mateo tentatively replied, not wanting to cast aspersions on Niki's preferred digestif.

"Just think, Mateo," Alex leaned toward him from his perch in the window seat, "you've expanded your repertoire from a steady diet of Modelo to cognac, sake, Scotch and now rare vintage port."

"And sushi ... and tonight, mussels," Mateo grinned, before turning to Ryan. "And some other things."

"I take full credit," Ricky pronounced, matter-of-factly.

"Is that right?" Juan responded, pulling Ricky into a side hug, gently, to avoid spilling any port. Ricky nodded.

"One word ... boxers." Ricky made lingering eye contact with Mateo, then glanced at Ryan, who looked confused. "Ask him later, Ryan. It's a good story."

"Speaking of ..." Luke said, "I think we should schedule a session in the turret room with another bottle of truth serum and have Hiroshi as our guest of honor. It appears Hiroshi has more than a few stories to share, and I, for one, would love to hear all of them."

"I second that," Raphael wiggled his eyebrows at Hiroshi.

"All in favor?" Greg joined the pile-on. Ten voices voted 'aye.'

"Do I get a vote in this?" Hiroshi amiably inquired, looking around the room.

"It's been my experience," Ricky smiled, a little sillily, and maybe a little inebriated at this point, "that the answer is 'No!'" Juan turned and kissed the shaved side of Ricky's head, then turned back to see Hiroshi smiling at the two of them. Hiroshi didn't have to say anything. His happiness for Juan and Ricky, was written all over his face. It seemed like a good moment to end the evening. Hiroshi rose and everyone else followed suit. Juan, with Ricky attached, approached Hiroshi and pulled him into a hug.

"Thank you again, Hiroshi, for being a part of my birthday 'ceremony,'" Juan said. "For being a part of this family. I hope you realize how much you mean to us." Hiroshi, a bit self-conscious, nodded at Juan. He hesitated a moment before replying.

"I think I do, Juan." As he pulled away, he addressed the rest of the room. "As always, this has been yet another very enjoyable evening. Thank you, everyone." As he started to turn, Mateo intercepted him with an embrace of his own. "Good night, amigo." Hiroshi pressed a kiss on the top of Mateo's head, then raised a hand in parting. "Matane."

"Matane, Hiroshi," Juan replied.

"G'night," Ricky added. Once Hiroshi had closed the back door, Ricky asked, "What does matane mean?"

"See you again," Juan replied. "Like when we say 'see you later.' A way of saying goodbye without saying goodbye."

"Well, I was never sure how it would all work out, but I think it's safe to say this has been a birthday to remember, Juan," Steve said as he approached Juan and Ricky. He pulled them into a brief hug, then issued his last instructions for the evening. "Why don't you take this sleepy fiancé of yours upstairs and put him to bed. We'll take care of clean up." Juan didn't argue as he turned and walked Ricky toward the foyer, and the stairs beyond. As they were clearing dishes from the dining room table, Niki started to pull one end of the table to free the extra leaf they'd added earlier in the day.

"Let's leave the leaf in, Niki," Steve suggested.

"And the extra chair?" Ryan asked.

"Yeah," Steve replied. "We might need it more often." Mateo smiled as he glanced at Steve, who didn't elaborate, nor did he need to.

Once they'd finished in the bathroom and snuggled into bed, Ryan and Mateo lay facing one another, close enough that they could feel each other breathing. Mateo reached down and repositioned Ryan's erection between his own thighs, so it pressed up against his balls. He liked trapping it there.

"You really like Hiroshi, don't you?" Ryan asked. Mateo looked deeply into Ryan's eyes, curious about what was behind this question.

"Uh huh. I do. He is nice. And kind. And in'resting." They continued to stare into each other's eyes. Mateo wrapped an arm around Ryan's back and tugged him closer, waiting Ryan out.

"Do you love him?" Ah. So that's it. Mateo dropped his gaze momentarily to gather his thoughts, and his words, before resuming eye contact.

"Yes, of course, Ryan, I love him." He paused only briefly before continuing. "I love everyone in our family. I am lucky to be here. So lucky I save the boxers." Ryan's brow knitted briefly in confusion. "Ryan," Mateo recalled the words both Juan and Raphael had spoken to him, separately, months earlier, words that had seemed abstract then but were perfectly concrete for him now, "I'm *in* love with you. I love everyone in the family. But now you are here ... I sleep only with you." He tugged again, reinforcing his commitment. Ryan's lips quivered ever so slightly before he leaned forward with a kiss, maybe to hide his threatened sob.

"I'm sorry," he muttered as he pulled his lips back, looking away briefly before resuming eye contact. "I guess I still haven't adapted to all of this ... you know. Living in this 'family.' Where it's okay for everyone to love everyone else, openly and naturally. To have loves and a lover. All at the same time. And for it to be accepted ... expected even. And healthy. I'm sorry. I was feeling a little jealous ..." Before he could continue Mateo leaned forward, his turn to plant a kiss and interrupt Ryan's apology.

"Is okay. I know. I had to learn, also, Ryan." A sexy smile spread across Mateo's face. "Is good, no? To have lots of loves ... and a lover, too?" Ryan chuckled and sniffled simultaneously. Mateo had never looked so sexy or sounded so profound. Or, maybe it was the bubbly and the port.

Regardless, Mateo was in his arms, professing his love, and that was all Ryan needed right now.

"Mateo, my prince, it's more than good. It's perfect. It's so, so perfect."

Across the hall, Alex and Greg were under the covers as well. Greg was on his back, propped up a bit on a couple of pillows; Alex on his side next to him, his head held up by his left hand, while his right hand was tracing up and down Greg's treasure trail.

"This was some evening, huh?" Alex glanced up at Greg.

"It was ... you guys did a great job with dinner, Alex," Greg teased, knowing that wasn't what Alex was referring to. "Did you make the goat cheese dip from scratch?"

"We did," Alex replied mockingly. "Of course. We even grew the mussels from larvae."

"Good for you," Greg played along. "I didn't realize you'd planned that far ahead." Alex squeezed a tuft of hair and pulled. "Owwww."

"You know that's not what I'm talking about, but yeah dinner was really good, thanks for saying so. It kind of paled by comparison though ..." Greg rolled onto his side and clasped a hand around one of the two butt cheeks Alex so enjoyed offering up to discipline.

"Yeah ..." Greg relented, "Juan and Hiroshi ... I have to say, I felt like a guilty voyeur."

"I know what you mean. It was, I don't know, intimate, raw ... explicit? Not that Hiroshi did anything gross. Well, there was the pee, but uh ..." Greg squeezed that butt cheek. "Hiroshi really knows his way around the inside of Juan's guts."

"And you thought you knew what it's like to have your ass pummeled." He reached a bit further and encountered the external curve of Alex's Thunderplug. "On second thought, maybe you know more about it than I was giving you credit for." Alex flashed a Cheshire smile.

"I, uh, don't think this is quite the same thing. Juan was pretty much in an altered state of consciousness, don't you think?" Greg nodded.

"Agreed. What do you think, Alex? Should we make a appointment with Hiroshi for you?" Alex groaned as he pushed Greg over onto his back again.

"Well, if I've learned anything in the last year or two, it's to never say never, but, for now anyway, I'll stick to my paddles and the Thunderplug if that's okay. Tried and true, you know."

"Fair enough," Greg smiled as he switched off the bedside lamp. He rolled toward the middle of the bed, where Alex was already positioned, for their night-long embrace.

Raphael had unwound Luke's fundoshi, after they'd entered their room, then wrapped it around his own head in an attempted turban. He was still wearing his fundoshi, in the traditional fashion, standing at the sink, brushing his teeth, waiting for a reaction from Luke, who was doing his best to pretend he hadn't noticed as he flossed. Both were just a little tipsy, as much from the happiness they felt for Juan and Ricky as from the evening's abundance of alcohol. Finally, Luke gave in.

"I guess it's true," he said before gargling.

"What's that?" Raphael asked before he spat. Luke waited until Raphael had rinsed.

"That you can pull off any look, even a silly one."

"It's not silly, Sir. It's audacious." He batted his lashes. "Isn't that your word?"

"Your ink is audacious, baby. Your get up, at the moment, is just plain silly." Raphael dropped his toothbrush into the holder, turned and ripped off both fundoshi. Dramatically, of course.

"Is this better, Sir?" Raphael demanded, before presenting his best demure smile. Luke pulled him tight.

"Much. Race you to the bed." Although they didn't race, they did end up there, and soon were settled into place, on their sides, Luke on the outside, Raphael enveloped in his arms. After a moment's silence, Luke quietly congratulated Raphael, "Baby, that was quite a finale you and Ricky planned. I don't know what surprised Juan more, Hiroshi's appearance or Ricky's proposal."

"That was all Ricky, Sir. All I did was help him with the ring. It was his idea, and considering how Juan reacted, it was a good one, don't you think?"

"He was channeling you, obviously. You have a way of doing that, don't you? Bringing Niki out of the closet. Inspiring Ricky to propose ... in a dungeon, no less."

"With an audience! I would have never had the guts to do that with you."

"What do you mean?"

"Well, Sir ... what if you'd said no? I would have been mortified. Not to mention devastated. For life." Luke raised up on his left arm to hover his face over Raphael's.

"You don't, for a minute, think I could have ever said no, do you?" He pulled away and rolled Raphael over onto his back, so they could see one another. "Baby?"

"Well ... I know that now. I was scared to death then. And a little messed up by what you'd just put me through. Kinda like how Juan was tonight, come to think of it. He must have been a little foggy, too."

"Yeah, but he was on the receiving end. You were the one in control, just like Ricky was tonight." Luke rolled onto his back, staring at the ceiling. "Interesting. In both cases it was the guy who was caged who made the proposal." Raphael snorted softly then rolled back onto his side, wiggling his ass in invitation for Luke to resume his place. Which he did.

"Which just goes to show," Raphael whispered after a moment of silence, on the edge of sleep, "it's always the bottom who's in control."

"I'm not sure I know what to think about what happened tonight," Niki said as he pulled the covers back and slipped into place. Steve crawled in from the other side of the bed and reached out to pull Niki close. They kissed softly, almost a chaste kiss, before Steve lifted his head, searching Niki's eyes for more. But, the man of few words held back.

"It was ... eventful." Steve offered in an open-ended reply. Niki sighed deeply and wiggled a bit, getting comfortable. "What *do* you think ...?"

"Well," Niki stared at the ceiling, "the easy part ... Ricky was awesome. He was so cute. And Juan ... giving him a hard time. I don't know how Ricky felt, but when Juan pulled his hand back, it freaked me out at first." Niki returned his gaze to Steve. "It was a terrific birthday present, I'll say that."

"And what about Hiroshi's present?" Steve knew that was what was weighing on Niki.

"Yeah ... I mean ... in the abstract it was sexy hot." Niki bit his lower lip in thought. "I've seen fisting porn, but in real life, up close ... like I said, sexy hot. But also, kind of scary." He put a hand on Steve's side. "Don't you think?"

"The word 'intense' comes to mind, yeah. Greg and I were concerned it might be scary for Ryan and Mateo, but it hadn't occurred to me that it might scare you."

"I guess I was thinking about what kind of damage somebody could do ..."

"Yes, Nurse Niki, but remember Hiroshi ... and Juan ... know what they're doing." Steve gave a short laugh.

"What's so funny?"

"Oh, just that I was worried about Ryan and Mateo, and you're the one I should have been worried about. Turns out Ryan actually seemed pretty fascinated by it." It was Niki's turn to chuckle.

"He was. Jeez, I hope he doesn't try something with Mateo."

"Mateo can handle Ryan, sweetie." Greg settled back into place.

"And then ..." Niki still had something on his mind. Steve rolled back to face Niki, but remained silent. "I still don't know what to think about Juan." Niki turned to Steve. "You know, getting fisted instead of doing the fisting."

"I see," Steve replied. He brushed his fingers through Niki's mohawk. "You think that was inappropriate?"

"Surprising is a better word, I guess."

"Do you think any less of Juan after tonight?"

"Oh, god, no!" Niki shook his head and reached over to gently rub Steve's belly. "He obviously has more guts than I do." Niki cleared his throat. "Pun intended. It's just ... surprising."

"Like finding out your lover is secretly a puppy?"

"Touché." Niki rubbed a couple of seconds longer, then moved his hand around Steve's side in an effort to hug him closer. "Like I said. I just need to process it. Okay?" Steve leaned down for a final goodnight kiss.

"Take your time. Maybe all you need to do is sleep on it."


"Did you enjoy your birthday, Papito? Was it a good one?" Juan was laying on his back, with Ricky snuggled at his side, both still on top of the covers after having completed their ablutions. Juan's right arm was wrapped around Ricky's neck and shoulder, his left hand gently brushing Ricky's side.

"No, I can't honestly say it was good." Ricky, fully accustomed to Juan's sense of humor, didn't react. He simply lifted his eyes to Juan's without moving his head. And waited.

"No. It was legendary." Ricky flashed a satisfied grin.

"Yeah. You and Hiroshi put on an amazing show." Juan chuckled at Ricky's effort at self-deprecation.

"Hiroshi was very good, yeah, but you, mijo ... you were the real show-stopper."

"Were you surprised?"

"I was." Juan bent his head down to press a kiss on Ricky's head. "I probably shouldn't have been, but yes, I was." He chuckled again. "I have to say you looked pretty nervous as you held out this ring." Juan lifted his left hand to admire the ring in the light from the bedside lamp.

"I *was* nervous, Papito! What if you said ... not yet?"

"What if I'd said no? Hmmm. Now that's an interesting question. What if I'd said 'not yet' to this beautiful man, a man so courageous and so impassioned that he was willing to walk into a bar with hundreds of people, displaying a chastity cage in see-through shorts, to beg me to make him my locked cock leather boy?" While Juan pondered, Ricky raised up into a sitting position and reached for Juan's left hand and tried tugging on the ring.

"Oh, no you don't," Juan laughed. "No backsies on your proposal, future Mr. Ricky Reyes. Or will it be Mr. Ricky Soto-Reyes?" Ricky giggled, but continued tugging on the ring.

"I'll be Soto-Reyes if you will, but, here, let me show you something, Papito." Ricky put Juan's ring finger in his mouth to lubricate Juan's finger, then he gently pulled the ring free. "Look inside." He handed the ring back to Juan, who turned to hold it closer to the light. There he read the engraving: 'Love u always, Ricky.'

"Hmm." Juan slid the ring back into place and pulled Ricky into an embrace. "Well, there's the answer to your question. How could I say no to the one man who, no matter what, has promised to love me always?" Juan held out his hand to again admire the ring. "You thought of everything, didn't you, mijo."

"Well, I had a little help from Raphael," Ricky muttered into Juan's chest. "So. You're really happy, you know, about having a fiancé?"

"Yeah ... I guess." He took a deep breath, lifting Ricky's head along with his chest. "It'll have to do for now. Until I have a have a husband. Rumor has it he's the World's Best Locked Cock Leather Boy, too, so yeah, I'm pretty happy." Ricky, nodded, without lifting his head off Juan's chest. He appeared to be settling in the for the night. "Are you happy, mijo?" Ricky nodded again.

"Two guesses, Papito ..."

Next door, Hiroshi was wiping down the cork puller and strainer funnel after rinsing them off. He was smiling, about the fact the port had gone over well ... and hadn't been corked after spending twenty-six years in the cellar. About sharing another delicious and entertaining evening with his 'bubble.' And not just a bubble really; Juan had reminded him they considered him a part of the family tonight. About performing a most intimate act with Juan again, after far more than a year's interim. Had it been just him and Juan tonight, he might have felt guilty, just a little, in doing so, but Ricky had been right there, the whole family had been. So, no guilt. Just a long-missed sense of purpose. Of fulfillment. He and Juan had connected again, and in a way, as if no time had passed at all. But time had passed. Much had changed. Juan, as of tonight, was engaged, and that, too, brought a smile to Hiroshi's lips. Ben was gone. But never forgotten. Ben would have been so very happy for Juan. And for Ricky, had he had the opportunity to have known him. In a very real way, Hiroshi honestly felt, Ben would be at peace knowing Juan and his family were there, bringing new life and energy to his home. He would have laughed had he known his passing would result in Hiroshi living next door to the House of the Locked Cock Brotherhood. No doubt he would have led in toasting the happy couple, the whole family, this evening. And certainly, he would have been happy for Hiroshi. So, as he climbed the stairs to his bedroom, Hiroshi thought, maybe it's time I felt happy for myself. I've lost Ben. Ben cannot be replaced. But I now have ten very kind, very handsome, clothing-averse, generous, sexy, caged and collared neighbors, who seem to have embraced me as one of their own. Family. Dare I say ... brothers? Much younger brothers, granted, but so much the better ... they will keep me young. Hiroshi unwrapped his fundoshi as he walked into the bath and tossed it into the shower, where he would hand wash it while he showered in the morning. He looked down at his cage, then into the mirror, and wordlessly asked himself if it was time. The smile he saw there was his answer. He pulled open the top vanity drawer and retrieved his keys.

Twenty-Nine

# RAPHAEL AND ALEX COLLABORATE AGAIN

"CHECK THIS OUT." RYAN was just heading out of his door when he encountered Luke topping the stairs on the way to his and Raphael's room. Luke had a towel over his shoulder, having just finished a workout. He followed Ryan back into his and Mateo's room and over to the window overlooking the back garden. Ryan looked down, then over to Luke, grinning. There, splayed across a couple of beach blankets were three bare-assed young men, nearly thigh to thigh, soaking up some summer sun ... since summer in San Francisco falls in September and October. Alex was in the middle, with Raphael on one side and Ricky on the other. Three full moons invitingly on display.

"You have a much better view from your room than we have from ours," Luke observed. "I guess we all miss the beach."

"You all used to go a lot, huh?"

"Many Saturdays just like this ... when the fog cooperated, yeah. That's where both Alex and Ricky learned to wear their cages proudly."

"And Raphael?"

"Oh, mostly the gym. He was shy about it at first, but it didn't take him long to become a sensation in the steam room. First him and later Niki. Kinda miss the gym, too, sometimes."

"Not from the looks of this," Ryan said admiringly, squeezing Luke's freshly pumped left biceps.

"We're making do, Ryan. Indoors and out, it seems." Luke turned back to the window and its view.

"You know what this looks like?" Ryan asked, chuckling. Luke shook his head. "This could be the opening scene of a porn flick. Then you, the outraged neighbor, storms into the garden demanding the sexy naked guys put on some clothes ..."

"And the sexy naked guys disarm, disrobe and seduce me and it turns into a raunchy foursome?" Ryan nodded, laughing. "You seem to know your porn, Ryan." Ryan looked sheepish, but nodded.

"I was there and Mateo was here. What was I supposed to do?" Luke nodded knowingly.

"Maybe I should go get my phone. *You* can be the outraged neighbor and I'll capture it all on video. Your chance to be a star."

"I don't know," Ryan pretended to consider it. "We'd probably need to do a few rehearsals first." Luke laughed. "But, seriously, aren't they worried about somebody calling the cops?"

"For what?"

"Public indecency?"

"Ryan, it's not illegal to be naked on your own property." Ryan's eyes widened.

"Seriously?"

"I was going to shower, but I think I'll join the party instead. Why don't you come down, too?" Luke headed for the hallway. "I'm going to grab some sunscreen. Come on. Grab a towel. You can surprise Mateo with a nice bronzy glow when he gets off work." As Ryan turned back to the window, the thought of laying out naked in the garden in the middle of the city, with four other guys was all it took to re-energize his rambunctious cock. He looked down in dismay. He'd just about decided to pass when Luke walked past the door on his way out. "Come on, pledge. Consider this an obligatory hazing." Before he lost his nerve again, Ryan pulled a towel off the closet shelf and followed Luke down the stairs, bobbing all the way.

Raphael was sitting propped up against the headboard, phone in hand, and most improbably, wearing a shirt, a navy locked cock polo previously worn only at the office. Back when people actually went to offices. Luke did a double take when he entered, before realizing, oh yeah. It's Sunday, and time for their monthly date with Angel and Mama. While Luke opened a drawer to search for a shirt of his own, Raphael's phone announced Angel's call.

"Hey, you're early," Raphael said. "Luke will be here in a sec."

"Hey, Raphael. Yeah, Mama's making us tea. I wanted to have a moment with you before she joins us."

"What's up, Angel?" Luke asked as he slid into place at Raphael's side.

"I want you to ... casually ... remind her of the importance of staying home and social distancing. I've caught her sneaking out to visit with her neighbor Rosa. Twice. I know she misses Auntie, and their weekly lunches. She misses coffees with all of her friends. She misses seeing you guys ... all of you guys. In the flesh. She hasn't hugged you since the wedding. The chats with you two and with Niki and Steve just aren't enough, I guess. I understand, but I'm worried about her. We've talked, but it might help if you guys ... and Niki ... back me up. Without it looking like we're ganging up on her."

"Gotcha," Raphael nodded. "Subtlety is one of my superpowers." Luke made a surprised face, producing a laugh from Angel.

"Mama's not alone," Luke said earnestly. "We've been dying for you two to come and visit and see our new home. You could even spend the night. We have that much room."

"Maybe you guys can at least give us a virtual tour today. Mama would enjoy that."

"Oooooh, not a good idea," Raphael grinned. "Remember, we live with eight other naked guys, half of them caged. We'd give Mama a heart attack."

"She might surprise you, but okay, fine," Angel looked disappointed. "Here she comes ..."

The next hour covered topics new and old, including family, current events, election politics and what little social life each had been able to enjoy. Luke bragged about Raphael's mussels for Juan's birthday dinner, thinking it might be a good lead-in to Angel's covert assignment.

"Yeah, Mama," Raphael took the baton. "We're lucky to be able to at least live together in our little bubble here with the people we love. It has to be very frustrating for you to not socialize like you used to ..." Mama sighed and glanced at Angel.

"I miss you boys so much. And I worry about all of you. Especially Juan, working in the hospital."

"We're all very careful, Mama," Luke said as reassuringly as he could. They'd never told her or Angel about Mateo's close call. "We worry about both of you, too. You have a lot more cases there than we've had here in the city. Are you both doing everything you can to stay safe?" Angel turned his eyes to Mama without turning his head, almost making Raphael laugh. Mama nodded as she spoke.

"We're being very careful, right Angel?" Angel screwed up his lips but said nothing, simply nodding.

"You must miss getting together with your friends and neighbors," Raphael probed. "And Auntie."

"Have you tried meeting any of them in the park," Luke added, "masked and socially distanced?" Mama sighed.

"It's not easy," was her only response.

"Maybe Angel could help arrange something like that," Raphael suggested, speaking past Mama to the man at her side, who gave Raphael a brotherly look of scorn.

"Well, Mama," Raphael concluded the intervention, "I know it's boring but you really shouldn't go anywhere, except maybe to the grocery. With Angel. And always with a mask. We all wear masks here every time we leave the house." He nudged Luke.

"We love you," Luke added with a genuine smile. "Promise you'll stay safe?"

"I'll be fine, boys," she maintained. "It's you I worry about." Angel rolled his eyes, just like Raphael, producing the same reaction from Luke.

"Angel, we're counting on you to protect Mama," Luke laughed.

"Maybe the two of us should just move up there and live with all of you until this is over," Angel countered, his eyes more mischievous than his smile. Fortunately, Mama laughed, put her hand on the side of Angel's face and turned his head so she could kiss him.

"I'm too old to be a house mother for a bunch of rambunctious young men, Angel," she declared. She then leaned a bit closer to the camera. "Maybe if this goes on too much longer, we can talk about it again." She winked to let Raphael and Luke know she wasn't serious. Almost as if maybe she knew more about life in the House of the Locked Cock Brotherhood than anyone realized.

It wasn't long after the call ended that Raphael received a text from Angel. 'Thanks guys. Not sure how successful we were. Pls brief Niki. XOX.' Raphael was tapping out a reply when Ricky stuck his head in the door.

"Dinner at six," he announced. "Hiroshi's going to join us, too."

"Cool," Luke replied. "What are we having?"

"Fish tacos. Black beans and coleslaw. Juan's making his secret mole sauce."

"Mole on fish tacos?" Raphael screwed up his face.

"Mexican mole, not Filipino mole," Ricky walked over and grabbed the hem of Raphael's shirt. "And what's with the shirts? You two have a hot date somewhere?"

"No," Raphael put his phone down, peeled off the polo and tossed it at Ricky. "We were talking to Angel and Mama."

"That's sweet," Ricky grinned. "Thanks for the shirt, Raphael. I'll wear it on my runs tomorrow."

"And you'll launder it and put in the second drawer on the left there afterwards," Raphael nudged Ricky out of the way as he slid off the bed. "Dinner sounds … interesting. Luke and I are off to the gym first though." He landed a quick peck on Ricky's cheek and headed out the door.

It turned out Juan's mole sauce was the perfect addition to fish tacos. Along with shredded lettuce and a little Pico de Gallo. Even Raphael thought so. As dinner was winding down Luke tapped his Dos Equis bottle three times with his knife, as if he were about to make a wedding toast.

"Ahem," he pronounced to a curious audience. "I don't know if any of you have noticed, but due to the pandemic, and the limited opportunities resulting from it, my lovely husband and I have had few opportunities to pursue our notorious hobby." Raphael turned to Luke, not sure what he was up to. He glanced around the table, and it appeared he wasn't alone. "However, and I have Ryan to thank for inspiring me ... I am ready to issue my next dare to Raphael."

"All right!" Alex reacted. "It's about time!" Raphael gave Alex the evil eye, glanced questioningly at Ryan, who looked clueless, then sat back in his chair alternating between glancing expectantly at Luke and looking down at his cage.

"Usually, but not always, we've revealed our dares to each other in private, but this time I wanted everyone to hear it. Since it's likely more than one of you may be enlisted to help Raphael fulfill what just might be my most wonderfully ingenious, and maybe most sinister dare yet. Who knows, Hiroshi, if you're lucky, maybe even you." Hiroshi nodded once, graciously, not quite sure what was unfolding.

"More sinister than your last one ... in the dungeon?" Raphael locked eyes with Juan, who smiled at the memory. Raphael turned his gaze back to Luke. "Oh, this can't be good."

"I think it's pretty good, actually," Luke said before taking a dramatic swig from his Dos Equis. He set the bottle down and looked lovingly at Raphael. Without speaking.

"Are. You. Going. To. Tell. Us. What. The. Dare. *Is*?"

"Baby ..." Luke looked around the table to insure he had everyone's attention, "your dare is to make and star in a porn flick. And post it online." Raphael looked as if his Zoom image had frozen. For several seconds he didn't react. Then he slowly turned to face Ryan.

"Ryan?"

"I ... I ..." Poor Ryan was speechless.

"Don't blame Ryan, baby. He had no idea when we talked yesterday that I would come up with this idea. He's innocent, totally. Now there are some parameters for this dare." Raphael closed his eyes and took a deep breath, still processing what Luke had just said. Then he shook his head and turned to Luke.

"Should I get a note pad? Sir?" Raphael chided. Luke laughed.

"No. Pretty simple, really." He looked around the table again to gauge everyone's reaction so far. He anticipated their ears would prick up shortly. "The film has to be at least five minutes long. You have to include at least two other actors ... no lame solo auto-erotica action. And I can't be one of them." Luke checked to make sure he'd made an impression. The look on Alex's face confirmed that he had. "I'll be happy to assist as sound man, camera, lighting ... whatever you need behind the camera." Raphael tilted his head back, eyes closed, and took another deep breath. Greg cleared his throat. Steve took a long swig from his Modelo. Both had been involved in previous dares. Would that make them exempt? Finally, Raphael lowered his head. And chuckled. Then, he started to laugh. Then, he looked back at Luke.

"You bastard. This really is ... sinister. And you just came up with it yesterday?" Luke proudly grinned. "So ... where online do I post it?"

"Your choice, baby."

"When does it have to be done?"

"Up to you. Just remember, until you complete this dare, you can't issue one to me." Raphael looked around the table with a slight smirk. With the exception of Niki and Mateo, everyone else avoided eye contact.

"With a minimum of two other actors?" Luke nodded. "But there could be more ..." Luke nodded again.

"Lordy," Ryan barely whispered.

"Including the guy who gave you this insane idea in the first place?" Once more, Luke nodded. Ryan whimpered. Raphael looked around the table again. Juan looked slightly amused. Alex was a deer in the head-lights. Steve was looking at Luke, brow furrowed. Hiroshi was looking peacefully at Raphael, with just the hint of a smile. "So, this ought to be fun, huh, guys?" Everyone rushed to say nothing. In this moment, it was as if Raphael was the teacher and nobody in class wanted to be called on. Or even recognized. Finally, Raphael said, "Well, there won't be any need for auditions. I've already seen all of you naked." Niki laughed, in spite of himself, which lightened the mood immediately.

"I think I need another beer," Steve said as he stood.

"Me, too," Ryan started to stand. Steve waived him back down as he headed into the kitchen. He returned with a twelve pack. Everyone but Juan accepted seconds. He was an on-call back up tonight. He studied Raphael a moment, who had fallen silent himself, trying to ascertain how Raphael was taking this dare. He didn't think the 'porn' part of it was a concern necessarily, given his openness not just about his sexuality, but about his kinks as well. Although that might be an issue, considering that an on-line posting would live on into posterity, depending on where it was posted. And reposted. He might be thinking about the requirement to include others who might resist, or even refuse to participate, and the discomfort that would produce, at least temporarily. Or ... maybe it was simply the logistical challenge of producing a worthy cinematic product that was weighing on Raphael, who was about as precise and perfectionist as anyone Juan had ever known.

"Raphael," Juan broke the silence, "I have to say you have one thing going for you in this dare." Raphael raised his eyebrows in a query over the upended bottle he was slowly draining. "You couldn't ask for a better location set for a gay porn flick. Think about it ... a gym, a *dungeon*, beautifully appointed rooms for contrast. A high-tech kitchen. Even a beautiful garden in back. You can take this in just about any direction you want." Raphael slowly lowered his bottle of Modelo, still focused on Juan. Then a smile grew as he turned to Luke.

"Kinda sounds like Juan just volunteered to be a part of this super fantastic dare of yours, Sir." Luke put an arm around Raphael's shoulders and looked across the table to Juan.

"Kinda does, doesn't it, baby?" Juan balled up his napkin and tossed it at Luke. No one else spoke for a minute, not wanting to draw attention to themselves.

"Just to be sure," Raphael said, looking at no one in particular, "are there any more parameters I need to know about before I start casting?"

"No, baby, the rest is up to you." Raphael locked eyes with Ryan.

"Okay, then. We'll ... uh, do our best to make you proud. Right, Ryan?"

"I ... uh ... lordy." Ryan turned to Mateo for support. Or, maybe for sympathy. All he got was an innocent smile. Luke stood and picked up his and Raphael's plates, sending the message that 'my work here is done.' Before anyone else moved, Hiroshi spoke.

"Well, my friends, you have outdone yourselves tonight. Each meal I share with you is always uncommonly entertaining as well as an epicurean delight. Raphael, I look forward to being invited to the premiere of what I am certain will be a cinematic masterpiece." Raphael stood and bowed.

"We won't let you down, Hiroshi. You have my word."


Not surprisingly, no one dared raise the subject of the dare in the following days. It wasn't until midway through their run late that Thursday afternoon, when Alex, Raphael and Niki had reached the Conservatory of Flowers in Golden Gate Park, that Niki couldn't contain his curiosity any longer. They'd slowed to a walk, for a breather, before turning back.

"Nice route, Niki," Alex said. "What are we doing today?"

"About three point six miles," Niki replied. He stopped to retie his shoe.

"Alex," Raphael turned and walked backward to face Alex and keep an eye on Niki, "did you train like this when you were a competitive volleyball player?"

"Yeah, I did. Not the weights like we're doing now, but we used to run. This is great. I'm glad we started doing this." Niki caught up with them.

"We can turn back now," he suggested, "or, we can turn back at the de Young and make it an even four miles." No one replied, and they continued walking, which settled that. "So, uh, Raphael. Have you thought more about Luke's dare?" Raphael sighed.

"Actually, I've been trying not to, Niki."

"Okay." Niki felt badly about bringing it up.

"I don't think we've ever had a dare where the guy on the receiving end has to create the dare. Usually, we just have to do what the other one tells him to do."

"Well, you had to come up with your tattoos," Alex reminded him. "You blew everybody away with that one." Raphael issued a non-committal mumble.

"Maybe. But that seemed easy compared to this. I just had to lay there and take it."

"Give yourself some credit, dude," Alex grabbed Raphael's arm. "Your ink is outrageous. Nobody else would have come up with anything half as bold as what you did. Front *and* back."

"He's right," Niki agreed. "You probably just need some time to think."

"I don't know," Raphael said dejectedly. "I feel like it's all been done. A thousand times. Most porn is *so* boring."

"It's boring to you because what we're living is a real-life porn flick, Raphael," Alex said. "A brilliant man once said those very words ... and not so very long ago."

"That, uh, brilliant man wouldn't be you, would it?" Raphael grinned behind his mask.

"Well, of course. But you have to admit it's true."

"So ... what? You're suggesting I just film us being us?" Raphael thought a moment. "I guess that would be easy enough."

"Raphael, you disappoint me." Raphael looked at Alex, a little hurt. "Raphael, you can do so much better than that." Somewhat assuaged, Raphael looked forward again. "I'm really surprised you haven't leaned on your in-house evil genius. You know, the one with the theater background. Costumes. Make-up. Singing. Dancing." Alex paused briefly. "Acting."

"Performing sex on camera?" Raphael locked eyes with Alex, the Alex who not so long ago wouldn't even appear naked at the Folsom Street Fair. "How far are you willing to go, Alex?" Alex didn't respond.

"Sorry, Alex," Raphael apologized. "I appreciate what you're saying, but ... I don't even know where to start. That's the problem." Alex grabbed Raphael's biceps once again and stopped their progress. He looked intently into Raphael's eyes.

"I do." He glanced at Niki who was silently enjoying the trajectory of the conversation, then back at Raphael. "I have an idea. It's crazy, but the more I think about it, the more I like it. Luke didn't say you had to script this alone. Did he?" Raphael shook his head. "In fact, he wanted you to include other people." Alex stepped back and spread his arms. "Mr. Malaluan, I hear you're looking for a screenwriter. Can we take a meeting?" Raphael looked at Niki, rolling his eyes and shaking his head.

"I think he's been taking lessons from you, Raffie," Niki laughed. "You can't say no to that."


"Where are you going?" Luke asked. He was exiting the bathroom after dinner as Raphael was heading out their bedroom door, his tablet in hand. "Are we decamping to the sitting room?"

"Actually, Sir, I'm off to a meeting in the turret room. Invitees only. Maybe you can watch some TV with Greg." Luke paused a moment before catching on.

"Oh. Gotcha. So, you'll be with Alex?" Raphael flashed a confirming grin. "Okay, you guys have fun." Luke wandered into Greg and Alex's room as Raphael headed up the stairs to the third floor and beyond.

"Alex said I might expect you," Greg looked up. "Do you know what's up?"

"My fault, maybe. They're either planning Juan and Ricky's wedding or they're working on my dare."

"Ah. Of course. Right up Alex's alley." Luke gave Greg a questioning look as he settled onto the bed next to Greg. "You know ... he loves to put on a show." Luke nodded.

"So, he's done video productions, too?"

"Well, nothing like what you've challenged Raphael with, but it's all theater in essence. Besides, they'll have fun collaborating. Maybe it'll be a documentary about the Chastity Brothers' life off the stage, or something like that."

"What have I done, Greg?" Luke turned a pained face to Greg. "It seemed like a good idea at the time."

"It was a good idea, Luke. We all need a distraction. Or two. Just remember not to laugh at whatever they come up with. Remember how hard they worked on the strip shows. They won't just blow this off."

"True. This is either going to be my most epic dare yet. Or, the lamest."

"It's out of your hands now, Luke. Don't stress. And try not to stress Raphael, either, if you sense he's struggling with it. You know, try not to bring it up, or exaggerate your expectations and pressure him. If I get any sense from Alex that this is overwhelming Raphael, I'll let you know."

"Thanks, Greg." He patted Greg on the thigh. "So, speaking of theater, what are we watching?"


Raphael closed the door behind him for added privacy and climbed the steep stairs up to the turret room. As he topped the stairs, he saw both Alex and Niki, on the floor, huddled over Alex's laptop. Both looked up and beamed at Raphael.

"Niki saw me coming up and asked if he could join us," Alex said as he patted the floor to his right. "He bribed me with some of his cognac, so I said yes." Niki poured an inch into a third snifter and reached past Alex to hand it to Raphael.

"The more the merrier as far as I'm concerned," Raphael took the snifter. "Thanks, Niki. Like I said, I have nothing." He took a sip and savored a moment, enjoying the warmth as it meandered its way into his gut. Then he leaned back in an attempt to see what was displayed on Alex's screen. "So ... what are you thinking, Mr. Screenwriter?" Alex closed the laptop and turned to face Raphael.

"Okay. Don't say anything until I finish. Okay? It's going to sound weird at first, but let me lay it all out before you react." Niki got up and carried his snifter over to Raphael's side, so they were both facing Alex. "I agree with you that most porn is boring. Derivative. And that's being kind. There's usually maybe one percent storyline, if that, then sex. Usually the same kind of sex. With both the top and the bottom limited to saying either 'uhh, uhh, uhh' or 'fuck, oh fuck, fuck.' Amiright?"

"Gee, Alex, have you watched much porn?" Raphael teased.

"Boys, I've seen it all. And I mean all. Remember, it's why I'm caged." Niki laughed into his snifter, acknowledging the veracity of Alex's point. "You know what's missing in porn? Actual entertainment. Real plot. And ... this is the evil genius part ... humor." Raphael turned to Niki, both of whom raised their eyebrows. Then in violation of Alex's request, he turned back to Alex and spoke.

"Tell me more."

# Thirty

# THE PLOT THICKENS. LITERALLY.

"So, what do you think?" Alex leaned back after methodically walking through his concept. Five minutes in, Niki had stretched out on his back, eyes closed, to better visualize what Alex was describing. Raphael had taken occasional sips from his snifter, but had hardly broken eye contact with Alex who had become more and more animated as he talked. Raphael was enjoying watching Alex's growing enthusiasm as much as he was absorbing his verbal storyboards. When Alex finished, Raphael turned to look at Niki, who sat up and took a sip of his own. He initially offered Raphael a non-committal continence that slowly morphed into a conflicted grin.

"It's either brilliant. Or insane. Raphael?"

"Well, you've both probably seen more porn than I ever have, but I guess I lean toward insane. It's not like anything I've ever seen." Alex reached over and squeezed Raphael's calf.

"And that's the point, Raphael. You said yourself most porn is boring. Does this sound boring?"

"No. It's ... it's ... well, I don't know what it is."

"Maybe this will help you understand what I'm going for. What I envision is not porn for porn's sake, but actual entertainment." He paused a moment. "I know ... one of the most successful 'horror' movies of all time is *Rocky Horror Picture Show*. Not because it was a great horror movie, not even close. It was camp. It was drole. Sometimes funny. I mean, it was a *musical* horror movie ... unexpected ... and it blew audiences away."

"Still does," Niki affirmed. "It's always playing somewhere."

"Yes. Yes!" Alex resumed. "Don't think of it as a porn flick. Think of it as Rocky Horror meets Bram Stoker meets Titan Men." Raphael closed his eyes and rewound some of what Alex had detailed. Alex offered more supporting evidence. "Like the scene when you first catch the burglars in the sitting room. And you cast the first spell. It'll be sexy as hell for the audience *and* they'll be cough-laughing their popcorn at the same time."

"Okay. I think I'm getting it. You really do have to kind of leave the whole porn idea aside, don't you?"

"Not aside. It's integral. But it's not the primary focus. It's sexy throughout. I mean, you are the sexy centerpiece, Raphael. Everybody in the audience will want to be you." Raphael looked down at his snifter, deep in thought. After a moment he glanced at Niki again.

"I changed my mind, Raphael. It's brilliant." Niki raised his snifter, indicating his judgement was final. Raphael turned back to Alex.

"It's growing on me. But ..." Alex chuckled.

"There's always a 'but.'" He looked past Raphael at Niki. "The thankless life of a screenwriter ..."

"No, Alex, not the concept. The casting." Alex looked disappointed.

"So, Mr. Client. Who am I going to have to fire?" Raphael laughed.

"No, no. A promotion. Juan should have my role. He would be perfect. I should be a burglar."

"God, he's right," Niki enthused. "Yes. Juan. Now it really makes sense."

"So, you don't want to be the star?"

"Oh, I'll be a star. Sal Mineo didn't get top billing in *Rebel*, did he? But, as far as I'm concerned, he was the star. I fell in love with him. But, seriously, don't you think Juan is perfect?" Alex dithered a moment.

"Yeah, but, guys, think about Juan's career. Remember, you have to post this online. Even if Juan was willing to do it, what if, you know ..."

"I already have that part figured out, Alex. Juan's career," Raphael turned to smile at Niki, "Niki's career, everybody's career will be safe. Rest assured." All three turned toward the stairs as they heard someone climbing them. Steve's head appeared.

"There you are," he said, looking at Niki. "Sorry, guys. Didn't mean to interrupt." He turned to leave, but Niki called out.

"Wait, Steve. Come back up." He looked at Raphael and Alex, raising an index finger to signal 'allow me.' Steve finished climbing the stairs and approached Niki.

"Is this one of the secret rituals you were telling Ryan about the other night?" he grinned as he settled in next to Niki. He picked up Niki's snifter and sipped.

"No, better," Niki said. "We're working on Luke's porn dare for Raphael."

"Oh, yeah? Good for you. How's it going?"

"Great," Niki grinned, glancing at Raphael and Alex. "Better than Luke ever imagined. I'm glad you're here, 'cause what Alex has come up with is way more elaborate than anything Luke was expecting. I think we all thought Raphael would be doing this on his phone, but, Steve, this deserves some real production values. The kind you bring to all the commercials you've produced. Would you be willing to help us out?"

"If I can, sure. What do you have in mind?" Niki turned to Alex.

"Alex can explain it better than me ..." Alex began. Now up to speed, Raphael interjected at times, too, embellishing the plot even further. Alex let him 'edit,' on the fly, knowing that there were still plenty of opportunities for ideas, good and bad, to be offered. And, if need be, rejected. He was gratified to see Raphael embracing his concept wholeheartedly. When he finished, Alex leaned back on both elbows, his legs stretched out behind Raphael. Greg ran a hand through his hair.

"Luke said five minutes. This is more like a short feature." Both Raphael and Alex continued looking at him, unfazed. "I guess if you really want to do this, there's never been a better time. Virtually all production has been shut down. It shouldn't be hard for me to get access to a good high-def camera, lights, baffles, and most importantly professional mics and audio gear. The most glaring flaw in a lot of amateur video is lighting and sound." Alex nodded knowingly.

"That's so true. I hadn't thought about it that way before."

"I suppose you'll want some needle drop, too. To add to the eerie atmosphere?"

"Needle drop?" Raphael asked.

"Background music. Pre-recorded ... unless you were thinking of hiring an orchestra."

"Oh, I hadn't even thought about music," Alex sat up. "Can we do that?"

"We can do whatever we want," Steve sipped again, before Niki took possession of the snifter. "If we're going to do this, we might as well do it right. Right?"

"I'm really starting to get excited now," Raphael beamed. "If this turns out the way I'm imagining it, we will blow Luke's mind."

"So, when do we start?" Niki asked. "What are the next steps?"

"This isn't going to happen overnight, guys," Steve regained possession of the snifter. "Alex, first you need to provide me with as detailed a script as possible. As much as you can, treat it as a screenplay instead of a stage script. Then, I'll come up with a shooting script." Both Raphael and Alex tilted their heads. "We won't be shooting this sequentially, like you would present a play, Alex. We'll shoot all the scenes that occur in the dungeon together, and all the scenes in the foyer together, etcetera. Saves time and effort. Likewise, we'll try to shoot all the scenes with the same actors at once to take advantage of their time. Then, in post-production, we'll edit everything into the right order."

"And that's when we add the 'needle-drop?'" Raphael asked confidently.

"Precisely. So, screenplay, shooting script, rehearsal, shoot, edit, review, re-edit, post and finally premiere."

"So ... Luke will get to see this next year?" Raphael looked disappointed suddenly.

"Don't look so sad, Raphael. You didn't build that body in a day, did you? Perfection takes time." Raphael smiled in spite of himself. "You want to keep this as much a secret as possible from Luke, I take it?"

"Totally," Raphael affirmed. "I want him to expect a lame smart phone flop."

"Okay. Well, depending on how long it takes Alex, and I'm guessing you, to deliver a finished script, and how many takes our novice actors will need in each scene, and we need to allow plenty of time in post to create some of these special effects ... considering that we're going to have to shoot around Luke's work days ..."

"What if we can keep him away all day every Saturday or Sunday?" Steve's timeline was weighing on Raphael. Steve reached past Niki and patted Raphael on the knee.

"That would help. Don't fret, Raphael. If all goes well, we could do this in a couple of months. Maybe less. I just don't want to over promise. It's not like we're doing a TikTok." Alex leaned in as if whispering in Raphael's ear, but spoke for everyone's benefit.

"There's no rush, Raphael. It'll be fun to keep Luke guessing, anyway, won't it?" A smile found its way to Raphael's lips. He picked up his snifter for the first time in a while.

"Good point, fellow burglar." He raised his snifter toward Steve and Niki. "Thank you, guys. I've never had this much help on a dare before."

"Well," Alex lifted his own snifter, "you've never had a dare in contention for an Oscar before, either."

"Oh?" Raphael turned to Alex. "For screenwriting, I assume?"

"You kidding? Clean sweep." Alex grinned at Steve. "Direction, acting, sound, set design. This is going to be fun." Steve stood up and reached out to take Niki's hand and pull him into a standing position.

"Keep me posted on how the script is coming, Alex. Meanwhile I'll check around and start lining up the gear we'll need." He headed down the stairs, with Niki following. Before he disappeared, Niki looked back and flashed his excited face.

"So, you really like it, huh?" Alex asked as he stood, then bent down to collect his laptop and snifter. When he looked over at Raphael, he could see Raphael was giving him an adoring look, much like the one he'd seen outside the elevator bank at the office, the day when Raphael was assuring him that everything between them was 'okay.'

"Alex, it's wonderful. It's ... well, it's on par with the wedding you orchestrated for us. Once again, you're proving you literally do know how to put on a show. Instead of dreading doing this dare, I'm pumped."

"All right, then," Alex grinned. "I'll start writing tonight. What are you going to do next?"

"I guess I'd better charm all our cast members into agreeing to participate." Alex headed for the stairs.

"And where will you start?"

"With the toughest one. Juan. If he says no, we're kinda screwed." Alex turned and looked up at Raphael, behind him on the stairs.

"When was the last time someone said no to you?" Raphael laughed.

"That would have been Mama, last Sunday, when we jokingly asked her and Angel to move up here with us until we have a vaccine."

'Mamas don't count."

"Oh, well in that case ... never."

"Thought so. Have fun with Juan."

Raphael cruised past Juan and Ricky's room after leaving the turret room, building his courage to approach Juan, but their door was closed. It was later than he'd realized and Juan, of course, had an early morning wake up Friday. In a way Raphael was relieved. He needed a little more time to put together his pitch. Luke wasn't in their room, so Raphael backtracked to Alex's room, where he found Luke and Greg sitting on the bed, watching TV. The door to their bath was closed, where presumably Alex was preparing for bed.

"Did you get everything figured out?" Luke asked as he began climbing off the bed.

"What do you mean, Sir?" Raphael played coy.

"Greg and I figured there was a fifty-fifty chance you and Alex were working on your dare. How'd we do?"

"What did Alex say?"

"He said 'ask Raphael.'"

"Well, there's a fifty-fifty chance you were right." Luke looked over at Greg and pulled Raphael into a hug.

"Looks like we both wound up with comedians, Greg."

"Lucky us." Greg agreed. Luke looked expectantly at Raphael, who looked at Greg, then back at Luke.

"Okay, yeah, we were working on the dare. You said I needed accomplices, so Alex is helping. I hope you're not expecting a lot, but we're going to give it a shot. That's all you get. For now. So there. Goodnight, Greg." Raphael headed for the door, pulling Luke behind.

"Goodnight, guys," Greg laughed as Luke disappeared around the doorway. Alex opened the door from the bath and bounded into bed. He leaned over and delivered a just brushed, fresh scent kiss.

"Raphael just dragged Luke away without a satisfying explanation of what you guys are up to."

"Oh, yeah?" Alex adjusted the covers and turned to face Greg who turned off the TV. "The plan is to keep Luke in the dark. You, too, until we need you."

"Need me? Am I going to be involved in this dare?"

"Everyone is, sweetie. Except Luke."

"You sound pretty sure about that. I haven't agreed to anything."

"You will. I have the perfect part for you." Alex reached over and squeezed Greg's balls. "Now, go brush and floss. You're going to be a star ... you need your beauty sleep."


Raphael had purposely timed his workout to hopefully coincide with Juan's anticipated return from work. Fridays were usually busy times for Ricky, so Juan typically worked out without him, as soon as he got home. Raphael was about half way through his routine when Juan appeared and nodded hello. Juan assembled a sixty-pound dumbbell and sat down on the open bench to begin a set of biceps curls. Raphael waited until he'd finished three sets before getting up and sitting down on Juan's bench, nearly thigh to thigh, but facing in the opposite direction.

"Hi, there," he said, as if they'd never met. He might as well have said, "Hello, sailor." Juan lowered the dumbbell to the floor as he turned to Raphael with one eyebrow cocked.

"I've been expecting you," he chuckled. Raphael tried to look innocent. He failed. "So, what's on your mind, future porn star?" Raphael pulled away far enough to put a foot on the bench, in an attempt to appear as casual as possible. And inadvertently prominently displaying his cage by doing so.

"We've been working on the dare ..." Before he could proceed, Juan interrupted.

"We?"

"Yeah. Alex has come up with an amazing concept. It's so cool, Steve is going to get professional gear so we can do it right."

"Huh. You're really into this? You didn't seem too thrilled the other night."

"It was kind of a shock. Don't you think? I didn't know ... But it's going to be amazing, Juan. Everybody's going to be in it. Except Luke, of course." Raphael lowered his voice. "He can't know anything. We're going to blow him away. Anyway, Alex is working on the script, and he's created a perfect character just for you."

"A script? A character? For me?" Juan's reaction was precisely not what Raphael had hoped for.

"Juan, we all agree you are perfect for the part."

"You all?"

"Yeah. Alex, Niki, Steve and me. Like I said, Alex is working on the script, but let me explain the concept. You'll love it." Raphael got up and walked to the door to peek around to be sure Luke wasn't eavesdropping from the other side. He scurried back to Juan's side. He hurried through a synopsis of the storyline just in case Luke might wander in. When he finished, Juan batted his eyes a few times in apparent disbelief.

"That sounds incredibly ambitious, Raphael. Steve really thinks you can pull it off?"

"*We* can. Yes. With you, Juan. You will be so sexy." Juan laughed.

"Raphael, that, uh, 'flattery will get you everywhere' thing isn't going to work. Come on. I'm no actor."

"Leave the acting worries to Alex and Steve. You'll be sultry and studly and sexy and menacing." Raphael trotted out his most adorable face. "Juan, we all agreed. You are prefect for this role."

"Raphael ..." Juan didn't want to hurt Raphael's feelings. But, besides the acting challenge, there was an even bigger issue. "Even if I wanted to do it ..."

"Juan," Raphael reached over and stroked Juan's taut thigh. "I know what you're thinking. Luke didn't think through his 'parameters' very carefully. Don't worry, amigo. No one will ever see this video except us. I guarantee it. You have my word."

"Yeah, but if you have to post it online ..."

"You have my word. Full stop." The intensity in Raphael's eyes was stronger than any notary seal. Juan made a pained face, clearly torn. "Okay," Raphael continued. "I was holding back, hoping I wouldn't have to use this."

"Oh, god, what now?"

"Juan. If you'll do it, we'll wipe out twenty of the dinners you and Ricky owe us. You know. Because of how much you owe us." It almost sounded like extortion. Juan looked down, deeply pondering Raphael's semi-imaginary offer. Then he turned to Raphael, eyes squinting.

"Thirty dinners. For a *tentative* agreement. I still need to see a script to be sure of what I'm getting into." Raphael leaned down and kissed

Juan's thigh. When he raised back up, he was beaming. "And no one else will ever see it?"

"No one. Which is a shame, Juan, because if anyone could see it, they'd never forget it. Everyone who sees it, will want to be you."

After dinner that evening during kitchen clean up, Raphael surreptitiously invited Ricky, Ryan and Mateo to the turret room. He was the last to ascend the stairs to the second floor, where Luke was standing in Greg and Alex's doorway, chatting with Greg. Luke was surprised when Raphael continued up to the third floor.

"Hey, baby ... aren't you? ..."

"Sorry, Sir. I have a meeting."

"Oh. Invitation only?" Luke looked genuinely disappointed.

"Yeah, but it'll be brief. I'll be down for our shave and shower in fifteen minutes or so. Promise."

"I'm beginning to question the wisdom of my dare," Luke said as he headed for their room.

"Oh, don't say that, Sir. It's turning out to be an excellent dare." Luke looked unconvinced. "I'll make it up to you tonight, Sir." Raphael blew an air kiss and disappeared up the stairs. He stopped by Steve and Niki's room to corral Niki for support. Again, not trusting Luke, he closed the door to the turret stairs behind them. Ricky, Ryan and Mateo were patiently waiting as they topped the stairs.

"Is this about your porn movie?" Ricky asked devilishly.

"It is," Raphael grinned as he and Niki sat and joined them. Raphael looked at Ricky. "Has Juan said anything to you?" Ricky shook his head.

"Okay, good. Remember when Luke said I needed at least two other participants? Well, I want all of you to help me. In fact, everyone except Luke will be in on it. Niki, Juan, Alex and Steve have already agreed. And Alex has come up with a plot that is so fun, I know you'll all want to help out." Raphael was giving it his best pitch. He figured his easiest sale would be with Ryan. "Alex is working on the script now, so I don't want to say too much before you can see it in detail, but Ryan, you get to play the part of a human pup." Ryan looked at Niki, who was grinning.

"Seriously? Me? A pup?" Both Niki and Raphael nodded. Ryan turned to Mateo, who was looking oddly shy. "You mean with a puppy hood and tail? And everything?"

'Yes, Ryan," Raphael grinned. "A total pup. With Niki. He'll be a pup, too." Ryan began displaying his trademark boner, indicating a successful sale.

"But I don't have any pup stuff."

"Niki has plenty to spare, Ryan," Raphael assured as he reached over and squeezed Ryan's knee. "How about it? Wanna be a pup?" Ryan looked again at Mateo, who was grinning now, either about Ryan's enthusiasm or his enthusiastic boner.

"Shh ... sure. I don't know what you need me to do, and I'll need some training. From Niki." He looked at Niki for encouragement.

"It's easy," Niki grinned, "but, yeah. It'll be fun to show you the ropes."

"Steve will be directing you, and the rest of us," Raphael continued. "You'll do fine." He turned his gaze to Ricky. "Ricky, you and Alex and I will be the 'bad guys.' Well, sort of the bad guys. Actually, we end up being victims, I guess. It's complicated, but you'll see as soon as Alex is done. The good news is, you'll have sex with Juan on camera, so there's that."

"I can do that," Ricky laughed. "It won't be the first time we've had an audience." He glanced conspiratorially at Mateo. Raphael laughed as he, too, turned to Mateo.

"Right ... the famous Juan and Ricky show."

"That we still haven't really heard about," Niki whined. Raphael put a hand on Niki's shoulder and squeezed.

"Which brings me to you, Mateo." Raphael wanted to comfort and encourage Mateo as best he could, so he'd saved Mateo's role for last, hoping the willingness of Ricky and Ryan would ease any hesitation. "You will play the part of Juan's lifelong companion ... more like a side kick. Like Batman's Robin."

"Or Don Quixote's Sancho Panza?" Ryan suggested.

"Yeah, thanks, Ryan. Exactly." The character Mateo would be playing was more servant than companion, but Raphael didn't want to characterize it that way this early in the negotiation. "You'll play the part of someone who has been living with Juan's character for many, many years."

"Will I have sex with Juan?" Mateo asked innocently. And so very logically.

"That's a good question," Raphael dodged. "I don't know. Alex is still writing."

"Oh, okay," Mateo replied. "Will I be naked?"

"At various times we'll all be naked, I think," Raphael asserted. "That's my guess, anyway. So, is that a si?"

"Si ... yes, Raphael." Mateo put a hand on Ryan's thigh, brushing against his boner. "If you think I can, I will try."

"Thank you, Mateo, you'll be perfect. You all will. Like I said, Steve is going to direct, and Alex will help us all, too. It's going to be a lot of fun, guys, and best of all, we'll blow Luke's mind. He has no idea what we're up to, and we need to keep it that way, so no matter how much he begs, don't say anything. Okay?"

"When are we doing this?" Ryan asked. "My schedule's a little intense right now." He looked meaningfully at Niki.

"It won't be a marathon, Ryan," Raphael assured. "We're going to try to shoot mostly on Saturday's. It'll take three, maybe four Saturdays. Maybe a bit on the days when Luke is working. We're still figuring that out. The next step will be when we all sit down with Alex's script. I'll keep you posted. But don't worry, Ryan. We'll work with your schedule." He turned to Niki. "With everybody's. You guys are awesome for participating. I can't say thank you enough."

With the meeting over, everyone filed down the stairs and headed in different directions. Since the session had gone quicker than he anticipated, Raphael decided to make one last pitch before joining Luke. He stuck his head in Greg and Alex's door to see Greg lounging on the bed and Alex at the desk, his back to the room.

"How's it going, Alex," he asked as Greg looked up.

"He can't hear you. He's wearing his noise cancelling, 'don't bother me I'm creating a masterpiece' headphones. Raphael chuckled as he entered and sat on the edge of the bed.

"That's okay, I wanted to talk to you, anyway." Greg muted the TV and put the remote aside to give Raphael his full attention.

"Let me guess ..."

"Yeah, I'm working on Luke's dare, too, Greg. Everyone else has agreed to be in it, and I was hoping you would too. Alex is writing a great part for you."

"Is he, now?"

"Funny thing is, yours is the only character who keeps his clothes on. So far anyway. Isn't that ironic?"

"So, I'm the one person in a porn flick who doesn't have sex? Not sure I'm interested, mister." Raphael laughed and climbed up next to Greg and began rubbing his chest.

"Oh, but you do get to play a big studly cop."

"So, I'm the spoil sport who breaks up the orgy? No thanks."

"No! You're the hero. You come to rescue the poor helpless victims. Kind of." Raphael began playing with Greg's nipple. "It's a very plum role." Greg continued looking unconvinced. "You'll get to wear a cop uniform. And ... don't tell Alex I told you already, but you're in the last scene. The finale."

"A uniform, huh? This is not a hapless Barney Fife character?" Raphael shook his head emphatically.

"Greg, you're the closest thing to a hero in this tale. Please say yes. Everyone else has." Greg glanced over at Alex. "Would it help if I arranged for you to have sex with the screenwriter?" Greg cracked up.

"I don't know ... what would Alex say?" He paused, momentarily torturing Raphael who was giving him a doe-eyed, pleading look. "Oh, okay. I'm not going to be the only one to tell you no." Relieved, Raphael leaned down and kissed Greg just above the crotch. At the same time Alex decided to turn around.

"Hey!" Alex pulled off his headphones. "What the hell?" Raphael sat up.

"It's okay, Alex. I was just finalizing the casting." Greg reached out and tussled what little hair Raphael had, as he smiled at Alex.

"I think I want your job," Alex laughed.

"Too late. I'm done. Everyone said yes! So, how's the script coming?" Alex stood and stretched, his cage glinting off the bedside lamp.

"It's coming. It's fun. I keep coming up with more ideas." Raphael looked at Greg.

"Remember, Alex, we want to finish this before the pandemic is over."

"Ha ha. I'm not making it longer. I'm making it better." Raphael began sliding off the bed to make his exit.

"When do you think you'll be done with the first draft? Everybody's asking." Alex shrugged.

"A week or two." He nodded at Greg. "Depends on how many blow jobs I have to give this guy."

"Well," Raphael said as he approached the door, "if it helps, I'll fill in for you, if it's okay with Greg." He disappeared before Alex or Greg could respond.

"Was that a dare?" Greg asked.

"More like a threat, I'd say." Alex sat next to Greg. "Let me know when you're feeling ignored, sweetie. You know how I can become obsessed with porn. Even if it's porn I'm writing." Greg grabbed him and pulled Alex on top of him.

"I'm feeling ignored." Alex pulled out of Greg's hold, stood and walked to the door, and closed it. He returned to the bed as Greg slid further down to reposition himself. Alex folded himself around Greg from the side, cupped his hand behind Greg's head and pulled him into a long kiss. Without completely releasing Greg's lips he responded.

"I'm here. For you." He reached down and fingered Greg's cock before grasping his balls. "Shall we dance?"

# Thirty-One

# PERFECTION TAKES TIME

BEFORE RETURNING TO HIS room, Raphael slipped downstairs and grabbed two wine glasses from the butler's pantry and a bottle of Chardonnay from the temp-controlled wine cabinet. Luke looked up from his tablet as Raphael entered their room, closing the door behind him. It might have been the wine bottle, or the closing door, but, as usual, Raphael's appearance produced a smile, overriding Luke's attempt at a pout.

"Is that a bribe?" Luke asked as he sat up straighter on the bed and put his tablet aside.

"What makes you think I need a bribe?" Raphael said, answering Luke's question with a question. He set the glasses on the night stand as he sat himself next to Luke, his ass against Luke's left thigh. He began cutting the foil off the bottle as he turned to Luke. "You know why I've been otherwise occupied." He pulled the cork free with the waiter's friend, set both aside, poured into both glasses, turned and handed Luke his glass with a cheeky smile. "It's all because of your dare." Raphael touched his glass to Luke's. "But my work is done for now, and I'm here. I'm all yours. Sir."

"So ... no more meetings in the turret room?" Luke asked after taking his first sip.

"Oh, I can't promise that, Sir. But not right away, no." Raphael leaned forward for a conciliatory kiss.

"I feel like I've created a monster. Who all have you roped into this anyway?"

"Well, Dr. Frankenstein, all I'm at liberty to say is ... more than your minimum of two. And it's not a monster at all." Raphael took another sip. "Although, it has taken on a life of its own." He reached down and fondled Luke's flaccid cock. "Turns out, it's a better than average dare, Sir. I think you'll be pleasantly surprised." He set his glass down, took

Luke's glass from him and set it next to his, then climbed up onto the bed and straddled Luke's legs. He stared into Luke's eyes a moment, then scooted further down Luke's legs, bent down and looked up at Luke appealingly. "Is it okay if I suck you off now, Sir, before we shave and shower? You can call it a bribe if you want." Luke sighed as Raphael leaned down, not waiting for an answer.

Raphael had decided he wouldn't be the one to bring up the script with Alex, not wanting to pressure him. The following week was a tough one 'at work' for both of them, due to several unanticipated challenges, including a couple of departures that dumped more work on both of them. Raphael figured Alex had put the script aside entirely, so he was surprised when Alex stopped in Saturday morning, while Raphael was still attempting to catch up on his To Do List.

"Here," Alex said, holding out a stack of papers, still warm from the printer.

"More bad news?" Raphael asked as he turned in his chair, still focused on work.

"No. First draft of the script." Raphael reached out eagerly.

"You're kidding? How did you ..."

"I've burned a little midnight oil. I think it's pretty good. See what you think and let me know." Raphael, still clutching the script, stood and hugged Alex. "I gave digital and hard copies to Steve, so he can begin putting together his shooting script."

"I'll dig in as soon as I finish up here. Thanks, Alex. You're amazing." Raphael flipped through the pages. "It's bigger than I expected."

"Well, it's triple-spaced. So Steve ... and you, I fear ... can make any edits. Even though it is a masterpiece, just as it is." Raphael buried it under a stack of folders on the desk where Luke wouldn't easily find it.

"I'll read it as soon as I finish work, Alex." Raphael was beaming. "I'm excited! Did Steve give you any idea when he'll finish the shooting script?" Alex shook his head.

"Hopefully by Monday. Let me know when you've read it." He lowered his voice. "And keep it between us until Steve's done. Then we'll do a big reveal to the whole cast."

It wasn't until Tuesday, when Luke as at work, that Raphael was able to read Alex's script, over a long lunch. Upon finishing it, he raced up the stairs, all the way up to Niki and Steve's room on the third floor. He knew Niki was in the library studying, and he couldn't wait any longer to compare notes with Steve.

"Excuse me, sorry, Steve ..." Steve swiveled around and waved Raphael in. He recognized the script in Raphael's hand and grinned.

"What do you think?"

"That's what I was going to ask you." Raphael sat on the edge of the bed, facing Steve. "Can we really do this?"

"I think we should try, Raphael. To be honest, I wish you really could post it online. I can see it winning prizes in gay film festivals around the country. Alex is breaking ground here."

"Well ... I promised Juan. And Niki. But you really think it can turn out that well?"

"From a technical standpoint, yeah. We should be able to do it justice. The challenge ... the real challenge, will be the acting. Alex is the only one with experience." Raphael nodded, realizing that he, too, would be called upon to perform in a way he never had before.

"I can't believe the ending. I blew tea through my nose when I read it." Steve nodded.

"Endings are the hardest part. He nailed it. It will leave the audience howling. Well, it would if there was an audience."

"You're used to millions of people seeing your work, Steve. Having an audience of ten must be frustrating for you." Raphael's sincere expression of regret wasn't lost on Steve.

"It's okay, Raphael. This isn't my first dare rodeo. It's fine. Besides, this will be fun. A lot more fun than any commercial I've ever produced. I'll have the shooting script done by the end of this weekend. But we don't have to wait for that to get everybody else up to speed. When do you want to do that?" Raphael put the script aside and rubbed his eyes, thinking.

"We need to do it when Luke's not around, obviously. Man. Hmmm. Other than evenings, weekend mornings are about the only time everyone is home. Sunday's out ... pancakes. If I can come up with a errand for Luke, maybe Saturday morning?" Greg nodded. "Let me make sure everybody can do it. Thanks, Steve." When he stood and turned, he saw the collection of gear in the corner beyond the door for the first time. "Whoa." He turned back to Steve. "We need all of that?"

"We do if we're going to blow Luke's mind. Right?"

"Right!" Raphael grinned. He paused at the door. "I haven't been this excited in a long time. You and Alex are saving my butt." With that he was gone, denying Steve the opportunity to respond with an apropos comment about his very photogenic butt.

Saturday morning, ten a.m. The family, aka the cast and crew, assembled in the dining room as Raphael had requested. He'd dispatched Luke to acquire a dozen preordered artisanal bagels from a pop-up shop on Fillmore. Luke balked, so Raphael decided there was no sense in playing games and told Luke his mission was necessary to allow Raphael's pursuit of the dare. They had an hour and half, maybe a bit longer before his return.

"Okay, guys, this will be a run-through of the entire script," Alex stood at the head of the table. "I have a copy here for each of you, and I've high-lighted your lines. We'll start at the beginning, and go through it once without stopping. Okay? We don't have a lot of time, so save your questions until we're done. I'll read the stage instructions, and of course my lines. Okay?" No one knew enough to argue, so there was silence as Alex walked around the table and distributed copies. He sat and began reading from the top. It was a testimony to Alex's script that it wasn't questions that interrupted what should have been a seamless reading. And it was really all Ricky's fault. He kept laughing hysterically. Which infected Mateo, who ended up face first in Ryan's lap at one point. Who was trying hard not to laugh, but was helpless in controlling his boner. It was porn, after all. Alex wanted to be irritated, due to the time constraint, but Ricky's laugh was infectious. More to the point, and gratifyingly so, they all got it. They appreciated the campiness, the tongue-in-cheek, but truly sexy through-line of the script. When they got to the final scene, in which he finally appeared, even Greg was whooping.

"I didn't realize this was supposed to be a comedy," he turned to Alex.

"It's not ... exactly," Alex replied. "It's still porn." Greg gave him an 'oh, really?' look. "Riddle me this. How long do you think this would stay up if we posted it to YouTube?"

"About seven nano-seconds," Niki volunteered.

"Exactly. It's porn ... with personality," Alex asserted.

"Greg," Steve said, "it's all in how we shoot it and how everyone performs. Especially Juan. If we treat this all matter-of-factly. Seriously. The campiness will be there for the audience, but for the actors, we should play it totally, pardon the expression, straight."

"Think 'Young Frankenstein,'" Alex suggested.

"Okay," Greg sat back. "I get it." He turned to Alex and put a hand on his thigh. "You amaze me." Alex responded wordlessly with a self-satisfied smile.

"We haven't heard from the central character," Steve prompted, look-ing at Juan. "Your fiancé seems pleased with the direction Alex has tak-en." Juan had been shuffling back and forth through the script while listening. He put it down and looked first at Raphael, then Steve.

"Well, when I told Raphael I'd consider doing this, I wasn't really sure what to expect. This is a lot more involved than what I anticipated. It's ... uh ... it's, well ... you've created a ... really a very nuanced character, Alex. Kudos to you. I like this guy Francisco, I'll admit. If you can produce on the screen what I see in my head, this will be unforgettable. But, like I told Raphael, I'm no actor. I ... I don't think I can live up to the character you've created here."

"Juan." Raphael paused to underscore what he was about to say. "Just be yourself. Only more so. You'll be," and he looked at Ricky, "legendary. It's why we picked you for the part." Ricky leaned over and wrapped and arm around Juan's neck and kissed his cheek. He whispered something in Juan's ear.

"I seem to be outvoted," Juan said as he unraveled Ricky's arm. "Okay. I'll try. But don't say I didn't warn you." Alex and Raphael exchanged relieved looks. "So, Steve, how do we do this?"

"Juan, how easy is it for you to get some time off, or maybe leave the hospital early on a day that Luke works? Here's what I'm thinking. We need to keep Luke away from the house on Saturdays for hours at a time for three, four Saturdays. Maybe more if we get bogged down. If we can shoot the last scene with you, Greg and Alex first, on a day when Luke is working, then Greg can be Luke's escort on Saturdays to insure he stays away." This assignment was news to Greg, who looked at Alex. Who tried to ignore him.

"Aren't we in that scene, too?" Raphael asked.

"Yeah, but we can shoot those angles later and edit them together in post," Steve explained. "I'm trying to keep this as simple as possible."

"I can try to trade some hours on a Tuesday or Thursday," Juan said. "How much time will it take?" He was looking at the last pages of the script. "This will be what ... a minute or two of the video?"

"Give or take," Steve agreed. "So, three to five hours of shooting." Juan's eyes weren't the only ones that widened at that. "Hey, don't look at me. I didn't write the script." Alex picked up his copy and held it up in front of his face. "Guys, it often takes twelve to twenty hours to shoot a thirty second commercial. Alex promised Raphael a slew of Oscars, so we're going to do this right."

"Let me see what I can do," Juan replied, at what turned out to be the end of the reading, as just then everyone heard the front door opening.

"Okay," Raphael stage whispered, "don't leave your scripts out where Luke can find them." He handed his copy to Alex and bounded into the foyer to make sure Luke went directly to the kitchen with the bagels. As everyone else dispersed, Alex joined Juan and Ricky in their room for what he suspected might be a necessary pep talk.

"Juan," Alex looked intently into Juan's eyes, "I'm sure Ricky has told you this a hundred times, but maybe you need to hear it one more time. You are one sexy dude, and the camera is going to love you. You are perfect for the role of Francisco. I wrote the parts of Francisco and Pablo specifically for you and Ricky. When you make love to him ... it will be genuine. When you look into the camera, don't see the camera. See Ricky. Make love to the camera, and you'll be fine. You'll be perfect. You'll be Francisco."

"He'll be legendary," Ricky seconded.

"Yeah, that, too. So, rehearse the scenes you have together in here and in the dungeon. Have fun. And don't forget to practice your Oscar speech."

Since elective surgeries were still pretty minimal, Juan was able to get the following Thursday off entirely. He and Ricky both hunkered down in their room until Luke left for work, none the wiser. Because the crew was able to set up and shoot first thing in the morning, Ricky and Mateo were able to play gaffer and best boy before their shifts, speeding things along. Alex had scheduled a PTO day so he could devote full time to both playing his role and doing everyone's makeup. Greg had stationed his laptop in the library, so he was able to split his time in front of the camera and doing a modicum of work. Niki gladly relinquished his study hall and did his class work in his and Steve's room for the day. In other words, it worked. They were able to wrap by three, in plenty of time to tear down and store the gear in Steve and Niki's room before Luke returned. The final scene was 'in the can.'

"When do I get to see your porn flick," Luke asked cluelessly Friday evening as he was perfecting Raphael's high 'n tight in the shower. Raphael snorted. "What? You must be done by now ... all the secret meetings." Raphael untangled himself from Luke's leg lock and scooted away a bit before turning around to face him. He took one of Luke's ankles in each hand and squeezed.

"Sir. I'm glad you brought this up. Beginning tomorrow, and for the next few Saturdays, you and Greg will be taking field trips somewhere ...

anywhere, to give me the time and space I need to complete your dare." Luke returned a blank stare. "You can take bikes to the Presidio and explore new trails. Hike along the Bay. Take scooters to Ocean Beach and watch the surfers."

"Watch the surfers?" Luke didn't sound thrilled.

"Volunteer at Open Hand? Look, Sir. You saddled me with a pretty challenging dare. Agreed?" Raphael waited until Luke finally relented and nodded. "I've never half-assed a dare, have I?" He waited again until Luke nodded. "So, give me the cooperation I need and I'll deliver on your dare. Now ..." Raphael turned and scooted back until he felt Luke's cock against his butt, "I believe you were making me beautiful." Luke leaned forward, resting his head on Raphael's shoulder in defeat. Raphael patted Luke's mohawk. "Remember this the next time you issue a dare." It was Luke's turn to snort before he sat up and reached for the shave gel.

The weeks passed, with work, studying, dinners, pancake breakfasts and most significantly, Saturday shoots. Some involved everyone. Some were limited to Juan and Ricky, or just Alex, Raphael and Ricky. A couple involved just Juan, Ryan and Niki. Ryan and Niki spent some time together on the days Luke worked, perfecting Ryan's puppy persona, and Ryan loved it. Later, after dark, he really got off on sucking off Mateo in full pup gear, and, to be honest, it was a turn on for Mateo too, giving his 'pup' his bone. But when Ryan tried to wear the pup hood and tail to bed, Mateo called a time out. He let Ryan keep the tail in a couple of times, but you can't kiss a guy wearing a puppy hood.

The shoots were a lot of work, setting up, tearing down, moving camera, lights, baffles and sound gear from room to room. At first, Juan would get frustrated when Steve would have him act the same scene, repeat the same lines four, five, six times, with Alex, and sometimes Steve, coaching ever so slightly different expressions or deliveries. Sometimes Steve would move the camera a foot one way or the other and want to shoot the scene again. But then, after one intense scene, Steve had the idea of showing Juan the first take and fifth take on playback. Juan could see the difference. Everyone could. It really was better. As they worked through the script everyone, Juan included, became more intuitive, more aware of what the camera wanted. They were learning how to act. That's when it was the most fun. So, in a way, it was a little disappointing, but a relief nevertheless, when Steve declared mid-day on their fourth

Saturday, "That's a wrap. Probably. Maybe. We'll see how it looks in post."

Post production, not surprisingly, didn't go as quickly as everyone had hoped, either. Even though no one outside the family would ever see the film, Steve applied the same detailed degree of perfection to the production as he offered to each of his agency's clients. So much so, in fact, there was, indeed, a half-day follow-up shoot to make one scene perfect. Alex had accompanied Steve to the first session in the edit suite, not that he didn't trust Steve, but since film was a new medium for Alex, he wanted to learn everything he could about it. On stage, in real time, there was no 'take two.' But on film, with hundreds of takes among all the scenes, the possible end results were ... endless. Now he knew why Steve kept so many notes during the shoots. He marveled at how Steve could even modify the footage after the fact, not just the special effects that he'd anticipated, but how at just the right moment, Steve could zoom in a little to reinforce an emotion on the footage that had been shot wider. Seeing the rough cut, in chronological order, even without the special effects and transitions Steve would be adding in subsequent sessions, made Alex emotional. Something he hadn't expected. All the hard work he and the rest of the family had invested had been worth it. Thanks to Steve, to Juan and everyone else, his creation had become 'art.'

It was nearly midnight when he and Steve got home after the first post session. The house was quiet as they stripped and headed for their respective beds. Alex was surprised to find Greg still awake, reading. He closed the door to avoid disturbing the others.

"You put in another full shift," Greg placed his book on the nightstand. "Did you guys finish?"

"No ... I wish." Alex crawled on top of the covers and snuggled up next to Greg. "God, there's so much to it." He looked coyly at Greg. "But we did get a lot done, and Greg, it's going to be amazing. I mean, you would swear all the characters were real. It looks like a studio release. I never realized how talented Steve is. Greg, we're going to blow Luke away. Hell, we're going to blow everyone away."

"Don't you deserve a little credit, too? You did write it, after all."

"Yeah, but Steve ... and everyone, brought it to life. I can't wait for you to see it."

"Which will be ...?" Alex chuckled as he sat up and squeezed Greg's thigh.

"I don't know. Like I said, Steve's making it perfect. Soon." He wiggled his eyebrows and leapt off the bed, and danced into the bathroom.

Steve wouldn't let Alex participate in any more sessions. He wasn't being difficult; he just didn't want Alex to get worn out watching the same scenes over and over as each little detail was worked out. He wanted Alex to enjoy the premiere as much as everyone else. To that end he had a little 'extra footage' to include that even Alex didn't know about. After a total of about twenty more hours of post production, over a span of three weeks, Steve was finally happy. He burned a single Blu Ray DVD, consolidated all the elements onto one USB drive, wiped all the files from the studio drives and carried his precious cargo home.

It was Tuesday of Thanksgiving week, good timing he thought. After dinner, he rounded up Alex and Raphael and the three of them gathered in his and Niki's room, away from everyone else.

"How's it going?" Raphael asked. Steve had been keeping him and Alex updated, to some extent. Steve picked up the DVD and held it between both hands, like the work of art it was.

"It's done," he announced. "I was thinking we might have the premiere Thursday, as a Thanksgiving treat."

"Yes!" Raphael reached out and took the DVD from Steve. The joy on his face was the reward Steve had hoped for. "Can I watch it? No, I want to wait." Uncharacteristically frazzled, he looked at Alex. "Should we?" Alex was amused. He was just as eager as Raphael to see the finished product, but was enjoying Raphael's emotional summersaults. Steve reached out and retrieved the jewel case.

"I think you should wait. Both of you. You'll enjoy it more if you see it first with everyone else. What's the plan for Thanksgiving anyway? I've kind of been out of touch." Raphael and Alex detailed the plan. Dinner at two. Turkey breast. Panko breaded sole for the pescatarians, since crab season had been delayed into December, thanks to the tardy whale migration. And all the usual sides. Hiroshi would be joining them.

"Perfect," Steve said. "I'm glad Hiroshi will be here. Alex, can we move your TV into the sitting room Thursday? We'll do the premiere there, after dinner, if that sounds good." Alex readily agreed. Finally. Luke's dare was complete.

"Let's not say anything to anybody about it for now," Raphael grinned. "Luke hasn't even brought it up lately. It's been so long." Everyone agreed, and the conspiracy was set. Finally.

## Thirty-Two

# NOW SHOWING

## IN A SITTING ROOM NEAR YOU

ANY OTHER THANKSGIVING, THE meal would have been the main attraction for everyone. And it was, for most everyone. Except for the conspirators. And Greg. Alex had clued him in – he had to – when he began disconnecting the cables to the television. The two of them spirited it down to the sitting room and set everything up while Raphael kept Luke distracted in the gym. They were counting on the likelihood that Luke wouldn't wander into the sitting room before the meal and spoil the surprise. During the meal Raphael and Alex kept exchanging furtive grins, hopefully disguised behind avid chewing and an unusually frequent use of napkins. When everyone finally refused one more helping of anything, Steve looked at Raphael and nodded once.

"We'll be serving dessert in the sitting room," Raphael announced, "so let's buss our dishes into the kitchen, then regroup there. We have fresh glasses there, too." Ricky and Juan were the first to enter the sitting room and Ricky's reaction telegraphed what was to come.

"Yea! The dare movie!" That motivated the rest of the family to beat feet into the sitting room to see what was what. In addition to the unexpected TV, across the room a bottle of Schramsberg on ice and an array of flutes were arranged on a console table. Platters of cookies and truffles were on each of two coffee tables. Luke looked hopefully at Raphael.

"Yes, Sir. We have completed your dare. And I do mean *we*. So, have a seat and get ready to be entertained." Steve pulled the drapes to darken the room as everyone found a spot and settled in. Steve sat a bit off to the side so he could watch reactions as much as the action on the screen. Alex, remote in hand, looked around to be sure everyone was ready, locked eyes one more time with Raphael, and pressed 'play.' Against a black background, the opening credits began to roll.

**Noe Street Films Presents**
*(fade)*
**A Locked Cock Brotherhood Production**
*(fade)*

## The House of Francisco

*(As title fades, haunting music begins)*

*(Open on dimly lit library, where, from behind, we see a seated figure with shoulder length hair, staring into the fire. Gender undetermined. The figure reaches to the left to pick up a snifter and drink, still not revealing a face. After a moment, a sound off-right is heard, causing the figure to rise and move toward it. In the dim light from the flames, we see it is a man, a handsome, olive-complected man. Camera pans right to follow him to a pair of closed sliding doors. He stops and listens, then silently parts the doors enough to peer into the foyer beyond.)*

*(Cut to foyer, where three men, dressed in all black, wearing full-face black ski masks and hoodies, bearing flashlights, are quietly creeping into the middle of the foyer from the entry. One of them, Pablo, bumps against a console table, producing a thud.)*

"Careful!" Adonis (Raphael) whispers.

"Chill, man," Pablo (Ricky) replies in a normal voice. "I told you. I've been watching this house for three days. Nobody's come or gone. It's empty."

"Who leaves a house like this unlocked?" Brady (Alex) asks. "People with a house like this aren't this careless."

"Maybe they all thought somebody else was locking up when they left," Pablo theorizes.

"Look, let's just get what we can, and get out of here," Adonis says plaintively. "In case somebody saw us coming in. This seems like kind of a nosey neighborhood."

"Why don't we start here," Brady suggests, turning to the doors to the library and sliding them open. "Aaaagh!" All three burglars step back at the sight of Francisco glaring at them from the other side of the doors. Francisco slides the doors further open and takes a step toward them. He is taller than all of them. We can now see he is wearing a skin-tight, open mesh body suit that reveals his well-built body ... all of it. *(Yes, his outfit from the wedding ... this was not a high-budget production, and besides, it's damn sexy on him.)* The three burglars are frozen in place. Francisco walks around them, inspecting them, and still they don't move. Except for their eyes, which try to follow his movements, in abject terror.

"Well," Francisco says. "What have we here?" He waves toward the ceiling, and the lights come up. He circles around them again, taking his time, clearly not concerned that they might attack him or flee. Once he has completed circling them, he faces them, looking very pleased.

*(Cut to view from behind the burglars, so we see Francisco facing them. After the special effects flash, follow with multiple close ups of Francisco and each burglar as he addresses him.)*

"How fortunate. How fortunate indeed." He takes a step back, gestures again, producing a blue flash of light around each burglar. After the flashes fade, the three, still immobile, are completely, bare-assed naked, their clothes, including the ski masks and flashlights, gone.

"Oh," Francisco says happily, smiling broader, if a bit menacingly. "Better than I thought." He steps toward Brady, cups his hand under his chin. Brady's eyes still projecting terror.

"Vanilla. A staple in every diet." Francisco turns to Pablo, whose face he cups in both hands. Pablo's eyes fix on Francisco's. "And Mocha. How I do love Mocha." Then, he moves over to Adonis. He brushes the back of his hand across Adonis' chiseled pecs.

"And to complete the menu, Spicy Asian. I haven't had Asian in ages." Adonis' eyes are looking up and down, taking in Francisco's barely concealed cock, his body, his face. Francisco steps back again to admire the three of them, all at once.

*(Cut to view from behind Francisco, so we see his thighs, ass and V-shaped back, his impressive mane and the three immobilized burglars in front of him. The angle is such that the audience is denied seeing their crotches. He gestures again with his right hand, freeing the burglars from the neck up so they can speak at last. They exchange anxious glances, then Brady speaks.)*

"We're sorry. We didn't know anyone was home. Please ... please let us go! We won't tell anyone. You'll never see us again!"

"What have you done to us?" Pablo pleads. "Why can't I move?" Adonis doesn't speak but has an intense look of anger. Of Bruce Lee just before he unleashes his fury. Francisco raises his hand to silence them, then concentrates on Adonis.

*(Cut to Adonis' intense, angry regard of Francisco, then back to Francisco's relaxed, smiling face.)*

"Yes. I was right about you, Spicy Asian. What say you?"

"You *must* release us. We meant you no harm."

"No harm?" Francisco chuckles. "You little fuckers were going to rip me off. If I was so weak as to need a gun ... I would have been justified in shooting you." Francisco pauses. "I could have called the police and had you all thrown in jail." He looks at Pablo. "Where you would not have lasted ten minutes before someone took ownership of you. And taken full advantage of you."

*(Cut to Pablo, and his obvious realization of how likely that would have been. Then back to Francisco as he leans down to come face to face with Adonis. The frame includes both*

*Brady and Pablo beyond as they turn their heads to watch,*
*still sufficiently terrorized.)*

"And ... Spicy ... surely you realize, you are in no position to tell me what I should do. But I respect your courage. I can't wait to indulge myself with what you have to offer." A look of confusion comes over Adonis' face as Pablo and Brady exchange nervous glances.

"I have a name. It's Adonis. You have to let us go. Like Brady said, you'll never see us again. You have our word." Francisco laughs, reaches out and brushes Adonis' high 'n tight.

"You have the look of a warrior, even the bravery of a warrior. Yet, it seems your parents knew your true destiny when they named you." Francisco glances over at Pablo and Brady and addresses them, as he continues to touch Adonis. "You see, Adonis was the god of beauty. Of fertility. And, most appropriately ... for me ... the god of permanent renewal." He turns his attention back to Adonis. "Yes. Renewal. All three of you were destined to come here. To me. This night was meant to be."

*(Close up of each burglar's face while Francisco speaks.*
*Slightly less terrorized, but still frightened, at least able to*
*look at each other, as well as at Francisco. End with POV*
*shot from the grand staircase with Francisco on the right,*
*Brady in the foreground on the left, Pablo in the frame,*
*Adonis beyond.)*

"Please ..." Brady whines. Francisco again raises a hand to silence him.

"You have no case, so stop pleading it. You will not be leaving. Not tonight. Not ever." Pablo begins to cry. Francisco bends down, catches one of Pablo's tears with a forefinger. And licks it off. He looks intently into Pablo's eyes.

"No need to cry, Mocha. I am not going to hurt you." He stands up straight. "I am not going to hurt any of you. On the contrary. You will receive the best of care here." He turns his attention back to Adonis, cupping a hand tenderly (threateningly?) around the side of his neck. "No, I want you. I *need* you. That is why you are here."

*(Cut to a wide view from the perspective of the entry, the*
*three burglars on the right, with Francisco facing them, the*
*grand staircase in the distance.)*

"Cadmael, I need you." Francisco speaks in the same normal, quiet tone of voice, but nevertheless it summons Cadmael (Mateo) who, seconds later, descends the stairs and approaches Francisco, seemingly unsurprised by the presence of the burglars. He, too, is wearing only a black mesh body suit.

"M'Lord?"

"Cadmael, we have visitors." Francisco looks lovingly at Cadmael. "Well, they *were* visitors. Now they will be staying with us. I need you to prepare three rooms for them."

"Yes, M'Lord." Francisco approaches Pablo and puts his hands on both shoulders.

"I will be feeding with Mocha now. When you are ready, please show Vanilla and Spicy ... *Adonis* ... to their rooms." Cadmael bows his head slightly in acknowledgement. "How rude of me. Gentlemen, this is Cadmael, my companion. My lieutenant, as it were. Cadmael has been in service with me for ... what? Sixteen hundred years?"

"One thousand, six hundred and fifty-seven, M'Lord." Francisco chuckles.

"Yes. I saved Cadmael's life. He was a star player in the revered Ulama game in his Mayan city. Oddly, the custom was to celebrate victory by sacrificing a player at game's end." Francisco shakes his head. "Such a waste." Cadmael looking at Pablo, simply nods. "I could not allow that to happen. Not to one as gifted as Cadmael. So, here we are."

*(During this monologue closeups and two-shots of the burglars show their reactions – increasing discomfort, bordering on terror again. As Francisco finishes, cut to wide shot from behind the burglars again, as Francisco pulls Pablo away from the other two. Pablo is suddenly able to walk. As Francisco and Pablo proceed to the far end of the foyer, past the stairs, cut to view from the entry again. Cadmael walks to the stairs and begins climbing. Francisco, without turning, addresses Adonis and Brady as he and Pablo pass by the staircase.)*

"Cadmael will show you to your rooms shortly. I will show Mocha to his room after we have finished."

*(Francisco and Pablo continue walking away, Pablo clearly walking against his will, but unable to resist. His steps are stilted but unwavering. Cut to closeups of Brady and Adonis*

*looking at each other, still unable to move anything below the neck. As soon as Francisco and Pablo are out of sight, they speak in hushed tones.)*

"Pablo really fucked up this time," Brady says. Then in sing-song mime of Pablo, "I've been watching the house for three days ..."

"Don't blame Pablo." Adonis is briefly angry with Brady. "We all willingly came in here. Now we're all screwed. Who is this guy? How can he paralyze us like this?"

"I think he's a vampire. You heard him. Over a thousand year's old? He said he's going to feed on Pablo. Adonis, I'm scared. If he kills Pablo ..."

"He said he wasn't going to hurt him."

"So ... what? He's just going to drink a *little* blood? Fuuuuck!"

"We need a plan. He released Pablo. At some point he has to release us, too. When he does, all three of us need to make a break for it. If just one of us gets away, he can go for help."

"And what happens to the rest of us?"

"Do you have a better idea?" Brady shakes his head no, on the verge of tears himself.

"Fuck!" Brady sniffs. "Now I know how a mannequin feels."

*(Cut to medium shot of Francisco and Pablo from behind as Francisco guides him to a sling in a dimly lit dungeon. When they reach it, Francisco takes him by the shoulders and turns him around, so he's facing Francisco, his back to the sling. The dark, moody music lightens slightly.)*

"Relax Mocha. There is no reason we should not both enjoy this." Pablo is looking around at the rest of the dungeon, failing to see any reason why he should be enjoying any of this. As Francisco takes his hands off Pablo's shoulders, Pablo slowly floats down and into the sling. He cries out in fear.

"Aaaaagh!" Once he is nestled into the sling, his hands and legs position themselves along the chains suspending the sling, again without any action on his part. He looks left, right, then up at Francisco who is standing between his legs at the base of the sling.

*(Cut to POV from beyond and just above Pablo's head, so we see his naked body displayed for Francisco, as well as*

*Francisco from the mid-thighs up. This is the first time the*
*audience has seen full frontal nudity of any of the burglars.*
*Francisco leans in and over Pablo as he reaches down with*
*one hand and begins to caress Pablo's remarkable abs.)*

"You are even more beautiful than I first realized." Francisco lifts his
eyes from Pablo's abs to stare into his frightened eyes. "This is not going
to hurt, Mocha. You have something I need. Giving it to me will not
hurt." He pauses, maintaining eye contact, willing Pablo to relax. "I
will never hurt you." He backs away very slightly, unzips enough of his
body suit to free his now rigid cock, produces a condom from nowhere
and installs it. He lubricates his cock, again with lube from no apparent
source, then advances on Pablo, slowly inserting his cock as Pablo, despite
himself, begins to moan.

*(Cut to foyer, POV from the entry, Brady and Adonis still*
*frozen in place on the right. Their conspiring whispers are*
*interrupted and they turn their heads to see Cadmael, with*
*great poise, descend the stairs. He pauses on the last step and*
*speaks.)*

"Your accommodations are ready. If you will follow me." He turns
and begins ascending as Brady and Adonis find themselves able to walk,
but, like Pablo, only in the direction Cadmael has allowed. Adonis tries
to turn toward the entry, but is unable to do so. Camera follows them up
the winding staircase. On the second floor Cadmael stops and turns to
face them at the doorway on the left. "I've prepared this room for you,
Vanilla."

"My name is Brady." Now ambulatory, Brady is feeling slightly braver.
Cadmael nods once in acknowledgment. He gestures to the right, to the
doorway across the very wide hallway.

"And you will find your room here, Adonis. If you require anything
further, simply speak my name. I will hear you." He begins to walk back
to the stairway as Brady and Adonis remain where they are. Cadmael
looks over his shoulder.

"M'Lord and your friend will rejoin you shortly." Cadmael descends
the stairs. Both Brady and Adonis enter Brady's room, which is dimly lit
with only the lamps from the bedside tables. They sit side by side on the
bed.

"Should we try to make that break now?" Brady asks, glancing at the
doorway.

"Yeah." Adonis glances around the room. "No ... not until Pablo's back." He looks at Brady. "I don't know, maybe we should. Then come back for him."

"If he's still alive," Brady says, to a look of sadness on Adonis' face.

*(Fade to dungeon. Sequence of shots, over building music – Francisco's theme – of Pablo's face, Francisco's face, Pablo's growing erection, rear shot of Francisco's clenched ass as he rhythmically fucks Pablo slowly, lovingly, steadily, Pablo's glistening abs as Francisco brings him closer and closer to orgasm. Pablo's moans increase, then he vocalizes.)*

"No!" Pablo cries out. Francisco pulls free, bends down and swallows Pablo's cock just as he begins to ejaculate.

*(Cut back to the POV from behind Pablo's head, as Francisco swallows Pablo, his hair falling around his head as he bobs up and down.)*

Francisco is ravenous, moaning over Pablo's protestations as he feeds. He slides his mouth up and down Pablo's cock, claiming every last drop, reveling in the bounty he has been denied for too long. Pablo, helpless, drops his head back in exhaustion and defeat. Finally, Francisco straightens, stands up and looks lovingly at Pablo as he licks his lips, then dabs at his mustache.

"Mmmm. Even better than I had hoped, Mocha. So much better." He takes a long, deep breath, then peels off the condom and replaces his cock inside his body suit and zips up. He extends his hand and raises it, which levitates Pablo up off the sling and into a standing position. Pablo looks confused more than frightened. "Come, let us join your friends."

*(Cut to POV from the far side of the bed where we see Brady and Adonis from behind as they rise and creep to the doorway. Cut to hallway as we see them exit the room and creep toward the stairs. As soon as they reach the top step, they both freeze. Close ups on each wary face as we hear Francisco's voice.)*

"We must do this again, Mocha. Soon." Brady and Adonis scurry back into Brady's room.

*(Cut to POV from far side of the bed again. Brady and Adonis return to their places just before we see Francisco and Pablo enter. Francisco has his left arm around Pablo's shoulders. As soon as they see Pablo, Brady and Adonis rush to him, pulling him away from Francisco.)*

"Pablo! Are you okay?" Brady asks fearfully. He is not so furtively examining Pablo's neck.

"Did he hurt you?" Adonis asks, looking menacingly at Francisco. Francisco gives Adonis a wan smile.

"I am sure Pablo will tell you everything, in detail, but as you can see your friend is unharmed." Francisco opens his mouth to continue, but Adonis interrupts.

"Look I don't know who you are or what you are, but this ends now! We're leaving, and you can't stop us!" Adonis starts for the door, clutching Pablo, when Francisco raises his hand, stopping them. A confident smile spreads across his face.

"Adonis. Adonis. We are going to have so much fun together." He waves his hand slightly, forcing the three burglars back and onto the bed in sitting positions. He steps in front of them.

"I am quite sure you will not be leaving. Allow me to illustrate why." Francisco puts his fingers to his lips and produces a shrill whistle. Within seconds two human pups bound into the room and position themselves on either side of Francisco. Both seem happy and eager, tails wagging. Both are sporting puppy hoods, mitts and furiously wagging tails. The Black one's cock is caged, the white one's cock is magnificently erect. The white one raises up on his haunches to better display his erection and puts his forepaws on Francisco's side, begging for attention. Francisco rubs behind his ears before motioning him to stand down.

"Allow me to introduce Sparky," Francisco nods to Niki, "and Bandit," he nods to Ryan. "Surely you realize by now that I exercise a great deal of power, of which you have none." He pauses to let that sink in. "These two pups were once young men, just like you. And each of them, at different times, tried to leave me. If you take one step beyond the threshold downstairs, this will be your fate." Sparky moves forward and sniffs the feet of the three burglars. Bandit pants eagerly, but stays at Francisco's side.

"As you can see, they are happy pups, but pups nonetheless. If you are so foolish as to try to leave ..." Francisco gestures to Bandit. Sparky returns to Francisco's side and the three of them walk toward the doorway. Before he reaches it, Francisco stops and turns while motioning the pups to go ahead without him.

*(Cut to POV from far side of the bed, the burglar's backs to us as they face Francisco)*

"One more thing," Francisco gestures, resulting in the three of them rising to their feet, their three asses, pleasantly on display again. Francisco nods and we see three flashes of light emanating from what must be their crotches.

*(Cut to Francisco's POV, so we finally see the burglars in full frontal nudity, revealing their newly installed chastity cages. All three look down in shock.)*

"What the fuck!" Adonis cries out. He looks up at Francisco. "Who the fuck are you? *What* are you?"

*(Cut to medium closeup of Francisco, who speaks in a confident, endearing manner.)*

"Who am I? I am Francisco. Your benefactor. You *could* say I own you now, but that sounds so ... so crass. What am I?"
"You're a vampire!" Brady asserts.

*(Closeup of Francisco, who chuckles, looks almost boyish and human as he smiles, then shakes his head. Cut to POV behind him, the three burglars facing him and the camera.)*

Francisco gestures and all three sit on the bed again, apparently against their will. Francisco pulls a chair in front of them and also sits, facing them. He looks at Brady.

*(Cut to POV from behind the three, then medium closeup of Francisco, occasional cuts to reactions of the burglars.)*

"This really gets old." He looks slightly peeved, another honest and uncharacteristically human emotion for the first time. "Brady, there is no such thing as a vampire. Well. Not exactly. When my friend Bram said he wanted to write about me, I tried to dissuade him, but he was strong willed, just like Adonis here. My mistake for letting him into my confidence. A rare, weak moment, I suppose. But, I did insist he change a few details, which actually made for a better story anyway, do you not think? I mean. I cannot fly. I can manipulate physical objects, as you well know, but no, I do not turn into a bat. I do not drink anyone's blood. That would be stupid. Counterproductive to kill those who sustain your powers. And what would you do with all the bodies? But, again, it does make for a great story. Oh, and I can see myself in mirrors." Francisco looks endearingly at Pablo.

"Comes in handy for when you want to look your best for those you care about." He pauses a moment, lost in his gaze at Pablo, who looks down sheepishly.

"What else? I have no issue with sunlight or crucifixes either, come to think of it. Oh, and you can forget looking for a wooden stake. Those do not work, either. And even though I can eat and drink just like you, it is not blood that sustains me and gives me my powers. It is your seed. Your semen. I think you call it cum these days. It is one reason I have settled here in San Francisco. The semen of young, healthy, vibrant men has always been extremely easy to obtain. Except in this pandemic. And to some extent in the prior ones. Although this social distancing practice has proven far more of a challenge this time around. Too much media in this century. That is why I am so very happy you are here. And not just for me. You will be of service to Cadmael as well. We have had to rely on one another for far too long. Which is why I have locked your cocks. So that you cannot waste your seed on each other. It is mine now. Mine, and Cadmael's." Francisco rises and replaces the chair. He reaches out toward Pablo, who hesitates.

"Come Pablo, I will show you to your room." Pablo rises and Francisco takes his hand. They walk toward the doorway. Francisco pauses, turns back to Brady and Adonis.

"You are all very precious to me. Cadmael and I will take very good care of you. Sleep well." Francisco and Pablo exit.

*(Cut to medium shot of Brady and Adonis who stand. Brady squats to examine Adonis' chastity cage.)*

"This is so fucked up, Adonis." Adonis looks down, reaches for the cage and lifts it up. Their eyes meet. Then Adonis looks over at the doorway, not knowing how much privacy they have. He sits on the bed as Brady stands up. Adonis reaches out and fondles Brady's cage.

"Did you notice," Adonis says, "one of the dog guys had one of these and one didn't? This is all so weird. I feel like I'm dreaming, Brady. I just want to wake up and know it's all over."

"Yeah. The dog guys. They weren't dogs, just dressed up like dogs. I think he's just messing with us. You know, so we won't escape."

"Maybe," Adonis replies. Brady sits down, just as Pablo reenters the room. Brady and Adonis stand and the three pull into a group hug.

"Guys, I'm scared," Pablo says, his face telegraphing his fear. "Can I ... can I sleep with one of you tonight?" The three move to the bed and climb on.

*(Cut to new POV, from beyond the foot of the bed, Brady and Adonis on either side of Pablo, who has his back against the headboard.)*

"What happened, Pablo?" Adonis asks earnestly, rubbing Pablo's arm. "What did he do to you?" Pablo turns to Adonis, hesitating before answering.

"He took me to some weird, dark dungeon downstairs. He moved my body into this thing on my back like I didn't weigh anything. He fucked me and when I came he sucked me off. Like forever."

"So ... you just had sex?" Brady asks, incredulously. Pablo turns to Brady and nods.

"Yeah. In a way, it was really sexy. I mean if he wasn't a vampire it would have been."

"So ... so he's telling the truth?" Adonis sits back. "All he wants is our cum?"

"I don't know," Pablo almost wails. "I guess. He was ... he was very ... gentle. I don't know. Guys, I'm really tired now. Can I sleep with one of you?"

"Let's all sleep in here," Brady says as he gets up and closes the door. "I don't think any of us wants to be alone right now."

*(Fade to black, then fade up title)*

## Two Weeks Later

*(Fade up on POV behind Cadmael kneeling at Adonis' feet in Adonis' bedroom, his left hand reaching up, fingering Adonis' pierced right nipple, his head obscuring Adonis' crotch as he appears to suck Adonis off. Cut to closeup of Adonis' face, clearly nearing climax.)*

"Ohhh. Noooo. Ohhh. Fuck. Fuck ..."

*(Cut to medium wide view as Adonis shudders in orgasm. Cadmael swallows and feeds. Adonis spasms several times as he comes then, a moment later, straightens in an attempt to regain his dignity. Cut to POV behind Adonis as Cadmael appears to re lock Adonis' cage.)*

"Thank you, Adonis," Cadmael slowly rises to a standing position and takes a step back, away from Adonis. Although he is shorter and smaller than Adonis, clearly, he is in control.

"You performed admirably today. I will let M'Lord know of your progress."

"Gee, thanks," Adonis replies. "So, when will you take this off for good?" He reaches down and lifts his chastity cage.

"Oh. I believe that is permanent, Adonis." We see from Adonis' face he is not pleased.

"Can I ask you a question, Cadmael?"

"Of course." Cadmael slightly nods in agreement.

"When can we get some clothes? We've been naked since we got here."

"M'Lord prefers you naked." He moves closer to Adonis and fingers a pierced nipple. "As do I, so ... no. No clothing is needed. It is much better this way." We see a subtle undertone of anger flitter across Adonis' face. Cadmael turns to leave.

"I have another question." Cadmael pauses and turns, looks expectantly at Adonis. "The dogs. Pups you call them. They're not really pups. They're just guys dressed up like pups. So, what gives?" Cadmael looks meaningfully into Adonis' eyes. Possibly reading his mind? Certainly, carefully forming his response.

"It pleases M'Lord that they retain the bodies of the sexy young men they were. Their minds, however, are those of puppies. They can no longer reason like a human. They think like puppies. They act like puppies. They *are* puppies. With sexy human bodies." Cadmael's expression communicates 'and that's that.' He turns and leaves.

*(Cut to a wide shot of the kitchen, where Brady and Pablo are eating lunch at the island. There is a veritable feast of items spread before them. Adonis enters and takes a seat on a stool next to Brady. Serene music undertone. Alternate closeups of each as they speak.)*

"You're late," Brady says to Adonis.

"Cadmael was feeding. Again." Adonis reaches for a prepared bowl of poke, chop sticks sticking up from the side. "I think I'm his favorite."

"Well, we certainly know who Francisco's favorite is," Brady says, actually smiling. He glances across to Pablo. Pablo sniffs and picks up his burrito and takes a bite and chews.

"Seriously, Pablo. How many times have you and Francisco been partying in the dungeon?" Pablo still chewing shakes his head in dismay.

"Yeah," Adonis says, also chewing. "And how come your chastity cage is prettier than ours? Yeah. You're his favorite. For sure." Pablo puts his burrito down, swallows and wipes his lips with his napkin.

"What if I am?"

"Fuck!" Adonis slams his chopsticks down. "Guys, this is messed up. We ... we can't stay here. Pablo's already falling in love with this ... this monster. We don't know what he's capable of."

"I am not falling in love, you prick." There is anger in Pablo's eyes as he faces Adonis down. "I'm just trying to stay alive."

"I asked Cadmael about the pups. He claims their brains are pup brains now, but they still have human bodies 'cause Francisco likes them that way. I don't believe him. I don't think anything will happen to us if we run. Right now." Adonis looks back and forth between Pablo and Brady. "How about it?"

"I don't know," Brady looks fearful. "You first?"

"Guys ..." Pablo seems unconvinced. "Maybe we should just ..."

"Fuck that," Adonis declares, standing up. "I'll get help." He heads out of the kitchen; Brady and then Pablo follow behind him.

*(Cut to POV from the library, panning as the three cross the foyer to the front doors. Menacing music rises.)*

The three are looking around and behind them, as Adonis slowly opens one of the front doors. He looks intensely at Brady as he extends his right foot across the threshold. Immediately his foot begins to glow before he pulls it back in shock.

"What?" Brady pleads.

"Aruuf! My foot ... it went numb. Then started tingling." Adonis slowly closes the door and turns to Brady and Pablo.

"Duuude!" Brady looks Adonis up and down. "Did you just bark?"

*(Cut to POV from the entry, the three burglars in the foreground, Cadmael at the bottom of the stairs in the background. As Cadmael speaks, cut to see the three turn and look at him in fear and awe.)*

"I will never lie to you, Adonis. I am so glad you did not try to leave." He starts back up the stairs, then pauses and turns. "We really do not need another pup." He takes another step, then over his shoulder says, "And I prefer you just the way you are." He proceeds up the stairs as the three put their arms around one another in solidarity.

*(Fade to a wide shot of a dimly lit bedroom, bigger and more ostentatious than what we've seen before. Francisco's theme fades up. Two figures are making love, one larger on top. Cut to tighter shot to reveal Francisco on top of Pablo, his elbows under Pablo's arm pits, his hands caressing Pablo's head, Pablo's hands on the small of Francisco's back. They are kissing passionately. Many closeups in the following scene.)*

Francisco slowly pulls his lips free of Pablo's. Pablo is looking intently into Francisco's eyes, his eyes darting back and forth, trying to read what is behind Francisco's eyes.

"Pablo, you cannot read my mind."

"Can you read mine?" A genuine smile forms on Francisco's face. His eyes close briefly, then open.

"Yes. And, yes, I am falling in love with you, too." A heartbreaking smile spreads across Pablo's face. Then, he nearly tears up.

"I've been trying hard not to. I want to hate you. But I can't." Francisco moves his right hand so he can brush his thumb across Pablo's full lips.

"I am glad you do not hate me, Pablo. I can control many things. But I cannot control your heart. Or mine, it seems."

"You must have had many lovers in all your years," Pablo whispers. Francisco sighs deeply. He briefly looks lost in thought, then resumes eye contact with Pablo.

"A few, yes. Something I have tried to avoid. For obvious reasons. Someone like me tends to meet many men."

"Did ... did they know ... what you are?" Francisco slightly shakes his head.

"Well. One, yes. But that is a long story." Francisco leans down and kisses Pablo, lingering a moment, then lifts his head again, smiling. "You are full of questions tonight." Pablo nods, with a slight smirk.

"I want to understand you. If I'm going to fall in love with you, I have to know who you are. What you are." He pauses, looking intently into Francisco's eyes. "I know you're not a vampire. But I still don't know *what* you are." Francisco rolls off of Pablo, positioning himself at Pablo's side, holding his head up with one hand, so he can still maintain eye contact. He lovingly brushes Pablo's abs with the other hand.

"We've had many names over the years. In different places. Different cultures. If the scientific community were to label us, perhaps we would be known as *homo semen*, as opposed to *homo sapiens*." Pablo chuckles faintly.

"I get it. So, you're funny, too." Francisco smiles. "You said 'us.' Are there ... are there a lot of *homo semen* around?" Francisco nods slightly, smiling.

"Yes, well, since we don't die off, we tend to accumulate."

"Were ... are your parents *homo semen*? Is that how you came to be you?" Francisco silently chuckles, amused.

"No. We don't propagate like *homo sapiens*."

"Then? ..." Pablo's expression shows he's trying to figure things out.

"Pablo," Francisco moves his hand lower, from Pablo's abs to his caged cock. "it's all about the semen. Your semen renews me. Maintains my powers. If you were to receive my semen, however, then you would be transformed. You would no longer be *homo sapiens*. That is why I always wear a condom when I enter you. Before the invention of the condom, we propagated much more frequently than we do today."

"That's it?" Francisco nods. "Does it hurt to ... transform?" Francisco smiles, slightly shakes his head. Pablo processes what he's just heard.

He reaches up and brushes Francisco's mustache, the bravest move he's made yet. "You're messing with me, right?" Francisco shakes his head again.

"No, Pablo." Francisco moves back on top of Pablo and leans down and pulls him into another deep kiss. Pablo moans through the kiss.

> *(Fade to a montage of obligatory porn flick 30 to 45 second scenes of Francisco fucking Adonis in the sling and feeding on his cum splashed belly, Cadmael sucking off Brady who is bound onto the St. Andrew's cross, Francisco with Brady in the sling. All with rhythmic music under. Then, the music slows, becomes moodier, the scene with closeup on Brady's dimly lit face dissolves to Pablo's. Shot widens to reveal Pablo with Francisco seated on the floor in front of the fire, which illuminates them, in the library. Cuts to many closeups as they speak.)*

"One month," Francisco says, before lifting a snifter to sip a rich colored cognac. Pablo furrows his brow and turns his head slightly, indicating a wordless question. He reaches out and fingers a pierced nipple through Francisco's mesh bodysuit. "You've been here one month tonight." Pablo smiles. "You weren't smiling that night, Pablo." Pablo silently chuckles.

"No. I was scared to death."

"And you hated me." Pablo nods, looking down, a neutral, conflicted expression on his face. Then he looks up into Francisco's eyes and smiles.

"I love you now." Francisco smiles and takes Pablo's nipple-teasing hand in his.

"Enough to spend eternity with me, Pablo?" Pablo looks seriously into Francisco's eyes and sighs.

"I wouldn't spend it with anyone else." Francisco pulls Pablo's hand up and kisses it.

"So, my love, you are ready to join me?" Pablo nods, then displays that adorable smile. He raises up on his knees, and playfully pushes Francisco over onto his back. He unzips his body suit enough to pull Francisco's cock out, then leans down and swallows.

> *(Cut to lingering close up of Francisco's face as we hear Pablo moaning, verbalizing as he sucks. Intersperse cuts of wider shot of both bodies and close ups of each face to show passage of time, ending with wide shot as Francisco partially*

*raises up in reaction to his orgasm. Pablo and Francisco are both breathing heavily. Cut to tight shot POV from behind Francisco's head as he reaches out and pulls Pablo forward and onto him. There is a small dab of cum on Pablo's lips as Francisco pulls him into a kiss. After several long seconds the sound of the doorbell silences Francisco's theme music.)*

"What can this be?" Francisco whispers as Pablo lifts his head. Pablo looks a bit dizzy. "Wait here." As Pablo climbs off of Francisco and sits up, supporting himself with his arms behind him, Francisco stands, crosses the room, opens the pocket doors, steps through and closes them.

*(Cut to foyer, POV from near the stairs facing the entry. Francisco walks to the front doors as he replaces his penis and zips up his body suit. He pauses, sensing who is on the other side. We see him straighten his shoulders, then pull the door open to reveal a uniformed officer (Greg). Multiple closeups in the next few exchanges.)*

"May I help you?" Francisco asks. The officer looks Francisco up and down quickly, assessing the fact that Francisco is essentially naked, while projecting professionalism. He nods curtly, and holds up his ID.
"My apologies for the late intrusion. I'm Officer Swanson, SFPD. We're investigating a series of burglaries in the neighborhood. I, uh, just wanted to ask if you've seen anything out of the ordinary? If anything of your own has gone missing?"
"Hmmm. Really? I don't *think* so ..."

*(Cut to Brady and Adonis, creeping out of Brady's room, Brady's arm around Adonis' waist. Adonis turns to Brady and whispers.)*

"This is it! This is our chance to escape!"
"But ... where's Pablo?"
"We have to go now, before he senses what we're doing and freezes us!"
Adonis bounds down the stairs, Brady on his tail.

*(Cut to POV from the officer's perspective. We see Adonis and Brady bounding down the stairs.)*

"Help!" Adonis shouts. "Help! We're prisoners. He kidnapped us!" Adonis' shouts rouse the pups, who come bounding out of the kitchen and enter excitedly barking from the far end of the foyer. Francisco raises one hand, freezing the four of them. Cadmael comes running after the pups from the kitchen and stops when he sees the officer.

> *(Closeup on Francisco, who turns his head to see the scene behind him, then turns back to the officer, revealing his guilty embarrassment.)*

"This is not what it looks like, officer ..." Pablo walks out of the library to find out what is going on, adding a third, young, naked, caged body to the scene. Still slightly dazed, he looks blankly at Francisco and the officer. Francisco looks back at Pablo, then back at the officer.

"Okay ... maybe it is." The officer reaches a hand toward his shoulder mounted radio. Francisco gestures, freezing the officer.

"What's going on, Francisco?" Pablo asks.

> *(Cut to POV from behind Cadmael, showcasing the entire unfortunate scene before him. Francisco walks over and puts a hand on each of Pablo's shoulders.)*

"It is nothing for you to worry about, my love. Go back to the fire, and I will join you shortly."

"May I stay? How else will I learn?" Francisco looks over at Cadmael.

> *(Closeup of Cadmael who faintly smiles and nods once, aware of what has happened between Francisco and Pablo. Medium shot from Francisco's POV as Cadmael rounds up the pups and the three return to the kitchen. Medium shot of Francisco and Pablo from officer's POV, frozen Adonis and Brady in the background. Pablo is looking up longingly at Francisco. When Francisco moves, camera pans and widens.)*

"Very well. No one as new as you has ever had an audience with an Elder before, I dare say."

"An elder?"

"Yes. Sometimes even I need assistance." Francisco steps away from Pablo, who starts to follow. Francisco motions for him to stay where he is. Francisco steps into the middle of the foyer, between the burglars and the officer and looks up over the burglars' heads and gestures with both hands. "Elder, if it pleases you, I, Francisco, request your counsel." A fog forms above and beyond the burglars. It grows denser as a cross-legged seated older Asian man (Hiroshi, of course) in a glowing yellow fundoshi, semi-transparently appears in the fog.

"I am at your service, Francisco," the Elder intones in a deep, echoing voice, as if he is present, but not quite present. He has a beatific continence. He looks around the foyer from his vantage point, pausing on the officer, then on Pablo, then the burglars, then finally on Francisco. "It has been many years since last we spoke."

"Yes, well ... I have not faced a challenge such as this before, Elder." Elder closes his eyes, then opens them as he smiles, possibly enjoying Francisco's dilemma.

"You do seem to be outnumbered, yes."

> *(While Elder and Francisco are talking, cut to Pablo walking up to the officer, then across the foyer, with closeups of Brady's and Adonis' eyes following him, stunned to see him not only moving freely but apparently collaborating with Francisco. He focuses again on the Elder before the camera cuts back to the previous POV that includes everyone but the officer, with closeups of Francisco, Elder and Pablo as they converse.)*

"I am at fault, Elder. I let my guard down." Francisco glances quickly at Pablo. "I have control of my charges, but I need your help in dealing with this officer of the law."

"Yes. I understand. You must let him go."

"Of course, but without any memory of what he has seen here."

"You know what must be done, Francisco. To take something from him, even if it is only a few moments of his life, you must grant him something of value. You cannot upset the balance of nature."

"Yes, I know. I am prepared. Will you lend me your powers to alter his memory, Elder?"

"Of course." Elder closes his eyes for several seconds, then opens them, glancing briefly at Pablo, then focusing on Francisco. "When he reaches the street, he will have no memory of ever having been here." Francisco sighs in relief.

"Thank you, Elder. I am in your debt."

"You can repay your debt by providing well for your new companion. I leave you in peace."

The image of the Elder fades faster than the fog, which collapses upon itself and disappears. Francisco walks over to Pablo and grasps each of his biceps.

"Pablo, we have to do something that will be painful for you, but as one who will now outlive everyone you have ever known, and ever will know, it is a pain you will experience many times. It is, in fact, our only real curse." A look of fear grows on Pablo's face.

"Who has to die?"

"No one ... not for a long time. But we will have to say goodbye to one of your friends. Wait here." Francisco moves back in front of the officer. He looks into the officer's eyes, closes his own eyes briefly, then opens them. The officer immediately drops his hand from his radio.

*(Cut to POV behind the officer, with the foyer before him.)*

"So!" Francisco says cheerily. "Which of these sexy young men would you like for your very own?" The officer moves forward as Francisco steps aside. The officer walks around Brady and Adonis, looking up and down, appraising them. He ruffles Brady's hair, runs a finger along and under Adonis' left pec. He moves back behind Brady, looks over at Francisco.

"This one." Francisco smiles and nods.

"A good choice. Good day, officer, and do take care." The officer reaches down and takes Brady's hand just as Brady regains the ability to walk, again reluctantly but unavoidably.

*(Cut to POV looking toward the entry from near the stairs, Pablo and then Francisco on the left, Adonis still frozen in the middle of the foyer, the officer and Brady approaching the entry as Brady glances fearfully back at Adonis.)*

As Francisco puts his arm around Pablo's shoulders and Pablo wraps an arm around Francisco's waist, the officer and Brady reach the entry. As they pass through it, a blue-white flash of light obliterates Brady. The flash fades to reveal Brady in pup form, tail wagging. His hooded pup face looks up at the officer and barks. The officer looks back at Francisco.

*(Closeup of Francisco, who looks pained.)*

"Oh ... sorry Officer Swanson. I ... forgot. His name is Brady. You will take good care of him, will you not?" The officer looks down at Pup Brady, reaches down and cups his snout. Pup Brady pants eagerly and barks, tail wagging.

"You bet. He's in good hands. Good day now." Officer Swanson and Pup Brady head across the portico as Francisco closes the door. He guides Pablo toward the library doors.

"Now, my love, where were we?" As they reach the door, he turns to the still frozen Adonis and gestures, freeing him. As he and Pablo enter the library and close the doors, Adonis collapses onto the floor in grief.

*(Fade to black. Credits roll over haunting orchestral needle drop.)*

# Thirty-Three

# THE REVIEWS COME IN

As STEVE'S TONGUE-IN-CHEEK CLOSING credits began to roll, Raphael grabbed Luke's wrist and held it up, displaying Luke's hand grasping a cookie.

"Before anyone says anything, I just want to point out that Luke is still holding the cookie he picked up when the opening credits began ... and he still hasn't taken a bite! Guys, I think we held his attention." He leaned over and took a bite out of the cookie himself before heading over to the console table and pulling the bottle of Schramsberg out of the ice bucket. He turned and nodded to Alex, who was high-fiving Steve, wordlessly asking for his help. As he poured and Alex distributed, Raphael glanced a couple of times at Luke, who hadn't taken his eyes off Raphael. Once he rejoined Luke, Raphael turned to him, raised his glass and said, "Your dare. Your toast, Sir."

Luke grinned, first at Raphael, then at everyone else, lingering on Juan and Steve. He turned back to Raphael, touched glasses and said, "I can honestly say I have never been more in awe of everyone in this room than I am right now. I'm ... speechless." Apparently, that was as good a toast as they were going to get, as Luke tipped his glass back and drank. When he lowered his glass, he turned to Juan. "You were fucking amazing!" Then, to Steve, "I've always known what you do, Steve, but I had no idea just how talented you are. That was ... epic!" Then he stood and walked over beside Steve so he could address everyone.

"You were all incredible. All of you. You obviously had the best acting coach this side of Hollywood." He knelt down by Alex and put a hand on his thigh.

"We had two acting coaches, Luke," Juan said as he raised his glass towards Steve. "This was all Steve and Alex."

"How did you ever dream this up?" Luke rhetorically asked Alex. "There's never been a porn flick anything like it as far as I know." He stood up. "Guys, you're all going to be famous. This is going to rack up a million views in just the first couple of days."

"Um, about that, Sir," Raphael set his glass down and walked over to Luke. He put a hand on each of Luke's hips in a kind of loving, 'there's something I have to tell you' stance. "There's something I have to tell you. Your 'parameters' were a little imprecise." Luke tilted his head. "You said I had to post it online." Luke nodded. "You didn't say where. Or how. Or for how long, so I posted it as an encrypted file in a password protected folder in a place no one would ever look, two days ago. And I deleted it yesterday." He looked over his shoulder at Juan before returning his gaze to Luke. "To protect Juan's, Niki's, really everyone's reputations and careers, so ... sorry, Sir, but no one outside this room will ever see it."

"But ..." Luke looked devastated. "What you guys did has to be the best gay porn flick of all time! You can't ... you have to ... seriously?" As Raphael led Luke back to their places, Luke gave Raphael a look only slightly less menacing than the one Francisco had first delivered to the three burglars.

"Sir. Don't let the online thing ruin your enjoyment of our fabulous production. Come on ... you know it's really for the best." He turned to Steve and picked up his glass for his own toast. "Steve, I don't know how you did it, but you made us all look sexy as hell. Or wherever it is that Francisco came from." Everyone followed Raphael's lead and toasted him. Steve stood and bowed.

"Thank you ... thank you. First let me thank my loving parents ..." Everyone laughed. "But seriously I couldn't have done this without Alex's script. Like all of you, I was truly inspired by his evil genius." He raised his glass toward Alex, who played along and stood for a bow.

"As long as we're handing out compliments, the script was just an idea. You all made it live and breathe. Like Luke, in a way I'm sorry no one else will get to see it, but I *would* like to say," and he turned to Juan and dramatically paraphrased Brady's first words. "Please ... please ... can we watch it one more time? We won't tell anyone!"

"Yes!" Both Ricky and Greg exclaimed.

"I want to see it again," Ryan chimed in. Alex grabbed the remote. Since Steve was the only one who had previously seen the finished product, this time each of them saw things they hadn't noticed in the first screening. Little details and nuances Steve had made sure to capture. The genuine distress in Pablo's tearful face. Adonis' earnest but failed attempt to prevent ejaculation at the hands of Cadmael. The inexplicable, but genuine delight on the face of Officer Swanson when he picks out Brady as his prize. The second time around everyone was laughing, groaning, complimenting others and munching down on the previously neglected treats.

"Hiroshi," Greg said as the closing credits rolled a second time, "you were perfect. And totally unexpected." He looked over at Luke. "That part wasn't in the script, Luke."

"That was my little contribution to the story," Steve explained. "Along with my co-conspirators Juan and Ricky. It's always fun to pull one over on the cast."

"I wish I'd written it in," Alex looked at Hiroshi. "You were preternatural, Hiroshi. Just what the story needed."

"Thank you, Alex," Hiroshi nodded. "I have to admit, I have mixed feelings about being cast as *The Elder*, but it was fun." He turned to Raphael and Luke. "I was pleased to be a small part of a Raphael and Luke dare." He grinned slyly as he reached for a truffle.

"There was one thing that disturbed me, though," Luke said, suddenly looking very serious. "I'm really worried about Adonis. Guys, my heart sank along with him when he dropped to the floor at the very end." He looked over at Alex. "What's going to happen to him? Will Francisco transform him into a *homo semen*, too? Or will Cadmael transform him and take him as an eternal lover? Or will they take pity on him and free him? Or, will he be a prisoner, a semen donor, for the rest of his life?" He looked over at Niki, then Ryan. "Or will he put himself out of his misery by becoming a pup? That scene broke my heart. Guys ... you have to make a sequel!" Steve and Alex exchanged shocked looks.

"Oh, no. No ... no ... no ... no ... no." Steve locked eyes with Luke. "You're the only one in this room who has no idea. How. Much. Work. This. Was. Cumulatively? At least a couple hundred hours. Probably more."

"Yeah," Ricky piped up. "You know the scene where Francisco cages us in Greg and Alex's bedroom? That took eighteen takes."

"And whose fault was that?" Steve prodded.

"I couldn't help it," Ricky laughed. "Just thinking about it makes me laugh." Steve looked at Luke as he tilted his head toward Ricky. "He kept cracking up. He was supposed to be shocked and sad."

"That was the hardest acting I did," Ricky confessed. "You know ... being upset about being caged."

"Yeah, it was a lot of work," Raphael said, "but we had a lot of fun, too, didn't we?" He looked appreciatively at Luke. "It was your dare, but we had all the fun."

"I guess so," Luke chuckled. He looked over at Ryan. "So, you got to be a pup for a day."

"Oh, more than a day," Ryan grinned. "It was awesome."

"Remind me to ask for my pup gear back," Niki looked conspiratorially at Ryan. "Whenever you want. No hurry." Ryan nodded, but said nothing, just turned to Mateo and planted one. Steve scooted over in front of the Blu-ray player and ejected the DVD. He secured it in the jewel case, then held it out to Juan.

"Juan, this is the only copy." Juan took the case. Steve reached back and picked up a USB drive and held it out for Juan. "These are all the elements that went into the finished product. I wiped the drives in the edit studio. No one will ever see this, unless you allow it." Juan nodded gratefully. "You were as perfect for the role of Francisco as Raphael predicted you would be. I appreciate your trust in me. In all of us."

"To be honest, I'm glad you talked me into it," Juan said. "I have to say, it's weird seeing myself ... seeing all of us on the screen, but thanks to your talent in producing this, I have to admit, I'm proud of what we accomplished."

"Juan," Luke leaned forward. "I'm not just saying this. If you ever get burned out in nursing, you can have a career in acting."

"Or, maybe it was just that sexy bodysuit," Ricky posed.

"Or, the sexy body in the body suit," Alex countered.

"Juan, do not lose that DVD," Luke continued. "We should make watching it a Thanksgiving tradition."

"Okay, sure," Juan played along. "I was thinking it would be fun to show the grand kids someday, too." He wiggled his eyebrows at Ricky.

"Yeah," Ricky grinned. "They'll really get a kick out of the love scene in dungeon, won't they?" Juan pulled him into a fierce sideways hug.

"Say, Ricky, I just realized," Juan said as he released Ricky. "I think you and I were the only ones who were actually compensated for our parts in this, thanks to Raphael."

"R a p h a e l?" Alex sat up on his knees and furrowed his brow at Raphael, who dismissed Alex with an eye roll.

"Yeah, that. I did what I had to do to persuade Juan to agree. No big deal."

"I don't remember getting anything," Ricky looked at Raphael, then Juan.

"I totally forgot, mijo. Raphael offered to wipe out twenty of the dinners we promised everyone." Juan glanced at Raphael before returning his gaze to Ricky. "I counter-offered for thirty."

"Woo hoo!" Ricky laughed. "You out negotiated Raphael! I love it!"

"Wait," Luke turned to Raphael. "You gave away thirty of the dinners they promised all of us without consulting anyone?" Raphael nodded confidently.

"It was worth every bite, wouldn't you say? Luke. Tell me. Are you satisfied with the results of your dare? Was it worth a few dinners?

Dinners that we all share now anyway? And was it worth all the 'away time' I had to put into fulfilling it?"

"Baby, I can't imagine, in my wildest dreams, ever coming up with another dare that will be as satisfying as this was. You guys didn't exceed my expectations. You obliterated them. Like I said, I am in awe. Of all of you." Raphael looked around at the group, nodding and looking self-satisfied. "But, having said that," Raphael returned his gaze to Luke, "nothing can ever make up for each and every moment we were apart. Not even sexy Francisco."

"Listen to this guy," Raphael looked at Juan, then at Hiroshi. "Excuse me, Elder, I beseech thee to alter time and return all our lost moments to Luke, so he can die a happy man." Hiroshi waved his hands dramatically in Luke's direction, then bowed from his sitting position.

"Any other requests?" Hiroshi looked around, but had no takers. He stood. "In that case, once again, I thank you for everything. For making this a most memorable Thanksgiving. I can honestly say you have all given me much to be thankful for." Before he could move, first Juan and Ricky, then Mateo, then Ryan, then everyone encircled him with a long and heartfelt Locked Cock Brotherhood matane hug.


As Greg and Alex were reconnecting cables to the television after returning it to their room, Greg looked up and saw Alex giving him a curious, smirky look.

"What?"

"I think I get to issue you an official dare." Greg looked confused.

"Remember? We agreed. If Mateo and Ryan started getting kinky, I'd issue you a dare and if they never did, you could dare me. Which is kind of unfair to me, now that I think about it, since we might never have been able to prove they were getting kinky, if they kept it hidden. Of course, when we decided this, we didn't know we'd be living across the hall from them, so ..." Greg stood up and put a hand on each of Alex's shoulders.

"What are you babbling about?"

"Months ago, in our kitchen. I remember it clearly. You said maybe Mateo and Ryan will always be vanilla. And I said we were doing a good job of corrupting them. Remember?"

"Oh, yeah. I do. Better than you, apparently." Alex pulled his head back in disagreement. "As I recall, you were claiming one or both of them would end up collared and caged. I haven't seen any new cages lately."

"But ... Ryan has been pupping out. More than once."

"You never mentioned snips or snails or puppy dog tails, darling. No cage, no collar … no dare."

"But …" Greg leaned in for a brief, but solid kiss to silence Alex. He pulled away displaying a triumphant grin.

"Like Luke, you've been hoisted on your own parameter petard." Greg glanced over at the bed. "So, it's not too late, and we have tomorrow off. What'll it be? Sex? Or a piece of that pecan pie nobody remembered to serve?"

"That's easy. Sex … then pie."

One way or another, the subject of the 'the movie' found its way into many conversations over the next couple of weeks. Occasionally, they'd even refer to one another by their character's names. Without coming right out and saying so, they were all, understandably, proud of how well it had turned out. What had initially seemed like an ordeal, one that Juan, especially, had dreaded, had instead become a bonding experience that they looked back on fondly.

"Come on, Brady," Raphael was coaching Alex on his flys in the gym early on a December Saturday afternoon. "Three more reps. You know it's the only way to tempt 'Franceesco' into keeping you captive instead of sending you off to be some random cop's pup." Alex resisted the urge to laugh. Indeed, the thought of avoiding permanent puppydom was the motivation he needed to pull off four more reps. Fatigued, he let the dumbbells slide from his grip onto the floor, then sat up. He looked down at his chest, then up at Raphael.

"So, Adonis … you promised me pecs like yours. Where are they?"

"Patience, Brady. Patience. And lots more reps." Alex broke eye contact with Raphael as Luke appeared in the doorway.

"Raphael." Luke looked oddly at Raphael. "Angel is on your phone. I answered when I saw it was him." He held the phone out to Raphael. As Raphael put it to his ear, Luke looked apprehensively at Alex.

"Angel!" Raphael answered. "What's … yeah … Niki's home. He's studying … okay, hang on." Raphael glanced at Luke, then, without saying any more, headed out the door. Alex looked up at Luke.

"Angel didn't sound like himself. I think something's wrong," Luke said before turning and following Raphael. Alex was right behind. Raphael was already in the library when Luke and Alex made it to the foyer. As Luke entered the library Alex hung back, not wanting to intrude, but unable to allay his curiosity and concern.

"Okay, Angel," Raphael had placed his phone on the desk and activated the speakerphone. "Niki's here. And Luke. What's up?"

"It's Mama," Angel replied, anguished. There was a fair amount of ambient noise. "I'm outside the hospital. They won't let me go in."

"What happened?" Niki pleaded. He and Raphael locked eyes. Luke put an arm around Raphael's waist. Meanwhile, as soon as Alex heard Angel's reply he headed for the stairs, ran up two flights and yelled for Steve before he got to his door. As he followed Steve back down the stairs, he peeled off on the second floor to round up Juan. When he and Juan got to the library door Steve was kneeling next to Niki, still seated at the desk. Angel was talking.

"She insisted she wasn't that sick. I finally wore her down and was able to take her temperature. I was right ... she had a fever. She was panting, just sitting there. I went all Raphael on her and was finally able to get her to let me drive her here to the emergency room. They basically took one look at her and took her away. Gave me some forms to fill out on a clipboard and shoved me out the door." As he listened, Juan realized what was happening and entered the library, to stand next to Raphael. Alex entered, too, and hung back, near the fireplace.

"Angel, it's Juan. How long have you been at the hospital?"

"I don't know. Half an hour. Maybe an hour. I don't know. I gave them the forms back maybe ten minutes ago. They're not telling me anything. I don't even know where she is now." Angel sounded near tears.

"Did you give them your contact information on the forms?"

"Yes."

"And name of her primary doctor?"

"Yeah, all her insurance info."

"Did she seem normal yesterday? Or was she coming down with a cold?"

"No, she seemed fine. Do you ... do you think it's COVID?"

"I think we need to be prepared for that, yes, Angel. What did they say when you gave them back the forms?"

"To go home. Don't stop anywhere. They'll call me as soon as they know more."

"How busy did they seem? How crowded is it?"

"Busy. Half a dozen ambulances have come while I've been here. Maybe more. I don't want to leave."

"Angel, I know exactly how you feel, but they're not going to let you in, under any circumstances. You should go home. They'll be contacting you in the next couple of hours. Hopefully. If Mama tests positive, she's exactly where she needs to be. If she is, then you'll need to quarantine and get tested. In fact, you need to quarantine anyway. You should get a call from a charge nurse, or someone like that. If you can, patch us in on Raphael's phone so I can talk to her or him, too. Okay?"

"Juan. How scared should I be?"

"Don't be scared, Angel. Be strong. I doubt you'll be able to talk to Mama today, but if by some chance you do, don't let her know you're worried. You need to be upbeat for her. They aren't going to have any answers for us for a while, Angel." Juan was looking at Niki as he spoke. "I know it's terrible not knowing, but they're doing everything they should. It just takes time."

"I don't want to leave."

"Angel," Raphael leaned over the phone and spoke in a measured, big brother voice. "You need to go home. If this is COVID, then you're vulnerable. You need to be thinking about yourself as well as Mama. Do it for her. Do it for me ... and Niki."

"Angel," Juan coached, "I want you to take your temperature when you get home and text it to me. I'll text you in a few minutes so you have my number. I want you to text me your temp every couple of hours. And let me know if you feel any symptoms. Mama could have been infectious for days, a week or more. I assume you've been at her place multiple times in last ten days."

"Yeah, almost every day. Like always."

"Were you both wearing masks?" There was a pause from Angel's end.

"Only when we went out. Shopping."

"Don't feel guilty, Angel. But it does make it more likely you've been exposed. Again, for Mama's sake if nothing else, you need to go home and look after yourself."

"I feel fine ... well, physically, I mean."

"And you said Mama felt fine yesterday," Niki rejoined the conversation. "Don't make us 'go all Raphael' on you, Angel. You're outnumbered." He looked up at Raphael with his best effort at a smile.

"Okay, okay. So, you said they'll call in a couple of hours, Juan?"

"It could take longer, Angel. Don't count the minutes. But patch us in when they do call."

"Okay. Later. Love you." Angel signed out. Raphael heaved a long sigh, still in Luke's side embrace. He looked across the desk at Niki.

"I'm going down. Angel shouldn't be alone. Wanna come? We can rent a car ..." Luke released his hold on Raphael and made eye contact with Juan as Niki nodded and stood up. Juan shook his head at Luke.

"Baby ... come here. Sit down." Luke guided Raphael to one of the fireplace chairs. "Niki, you, too. Come here." Alex sat down on the hearth, now in the thick of things. Juan sat next to him as Luke and Steve each settled in on the floor next to their husbands. Raphael looked at

Luke with his best 'Spicy Asian' look of defiance. He started to open his mouth, but Juan cut him off.

"Raphael, you made me a member of this family, so I'm going to take full advantage of that to exert a little authority. Professional, experienced authority in this case." Raphael closed his mouth and glanced at Luke, hoping for support, but getting none. "I know how you feel, both of you." He glanced at Niki. "The last thing Angel would want is for him to infect either of you. Or both of you. There's a very good chance of that happening if you were to go to him." Juan paused to let that logic sink in. "Whether your Mama has COVID or not, you won't be able to enter the hospital to see her. They'll only let you communicate on a phone or tablet. Taking a trip ... staying in a hotel ... you'll only increase your risk of exposure to yourselves. There's a lot more virus circulating down the peninsula than here ... you know that. Think about Mama. The last thing she needs right now is to have all three of her boys sick with COVID."

"He's right, Raphael," Alex reached over and squeezed Raphael's knee. "I know it sucks, but he's right." The defiance in Raphael's face dimmed, but hadn't completely faded when they heard the front door open. Greg entered, lugging three tote bags filled with groceries. Alex flashed a tight smile at Raphael, then at Niki as he jumped up and headed out to fill in Greg while helping him unpack the groceries.

"Baby ... Niki," Luke moved in front of both of them, "let's not make any decisions until we know more." He reached back to lay a hand on Juan's knee. "Juan will help us understand what's going on and make the right choices. Okay?" Neither Niki nor Raphael responded. "Can we do that?" Finally, Raphael nodded, giving in to the logic he couldn't reasonably refute.

It was more, much more, than two hours later when Raphael's phone finally rang. He and Luke were in their signature positions at opposite ends of one of the couches in the sitting room, each with a tablet, and each with a foot firmly planted in the other's crotch. Juan was stretched out on the other couch, nodding off, with Ricky sitting on the floor, scrolling through his phone, his head near Juan's slowly rising and falling chest. Niki was in the library, but rather than studying, he, like Raphael and Luke, was searching for everything he could find on COVID, its effects and treatments. Although he was surrounded by hundreds of books, none of them contained any answers to their current crisis. When the phone rang, Juan jumped up, nearly knocking Ricky's phone out of his hand. Niki slid into place next to Juan on the other side of the coffee table from Raphael as he answered.

"Angel ..."

"Raphael, I have Mama's nurse here. Is Niki there, too?"

"We're all here. What do we know?"

"Hello, everyone, I'm Elena, one of Ms. Malaluan's nurses. I'm the charge nurse on duty this evening. Good to meet you. What we know for certain, is that your mother is SARS-CoV-2 positive, and she is presenting moderate symptoms.

"Elena, this is Juan, I'm also a nurse. What are her vitals? Is there hypoxia?"

"Yes. Her oxygen level is between 92 and 93." Juan's face froze. "We have her on supplemental oxygen for now, and we've administered Remdesivir, which she is responding well to. Her vitals are stable."

"What about dexamethasone?" Juan asked.

'We've not seen any indication of cytokine storm, fortunately. We're hoping that will not be necessary. As I said she's stable and resting comfortably. When I told her I would be calling you, she said 'don't tell them it's COVID, or they'll never let me leave the house again,' so that's a good sign. She still has a sense of humor. You should all be optimistic."

"And it's probably too late for monoclonal antibodies?" Niki asked, exercising some of his newly acquired knowledge about COVID treatments.

"That's right. We're already administering oxygen. Juan, Angel, compared to many of our patients your mother is doing reasonably well. Please try not to worry. Unless you have any other questions, I should go for now. You may not hear from us again tonight, but we'll keep you posted."

"Okay," Juan replied. "Thank you, Elena." Elena rang off. Luke looked wryly over at Juan.

"Looks like you really are a member of the family ... she thinks you're one of Mama's own." Juan nodded and smiled.

"She's probably not used to families quite like ours." Juan made eye contact with Raphael, who looked more anxious than relieved. While Juan and Elena had been talking, Mateo and Ryan had entered the house from the daylong field trip they had taken. They were surprised to see most everyone in the sitting room, so they stood in the doorway as they stripped, listening silently.

"So, Juan, what does all this mean?" Angel asked, still on the line.

"Yeah," Raphael said. "What are we supposed to think about what you two just said." Juan took a few seconds to gather his thoughts. Meanwhile, after a whispered conversation between Mateo and Ryan, they had pulled their clothes back on and headed out again.

"We have to trust Elena's judgement. She's right there. Sometimes you learn as much about a patient from their body language and their eyes as you do from the monitors. The fact Mama's joking is good. I'll be honest, I'm concerned about her oxygen saturation. I was hoping it would be higher. So, there's already some involvement with her lungs. The Remdesivir should help. It sounds like they won't hesitate to administer dexamethasone if her numbers drop. So ... listen guys. If Mama had to get COVID, it's so much better it happened now and not six or seven months ago. We've learned a lot. About how this virus attacks in different ways in different people. We know what does and doesn't work in treating it. The next two or three days will be critical, but like Elena said, we probably shouldn't worry too much. How are you doing Angel?"

"I'm a wreck. Other than that, I'm fine."

"You should know," Luke said, "if we hadn't tied Raphael and Niki to their chairs, they would already be down there with you."

"Yeah ... and they're probably enjoying the heck out of being tied down, too, aren't they?"

"Riiiiight," Raphael replied.

"We're worried about you, Angel," Niki confessed. "We can be there in a couple of hours."

"Huh uh. As much fun as it might be to be quarantined with you two for two weeks, please, stay right where you are. I mean that. Luke, if you have to tie them up, please, do it."

"Roger that, Angel," Juan laughed. "Do you know where and when you can get tested?"

"They're sending me an email, doc. By the way, temp is still normal." Juan put an arm around Niki's shoulders and tugged before standing up.

"Good. Let's hope it stays that way," Juan replied. "Doctor's orders." He offered an optimistic smile to Raphael who was signing off with Angel.

"So," Luke looked up at Juan. "Good news? Okay news?"

"Pretty good news," Juan replied. "I think she's in good hands. We should all feel fortunate." Ricky, who hadn't left his spot in front of the couch, ambled over to Niki and Juan on his knees, phone in hand.

"Mateo just texted. He and Ryan are bringing home pizza for everyone, so we don't have to cook. He says forty minutes."

"Oh, yeah," Niki reached between Juan's legs to squeeze Ricky's thigh. "I guess we should eat. That's sweet of them." Luke stood and reached down to take Raphael's hand.

"Let us know when dinner arrives," he smiled at Ricky. "I'm going to take my husband upstairs for a little quiet time together." As they headed for the foyer, Juan reached down and lifted Niki into standing position, then hugged him from behind. Ricky stood on his own.

"It never gets any easier, Niki. Dealing with the emotions and fears of patients and their families. And your own emotions." Niki sighed. "In many ways it's the hardest part of the job."

"Seriously?" Niki turned to face Juan. "It never gets easier?"

"No, but you learn how to manage it. When you stop caring ... if you stop caring, then it's time to find a new profession." Niki nodded and pressed his forehead into Juan's chest a moment, then slipped out of Juan's embrace, brushed his hand along Ricky's abs with a smile, and headed to the foyer and the stairs beyond.

Dinner was a quick and somber affair. Unlike when Mateo had his COVID scare, this wasn't just a threat. It was the real deal. Most of the conversation, what little there was, consisted of everyone grilling Juan with questions about Mama's treatment and what, if anything, Angel could do in advance of learning his status. Everyone thanked Mateo and Ryan for their thoughtfulness, then began clearing the table and transporting dishes and pizza boxes into the kitchen.

"What's this?" Alex exclaimed, as he plopped a stack of plates near the dishwasher. Strategically spaced in the middle of the island were three tall, narrow tumbler sized decorated glasses with a candle burning inside each.

"Veladoras," Mateo said, glancing shyly at Raphael, then Niki.

"You guys!" Ricky went to Mateo and pulled him into a hug. "You got those before the pizzas? That's so cool. I wish I'd thought of that." Alex was slowly turning one of the candles, examining the strange images screened on the glass.

"So, what are they for?" he asked.

"They're devotional candles, Alex," Juan said quietly as he, too, examined one. "Ah, amazing, Mateo, Ryan. These are Doctor de Plaga candles. How did you ever find them?"

"I'm still in the dark," Alex continued, perhaps ironically. By now Raphael and Niki had surrounded Mateo.

"They're seven-day candles, Alex," Juan continued. "You let them burn to help you memorialize an event or achieve whatever you're praying for. These are designed specifically to help deal with a plague ... with COVID." He turned to Mateo and Ryan. "I can't believe you found these. But why three?"

"One for Mama, one for Angel and ... one for Niki and Raphael hearts," Mateo explained quietly, glancing furtively at Niki.

"We had to go to three shops," Ryan grinned. "Mateo was on a mission. In the Mission." Niki, as was his nature, teared up as he planted one on each of Mateo's and Ryan's cheeks. Mateo smiled at Niki.

"I don' know what else to do."

"This was the perfect thing to do, Mateo ... Ryan," Raphael whispered, not wanting to risk choking up. He cleared his throat. "We'll need to take a vote, but I think you two are ready to be promoted from pledges to full-fledged members of the Locked Cock Brotherhood fraternity." Mateo and Ryan grinned as if that was a real thing.

## Thirty-Four

# A SHAMAN APPEARS

ANGEL AND MAMA WERE nearly as present for breakfast Sunday as if Ricky had griddled pancakes for them as well. In fact, there were a couple of 'cakes left over, anxious appetites being what they were. That had never happened before. Even Steve passed on them. Juan had checked in on Angel's temp by text, and that's how they knew that he had yet to receive an update. Juan had discouraged him from calling the hospital himself, suggesting that no news was almost certainly good news.

Then came the news.

Early afternoon, Raphael's phone rang. He and Niki were in the library; except for sleeping, they'd rarely been more than a few feet apart for the past twenty-four hours, just in case. Luke and Steve were playing, attempting anyway, a game of chess in the sitting room, where Juan was reading with Mateo, working on his English. Raphael looked hopefully at Niki as he picked up his phone. Luke and company appeared in the doorway before he'd finished greeting Angel.

"Angel ..." Niki said, to let him know both he and Raphael were listening.

"I have Carla on the line, guys. Umm," Angel sighed uncharacteristically. "Carla, go ahead again."

"Hello, everyone. I'm calling about your mother, Ms. Malaluan." Niki gave Raphael a 'yeah, we know, get on with it' look. Juan led the others into the library and sat on the hearth, between Niki's and Raphael's feet. Luke and Steve sat next to their husbands, while Mateo, not wanting to intrude, sat behind them all at the desk. "We've decided to take a more aggressive approach to your mother's treatment. She has not been responding to the supplemental oxygen as well as we'd hoped, so we've begun a regimen of dexamethasone."

"What does that mean?" Angel asked from his end.

"It's a steroid, to help prevent and control inflammation," Carla calmly explained.

"Carla, this is Juan, a nurse. So, her oxygen isn't improving?"

"That's right. It has declined. We've starting administering six milligrams of dexamethasone."

"Oral or IV?"

"IV. She's responding well to that so far."

"And you are continuing the remdesivir?"

"Yes, for now. As you probably know the dexamethasone is a ten-day course." Raphael, who had been watching Juan's face for clues, widened his eyes in surprise.

"Can we talk with her, Carla?" Juan asked, already certain of her answer. Carla paused.

"We should give your mother some time to respond to the steroid. It would be difficult for her right now." She paused again. "Maybe tomorrow." Niki slumped in his chair. Steve took his right hand in both of his and squeezed.

"How scared should we be?" Raphael asked. Another pause from Carla.

"These therapeutics are proven. We have every reason to expect a good outcome. It will just take some time. I can tell your mother is a fighter. That is the most important thing. I'll tell her she has a whole team rooting for her. Do you have any other questions?"

"This is Raphael. Just tell her, we expect her to be well enough to talk tomorrow," he said with conviction. "'Or else.' She'll know what that means."

"Yeah," Angel almost laughed. "She'll know." Niki reached over and grabbed Raphael's wrist.

"I can do that. We're doing all the right things, gentlemen. Like I said, this will just take some time. We'll be in touch." Carla rang off. Raphael heaved a major sigh. He looked at Juan.

"So?"

"So," Juan replied. "It's not the news we wanted, but it could be a lot worse. She's awake. She's not on a ventilator. They're not waiting around … they're acting fast, as I would expect them to do. I meant to ask exactly where Mama's oxygen is now, but … that's kind of irrelevant." It was Juan's turn to sigh heavily. "Like she said. We just need to wait. Give the drugs time to work. And count on your Mama's iron constitution." He looked up at Raphael. "If it's anything like Raphael's, I wouldn't bet on the virus." Juan turned his attention to Raphael's phone on the table between Raphael and Niki. "Angel, what's your temp?" Angel didn't respond.

"Angel?" Niki asked. "You still there?"

"Yeah, I'm here." Another pause. "It's a hundred point one."

"FUCK!" Niki whispered. Juan rose to his knees and moved closer to the phone.

"Okay, Angel. Do you have acetaminophen on hand?"

"I think so."

"Go check. We'll wait." They could hear Angel carrying the phone into another room, where he pulled open a couple of drawers and rattled around a few containers.

"Yeah. I have regular and extra strength."

"I want you to take two every four hours. Regular strength for now. How's your chest? Any cough?"

"That's fine. I feel tired, but I haven't really been sleeping."

"Do you have melatonin?"

"Yeah. Right here. I forgot I had some."

"Take it an hour before bed. You need to rest. Drink lots of water. All this will increase your chances of having a mild case."

"Should I go get tested?"

"I think it's too late for that, Angel. Like I said, you need to rest. As much as possible. I want your temp once every hour now, Mister. And don't sugarcoat it? Are we clear?"

"Yes, doctor."

"I'll be counting the minutes."

"Okay, okay. I promise. This really blows, guys."

"Angel," Raphael said, "you should know by now. Never say blow to gay man."

"So ... I should say this sucks?"

"Nope. That's even worse."

"Goodbye, guys. Juan, I'll text you in an hour. Promise." Angel rang off. Raphael was looking dejectedly down at his feet as Luke rubbed his forearm.

"Raphael ... Niki," Juan said as he sat back on the hearth, "this is why I didn't want you to go to Angel. Your hearts are in the right place, but Angel's young and healthy, and he should get through this just fine. He's also totally capable of exposing both of you. In fact, he might be the one who exposed your Mama."

"No." Raphael lifted his gaze and looked into Juan's eyes, then at Niki, then back to Juan. "Mama was sneaking out to visit with a neighbor recently. Angel told us and asked Niki and me to shame her into stopping. We thought we had. Obviously not." He held eye contact with Juan a moment longer. "Is there anything we can do for Angel?" Juan smiled.

"Just stay in touch. Let him know he's not totally alone. Try to keep his spirits up. The 'blows' comment was a good touch." Juan turned to Niki. "Be the brothers you've always been. Only more so." As Juan rose to his feet, Mateo climbed out of his chair and came around to take Niki's hand in one hand and Raphael's in the other. He didn't say a word, but he didn't need to. Then, he let go and followed Juan out of the library. He found Ryan in their room, at the desk, studying. Ryan turned at the sound of him entering the room.

"What's wrong," Ryan asked, reading Mateo's face. Mateo plopped onto the bed and sighed. Ryan sat next to him and ran a hand across Mateo's chest. Mateo filled Ryan in.

"That doesn't sound good, does it?" Ryan asked. Mateo shook his head.

"I guess we are lucky. Is better here." Ryan nodded.

"Juan was right. To keep Raphael and Niki here," Mateo said, looking up into Ryan's eyes. "I hope your madre and padre are careful."

"I know," Ryan replied as he stretched out next to Mateo. "I've been thinking about that. I should call them. Let them know about Mama and Angel. It might help motivate them to stay diligent."

"Diligent?"

"To follow the rules. To stay safe."

"Diligent ..." Ryan chuckled and leaned down to deliver a gentle kiss.

"Yeah, diligent. Today's word of the day." He sat up. "I'm going to call them now. Thanks for the suggestion." Ryan slipped in his AirPods and dialed. While Ryan was talking, Mateo had an idea of his own. He grabbed his phone and texted Hiroshi.

Once again, the main topic of conversation at dinner was the family's all too personal relationship with COVID. Everyone was now up to speed on Angel's and Mama's status, not that there was anything anyone could do, but worry.

When Juan turned in at nine, Angel's fever had fallen slightly, giving everyone something to feel good about. Niki and Raphael had briefly debated taking over for Juan on fever watch, but they had to admit waking Angel from a much-needed sleep would not go over well with Angel or Juan. A night nurse in the hospital would have no qualms doing it, but neither of them qualified. Not yet anyway. So, by ten, the house was quiet.

It was nearly two a.m. when Raphael admitted defeat. He was pretty sure he hadn't slept ten minutes, and he felt guilty about disturbing Luke's sleep. He delicately slipped out of Luke's hold and lowered his feet to the floor.

"What ...?" Luke muttered. "Where are you going?"

"Go to sleep. I'm just going down to get some milk. See if it'll help me sleep." Raphael shuffled to the back stairs and down into the kitchen. When he got to the door, he was startled to see Mateo and Ryan on adjoining stools at the island. Mateo's head was bowed, his hands clasped on the counter in front of him. Ryan looked up at Raphael with a sheepish smile and put a finger to his lips. The three veladoras in the center of the island were the only source of light. Raphael realized immediately that Mateo was praying. He'd come to the candles to pray for Mama and Angel, and Ryan was keeping him company. Raphael teared up, and his chest grew tight with emotion. The milk forgotten, he quietly slid onto the stool next to Mateo, who was muttering under his breath. Raphael stared at the veladoras a moment, then, not sure what might or might not be appropriate, he reached over and wedged his left hand between Mateo's clasped hands, intertwining his fingers with those on Mateo's right hand. Mateo squeezed, but continued praying, without looking up. Inspired, Ryan took Mateo's left hand in his. At first Raphael assumed Mateo was praying in Spanish ... it certainly wasn't English. As he sat there, holding Mateo's hand, letting Mateo's rhythmic whispers soothe him, he realized it wasn't Spanish. It wasn't a prayer.

"Nam Myōhō Renge Kyō," was what Mateo was whispering over and over. Methodically. Hypnotically. Actually soothing Raphael. Slowly Raphael recognized what he was hearing. Mateo was chanting Hiroshi's mantra. The one Hiroshi had employed when Mateo was quarantined himself. The realization swelled in Raphael's throat ... that Mateo was sitting here, in the middle of the night, chanting before the veladoras, paying forward the love and concern that had been employed to assure his own health, in hopes of protecting Mama and Angel. His eyes closed, Raphael listened and then, first silently, then in his own whisper, he began chanting along with Mateo. "Nam Myōhō Renge Kyō ... Nam Myōhō Renge Kyō."

Sensing something missing, Luke roused just enough to reach out for Raphael. Then he reached further. He lifted his head and opened his eyes to find himself alone in bed. He'd drifted off again, maybe not for long, but long enough that Raphael should have been back by now. Curious more than concerned, he crawled out of bed and headed downstairs. He heard the chanting before he got to the door, which combined with the dancing candle light spooked him until he saw the three naked men, heads bowed, hands clasped, chanting. He didn't really understand what was happening, but even in his half-awakeness, he knew better than to interrupt. He watched silently a moment, then walked over and slid back the stool next to Raphael and sat, taking Raphael's right hand in his left. He stared into the candles for a moment before studying the dimly lit face of his husband. He glanced at Mateo and Ryan, both seemingly

oblivious to his arrival. He bowed his head and listened to the chant.
"Nam Myōhō Renge Kyō. Nam Myōhō Renge Kyō."

The sound of Luke's stool woke Niki, who had decamped to the
library a couple of hours earlier. He, too, had been unable to sleep, or
so it seemed, so he'd wandered down, ignited the fireplace and stretched
out to soak up the warmth. And hopefully not think. Apparently, it had
worked. He sat up, momentarily disoriented, then stood, extinguished
the fire and headed for the main staircase. Before he reached it, he heard
something coming from the kitchen and could see the dancing, dim glow
reflecting off the wall. Oh yeah, he thought, the veladoras. He detoured
into the kitchen and like Luke before him, and Raphael before Luke,
he encountered a most remarkable sight. For a moment he simply stood
in the doorway, marveling at what he saw. It was magical in a way. It
would have been sexy under other circumstances. He wasn't sure what
was happening, but he didn't want to interfere. As he started to turn
away, Luke turned his head and smiled and motioned him over with
his free hand. Niki hesitated. Luke motioned again, so he approached,
quietly slid onto the stool next to Luke. He studied each of the candlelit
faces, fascinated, but not yet comprehending exactly. Luke grasped his
left hand and bowed his head. Niki listened to the whispered mantra,
finally beginning to understand. He reached across the island with his
right hand, tentatively offering it. It wasn't until he joined the chant,
certain now of the words, that Ryan looked up, saw Niki's hand and
reached over and took it in his own. It was then that Luke decided there
was a reason for this extraordinary moment and a vehicle to add to its
power. He slowly extricated his hands from Raphael's and Niki's grasps,
slid off his stool and made his way up and into Steve and Niki's third
floor room.

"Steve ... Steve ... sorry, but you need to get up." Luke was discovering
that Steve was a sound sleeper. He sat on the side of the bed and bounced.

"Whoa ... what the ...?" Steve, barely awake, looked crossly at Luke.

"Steve, I'm sorry, but you need to come downstairs and take some
pictures with your phone."

"What? What's the matter?" Steve looked over at Niki, only to discover he was alone in bed.

"Quick, before it ends. Just come down and capture it. Be sure to
silence the shutter sound first. Just give me thirty seconds." At that,
Luke stood and dashed out of the room. Steve sat up, rubbed his eyes,
and probably would have laid back down again, had it not been for the
fact that Niki was missing. He glanced at the bedside clock. This was all
too weird. He slid out of bed, fumbled his phone, and silenced it as he
meandered down the stairs. He approached the library, assuming that
was where he was supposed to go, but it was empty. When he turned, he

saw the dim candlelight from the kitchen and headed there to discover what Luke intended him to find. Five of his family, including Niki, holding hands, heads bowed around the veladoras, quietly chanting.

"Nam Myōhō Renge Kyō." Steve got it immediately. Luke wanted to be able to show this to Mama. And to Angel. To let them know they had immense, if physically distanced, loving support. Steve made a couple of setting adjustments and carefully, quietly crept around the kitchen as he took shot after shot. Once he'd captured a dozen stills, he switched to video and did his best to 'truck' around the island several times, to capture the live action, including the flicker of the candles and the soothing chant. Once he was satisfied, he put his phone down on the counter. The circle was already perfect, so he simply moved behind Niki and Luke and put one hand on Niki's shoulder and one on Luke's. After listening a moment, he bowed his head and joined in the chant. "Nam Myōhō Renge Kyō. Nam Myōhō Renge Kyō." Along with the mantra, at least one of the participants was praying, one, for certain, was visualizing and one was bargaining with the fates.

Steve had only been contributing a couple of minutes before Mateo straightened his back, looked around and fell silent. One by one, around the circle, the chanting ceased. Raphael, inhaling deeply, turned to Mateo, his eyes glistening with captive tears.

"Thank you, Mateo. For Mama. For Angel, for me." Mateo smiled and blinked.

"Is all I know to do."

"Oh, I think you knew exactly what to do, muchacho." Raphael leaned in and briefly pressed his lips against Mateo's. "Ryan was right. But I think you're more than a prince. You are a medicine man. A shaman. And this was a moment I very much needed." He glanced across at Niki. "That we all needed. Thank you." At the word 'prince' Ryan's eyes widened, but Raphael, sleep deprived and momentarily ingratiated to Mateo, missed it. As everyone stood and pushed their stools in place, Niki came around and hugged Mateo, then Ryan.

"I don't know if what we just did will help Mama or Angel," Niki said quietly, "but, like Raphael said, it sure helped me."

"Oh, it will help Mama," Mateo replied with certainty. "It will help Angel. Hiroshi tol' me." Raphael put an arm around Luke's waist and started pulling him toward the back stairs.

"Did you get your milk, baby?"

"Like Niki said, I got something much better, Sir. Come on, let's go to bed."

As they snuggled together, back in bed finally, chest to chest, cock to cock ... the only couple in the house still able to do that ... and lips to lips, Ryan debated whether or not to bring up what was on his mind. Mateo's fingers playing a chord along his back gave him the courage to ask. He pulled his lips free.

"Mateo. Did you tell Raphael about me and you? About me being your servant. And you, my Prince?" Mateo's eyes tracked back and forth, rewinding and replaying past events.

"I think ... si ... yeah. Once. I ask how to be your prince. Is okay?" Mateo employed that adorable smile that could disarm far more resistant men than Ryan.

"It's kind of embarrassing, I guess." Ryan reached into Mateo's hair and fondled his left ear, massaging the lobe.

"They think it was cool."

"They!?"

"Raphael and Alex. Only Raphael and Alex." Mateo closed his eyes while Ryan continued caressing his ear. "Sorry. I didn' know it was secret." Ryan pressed his lips to Mateo's again and held them there. They were both very tired. Ryan responded, his lips moving Mateo's as he spoke.

"Well, if they thought it was cool, I guess it's okay. I mean, these guys don't think Pup Niki is weird. I guess I shouldn't be embarrassed to make you my Prince." Mateo grinned, moving Ryan's lips with his.

"Your Prince wants servant Ryan to sleep now." He pressed his lips harder into Ryan's to punctuate the command, then, rolled over and backed up into Ryan's warm embrace.

Raphael moved his laptop and some files into the library, so he and Niki could work together in the same room. Niki ceded the desk to Raphael and settled into his chair to study. Neither of them was working at peak efficiency, but neither cared. It just helped not to be alone with one's thoughts. Mid-morning Alex made a fresh pot of coffee and talked them into taking a break. While the three of them were sitting in front of the fireplace, and since they hadn't heard anything, Niki texted Angel for his temp. It was still under 100, a good sign that his body was winning the battle. Angel confirmed he hadn't received a call from the hospital, but that he'd been texting his temp to Juan diligently, knowing full well that Juan was probably unable to read or respond while in surgery. Niki texted back a crooked smile emoji.

"Would you like to see what I was able to capture, while half asleep last night?" Steve said as he wandered into Luke's room, laptop in hand.

"Sure," Luke replied, enthusiastically. "I apologize again, Steve, but ..." Steve waved Luke's apology away.

"No, I'm glad you woke me, Luke. It was a scene worth documenting. If we can get Mama and Angel on a Zoom call, I think it will be pretty powerful. Here, watch." Steve sat on the bed next to Luke and played a sixty second video he'd compiled.

"That's amazing," Luke agreed. "Play it again." Steve did. "Damn. Everyone looks so ..."

"It's the lighting. And the mantra. Even you look angelic." Luke laughed.

"I do, don't I? Damn, you're good. I think we should lobby the nurse hard the next time we talk. Mama would love this. I know she would." Steve nodded as he stood.

"Wanna go show it to Raphael and Niki?" Luke grinned, but shook his head as he stood.

"No. Let's surprise everyone. Once again, I'm in awe, Steve. You did great."

"It was your idea, so you deserve half the credit."

"Fair enough. But I insist you take top billing."

Angel finally called, with Nurse Elena, late in the afternoon, but before Juan retuned home. Mama was stable, marginally better, certainly no worse. Once again, she deflected Angel's request to Zoom with Mama.

"She's very weak. I know it's frustrating, guys. She knows you want to see her, and that's helpful. It really is. Maybe tomorrow."

"You keep saying that," Raphael protested, then sighed.

"I'm sorry. Give her just a little more time, okay? It's frustrating for us, too. Believe me."

"We know," Niki said, doing his best to fill in for Juan. "We appreciate everything you're doing. We really do."

"I know you do. Stay safe everyone. We'll be in touch. Soon."

When Juan entered the foyer, he stopped at the library door, still dressed, to check in. Raphael and Niki debriefed him. He nodded, gave a thumbs up, then stripped and placed his scrubs in the washer on his way upstairs to decontaminate. He was surprised when he exited the bath to find Luke and Steve sitting on his bed, waiting for him.

"Guys ..." Juan smiled.

"Juan, we want your opinion and maybe your inside knowledge and access," Luke moved to make room for Juan between him and Steve and patted the bed, inviting Juan to sit. Once he'd settled in place, Steve picked up his laptop, opened it and played his video. Juan was clearly affected.

"When did you do this?" he turned to Steve. Steve and Luke walked Juan through the events of the previous night.

"Juan," Luke continued, "wouldn't it be helpful if Mama could see this *now*? To know her boys and their family are pulling for her to recover? Mateo made this happen in the middle of the night. Totally spontaneous."

"Well, we don't know everything the staff is dealing with. I'm sure it's not as overwhelming as it was when I was in New York. Still, we can't ask them to take time away from critically ill patients. This would need to be coordinated and scheduled around everything else. But, yeah, this would lift Mama's spirits for sure."

"Would it hurt to ask?" Luke pleaded. "Whenever they can ... but as soon as they can? You know how to work this, Juan. Just ... ask. If they say not now, at least we tried." Luke and Juan held each other's gaze a moment, not so much a test of wills as a wordless exchange of desire versus reality.

"Let me see what I can do. Don't get your hopes up." Juan stood and walked to the desk, picked up his phone and texted Angel. He sat in the desk chair, read the response and dialed the number of the nurses' station that Angel had forwarded. He left a message for Elena to call back at her convenience.


Juan's phone rang about forty-five minutes later. He thanked Elena for calling back and quickly relayed the request. No need for Mama to be able to talk, they just wanted to say hi and show her a one minute get well video. Pretty please. Elena put Juan on hold, giving him time to run downstairs to the library. He sat on the hearth in front of Niki, holding up his phone. Raphael came around from behind the desk and sat in the other chair.

"What is it?" Raphael asked. Juan held up his free hand, listening.

"We'll be ready, Elena. Thank you. What's your favorite flower? No, I'm serious." Juan nodded. "Thank you. Thank you. Bye." Juan set his phone down and looked at Niki and Raphael. "Zoom call with Mama and Angel in thirty minutes. Go put a shirt on!"

## Thirty-Five

∴◎∴————————∴◎∴

# RYAN'S BARGAIN

"I SEE YOU GUYS dressed for the occasion," Angel greeted the family. Everyone had joined the Zoom session with the credentials Elena had given to Angel moments before, everyone except Mama. Elena wanted everyone else logged in first to save time and conserve Mama's strength. To minimize the number of thumbnails Mateo, Ryan, Alex and Greg were on one laptop, Luke, Raphael and Ricky on another, and Steve, Niki and Juan on a third. Angel's made four.

"Yeah, the top half anyway," Niki joked as he stood up to illustrate he wasn't kidding. He dropped instantly as he realized Elena might be able to see his video even though he couldn't see anything from her end. "It's *really* good to see you, Angel. How are you feeling?"

"Tired, a little achy, but you won't hear me complain. I think I'm going to be one of the lucky ones." Niki held up his right hand with his fingers crossed. Video from Elena's end appeared along with the background cacophony of multiple medical machines. Elena's face filled the thumbnail. What they could see of it, beneath all the PPE.

"Is everyone here?" she asked.

"We're all here, Ma'am," Raphael smiled. "Nice to finally meet you."

"Nice to meet all of you, too. Wow. You're all Ms. Malaluan's family?"

"We are," Niki affirmed.

"Which one of you is Juan?" Elena asked. Juan raised his hand.

"Hi, Elena. I'm Juan." Elena smized.

"I'm glad you asked to do this, Juan. Ms. Malaluan told me she had a brood of handsome boys, but I thought it was just a mother's pride talking. Seeing all of you now, I can see she was right. She was very excited when I asked her if she was up to this. She won't be able to talk much, if at all, with the oxygen mask, but I'm going to put headphones on her so she can hear you. Okay? I just need to mount this on this bracket here ..." For a moment, the view from Mama's room was of the instrument clutter

on the wall above and alongside her bed, but Elena quickly positioned
the tablet over Mama's torso, and tilted it to bring Mama's face and
upper body into view. She looked so small in the bed, with wires and
IVs going in multiple directions. She looked tired, and really not much
like herself. She raised her right hand in greeting and said something, but
it was swallowed by the oxygen mask she was wearing. Elena positioned
the headphones onto Mama's head and said something to Mama, and
Mama nodded. She smoothed Mama's hair with a touch anyone of the
family would have paid dearly to be able to do themselves. Then, Elena
looked into the tablet's camera. "Go ahead, she can hear you now."

Everyone talked at once, then everyone stopped. Typical Zoom inter-
action. Then, Angel spoke.

"Mama, we miss you. So much! They won't let me come to see you."
Mama nodded.

"I'm so glad you're feeling well enough to do this now," Raphael followed up. "Juan had to twist Elena's arm. But this means you're getting
better. Right?" Mama nodded and slightly raised her right hand again.

"You look beautiful, Mama," Niki spoke. "I love what you've done
with your hair." Mama gave a short laugh, followed with coughing,
making Niki feel miserable. But it didn't seem to faze Mama. She raised
her hand again and wagged a finger at the tablet, and presumably at Niki.

"Mama," Luke spoke up. "You remember Mateo? From the wedding? Mateo wave to Mama." As Mateo waved, Mama nodded and said
something else that was lost to the oxygen mask. Raphael glanced at
Luke, wondering why he was mentioning Mateo. "Mama, something
very special happened in the middle of the night last night, and Steve
captured it on video. We wanted to share it with you. Is that okay?"
Mama nodded. Steve pressed a key and the video filled everyone's screen
and began to play. As it began Niki, surprised at Luke's words, reached
down and squeezed Steve's thigh in reaction, without taking his eyes off
the screen.

The video began with an establishing shot as Steve circled around
the group, the veledoras always in the center of the frame, the faces
highlighted by the candles, the background lost in shadow and nearly
black. The audio was clear, but subdued. "Nam Myōhō Renge Kyō."
Then, a dissolve to a still of Niki's face, head bowed, over the audio,
then a dissolve to a still of Mateo, then more circling video, all over the
uninterrupted audio. "Nam Myōhō Renge Kyō." Dissolve to a still of
Ryan, then of Luke, not bowed, but looking to his left. Dissolve to a
two-shot of Luke and to his left Raphael, head bowed, dissolve to a
closeup of Raphael, dissolve to another still of Niki, dissolve to another
still of Mateo, dissolve to another still of Raphael, eyes closed, head
bowed, his lips parted in mid-chant, then dissolve to a continuation of

the circling video for another ten seconds before audio and video faded to black. Steve had cropped the stills and video so that, although all of the men were clearly bare chested, there was no reveal that they were, in fact, completely naked.

All the thumbnails refilled the monitors. "Mama ... and Angel," Luke continued, "Mateo taught us all how to send you both special prayers with an ancient Buddhist mantra last night. We wanted to share it with you. So you would know, even in the middle of the night, we're with you, and we want you both to get well very soon." While Luke spoke, Raphael leaned his head on Luke's shoulder as he gazed into the camera, so Mama would see his pride in Luke. At the same time Niki was rubbing out a sniffle next to Steve before planting a grateful kiss on Steve's cheek.

"That was beautiful, guys," Angel said, leaning into his frame. "Wasn't it, Mama?" Mama nodded and lifted her right hand again in gratitude. She looked to her right as Elena reentered her frame and took hold of Mama's hand and patted it. She bent down and listened as Mama said something, then turned to the camera.

"She promises to get well soon so she can properly thank you all." She bent down again. "Especially Mateo." In their frame both Alex and Ryan were grabbing Mateo by the shoulders and shaking him.

"We'll hold you to that, Mama," Raphael said, before his lips started quivering. As Luke wrapped an arm around Raphael's shoulders, Juan spoke again.

"We really appreciate your doing this, Elena. We can't thank you enough; we know you have plenty to do." Elena released the tablet from the bracket, and moved away from Mama's bed. Her face now filled the frame.

"Juan, as I'm sure you know, this is the part of the job that's most gratifying. What you just did is the best medicine anyone could provide your mother." She glanced over toward the bed. "I'm just sorry this is as close as you can be right now. Stay safe everyone. We'll be in touch." Elena ended the call.

Within seconds of the Zoom chat ending, Raphael's phone signaled a call from Angel.

"Okay, buddy, what was that?" Angel spoke before Raphael could even say hello.

"Um ... that was the first time I saw that myself. I only know part of the story. Hang on. I'm going to run up to Steve and Niki's room." As he stood, Raphael cupped the back of Luke's head. "Always full of surprises.

Sir." Luke and Ricky followed Raphael, who continued talking to Angel in the hall. "I had no idea we were being videoed, Angel." Raphael stuck his head in Greg and Alex's door. "Mateo, Angel wants to know what we were doing in the video. Can you come and tell him about the mantra?" Mateo stood and started toward the door. Not to be left out, yet again, Alex was right on Mateo's tail. Ryan, along with Greg, who was also in the dark, followed behind. The convoy met Niki, who had been on his way down to Raphael and Luke's room, at the top of the stairs. "Is Steve still in your room?" Raphael asked. Niki nodded. "Angel's on the phone. We're going to fill him in on last night." Niki turned and followed Raphael, who looked over his shoulder and announced, "Y'all look pretty silly in shirts but no pants. Just sayin'." Clearly, seeing Mama and being able to interact with her, if only partially, had lifted Raphael's spirits tremendously.

Steve started to stand as the family invaded his room, but Raphael motioned for him to resume his seat at the desk. Raphael sat on the edge of the bed next to Juan.

"Angel, Steve and Mateo are both here. Well, everybody's here, actually. I think everybody has the same questions as you." He motioned to Mateo. "Mateo sit here next to me so Angel can hear you." As Mateo sat, Raphael addressed his phone again. "Before Mateo explains what we were doing last night ... Angel, what did you think about Mama? Did she look that sick when you two went to the hospital?" At that, Mateo put an arm comfortingly around Raphael's waist. Raphael followed suit, pulling Mateo closer, thigh to thigh.

"Well, she didn't look so great Saturday, but she did look pretty awful just now, yeah. What did you think, Juan?"

"I thought she looked pretty good, considering, Angel. I briefly caught a glimpse of the monitor next to the bed when Elena was adjusting the tablet, and things didn't look too bad. We should be optimistic. Nobody looks like themselves after several days in a hospital bed."

"Okay." Angel paused. "If you say so, Juan. So ... about that video."

"Let me start," Raphael began, since he was holding the 'talking stick.' "I went down to the kitchen to get a glass of milk. I couldn't sleep. It was like two a.m. And I found Mateo and Ryan sitting at the island, with the veladoras. At first I thought they were praying." Raphael turned to Mateo. "Tell him about the veladoras, muchacho." Mateo smiled and needlessly leaned slightly toward Raphael's phone.

"When Ryan and I hear your Mama was in hospital, and you may be sick, too, the only thing I thought was to get veladoras. My family always does for times like these. I want to help. Then when we learn your Mama was ... worse?" Raphael nodded. "I think the veladoras are not working so good. So, Hiroshi tell me his mantra. He use it to help me."

"Angel," Raphael butted in. "Or friend Hiroshi is Japanese-American and Buddhist. He told us about this mantra when Mateo was exposed to COVID and had to quarantine."

"Mateo had COVID?!"

"No, thankfully. But he was exposed at work. Anyway, Hiroshi told us afterward that he had employed this Buddhist mantra to basically send good vibes to Mateo to help him stay well. It worked. Mateo was negative. And that's what Mateo and Ryan were doing when I found them in the kitchen. They weren't praying at the veladoras. They were chanting the mantra. Right, Mateo?"

"Yes. I think Hiroshi's mantra maybe help."

"Luke told Mama you were sending special prayers, and I thought, Raphael ... special prayers? So, you weren't praying. You were reciting a mantra?"

"I wanted to keep it simple," Luke spoke up. "Mama understands prayers." Raphael nodded as he looked over at Niki, who smiled.

"So, yeah," Raphael continued, "I figured I'd do anything to help you and Mama, and in the moment, seeing Mateo and Ryan with their heads bowed, chanting ... it just made sense I should join them. At first, I was just visualizing you both getting better. Listening to them chant was ... soothing, I guess. It helped me, that's for sure. So, after a while, I started chanting the mantra, too. At some point I felt Luke take my hand. Then, later, Niki showed up."

"They weren't the only ones who couldn't sleep," Niki chimed in. "I sat next to Luke."

"I suddenly realized," Luke rejoined the narrative, "a few minutes after Niki took my hand, that what we were doing for you and Mama was one thing, but showing it to Mama ... to let her see how much love we were sending her way, might be helpful. So. I left the circle, woke up poor Steve, our resident photographer, and, well, what you saw was the result of his sensitive, artistic genius. I was just expecting him to snap a couple of pictures."

"Steve?" Angel probed.

"Yeah, I'm here," Steve replied.

"That was very ... powerful." They could hear Angel sigh deeply. "And you did that in the middle of the night? You should be very proud. You guys ... you all looked so, I don't know, reverent. What was that mantra again?"

"Nam Myōhō Renge Kyō," Mateo replied.

"Steve, is it weird if I ask for a copy of that video? Especially considering that you were all naked?"

"Angel," Steve laughed, "if it'll help you get well, I'll send you the raw footage that *proves* they were all naked."

"That's okay. I've already seen you all naked. Hell, you've all seen me naked. Except. Is this guy Ryan there?"

"Yeah. Hi. I'm Ryan."

"Ryan is Mateo's boyfriend," Raphael explained. "He was at the second wedding as a guest, so you may not have met him. But, yeah, he's seen you practically naked." Raphael glanced at Ryan. "When you see *him* naked, and hopefully that will be sooner than later, you'll see his naked glory comes with an added bonus."

"Oh ... kay," Angel replied. "Assuming Mama and I do get over this, maybe we can think about doing that. After all, I guess we'll both be immune and able to travel."

"Angel," Juan spoke up. "Mama is going to be fine. Between the skill of Elena and her team and Mateo's mantra, her prognosis, like yours, looks pretty good to me."

"You're not just saying that?" Angel asked tentatively.

"I feel good about this, Angel," Juan assured him.

"Thanks. Thank you, Juan, Mateo, the mysterious Ryan. The whole mantra crew. Love you. Talk to you tomorrow."

"Love you, Angel," Niki and Raphael said in unison as the call ended. Raphael turned and planted one on Mateo's handy cheek. "You were the star of the show, Shaman Prince, master of mantras and provider of powerful veladoras. Thank you, Mateo. So much." Raphael's eyes were glistening again. Mateo smiled humbly as Ryan pulled him to his feet. As everyone was filing out and toward the stairs, Alex turned to Juan.

"What do you think, Juan? Do we have to start sleeping on the stairs to be included in middle of the night seances around here? You and Ricky want the front stairs? I'll take the back?"

"I'd might be up for it ... before nine, but after that, I'd rather sleep in my own bed, thanks."

Dinner, for the first time in several nights, was more lighthearted, still more subdued than usual, but more normal after the tension relieving video chat with Mama and Angel. Everyone apparently was taking Juan at his word that Mama just might beat COVID after all. When Greg stood to start clearing his place, Alex grabbed his wrist.

"Wait, honey. Sit down. We're not quite done." Greg looked at him questioningly, but sat. "Ricky," Alex said as he himself stood, "I need a hand." Ricky stood and followed Alex through the butler's pantry, with all eyes following them. More than one was anticipating a surprise dessert, but when Alex returned, he was gingerly bearing two of the veladoras, which he was trying to not extinguish. Ricky followed with the third.

"What's going on, Alex?" Niki asked. Alex placed one of his two veladoras in the center of the table, then the second half-way to the end, where Steve was sitting. Ricky placed his on the other side, half-way between the center and where Juan was sitting, then he returned to his seat next to Juan. Alex turned off the chandelier, then returned to his seat, and pushed his placemat forward, away from the edge of the table.

"We may not have made it into Steve's latest production," Alex quietly explained to Niki, "but, it's not too late for the rest of us to do whatever we can to send healing thoughts to Mama and Angel. What you guys did last night made Mama and Angel feel better if nothing else. If the rest of us can join you one more time, it'll make us feel better, too. I know it'll make me feel better." Greg reached over and squeezed the back of Alex's neck, then slid his hand down until he took hold of Alex's right hand. He pulled it up onto the table top, pushed his own place mat forward, then reached over for Steve's left hand. He made eye contact with Raphael as hands were joined around the table. "Mateo," Alex continued as he bowed his head, "why don't you start us off." Mateo bowed his head, paused a moment, then began.

"Nam Myōhō Renge Kyō ..." He paused only a moment, then repeated, with the chorus joining him, "Nam Myōhō Renge Kyō ..."

The veladoras remained in the dining room, where they continued to burn. Where they inspired recitations of Mateo's mantra after dinner for two more evenings. It seemed to be working. Angel's fever was under control, and in the brief Zoom chats Elena allowed late each afternoon, Mama seemed to be growing stronger. Progress was undeniable on Thursday when Mama joined Niki, Steve, Angel and Raphael on Zoom and greeted everyone without her oxygen mask. Luke was still at work.

"Look, boys!" she clearly said, smiling. "I can say 'I miss you' at last, and you can hear me." She looked more like herself, bedhead and all.

"Cool!" Niki rejoiced. "So, no more supplemental oxygen?"

"Not all the time, no," Mama replied. "They tell me when I need to use it, but not all the time today." The conversation was brief, like all the others, but tentatively hopeful, even cheery, a little bit like the monthly FaceTime calls they were used to. When she ended the call, Elena looked into the camera after detaching the tablet from the bed.

"Thank you for the bouquet of flowers, boys. Everyone on the floor loves them. We brought them in to show your mother what a thoughtful 'brood' she has, but we can't keep them in here, so they're on display at the nurses' station. It was really sweet of you." She ended the call before anyone could ask for details.

The Zoom chat had been promising enough to motivate Raphael to start out dinner that night with a bottle of celebratory Schramsberg. Predictable behavior for him, and always appreciated. After he and Niki had shared their takes on how well they thought Mama was doing, Raphael posed a question.

"At the end of the call, Elena thanked us for the flowers she said we sent. Angel says it wasn't him, so everyone who didn't send flowers to the hospital ... raise your hand." Nine hands went up. Then all eyes focused on Juan. Who grinned, a Cheshire grin, almost as good as Luke's.

"Well, she did us a favor, guys. A big one. I wanted to thank her, and everyone there taking care of Mama. I know how much something as simple as a surprise flower arrangement can mean when you're dealing with what they're dealing with day after day, night after night. It was my little contribution." He turned to Mateo and winked. Raphael raised his glass toward Juan.

"To Juan, winner of tonight's Classiest Member of the House of the Locked Cock Brotherhood award." Juan shook his head, deflecting the praise, silly as it was. Raphael turned to Luke. "What do you think? Should we shave off another hundred or so dinners for that? We all got credit for it, you know."

"What kind of flowers were they?" Niki asked.

"Bird of Paradise and Calla Lilies," Juan replied. "Elena said she likes Calla Lilies. The Bird of Paradise were my idea. I love the one's we have in the garden."

"In that case," Niki turned to Raphael, "we should probably shave off two hundred dinners." Raphael nodded firmly, as Luke just shook his head, not daring to challenge this particular vote.

The veladoras flickered out the following day, Friday. Not ready to let them go just yet, Niki collected them and lined them up on the desk in the library. The recitations of what was now officially 'Mateo's mantra' came to an end, at least as an after-dinner group ritual. Although much better, Mama had not completed her regimen, and wasn't home yet, so sometimes before bed, at least once in the gym, and even while cleaning up after a meal, more than one member of the family could be heard to quietly mutter, "Nam Myōhō Renge Kyō." Just for good measure. Life began slowly returning to normal. The new normal. Raphael resumed working from the desk in his room, since he and Niki were no longer on edge about the prospect of an unexpected call from Angel. They were able to continue Zooming with Mama once a day. It was on Sunday afternoon, at the end of their four-way call, when Carla delivered the news.

"Angel, if you aren't too busy tomorrow morning," she peeked around, sharing the frame with Mama, "if you'd like to come by the hospital, we'll be ready to discharge Ms. Malaluan." Distorted shouts from the five other participants erupted. Mama reached up and grasped Carla's wrist in appreciation. Carla smized at her, then turned back to the tablet. "Understand, she's going to be very weak, and far from her old self for a while. We'll need you or someone to stay with her twenty-four seven for at least a couple of weeks. I understand you're still recovering, too."

"Not a problem, Carla," Angel grinned. "I'm working from home, and I can do that from Mama's as well as from my place. I'll move some of my stuff over today. Just tell me when to be there." Carla gave the tablet a gloved thumbs up.

"Someone will call you later today, Angel. We'll meet you at the south entrance with Ms. Malaluan at the appointed time tomorrow, probably around ten or eleven." She looked back at Mama for a moment then back at the tablet. "I'm so glad we've come this far. There were some tense moments ... but you all proved stronger than this virus. Especially you, Maricel. We're all very proud of you." As she turned back to Mama, she patted her hand.

"Oh, no, you get all the credit," Mama said quietly. She nodded toward the tablet. "My Niki is studying to be a nurse, too, you know. We're all proud of him, too." Carla turned back to the tablet, to see Niki blowing Mama a kiss.

"Niki," she said in closing, "study hard and study fast. We need all the nurses we can get ... yesterday. Say goodbye, guys." As everyone waved, Carla ended the call.


Raphael and Niki were jazzed. After they shared the news with everyone else, except for Mateo and Ricky who were both out working, they invited Alex along for a run. They hadn't run for over a week, too focused on Mama and Angel to think about their own physical fitness. Besides, they were out of bubbly, and tonight, of all nights, demanded a celebratory pour before dinner. It was while they were out that Ryan found Luke in his and Raphael's room.

"Hey, Ryan," Luke looked up from where he was sitting on the floor, conditioning his and Raphael's body harnesses. They, too, had been abandoned the last few days, and Luke knew Raphael would be pleased to find his harness supple, smooth and shiny.

"I wanted to ask you a favor," Ryan said shyly. He walked over and plopped down next to Luke. "I'll understand if you say no, but I guess I kind of got ahead of myself." Luke set the harness down and gave Ryan his full attention.

"What do you mean? How can I help?"

"Um ... well ... I was hoping ... can I borrow your cage?" Luke reached up and rubbed his mohawk thoughtfully as he processed Ryan's words.

"My cage?" He paused. "Sure. I guess. But ... why?" Ryan, a little embarrassed, took a deep breath.

"That night. In the kitchen, around the veladoras? While we were reciting the mantra? Whenever I've wanted something really badly, I've made a promise to myself. To the fates, maybe. Well, more like a bargain. 'If you'll let this happen, I'll do that' kind of thing. Anyway," he took another deep breath, "I promised to be caged for a week if Mama and Angel would be okay. I mean, Mateo was doing so much, and I felt kind of useless."

"You weren't useless at all," Luke soothed, reaching out and grabbing Ryan's nearby foot. "You were right there with Mateo. You guys made Raphael and Niki feel so much better."

"Yeah, but ... anyway, I promised the fates I'd be caged for a week ... like you were, if they got better. So, I have to be caged. I promised. But I wasn't really thinking. I don't have one."

"Of course, you can borrow it. But are you sure? I mean ... you know ... with your boners? You won't believe what it's like when you're caged. For a week?"

"Um, well, actually, when Mama got worse, and we did the mantra after dinner? I upped the ante. To a month." Luke starting laughing. He tried to stifle it, but he couldn't. He put his hand over his mouth and looked at Ryan, his evil eyebrows dancing.

"I'm sorry. Sorry, Ryan. A month? You? Caging your boners?" He dropped his hand. "I don't think you can." Ryan looked defiant, and a little insulted.

"Alex has been caged for years, Raphael and Niki, too. I can do a month, Luke." Luke opened his mouth to argue, saw the look in Ryan's eyes, and stopped. He closed his mouth and nodded.

"Okay. I respect what you're doing. Believe, me, having been there. Twice. I have nothing but respect for you." He stared into Ryan's eyes a moment. "When did you want to start your lock up?"

"Now. Right now. Can you help?" It was Ryan's turn to be on a mission.

"Man, when you make a bargain, you don't kid around do you?" Luke stood and walked into the bath. A moment later he returned with the familiar little brown translucent case and an unfamiliar plastic bottle. "Okay, Ryan, stand up. It'll be easier." Luke opened the case and pulled out the cock ring, tube and keys. Ryan's cock began to rise. When Luke looked up and saw it, he laughed again. "You're not going to make this easy, are you?" Luke sat back, reached up and ran his fingers through Ryan bush. "Did you want to be clean shaven like your locked cock brothers? It'll be easier if we do it now, before I cage you." Luke was thinking the shave might give Ryan's boner time to subside. At least a little, maybe.

"I guess I hadn't thought that far. I probably should, shouldn't I?" His erection grew bigger. 'So much for that idea,' Luke thought.

"It'll look better, and it'll feel better, too. No hairs for the cage to pull on. Let's go in here." Luke stood and returned to the bath, with Ryan behind him. Luke assembled clippers, razor, cartridges and shave cream on the vanity, while he began running the hot water. He placed a towel in the middle of the floor and motioned for Ryan to step onto the middle. "Okay, spread your legs." As Luke got down on his knees and began to work, he was pretty sure he heard a moan over the sound of the clippers as he carefully denuded Ryan's crotch. He looked up and saw Ryan's eyes were closed, his arms crossed. Ryan opened his eyes when Luke snapped off the clippers. He reached down and ran his fingers over his new stubble, and smiled.

"Feels cool."

"You never shaved your pubes before?" Ryan shook his head.

"Get ready for a treat." Luke squeezed out the wash cloth he had soaking in the hot water and rubbed it all around Ryan's pubic bone, cock, balls and taint.

"Mmmmm." Ryan looked down at Luke, his tongue briefly licking his upper lip. "This was a good idea."

"What? The shave or the caging?"

"Well, the shave for sure." Luke ran a finger back and forth on the underside of Ryan's horizontal cock.

"Your cock certainly thinks so. Maybe you and Mateo should consider keeping you shaved, caged or not. Raphael and I buzz and shave our heads every night, and each other's crotches a couple times a week. Feels good, doesn't it?" Ryan nodded, still smiling. Luke began applying the lather, and just for fun, he made sure to smear some up Ryan's taint and into his rosebud.

"Oh, god ..."

"Sorry ..."

"It's okay." Yeah, Luke thought. This is definitely going to be a regular thing for Ryan and Mateo. He clicked a new cartridge into the razor and went to work. First the pubes, then Ryan's balls, then the shaft, which was only hairy about a third of the way down, and that was fairly sparse. He looked up again to see that Ryan's arms were still crossed, and his eyes closed, but his forefingers were busy massaging his nipples. It wasn't really necessary, but Luke decided, since Ryan was enjoying this so much, to shave his taint as well. Ryan sighed deeply. When he finished, Luke reapplied the hot, wet wash cloth a couple of times, all around Ryan's newly smooth skin. Then he stood and reached around to cup a hand on Ryan's left butt cheek to bring him out of his reverie. Ryan's eyes popped open to find Luke's smile inches away.

"All done." Ryan looked down to admire Luke's efforts. "Do you want to touch it one last time before we lock it away?" Ryan returned his gaze to Luke. His eyes flicked up briefly in thought, then centered on Luke's. He shook his head.

"No. I made a promise. Mama and Angel made it through. I don't deserve to touch it again. For a month." He took a deep breath. "Let's lock it up, Luke." Luke chuckled.

"Well, just remember, you still have Mateo's no doubt very tasty cock to worship. Oh, and you'll also have these to play with for the next month." He reached out and lightly brushed Ryan's left nipple, producing a gasp. "These may become your favorite erogenous zone, now that you won't have a cock to play with."

"Luke, lock me up before I try to touch myself!" Luke grabbed Ryan's biceps and led him back into the bedroom. He tried slipping Ryan's balls through the cock ring first, then the cock, what he considered the normal way, but Rigid Ryan made that a challenge. He started over, first the cock, then, one at a time, the balls. He was worried he was squeezing them too hard, but Ryan persevered. If anything, the pain helped to tame his cock a little.

"Okay, buddy, I need you to cooperate or this isn't going to work," Luke pleaded as he smoothed coconut oil around Ryan's cock. He wiped his hands on a towel so he could maintain a good grip on the tube and began rotating it back and forth as he pushed it toward the cock ring. The force caused Ryan to stumble back a step, but he solidified his footing and pushed toward Luke. "I don't want to hurt you," Luke muttered through gritted teeth.

"It's okay ... just *do* it." Ryan took a couple of quick deep breaths, his eyes squeezed tight, and then, somehow, the tube met the ring. With his free hand Luke grabbed the lock and key and seated it before Ryan's exuberance forced the tube away from the ring again. Luke pulled on the left and right sides of Ryan's scrotum, and the back, to seat the cage up tight against Ryan's smooth body. Satisfied, he stood.

"We did it, Ryan. You're a locked cock brother now. I'm proud of you." Ryan looked down, a little surprised, a little proud himself, and definitely relieved.

"Thanks, Luke! It was worth it. To help Mama and Angel. Thanks." Then, uncharacteristically for Ryan, he leaned forward with a kiss. Luke pulled him into an embrace, which allowed him, weirdly, to feel his own cage press against his cock. When they pulled apart, Luke looked down to admire his handiwork once again.

"How does it feel, chastity boy?"

"You were right. It hurts like hell." Luke laughed as he reached down and gathered up the case and coconut oil. He held out the keys to Ryan.

"You'll get used to it," He consoled. "I'm no expert, but it's been my experience the worst will be when Mateo sticks his tongue down your throat. You've been warned." Ryan reached for the keys, then thought better of it.

"Why don't you keep the keys, Luke."

"Whom don't you trust?" Luke smirked as he dropped the keys back into the case. "Mateo? Or yourself?"

"Neither one of us, I guess. I hope Mateo's okay with this." Luke put a hand on Ryan's shoulder.

"Mateo loves you. He'll be fine with it. After all, it's only for *a month*." Luke's verbal emphasis on 'a month' brought grins to both of them. Only a month. Four weeks. Twenty-eight days ... and nights.

## Thirty-Six

## SHOW AND TELL

RAPHAEL THOUGHT THE BUBBLY would be the center of attention at dinner that night. But Ryan and Mateo's entrance, no matter how nonchalant Ryan tried to make it, upstaged his plans. Hot pink adornments have a way of doing that.

"Whoa, whoa, whoa," Niki exclaimed before Ryan made it to his chair. "What spectacular turn of events is this?" He and Alex, abandoning his duties distributing filled flutes, surrounded Ryan. "It's as pretty as Luke's," Niki pronounced. Alex looked into Mateo's eyes.

"Has our Prince officially added a dutiful eunuch to his court?" Ryan winced.

"Shaman Prince!" Raphael corrected, over his shoulder. Once everyone was seated, Luke raised his glass.

"My toast tonight," he said as he turned to Ryan. "Here's to bargains. And the good they bring to others and the adventures they bring to the ones who make them." After the hear-hear's and the subsequent sips, Raphael spoke next.

"Interesting toast, Sir. Does it come with an explanation?" Luke smiled smugly and took another sip.

"Ryan," he finally replied, "you have the floor." After Ryan told his story again, leaving out the potentially embarrassing details of Luke's shave down, Raphael glanced at Niki, then the two of them were out of their chairs and on either side of Ryan. A couple of cheek kisses and an awkward seated hug later, they were back in their seats and dinner resumed.

"A month, huh?" Alex said, not really a question. "You. Rigid Ryan." He shook his head.

"Be nice," Greg smiled at Ryan, then Mateo. "I think Ryan is one upstanding young man."

"We'll ... I can think of one thing that won't be 'up standing' all right," Alex continued. When Greg gave him a 'hush' look, Alex continued. "I'm not trying to be mean. I think it's amazing. Really. And so thoughtful. But I just remember what my first few weeks were like. Man!" He looked directly at Ryan. "I couldn't look at porn for weeks."

"That was the whole idea, dear," Greg replied, without looking at anyone.

"Okay, I'll say just one more thing, then I'll shut up." Alex looked at Mateo tenderly. "Be gentle with him, muchacho. Your kisses could be deadly for the next few days." Luke guffawed.

"That's exactly what I told Ryan." Mateo looked worried. He glanced at Ryan and comfortingly put his hand on Ryan's thigh, producing a groan.

"I remember those days," Niki added to Ryan's dismay. "Fortunately, I was so wrapped up in learning how to be a pup, I was too distracted to dwell on the pain. It was worst at night, curled up around another naked pup."

"STOP!" Ryan burst out. He literally bit down on his closed fist. "Sorry, Niki. You know how sexy I think Pup Niki is. The last thing I need to envision right now is Pup Niki, naked in a cage with another pup. Owww. Owww."

"Ryan," Steve offered, "after dinner, why don't you and Mateo take a long soak in the jacuzzi tub in our bathroom. A nice hot soak might help, at least for a little while."

"Yeah," Niki seconded. "I'll get it ready for you." He turned to Steve. "Good idea!"

"I really do think what you're doing is a noble thing," Alex said, breaking his promise. Then he turned to Greg. "What a very *daring* act of compassion and sacrifice it is, don't you think? Dear?"

"You bastard," Greg whispered as a sly grin spread across Alex's face.


The jacuzzi soak did help. About twenty minutes in, Mateo decided to test the waters by sliding over and on top of Ryan, facing him. First, he just pressed his lips against Ryan's and wiggled them a little. Not hearing any groans, he pressed harder and separated Ryan's lips with his tongue, expecting Ryan to resist. He didn't. Like every other time, Ryan parted his lips and invited Mateo in. Mateo made it almost all the way to Ryan's uvula with only a thank you moan. He slowly withdrew and slid off Ryan and reclaimed his seat next to him.

"Was that a test?" Ryan asked, looking amused and a little bit relieved.

"Yes," Mateo grinned. "You pass. We pass. Is okay?"

"Either that or I'm already getting used to it. It's hard to tell." Ryan reached down and squeezed Mateo's very available cock. "Maybe, to be sure, you should do another test." He didn't have to ask twice.

Half an hour later, two very relaxed pledges dried off with the bath sheets Niki had laid out for them. They drained and wiped down the tub, then headed down to their room. As they approached their door, Mateo veered off and down another flight to the library to let Niki and Steve know they were done. When he returned, he found Ryan sitting on the bed, holding a note. A steel chain puppy collar rested on the bed next to him.

"Close the door," Ryan looked up, grinning. Mateo did, then he joined Ryan on the bed and picked up the collar.

"From the movie?" he asked. Ryan nodded.

"Yeah. It's the one Niki loaned me." He turned to Mateo. "Alex wants me to wear it tomorrow. It's a joke between him and Greg. He says he'll explain later."

"Hmmm," Mateo muttered as he examined the collar. "Maybe you can wear it now?" He looked up and smiled. Ryan delivered a medium-sized kiss that Mateo interpreted as a yes. In addition to the padlock, which Alex had conveniently left unlocked, the chain sported a red dog bone shaped tag. The tag was plain, with no puppy name engraved like the one Niki wore. Once he'd locked the collar in place around Ryan's neck, Mateo fingered the tag. "If you wear it permanently, we will put your name here."

"Permanently? Are you collaring me permanently?" Mateo tried to look thoughtful, thoroughly enjoying the moment.

"Maybe for as long as you are caged." He stroked Ryan's cage, his fingertips lightly brushing Ryan's newly shaved balls in the process. Ryan moaned. "Si, Shaman Prince says as long as you are caged." Ryan reached over and pushed Mateo onto his back, then the two of them wriggled up fully onto the bed. Since Mateo was already on the bottom, Ryan scooted down and swallowed Mateo's cock. As Mateo grew hard, Ryan, already relaxed from the soak, quickly entered the head space he had once tried to describe to Niki. With each breath stolen between thrusts up and down on Mateo's cock, Ryan became less and less consequential and more and more an appendage of Mateo. Mateo's cock was his cock, his only cock, his reason for being in this moment. It sounded cliché, but true to his words of weeks ago, he was here to worship Mateo. Or more specifically at this moment, Mateo's cock. He massaged the underside of it with his tongue, memorizing where each vein wrapped around it. He alternated suction with partial release, so that he could slide free just enough to roll his tongue into the slit offering droplets of pre-cum. Savory pre-cum his

Prince was providing just for him. Ryan's boner was raging now, pressing against the cage, attempting its escape. Ryan didn't care. He was here for Mateo. His Prince. His beautiful, inspiring, Shaman Prince.

Ryan moved his body further down the bed, no longer supporting himself with his arms, so he could move them up Mateo's body without releasing his hold on Mateo's cock. He slowly slid his hands up to Mateo's hip bones, where he paused, reaching his fingers down to massage the sides of Mateo's ass. Then, past his belly, and further up until his thumbs found their prey, Mateo's sensitive nipples. As he began brushing them, moving in gentle circles, clockwise on the right, counter clockwise on the left, Mateo grabbed each wrist, not to stop Ryan, but to more fully engage with him. The well-practiced circuit was completed. After Ryan made a few more revolutions around his nipples, Mateo bucked, cried out and rewarded Ryan with a warm, creamy offering, a sort of Shaman Prince communion that any worshipper, lucky enough to be allowed an audience, might aspire to receive. Once Mateo was finished, Ryan, throwing caution to the wind, slowly crawled up Mateo's body until their lips finally met, then parted. Mateo, always one to listen to his brothers, was tentative at first, but Ryan, still furiously erect and too horny to fear promised consequences, invited him in. Dared Mateo to inflict upon him what was, so far, the longest, sexiest, most savory ... most painful ... and most gratifyingly objectifying kiss of Ryan's life.


Greg was buttering his toast when Ryan and Mateo wandered into the kitchen. He took one look at Ryan and barked a short laugh, surprising both of them.

"'Morning Greg," Ryan smiled. Mateo grinned, self-consciously proud of his caged and collared acolyte.

"Let me guess," Greg turned away from his toast, one hand on his left hip. "Alex gave you that collar, didn't he?"

"Yeah," Ryan replied over the mug of coffee he'd just poured. "I'm not sure why."

"I know exactly why, Ryan." Greg shook his head and snorted before picking up his toast and settling onto a stool at the island where'd he'd already placed his coffee and juice. "You and I have both been had." Ryan's confused look begged an explanation as he sat across from Greg. Mateo, splitting a couple of English Muffins next to the toaster, paused to listen.

"Alex has been trying to get me to agree to doing dares with him. Like Luke and Raphael do." Greg took a bite of toast and munched, adding a dramatic pause to his explanation. "He more or less bet me that if either of you ever ended up collared and caged, we'd have to do it. I thought I was safe." Greg half-laughed. "But here you are. Collared and caged."

"Well, that's not fair," Ryan asserted. "The cage was my doing, but not the collar. Alex cheated. You shouldn't have to lose the bet if he's the one who collared me."

"I collared you," Mateo grinned, as he slid a glass of juice next to Ryan's mug. He slung an arm across Ryan's shoulders and looked meaningfully at Greg. "He is collared as long as he is caged. One month!" He planted one on Ryan's cheek and returned to the toaster to retrieve their muffins. Once he'd plopped onto the stool next to Ryan and begun slathering blueberry jam on his muffin, he glanced up at Greg.

"You said 'either' me or Ryan. So, maybe I would be caged, not Ryan?" Greg nodded drolly.

"Alex didn't care which one of you was caged, or even if both of you were caged. Just so one of you would be. To be honest, I didn't expect either of you to be caged." Mateo looked thoughtful as he munched.

"Either way, I still think Alex cheated and you shouldn't lose the bet," Ryan maintained. He absentmindedly fingered the collar as he bit into his muffin. When he glanced back at Greg, he was surprised to see Greg smiling broadly. "What?"

"You're right, Ryan. Alex cheated, and he should pay. You two are my witnesses. Instead of Alex daring me, I should get to dare Alex, don't you think? Wouldn't that be fair?" Both Ryan and Mateo nodded. Once he swallowed, Ryan agreed.

"It should be something awesome, Greg. Raphael and Luke have regular dares and mutual dares and flash dares. You should come up with a punishing dare." Greg's eyes lit up.

"A punishing dare. Ryan, I love it. Maybe for once, I'll be the evil genius. And come up with something that hopefully will end the dares before they even begin." He stood and carried his glass and plate to the dishwasher. As he walked behind Ryan and Mateo, he put a hand on Ryan's shoulder and squeezed as he leaned in. "For what it's worth, though, the collar looks as good on you now as it did when you were a puppy in the movie." As Greg headed toward the back stairs, Ryan turned to Mateo with a pained look.

"Boner?" Mateo asked. Ryan nodded.

"He said puppy."

As soon as Niki heard Juan coming through the front door, he jumped up from the desk chair to meet Juan at the library doorway.

"Hey, Niki," Juan greeted him as he slid his street shoes into his cubby and began pulling off his scrubs. "Did Mama get home okay?"

"She did!" Niki beamed. "Listen, as soon as you've showered, can you come back down for a couple of minutes? Raphael and I have some questions for you."

"Sure," Juan nodded. Scrubs in hand, he headed for the washer and the back stairs as Niki retreated to the library. When Juan returned, Niki was in his fireplace chair and Raphael was perched on the hearth. He motioned Juan to sit in the companion chair. Juan himself started the questioning.

"Did you guys get to Facetime or Zoom with Mama and Angel?"

"We did," Raphael looked more intense than gleeful. "She was in her easy chair instead of at the dining table like usual. She looked ... better, I guess, but kind of wasted." Juan nodded.

"Guys, it's going to take a while for her to recover." While grimacing, Niki got right to the issue.

"Raphael and I want to go down and visit her and Angel. We wanted to know what you think."

"When are you thinking?"

"Friday night," Niki replied. "Stay the weekend." Raphael was nodding while making hopeful eye contact with Juan. Juan leaned back and took a deep breath before responding.

"That soon?" He waited for a response, but neither brother answered. Juan brushed his mustache thoughtfully as he chose his words, knowing he was up against two very strong willed and devoted sons. "I know how you feel, but, guys, it's possible that both of them are still shedding virus. And we already talked about the risk of traveling." He looked into each of their eyes, reading the firm intent there. Knowing they'd already made up their minds, Juan's best hope was to moderate their plans. "Does your Mama have a patio, or porch? A good outdoor space?"

"A patio," Raphael replied unenthusiastically, as if it were a confession.

"You asked, so what I would like you to do is make it a day trip. Don't stay in a hotel or at Angel's or Mama's. Meet them outdoors. Masked and distanced." He read Raphael's reaction. "I know ... you want to hug them. And eventually you can, but if you want to go now, this soon, that's my recommendation." Neither Raphael nor Niki responded. "Guys, how would Mama feel if she was the one to give you COVID?" Raphael stared at Juan's feet. It was Niki who finally answered.

"She already blames herself for giving it to Angel." He met Juan's non-confrontational gaze. Juan nodded.

"Your Mama's been through a lot ... as you well know. Spending a couple of hours with you outdoors is about all she can manage right now, anyway. You don't want her to feel guilty about not being able to cook for you, or even make a pot of tea. Just driving down and spending some quality time with her without a screen between you will show her how much you love her. She'll be exhausted but happy. You'll feel better. And nobody will be at risk. In a month, hopefully, she'll be up to entertaining company and maybe then you *can* make a weekend of it." Juan waited for Raphael to react. When he didn't, Juan wiggled his toes, which shook Raphael out of his reverie. He lifted his gaze to Juan, then to Niki.

"Juan makes sense," Niki, the aspiring nurse, relented. Raphael shifted his body, then turned back to Juan.

"Thanks, Juan. I know you're looking out for everyone. I don't like it, but you're probably right. Mama did look pretty tired." He looked back at Niki. "We don't want to make things worse, I guess." He stood. "We were thinking of taking Luke and Steve ..." He already knew the answer before Juan spoke.

"When Mama's stronger, Raphael, that would be a great idea."


Raphael and Niki weren't the only ones running errands Friday afternoon. They left to pick up the car Raphael had rented so they could hit the road first thing Saturday morning. An easier to obtain Zipcar was out of the question, considering the duration of their trip. But with the pandemic, and the loss of tourists, they had their pick of national rental cars. While they were out, Luke and Steve, along with some additional cash from Greg and Alex, had snagged a picnic basket which they filled with a bounty of food, sweet and savory, as their way of sending well wishes, as well as holiday greetings, to Mama and Angel. On his way home from the hospital Juan picked up a bouquet as the contribution from him, Ricky, Mateo and Ryan. It was all everyone could think to do.


Mid-morning Saturday Greg was on his way down to the gym, where Alex, Juan and Ricky were already working out, when the doorbell rang.

He changed course into the foyer, approached the front door and peered through the peephole. A masked, middle-aged Black woman was on the other side. Anticipating some sort of solicitor, Greg was first tempted to just open the door as he was, in hopes she'd immediately flee. But his mid-western instincts over-ruled, and he pulled his shorts and a mask out of his cubby and slipped both on.

"May I help you?" he asked as he pulled open the door. Despite his efforts, his half-nakedness seemed to startle the woman.

"Yes ... um ... hello. Is Nicholas home?" She leaned her head to her left and peered past Greg into the foyer.

"I'm sorry, you must have the wrong address," Greg replied. She didn't react, so he continued, "There's no one here named Nicholas."

"Oh ... I mean Niki. He goes by Niki now." Greg looked more carefully at the woman, realization beginning to dawn.

"Niki's not here right now. He and his brother Raphael are out of town, visiting their Mama." The woman's head swiveled abruptly, as if in disbelief.

"*I'm* his mother," she replied.

"Excuse me?" Greg wasn't sure how to navigate what was quickly becoming an awkward exchange. The woman looked flustered behind her mask. He couldn't really read the look in her eyes, a combination of sadness and frustration. "Oh. I'm sorry ma'am. Are you Niki's birth mother?"

"Birth mother? I'm his only mother." She started to turn away. "Sorry to have bothered you."

"No, wait," Greg stepped through the door and joined her on the portico. "Forgive me. My name is Greg. You're Niki's mother?" He decided to drop the 'birth' adjective in hopes it would encourage a less emotional dialogue. She stopped and turned. Her shoulders slumped.

"Yes. I am. I'm Gladys Johnson." She paused for an uncomfortably long time. "I was hoping to talk to my boy." Greg nodded.

"I'm sorry you missed him. Any other time he would be here, but his Mama ..." Greg took a deep breath unsure how to explain reality without offending the woman. "His adoptive mother and his brother Angel are recovering from COVID, and he and Raphael are visiting them today. She just got out of the hospital earlier this week." She absorbed Greg's words, then accepted them.

"I'm truly sorry for them. That's ... so they're getting better?" Greg nodded.

"It was very serious for a while, but we're hopeful everyone will be fine." After another awkward pause, Greg had a thought. "Why don't I get your number. When he's back, Niki can give you a call. Be right back." Without giving her the opportunity to decline, he dashed into the foyer and on into the kitchen. The woman approached the door and peered in again, further this time, catching glimpses of the sitting room, library and the grand staircase. She backed up as soon as Greg came through the kitchen door.

"Your number?" he asked as he rejoined her, pen and paper in hand. Once he had the number, still unsure how to handle the situation, Greg invited her in for coffee or tea.

"Thank you, no, you're very kind. I'll be on my way." She glanced up at the staircase again. "So, this is where my Nicholas lives." He's *our Niki*, Greg thought, and chose his closing words carefully.

"Yes, in fact it was Niki who chose this house for our little family. I hope it reassures you to know he's very happy here." She nodded slightly, then turned and descended the steps.

"Well, look who's finally here," Alex snarked as Greg entered the gym.

"You guys won't believe what just happened," Greg said, ignoring Alex. "Niki's mother was here, looking for him."

"His birth mother?" Juan asked. Greg nodded. "How ironic ... to show up on the day he's visiting Mama."

"What did you say?" Ricky looked unnerved. Greg reported the conversation as he sat down next to Alex on the bench.

"She seemed to have trouble accepting the fact that Niki has another, closer mother in Mama."

"What the hell did she expect?" Alex put a hand on Greg's shoulder. "I'm glad you gave it to her straight. She needs to know Niki's doing great. Well, as great as any of us are, considering."

"To be honest," Greg turned to Alex, "she seemed pretty sad. Maybe remorseful." He looked at Juan. "I don't know. But I got her number in case Niki wants to follow up."

"So, Greg," Ricky asked. "How did she find out we live here ... that Niki lives here?" Greg looked surprised.

"Good question, Ricky. I didn't think to ask. Once I told her Niki wasn't here, she was in a hurry to leave." He held eye contact with Ricky a moment longer. "Creepy. Huh?"

"What time did you guys get back last night?" Ricky asked as he slid Niki's plate of 'cakes in front of him. Greg and Alex were helping distribute pancakes as well.

"Around eleven, I guess," Niki replied. "We took Highway 1 part of the way, just for fun. And for the view."

"Yeah, we weren't in any hurry coming back," Raphael explained. "Oh, here ..." Raphael slid out of his chair and grabbed a stack of envelopes from the sideboard and handed them out to everyone except Niki. By the time he got back to his seat, several had already opened theirs and were 'awing' and 'oohing.' "Mama keeps a stash of cards on hand 'just in case' and she spent about an hour writing those out for you guys."

"She didn't need to do that," Juan set his card upright, on display, in front of his placemat. "So, tell us everything. How are she and Angel doing?"

"She was really touched," Niki offered. "Angel, too. They really appreciated everything." He turned to Steve. "Including the mantra video. Angel played it again while we were there." Then in answer to Juan's question, he and Raphael took turns recounting the visit and their observations of Mama's and Angel's recovery.

"You were right, Juan," Raphael concluded. "By the time we left, Mama was clearly exhausted. But she was really happy to see us. I'm glad we went."

"Yeah," Niki added. "You can't believe how hard it was not to hug and kiss her. Or Angel." He wiggled his eyebrows coquettishly as he spoke Angel's name.

"Well, as long we're doing show and tell, Niki, I have something for you," Greg said. He walked into the foyer and returned with a slip of paper, handing it to Niki.

"Whose number is this?" Niki innocently asked.

"Your mother stopped by yesterday," Greg replied, knowing how those words would land.

"What?!" Niki, shocked, looked at Greg, then at Steve, then Raphael. "No. But, how ...?"

"She wanted to talk to you. I told her where you and Raphael were. I don't think she knew how to take the news that you were visiting your Mama and your brother Angel. With your other brother Raphael. I kind of blew her away." Niki didn't speak, just looked at the paper again, then back at Raphael.

"Why would she show up after all these years?" Raphael asked rhetorically.

"And," Ricky reiterated once again, "how did she know we live here?" Once again Raphael and Niki locked gazes. Steve cupped the back of Niki's neck with a warm, loving hand, then rubbed his back.

"You don't have to call her if you don't want to," Steve counseled. Niki took a deep breath and sighed. He turned to Steve.

"I know," he said quietly. "Thanks."

# Thirty-Seven

## THE TRUTH IS OUT THERE

"HERE'S TO NEW YEAR'S Eve, 2021," Alex, in his regular place at the dinner table, held his flute higher than usual. "We say goodbye to the suckiest year since 'Franceesco' and Cadmael had to forage their way through the Black Death. And here's to the lamest New Year's Eve ... maybe until we're in our nineties ... that we'll ever celebrate together."

"Well," Steve raised his glass, "on that happy note."

"We've got to stop letting Alex make toasts," Raphael agreed. Alex lifted the silly hat he was wearing, and let the elastic band under his chin pull it back into place.

"So, what's so lame about it, Alex?" Ricky asked. The hats had been Ricky's idea.

"Oh, nothing about what we're doing now," Alex assured. "Good food, good wine, excellent company," he nodded to Hiroshi, the evening's special guest. "And we're all stylin'." He tapped his hat. "I mean, we do this all the time. New Year's Eve should be parties, noisy bars, crowded streets, drag queens. At least, I guess, we have a few leather men." Greg snorted as Alex sighed.

"Well, you know," Ricky beamed, holding up his flute, "I'd rather be here with all of you," he turned his gaze to Juan, "than in any old bar." He turned back to Alex. "But, if I can borrow one of your outfits, Alex, I'll be your drag queen for the night." That got a howl from around the table, the loudest from Greg.

"You kinda walked into that one," Raphael grinned at Alex.

"God ..." Alex pretended to bite his tongue. "How do I keep doing that?"

"I don't know, sweetie," Greg passed the bowl of crispy brussels sprouts to Alex. "But we hope you never stop."

"I have an idea," Niki spoke, then continued before Alex could remember the torment he and Raphael inflicted on him the last time those words were spoken. "Luke, maybe New Year's Eve is the perfect time for that next session in the turret room, with another bottle of truth serum. We promised Hiroshi we'd do it. Remember?" Several pairs of eyes lit up. "Steve and I will pay for it."

"How about it?" Luke looked around the table. "Is this a good night to delve deeper into the mysteries of The House of the Locked Cock Brotherhood?" No one objected. Luke turned to Niki. "Niki, you can pay for it by doing the cleanup tonight. Deal?"

"Deal!"

Niki and Ricky helped Raphael with the glasses this time. In keeping with the celebratory nature of the evening, in addition to the bottle of Aberlour A'bundah Alba that Luke was bearing, Hiroshi carried up a platter of beautifully presented kagami mochi he'd made in the Oshougatsu tradition. He'd intended them for dessert, but had not anticipated pairing them alongside 'secrets' in a turret room session centered around 'truth serum.' Once again, dinner with his friends in the House of the Locked Cock Brotherhood included a side course of drama. While everyone settled into place, Luke opened the bottle and explained to Hiroshi what they were up to. As Luke began pouring, Hiroshi turned to Ricky.

"This definitely sounds like more fun than a crowded bar," he grinned. "My friends, you never disappoint."

"Well, we'll see if this time is as productive as last time," Raphael replied to Hiroshi. "That night Niki made the best use of the truth serum, I think. So, we'll see ..."

"Okay," Luke said as he took his place next to Raphael after pouring the round, "everyone take a dose." He raised his glass toward the center of the circle, then sipped.

"I have maybe a good one," Mateo volunteered, to the delight of everyone. Alex clapped. Niki woofed. Mateo rose up on his knees and faced Juan and the partially entangled Ricky. Then he hesitated and turned to Luke. "Is two questions okay?" Luke smiled and nodded. Mateo turned back toward Juan and Ricky. "Juan, when Ricky ask to marry you, you say only if your engagement is short. How long is short?" The look on Juan's face was priceless, but no one had a phone handy to capture it. Ricky untangled his arm from Juan's waist, pulled back a bit and looked intensely into Juan's eyes as his heartbreaking smile bloomed. Juan actually closed his eyes to protect himself. Ricky looked across the circle at Raphael, his co-conspirator in the proposal, aiming that smile at him.

"Wow," Steve spoke. "No warm up questions this time." As Mateo settled back, thigh to thigh with Ryan, Juan set his glass down and pulled Ricky closer.

"We've talked." He and Ricky made meaningful eye contact. "We weren't ready to make it official yet, but now that I think about it, Mateo, in his role as Shaman Prince, has maybe chosen the perfect time for an announcement. Raphael, didn't you propose to Luke on New Year's Eve?"

"Or New Year's Day, yeah. It was about exactly midnight." Juan nodded.

"Not that we're copy cats or anything," Juan continued as Ricky wiggled his eyebrows at Niki and Steve, "but, uh, we were thinking of getting married on Valentine's Day."

"Yeah!" Ricky interrupted. "You know, so most of us wouldn't forget our anniversaries."

"Perfect!" Niki exclaimed, rising up and pulling Steve into a quick, but passionate kiss. Raphael and Luke clinked glasses in approval.

"I ..." Alex leaned forward but before he could continue, Juan held up a hand, with a smile.

"I know what you're going to say, Wedding Planner of the Century. Yes, we welcome your contribution to what will be the second biggest day of our lives. But you will have to agree to work with a collaborator." Alex furrowed his brow as he sat back and lifted his glass to his lips. A collaborator? "We've asked Hiroshi to officiate a Buddhist ceremony for us. In the back garden."

"Hiroshi!" Niki exclaimed again. "You ... dog! You guys ..." He looked back and forth between Hiroshi and Juan and Ricky. "This really was a secret to reveal." He turned his gaze to Mateo. "Good job, Mateo." Mateo grinned as Ryan massaged his thigh, smiling alongside him. Meanwhile, Alex alternately eyed Hiroshi and Juan, pondering his options, with his glass still at his lips.

"Mateo," Luke asked, "you said you had two questions?"

"Yes," Mateo cleared his throat after a bigger than intended sip of truth serum. "Ricky. What is up with your pezones?" It was only by sheer luck that no one wasted precious single malt Scotch in a spit take. Ricky's eyes widened as he looked down at his chest self-consciously. Then he looked at Juan, sheepishly at first, but seeing the confident, possibly proud look on Juan's face, he turned back to Mateo with his signature, adorable grin.

"Well, you know, I've been doing my leather boy training lately. Juan and I discovered my nipples have a lot of potential, so we've been training them. Do you like them?" Mateo nodded with a grin. Raphael crawled across the empty center of the circle and gently fingered Ricky's left nipple. A firm, perky, plump nipple that was lotion smooth to the touch. Ricky imperceptibly shuddered. Raphael withdrew his arm and sat back to better admire Ricky's pecs.

"Damn," he pronounced as he and Ricky locked eyes. "I guess I hadn't noticed. Are you going to get them pierced?"

"Maybe. Probably." Ricky turned to Juan. "Juan and I haven't decided for sure. Maybe four piercings are enough."

"Yeah," Raphael countered, "but your earrings, septum and labret are fashion ... beauty piercings, not erotic piercings." He reached out and lightly brushed Ricky's right nipple. "I don't know ... these would be beautiful with little gold beaded barbells, to match all the others, too." As Raphael returned to his spot next to Luke, Hiroshi spoke for the second time since the session began.

"How big are you hoping to train them?"

"Not sure," Juan replied. "Right now, we're just enjoying the journey." He reached over and duplicated Raphael's gesture, producing another shudder in Ricky. Ricky turned to Hiroshi.

"I love living naked, but I never thought wearing a shirt could be so ... sensual before. I actually look forward to going up and down stairs on deliveries now."

"Wait 'til you get them pierced," Raphael teased. "I avoided elevators at work for weeks after that."

"And here I thought you were just working on your glutes and quads," Alex laughed. "I should have known you were secretly getting off by taking the stairs." He looked at Luke. "I have a question for Mateo and Ryan, although, I don't know, Mateo's set the bar incredibly high." Luke nodded and motioned his head toward Mateo and Ryan in invitation.

"Mateo, those really were excellent questions. My question for you two is sort of a follow up to the one Raphael asked the last time we were up here: How's it going for you, now that Ryan's been locked up for a couple of weeks? And don't hold back." Niki woofed again as Ryan put a hand in front of his mouth in mock, or maybe genuine embarrassment. Then he and Mateo exchanged a long glance, silently negotiating how much to reveal and who should reveal it.

"I'll go first," Ryan said, "since I really didn't give Raphael much of an answer last time." He glanced guiltily at Raphael before returning his gaze to Alex. "I can't say for sure why I promised the fates to lock up if Raphael and Niki's Mama got better, but I blame all of you guys." He looked around for reactions, but no one seemed willing to accept responsibility of any kind. "It was the best I could come up with, sitting there chanting the mantra with two locked guys, Raphael and Niki, and with my Prince. I guess it was as close to a human sacrifice as I was willing to make. It, uh, has been a sacrifice. I don't know how you guys have done it. The pain is slowly getting better, but ... lordy ... I want to touch my cock so bad!" He turned his gaze from Alex to Mateo, who was hanging on every word. "So, all my attention now is focused on this guy and his cock. I hunger for it, Alex. Just seeing it makes my cage ache. And my ass. I want his cock in my mouth and ass at the same time. The best I can do is suck him silly and then sit on his cock and suck his tongue and savor ... those ... beautiful ... lips." He paused, staring a long moment at Mateo before shaking his head, coming out of the daydream the two of them seemed to be sharing. "Um, sorry." He turned his gaze back to Alex. "It's been painful. Frustrating. Horny beyond anything I've ever experienced. Humbling, for sure, and yet unexpectedly gratifying. I truly know now what it means to worship Mateo." He paused a moment, looking to Niki, then Raphael. "Plus, I'd like to think doing this really did help Angel and Mama recover." He placed his right hand on the back of Mateo's neck and pulled him closer. "And my Prince has been very, very, very understanding." At that, Mateo grinned and looked down at Ryan's cage, then back up at the group.

"We learn a lot," Mateo said succinctly.

"Okay, I'm just going to say it," Alex said. "I'll pay next semester's tuition if the two of you will give us a demonstration of what you just described right here ... right now." In an uncharacteristic move, Hiroshi reached over and pushed Alex's shoulder, causing him to bounce off of Greg. Ryan took another sip, before looking at Raphael again as he responded.

"I think we'll follow in Raphael and Luke's footsteps ... no demonstrations in the turret room." Alex pretended to be massively disappointed.

"Fine. But thank you for that evocative answer to my question, Ryan. Do you have anything to add, Shaman Prince?" Mateo slowly shook his head with a subtle, wry smile.

"No, Alex. Everthing is good. Really good." He reached down and jiggled Ryan's cage. No one spoke for a moment, sipping Scotch and mulling over what Ryan had so willingly revealed. Then, Juan spoke.

"Now that Alex's question has raised the temperature in the room, I have one for him. Not quite so personal, but ..." Alex, eyes closed and grinning, turned in Juan's direction.

"I'm all yours, Francisco."

"Funny you should put it that way," Juan responded. Alex opened his eyes. "I guess, in a way this is a question for you and Raphael. I was wondering if it would be okay if I stole a little intellectual property from you two. Well, maybe, a lot." Raphael and Alex exchanged clueless looks. "I know I resisted getting involved in the movie, but after watching the amazing job Steve did, that we all did, I've really become more and more, shall we say, enchanted with your story. I'd like your permission to try writing a full-fledged novel about Francisco, Cadmael, Pablo ..." Juan tossed a glance at Raphael, "Adonis, the Spicy Asian, and all the rest. I think there's a lot of material there just waiting to be explored."

"Seriously?" Alex sounded astounded. He looked at Raphael. "Raphael, I think we should be flattered."

"Perhaps," Raphael replied, turning to Juan, "but more importantly, we should discuss royalties." He turned back to Alex. "Don'tcha think?" It was Luke's turn to nudge Raphael's shoulder. "Have we had any other offers, Alex?" Raphael continued.

"Well, there was that one from Spielberg, but that was for film rights, not a novel." Raphael nodded dramatically, then sipped again, grinning at Juan over his glass.

"You're seriously thinking of writing a novel, Juan? I'm impressed."

"Well, I took a creative writing class in college," Juan put an arm across Ricky's shoulders as Ricky casually slid his right hand across Juan's thigh and down over his crotch. "I explored a little before I zeroed in on medicine. Anyway, I never seemed to have any compelling ideas to pursue until Francisco and the gang came along. So, yeah, I'm feeling inspired."

"Well. Okay," Alex relented, meeting Juan's gaze seriously this time. "No acknowledgements. We want to be in the dedication." He saw Ricky's reaction. "Of course, we're willing to share it with Ricky."

"And that, my friends," Raphael concluded the exchange, "is how you negotiate." Raphael tipped his glass up and drained it to punctuate his point. As Luke refreshed his glass, Steve held his out toward Luke as well. Once Luke had poured, Steve took the floor.

"Although Niki here is famous, or at least was, for being a man of few words, Luke, you come a close second. These revelation sessions with your father's truth serum were your idea. I think it's time we heard from you. How are you, brother-in-law?"

"Yeah," Greg seconded. Raphael turned ninety degrees in his spot, leaned back and rested against Niki, giving Luke his full attention and making himself very comfortable.

"Yes, Sir. We're all ears." Luke shook his head, a typical reaction to Raphael's all too frequent entreaties. Clearly caught off guard, he closed his eyes and rubbed his forehead in thought. Finally, he looked up at Steve as he reached over and squeezed Raphael's ankle.

"It seems longer, sometimes, but it was two years ago tonight that I took a risk." He glanced at Raphael, before spreading eye contact around the circle. "A big risk. I was dating the sexiest guy I'd ever met and it felt like it was actually getting serious. More serious than I'd ever experienced. You all know the story. I tied him up and introduced him to what life could be like as a leather boy." He returned his gaze to Raphael and held it there. "The truth is, I really didn't care if he became my leather boy or not. I just wanted him to be mine. And the funny thing is, at the end of the night, it was Raphael who made me his. He dared me to accept his ring. To marry him." Luke returned his gaze to Steve. "I thought I was being the daring one. The dominant one. But it was Raphael who took ownership of me." Luke paused and took a deep breath.

"When I think back over the last two years, it's hard to believe how rewarding they've been. To become Raphael's husband. Your and Niki's brother-in-law. Family with all of you. Including you, Hiroshi. I don't know what I did, or maybe am destined to do, to deserve all of you, but, I'm stupefyingly grateful." Raphael leaned his head back and looked up into Niki's eyes.

"Once again, it's getting pretty deep in here, Niki," he said, deflecting his embarrassment and producing a rare chuckle from Niki. Luke shook Raphael's ankle and released it in mock rejection.

"No, Raphael," Alex came to Luke's defense. "I want to hear more. You told me once what a softy Luke really is, and I wasn't sure if I believed it, but ... you were right." Alex slid his glass forward, seeking a refresher from Luke. "Truth is, Luke, you and Raphael have been more than just an inspiration to the rest of us. You two are the center of our little universe." Raphael sat up as Luke poured into Alex's glass, and before Alex could reach out for it, Raphael crawled forward and grabbed it.

"Come get it," he demanded of Alex, who was only a couple of feet away. Alex leaned out for the glass, and when his hand wrapped around Raphael's hand and the glass, Raphael leaned further forward and planted one, a lip-on-lip kiss. Alex looked surprised, but didn't resist. Quite the opposite.

"I thought there wouldn't be any demonstrations," Ricky giggled. Both Alex and Raphael returned to their spots next to their husbands.

"I was just thanking him for saying the sweetest thing about me," Raphael explained.

"About us, O Center of the Universe," Luke corrected him. "Now what's this about me being a 'softy'?"

"Like everybody didn't know that," Raphael deflected, while giving Alex the evil eye. "Next!" he announced before Luke could pursue the issue.

"Me! Me!" Ricky insisted. "I haven't had a turn." He leaned forward to look around Juan at Hiroshi. "Thank you for the mochi, Hiroshi. I love everything you make and do. You're the most amazing friend, not just because you're a wonderful person, but I'm always learning something new when I'm around you. And I've wanted to ask you for a while, now, but I didn't know how to." He looked over at Luke, then back to Hiroshi. "Anyway, maybe with the truth serum I have the courage to ask." He paused, and Hiroshi smiled and nodded an invitation to proceed. "I've noticed you aren't wearing your cage anymore. Does that mean you're in a better place now?" Alex reached over and cupped Hiroshi's knee, a move he never would have made had he not consumed his own share of truth serum. A genuine, wide smile spread across Hiroshi's face as he placed his hand over Alex's.

"Ricky, thank you for asking." He looked around the circle, where all eyes were focused on him. "Since we are drinking truth serum, I guess I cannot hold back, is that right?" Everyone nodded. "After Ben died, I was not sure I would ever be happy again. I felt like my life was behind me. A good life, no regrets, you understand, but I was certain all my good times were in my past." He paused, looking thoughtfully out the window beyond Mateo's head, before refocusing on Ricky. "Then this crazy band of friendly, naked, unbelievably uninhibited, and adventurous young men, one of whom I had actually once had the great fortune to know quite intimately, appeared out of nowhere and took possession of Ben's house. Apparently, all just to rescue me." He turned to Niki. "I know ... I know. You think you found this house. But, actually, this house ... the spirit of this house, the soul of this house if you prefer, found you. Sought you out and brought you here." He turned his gaze to Steve. "Seriously. How to explain that Ben's grandson reached out to Steve, who is married to a man of impeccable taste?" Niki smiled and looked down shyly. "Who has a brother who does not know how to take no for an answer? And knows how to make the most improbable things happen?" Raphael and Luke both nodded knowingly. "Some might say it was simply The Force manifesting itself in our lives. Whatever it was, I will be eternally grateful, because, yes, Ricky, my friend, despite everything, thanks to all of you, I am in a very good place."

Juan set his glass down, and stood, pulling Ricky with him since Ricky was still attached. He reached down and offered a hand to Hiroshi, who reached up so Juan could pull him to his feet. Juan and Ricky wrapped their arms around Hiroshi in a traditional House of the Locked Cock Brotherhood group hug. One that immediately grew with the addition of Mateo at first, and then Ryan. They lingered a moment, as the rest of the family exchanged smiles. "This," Hiroshi said quietly as the huggers dispersed and he sat back down, "being here with all of you, is more than any one should ever expect. I do not believe in an afterlife. But, if there is one, it would not surprise me if Ben himself had arranged all of this to make sure I would be happy in his absence." He lifted his glass and sipped, signaling the end of his answer to Ricky.

"Wow," Raphael quietly uttered. He smiled at Hiroshi. "When you look at it that way, it really does kind of make sense." He met Niki's gaze. "What do you think, Niki? Were we in charge? Or not?"

"I don't know," Niki answered. "I thought we were. But, the very first time Steve and I entered the foyer, I don't know, it … it just felt right. I felt like I was home. I mean, each room spoke to me." He paused, then looked across at Juan. "And we didn't even know about the dungeon. Or about Juan's connection to the house and to Hiroshi."

"Or Juan's connection to Ricky when we made Ricky a member of the family," Alex offered.

"Okay, guys, you're weirding me out," Greg said. Hiroshi, Luke and Juan all laughed. Luke tipped his glass toward Greg.

"Well, Greg, after all, we have been drinking truth serum," he explained. "The truth is out there." Raphael groaned, then sat up, folding his legs beneath him, making himself as tall as Luke.

"Hiroshi, you are the deepest person I've ever known. Grandpa Ben … The Force … the house's spirit, any or all of them may be why we're all here together. But here are some truths I do know." He cocked a disdainful eye at Alex. "Rather than a question, I'd like to offer an antidote to Alex's earlier condemnation of 2020, which, I agree, left a lot to be desired. But … it wasn't all bad.

"Think about it! Niki, Steve, Luke and I got married." He glanced at Ricky. "In two wedding ceremonies, one of which, rumor has it, was legendary. And like we were just saying, we're here, under one roof. We're a real family. Niki has found his calling and is studying to follow in Juan's footsteps. Mateo, our Shaman Prince, with Hiroshi's help, successfully led us, along with Juan's guidance, through our personal dark days of COVID. And he and his sex slave Ryan are together at last. Ricky proposed to Juan, who accepted. We found out how incredibly creative Alex and Steve are in the production of the best gay porn flick no one will ever see." He paused a moment to let his contention sink in. "In 2020 we saw millions of people, from all walks, stand up and march for Black Lives, and we were able to add our own voices. Those same people, along with millions more, made sure that the last four years of insanity and cruelty in the White House are finally coming to an end. We've been able to recreate a fitness routine. Ricky's nipples are perkier." He turned to Luke. "Luke is more handsome than ever." Raphael put his right arm across Luke's shoulders as he raised his glass in his left hand just as fireworks boomed in the distance, announcing the arrival of the new year. "Here's to 2021. To even better days. For each and every one of us who call the House of the Locked Cock Brotherhood home."

Niki reached over and rubbed Raphael's thigh in appreciation. Greg started to stand, figuring Raphael's soliloquy was the perfect exclamation point to the evening, but Alex grabbed his hand and pulled him back down.

"Raphael's right," Alex confessed. "I want to retract my snarky toast at the dinner table. And to make up for it, if you will all indulge me, I'd like to lead us all in a Hiroshi inspired greeting to the New Year." He reached out his left hand to Hiroshi, who took it, not quite sure what Alex was referring to. Alex took Greg's hand in his right hand, then looked expectantly around the circle until everyone caught on, and took the hand of the men sitting on either side of them. Mateo was the first to realize what Alex had in mind. As Alex bowed his head, both he and Mateo quietly spoke. In unison. "Nam Myōhō Renge Kyō." A smile broke out on Hiroshi's face as he bowed his head, squeezed Alex's hand, and joined in. "Nam Myōhō Renge Kyō." On the third incantation, everyone joined. "Nam Myōhō Renge Kyō."

# THANK YOU

I HOPE YOU ENJOYED following the continuing exploits of this daring chosen family now inhabiting the House of the LCB. If you did, first, I hope you will leave a favorable (spoiler-free) review with your favorite retailer.

Secondly, I hope you will seek out *Double Dare III, Hiroshi's Gift*, which concludes the trilogy. In this third volume, members of the family face heartbreaking trials and breathtaking opportunities they never would have imagined.

You can find more information and links to all three books and interact with me at:

www.macinsf.com.

To pique your interest, a sneak preview of the first chapter of *Double Dare III, Hiroshi's Gift* is included here. I hope you find it compelling enough to continue reading the trilogy.

# ACKNOWLEDGEMENTS

My humble gratitude goes to: Ron Bedford for his EMT expertise. To Carlos Hickerson for perfecting my Spanish. To the many early readers, too many to mention, for their encouragement and patience. Most especially to Ms. Conner, sophomore English teacher, who took me aside after class and told me I should become a writer. (After reading my short story to every one of her classes that day.) Teachers who inspire their students deserve pedestals. And better pay.

To the city of San Francisco and it's lovely people who inspire me to write. It never ceases to amaze.

And to the men I've known and loved who inspired many of the characters in this trilogy. They are by no means 'too many to mention.' But each of them taught me much and left me a better man.

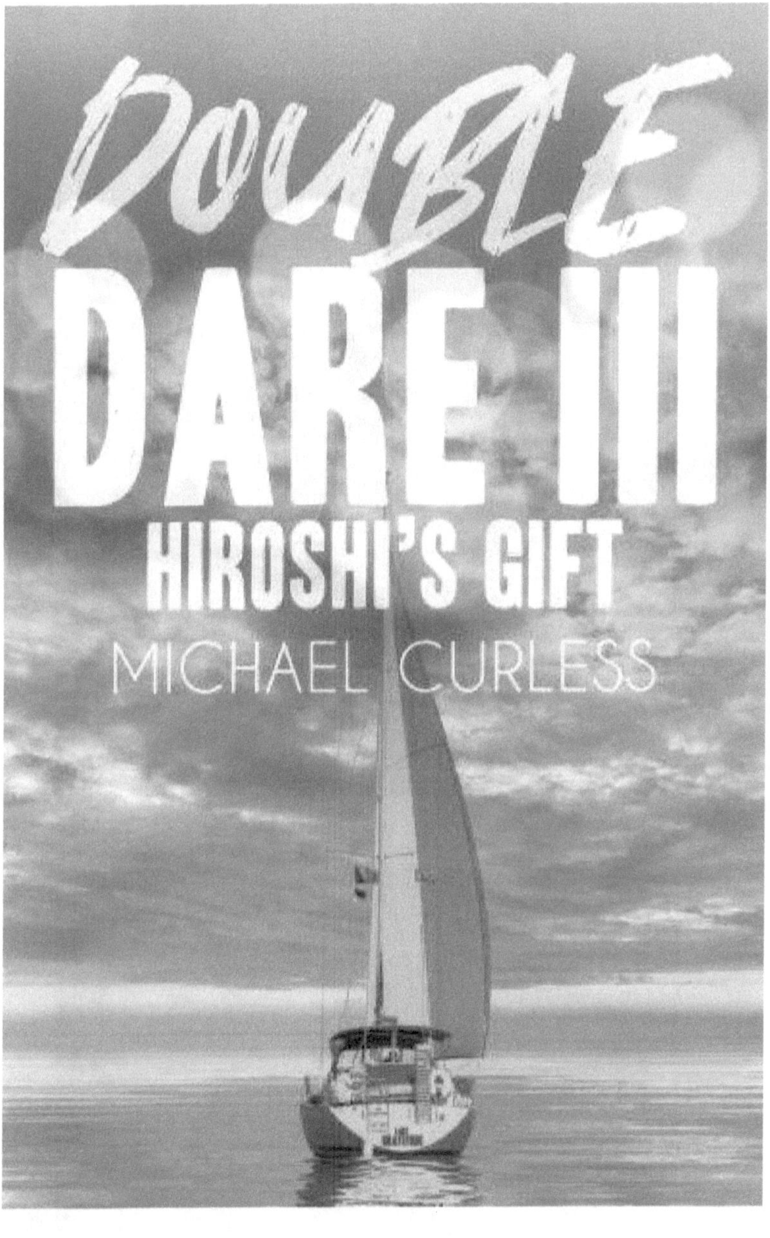
DOUBLE
DARE III
HIROSHI'S GIFT
MICHAEL CURLESS

# THE COLLABORATORS

"KNOCK. KNOCK." ALEX CALLED out as he stood at Hiroshi's open back door, debating whether to just walk in or wait for an official invitation.

"Come in, my friend," Hiroshi called from inside. "Do not stand on ceremony." Alex wandered in through the mudroom to find Hiroshi in the kitchen, pouring steaming water into a black iron teapot. Hiroshi looked up and smiled. "I'm preparing tea for us, specially blended to promote our creative juices." Alex approached the counter and sniffed.

"Mmmm. I feel more creative already, Hiroshi." Alex smiled as he spied the plate of individually wrapped senbei on the tray with the teapot.

"Well, Alex, we have seen just how creative you can be as a screenwriter, so I am confident you do not need any herbal help. In fact, I have been looking forward to working with you in planning Juan and Ricky's wedding." Hiroshi picked up the tray and headed toward the front of the house. "I thought we would work in the study." Alex followed Hiroshi through the dining and living rooms, across the entry into Hiroshi's study, marveling at the meticulous braiding of the gauzy rokushaku fundoshi Hiroshi was wearing. No matter how many times he'd tried, he could never get his own fundoshi to come out as perfectly as Hiroshi's always were. Which is why he hadn't even tried today and had come through the back garden harnessed and caged, but otherwise naked, as always. Hiroshi set the tray on the desk and poured two cups as Alex pulled up a side chair, set his phone on the desk, and settled in. Hiroshi handed a cup to Alex then placed the plate of crackers between them. As Alex tore open a nori senbei, Hiroshi sat back in the desk chair and sipped from his cup, enjoying the sight of Alex savoring his favorite snack.

"I've done a little research, Hiroshi, but I still don't have a good sense of what a Buddhist wedding ceremony should be. Where do we start?" Hiroshi set his cup down.

"Let us start with what you do know, Alex."

"Well, it's not a religious ceremony, typically there aren't any vows, it's mostly the monk chanting from sacred texts or mantras. Sometimes incense is burned. Not a lot of the pomp and circumstance of weddings here." Hiroshi had peeled open a cracker and munched it while Alex was talking. He picked up his cup and sipped.

"Sounds pretty boring, eh, Alex?" Alex struggled to find a non-judgmental answer.

"It maybe sounds dry on paper ..."

"Was your ceremony for Niki, Steve, Raphael and Luke a typical American wedding?" Alex laughed cracker crumbs onto his lap.

"It was more of an over-the-top production, Hiroshi. I kinda got carried away." Hiroshi nodded.

"From all accounts, your efforts were appreciated by all who were in attendance. I see no reason why we cannot make Juan and Ricky's wedding unique and memorable as well, even if it is a more intimate affair. Alex, I don't think they asked me to officiate because they wanted a traditional Buddhist ceremony or a Japanese ceremony, which are two different things, really. I think they just wanted a simple but meaningful ceremony, blessed by the presence of the people who love them." Alex nodded his agreement. "Here is my suggestion, if I may. We should put together an eclectic ceremony that borrows the best from several cultures, considering the diversity of this unique and wonderful family. What do you think?"

"That's a great idea, Hiroshi. So, we can pretty much do whatever we want?" Hiroshi smiled and nodded. "I mean, within reason. What is the best of the Japanese Buddhist tradition that we should include?"

"Since the setting will be somewhat informal, your garden, I thought the clothing should be rather dramatic. Is it okay with you if the wedding party is wearing clothing, Alex? Unlike your last wedding?" Alex looked self-consciously down at his cage, then back at Hiroshi with a wry grin.

"Like I said, that was something of a spectacle. Intended to honor the kinky lifestyle of the four grooms. If we go multi-cultural, with an emphasis on Buddhist-Japanese influence, I agree, nudity, as much as we all enjoy it, may not be appropriate. Besides, I don't want to be pegged as a one-note wedding planner." Hiroshi laughed. "So, what are you thinking? Will everyone be wearing off the shoulder orange robes?" Hiroshi laughed again, eyes closed, shaking his head.

"No ... no orange robes. Here, what do you think of this?" Hiroshi woke his laptop and the connected larger monitor to display a handsome young Japanese man dressed in a dark, floor length garment. "This is what I was thinking for Juan. It is a yukata, in the keisho kanji print, which represents 'fortunate event.' Not a traditional kimono for a wedding, perhaps, but, as we agreed, this will not be a traditional wedding."

"No," Alex replied, projecting a mix of surprise and joy, "but it will be a fortunate event. We'll see to that, won't we?" Hiroshi nodded with a smile. "That's kind of sexy. I didn't know men wore kimonos. I thought only women wore them … mostly geishas."

"No, Alex, men and women both wear kimono and yukata, and perhaps you may not have known this, but the first geisha were actually men." Hiroshi lifted one eyebrow to Alex's delight.

"Of course they were," Alex grinned, wiggling his eyebrows in reply. "I like it. Do you think studly Juan will wear that? It's, well … it's sort of androgynous."

"Only to an American eye, Alex. I am confident Juan and Ricky will go along with whatever we decide. Afterall, they did put us in charge, did they not?"

"They did!" Alex replied. As he tore open another savory senbei, he looked mischievously at Hiroshi. "Okay, now I'm getting excited." He popped the cracker into his mouth and munched. "So, what do you have in mind for Ricky?" Hiroshi clicked on another tab, bringing up an image of a navy blue kimono emblazoned on the front with two small gold embroidered kanji symbols, one over each pectoral. He clicked to display another image showing the back, with a larger embroidery of the same symbol centered between the shoulder blades.

"Mmmm. Very classy," Alex opined. "What does that symbol represent?"

"Long life and happiness." Alex looked pleased.

"They'll look stunning dressed in these kimono, Hiroshi. Do they have any idea this is what you're planning?" Hiroshi shook his head, delivering his own mischievous smile.

"No, my friend. Not what I am planning. What *we* are planning. We will share the credit, and any blame. Agreed?"

"Agreed," Alex grinned. "Will there be anyone else in the wedding party like we have here … best man, groomsmen … maid of honor?"

"I spoke with them about that. In a typical Buddhist ceremony, no. But since we are choosing from different cultures, that is one we will add from the Western world. Alex, it is a testimony to how much love and respect there is in this family that choosing two best men was nearly impossible for them. But they finally decided that since you and Greg had taken Ricky in and protected him from harm, that the two of you should have the honor of 'best men.'"

"Whoa. Really? That's … I thought they'd pick Raphael and Luke." Alex looked pleased and humbled.

"As I said, it was not an easy decision for them. But I think they made the right choice. Here, take a look at what I suggest you and Greg should wear." Hiroshi clicked on yet another tab to reveal another kimono. He turned to Alex with an expression silently asking, 'what do you think?' Alex studied the image a moment longer.

"For both me and Greg?" Hiroshi nodded as he clicked to display the front and back images of a black kimono decorated with colorful embroidered dragons, smaller ones over each pectoral on the front, and, similar to Ricky's, a larger embroidered image on the back. "Very elegant. I assume there is symbolism behind the dragon?"

"Of course. This is the Kaenryu design, called a flare dragon because it is flying through a 'flare' cloud, these little red wisps. The dragon is thought to prevent evil and bring good fortune."

"So, we'll be more than best men, we'll be good luck charms, too?" Hiroshi laughed again, more heartily than before.

"I *like* that interpretation, Alex. Yes, let us go with that. Would you like to explore other possible designs?"

"No," Alex shook his head and lingered on the image on the screen. "I defer to your expertise on kimono. I think we'll all look stunning, not to mention surprising. Not that we'll have a very big audience. Will these be hard to get?" Hiroshi shook his head.

"Not if we act soon, Alex. I'll just need shoe sizes for everyone for the zori, the traditional sandals. Can you do a little sleuthing to find that out for us?"

"No problem." Alex reached for another senbei. Hiroshi refreshed both tea cups.

"Now, to your expertise, Alex. Since the ceremony will be outdoors, I thought we might introduce an element from your culture."

"Hmmm?" Alex queried through a closed but cracker filled mouth.

"I thought we might erect a chuppah as the focal point." Alex's eyes widened as he swallowed.

"A chuppah? For a Buddhist ceremony?" Hiroshi slowly nodded with a faint smile. "You weren't kidding about mixing cultures, were you?" Hiroshi just maintained the smile. "How did you know I was Jewish? I'm not the only one in the family without a foreskin."

"On one of the days when we were marching for Black Lives, in all his sweet innocence, Mateo asked me if Buddhism and Judaism are similar, since neither worships the Christian savior. A deep subject on a very momentous day. He wants to understand each of us, I think, and emulate the best of us. A remarkable young man."

"What did you say? This ought to be good ..."

"It was not the best setting for a deep philosophical discussion, as I am sure you recall. So, I simply said that most religions and spiritual philosophies, at their core, are more alike than different. When I asked him why he was asking, he said that I was the only Buddhist that he knew, and that you were the only Jew. And that he wanted to better understand our two cultures." Alex leaned back and sighed.

"I don't remember ever talking about being Jewish with Mateo." Alex held eye contact with Hiroshi for a moment. "He must trust you more than me."

"He reveres you, Alex. Maybe he just felt comfortable enough to ask me what had been on his mind in that moment. With us holding hands and 'making good trouble' in support of his Black brother. As with Ricky, you and Greg provided Mateo with safe harbor and he will always be in your debt. He trusts you Alex, more than almost anyone else in the world." Alex had a studied look as he processed what Hiroshi had said.

"What do you think ... about the chuppah idea?" Hiroshi brought Alex back to the task at hand.

"Aesthetically, I like it. I agree it would be a nice focal point. I can see you, Juan and Ricky standing under it, with flowers twined around the posts. I already have an idea how to embellish it. They don't even have to know it's a Jewish tradition." Hiroshi tilted his head questioningly.

"Why not, Alex? Is it not expected in a Buddhist-Japanese-Jewish-Catholic-Atheist-Black-Latino-Filipino-Caucasian family wedding?"

"Well ... when you put it that way." Alex looked slightly pleased. He leaned toward Hiroshi. "What will you be wearing? A Japanese-Black-Latino-Filipino-Caucasian suit? Or something from the rainbow couture?"

"There is that over-the-top wedding planner I have heard so much about," Hiroshi smiled. "No, my friend, I have a subtle black kimono, with a pale grey obi that I thought I would wear. I do not wish to compete with the wedding party."

"Obi?"

"This," Hiroshi pointed to the wide belt in the image on the monitor. "It serves as a belt on the kimono, but it is actually a long piece of fabric, much like the fundoshi." Alex dunked his head in appreciation.

"That's what I think I most admire about Japanese culture, Hiroshi. Everything is so precise, so beautiful, well planned and executed, yet so very simple." Hiroshi gave Alex a doubtful look. "I mean, look ... no gaudy buckle, no belt loops ... a simple strip of fabric that does the job." Before Hiroshi could respond, Alex's phone vibrated. He looked at it, glanced guiltily at Hiroshi and picked it up. "A text from Raphael. We're supposed to run with Niki this afternoon." He tapped out a reply. "I told him I'm here with you and I'll be home in a few. What else should we discuss today?" Before either of them could speak, his phone vibrated again. Alex looked at the notification displayed without touching the phone. He looked at Hiroshi. "Oh, oh. He says he's coming over."

"We will need more tea," Hiroshi said as he closed his laptop to conceal the display, picked up the teapot and headed to the kitchen. Alex rose and began taking in Hiroshi's study. Unlike the library in the House of the Locked Cock Brotherhood, aside from a couple of bookcases, the door, and the street-facing window, most of the wall space was open, and much of it was covered with framed photos, artwork and ephemera. Some of the photos were of small groups of mostly men in party settings, outdoor venues, tables in restaurants. Many had been taken years ago, yet it was easy to spot a young, bespectacled and studious-looking, but arguably very cute Hiroshi.

"Oh wow," Alex muttered under his breath as he came across a photo of Hiroshi standing next to a taller Caucasian man with shoulder-length hair, his arm slung around Hiroshi's shoulders. They were at a gathering, a demonstration of some sort, both smiling into the camera. Behind them, towering over them on a platform, was a man with a bull horn ... Harvey Milk. So, Alex thought, Hiroshi hadn't just participated in the White Night demonstrations to go along with the crowd. He'd been a supporter of Milk, possibly throughout his career. Perhaps they'd even been acquaintances. Maybe even friends. That could explain why such an otherwise gentle soul clocked a cop. Alex was perusing other photos for familiar faces when Hiroshi returned, teapot and cup in hand and with Raphael by his side.

"Very nice," Raphael remarked, looking around the study while Hiroshi poured tea into the third cup. Hiroshi pulled up a chair for Raphael between his and Alex's, then sat. "Someday you'll have to tell me what other brilliant things you do in here when you're not planning a wedding with your collaborator, Hiroshi." Raphael looked at Alex as he sat and took the tea cup Hiroshi offered him. "I hope you haven't finalized the ceremony yet." Raphael took a sip of tea, glanced at the dwindling plate of senbei, then did his best attempt at a 'Brady' impression. "Please, please, may I have a cracker? I won't tell anyone." Alex rolled his eyes and held the plate toward Raphael.

"If you promise to leave right now, you can have them all," Alex replied. He addressed Hiroshi. "Clearly I knew what I was doing when I cast myself, and not this guy, as Brady." He turned back to Raphael as he set down the plate. "Are you just here for the crackers, or ...?" Raphael slowly munched his cracker, smiling and purposely delaying his answer to irritate Alex. He glanced at Hiroshi a couple of times without turning his head to make sure Hiroshi was appreciating this brotherly standoff. He swallowed.

"I'm not here to interfere. I'm sure Juan and Ricky's wedding is in the most capable of hands. But ... I do have a couple of suggestions, no, requests that I hope you will incorporate into the ceremony. I wanted you to know about them before you finalize everything." Raphael turned to Hiroshi, anticipating more deference from him, since Juan and Ricky had chosen him to conduct their ceremony. And since he wasn't Alex.

"One should always be open to good ideas, eh, Alex?" Hiroshi replied. Alex nodded, a bit apprehensively.

"Good," Raphael began, "because I sort of made a promise to Ricky, well, actually he made a request of me at our second wedding, produced by *you*, Alex. He asked me to be his ring bearer when he and Juan got married. I think he already knew in his heart that this day would come." Raphael momentarily met Hiroshi's gaze. "Hiroshi, he was naked, completely covered in glitter and was wearing a glowing baby blue cage in a room filled with a couple hundred strangers. To honor us on our wedding day. There was no way I could say no. So ... Alex, I need you to make me Juan and Ricky's glitter covered ring bearer." Alex stared at Raphael as if he hadn't understood a word he'd said. "I promised," Raphael pursued. Alex looked to Hiroshi, hoping for support.

"Are ring bearers traditional in a Buddhist ceremony, Hiroshi?" he asked, anticipating a 'no.'

"I believe they are now, Alex," Hiroshi grinned impishly as he reached out and patted Raphael's naked thigh. "Another adopted tradition for what is destined to be the second most memorable wedding of the century."

"Hiroshi," Alex protested, "you guys ... you don't know what you're asking here." He turned to Raphael. "It'll take forever to coat you in glitter. And afterwards, it'll take forever to clean you up. And assuming you want to be the *surprise* ring bearer, you'll miss virtually all of the ceremony." Raphael shrugged.

"I have an idea," Hiroshi said. He looked meaningfully at Alex. "It will help to prevent marking you as a one-note wedding planner." Alex looked suspiciously at Hiroshi, then Raphael, not sure what was coming. "Maybe this will help you fulfill your promise to Ricky, Raphael. Just give me a minute." Hiroshi pulled his laptop onto his lap and spent a couple of minutes clicking around while Alex and Raphael laid waste to the plate of senbei. "Okay, here," Hiroshi announced as he reactivated the large monitor. On the screen a young Asian man appeared, naked, and completely gold-plated head to toe. At first, Raphael and Alex assumed it was a statue, but as the video advanced, it was clear it was a living, moving human, one who was, in fact, pleasuring himself.

"What the hell?" Alex asked.

"Whoa," Raphael leaned forward. "He's beautiful. How is that possible? Is it permanent?"

"Spray paint?" Alex assumed.

"Not exactly," Hiroshi explained, "he's coated with a mixture of powdered gold paint and coconut oil." Hiroshi brought up another video that showed two men, both completely golden skinned, enjoying sex with one another." Alex and Raphael both watched, rapt. After a moment, Alex turned to Raphael.

"You could never do that coated in glitter." Raphael laughed.

"Is this easy to do," he asked Hiroshi.

"Much easier, I suspect, than coating you in glitter. And easier to remove, as well. Alex, we could gold plate Raphael from the neck down, dress him similarly to how the rest of the wedding party will be outfitted, along with gloves, so the gold is hidden until time for the rings. Perhaps have some role for him in the beginning of the ceremony. Then, while Raphael retreats inside the house to strip and retrieve the rings, we could continue the ceremony. On cue, over an appropriate musical accompaniment ... and the visage of a naked, golden Raphael would certainly demand accompaniment ... Raphael, the ring bearer, could make his entrance and approach the grooms under the chuppah." Alex looked thoughtful a moment.

"Okay," he actually smiled at Hiroshi. "If you think we can pull this off, Hiroshi, it does add a little spice to the ceremony." He glanced at a beaming Raphael. "Looks like this ceremony won't be entirely nudity-free after all."

"No," Hiroshi chuckled, "but it is a sacrifice we will make to honor Ricky's request. Somehow, we will all just have to suffer through having a living, breathing, golden Adonis in our midst." Raphael raised a clenched fist to celebrate his victory.

"But what about Raphael's head?" Alex worried. "Will he have time to coat it in this paint stuff while he's out of sight to strip and get the rings?" He turned to Raphael. "I still think this means you'll miss a lot of the ceremony."

"Not necessarily, Alex. Raphael could wrap a sheer gold lamé scarf around his neck and head to blunt the disparity between his golden body and his flesh-colored head."

"A veil, in other words," Alex agreed. He glanced teasingly at Raphael. "Let's hope no one confuses you for the bride."

"Not much chance of that, since this," Raphael jiggled his cage, "will be on full display. It'll be gold plated, too, I assume?" Hiroshi nodded, wiggling his eyebrows, clearly delighted with Raphael's contribution to the ceremony.

"You had a second request for us to consider?" Hiroshi asked.

"I wasn't sure whether to bring this up to Juan and Ricky or you two. I'd like to invite Mama and Angel. I think Mama will be ready for a little road trip by Valentine's Day. It'll be a good reason for them to finally see the house, and it would be the perfect opportunity for her to thank Juan and Mateo in person for all the support they provided to her and Angel while she was in the hospital."

"I think you should ask Juan and Ricky," Hiroshi counseled, "but I am sure they will be honored. I would love to meet the rest of your family. In fact, I am not sure which I most look forward to ... a gold-plated ring bearer or meeting Raphael and Niki's family. What do you think, Alex?"

"It sounds great to me. Except." Raphael scowled at Alex. "Raphael. You just told us you want to be the bare-assed naked ring bearer. At a wedding attended by your mother."

"Oh. Yeah," realization dawned across Raphael's face. "Well ... she's seen me naked a thousand times."

"As a baby ..."

"An ass is an ass ... even if it's gold plated."

"And a cage is ...?" Raphael's eye widened. "And what about that audacious tattoo above your cage?"

"Oh. Damn ..." Raphael looked down at the tattoo above his cage, teetering on the horns of his dilemma. He painfully looked up at Hiroshi.

"What if ..." Alex proposed, "how about you wear just a fundoshi?" He turned to Hiroshi. "Can we find a gold color fundoshi?"

"Good idea," Raphael smiled, "but, no. I have to be naked, just like Ricky was ... in front of hundreds of strangers. I can't wimp out." Hiroshi, who had been ruminating thoughtfully, smiled and stood.

"Elder has your answer, Adonis. Wait here." Hiroshi left the study.

"Thanks for letting me invade your planning session, Alex," Raphael said. "Ricky will be so surprised."

"Yeah, and so will Mama," Alex cackled. Raphael knitted his brow, then laughed in spite of himself.

"Is this what's known as painting yourself into a corner?" Raphael asked. Alex nodded sagely.

"Ahem." Hiroshi appeared in the doorway, balancing a small toss pillow in both hands at waist level, over which he had draped his unfurled fundoshi, which hung down over the front and back of the pillow, past his knees. He ceremoniously paraded in a circle, approaching Alex and Raphael, then retreated back to the doorway. "Adonis, you said a bare ass was fair game. But, if I was wearing one, would you be able to see my cage?" Raphael shook his head, grinning. He turned to Alex and raised his right hand for a high-five.

"Brady, Elder has once again saved the day. And my ass." Hiroshi laid the pillow and fundoshi aside and approached Raphael and kneaded his shoulders from behind.

"Yours is an ass worth saving, my friend. I think I speak for Alex, and for the grooms, when I say both of your requests will enhance the ceremony greatly. Thank you. Alex, you and I should reconvene soon to continue our planning. But for now, my special powers tell me Niki is eager for the two of you to join him for your run." Alex and Raphael stood and pulled Hiroshi into a brief but firm hug.

# About the Author

AFTER SPENDING MANY YEARS, maybe too many years, in the advertising game, sometimes writing copy for print, radio and television, which followed a period of feature writing for a periodical during his undergrad years, the author took a break from all that to take over a bed and breakfast, as one does. And where he collected enough anecdotes and personal stories to fill a six-story bookstore.

That was interesting.

Now, he's back to writing. And reading. Full time, as it were. And incorporating a few of the lessons he's learned on the path to the life he dreamed about living all those years when he was doing something else. He doesn't teach writing, like many writers. He just writes. Although he was privileged to sample the offerings at the esteemed University of Iowa Writers Workshop. Maybe it helped. You be the judge.